Cleelok, Book II
The Cabal of Lochom

by

Sean Nuber

FRITTER AND
BOONDOGGLE

ISBN-13: 978-1-7359696-4-0

Contents

Chapter 1

Clerin Toswin was a Fluen living in the Pyran realm. Her long blonde hair and pale ice-blue eyes were out of place almost as much as her height. But she was amazed and enthralled by the Pyran realm. The plateau was dry and rocky with few plants and fewer animals. But it was full of life. The first week after Trela defeated Qizern was one giant celebration, but then it quieted down until the first festival. Trela had wanted to prove herself as a force for change, dedicated to her promises and to her subjects. She quickly faded into the minutiae of rule. That left Clerin to absorb the Pyran life. The peaceful Pyran life. And it was filled with festivals, about one every three weeks. She thought that it must have something to do with how quickly life could end there, how difficult life was for those who lived off of the barren landscape. She liked to think that this was the norm and that life on the road, amongst Trela's warpack and the constant struggle, was the rarity. She could not be sure but she felt that the former held more truth.

Trela rewarded her loyal warriors handsomely before they dispersed. Less than a third stayed, which somewhat surprised Clerin. The others, those that fought against Trela, swore fealty immediately and went back to whatever they were doing for Qizern. The transition was quick and seamless. It was as if their loyalty was to the Throne, the institution, not the ruler. Trela did not worry that any of the Guard would try to assassinate her or rise up against her. Lishean did not worry. Estfale, Rewista, Serghno—none of them worried. Trela had defeated Qizern and was now the Queen. That was that. No hard feelings. She had even kept some of his Seconds around as advisors. "Why waste such talent," had been her simple response.

In the Fluen realm everything was weighed down by so much history. Nothing happened very quickly there due to the inertia of the past. A new ruler could not just pop up from some tiny backwater village, unheard of and from an anonymous family; they would need to be vetted and vouched for, to be able to call in favors, have a verifiable reputation, have backers and old relationships with even older families. Clerin understood how the Fluens thought of the Pyrans. When she first arrived and saw all of the destruction and mayhem that the warpack system wrought upon the land, and how none of its denizens thought it odd, she thought of their way of life as barbaric. She would never admit it, but she had felt superior about the Fluen system. Now, however, after immersing herself in the most violent aspects of it, she was able to experience the other side. The peaceful, fun-loving, carefree side. Where any lowly commoner could speak with and (gasp) even eat with royalty. Where any lowly commoner could *become* royalty. It boggled the mind.

Clerin joined in the festivals as much as she was able; many of them had specific dances and games which she knew nothing about. The Pyrans themselves were surprisingly eager to teach her, however. They were proud of their traditions, proud of themselves and of their way of life. If Clerin showed even the slightest interest in something, they would go out of their way to show it to her, to explain it to her. Not just because she was Trela's Fluen princess, not for any stature or to gain any favor, but because they truly enjoyed showing it off. They were truly proud of their own traditions. Clerin promised herself that if she ever got back—no, not if, but when—when she got back to the Fluen realm, she would explain the Pyrans to her fellows in a fair and loving manner. Truthfully, honestly, without any sugar coating, but with the same pride that they themselves explained their ways to her. It was the least she could do.

It was at one of these festivals, the Siloha festival, to celebrate the first full moon of summer, that she met Yihrum. He was young, younger than she was, and he had curious green eyes. They reminded her of a cat in their color, shape, and attentiveness. The rest of his body had feline qualities to it as well. Strong, yet supple with flexible limbs and spine. He was a dancer and a juggler. She first saw him while he was juggling on a tightrope. Cat eyes staring up at the spinning balls, feet twitching back and forth to keep himself balanced while his hips were somehow immobile. His short brown hair was plastered to his forehead due to the heat of the day. With a quiet rush of adrenalin, she felt a small fear that he might fall. And, behind it, a curious childlike glee. It was as if she were a girl again, in a large town for the first time, watching the entertainers with wonder and surprise.

After being enthralled at the performance for what seemed like too long, Clerin had wandered away into the thick of the festival with her mind on nothing more than finding food that did not wholly consist of some type of meat on a skewer. Her absentmindedness made running into Yihrum amongst the throng a little shocking. And behind that the curious glee.

"If you are lost, may I offer my expert services as a guide." His grin seemed to be too wide to be just for her, like he was still on the rope attempting to wring more coins from the audience.

"How can one be lost at a festival? Is not the point to wander about where your fancy takes you?" She smiled back at him.

"But if you are aimless, you may miss the best parts." His arms tried to cross themselves, but he placed them at his sides instead. Their palms were facing Clerin however, as if he was about to raise them with a flourish.

"I thought I had just caught the best parts. Surely there is nothing greater than juggling on a tightrope." Something about him made her feel mischievous.

"Quite true, quite true. But the personal touch of a good guide can make the more mundane parts of the festival come alive." With that his right hand did come up with a flourish. It snapped up quickly but then slowed and turned at its apex.

The earnest cuteness was almost too much for Clerin. She had known similar personalities back in the Fluen realm. Their attention was rapt enough at first, but was often lost to the next shiny bauble that inevitably came along. But that audacity, that chutzpah, made it all the more irresistible. There was a little nostalgia that accompanied her decision to follow Yihrum that day. If she were honest, there was a little bit of boredom that she was hoping he could shake off as well. So, against her common sense, if not quite against her judgment, she acquiesced to his offer.

Clerin spent several meaningless, but quite enjoyable, moons in Agoge and the surrounding countryside. Oddly enough, she thought she was tiring of Yihrum faster than he was tiring of her. She had not spoken to Vrric for some time, nor any of the others really, except for Croy and, occasionally, Knill. The Gaens were steadfast friends and were almost always available. The Luften warriors, on the other hand, had been absorbed like long-lost comrades. They would spar and train with the Pyrans just as they had done in the warpack, but seemed more aloof than before. They had made their tight circle of Pyran friends there at Agoge and they were all warriors. The Pyrans of the warpack that Clerin might know were either assisting Trela, and therefore as difficult to find time with as she was, or they had left to return to their own respective families. Clerin thought about skulking around the medical buildings and chambers but was a little worried that Nochiel might be around. She seemed unable to let go of the Haswyxe incident and blamed Clerin for even "putting Croy in that position." To top it all off, Vrric and Gyllhelon were spending most of their spare time together. Clerin told herself that this did not bother her, that he was free to make his own decisions and that she had Yihrum to hang around with anyway. Except that she was getting bored with Yihrum.

For most of her time at Agoge she thought little about the Temple. In truth, the messages she carried had quieted down a little, letting her relax. Or maybe she had finally gotten used to their vibrations, she was not positive. What she was sure of, however, was that Trela had been given more than enough time. Clerin felt that the time had come to visit the Pyran Temple and finish her quest. But no, there was little chance of that. She would not be finishing anything. She needed to continue her quest. This was what bothered her about visiting the Temple and the main reason that she had been putting off the meeting. Who would accompany her to the Gaen realm? What if Gorbanax wished to communicate with Linchon again, before communicating with Gunzgak? What if she needed to go to the Fluen realm and back? She did not want to travel alone, nor with a bunch of strangers. It was fear that held her back. It was discontent and discomfort that pushed her forwards. Luckily for her, the fear was finally weaker.

Clerin was quartered in the third western wing of the castle. The castle complex, all the buildings and spaces that were encompassed within the original defensive walls, was formally called the Blaze of Agoge, but most of its denizens just referred to it as the Blaze. She had gotten to know many of the public corridors during her wanderings, but there were many more secret doors and passageways that she had only heard about. The Blaze was a giant maze, a full city within its imposing stone walls. There were numerous paths, courtyards, solariums, and open-air spaces. Some of these were filled with makeshift shelters, stalls, and gardens. Others were wide open with trees, benches, and wildlife like the parks Clerin recalled from Tureyn. Amazingly enough, a little over half the area was roofed. At some locations it was obvious where one building had melded into another, maybe within the last hundred cycles. At other locations the melding had happened so long ago that there was scarcely a discernable seam between their walls. All the walls were made of carefully chiseled stone blocks and appeared to come from the same quarry. The roofs, however, appeared to be haphazardly placed. Some were slate, some clay, and some were even thatch. Clerin wondered what it must look like from above. The back of the castle had been carved into the basalt walls of the volcano, defining its southern edge. Agoge, the city proper, included the Blaze and was about ten times larger. It spilled forth a little to the east and west of the Blaze and quite a bit to the north. Those parts not confined within the mighty castle walls were considered the "new city," though much of it was quite old. The new city was cut further into eight boroughs, each surrounded by a smaller wall that had various gates crossing into the adjacent boroughs. It made her nostalgic for the open palaces and sprawling cities, with their grass-lined canals and winding streets, that made up her home realm.

Clerin began the day with purpose, to gain audience with Trela. That was her only goal. She was raised around royalty and bureaucracy, however, so she instinctively understood the magnitude of her undertaking. She packed a light satchel with hard meats, cheeses, an apple, and some crusty bread. She wore clothing that would allow her to move freely and would breathe in the heat. She chose her most comfortable pair of boots. She was prepared to get lost and be stymied.

Clerin only got lost once on the way to Trela's antechambers. She had gone up a short flight of stairs when she should have gone down. When she opened the door at the landing, it opened to a catwalk at one of the castle walls, so she immediately knew that she was in the wrong spot. It did not take her too long to find where she was going and it was barely afternoon when she finally arrived at the antechambers.

"I seek audience with the Queen." Clerin had learned quickly that using the name Trela did not speed up the process as it typically would in the Fluen realm.

"The Queen is not seeing anyone today." The nondescript Guard was bored, but polite. His purple cloak looked hot even though it was the lighter, peacetime style. It was the only thing indicating he was not just a guard, but one of the Guard.

"You don't understand, I really must see her today." Clerin put on her most gracious smile.

"Listen, I am under strict orders…" The smile that the Guard wore looked almost pained.

"Please, just let her know that Clerin Toswin is here to see her." She missed the days that she knew all of Trela's support staff. She wondered briefly why it had taken her so long to return. Her first tour of the Blaze had seemed so glamorous, a huge castle complex and she knew the Queen, but now it seemed tied down in tedious bureaucracy. The scenery had not altered much, so she rightly assumed that it was her mood that had changed, not the antechamber.

"Well, you are going to have to await my replacement. I cannot leave my post unattended." He gave her the pained smile again.

Rather than argue with him, she sighed and wandered over to one of the benches. She slouched down and brought her feet up onto the bench in front of her. More to keep her hands busy than any actual hunger, she began to root through her satchel. Finding nothing unexpected, she sighed again.

"How about if I watch your post while you run off and tell Trela that I am here. It shouldn't take any time at all. And... well, there is no one else about." She half-heartedly batted her eyelashes at him. She was not even sure if he could see her eyes from that far away and she doubted it would work anyway. The members of the Guard were notorious for following orders to the letter, no matter how foolish or mundane.

"I have been expressly forbidden to leave my post until my replacement arrives. If you like, I can give your message to the Queen later today and you can return tomorrow for an audience." His smile was a little more relaxed.

"No thank you. I have resigned today to the cause." It was not that she did not trust him, but... the only way she could be sure that her message would get to Trela was to wait and remind him once the replacement arrived. She only wished she had thought to bring a book. "So, tell me about yourself. Were you involved in the campaign?"

"I am not allowed to fraternize." His brow furrowed and his smile dropped from his face.

Clerin could tell when she was beaten, so she settled in for the long wait. It took several hours of mind- and butt-numbing boredom before the Guard's replacement arrived. During that time not a single other derlian attempted to gain audience with Trela.

"Do not forget my message." Clerin had hopped up to interrupt the Guards' customary chatter. They both glared at her, but she just beamed a smile back at them. Eventually the first Guard nodded and walked off. Clerin smiled at the remaining Guard. "I am waiting for an audience with the Queen…"

"I am not allowed to fraternize." He glared at her much in the same way the first Guard had. It made Clerin wonder if they were taught that phrase at some point. She almost felt like she was back in the Fluen realm, with so much petty functionary angst and power wielding. She sat back down.

It was not long before Clerin could hear a slow but steady rhythm of boots coming down the hall. Much to her delight, Trela strode into view with the first Guard trailing afterwards, wringing his hands unconsciously.

"Clerin, darling! I cannot believe you were kept waiting." Trela cocked an eyebrow and turned her head towards the Guard slightly. He looked embarrassed but was professional enough not to offer any stammered excuses. Her red hair and yellow eyes always seemed to give her a feral edge to Clerin, even if she was being nice.

In a whirlwind they were headed back into the throne room, Clerin's long legs the only thing allowing her to keep up with Trela's pace. They did not speak on the short walk down the dim corridor. Once at the magnificent doors, Trela pushed them both open with a flourish.

The throne room was quite large and a little garish. There was a gigantic topographic table map that looked even more detailed than Vanelia's. Against the back wall, upon a tiered dais, were two large, ridiculously ornate thrones. They had high backs; one had a golden sun centered above and the other a silver moon. The fabric appeared to be a red velvet, the arms had carven lion's heads, there were spires and turrets jutting out at the shoulders, and there were even crossed halberds on the wall behind each one. There was red carpet leading up to the thrones, red velvet ropes around the dais, carved wooden benches along each wall, one gigantic and two smaller chandeliers, paintings and tapestries ringing the room, and five ornate stained-glass windows. Clerin slowly walked into the room and gawked. She wished she had seen the throne room of Tureyn, just to try to compare them. Now that she thought about it, she had only seen the small throne room in the Ariellyna. Surely the main throne room was much more impressive. She really had nothing to compare this one against.

"You really must forgive my Guards, they are on strict orders not to admit anyone today. They can take their orders quite seriously, especially during this transition period." Trela laughed lightly and stood before her map. This was how Clerin always saw Trela when she thought of her, standing in front of a map. The doors closed themselves quietly.

"You have done well for yourself…" Clerin waved vaguely around the room.

"It's just meant to be imposing, really." Trela was looking down. She took a deep breath and smiled at Clerin. "So, how is Feyazki?"

"How should I know?" She did not mean to sound like she did. Rather than get into a long conversation, however, she decided to get to the point. "You know why I am here, don't you?"

"Of course, of course. You wish to commune with Gorbanax in the Temple of Fire." Trela's smile did not slip for a moment. Not even when Clerin had snapped at her.

"I need to. This is not about desire." Clerin breathed in deep. She was not sure where her agitation stemmed from.

"This was my promise to you and you have certainly waited long enough. When would you like perform your duty? Tomorrow?" She had her back to the topographic map now, leaning on the table.

"Yes, the sooner the better. Tomorrow will be great." Clerin made an unconscious shallow curtsey. She felt herself turning to leave.

"Then you will dine with us tonight. I have the greatest chefs in all the realm at my disposal. You must try my hospitality." Trela did not move, but stopped Clerin all the same. "Plus, it will do Knill some good. He doesn't even spend much time with Tumu anymore now that Lishean is the leader of the Guard. It will be good for us all."

The dining hall was massive with echoes. The three of them huddled at one end of a table meant to comfortably seat and impress hordes of dignitaries. Trela sat at the end, while Clerin and Knill sat opposite each other. Knill was on Trela's right. The five-course meal was fantastic, the grog was both flavorful and strong. It started with canapés and a small pilaf, then a salad, a perfectly cooked and seasoned slab of beef with sides of small red potatoes and asparagus, then a form of pie that had a mix of strawberries and something tart.

"Rhubarb. I had never even heard of it before. I do not think it would be great alone, but mix it with a jellied fruit and it is just amazing." Knill was talking excitedly about the meal.

Knill was curious to Clerin. He seemed like the type of derlian that would just curl up and die if left alone for too long. He was very... sociable. He was certainly gregarious and fun to talk with. But there was a need... a hunger in his conversation tonight. It made her wonder how much time Trela spent away from him. So she spent most of the evening in pleasant, if a bit meaningless, chitchat with Knill. She doubted she had even spoken twenty words to Trela. She had wanted to plan out tomorrow's trek during dinner but figured it could wait. She took another sip of grog and a last bite of the wonderful pie and sat back, smiling. She felt even more relaxed and contented than on a lazy day with Yihrum.

The meal passed quickly and easily. After the glow of the food and grog began to fade, Trela excused herself. Clerin thought it odd that they did not all leave at once, but both Knill and Trela seemed unperturbed. Like it was typical. Routine. She let Knill ramble for a while about camp life during the campaign, he seemed very nostalgic for that time. Eventually, though, she got tired enough to say something.

"Thank you for a lovely dinner. And you must thank Trela for me as well. But, I ah... should be heading towards my quarters." Clerin slowly stood.

"Here, let me walk with you." Knill hopped up and walked over to her side of the table.

They walked for a while as he continued to ramble. Clerin was not really paying attention to what he was saying. Eventually they arrived at an open air park area. Knill led her over to a large birch tree, with leaves that shown in the moonlight. He stopped and began to look around nervously.

"We are alone, are we not?" He spoke in a conspiratorial tone.

"I... I think so." Clerin was not sure why, but she also looked around nervously. The feeling was contagious.

"I am probably just being paranoid, but... Tumu wants to send you a warning. You must not go too far into the Temple of Fire. You are supposed to commune, I think, but do not accept anything

10

from Gorbanax. Something large is afoot, something that has given Tumu fits and nightmares. I do not know what it is or how it involves you, but Tumu was adamant that Gorbanax wants to hurt you. Just… be careful." Knill was bobbing his head up and down slightly.

"Be careful? How do you protect yourself against a Beleg?" Clerin was flummoxed. She had not been feeling nervous about her meeting, or at least not any more nervous than she had been to commune with Linchon, but now she was worried.

"It has something to do with proximity, but I am not sure. Tumu had a difficult time explaining himself. He's… it has been very traumatic for him lately. He has not been sleeping well." Knill kept his voice low and looked around some more.

"Does Tumu dream?" Clerin had not talked to him much during the campaign.

"No, he has different talents than Croy. Hmm… Maybe I should have visited Croy, I have not seen him for almost a moon. Maybe he has been dreaming." Knill cocked an eyebrow inquisitively.

"Trela told me that you were not spending a lot of time with Tumu either." Clerin wondered herself if she should try to speak with Croy. She also wondered about speaking with Tumu. So many things could be lost in translation.

"How would she know how I spend my time?" Knill's voice became steely for a moment but then, almost immediately, his face relaxed. "I know that I am not much help and I certainly do not know how to protect yourself from a Beleg, but I wanted to give you the warning."

Knill ducked out and disappeared quite quickly, leaving Clerin standing alone next to the birch tree. She stood there alone for a while, listening to the quiet nothingness of the night. She appreciated Knill attempting to help her but there was really not much she could do to prepare for tomorrow's meeting, at least not much differently than she had already planned. It was as if she were a loosed arrow, already in flight. She suddenly felt very small in a large world, like an ant crawling up the trunk of a tree.

Clerin awoke early enough to have a long bath and nibble on a salad and some fruit. She put what herbs and oils she could into the tub, trying her best to remember the scent of her bath at the Liar's Lyre so long ago. She could easily find lavender, cedar, and sage, but had difficulties finding some of the others. She had done nothing for Linchon, however, so she did not think Gorbanax would begrudge her a few herbs. Did Gorbanax like the same herbs as Lembin? Did it even want herbs at all? Deep down she believed it was the thought, the attempt, that counted. Of course, she would not know until she arrived at the volcano to commune.

It was nice of Trela to accompany Clerin to the entrance to the Temple. It was, as she had stated, "the least she could do." It added gravitas to the journey and aided immensely at every checkpoint. It seemed that every Guard personally recognized Trela. They would back out of the way, bowing and scraping as they moved. Occasionally, Trela would ask simple directions to make sure that they were still on the right track, but typically the only words spoken by the Guards were "my Liege" or "my Queen." It made Clerin feel special, riding atop Riverlightning and staring down at bowed heads and caped backs. She could only imagine how it made Trela feel.

They rode for quite some time. They had started at dawn at the royal stables. Clerin really enjoyed getting her own horse ready, she had almost forgotten that. Checking the shoes, tossing the thick blanket over, struggling with the pungent leather saddle, combing the mane and tail. Sure, back in the Fluen realm, after a long ride she had never minded handing the reins over to Gymnie and letting him rub Ranger down with dry straw, pull all the stickers and brambles off and feed and water the horse. However, during the long campaign Clerin had no such assistance and she had become quite accustomed performing all of her own duties. She also thought it strengthened the bond between herself and Riverlightning, and there seemed to be no lessening of that bond over the last several moons that she had neglected him. It was almost noon and they were now crisscrossing up the side of the volcano. She wondered briefly if she should have brought a donkey instead, but Riverlightning was very sure-footed on the rocky path. Another two hours of slow going had finally brought them to a gigantic ledge.

Clerin dismounted, letting a Guard take Riverlightning's reins, his purple cape flowing about him. Though it gave her a bit of vertigo, she stared over the ledge down upon all of Agoge. The Blaze still looked massive from this height, but it paled in comparison to the city that sprawled out beyond it. Clerin had spent so much time in the Blaze proper, she had really only ventured out into the city for festivals, that she had not really considered the scale of it all. She wondered if it was larger than Tureyn. From the image below her, she guessed it might be, but she had never seen Tureyn all at once from a great height.

She turned and examined the large cave entrance. It was a fairly symmetric round-topped arch. There were no doors, only a bevy of Guards standing around. There was discernable heat emanating from the cave, but it was quickly removed by the constant wind blowing by the ledge. Trela was whispering amongst some warriors as Clerin walked up.

"…and I want no interruptions, understand? Ah, Clerin, perfect. I hear that the volcano has been rumbling. It appears that you are anticipated." Trela smiled, a bit maniacally. "Fregonal will be guiding us." Trela pointed to a scarred, wiry, tough-looking Pyran. It made Clerin wonder for a moment. All of the Guards seemed to be skinny. Well, maybe not skinny—they were certainly all muscular—but not one was incredibly large, certainly nothing approaching Torpalin's size.

They walked in and it quickly it became dark. It took a while before Clerin could get her eyes to adjust. Luckily, they walked straight for quite some time with the sunlight seeping in from behind them. Eventually they took a turn and that was where the torches began. There were occasional offshoot tunnels that led to small chambers, filled with beds as far as she could tell. It appeared that the complex was a small garrison. She wondered how often some undesirable snuck past the numerous checkpoints and made it all the way to the ledge. There appeared to be a lot of warriors guarding the path to one of the most powerful beings in existence, as if the Beleg would be unable to protect itself. It was getting noticeably warmer, and she realized that the warriors they passed were no longer wearing any cloaks. This made her wonder if they were all Guards up here, or if there were regular guards mixed in with them. She had no idea how to tell them apart without the cloaks.

They walked much farther than Clerin would have assumed possible, with multiple twists and turns extending their path. As they neared the center of the volcano the heat became quite intense, making her break out in a light sweat. They finally arrived at a pair of doors. There were two cloakless Guards leaning on pikes in front of the doors. She knew they had to be Guards just because of the door they were guarding. They instinctively recognized Trela and bowed deeply.

"The Queen and her companion wish to commune with Gorbanax. Step aside." Fregonal projected his voice from his diaphragm. Clerin felt the tunnel they were in was much too small for that amount of pomp, but she supposed that he rarely had a chance to speak like that.

The Guards instantly straightened their spines and did their best to step aside. Their heads were stiff and they stared directly at each other. Fregonal opened both doors with a flourish. He bowed deeply as Trela and Clerin passed him, and then shut the doors behind them.

The room was quite long and opened up at the far end. It had a perfectly rounded top and bottom, seeming more like a tube than a room. There were four more cloakless Guards and a Pyran in long dark robes that Clerin assumed was a mage. They all bowed deeply and stayed bent over. At the end of the tube was a lake of lava, and it appeared that the roof opened up above it; Clerin could not be positive from this distance. There was a background hiss and bubbling, but Clerin's ears seemed to be stuffed with cotton. It was hard to hear anything. The heat was almost unbearable.

"Rise." Trela's voice carried oddly. It seemed to have a small echo at first, but died out quickly.

"Will you be communing today, my Queen?" The mage stepped forwards.

"No, not I. Only my companion." Trela nodded sideways to Clerin.

"Will you be requiring a protection spell?" The way he asked made Clerin wonder how often Gorbanax was visited. Lembin was visited quite often, and there were several mages always on hand to provide the necessary spells. Linchon, however, was visited so rarely that only the King had known where the Temple was located. Gorbanax appeared to be somewhere between the two extremes.

"Yes, but… I must disrobe to commune." Clerin was not necessarily shy, but there were just so many others in the room.

"Oh, of course. You four, leave us." Trela waved at the warriors. Once they had left, Trela turned her attention back to the mage. "You must cast your most perfect spell today, mage. You must protect her as if she were me. Any pain or damage that she receives will be visited ten-fold upon yourself. Do you understand?"

"Of course, my Queen. I had protected Qizern many times in the past and, as always, I will strive to perform my best." His eyes were held down. Clerin was sure it was out of respect, but she would have preferred to look directly into his eyes. Just to see what she could see. Knill's warning came back to her unbidden at that moment.

There was not much else to be done, however. She could not cast a spell powerful enough to protect herself. Her mind wandered to why Trela had not brought Vrric with them while she undressed. There was surely a reason, and besides, if this mage had protected Qizern, he should be quite proficient at the spell he was about to cast. Soon Clerin handed her pile of clothes to Trela and stood naked before the mage, her skin shimmering with a light sheen of sweat.

"Lumtecpiarc!" His voice was deep, even, and confident. He took another breath. "Narteclufarc!"

A soothing wave washed over Clerin which removed the excess heat and gave her a feeling of comfort that was unmatched by anything she had felt before. She felt more relaxed than sitting in a warm bath after a long day's ride. She breathed in deeply with an unconscious smile upon her face. There was really nothing else to be done, other than to walk into the lake of fire. She began the long stroll down the tube towards the glowing lava.

Clerin stood in front of the lake for a moment. She was trying to think of Knill's comment on proximity. She wished she could have spoken with Tumu. She stared up and saw the sky peeking down. There were a myriad of holes above her and, about fifty rods further, it appeared to open up completely. She took a deep breath to steady herself.

She took her first step and her foot sunk into the molten rock. She took another and another. Then, suddenly, she dropped. She had sunk to her shoulders. The floor beneath her felt like soft mud. As she sifted her feet, attempting to keep her head above the lava, she slid further down. The mud shifted and parted under her weight. She had stopped moving forward but she continued to drift downwards. Slowly. It was just as the lava slipped over her eyes that she felt the most panic. She wanted, more than anything, to scream. To yell and cry and shake her fists. She could see nothing but a pale yellow-orange before her. It felt like her hair was floating, but she could not be sure.

There was a low rumble that she heard, yes, but more than that, she felt it. As if she were laying in soft mud next to a road that had a hundred horses thundering along it. She could feel the hoofs shaking her. She could feel them through her. Her whole body vibrated with them.

She did her best to stay where she was. She tried to keep her feet up on the surface of the mud. She tried to tread the lava. She did everything in her power not to move forward. She had a strange sense of horizontal vertigo and could not tell if she was shifting or floating or holding completely still. It was incredibly disconcerting.

An image of crossed pikes appeared before her, obviously barring her way. They were flat black against the yellow-orange background. She wondered if Gorbanax did not want her to be in proximity either. *What if Knill's warning was for the Beleg, not because of it?*, she thought.

A flat black silhouette appeared. It was a crude, almost shapeless shadow, but had hair that flowed the same length as Clerin's. She raised her right hand. It raised its mirrored hand. She raised her left and it mirrored that as well. She made several gestures, just to make sure, and it followed her exactly. Clerin understood that the silhouette represented her.

Then a large flat black image of a bonfire appeared. It was gigantic and the "flame" moved in a herky-jerky manner, stilted and choppy. The bonfire encompassed the majority of the view behind the pikes. Then it moved back or got smaller, it was impossible for Clerin to tell, and the silhouette floated over to it. Suddenly, two large crossed pikes appeared between the two images. Everything stopped for a moment. Then, slowly, the silhouette moved towards the bonfire. Suddenly the pikes swung together in unison, like scissors swiveling at their center, and they struck the silhouette. At that same moment, Clerin was unable to breath. Her chest tightened and would not move. Her diaphragm seemed to be made of stone, it was so unresponsive to her will. It took several moments before panic set in. Had she gotten too close? Was Gorbanax going to kill her right there? Stars began to dance in front of her vision. Before it got black, however, she began to flail about. It was a useless, but natural, gesture to try to reach the surface. To reach the air.

The asphyxiation stopped as abruptly as it began. The bonfire and the silhouette disappeared. Clerin was able to breathe normally under the lava again.

Another flat black image appeared, this one of a small fire. It was a caricature of fire, with its sharp peaks frozen in time which did not move like the bonfire's peaks had. It reminded Clerin of the puppet shows that she watched as a little girl. They would have symbolic crude cutouts of items that would shake around animatedly, but would, of course, never change their shape. The fire image shook around for a moment behind the large barring pikes.

Then a crude cutout image of a derlian appeared. It was too crude to tell what race it was supposed to represent. Clerin assumed a Pyran. The derlian's arms suddenly popped upwards. Then back down. Then up again. The fire image turned into a sword image. Then agonizing pain shot through her. It was as if she were being burned alive, as if the mage's spell had ended and the lava was finally encroaching upon her flesh. She tried to scream through the lava but it was too thick. Then the pain stopped. Two smaller crossed pikes appeared before the sword. They flashed in and out of existence. Blinking.

Then more derlian cutouts arrived. They circled in front of Clerin for a while, though still behind the large pike image. They seemed to be of various sizes. Seemed to be a group, a diverse group. After they circled for a while, they too raised and lowered their arms. The sword image appeared to shatter, but the flame image did not reappear. Then the group descended upon the original derlian image. They shook up and down in front of it, obviously very agitated. Then they parted and the first image turned on its side, then floated up and out of view. The group then shook up and down again for a brief moment.

It was then that the silhouette reappeared. It moved forward slowly and the pikes separated, allowing it to slide pass, then re-crossing. The bonfire image and the silhouette moved together, as if dancing. Then the silhouette put out its hand and the bonfire, amazingly, put out a hand as well. They shook hands slowly in front of Clerin for some time.

"I understand that I have much to do before we may truly commune and I may give you my messages. I shall not bother you again until I have accomplished what you require." Clerin did her best to bow, but dared not get too close to the crossed pikes. She waited for a while but they did not disappear, nor did any other images come before her. So she swam her way back to the thick lava that felt like mud and, eventually, was able to bring her head above the surface. She crawled out and lay on the solid stone ground for a moment. The mage's spells still comforted her. She did not even feel the hard and somewhat jagged stone beneath her.

"You must shake any lava off before you come any closer." The warning was yelled over by Trela. Since Clerin had not been moving, she assumed that Trela was warning her that the spell was nearing its end. Dutifully, she stood and brushed herself off as best she could. There was not much lava on her anyway. It had sort of pooled under her as she had lain. With a deep breath, Clerin walked the long walk back to Trela and the mage.

"Were you able to commune as you needed?" Trela was holding Clerin's folded clothes out for her.

"No... Yes... I am not sure. I need some help interpreting what was being communicated." Clerin began to dress and talked into her shirt. "Gorbanax will not fully commune with me until I perform some task. So, while I understood much of what our communication intended, which was helpful, I was unable to complete my mission." Her voice trailed off.

"Do you need to rest a while? I could have someone fix up a meal." Trela had started walking towards the doors, ignoring the mage.

"No, I think I would rather head back as soon as possible. Besides, Riverlightning will do most of the work." She smiled wide.

"Can you *whisper* to the Blaze and let them know we are headed back and will need a meal and a bath prepared for our arrival?" Trela had one of the doors open but was looking back at the mage.

"Of course, my Queen." He bowed low.

Clerin took a deep breath as she exited the chamber. This was not the end either. There was no telling exactly what Gorbanax required, but she was surely not going to be able to deliver her messages for some time. First was the interpretation. She certainly needed help with that. And though she had no conscious reason why, she had a gut feeling that Croy was the derlian to help her.

The ride was long, but not arduous. Once they arrived at the Blaze, Clerin went straight to the bath. Somehow bathing always made things better.

"Could you invite Croy to the meal? And bring Knill." Clerin rarely gave orders, or even requests, to Trela, but she did not hesitate for a moment in her response.

"Of course, everything shall be prepared once you have bathed." Though Trela certainly did not bow, there was an odd nod that her head made. "Take your time."

The bath was utterly fantastic; it was just what Clerin needed. Though it was effective at washing the journey's grime from her, it was the soothing and relaxing aspects that she enjoyed most. Her mind did not even concentrate on the task at hand. She did not think about Gorbanax or what its vague requirements of her might be. She kept her mind blissfully blank. That nothingness had an amazing restorative power over her. She wished she could have stayed in the tub all night.

The meal was held in the same oversized dining hall that she had eaten in the night before. Trela, Knill, Croy and Vrric—no, Feyazki; she had to remember that he had changed his name—were all standing around, nibbling on canapés and quietly conversing. The table was set and it had some food on it, but was bare of the main course. Clerin wondered how long they had been waiting for her.

"Ah, there you are. We were beginning to get worried." Trela smiled at her. "I thought I was going to have to get Feyazki to check up on you." Clerin and Vrric both looked at the ground and the silence started to get palpable. "Here." Trela pulled a chair out from the table for Clerin. "Sit. Relax. We will be enjoying our meal shortly." Everyone chose their chairs and sat down. Trela was at the end of the table. Clerin was at Trela's left hand, while Knill was at her right. Croy sat next to Clerin and Vrric sat next to Knill. The more derlians that were around the table, the more comfortable Clerin felt. She wondered what it was like when the entire hall was full.

They ate, drank, and were merry. It was an easy meeting amongst old friends. They told stories about the campaign and jokes about those they had traveled with. They even joked about each other, giving each of them at the table a good ribbing in their own turn. And they laughed through it all. Clerin had forgotten what a good cook Torpalin was until Croy brought it up. Vrric performed an amazing impression of Elange, his former mentor's mad mentor. Knill told of his pretending to be a ghulzan while he did not understand what a ghulzan was. Trela talked about how she had no clue where the Luften Temple was hidden, even though she had promised Clerin that she knew how to find it. And Clerin, for her part, told the story of accidentally stealing Riverlightning. They chatted and drank and reminisced and ate and laughed for well over an hour. Finally, the reverie died down and all eyes turned to Clerin.

"I am sure you are wondering why I wanted to speak with you all. I communed with Gorbanax, but am not sure how to interpret the images that were shown to me." Clerin then explained, as thoroughly as her sharp memory allowed, everything that she had seen. Silence answered her for some time, as almost the entire party furrowed their brows in consideration. Croy, however, was staring into his cup.

"You were the first I thought of Croy. What do you think it all means?" Clerin gently prodded him.

"Well… I certainly would not know why, and I am not even sure that I know at all, but…" He trailed off.

"Don't hold back, Croy. What's your interpretation?" Trela raised her eyebrow and then her glass.

"I think it represents the Cabal of Lochom." He looked around, but no one interrupted. "I have not mentioned this before, but… The reason that Ilana and I went into the desert, besides destiny obviously, was to commune with the Vijen about the increase in Tlana along the desert border. The Vijen that we found was not very helpful at all." Trela added a laugh to Croy's speech at that. "The expedition was led by a Gaen named Aedon. None of us knew at the time, but she already had a theory about the increase in Tlana before we left Serif. You see, the Cabal practices Yavencide. As you know, all magic is based on chaos and, therefore, ephemeral."

"All magic is transitory," Vrric said quietly, almost unconsciously.

"What is Yavencide?" The question was posed by Knill.

"The Cabal traps a Yaven into an item to make that item permanently enchanted. From what I hear, if you trap a Pyran Yaven into a sword, that sword will be forever sharp and able to slice through armor, flesh, bone. It is not necessarily ablaze, you may not be able to sense it, but it has a power beyond our world ensconced inside. I believe, well Aedon believed, that the Cabal was making these items, and that the evil of it attracted more Tlana." Croy paused and licked his dry lips. "When you spoke of the image of the small fire getting absorbed, that was the first thing I thought of. I believe that Gorbanax wants you… wants us… to destroy the Cabal."

They sat in silence for a long moment. Croy's words sunk into Clerin and she pondered the issue. It had never entered her mind that a Yaven could be killed by a derlian. Especially here, in the derlian realm. She had always thought they just got sent back to their own realm if they were overpowered.

"I would assume that the possibility of Yavencide is ultimately abhorrent to the Belegs. It would be like watching your children murder your siblings. It would be the ultimate betrayal. The ultimate evil." Trela spoke up while looking down at her empty plate.

"They don't seem to mind if derlians die." Vrric's voice had an undercurrent of vehemence.

"Derlians die all the time. It is unavoidable. It's… natural." Knill cocked an eyebrow at Vrric. "Yavens can live for eternity."

"But they *can* die. At least in their own realm from what I hear." Vrric took a draught of grog.

"I do not think it is just the death. I do not even know if it causes death." Croy spoke up. "It's the entrapment. They are stuck, forever, without being able to do anything. Unable to move, unable to communicate, unable to sense. Imprisoned forever, silently screaming in agony. From what I hear, they die when the item is destroyed. I think that death is the release." Croy took a deep breath. "I would think that the Belegs, all of the Belegs, not just Gorbanax, would want all of these items destroyed. They would want us to give succor to those already abused. They would want us to kill them, kill them all. The trapped Yavens, the Cabal itself, and anyone with any knowledge of how to perform the atrocity. Wipe the slate clean."

Clerin had not heard Croy use such strong imagery before. He was typically so soft spoken and shy. Most of her conversations with him revolved around the healing arts, not killing.

"Is that how you interpret your communication with Gorbanax?" Trela glanced from Croy to Clerin.

Clerin took a moment to think about it. Croy's explanation matched up with everything she had seen under the lava. It synched with the image of the fire cutout turning into a sword perfectly. The agonizing pain that she had felt during that flash certainly carried the connotations of great evil. She was not in the least bit confused about how Gorbanax felt about the cutout turning into a sword. The anger, the rage, the near nemesis had been palpable.

"Though I had never heard of this Cabal before, I believe that Croy's interpretation is correct." Clerin took a drink. "I do not think that Gorbanax will allow me to commune again until the Cabal is destroyed."

"Then we should all go." Knill spoke quickly. "Croy is needed to find the Cabal. Feyazki is needed for the Tlana. Clerin is needed since this is her quest. We will need some warriors and mages. And we will need Trela to lead the expedition." He looked happier than Clerin had seen him in quite a while.

"I cannot go." Trela looked down and spoke quietly. "I have just started my reign. There is... there is too much to do."

Not only was Trela's refusal stunning, but the awkwardness afterward was stunning as well. No one spoke the whole time Knill attempted to glare a hole through her skull. They all chewed on their lips and stared at their empty plates.

"You must talk to her, she will not listen to me." Knill was emphatic. He had walked her home just for this conversation, Clerin was sure. "You must convince her that she is necessary for us."

"But, how do I know that she is? She has spent her entire life working towards becoming Queen. How can I talk her into walking away from that? Even for just a little while." Clerin was curious as to where his passion came from. She, herself, had thought that having Trela come along would be quite beneficial. Trela could bring any warriors, mages, equipment, horses—anything and everything to help make the mission successful. She would be incredibly helpful crossing any towns or villages along their way, anywhere at all in the Pyran realm and maybe into the Gaen realm as well. She was, in her own right, a consummate warrior. Surely, talking her into coming would greatly enhance their chances of success. Clerin did not think that these were the items that Knill was concerned with, however. The tone in his voice, the urgency of his argument... it all hinted at something else. She just did not know what. Well... not exactly.

"Kriishan. She has spent her life fulfilling the destiny of the Kriishan. Becoming Queen was part of a larger whole." Knill looked her in the eye. His brown eyes, which used to remind Clerin of a deer's, looked slightly feral. "You need to convince her that this quest, your quest, is part of her larger Kriishan destiny."

"Why?" Clerin stared back.

"Because it is." Knill seemed to become more sedated. Then he took a deep breath and let it out slowly. His eyes were suddenly brimming with emotion. "She doesn't need me anymore.

Do you know what that means? She does not want my advice on how to run a realm, what laws to pass, what projects to start. I am not even her ghulzan anymore. I am something that only gains attention because I need it—like a forgotten puppy—and I am begrudged the little attention I do get. I am a mere distraction."

The thought stopped Clerin from her prepared flippant response. She could see him as a forgotten puppy, one whose only avenue to gain attention was to piddle on the floor or chew apart a book. Only negative attention was available. It shamed her to think it, but Knill was always so stolid and steadfast that she had not really considered that he had emotional needs. He had always seemed unflappable and indefatigable. On the campaign he had always seemed to be in a good mood, always eager to please and to help. She was never sure what he had gained by his relationship with Trela and had erroneously, obviously, assumed that he needed nothing. Apparently what he needed was the feeling of being needed.

"I will do what I can." She meant it, but was unsure of what it actually meant. She would truly do what she could, but what could she really do? What argument could pull a Queen away from her subjects, from her realm? It was a hollow promise made to a desperate derlian. "Why don't you tell her that Tumu has foreseen it?"

"Don't you think that I have tried that?" A little anger crept into his voice but quickly faded. "It must be you. Please. She will not listen to me."

The conversation with Knill weighed heavily on Clerin's mind. She wanted to have a solution before speaking with Trela but could think of nothing. Three days had passed and she was sure that Knill would be getting antsy. Nothing useful had come to her.

Clerin awoke with the awful understanding that she must speak with Trela sometime that day. It was with heavy heart that she bathed, dressed, and began her journey into the heart of the Blaze. She was immediately accosted by Croy.

"Have you spoken with Trela?" His voice was quick and his face was slightly sweaty.

"No, not yet. Did Knill send you? I told him I would do my best." He gave her quite a start. Clerin had barely closed her door when he'd arrived.

"No. Well, yes, he did want me to speak with you. But, no, he is not the reason I need to speak with you." His breath was ragged, as if he had been running. "I had a dream. It was specific and… scary. Anyway, I cast what you told me to in the dream. I cast 'Losidtotarc' while dreaming and… and I can't explain it. I think a Yaven spoke to me. I think the Yaven wants you to summon it. I… its name is Taglochprefwaskintruld. It wants you to summon it while you are talking with Trela. It wants to speak with her."

"I can't summon a Yaven, are you mad?" Clerin's mind raced as quickly as she imagined Croy's heart was beating.

"But you can. It wants to be summoned, don't you see. By you, to talk with Trela." He pulled a piece of paper out of his pocket. "Here, I tried to write it down. Can you cast a Mek power level?"

Clerin looked at the folded parchment. The name Taglochprefwaskintruld was written in a shaky hand, but it was readable. She folded it back up and put it in her pouch.

"Yes, I think so." Her mind was wandering slightly due to the shock.

"Good. You need to cast Mek - Sid - Pi - Arc." He spoke slowly, separating each syllable. It was a little frustrating since Clerin knew all of the Majora quite well, it was just that she could not cast powerful spells. "I must run, I have another errand. I cannot believe my luck in just catching you." He grinned mightily and ran off.

Clerin stood there quietly for some time. She was sort of thinking, but was mostly attempting to recuperate from the shock. She did not know what to make of it, nor had she any idea of what she was going to say to Trela. She walked the entire way to the antechambers with a furrowed brow.

Due to the fiasco last time, Clerin had asked for an audience with Trela for later in the day, thinking it would give the Guard enough time to set something up and give her time to think of what she was going to say. To her great surprise, he said that Trela was waiting for her. Expecting her.

Clerin walked into the throne room to find Trela seated and encumbered with the trappings of royalty. She had a mantle, a crown, a scepter; she appeared unlike Clerin had ever seen her before. In fact, the complete opposite of how Clerin was used to seeing her. Her back was straight and her wolf-like eyes were haughty.

"The answer is no." The doors had not yet shut behind Clerin.

"You have yet to hear what I have to say." Clerin slowly strolled along the long carpet leading to the throne. Though she was not wearing skirts, she curtsied low and demurely.

"You have come to ask me to leave my subjects. To leave my realm. To leave my reign. To give up all that I have worked so hard for." Trela waved her bejeweled hand in a wide circle.

Clerin laughed. Heartily. She had not wanted to, it just popped out. The nervousness of the situation, the seriousness of the situation; the laughter was incongruous and, she doubted, very helpful. It was all just too much. Too much pomp, too many jewels, too many ostentatious trappings.

"Pardon me, but you appear the buffoon." Clerin half-heartedly wiped an eye. "This is what you worked for? This?" She waved her own hand in a wide circle. "I do not think I have ever seen you out of traveled-stained breeches, but here you are in silk. And where is your sword?" Clerin regained some composure. "All you need is a court full of pompous sycophants, bowing and scraping, to complete the image. I had never, in all my time knowing you, realized that *this* was what you were working for. To be honest, I am appalled." Trela opened her mouth to speak but Clerin cut her off with a wave of her hand. "I had thought you were working for something noble, no pun intended. I thought you were sacrificing yourself for the good of all Pyrans. I thought that you were an agent of destiny. The Kriishan. But now you do not want to leave your own throne room."

"I am working on a canon of laws to bring justice to the entire realm. I am working on the hierarchy of command needed to implement these laws. I am working on which order of civil projects will be best for the entire realm. It may not look like it, but I am constantly working for the good of my subjects." Trela looked quite angry. "You would not believe how much time I have to take to listen to others who would spend my time differently."

"Your destiny is larger than this room. We both know that." Clerin thought of something else. She was getting the order wrong. "Listen, you deserve a rest. You have earned some time, certainly not relaxing, but some time here, amongst all these comforts. You have more to do, of course, but you deserve to be able to do it here. Out of the rain, out of the cold, out of the hot sun. Could you imagine not having to hoist yourself into a saddle every day? To be able to sleep in a bed made of feathers that feels just like a cloud? Can you imagine sitting on a throne with a jewel encrusted crown?" Clerin took a breath. "You have much to do and your realm needs you. And these are not bad things. These are things that you truly have earned. But..." She took another, deeper breath. It was now or never. "Destiny is not done with you. Destiny has not finished guiding you, needing you, demanding of you. This is not the end of the path, at least not for now. Gorbanax, a Beleg, *your* Beleg, needs more from you. Has asked me to ask more of you. There is a great evil that walks this world. It destroys our parents and makes our creators weep with suffering and rage. It is an evil so great that it somehow creates more Tlana in the desert. It is an abhorrent twisting of magic and nature, a true abomination. It is a blight upon our world that must be eradicated. And it must be eradicated by you. You are the right hand of destiny, Trela. You are the Kriishan. But do not take my word for it..." Clerin breathed in deeply, one more time. She pulled the parchment from her pouch but had her eyes closed. She breathed in as much energy as she could, as much magic as she could muster. For a brief moment she was terrified. "Meksidpiarc! Taglochprefwaskintruld!"

There was a loud boom and a blinding flash. A stench of sulfur permeated the air. Clerin was not sure if it was the smell or the casting of the spell, but she felt extremely lightheaded. She bent over and held herself up with her hands on her knees. Then she noticed movement off to her right.

It was an inferno. The roar, the sight, the smell, there was no other single word to describe it but inferno. The fire sounded like wind shooting through a narrow tunnel at high speed. There was no crackle of wood, no hiss of steam, just the low rumbling of fire. It sounded to Clerin like a giant cat purring on top of a timpani drum. She was not sure if seeing Wil form in front of her, so long ago, tainted her idea of what a Yaven looked like. But the fire was so chaotic that it appeared to be boiling to her. It rolled over itself and twisted and turned. It was not a simple fire, tamed by the hearth. It was a bonfire that licked the ceiling but, curiously, gave off little heat.

As soon as it raised to its greatest height and girth, it quickly reduced itself. Legs split from the base, arms from its sides and a rough approximation of a head appeared, though the neck was so thick as to be non-existent. It bowed to Clerin, then bowed to Trela.

"Greetings, great ruler. Gorbanax sends congratulations through me for your just and powerful defeat of the one known as

Qizern. You may call me Taglo, as I am called in this realm of chaos. I knew Gorbanax before it changed into a Beleg and created you. I have been here many times before but never with so urgent a message. This message comes straight from Gorbanax, who was concerned that such a complicated understanding of events would become confused by the forced dispersal of communication required of direct exposure to derlians. This other derlian, the Fluen, is the communicator, is she not?" The flames roiled about the outline that suggested a derlian form. It held the attention such that it even made the simple act of listening difficult for Clerin.

"Yes, I communed with Gorbanax three days ago." She bowed to the Yaven, not knowing what else to do. A curtsy did not seem appropriate.

"What did your small mind perceive about the intent of Gorbanax?" The roar had faded somewhat and the sulfur smell had abated, but Clerin could not get over the constantly shifting image of conscious fire that stood before her.

"That there is an evil cult of derlians, known to us as the Cabal of Lochom, that commit Yavencide by trapping your kind into items in an attempt to affect chaos eternally. Gorbanax wishes this Cabal to be destroyed, all of their knowledge to be destroyed and all of the items to be destroyed. Gorbanax wishes a varied group of derlians to accomplish this task." Clerin tried to be as succinct as possible.

"Well done. You accomplish much with the faculties at your disposal. More than Gorbanax assumed, I may tell you that. The evil is real and must be destroyed. The knowledge must also be wiped from this world, no matter its form or location. The items are still a conundrum. Most often hopes are greater than reality, but another option would surely be sought, though if not found in a timely manner, then yes, the items will need to be destroyed also. We do not know the final configuration of the group to be successful. This realm swirls with chaos, which makes this difficult to foresee. We shall decide together what best options are available." The Yaven appeared to glance between Trela and Clerin. "And I? I am here as a guide. I am here as the grand assistant. I will ensure the success of this endeavor before I will leave this realm. I am at your disposal, but you are also at mine."

The Yaven's speech pattern was so different than Wil's that it took Clerin a bit aback. It was still somewhat emotionless, but there was a long-winded urgency behind it. The words seemed to ramble and tumble and wobble. Like a spinning top that was heavily unbalanced on one side.

"You have been to our realm many times?" Taglo nodded to Clerin. "I know this is not the time, but may I see your Menel?"

If fire could flare into a grin, this inferno did so. "You are quite correct that times like these should be filled with the urgency of the required deeds. However, I understand that our time here will take longer than wished no matter the amount of urgency. No offense is meant by me, but you have the weakest summoning voice I have ever heard whispered across the veil. If not for my intensive attentiveness and desire, I may not have even heard you. Have you actually seen a Menel before?"

"You are correct that I am not a summoner. I am not even much of a mage. But yes, I have seen a Fluen Yaven's Menel, owned by one who I knew as Wil." Clerin thought with all of her might, but was unable to think of more than Wil. The name was just so long and it had been quite a while since she had heard it.

Taglo turned to face Clerin. As the fire raged all around, a small dark circle appeared in the depths. The circle grew as it neared the surface of the fire and, just at the edge, the fire seemed to pull back around it. The amulet was quite large. In diameter it appeared to be about the same size as Wil's Menel. However, when Clerin looked at it askance, she was able to see the thickness. It was over two fingers thick. Less than double what she remembered Wil's was, but it was certainly thicker. The amulet itself appeared to be made out of a dark gray metal. There were three sections, one for each element besides fire, and each had a defining symbol embossed upon it. There was also the same curious carving on the surface that she had noticed on Wil's. The firelight danced over the dark gray, giving a hematite shine to the amulet. It was quite beautiful.

"That light carving, are those words?" Her face glowed softly in the firelight, purely intent on the item before her.

"Though the written Pyran Yaven language fades over time in our own realm due to the shifting environment, it is strangely permanent in this realm of chaos. Also, it is unable to be printed on a flat surface. See?" The Menel turned slightly and Clerin could see the carving swirl into the face of the amulet and keep twisting and turning. Much to her surprise, Trela appeared next to her and also peered in fascination at the Menel.

"What does it say?" Clerin assumed that if she asked something inappropriate, Taglo would inform her.

"This is part of the personalization aspect of the Menel. I prefer to write about what happened when I gather the elemental gel. I prefer to wait to collect the gel until something great has happened. This means I must usually wait until close to the time of return, the time of unsummoning. In fact, I have been returned so quickly before that I was unable to collect anything and, therefore, had a trip that did not benefit my Menel. I know Yavens who will collect their gel in the first moments of their summoning, just so they do not return without benefit. However, I like to write something of meaning to me upon my gel as it hardens into another layer of the Menel. Therefore, I prefer to wait." The Menel spun slowly so that Clerin could examine the sides and the back, as well as the front. The back looked like flat and unadorned gray metal.

"How thick is each gel layer? After it hardens." Trela's strange yellow eyes were wide open and staring intently at the fat spinning amulet.

"Less than the thickness of a derlian hair." Clerin's mind boggled at how many times Taglo must have been summoned. She could not even fathom the amount that Wil had accumulated, how could she wrap her mind around Taglo?

"You must have been here countless times." Clerin spoke softly.

"By definition that is incorrect. The Menel itself is a device used to keep track of the many times I have visited. I was amongst the pioneering firsts to allow ourselves to be summoned to your realm. It was I who perfected the notion of surrounding ourselves with the Void to protect against the constant Chaos that your realm is saturated with. At least for the Pyran Yavens. I have not met many other Yavens during my times here, however. Those few that I have met are almost exclusively Pyran, though I have had the pleasure of meeting two Gaen and three Luften Yavens amongst my many journeys." The Menel stopped spinning. "I have never met a Fluen Yaven. You must promise to summon the one that you knew before later if you are able and it is amenable to the one you call Wil."

Trela's cheek was close to Clerin's. They were both somewhat hunched over to be able to examine the disappearing Menel. As Clerin glanced over she noticed a glint in Trela's eye. There was a deep and wide intensity just behind the glint. Trela's cheeks were tight and she had a large, seemingly unconscious smile on her face. Clerin smiled in response. Trela was not done with adventure, not by a long shot. She was still too fascinated by the unknown, too intrigued by the curious nature of life. All Clerin had really needed to do, she realized, was to summon the Yaven. Her speeches had not made a dent in Trela's will to stay and govern. She may as well have been a braying donkey, she had been so ignored. But Taglo… Just the presence of Taglo had broken Trela's desire to stay cooped up in a castle. Though she had not agreed to accompany them yet, Clerin knew that it was only a matter of time. Trela would be unable to resist.

"I will certainly do what I can but, unfortunately, I am unable to recall the Yaven's full name." Clerin straightened herself as the Menel disappeared back into the central depths of Taglo.

"You must take me to the proposed initiates. I wish to speak with all members of the party and even the non-members of the party. I must convince the destiny of those that are willing but unnecessary just as much as I need to convince the destiny of those that are necessary but unwilling." The inferno shrunk a little and Taglo looked more derlian shaped and sized. "You realize that you both are necessary, do you not?"

"I am… I am needed here." Trela spoke softly towards the ground.

"I will not argue with truth. I will say this, however. You are needed elsewhere much more. Your destiny is greater than you give it credit right now. I have only seen one other whose destiny encompasses a larger sphere of influence. We do not have to converse now, we will do so later. Think about this decision. Do not make your decision based in haste or in reflex. Do not base your decision upon who you were an hour ago, or a second ago. Your decision must be based upon who you are now and who you wish to be in the future." Taglo turned towards Clerin. "You realize that you are necessary, do you not?"

"I do not feel that I am truly necessary. I do not bring any unique or powerful skills, but I will certainly give what aid I can. I humbly offer my services for this journey." Clerin bowed deeply.

"No." Taglo's deep voice echoed throughout the throne room.

"But…" She kept her head down. She could not, for the life of her, figure out why her assistance would be refused.

"Do not hide behind modesty or shyness or self-deprecation. These are confusing derlian traits to Yavens. Do not confuse the situation by negatively affirming yourself to this task. If you are to affirm yourself to the task, do so without subterfuge." The inferno flared up slightly. "Do you realize that you are necessary?"

Clerin stood straight and looked at Taglo head on. "Yes."

"Good. We are done with this location." Taglo turned towards the double doors. "Lead away."

Chapter 2

Croy somewhat missed the campaigning that encompassed the warpack life. The routine, the traveling, mostly the camaraderie. He certainly did not miss the violence, the tents, the bland camp food. It was with a mix of emotions that he began to fall into a new rhythm. After Trela's defeat of Qizern there was an entire week of celebration. There were pockets of festivities inside the castle they called the Blaze of Agoge. And there were pockets outside the Blaze's imposing walls, but inside Agoge's low walls. Even the perimeter, outside of the low walls, was surrounded by celebrating Pyrans. They danced in the streets. There were parades with Trela's army snaking through the winding roads. It was certainly a grand week, but Croy was happy when it was over.

The next several moons he spent relaxing. He did nothing useful, but nothing detrimental either. He did not go to the various festivals with Clerin, nor the wild mage's guild "meetings" with Feyazki. He did not attempt to create and modify the leviathan bureaucracy of government with Trela. He did not set up shop with Nochiel. He was re-learning how to live alone, without Ilana, but he did not want to forget her. Her memory could not be watered down with so much grog, but it could also not be swept from his mind with numbing daily drudgery. He wrote bad poems and attempted to learn how to draw, but he could never sketch her face as he remembered it. As it was before they had found the well.

Croy lived in the back of the Blaze, towards the towering volcano. His room was nested with many others, a sort of non-military barracks. His neighbors were bureaucrats and functionaries. They all assured him that what they did was essential to the smooth operation of the realm, but he was never really sure what that was. As far as he could tell, they merely kept track of things. There were many similar workers in Serif, even though he was never exactly sure of what they did there either. Croy was comfortable with the thought of thousands of unseen hands ensuring smooth operations of unknown tasks, and they made him feel more at home.

The building that Croy lived in was made of stacked and chinked rock. The masons in the Pyran realm did not seem to have the expertise, or maybe it was the time, that he had become accustomed to in the Gaen realm. Even the dry stack walls that penned the sheep on the hills outside of Serif fit together more tightly.

Young Gaens would be out there, sitting on the ground with chisels and small mallets, shaping each stone before it was gently placed into its final resting place. The wind was minor and he had yet to experience cold or snow here, so he thought that maybe it was just not a concern for the Pyrans. The building was low and had a finely thatched roof, which somewhat made up for the shoddy wall construction.

Croy's actual quarters were somewhat bare. He had a rope bed in one corner with a comfy, but scratchy, straw-stuffed mattress. During the hot nights, he would place his blanket under him for extra padding. There was a dilapidated dresser, a small writing desk with a simple wooden chair, and a tall, rickety wardrobe with a full-length mirror attached to the interior of one of the doors. His neighbors told him how lucky he was to have both a dresser and a wardrobe, even if the mirror was slightly warped and cloudy. The other luxury was that his floor was made out of sanded wooden planks, with a giant, somewhat ornate, circular rug centered in the room. Some in the same building had dirt floors and others would complain about the constant splinters they would get in their feet. There was a row of latrines a quick courtyard away and he had a chamber pot if he was pressed. Croy was a simple Gaen and did not mind the simple living. It was certainly more comfortable than the tents he had been living in during the campaign.

More than anything, he was getting bored and felt slightly ashamed at not having to contribute. Not having anything *to* contribute. Pyrans were, by nature, exceptional herders. It assisted greatly with their nomadic lifestyle and many Pyrans were at least partially pastoral. Here at Agoge, however, was the defined sedentary life of a huge city and the seat of government to boot. He finally decided that he should walk the perimeter of the city and see if there were any herds nearby that might need an additional shepherd. Something simple that would let his mind wander, but would let him feel that he was working and not just living off of Trela's largesse. *Yes*, he thought, *that is exactly what I need.*

Croy packed with purpose. He had enough hard meats, cheeses, and breads to survive for two days alone on the plateau. Of course, he only had enough water for one. He let himself wander through the Blaze, marveling at its many gardens. So much so, that it took almost two hours to get to the city proper. He immediately became lost within the maze of buildings and streets. He tried to look to the sun for guidance, but it was nearing noon. He was not sure which direction would lead him to where he wanted to go anyway. So he wandered through Agoge for another two hours. After chatting with several locals in the various markets, he got a direction that would lead to the closest thing that the plateau had to meadows. At last he had finally left the city.

It was afternoon but the sun was still high and beat down pleasantly upon Croy's brow. There was a small river that collected the snows from the mountains behind Agoge. It was along these banks that a bright greenway formed. Croy wandered for a while until he finally found a Pyran peasant.

"What do they call this river?" Croy walked up to the Pyran, who was carrying two pails of water. He had a curved wooden yoke that spread out from his shoulders like wings and had a rope at each end tied to the handle of a pail. It was a curious contraption. Croy instantly took to its usefulness and the ingenuity it took to build, but he knew that something that wide would never work in the narrow halls of Serif.

"Woadell. They call the stream Woadell." The Pyran looked quite young and had a heavy bead of sweat forming on his brow. His clothes were simple and somewhat ragged, with an open jerkin and a rope for a belt holding his too-high trousers in place. His hair was a dusty brown and the parts not pasted down with sweat looked quite disheveled. His eyes were a simple brown, but had a bit of sunburst in the center if you looked close enough.

"Do you know of any herders that need some assistance?" Croy was sure that he was bothering the Pyran but did not know by how much.

"My uncle is a herder, but I am not sure if he can afford such an extravagance." The Pyran began veering off towards some trees. Croy followed diligently, talking all the while.

"I am willing to work for very little. I just… do not have many skills to offer." Croy's hands wanted desperately to take one of the pails to be helpful, but his mind knew that would unbalance the yoke.

The Pyran grunted non-committedly. He seemed to speed up his pace a little. Croy hoped that it was just to set down his burden at the trees. Once they arrived, the Pyran dipped down until the pails rested upon the ground, then wormed out of the yoke.

"My name is Vectuley." He held forth a dirty hand. Croy gratefully took it and shook heartily.

"I am Croy Sie'tin, a Gaen from Serif." It may have been a bit overdone, but Croy wanted to get everything out at the beginning.

"You must be one of the foreigners that came with Queen Trela." He bowed a little which made Croy uncomfortable.

"Yes, I traveled with her and her mighty warpack, but you do not have to bow to me. Truly, I am no one of consequence." Croy smiled widely while Vectuley still looked nervous. "Would you like some lunch?"

Vectuley looked around, as if he were being spied by someone. His right hand unconsciously rubbed the back of his neck. His eyes, however, were quite wide and eager. As is often the case, hunger won out.

"That would be grand." Suddenly he smiled. It was a warm smile that lit up his face under the mask of dirt.

They sat for almost an hour, chatting and working on the food. Croy learned an amazing amount about Vectuley's family. His mother had died a long time ago, so he was basically raised by his father, Uldun. Though his father was generally kind and obviously loved him, Uldun did not understand children at all. To make matters worse, Uldun's brother, Ertyin, never had children of his own. The brothers did their best raising Vectuley and his two sisters, Wexin and Breawath. However, they were quite poor and, therefore, were constantly working. As soon as Vectuley was old enough to haul wood, he began his chores. He assumed he would become an old bachelor like his uncle, working from sunup to sundown. His sisters ran the homestead. Finally, now that their daily routines were running exceptionally smoothly, Wexin was old enough to get married and leave. And she appeared to be wanting just that. How could you begrudge her a little happiness after so many sun cycles of finger numbing work? You just couldn't. That did not make Vectuley any happier, though. Breawath was only a couple of cycles younger, and she did not have half the work ethic her older sister had. There was constant bouts of bad weather or bad luck that had kept them at the threshold of starvation, but Vectuley loved his family mightily and would do anything to help them thrive.

It was during this long conversation that Croy again interjected his desire to assist in herding. Except this time he did not mention payment of any kind. He knew that Trela would take care if his simple needs until the end of time if he wished it. He did not want to burden her with other families, of course. He could probably find hundreds of destitute but deserving families within a stone's throw of Agoge, but he felt he could not leave this family after hearing such a story. Besides, all he really wanted to do was wander with some sheep. Take them to pasture, then to the stream to drink, then back to their pens. It seemed like a win-win situation.

Croy followed Vectuley back to the tiny cabin to speak with his uncle. It was getting towards dark once they arrived. Though at first Ertyin was sore at Vectuley for arriving so late, once Croy offered his free services, he had a quick change of heart. They arranged to meet the next day.

Croy walked back to Agoge in the dying light. It was quite dark once he reached the edge of the city but, luckily for him, they would not seal the gates for another couple of hours. As he wandered through the city an odd feeling came over him. It was as if he were being watched. He shook it off.

It was not until the fifth day that he realized that someone truly was following him. The strange sensation of being watched, an ominous but vague foreboding feeling, dogged Croy each day. There was a low feeling of unease in all that he did. He found himself looking over his shoulder at random intervals, for no reason known to him. He had been herding the sheep back to pasture when he caught an image of a derlian behind a tree in the distance. It was a tall rowan tree, with a proud mane of leaves and only one thick trunk to hide behind. He ran towards it and yelled the whole time, watching the tree for further movement. Once he arrived, there was no one there. Croy had certainly not seen anyone leave. It was unnerving to both himself and the stunned sheep, but they quickly forgot about their screaming master and remembered to nibble at the grass. He was vexed but did not feel that he was going crazy. He *had* seen something; he knew it with every fiber of his being. Whether or not it was a derlian, he was no longer positive.

Since the sheep were successfully ignoring him, Croy sat down at the base of the rowan tree. He rooted through his pouches and discovered some lunch. He nibbled and stared at the sheep amongst the grass. They were nicely bunched up and docile. He ate his fill and then leaned heavily against the rough, but comfortable, bark. He did not want to, in fact every tiny fraction of him cried out against the folly of it, but somehow he fell asleep leaning on the tree. And he dreamed.

It started out as many of his normal dreams of late had started. Croy and Ilana were walking side by side in the close tunnels of Serif. They were always chatting and laughing. He never remembered any of their conversations, but was always reminded of the warm comfort of their being together. It was like a soothing balm cooling an itchy wound. It was calm and peaceful.

Then something happened to make Croy think this was not a normal dream. They were suddenly walking outside in a sandy desert. It was still cool about them since they were walking through a colonnade of Vijen trees, except they were shaded by green instead of golden boughs. The tunnel effect of the trees made the transition from cave to desert comforting. The wind began to softly blow through the leaves. There was a hint of jasmine and sage in the air. The two starkly contrasting scents somehow melded pleasantly. The wind was blowing from behind. It began to pick up speed and veracity. Croy turned to Ilana, to laugh about the odd wind, but she was no longer smiling. She looked worried, with her brow furrowed in that cute way that made her nose crinkle at the top. She walked over to a Vijen and pulled a large dagger out of its trunk. Croy was shocked that he had not noticed it before she touched it. The dagger was serpentine shaped and had blood coating the point that had been embedded in the tree. Blood shot out of the tree trunk and a great howl crashed forth. The wind began to whip around mightily, making it difficult to stand. Croy suddenly realized that all of the Vijen trees had curved serpentine daggers sticking out of them.

"Remove the daggers!" Ilana's voice was barely perceptible over the howling wind and howling tree. "Help me, you must help me remove the daggers!"

Croy began to move frantically, removing as many daggers as he could. At first he yanked them out and tossed them to the ground, grabbing another an instant later. After several of them, however, he noticed that they did not stay on the ground. He was not positive that they were being reinserted in the trees, but they were certainly vanishing while he was not looking. He switched his tactic and began to hold as many daggers as he could in his left arm, while removing more of them with his right. At first he had tried to dodge the spurting blood after removing a dagger, but soon he was covered anyway. His hand began to get slippery and it became more and more difficult to dislodge the daggers. The howling was deafening.

"Faster, we must remove them all!" Ilana had a large bunch of daggers in her left hand as well.

Croy was not sure if speed was the answer. What he felt he needed was a place to put the daggers. Then he could use both hands to remove them. Just then he noticed a large hole in the ground at the end of the colonnade. It was not very large in circumference, but it was dark, which appeared to indicate depth. He yelled with excitement but the sound was torn from him by the frenzied wind. He dislodged another dagger and struggled to run towards the hole. Though he had not thought it possible, the wind picked up velocity and pressure. Suddenly it was an exhausting struggle just to place one foot in front of another. He kept his head down, squinting through the windborne dust, and clutched his sharp and dangerous cargo to his chest with both hands. Placing one foot in front of the other. It was agonizing.

When he looked up, Ilana was standing at the hole, tossing her daggers in, one by one. A small dark cloud shot up out of the hole each time that she dropped one in. He struggled forwards and ducked his head again.

Croy felt an arm on his, tugging lightly enough not to dislodge any of the daggers, but hard enough to help him against the wind. He looked into Ilana's face. Her freckles and green eyes stopped all sound. The wind still pushed on him, he could feel it, but it no longer howled. She smiled at him, at his struggles.

"It will be okay. You are almost there, my love." She tugged lightly on his arm again.

Croy finally arrived at the hole. He began tossing the daggers in as quickly as he could. Ilana lightly touched his arm.

"Not so fast. One at a time." She was so calm and serene that it soothed Croy just to hear her. In the back of his mind, he thought it odd that he was covered in blood but she was not stained at all. She appeared untouchable, pure.

For every dagger dropped there was a jet of smoke or mist, Croy could not tell which, that shot forth from the depths of the hole. It was as if the daggers were vaporized, sublimated straight to a gaseous state. As each dagger was consumed, the wind pushed a little less. The silence appeared to lengthen time, but Croy felt that the feeling was probably an illusion. Finally he had thrown down his last one.

"There, was that so hard?" Ilana smiled and kissed him on the cheek.

Croy laughed a little at that, it all seemed so calm. Then he turned back to look at the colonnade. The trees were on fire. The sound came rushing back in. The screaming began anew. He was shaken awake.

A wild-maned derlian had his face near Croy's. The derlian's hands gripped his shoulders like iron vices. There was a slice of scar tissue through the derlian's left eyebrow and the nose looked like it had been broken before. Croy thought that, vaguely, in the distance, he should recognize this creature that had pulled him from the depths of dream.

"Croy. Croy! Wake up!" A sudden realization came with the voice.

"Haswyxe? What are you doing here?" Croy shrugged the vices from him.

"You were screaming bloody murder, I had to do something. Are you all right?" He sat back on his haunches.

"No, I mean here." Croy pointed down to the ground below him. "Why are you away from Agoge? What are the odds that you would be in this same field?"

"I... I have been shadowing you, Croy." His face scrunched up in an emotion. Maybe shame?

"Why? I don't understand..." Croy wanted to stand, the bark of the Rowan tree was no longer as comfortable as it had once been. Haswyxe, however, was too close for him to be able to stand comfortably.

"You shouldn't go out alone like this, Croy. I know you like sheep and all, but... It could be dangerous." The emotion was not shame. It was more properly sheepish.

"But I..." Croy was swiftly interrupted.

"I owe you my life, Croy. I know what happened in that tent with Nochiel. I cannot let anything happen to you while I am still in your debt." Now the shame appeared in his countenance.

"Gaens do not have ghulzans." Croy did not know what else to say.

"Neither do Luftens. And yet... the debt is here all the same." He stood and stepped back. This allowed Croy to rise as well.

"How long have you been following me?" Croy dusted himself off as best he could.

"For several days now. Maybe... five?" Haswyxe's eyes rolled upwards as he thought. "I was wandering through the outskirts of Agoge, looking for... well, I never found what I was looking for. And suddenly there you were, wandering through the western gate as if you didn't have a care in the world. I skulked around you, then decided to follow you home. You do not pay very close attention to your surroundings, do you?"

"It had suddenly gotten dark that night and I had a lot on my mind." Croy tried to think up an excuse. That was the best he had.

"Oh, not just that night. There were times during the day that I would see how close I could get to you before you noticed. There were times that I could have reached out and tweaked your ear." Here he smiled wide and warmly. "That is what started it, your obvious inattention. I thought that you might need some extra protection. It soon became obvious to me, however, that no one wants to harm you. Though you notice little, others do not notice you at all. Your benign stature and benevolent face allow you to walk through the streets of Agoge as if you were invisible. And you are a Gaen! Even out here, in the middle of nowhere, others do not look upon you as a dangerous stranger. You are like a deer bounding through the forest." His smiled turned into a small frown briefly. "I still could not let you wander alone, however. Even though I knew, in my heart, that there were none who wished you ill, I worried about an accident. Maybe you would fall down a cliff, or get attacked by an animal, or even get mugged by someone not realizing that you have nothing, or have a bad dream and scream until you draw a crowd of passersby."

"I guess I cannot argue the last point." Croy looked around in case there really was a crowd, just out of vision.

"Do you dream a lot?" His smile returned easily.

"That depends upon what you mean by dream. I have many simple dreams, sometimes more than one a night." Croy found himself unconsciously nodding. "I look forward to those, truly.

There is a simple passivistic beauty to them. But I also have deeper dreams. Dreams that, while in them and while unable to consciously change them, I do have this realization that they are different. I know, somewhere in the back of my mind, that *this* dream is not normal. It brings with it a feeling of foreboding, of nervousness. Something about it makes me think I have dreamt it before, even though that is rarely the case. It is a vague feeling that I almost know what is about to happen. Almost. But that I am unable to veer out of the way, even if I were to actually know. I pull on the reins but my mount will not obey me. It is all very disconcerting. I guess it could be likened to falling off a cliff. You see the ground approaching, but try as you might, you are unable to avoid it. Except that I cannot actually see the ground, I can only feel its high velocity approach."

"But they mean something, right? That's the difference. You are given an edge over a derlian who does not dream as you do." His smile was somewhat infectious.

"They are rarely that simple, however. When I awake, it is mostly to confusion." Croy gave a warm smile back to Haswyxe. "Don't get me wrong, there are times when it is obvious. Times when I feel I am being shown something. Something external and unbeknownst to me before. Something that can be proven to come from somewhere else, from outside of me." Croy glanced down, then back up again. "But most of the time it is just confusing. Then I wonder, was that a normal dream? If I am unable to interpret them, if I do not understand what they are trying to tell me, then maybe they were not telling me anything at all. Maybe it was just the feeling that confused me, making me think the dream was more than it was. Maybe my dreams do not mean anything, but I confuse the feeling of them and make up an interpretation that explains them as something more."

"What was your most prophetic dream? Which dream had the most information that was 'from outside of you'?" They began to walk towards the wandering sheep. Croy always enjoyed walking and talking.

"Well… I dreamed of the location of the Fluen Temple." He had not wanted to say that one out loud, but it was the most specific one he had ever had in his life.

"I had thought Trela knew where the Temple was?!" Haswyxe's jaw dropped and he stopped in his tracks. They were still in the shade of the rowan.

"She had no clue. Just a solid belief in her own destiny." Croy's grin split his face. He knew he would regret slipping her secret, but watching Haswyxe's response was incredibly enjoyable. "You mustn't tell anyone, however."

"Then how do I know it's true?" His eyes narrowed.

"I would not lie about that, but... Ask Clerin or Feyazki. They also know." Croy started them walking towards the sheep again.

"I trust you, but I just might ask one of them." Haswyxe looked pensive for a moment. "You see, how can you not trust your feeling during your dreams? My dreams do not show me anything, certainly not something as amazing as the location of a Beleg's temple. Wow."

"It's nothing special." Croy put his hand up to ward off Haswyxe's immediate rebuttal. "Maybe it is, but I have never trained for it. I did not try to gain the ability or spend the effort to practice a skill. It just happens to me." It was Croy's turn to look pensive. "I do not feel special."

And he didn't. Croy had always felt average and small. Mundane and mediocre. A quiet voice in a clamoring concert hall. More than anything, he was just trying to keep up. Trying not to get hurt or killed. Oh sure, he tried his best at everything he did, but he never really excelled at anything. He had no indispensable skills, no great contributions of strategy, nothing that anyone else in Trela's warpack could not have provided. He was only part of her inner circle because he had found her. So long ago it seemed. He had stumbled across her and, of course, Synde, and that had changed his life. That had been that. It was always happenstance, or maybe Trela was right and it was destiny, but it was something unlooked for, unknown, and unwanted. Croy had not yearned for great things. He had not strived for a life of wide travels and fantastic adventure. He had only wanted a simple existence with the love of his life. And even that had been taken from him. More than not feeling special, which was a true statement if he had ever thought one, he did not want to be special. Whatever glamour had originally shone on Croy's adventures was gone. He wanted nothing to do with special.

"I do not feel special," he said quietly once more for emphasis. Like most things, however, it did him no good. It only reinforced what he already thought about himself. It certainly did not change the way the world viewed him, or even Haswyxe, for that matter. "I'm just glad I'm here." Croy had meant being there, with the sheep, having a life as close to his old one at Serif that he could. Quiet and uncomplicated, at least when he wasn't dreaming. But Haswyxe misunderstood him.

"Agreed. I'm glad I was chosen to escort Clerin to the well. So much has happened since then. Not all of it great, mind you, but all of it amazing, truly amazing. I've seen things beyond my imagination, and for that I am grateful." Haswyxe looked almost wistful.

"You know, I've never heard. How *were* you chosen?"

"Well, did I ever tell you how I met Malghain?"

"No, never."

"Well, I met him in a dirty tavern, down in the mud at the base of a helioarc tree. I was a mercenary for hire then, but had never spoken to anyone in the Royal Branch at all, certainly not to someone like Queen Vanelia or King Hulgert. In the Luften realm, if you tie a red ribbon around the hilt of your sword, you're indicating that you're for hire, so he could tell I was a mercenary because I was advertising. In those days I was always advertising, taking small bodyguard jobs to pay for my humble abode and my mead. So he sits down next to me and buys me a goblet of mead and we start chatting, just two warriors trading stories. We were well into our cups when we heard someone start yelling. There was a huge Luften, similar in size to Torpalin, and he was pulling on the arm of a tiny slip of a thing, and she was screaming her head off. Both of us jump up. There's something in me that boils when a lady screams like that, and I suppose that's in Malghain as well. She was surely not going to get raped there, out in the open, but she screamed as if she thought that was where she was going to end up. She didn't want to leave with that Luften, didn't want to go to any secondary location. I've got no patience for even the thought of rape. First, there's nothing sexier than consent. Am I right? You know I'm right. Second, it is, pure and simple, the torture of an innocent. So we walk right over there and it seems he has a bunch of friends. There's about eight of them around us, all standing and looking menacing. She's stopped yelling, but he still has her by the arm and her eyes are wide and terrified. In my mind, there was no way to kill them all before they get to us, or at least hurt her. I hadn't known just how dangerous Malghain was at the time and I was feeling a little drunk and off my game. So, instead of pulling my sword and getting us all killed, I walked straight up to the huge Luften, jumped on his chest, grappled his head and bit his ear off. I land in front of him, look up to the ceiling, and spit the bloody thing as far up as it'll go. I've got blood down the front of me, the huge Luften is screaming and clutching himself, and the lady escapes past us. Everyone pulls their weapons and starts growling. Malghain has two swords, a regular sized one in his right hand and a short one in his left, and he slashes the two Luftens between us and the exit quicker than a snake, and we run as fast as we can out the door. We don't stop running for at least ten full minutes. I had no idea where we were at the end of it, panting like a race dog and half doubled over. We never did see the lady on the way out, though I must say I wasn't looking sideways. Whew!" He seemed out of breath just retelling the story.

"So Malghain asks me how I thought of that so quickly, and I told him I don't think while I fight. He laughed his head off at that. He tells me that he's been hired by the Queen and he needs some trustworthy warriors that don't think while they're fighting. And so he got me the best job I'd ever had. Not always steady work, but the pay was quite good. We worked together for a couple of sun cycles before Clerin arrived. I have to tell you, after seeing countless fights and participating in many of them, there is no warrior that is more dangerous than Malghain. None that I have ever seen. I hate to admit it, but I think it's because he thinks while he fights." He had a huge grin on his scarred face when he said that last sentence.

"That fight sounded... ugly." Croy did not mean that he thought what Haswyxe did was ugly. On the contrary, it could have been considered brave at best and foolhardy at worst, but not ugly. Doing nothing would have been ugly. He had meant that it was terrible, that it was a rough spot to be put in, that the situation itself was ugly. But Haswyxe misinterpreted Croy's poor choice of words.

"Fighting, in its purest form, *is* ugly. If you're in a true knock-down, drag-out fight, no weapons, no forethought, no strategy; if you are trapped away from your friends, surrounded and outnumbered, what can you do besides play dirty? There's no honor in death. No, you must show your enemy that you are willing to go farther, dig deeper, scratch, bite, spit, tear, aim for the balls and the eyes, gouge, and maim. You must, in essence, show them that you are uglier than they are. Most derlians don't want to be thought of as ugly, don't want to *be* ugly. It's instinctual. It's why civilization exists. But I've never been afraid to use it. Ugliness is my asset. This is where Malghain and I differ."

"So, if you have to be ugly to cut to the quick, you're saying that beautiful derlians are not dangerous?" Croy was a little confused but happy that Haswyxe had not taken offence.

"No, no, you misunderstand. Gyllhelon is one of the most dangerous derlians I've ever met. You just don't realize it because Malghain is so dangerous and I'm so ugly and she gets forgotten in the shuffle. It is precisely because she is so beautiful that she is so dangerous. Some beautiful derlians decide that their lives should be easy and they parade around for anyone who will keep them in comfort. Not Gyllhelon. She truly reviles those types of derlians. She worked hard, every day, for all of her youth, through all of her practice and her training, to become dangerous. She works hard straight through to this day to remain dangerous. She just happened to be born beautiful. And she is dangerous enough to stay beautiful." Haswyxe was smiling throughout his description of her. "Derlians naturally assume she is as useless as an ornament, a work of art to be displayed to the world. The Luften realm can be quite cruel when it comes to beauty. It's often joked to be the inverse of a derlian's intelligence. I'm not sure how it is in the Gaen realm." He looked down and thought for a moment before continuing. "Her dedication to her craft is unparalleled. And I truly believe her drive is so phenomenal exactly because no one expects it of her. It's that lack of expectation that fuels her desire to prove them wrong. I'm not sure if it angers her, because she always seems to be in a good mood even when everything is falling apart, but it certainly fuels her."

"And what fuels Malghain?"

"I'm not sure… But if Gyllhelon was born beautiful, Malghain was born dangerous." Haswyxe gave a deep throated chuckle. "Maybe he doesn't need fuel, he just *is*."

The daily work was fantastic. It was just what Croy needed. He did not dream again for some time and the herding gave him plenty of time to relax and think of Ilana. He had to wake quite early, just before the sun. Then he would wind his way through sleepy Agoge and escape its boundary walls to the sweet-smelling countryside. Sometimes he would run into Vectuley or Uldun, but mostly he would nod at Ertyin as they passed each other at the pens. Croy would gather up his allotment of sheep and head down to the Woadell. First drink, then graze. Ertyin would gather up the rest of the sheep and head towards the far pasture. First graze, then drink. It was not ideal, keeping the sheep on opposite schedules and differing pastures, but it certainly made splitting the chores, and the sheep, simple. After the day had ended, Croy would bring them back and pen them in. It was a simple and relaxing routine.

There were certainly times that Croy wished he had a horse or, better yet, a dog to assist him. Maybe it was the fact that Croy worked for free, but Ertyin always took the larger group of sheep. He may have taken the unruly ones as well. There were a couple of wanderers that you had to keep your eye on in Croy's group, but there were not any runners.

Haswyxe would often openly accompany Croy on his rounds. He refused to do any "farm work," as he called it, but would often help out if Croy needed. Most of his time was spent with his short sword, spinning in the sun, practicing. Sometimes he would set up a small target to practice his aim with his bow. And some of the time was spent just chatting with Croy. But he gave Croy his space, as much as was desired. There were days where Croy did not even see Haswyxe, but thought he could feel a presence. Mostly he assumed that feeling was Haswyxe skulking out of sight, but sometimes he merely hoped it was.

There was an odd disconcerting feeling that Croy would sometimes get. A small itch of something in the back of his mind. Not just of being watched, but of being studied. As if detailed and meticulous notes were being taken about him. As if his actions were weighed and even his non-actions were being judged. He would pick himself up and wander out in the open when he got that feeling. Giving as little cover to the culprit as he could. But he never saw anyone. Not even Haswyxe. So he made soothing assumptions about his imagination running wild now that he was not surrounded by the bustle of the warpack. The quietness and solitude that he had consciously sought out were playing tricks on his mind. He had always been prone to flights of fancy. And besides, it was probably just Haswyxe keeping an eye on him. These were feelings that happened alone, not around others. He told himself that he was just being paranoid. Of course, earlier, when he felt that he was being followed by Haswyxe, he was actually being followed—there had been no paranoia that time.

Several more weeks passed. He was enjoying the work and was fully appreciated by Vectuley's family. They offered him meals and had even offered a place for him to sleep if he did not want to travel all the way back to Agoge at night. Since his room and meal stipend were provided by Trela, however, he did not need to impose upon their hospitality. Besides, he quite enjoyed his walks to and from the countryside.

It was a typical day. Haswyxe arrived after noon and they chatted amiably while eating lunch. Croy had taken to nibbling on food throughout the day, so he could easily picnic whenever anyone showed up. As they talked he noticed Haswyxe squinting at something up in the sky. Croy also squinted. There was certainly a black dot floating around up there, but Croy could not make out what it was.

"What type of bird do you think that is?" Croy had spoken more to break the uneasiness rather than any real curiosity.

"That is no bird. See how it shifts from forward momentum to sideways without turning? Birds don't do that." Haswyxe had put down his chunk of bread.

"Hummingbirds do." Right as he said it, Croy cringed. It just popped out.

"Look how far away that is. That is no hummingbird." Haswyxe cocked an eyebrow at Croy.

"Of course not, sorry. What do you think it is?" As he spoke he began to get a small tingling feeling.

"I'll tell you what I'm worried it is." Haswyxe stood up.

"It is definitely a mage." The tingling turned into a kind of sick feeling. Then he thought he heard something. It was very quiet, but it sounded like someone calling his name. Croy stood as well.

"Nufintotarc! Feyazki?" He had meant to say it all quietly, but Haswyxe obviously heard it.

"Ah, Croy, I have been looking for you. Where are you?" Feyazki's voice came strong through the *whisper* after Croy's simple spell.

"It's Feyazki, don't worry." Croy made a small downward motion with his hand.

"Are you sure it's him? What if it is a trap?" Haswyxe had a hand on the hilt of his sword.

"Who else could it be? Besides, it sounds like his voice." Croy began waving both his hands in the air and walking towards the center of the pasture. He watched the dot grow larger. It did not take long for Feyazki to find them and land once he had a lock on Croy.

"Haswyxe? Good to see you." The name was posed as a question, as if Feyazki were wondering why he should be with Croy. The statement was lively and full of warmth, however. Two old friends meeting unexpectedly. They shook hands vigorously, then Feyazki turned towards Croy.

"What are you doing out here? I figured you would be enjoying the comforts of Agoge." He smiled white and toothy. It was infectious.

"I am herding sheep." Croy swept his hand in a wide arc to encompass his flock. It was a bit of a grand gesture, as if he were protecting priceless works of art.

"Yes, that sounds like you." Somehow his grin got larger.

Feyazki glanced around, as if looking for a place to sit down. Finding none, he clasped his hands behind his back. He glanced once more at Haswyxe before turning towards Croy.

"I have a friend in the mage's guild here who would like to speak with you." His chest deflated a little, as if he had been holding his breath.

"About what?" Croy was stunned that someone even knew of him, let alone wanted to speak with him.

"About the well. You know about that more than anyone. There has not been a derlian to live amongst the village and still be able to leave. At least not within Pyran memory. Any knowledge that the Pyrans do have of the well is spotty at best and rumored to be mere rumors." Feyazki held up his hand to ward off any of Croy's oncoming protestations. "I understand you may not wish to divulge anything. However, I lost a bet and made a promise that you would at least hear the mage out."

"Wait, you lost a bet and I have to do something?" Actually, Croy had been about to agree. There was no reason not to speak about what little he knew of the well and its surrounding village. His only concern had been that his knowledge was too limited to be of much use. That was until Feyazki's last sentence.

"You just have to speak with her. Please, as a favor to me." Feyazki's smile seemed just as sincere as it did a moment ago. The smile had not changed at all. Croy's attitude about it is what had changed.

"I don't know..." Croy was not really annoyed, but did not want to acquiesce too quickly. Luckily he was interrupted by Haswyxe.

"Did Croy show you where the Temple of Air was?" It just blurted out of him, almost violently. If it had consisted of more corporeal ingredients, it would have been vomit.

"Well..." Feyazki glanced sideways at Croy. Since Croy did not want Haswyxe to think that he was leading Feyazki, he just crossed his arms and stared silently back. Hard. "Truthfully, yes. He said that he had dreamed it. Knew where it was even though it was hidden, knew the way through the caverns and everything." Feyazki barely paused. "Why do you ask?"

Haswyxe stared at both of them for a long minute. "Just making sure. Carry on."

"Please. As a favor." Feyazki shook off Haswyxe's bizarre interruption and focused back on Croy.

"Well, I suppose. I cannot stay mad for long over something so simple." Once he said it, he realized it was true. He was glad that it was true, but for some reason he did not want to let Feyazki off that easily. "But you owe me one."

"Duly noted." He unclasped his hands and brought them forward. "I assume you will need to finish with the sheep today. What would be your earliest convenience?"

Croy had not thought Feyazki would take that so simply. He had helped him so much during the warpack campaign. Gave him encouragement and advice in spell casting and magic in general. He was proud to call Feyazki his friend. Croy suddenly felt ashamed at not agreeing to help him out immediately.

"Three days from now." Croy had no idea why he chose that amount of time, but he had said it with such deliberation that he felt he could not change it. Feyazki, sincere grin still intact, merely nodded.

"You see Croy, you are special." Haswyxe laughed heartily.

The three days passed quickly. Croy had arranged to hand over his shepherding duties to Vectuley while he was gone. Ertyin probably could have handled it all by himself for one day, he was certainly used to it, but it was decided that it was best to keep the sheep on the same schedule. Besides, as Croy promised, it would only be for one day.

Feyazki came to Croy's small apartment to pick him up. He was a little early, so they had some time to waste. He walked around the room examining everything in view. This only took a few moments.

"You should really think about joining the mage's guild here. The quarters, even for apprentices, are much more roomy and comfy. For one of your stature and skill, they would probably provide a room twice this size." He raised his eyebrows invitingly.

"I like the freedom here. I can come and go as I please." Croy sat on the edge of his bed, leaving the chair for Feyazki.

"There is not a lot of responsibility or onus involved, really. Think of it more as a fraternity or club." Feyazki stayed standing. "Plus, there would be plenty of time for practicing your skills. They have sparring arenas, study halls, meditation centers, herbal classes, and healing. You would have plenty of time to practice your healing."

The talk of practice and of healing made Croy think of Nochiel. He immediately saw her face framed with her short wavy brown hair. The way she would stomp around the medic tent. Her voice... He tried not to think about her. Ever since the situation with Haswyxe, something had become lost between them. Once they were at Agoge she had tried to reconcile. She had offered him a position at her practice; she had become quite famous as a healer. The greatest healer in all of Trela's mythical warpack. Her practice would be busy, he was sure. And she had sounded earnest in her offer. It was an olive branch of peace that she offered, as well as a paid position. He had felt unable to take it, however. He did not think he could stand next to her all day long and remember what had transpired that day. She had told him he would have to choose ten derlians to let die if he wanted to save Haswyxe. He had dodged the responsibility by pretending that he did not compromise his capabilities by saving a friend. But he *was* slower. When he was honest with himself, he admitted that he had been compromised, at least a little bit. She had not spoken kindly to him for over two moons after that. Yes, something had certainly broken between them. He felt that he could not learn any more healing skills under a different mage, but he did not think he could learn from her anymore either. Not while there was this rift. It had made him stop healing, which was sad really, his own self-imposed exile. Healing had been the only branch of magic that he had shown true promise with. He knew that it was his decision, his fault, for she had attempted to reconcile. But there he was, stuck. He did not want to learn from another and could not learn from her. The impasse in himself was a sore spot, like a bruise, that he might push on while alone and bored, but was quick to annoyance if another attempted to do the same.

"I do not heal anymore." It was a terse statement that sounded more vitriolic than he intended. At least it had the effect of making Feyazki quit the subject.

"Just a suggestion…" Feyazki looked slightly offended. And he was quite difficult to offend. It made the situation more shameful since Croy's annoyance was with himself, not really with Nochiel and certainly not with Feyazki.

"I apologize. Nothing to do with you." Croy motioned for the exit. If he was going to embarrass himself, he may as well do it on the road.

They walked through the maze of buildings while Croy racked his brain to think of something light and airy to speak about. Not something as obvious as the weather, but something to switch the subject up. They had reached an exterior garden courtyard before an idea popped into his head.

"How is Clerin doing?" It seemed like an innocent question when it entered into his mind.

"I'm not sure." Something passed over Feyazki's face but it was gone before Croy could put his finger on what it was. "Last I heard she was going to festivals with some Pyran named Yihrum."

Feyazki had stayed passive and in control during the sentence, but Croy realized that it bothered him quite a bit. It was a shame. Of all the members of Trela's inner circle that Croy had thought would make a good pair, it was Clerin and Feyazki. It was the way they would huddle together and talk. The way their faces lit up in each other's company. The way they talked about the other when they weren't around. It made sense. It had seemed natural. And, to be honest, Croy had assumed that something had already happened. But maybe not. He would have to pay more attention to the situation.

"We should be going. Mekkinderclo!" The force of Feyazki's magic, even the small and mundane spells, always shocked Croy. He could fly himself now, though he rarely did, and he had flown with several other mages. Even if the same power level was being cast, there was a different feeling with Feyazki. It made Croy think of water exiting a pipe. If the valve were set to a trickle, like a low-level spell, then the same amount of water would come out of the pipe no matter the size of the reservoir behind it. There should be no way to "feel" the size of the potential behind it. But that was what magic from Feyazki made him think of. That no matter how meager the trickle, there was a giant ocean sitting behind that pipe. Just waiting to burst forth. It gave Croy the tingles.

They flew briefly, both in distance and in time, but it would have taken quite a while to navigate the maze of buildings and paths if they had walked. Soon they were in front of an impressive stone facade. They were in another open-air courtyard, facing the Pyran mage's guild hall. Though the portcullis was small compared to a true keep's, the double doors were impressive. And the building itself was quite large for something housed within the Blaze. There were two small turrets in the front that protruded from the otherwise flat building face. They had rounded windows placed at odd intervals of elevation. *Must be stairs*, thought Croy. The other windows, those in the main stolid section, were large and rectangular, with thin bars crisscrossing in front of them.

Feyazki walked towards the doors which had giant brass lion heads with heavy rings held in their mouths for the knockers. He lifted one and crashed it down on its striker plate several times. The sound, though a bit hollow, filled the air around them. Croy was staring at the massive iron hinges as the door swung open. They worked so silently that he wondered how often they were oiled.

There, before them, stood a young mage in flowing white robes. She had bright eyes and a quick smile, but she buried them downwards quickly as she recognized Feyazki. Croy knew that supplication was supposed to be a symbol of respect in the Pyran realm, but he had never really gotten the hang of it. Feyazki, for his part, did not appear to notice.

"You are expected." The neophyte spoke into the floor.

"I know the way." Feyazki waved a hand towards another young mage dressed in bright white who had been walking towards them.

Croy had to pump his little legs to keep up with Feyazki. It was not usual that Feyazki strode with such purpose, and it made Croy slightly frustrated to have to keep up. They vanished from the large two-story hall into a much smaller hallway. Thankfully, the close walls seemed to slow Feyazki a little. They turned this way and that. Went up some stairs and down others. Croy had begun with a mind to keep track of the way out but gave up after a while. By the end of their quick journey he was not even sure which direction the volcano lay. They halted in front of a nondescript door.

"I am not sure if Ryshial will be alone or not. She is the one that you will have to speak with. If there are others there that you do not feel comfortable with, just let me know and we can clear the room if you like." Feyazki was smiling sheepishly.

Croy had decided that there was no reason to be shy. He owed Feyazki far more than a simple storytelling. He was not even sure why he had been reluctant in the beginning.

"It is fine, really. The story will not take long to tell." Croy nodded towards the door.

Feyazki opened the door without knocking. The room was quite large compared to the tiny door in the tiny hallway. There were many chairs surrounding a wide circular table, but only one was occupied. The lady sitting down smiled up at them. Her smile was wide and genuine, and it reminded Croy slightly of Clerin's. She had brown flowing hair with shades of chestnut in it. Her eyes were drawn back, somewhat almond shaped. She had long fingers and straight shoulders. Her brown eyes sparkled with delight as they entered, as if she had been waiting eagerly for them. And maybe she had. There were three full glasses of grog arranged around her.

"I am so pleased that you have arrived." Her voice was light and lilting. Since she kept glancing between them, Croy could not figure if she was speaking to him or Feyazki. He naturally assumed Feyazki.

They walked towards her end of the table, Feyazki from clockwise and Croy from counter. He was not sure why he had not just followed Feyazki, but the glasses were set up opposite each other. She held her hand out to Feyazki, fingers loosely held down with her knuckles towards him. He kissed the top of her hand gently.

"Ryshial, you look as radiant as ever." He had one eyebrow cocked upwards. "May I introduce to you Croy Sie'tin, the Gaen dreamer." For some reason, Croy felt a little shy at the title bestowed upon him.

"I have heard so much about you." She held her hand up to him as well, so he kissed the spot that Feyazki had. They sat down in front of their glasses. "I cannot believe that I am sitting with someone who has visited the well and returned to tell the tale."

"Well… Feyazki has visited the well also." He felt a little unprepared. He had heard nothing about her until he had arrived at her door. He was glad that the room was not full of Pyrans, though.

"Barely." Feyazki put up his palm.

"Trust me, I have already picked that bone clean." She laughed liltingly. "You traveled with the village? You spoke with the guardian of the well?" She hid herself behind her glass, letting the empty air draw Croy out.

"Well, yes. My wife Ilana and I had gotten lost in the desert. She was deathly ill, you see. It got to the point that I did not think she had another day's worth of travel in her…" Croy took a sip of his grog. The others were leaned back in their chairs, settling in for the tale. "We came upon the well by chance, really. We were very tired and, as I said, Ilana was sick. So I gave her some water and then I tried to heal her, but just ended up passing out. When we awoke, the guardian of the well, his name is Lemniscate, was standing over us. At first he would not explain the well…"

Croy told as much as he could remember. Ryshial listened leisurely and attentively without a word of interruption. If he stopped for too long, she would smile and nod at him until he started back up. It took longer than he had thought it would, but he did not want to leave anything out. He finally finished his tale.

"You said that Lemniscate was a Fluen Yaven and that he knew Lembin before our world was created, correct?" Croy nodded slowly. "You also mentioned that he 'begged' for the well?" Croy nodded more slowly. "Did you get the impression that Lemniscate directly procured the well from the Belegs?"

Ryshial had the most amazing memory for detail that Croy had ever witnessed. Each sentence that he had originally spoken during his uninterrupted telling was brought back by her to be scrutinized. She delved into and explored each word like a deep and dark cave. She made him rethink what he had said, and if he said it even slightly different the second time around, or the fourth time around, she would remind him of his earlier wording. She would ask why it had changed. She would dig and dig to bring a more clear light to the tiny underground world of his story. She was relentless. Each detail did interest her, and she indeed pulled any hidden truth from the shadows that she could find, but it was Lemniscate that truly fascinated her. Ryshial would ask things that Croy had not even noticed, and had a difficult time remembering, about his conversations with Lemniscate. Like facial expressions. She was intently focused on what Croy thought Lemniscate was thinking while they were discussing themes such as time. And if Croy had no immediate opinion, which was often the case, she would ask more and more about any tiny detail that he remembered that she might be able to use to reconstruct what Lemniscate might have been thinking. It was exhausting. By the end of it, Croy had come back around to thinking that Feyazki owed him big. It had not been a quick and friendly storytelling. It had been friendly, as long as Croy appeared to be cooperating and thinking hard about Ryshial's questions. But as he flagged under the crushing fatigue of repetition, she became a little more agitated. There were times that Feyazki would speak up in Croy's defense, telling her that no one could remember that much detail. But for most of the conversation he was silent. He looked pained and embarrassed whenever Croy would plead with him silently, with large wet eyes and small hand gestures, but he did not always come to the rescue. That was what annoyed Croy the most.

It did finally come to an end, however. Ryshial eagerly thanked him for his time and effort, with that boundless energy that she seemed to own. Feyazki breathed heavily and stood, waiting for Croy. It took Croy a little while to stand, even though he wanted nothing more than to leave. He was utterly fatigued. He finished his third cup of grog—she had started to ration it after he had finished off his first—and slowly got to his feet. She thanked him once more and pressed a small, worn, supple leather pouch in his hands. It felt lumpy and heavy. He was too tired to do much with it besides tie it to his belt.

They left the way they came, with Feyazki leading through the maze of small corridors that encompassed the guild hall. At the high-ceilinged entrance—*now the exit,* thought Croy—the white-robed young acolytes scurried around them, attempting to be helpful and somberly supplicant at the same time. Finally they were outside in the refreshing courtyard. Croy stood in the center and breathed slowly in and out with his eyes closed. He was not sure how long he stood there, it was certainly quite a while. Feyazki, for his part, stayed completely silent. He did not bother, pester, or even attempt to talk to Croy. Croy was not even sure if he moved. Even his breathing was silent. Eventually, however, Croy had to reopen his eyes. He was only delaying what he had wanted all along, a quick flight back to his sleeping quarters. To his humble home in the Pyran realm. He was suddenly awash with homesickness. For his cave, for Serif. For Ilana. Properly analyzed, it was a mixture of different nostalgias, but he was sure that he would not be feeling this way if Ilana were with him. In essence, she had been his home.

Croy was once again surrounded by humble sheep. The sheep did not demand much of him. He moved them along in the proper direction during the proper time. He did not have to bring them water, bucket by bucket. He did not have to gather their hay, or haul any bales. They were not close to shearing season, so he did not even have to gather wool. He had missed their lambing season, so he had not needed to help with that. They walked, under their own power, everywhere they went. He just kept them from wandering off. He was like the sun. Essential but passive.

Haswyxe had stopped coming to visit every single day. Or, at least, he did not make himself visible each day. Croy could not be sure. Though his visits had already shifted slowly to becoming more periodic, it seemed to have started in earnest soon after Feyazki's fateful visit. Croy might not have even noticed, but after his conversation with Ryshial he had been looking forward to chatting lazily with Haswyxe amongst the sheep.

Though he was not necessarily supposed to, he took to catching a nap during the heat of midday. His habit was to nap under the same rowan, in the same meadow, where he had first run into Haswyxe. The shade was just right and the ground was a perfect resiliency. After a hearty snack of bread, meats, and cheeses, Croy would lie back and drift into blissful dreamless sleep. Except for this time.

It began as many of his dreams did. With darkness, emptiness, and desolation. But this time no movement came. He did not fly anywhere, he did not float anywhere. It did not even feel like he was drifting. How, then, did he know he was dreaming?

There was a low and unintelligible murmur in the background. Like conversations in another room. There was a feeling of heaviness, like being swaddled in thick black velvet. And there was a vague feeling of pain. It was a sort of ache, deep within the middle of him. It was a crushing feeling, of the middle of him being compressed down to the size of a pebble. Like a fist gripping some internal organ and squeezing. The pressure was constant and symmetric. It was a perfect sphere. It did not pull, it did not cut, it did not burn. It was not really that painful, even. Just constant.

Croy futilely tried to move. At first it was basic. He tried to wave his arms around. He tried to walk or to swim. But he could feel nothing. He then tried to think about movement. Tried to will himself to fly through the abyss. He thought about casting magic. Surely willing himself to fly in a dream would be enhanced by a flight spell. He opened his mouth to speak but nothing emerged. That was when he wondered if he was able to open his eyes. Maybe he was in a well-lit dream, but it only seemed to be dark since his eyes were closed. He willed his eyes open. Nothing changed. He willed his eyes closed—and nothing changed. He then shut his eyes as tight as he could, so tight that he felt the scrunch of his face in his skin, and moved his hand over them. Nothing. He could not feel his own face with his own arm. He then tried to pat his chest. Nothing. He could not feel his own chest. He began to flail around wildly. He tried to tap his feet together, grip his own hands or bite his own shoulder. Nothing. He did feel a tiny bit of sensation. When he tilted his head back, way back, he could feel the stretch in his throat. But he could not feel any part of himself with any other part. That is when the panic began to set in. His silent screams scratched his throat raw.

Then, out of nowhere, searing light blinded him. It burned him and cut him. He silently screamed anew, but with the vigor of excruciating pain behind it. It was like nothing he had ever felt before. Like every single tiny part of him was on fire. Like he was being torn apart, piece by tiny piece. Like he was being pushed through a fine mesh sieve made of razors by horses trampling on his back. This lasted so long that he was unable to scream anymore. It was not that he was numb, just that his throat felt so swollen that it had shut itself. His eyes watered, but he felt no tears on his cheeks. His fists clenched so tight that he felt his forearm muscles vibrating, but could not feel his fingernails digging into his palms. He tried to beg and whimper for his freedom. He tried desperately to wake himself up. He tried to will his heart to stop, to drop dead. Anything to alleviate the pain, even just a little bit. But... Nothing.

Then, after what seemed an eternity, the pain eased and the darkness returned. He felt his chest heave in silent wracking sobs. But, of course, could feel nothing else.

This cycle happened over and over. Again and again. Croy felt that a lifetime had passed. He forgot that he had another lifetime. He forgot he was dreaming, that he was a Gaen, that he was alive. There was only darkness and nothingness, or light and incomprehensible pain.

Then, mercifully, he woke up. He could feel the grass under him, and the sun that split through the tree leaves was warm on his face. He was lying on his side in a pool of his own vomit and blood. It shocked him enough that he pushed himself upright. He tried to talk out loud, just hear himself, but his throat was too dry and raw. He breathed slowly through his nose. His tongue felt weird as well; he spit blood down onto the grass. It felt like his tongue was lacerated and swollen, like he had bitten it while dreaming. He staggered up and hobbled towards his waterskin. It took quite a while and most of his water before he felt normal enough to cast a small healing spell. Then he cast a slightly larger one, and so on. It was getting towards dusk and he was already late returning the sheep to their pen. To his great astonishment and thanks, none of the sheep had wandered off too far during his dream. He swore to himself to never doze while herding again.

Croy looked so bad that Ertyin and Uldun refused to let him back for at least three days. He had tried to talk them out of it, to explain what had happened, but he was still finding it difficult to speak. If he were honest with himself, he was afraid to go back anyway. He thought that a couple of days off would do him some good. More than anything, he just wanted to lie around and heal. Not sleep, mind you. But to relax and heal. He almost went to Nochiel.

During his recuperation he was visited by Knill. The Gaen had aged somehow. He was still quite young, much younger than Croy, of course. But something had happened to place weary lines on his face. Croy had assumed it was the campaign. All that violence and worry had to take its toll. But it was not that easy. It rarely was.

"It is Trela." It was a sigh that heaved up and over the barricade of Knill's mouth. Those three words were heavy with meaning and sentiment. Even if Croy had no idea as to what the actual issue was, or issues as it were, he understood enough of the feeling from hearing that three-worded sigh. Without a word he walked over and hugged his friend.

They commiserated for quite a while. It had been some time since he had last seen Knill, and he felt bad for it. The end of the campaign split a lot of them farther apart. Croy thought that he had just been avoiding the life of royalty and politics, but now realized that he had been avoiding more. He had spent more time with Knill than anyone else, except maybe those in the medic tent. As they talked, he realized how much he missed their little chats.

As for the subject at hand, Croy had little advice and none of it very useful. His own reality was such the opposite that he had difficulty coming up with decent solutions. All he could truly offer were condolences and camaraderie. Luckily that was enough.

Just before Knill left, one hand on the door jamb, he turned and smiled warmly at Croy. "It has been so nice to talk with you that I forgot the real reason I stopped by." Croy had thought it was just for the talk itself. "Clerin and Trela are putting on a dinner and you are invited." He laughed lightly. "Maybe invited is not the right word. You are requested to attend." He laughed again. "Maybe requested is not the right word either. I guess…" He paused for a long moment. "Required. Yes, required sounds about right."

The dining hall was gigantic. The walls were shrouded in tapestries, but there was still an empty echo that hung in the air as one spoke. The table itself was meant to seat at least fifty comfortably. It appeared to be made of one incredibly long and thick plank. Croy wondered how it had fit through the doors and halls to arrive in the room. It did its best to compete with the massive hall that housed it. Certainly a smaller table would have been swallowed whole.

Croy had been chatting with Feyazki about Ryshial, eating toasted bread with crushed olives and cheese melted on top, when Clerin finally showed up. He had not really wanted to bring up the subject of Ryshial, he had wanted to bury the whole experience away from his mind, but Feyazki had tried to apologize and would not let the subject go.

"Ah, there you are. We were beginning to get worried." Trela smiled at Clerin. "I thought I was going to have to get Feyazki to check up on you." When nobody spoke, Trela pulled out a chair for Clerin and invited all of them to sit. Croy sat down next to Clerin to avoid sitting next to Feyazki.

The dinner conversation was pleasant. There was a comfortable feeling of camaraderie. After sharing so many bizarre hardships they had much to joke about. For Croy, it was one of the most entertaining evenings he had experienced at Agoge. He was grateful to have been invited.

After the food was eaten and some of the grog was drunk, Clerin explained that she had requested all of their presence and told her long story of communing with the Beleg Gorbanax. Croy listened half attentively until she began speaking about the images that Gorbanax gave her. As she was speaking, as she was explaining the silhouettes and crude cut-out figures, Croy began to feel a hum. It was just below hearing and not quite a vibration. When she spoke of the fire image turning into a sword image, he began to feel ill. There was only one interpretation that entered his mind, and he was sure he was right. In his mind's eye floated Aedon, speaking of the Cabal of Lochom around a campfire. How they could trap Yavens into inanimate objects—the painful clash of impossibilities—infinity divided by zero.

Suddenly Clerin had stopped talking, and he realized she was asking him a question. "What do you think it all means?" All eyes shifted from her to him. They were heavy gazes.

Croy did his best to explain. Not only about the Cabal and Aedon's reason to find the Vijen, but also about the horror of Yavencide. It was difficult to explain why he thought it was worse than the death of a derlian. After all, he was a derlian. They were all derlians. And yet… Yet, there was something eerily wrong about the death of a Yaven. Something… unnatural. He did his best to explain, with the horror of his most recent dream on his mind but unspoken, but he was not sure if it got through. At least he was not sure if it got through to Feyazki. And Trela, though she commiserated, did not want to leave Agoge no matter how important the quest or how grave the task. He did his best to create a sense of urgency, but he felt that he came up short.

"Then we should all go." Knill spoke happily and quick. Croy thought it was almost giddy.

But Trela refused. She would not be moved. Feyazki stayed silent, but Croy thought that he might be difficult to convince as well. Knill glared at the side of Trela's face as she ignored him and made her excuses to Clerin. Luckily the awkwardness was short lived and soon they all went their separate ways.

Another few days passed and Croy recuperated nicely. Knill had not visited again, no one had, but each night he felt more and more refreshed. It was not until the third night from the dinner that he dreamt again.

He could feel that he was dreaming in his seemingly comfortable bed, but there was no pain, no darkness, no fear this time. Croy floated amongst the clouds for a while, hither and yon. It was nice not to be pushed or pulled. Eventually he picked a nice landing area and wandered around. It reminded him vaguely of the meadow that he fed Ertyin's sheep in. There was a myriad of wildflowers amongst the short grass. As he meandered, he noticed smoke in the distance. It was not alarming, certainly not a large fire, but maybe a campfire. His curiosity slowly tugged him in that direction.

It did not take long for Croy to arrive at the small fire. He half expected someone to be there, tending the fire. But he was alone. It had a nice ring of cobble-sized stones surrounding it. It was about knee high and flickered erratically. He walked around it slowly, circling it. There was something about it. Something he should be paying attention to.

Croy squatted low to better stare into the flames. It appeared that there was a small figure in it, dancing erratically. Yellow with orange outlines spinning together with a definite derlian shape to them. The arms were upraised, then swung down. The feet twisted and swirled as the flames curled upwards. Croy sat down to better examine the figure. That seemed to startle the figure because it suddenly stopped and turned towards him. There seemed to be tiny glowing eyes peering out at him. Croy squinted and pushed his face forwards as far as the heat would comfortably allow, trying to examine the minute detail of the figure. It was quite beautiful.

The figure began to gesture to Croy. It attempted to pantomime something. It kept cupping its hands towards its mouth, as if the reason Croy could not hear it was that it was too quiet. Suddenly, completely unbidden, the thought of Clerin popped into Croy's head. It was her face and she was saying something. They were walking their horses or maybe riding them. What was she saying? Why was it so important to remember? Croy struggled to remember anything at all. Wait! It was something about communicating in a dream. There was a spell she had suggested he cast...

"Losidtotarc!" It finally formed in his mind and he immediately spoke it. The figure appeared to smile.

"Greetings, great dreamer. I have long been rummaging through the local derlians. Few of them are reachable, fewer still remember, and only a tiny amount understand enough to realize that all communication, even dictation, must travel in more than one direction. I have been told that you are one such derlian." The figure grew as it spoke and Croy stood along with it. Its feet were still firmly planted in the campfire, its head was held at Croy's height. "We have much to discover together."

"I... Who told you that?" Croy was wondering about so much more, but that was all he was able to vocalize. It was a feeble swipe at truth.

"Though you may not know others, they may know you. And even if you did know, you would not understand." The arms disappeared into the figure's sides when not in use. "But I did not come here to discuss this. My presence is much more determinate. You need to convince the great communicator to summon me at the appropriate moment."

"You... you are really a Yaven?" Croy's mind was reeling.

"Yes, and you are really a derlian." There was an impatient rumble that accompanied the statement. "Are you a derlian who summons?"

"No, I have never summoned." Croy decided to try to keep his conversation on target and succinct.

"But, you are a mage...?" The voice trailed slightly at the end.

"I can cast spells." Croy was not sure what he was, but he did not think he could call himself a mage. Not after he admitted to never summoning a Yaven.

"That is what a mage does." The fire seemed to be burning hotter. The warmth had felt good against Croy's cheeks, but now it was getting a little uncomfortable. "I wonder if I was given misleading information. No matter, it is too late now. You need to tell the communicator to summon me tomorrow. Around noontime. I will allow her to cast at a Mek level. She will need to cast Meksidpiarc and then say my name to summon me. Do you understand that spell?"

Croy closed his eyes and repeated it several times in his head. He breathed in slowly and opened them. He nodded slowly and deliberately to the figure.

"Good. Is there anything you wish to ask me? Anything that you would like to discuss before waking?" The flames had lowered slightly.

"Will you be in this realm for long, and will I be accompanying you?" He snuck two questions into one sentence.

"I will be there for as long as it takes. This will probably be considered long by your understanding." The figure tilted its head. "It is my belief that your presence will be necessary for this mission. I will attempt to persuade you to accompany us."

"Then I will save my questions for a later time." He wanted his statement to appear spoken out of respect, but in truth he was worried about not remembering the spell he needed to tell to Clerin. He bowed to the figure.

"Then you must know my name." The figure reached a flaming arm out to Croy. It appeared, and felt like, the hand entered his skull. It was excruciating and, at the same time... poignant? There was a thunderclap of shockwave surrounding Croy. "Taglochprefwaskintruld!" The name was repeated, along with the thunder, five distinct times. It echoed through Croy's mind, his spine, and his awakening.

He shot bolt upright in his bed. Sweat stuck the sheets to his small body. Immediately he reached for a quill and inkwell. He had to write the name down before it faded. He slept an invigorating, dreamless sleep for the rest of the night. It was quite refreshing.

Croy awoke slowly and comfortably. As his mind wandered to the note that he had scribbled to himself in the middle of the night, however, he began to feel a twinge of panic. Quickly he washed himself as well as he could with the utensils at hand and got haphazardly dressed. He ran from his tiny abode to find Clerin. He knew that he had to give her the message before its urgency wore off.

Chapter 3

Trela's acceptance as ruler was swift and absolute. She had her opinions of Qizern and knew that she had been destined to defeat him, but she had only heard stories about his rule from outsiders. Most of those who were in her warpack had never met Qizern. Even for those who had, it had usually been at some public event, merely brief official encounters. There was Synde and Lishean and a few others, of course, but she did not know many who had worked with him daily. The members of his court and his Guard all lined up to swear fealty to her during those first few days. They were all very formal and gracious at first, and then quietly told her how much they had hated Qizern and his ways. It was an odd sensation. They would denigrate him behind the backs of their hands as they smiled across their palms. If she let herself, she felt that she could become paranoid of how they would speak about her if she was ever overthrown. Or, more to the point, when she was overthrown. Though their jobs were predicated on their perceived loyalty, Trela did not think they were lying about their distaste for Qizern. There was a sad sincerity to their words. It was when she was alone with someone that the real horror stories came out. Stories of Qizern torturing confessions out of innocents who had angered him. He would take all their possessions. He would hang them from the Blaze's walls so that all the town could watch their bodies decompose. In public she heard the petty grievances, the small slights and, at worst, his incomprehensible mood shifts. It was in private that she would hear what a complete monster he was. And these stories came from those who knew him best. Those who had sworn fealty to him and had done his bidding on a daily basis.

The days that it took swearing her in, taking the oaths from her subjects, solidified her idea of Qizern. It vindicated her own anger and resentment. She had seen what he was capable of, she had seen the look of unreasoning rage in his eyes. She had been chased out of the Pyran realm, had narrowly escaped his clutches, had faced him in single combat. But it had taken an enormous amount of bloodshed to dispose of him. She needed to feel that there was a reason for it. A justification. Speaking with those who worked with him gave her that justification. It made it all the sacrifice seem palatable. No matter how much pain and suffering she had caused in her relentless campaign to topple his reign, it was worth it. She was told that by countless Pyrans who swore their undying loyalty to her. That it was worth it. It was a completely redeeming feeling.

It took three days for all of the oaths and introductions. Outside, amongst the ordinary citizens of Agoge, the celebration was raging. She could hear the music and laughter from her windows. At night she could see the torches and fires from her ramparts. She felt oddly removed from a celebration that was honoring her but that she could not attend. It was as if it was not quite real. Not real for her, at least.

It was not until the fourth day that the parades began. Then the reality set in and made her giddy. Though Trela did not lead any of the parades, she was always near the front. The bands, flags and fanfare strode before her and her warpack rode behind. It was, as she explained to Knill later, pleasantly exhausting. She rode on her horse, or in a carriage, or on the back of a gigantic cart and waved. There were two parades each day and though there were countless cheering citizens lining the streets of Agoge on the morning of the first day, there were just as many at dusk on the last day. The route was a shifting snake along the broadest streets in the city. Though coins and candy were tossed to the cheering watchers, Trela liked to believe that they were there to see her. To express their gratitude of removing the fickle rule of Qizern from their lives. Like most things seen at a distance from horseback however, she could never be sure.

The last four days of the celebration were some of the most fantastically joyful of her life. Though she was unable to mingle amongst the crowd to watch the street performers, she did have a seat reserved for her at every large sit-down event. Since she could only be at one place at a time, she pondered the usefulness of several empty chairs at the other events while she was enjoying some play or acrobatic ensemble somewhere else. Against tradition, she ordered those seats to be given to whichever ordinary paying citizens were first in line. It meant that she had to provide each venue with her itinerary and that she could not leave an event halfway through if she were bored. Once it was realized what she was doing, it created a small frenzy of excitement as Pyrans camped out in front of their favored entertainments to try to get the best seats in the house. For free.

Trela had inherited a bevy of advisors as she assumed the throne. Most were useless, merely agreeing with her statements and bowing in a sycophantic way. Some offered decent opinions, and she tried to listen to these intently. One, however, rubbed her the wrong way. He was a haughty, thin Pyran by the name of Linloy. He was thin, almost emaciated, with long brown hair and a clean-shaven face. His arms looked too long, his legs too short, and he walked with a slight limp. Somehow, even this was infuriating to Trela since it meant that she had to slow her pace while walking with him. Linloy had a very concrete idea of what it meant to be a queen. For as long as Trela was to know him, he offered no advice upon policy or military matters. His only concern was her image that was projected to the citizens of Agoge. To him, tradition was the epitome of sophisticated style. Her idea of giving away seats to common citizens made him positively apoplectic. That probably gave her more enjoyment than anything else that day.

In between the parades, she would go to various planned events. Therefore, she missed much of the small parts of the festival. She missed the press of the crowds and the hidden corners of ecstatic celebration. But the nights inside the Blaze were filled with enough revelry to more than make up for what she missed in the streets. The pageantry was beautiful and she enjoyed every moment.

Then it ended. During the week, time slowed to molasses on a cold winter's morning. Each moment seemed to last forever. Her face actually hurt from smiling so much. Somehow, however, it all ended too soon. The streets quieted down so much that the only thing to be heard were the brooms sweeping the cobbled streets. The city spent the two days after the celebration in a quiet and collective haze of hangover. It was as if an invisible fog hung dank and heavy over the entire town. It muffled noises and shortened sight. But that too soon passed. Nine days after arriving at Agoge triumphant over Qizern, Trela began the rest of her life.

The first day was spent deciding how to divide up the rest of her days. She did not want to follow Qizern's pattern of daily events but she had none of her own. She ordered her inherited advisors to list out their own itineraries for each day of the week and what they thought Qizern did during those times. Between the seven of them, she found a basic pattern that should fit any ruler. She then re-ordered them, both hourly and daily, so that she could call her schedule her own. This meant, of course, re-ordering the advisors' schedules as well. She had expected some complaints but none were to be had. It seemed expected that she should shake the routine up. The disruption was enough of a tradition to make them all comfortably happy with the change in their schedules. It was a way to demark the shifting eras. They were now entering the epoch of Trela.

There was much to learn and it took her a while to get into the swing of things. Eventually she was able to have some spare time during her work day. At first it was just a few minutes, which she took up in rest. Eventually, it lengthened enough that she felt she had to find something to do. She meditated on what makes a realm. What is the one thing that a ruler can affect that would benefit the largest swath of her citizens? What could be the sharpest departure from the style that Qizern ruled with? What would resolve his greatest failures while, at the same time, give her a great triumph? It had to be the rule of law.

To be able to affect the law, however, she needed to know what it was currently comprised of. When she asked for the actual codified law from her advisors they seemed a bit confused. They thought and scratched their heads and then they each left in a seemingly different direction. They returned, one by one, each with a different book. Some had several smaller books. Some had scrolls. Two had giant tomes that covered almost half of her writing desk. Each.

"Which set has the laws in them?" Trela was dumbfounded by the amount of parchment in front of her.

"Well, they all have some laws in them." It was Linloy who spoke first.

"Which one has the current laws?" She squinted her eyes at him. He heaved a heavy sigh as if he were an old teacher explaining something simple to a thickheaded child.

"That one there" —he pointed to a gigantic, ancient-looking tome— "is the first book of laws. There are many laws in there that make sense, say 'do not steal' and the like. Some of the laws make a little sense, such as 'you may not sleep on a park bench.' Some them make sense, but are unenforceable, such as 'you may not spit in the street.' And there are some that do not make any sense at all, such as 'you may not exchange money on Moondays.' Those over there" — he pointed to a small pile of scrolls— "were addenda and commentary for the first tome. These over here" —he pointed to a group of books— "attempted to be an omnibus guide. However, it is believed that some of the laws were removed and/or edited at the author's discretion. Which ones were removed? Which ones were edited?" Linloy cocked an expressive eyebrow and shrugged his shoulders. "Each ruler adds laws that they deem invaluable, but most are afraid to remove laws they disagree with. If a law is not considered useful to a ruler it is usually just ignored, rather than erased. So, you see, it is impossible to tell which book is the correct book because they are all correct." Then he smiled widely. "They are all correct seen through the eyes of our Queen."

Trela was stunned, truly stunned. She stood there quietly staring at all the different books and scrolls piled in front of her. She tried to make sense of it all. Surely all the really necessary laws, those that anyone would agree with, should take up less room than even the mightiest of the tomes before her. How could each book contain separate information? It boggled her mind.

She sat down heavily. How could she even begin? "I will need several scribes."

Trela decided to go through the various law books in order and pick out every law that sounded remotely reasonable. She would then have the scribes transcribe the law onto a separate sheet of paper. It would be numbered and a long scroll, or scrolls, would contain the index. She could then decide which were the ones that were not necessary, or redundant, or poorly worded. She would winnow the laws down to a manageable size, hopefully one thick book would be sufficient, and finally, she would re-order them into a logical list. If all went well, she could then have the book transcribed and sent to every guard station, every magistrate's office, and every library in the realm. Then, and only then, could she say that every citizen lived under the same rule of law. All of this effort was to be able to state that she was governed by the exact same laws as her subjects. It was a lot of effort but it needed to be done. She needed to prove that she was unlike Qizern. That she was the opposite of Qizern. And that needed to start with a form of legal equality. She had so many more ideas. So many ambitious plans. But they would all be for naught unless this first stepping stone were laid straight and plumb, on a solidly packed bed of soil. She had not realized the length of time even the simplest things could take in the midst of bureaucracy, let alone something incredibly complicated.

"Not for a couple days, but I will need several very dedicated, trustworthy, and hardworking scribes." A large unconscious sigh deflated her slightly.

"Would you like us to ensure that you have a copy of all the written law books in Agoge, just to make sure that there are no others out there?" An advisor named Hunvarb spoke up. She was somewhat squat and dowdy, with long brown hair and chubby cheeks. Her brow always seemed to be drawn in thought, or maybe worry, Trela was never fully sure.

"Yes, of course. I will need at least one copy of every book, scroll, tablet, or scrap of paper that has a law on it. In this first stage, completeness is of the utmost importance." Another large sigh escaped Trela's lips. More? How could there be more? "That is enough for today." She waved her hand at the advisors to send them on their way. She knew that they all probably had further plans for her, but she did not want to think about anything else right now. They left quietly, without a word of protest.

Trela looked around her study. It was quite large, but was bereft of books. She had taken to having her meetings with her advisors there since there were three large couches. She liked to pace while talking, and it helped her that they had to sit and watch her move. There were five separate and quite cushy chairs, with small pillows on some of the larger ones. There were two separate desks. One was small but very tall, almost a podium really. The other was double sided with a chair, writing surface and drawers at each end. There was only one window opening, but at least it was quite large. The room had vibrant tapestries depicting epic battles over the ages, nothing as intricate as in the throne room of course, but many were still quite impressive. There was one in particular, it showed a hunting scene with hounds baying at a large four-point by five-point deer; its eyes were so realistic you could almost see them rolling. There was a hunter with a bow on a horse on the far right of the tapestry, but it almost seemed added as an afterthought. Trela could stand in front of it all day, staring at the amazing detail of individual hairs on the hounds or the long lashes on the deer. But she did not want to dally today. She got the large, oldest tome laid out on the opposite side of the desk than she usually sat at. With one last big sigh, she opened it up and began to read.

She spent several days attempting to get ahead on the laws. Each day had its own rhythm of requirements. Functionary meetings during the morning hours, the specific day's task around noon, lunch, and then audiences with her citizens during the afternoon. That left the evenings in which she tried to read the ancient law books and mark what passages seemed appropriate. Unfortunately, this left very little time for her and Knill to chat and relax. More than once she had arrived at their lush quarters later than she had promised. Though he would never say anything out loud—for in truth what could he say, could he really get angry that she was spending her time ruling her realm—he would have a look that combined frustration and petulance amazingly into one countenance. He would smile with pursed lips. Though he did not give her the full silent treatment, he would be unusually terse and taciturn. Nodding and grunting in response to her half-hearted apologies. There were times that it was so subtle that she was not sure if he was intending it or not. Maybe she was being paranoid and creating it out of thin air. At other times he was obviously annoyed, there could be no mistaking his mood. To be honest, it made her want to stay in her study and work even longer. Anything rather than stare at those large, wet, and pained eyes.

What was even more frustrating was her own lack of progress. Each day was a tiny half-step, an aged derlian's shuffle, towards her goal. She needed to be running, or jogging, or in the least, walking steadily. But no, she merely hobbled along, stopping for frequent breaks lost in a dense fog. Maybe some of her annoyance with Knill was misplaced. Maybe some of that should have been directed at herself. Either way, she could not stand looking at his pained eyes.

Trela had arrived late yet again and Knill was there, sitting in front of cold food. It appeared as if he had pecked at it at least. The meat showed some cut edges and the peas were scattered about the plate. But he was staring at her across the table with his arms crossed over his chest. He was prepared for something.

"I'm sorry that the food has already gotten cold." At least the anger masked the pain, but Trela could not believe that his opening move was a veiled apology. Or was it a veiled attack?

"I've already eaten." Trela felt tired.

"I wish I would have known, I would not have had Kolaf make so much food." He was not backing down. Bringing up their chef's name was surely an attempt at escalation. Kolaf had been her faithful chef in the warpack, during her campaign. Trela kept him for personal assignments, but she used Qizern's chef, a large Pyran by the name of Glinwy, to cook for large groups. No one in Agoge knew the royal kitchen as well as Glinwy did. There were times, such as this night, that she would order some tidbits brought to her study from the kitchen to tide her over. She thought it harmless but tried to make a mental note to make sure that Kolaf was not concerned by her missing his meal.

"I did not want to send a messenger and I kept thinking I was almost done. It just... I was almost done for quite some time." Trela felt old.

"How many messengers do you send out on petty errands each day?" He truly was rearing for a fight.

"I am sorry, all right? Truly, deeply, and embarrassingly sorry." She did not usually back down from conflict, but she just did not have the energy. And she thought utter capitulation would end it. "It is my fault and I will try not to do it again."

"One, that is not a sincere apology. Two, you *will* do it again. Probably tomorrow. If you spent just one tenth..." Trela started walking away and his voice faded into the distance. At least he was not following her.

Trela was starting to get the hang of her constant duties. She would walk briskly to each different locale, various Pyrans would bombard her with questions, and then she would walk to a different locale. Each evening she spent one hour working on the laws, then she would promptly return to her quarters to a waiting Knill. He was not happy, but he was not unhappy. They had seemed to reach an equilibrium of sorts. She was in the throne room and had just finished with a small audience of farmers when a Guard arrived to tell her that Clerin was seeking audience.

"I stalled her for as long as I could, but she does not appear to be leaving anytime soon." He tried to smile. It appeared difficult for him.

"You should not have stalled Clerin. She is my Fluen princess." Trela immediately strode out of the throne room.

"But... you were in the middle of a meeting." The Guard trotted after her. Trela knew it was mean, but she did nothing to assuage the Guard's concern. She tried to remind herself to comfort him later. After all, he was just doing the job she had asked him to do.

"Clerin, darling! I cannot believe you were kept waiting." Trela cocked an eyebrow and turned her head towards the Guard slightly.

They strode briskly back to the throne room. Trela tried to make excuses for her Guard as Clerin surveyed the room.

"You have done well for yourself…" Clerin waved vaguely around the room.

"It's just meant to be imposing, really." Trela wondered what Clerin saw in the room. There were so few that Trela knew who had actually seen another throne room. There were few who had even seen this room before. Did Clerin think it gaudy, or apt? Pretentious, or simple and mundane? From what Trela had heard, nothing could compare to the opulence of the Fluen royalty. This probably looked like a sad rundown backwater room to Clerin. Trela decided to change the subject to something that Clerin should enjoy. "So, how is Feyazki?"

"How should I know?" Clerin sounded put out, almost angry. Trela marked the emotion in her mind. She would have to investigate its root cause later. "You know why I am here, don't you?"

"Of course, of course. You wish to commune with Gorbanax in the Temple of Fire." Trela kept her smile steady.

"I need to. This is not about desire." Clerin took a deep breath.

"This was my promise to you, and you have certainly waited long enough. When would you like perform your duty? Tomorrow?" Trela had much to do tomorrow, but she had known this day would come. It was best to resolve it now and then get back to the work at hand.

"Yes, the sooner the better. Tomorrow will be great." She made a shallow curtsey and turned to leave.

"Then you will dine with us tonight. I have the greatest chefs in all the realm at my disposal. You must try my hospitality." Clerin stopped in her tracks at Trela's words. "Plus, it will do Knill some good. He doesn't even spend much time with Tumu anymore now that Lishean is the leader of the Guard. It will be good for us all." And she meant it. Knill would be thrilled at having a full, relaxed meal. Plus, Knill liked Clerin and should enjoy the evening on that premise alone. She was so effervescent, everyone liked Clerin.

The meal was pleasant and the company even more so. However, the law books beckoned to Trela from across the castle. She could hear their irresistible soft song during the entire meal and, finally, she could take it no more. Ashamedly, but briskly, she excused herself and wandered the quiet halls back to her study. Once she opened the door the smell hit her. The smell of musty old books. The odd mixture of heavy paper, stale ink, and a slight hint of something moldy. She had not always been much of a reader, but she was learning to enjoy that smell. She pulled open her heavy tome with something akin to glee.

Trela awoke before dawn. Though she was putting much on hold for the day, it felt truly invigorating to be putting on her riding breeches while still half asleep. As she walked towards the stables with her heavy leather boots ringing out against the cobblestones, she felt fully alive. The air smelled of adventure. Though the chore could not have come at a more hectic time and was completely obnoxious, and she had not gotten enough sleep last night, and it would take all day, and, and, and… The warm thrill of nostalgia poured through her veins, rousing her sluggish blood. She was on the move again. She was the Kriishan.

Their ride up the mountain was long and quiet. Much of it had to be traversed in single file, making chit-chat difficult. During the times when they easily rode side by side, Trela would try to think of conversations to start, but she kept thinking of Feyazki and she knew that Clerin did not want to talk about that. She did not mind the silent ride as it allowed her mind to wander unfettered. Clerin did not seem to mind either.

They finally arrived at the gigantic ledge that encompassed and defined the Temple's entrance. There were almost twelve Guards standing around the round-arched entrance. Trela wondered what the normal contingent was. Surely they added several just for her arrival. She wondered how many there would have been if she had not warned the captain of her coming. It was a curious but fleeting thought. Sneaking around and trying to catch her Guards off guard sounded like something Qizern would do.

"My Queen, we are pleased that you have arrived. I hope that all is in order." Trela racked her brain trying to think of the captain's name.

"Of course, Captain Devonsar. This is quite a... group." Trela finally came up with the name. She hurried to finish her sentence so that she would not be in the middle of dismounting while she was talking.

"It is larger than normal for the royal visit." He looked a little pained when he spoke. Like he had pondered about how many he should have waiting at the entrance. Trela wondered how many Guards Qizern would insist upon seeing everywhere he went. She knew she had to be cognizant of her subjects trying to gauge her desires and probably erring on the side of tradition. However, she certainly did not need or want such a large welcoming committee everywhere she went. Her desires needed to be communicated somehow.

"No harm done. You obviously keep tight control over your station, as is required of such an honorable post. You are the gate to Gorbanax. However, when you are merely greeting me at that gate, probably only half as many Guards are required." Trela shook her hand slightly, fingers splayed, to show that there was no specific number that she had in mind.

"Of course, my Queen." Devonsar bowed deeply. "Do you and your companion require a guide?" Trela nodded as he turned towards one of his Guards. He obviously anticipated her need. "Fregonal, front and center." It was spoken with a snap.

A thin and wiry Pyran appeared, back held perfectly straight. He had several shallow scars on his face but had quite a few deeper ones on his forearms. Mostly his left. Trela assumed that he had seen a lot of knife fights, and he was obviously right-handed.

"The lava has been bubbling quite energetically this morning, my Queen. I think Gorbanax is anxious." Fregonal bowed deeply to her. Trela, however, wanted to give one more pat on her captain's back.

"Very good, Devonsar. I thank you. As I say, you keep tight control over your station. While we are in the Temple I want no interruptions, understand?" Trela realized that Clerin had finally wandered over. "Ah, Clerin, perfect. I hear that the volcano has been rumbling. It appears that you are anticipated. Fregonal will be guiding us."

As they wandered through the caverns Trela marveled at how many Guards were about. She wondered how many were necessary. How many times had an interloper actually tried to gain unwanted access to Gorbanax? She was certainly not planning on attempting to commune with Gorbanax today, but thought she might ask if it was worried about unwanted guests, or an attack, or if she could shrink the amount of protection around the Temple. She filed it in the back of her mind. It was certainly not a pressing issue.

It became warmer and warmer as they neared the center of the Temple. As Trela was wondering how much farther they could go and how much hotter it would get, they finally arrived at a pair of large doors. They were wooden, which made Trela wonder slightly; iron could get too hot but it wasn't flammable. Though she did not recognize the Guards at the doors, they immediately knew her and bowed deeply.

"The Queen and her companion wish to commune with Gorbanax. Step aside." Fregonal spoke firmly and clearly. Trela wondered if the verbiage had any tradition to it. As they entered, Fregonal bowed deeply as well, then swung the doors shut behind them.

The room was a long tube, hollowed out by molten rock long ago. There were more Guards and the mage. She made the Guards leave and warned the mage, quite sternly, that no harm was to come to her Fluen princess. Clerin disrobed and the mage cast his spells with his eyes downwards. Trela watched as Clerin strode naked down the tube, hesitated slightly, and then slipped quietly into the glowing lava as if it were a placid pool of water. It always amazed Trela that Clerin did not seem to be aware of her own beauty, or even its effect on others. The mage looked uncomfortable as he stared intently at the floor. For some reason Trela felt mischievous.

"She is stunning, is she not?" Trela tried to will the mage to look up, but he did not.

"I would not know, my liege." Somehow, he looked even more uncomfortable.

"You just cast several spells on her, how could you not glance?" Trela wondered if it really was just social station that caused the mage's embarrassment. Would he have behaved thusly if she had stood naked before him? If Qizern had done the same? Certainly he would not have become so flustered with grizzled old Qizern standing before him, even if Qizern was his king. Wouldn't he?

"I am only here to perform my duty to the throne." His throat sounded a bit strangled.

It made Trela feel somewhat sorry for him. She positioned him such that his back was towards the lava pool and engaged him in soothing, meaningless chatter. By the end, he was looking up into her face as they talked and appeared much more relaxed. Soon Clerin had finished and they were riding back towards Agoge.

At Clerin's urging, Trela had an extravagant meal prepared. She had it set up in the large dining hall. Knill was beside himself with excitement. Almost giddy.

She chatted with Feyazki about the mage's guild while Knill and Croy were laughing amongst themselves. It felt good. She decided to try to take more time to socialize amongst friends. Currently she was doing her best to get Feyazki to join the guild elite. She had spoken with Ryshial and the other guild masters about Feyazki, and they had seemed quite receptive.

"You really should join up. They could use a mage as skilled as you are." Trela was nodding to herself.

"I have joined. I spend most of my time there, trust me." Feyazki was grinning broadly. It made Trela's heart light to see him like this, he had been so broody the last couple of times they had crossed paths.

"No, not the just the guild. You could never be just some neophyte apprentice or thane, but a teacher or seneschal. In fact, you should petition to become a full master." Trela had wanted to make the idea his own. To plant a seed so small that it went unnoticed until it bore fruit. However, she found that she did not have the patience for something that complicated this evening. Besides, she did not want Feyazki to think her manipulative, especially for something so minor. So she had decided to be blunt.

"You know that I am not even allowed to apprentice. I am not a Pyran." He was still grinning. "They would never accept me as a master." He glanced over her shoulder briefly, at something behind and beyond her. "Oddly enough, they *have* asked me to teach." Just then Clerin arrived and interrupted them.

"Ah, there you are. We were beginning to get worried." Trela smiled at her. "I thought I was going to have to get Feyazki to check up on you." Clerin and Feyazki both looked at the ground. Silence. Pure, heavy, black, palpable silence. She cursed herself for being so ham-fisted. Quickly, she pulled a chair out from the table for Clerin and they all sat down.

She sat at the head of the table and let the others sit where they were most comfortable. Not that it mattered, but in her mind she had assumed that Croy and Knill would sit beside each other. It seemed like she was just a little off this evening. Maybe it was because her mind kept wandering involuntarily to the musty law books. She told herself to pay more attention to the here and now.

The dinner conversation was quite engaging and entertaining, and yet it was a little banal. They all enjoyed themselves, but it turned a bit hollow for Trela. She felt she should be doing something more concrete, more helpful. More required. It all seemed a bit frivolous. She felt like two different derlians. One part of her really needed to chat about nothing and connect with her friends. One part of her really needed to be back in her study, hunched over her books. It was an unwanted conflict that distracted her. It made the time flow by.

Soon Clerin was repeating her story of Gorbanax. Then Croy made his case about the Cabal. Then Knill seized the moment with the grip of a murderer on a victim's throat. There was something fanatical in his eyes. Joyful with a light form of excitement, but definitely something fanatical as well. It was as if he had found something to trap her with. Some magic rope or net. The two derlians within her merged into one—the one who needed to be back in her study.

"I cannot go." Trela stammered meekly. "I have just started my reign. There is… there is too much to do." The silence was worse than when she had joked about sending Feyazki to find Clerin. There was an underlying anger to Knill's stare. She had known it would appear before she spoke. And yet she was unable to say anything else. How could she just agree? How could she just up and leave her throne? *Her* throne! The pained silence from the others was bad enough. She could not believe the nerve that he showed by being angered by something he knew she could not agree to. He *knew* that she could not leave. His anger made her angry, though she did her best to hide it. How could he even ask her to leave everything that she had fought for? Did he not know her?

✳✳✳

It was while Trela was rummaging around in Qizern's old desk that she found it. It had been a long, slow day, full of meetings and squabbles. She had been taking her meals in her study, partly to avoid Knill, so it was typically quite late when she would finally arrive at her bedchambers. She sometimes even took naps on the couch. She practically lived between her study and throne room. Yet somehow, for moons, she had overlooked it.

While getting frustrated during her rummaging, she had by then forgotten what she was originally looking for, one of the small drawers at the top part of her desk was pulled out too far. It immediately pivoted in her hand when it was no longer supported by its runners and it came crashing down to the ground. There, held to the bottom of the drawer with wire, was a small brass key. She stared at it for a while, slightly stunned at its existence, before reaching out to touch it. It had a vague tip, with an oddly shaped fin and hollow core. The thumb and forefinger end was heavily filigreed and quite complicated, but it was not as exotic as the end that entered the lock. She sat there, amongst the detritus of the spilled drawer contents, for some time. Holding the key and turning it slowly in front of her, as if she were memorizing its shape. As if she would need to describe it to some locksmith. She could not think of a lock in the entire Blaze that was missing a key. How many closed doors did she walk by in a day? How many cabinets? There were certain doors that she opened and closed all the time, but there were many, many more that she never touched, let alone all of those that she never saw. For the first time in over a moon, she forgot about her law books.

Trela carried the key with her on her way back to her chambers, searching for the specific lock that would be its mate. The key was smaller than a large door's, certainly smaller than a prison door key. However, it seemed larger than a jewelry box's key. The more she examined it, the more she thought it must belong to some large cabinet. Either that or some small interior door, like a closet of some sort. There were very few viable doors on her way back through the halls, so she hurried home.

She entered her chambers with fresh eyes. There was her giant four-posted bed against the far wall; its silken drapes engulfed the bed with their billowing embrace. On each side of the bed was a nightstand, and each nightstand had a drawer that could lock. There was a desk to the right of the bed, pushed up against a window. The desk was a roll-top with assorted drawers that might lock. To the left of the bed was a large armoire, which she could not recall having a lock anywhere on it, but it would have to be checked as well. There was a vanity dressing table with its oversized mirror, two closets, three dresser drawers, and various small chests and jewelry boxes stuffed throughout the chamber and closets. She would have to try them all. Though she could not recall coming across anything locked, just the anticipation made her excited.

Knill was out for the evening visiting Croy, she thought, or maybe Tumu. She could not really be sure. Either way she was glad of it and began to meticulously circle the room, examining every lock. The key might fit a lock that was already open for all she knew. Most of the locks were too big and a couple were too small. There were several that seemed the right size, but they did not have the curious post that should fit the key's hollow core. She was not quite sure if that was a requisite, but the key did not turn any of the locks that it was sized close enough to enter. Though the chambers were quite large, she had not originally thought it would take her the hour it took to scour the place to her satisfaction. Or, more correctly, her dissatisfaction. Though it had not been difficult work, she felt exhausted.

She had already checked the study. The throne room had almost no furniture, certainly no locks that she could think of. There were several other rooms that Qizern may have lived in, or at least frequented, that she might try. It might very well be to something as mundane as a lock in the kitchen, for the tea or sugar, or perhaps even the grog cellar. Maybe Qizern had a mistress kept away somewhere in the Blaze, or even elsewhere within Agoge, and this key was to her door. Or maybe it would unlock a secret passageway that led to his mistress's door. The possibilities seemed so utterly endless as to make the quest quite frustrating.

Clerin arrived in her throne room for another meeting. But from the start, this one seemed much more confrontational. She knew that Clerin was there to convince her to leave her Pyrans, to leave her realm, to leave her throne. She needed to show Clerin that she was not to be budged, so she allowed an immediate audience.

Trela explained she was not planning on leaving and Clerin had called her a buffoon. A buffoon! Clerin told her that she was afraid to leave her throne room. Clerin told her how much she loved her jewel encrusted crown. She expected this type of language from Knill. She had not expected it from her Fluen princess. She felt somewhat betrayed. There was an ugly, bile-filled anger that began to boil up in her. Her right hand itched for her sword. There was a rush of adrenalin fueled emotion that threatened to overwhelm her. Later she would feel a twinge of shame at the brief vitriol that had filled her, but it was all over in a moment.

"Meksidpiarc! Taglochprefwaskintruld!" Clerin spoke clearly and strongly. She had not thought Clerin could summon. It was impressive.

There was a loud boom and a blinding flash. A stench of sulfur permeated the air and a gigantic inferno stood before them. Flames shot in every direction and, for a moment, they seemed to get larger. Then, almost as quickly, the flames decreased in size and took on a more derlian outline. It bowed to each of them individually.

"Greetings, great ruler. Gorbanax sends congratulations through me for your just and powerful defeat of the one known as Qizern. You may call me Taglo, as I am called in this realm of chaos. I knew Gorbanax before it changed into a Beleg and created you. I have been here many times before but never before with so urgent a message. This message comes straight from Gorbanax, who was concerned that such a complicated understanding of events would become confused by the forced dispersal of communication required of direct exposure to derlians. This other derlian, the Fluen, is the communicator, is she not?" It was strange, but no heat was given off by the Yaven.

Trela opened her mouth to speak but was interrupted by Clerin. The Yaven asked for her version of the conversation she had with Gorbanax, and she gave it. Taglo, for its part, seemed pleased by what it heard.

"And I? I am here as a guide. I am here as the grand assistant. I will ensure the success of this endeavor before I will leave this realm. I am at your disposal, but you are also at mine." Taglo's voice was somewhat monotone, but became quite menacing at the last statement. "You are also at mine." It reverberated in Trela's ears. Was Taglo truly in this realm to due Gorbanax's bidding? She steeled her resolve for she knew what was coming.

Suddenly the subject shifted to Menels, something that Trela had heard about but had no direct experience of. They spoke at great length about them and then, much to Trela's delight, Taglo produced its own for them to look at. It was a dark gray amulet that appeared from its depths and slowly surfaced. Or maybe the fire receded. The Menel was very thick, though she had nothing to compare it with, and had three sections to it, each with its own symbol carved on it. It took her breath away. She had not realized how hunched over she was, face nearing the great flames that made up the Yaven, until she saw how close Clerin was to her. It was all so fascinating that she forgot everything else around her. Even the fact that she was Queen.

"You realize that you both are necessary, do you not?" The thunderous words brought Trela back to reality.

"I am… I am needed here." She spoke meekly.

"I will not argue with truth. I will say this, however. You are needed elsewhere much more. Your destiny is greater than you give it credit right now. I have only seen one other whose destiny encompasses a larger sphere of influence. We do not have to converse now, we will do so later. Think about this decision. Do not make it based in haste or in reflex. Do not base your decision upon who you were an hour ago, or a second ago. Your decision must be based upon who you are now and who you wish to be in the future." Taglo turned towards Clerin. "You realize that you are necessary, do you not?"

Clerin quibbled, but then agreed. They left. There was an all-consuming emptiness left behind. Words tumbled through Trela's brain like buffeting rain. They pushed sideways, they fell in sheets, they pushed her from top to bottom. "Necessary," "influence," "future," and, of course, "destiny." She could discount many things. She could ignore all sorts of opinions. But omens? But destiny? Destiny had been her entire life, had led her from ignominy to grandeur. She did not want to leave Agoge, did not want to leave her realm, her duty, her throne. But was she destined to? The thoughts clashed and buffeted for some time. She was alone, in her vast throne room, for what seemed like forever. Listening to the rain and wind of her mind howl in frustrated quandary. There was not just a storm brewing, there was one that already existed.

It was difficult for her to get back into the swing of things. The musty law books did not have the same pull as they did earlier. Her mind kept wandering, kept wondering. The meeting with the Yaven… No, the meeting with Taglo, Trela told herself, stood out in her mind, amongst her chaotic thoughts, like a powerful beacon from a lighthouse. She would be listening to one of her subjects complaining about something or other, and flash!, suddenly Taglo's fiery visage would float before her in her mind. The word "destiny" would echo between her ears. It was almost impossible to concentrate.

She tried to fill her days with meetings, because it was ten times worse when she was alone. Alone, her mind was adrift like a ship without a rudder. At least when she was around others there was a constant need to focus elsewhere. Whether or not she always accomplished that was up for debate.

She wanted to fight against this. She needed to stay Queen, stay current in her position and keep vigilance upon her throne. More than anything, to be present. There was much to do, truly. But much of her reasoning hinged on the image of it all. She needed to cultivate an image of her rule, one that was strong enough to last during any future absence. The image that she wished to project, more than anything, was one of dedicated compassion. She wanted to be there for her subjects. She wanted them to know that she cared about them, that she would listen to them. She wanted to be able to help each and every one of them with their individual problems. If she was honest with herself, what she really wanted was to be loved. To be loved by the entire realm. She had already come a long way in that regard, at least that is what her advisors told her. But she needed to do more than just not be Qizern. She needed to accomplish great things. To do this, she needed to be present. Therefore, she was unable to join a grand adventure. Even if it was at the request of a Yaven. Even if it was at the insistence of a Beleg. Even if it was her destiny. During the moments when she could focus and concentrate, she felt herself splitting apart.

Trela wanted to talk with Knill about this, about Taglo, but knew she could not. His answer was known before Taglo had arrived. She thought about talking with Croy, but for some reason she felt that he was too close to Knill. She could certainly not speak about her quandary to Clerin, not after their last argument. She thought about bringing it up to Feyazki, but did not think she could. She respected his opinion greatly, but he had a blasé attitude about some things that could be infuriating if discussed at the wrong time. She pursed her lips unconsciously. His face kept sliding into her vision. It must be Lishean. He could be trusted to understand the importance of these matters. He was one of the few that could understand both sides of her problem. She drew a deep breath and set out to find him.

It took a little while to find Lishean, though it was still morning by the time she did. He was not at his quarters or in the Guard meeting hall or with any of his Seconds or lieutenants. When Trela found him, it was in one of the larger courtyards of the Blaze. It was large enough that there was a small stand of alder trees in the corner, with benches for respite in the shade, that did nothing to impede the courtyard's main use. There were some small units, partial cohorts that maybe consisted of fifteen or so warriors, a couple of even smaller groups, and a myriad of individuals spread about the open portion of the courtyard. Some were practicing formations or performing drills, but most were simply sparring. Lishean was striding back and forth across a small platform like a harried symphony conductor during the warm-up scales, before anyone played anything coherent. He would occasionally yell some encouragement or some more poignant advice out into the sparse crowd. He would point or make some exaggerated gesture to help convey his meaning. The courtyard looked well trampled and the active participants appeared to be bathed in sweat. It made her proud.

Instead of walking towards the platform boldly through her many warriors, Trela skirted the catwalked wall. She would pause and lean back, feeling the cool shaded stone against her back, and watch in earnest as a particularly energetic sparring match was coming to a close. Then she would move on, hugging the shadows along the wall. She passed through the stand of alders about midway. Though it was tiny, it smelled different than the rest of the courtyard. Not that it had an identifiable smell, but there was a freshness that contrasted with the sweat and packed dirt, contrasted with the mineral smell of the stone walls. It almost felt like forest, like a campaign, like adventure. She shook her head slightly to clear her mind and decided not to sit on an inviting bench. She forced herself to watch the courtyard, to watch her warriors practice, and moved on from the peaceful alders and into the clanging open area. She leisurely took her time, stopping and starting along the stone courtyard wall, before she got to the edge of the platform. Still, no one had noticed her, or at least no one had announced her presence. She stayed rooted to the ground, at the back of the platform, watching Lishean pace back and forth like a large angry cat. Finally she could wait no more, and she hopped up and strode across the creaking wooden boards with purpose.

"Lishean, may I have a word with you?" She stood a couple paces behind him with her hands held behind her back.

"I was wondering when you would show yourself. Took your sweet time strolling around." He turned towards her briefly, flashing his grin and blue eyes, before he turned back and yelled some more at the warriors below. She was always amazed at how his white hair contrasted with his chiseled body. The hair showed his age and wisdom, but his body had lost none of its vigor through the long cycles. Luckily for Trela, his mind had lost none of its vigor either. "Did you like the way I had Delft and Ingohan spar for you? They are amazing to watch, are they not?"

"Which two were they?" Trela hated to admit it when she did not know which Guard was which, but she could not know everyone all the time.

"They were sparring when you were over against that wall." Lishean pointed over Trela's left shoulder. "Just before you got to the stand of trees."

She squinted to where he was pointing and then back at the place he had pointed. She walked towards Lishean and the front of the platform as he walked towards her. She was trying to triangulate from where he indicated she was from where he was standing. If it was the bout she was thinking of, the two had split up and were sparring different warriors at this point.

"Hmmm. Him and… him?" Trela pointed to the two that she guessed. A bright grin lit up Lishean's face.

"Yes, well done." He unconsciously wiped the sweat from his own brow. "I will tell them you recognized them immediately."

"Tell them I was impressed by their ferocity." It was true, if a bit belated.

"I will, my Queen." He rested his fists on his hips and looked at her askance. "But you did not come here to watch your warriors spar, did you?"

"Observant as always, Lishean. No, I came to speak with you." She looked around and, though there was no one within earshot, felt a little exposed standing on the platform. "In private, if that is okay?"

"Of course, my Queen, of course." He bowed deeply to her.

"Lead the way, my General." She did not mind being called queen, but it was odd to hear it so many times in a row from him. Lishean laughed politely.

"How is Elzie doing? I have not seen her for some time." Trela turned to follow him.

"She's doing well. She'll be glad to know that you asked about her." He smiled over his shoulder quickly. "I'll tell her you're impressed by her ferocity." They both laughed.

They wandered into a nearby tower and began the slow spiral ascent. The stairway suddenly reminded her of Parthia. She stared at her feet as they wound their way upwards, lost in nostalgic thought. Her mind drifted from the warpack's cries of victory to a quieter time just before the raid. She did not know why, but she thought of Estfale, drinking grog across from her in the crowded bar. She thought of Dartsyle too, but there was something about Estfale's smile that night. Something mischievous. She had not seen him for over a moon and wondered why he should implant himself in her mind at such a time. Nostalgia had a strange way of breeding memories in Trela.

Eventually they reached the top. Lishean grunted the trapdoor open and they climbed up and through. The tower top was simple, but the view across the crenellated wall was magnificently complex. She walked over to the edge and peered out at Agoge. *This is mine*, she thought, *and one day I will suddenly wax nostalgic about this very moment.* The thought made her smile.

"It is an amazing sight, is it not?" Lishean leaned across the crenellation next to hers.

"Can you believe how far we came? As a young girl I used to dream of what Agoge was like. I think I imagined something more slender and graceful and maybe a little less…" Trela looked out across all the walls, beyond the Blaze and towards the squatty low warehouses and dirty streets, trying to think of the right word. "…brutal. But it is certainly more amazing than I had ever imagined. So vibrant. And it is no less beautiful for its brutality."

"Barely. I can barely believe that we did not perish on the way here. All the battles, the marching, the hunger. I can barely believe that we were able to take Dun Oengen, that we were not crushed on the Dekhan Plateau, but what I really cannot believe is that this is what you needed to discuss. Now, what was so important that you had to drag me all the way up here?" His smile was wide and genuine.

"I am being pulled into two different directions. I worked so hard, I fought so hard, to become Queen. And there is much to do and it is as rewarding as it is challenging. I could spend the rest of my life working for this realm from this very spot." Trela turned from the beautiful view and rested her back on the warm stone, the sunlight beat down on the turret and her alike.

"And the other direction?" He kept his gaze out towards the city.

"Clerin communed with Gorbanax. She feels it gave her a quest. They all want me to go but, of course, I told them I could not. However…" She looked up at the lazy clouds, motionless amongst the azure morning sky. "She summoned a Yaven to convince me, Lishean. I stared into an Eternal's eyes and told it that I could not join the quest. It told me that it was my destiny to join, and I still refused."

Lishean did not move but stayed staring into the distance. "And when did you meet this Yaven?"

"Three days ago. I have been unable to think of much else. The Yaven said it would speak with me again about it and I do not know what to do." She took a deep breath and let it out slowly. "I need to finish what I started here, but…"

It was quiet for some time. He seemed to be waiting for her to say more, but she did not know what else to say. The problem was not a complicated one, just a difficult one.

"But you wish permission to leave?" There was a ghost of a smile on his face.

"I don't need permission, but…" She was not really sure what she needed.

"More than anything, you are a creature of destiny. More than anyone I have ever known, seen, or even heard about, you are moved by destiny." He turned and stared hard into her. "Do not listen to Clerin, or to me for that matter. Do not listen to Yavens. Or even Belegs. No! There is only one thing you need to know. On which path lies your destiny? No other thing matters, not to one like you. There is only one being who can tell you what you need to know. And that is yourself. All you need to do is figure out which is the correct direction of pull. Then you push."

"That is exactly my problem, however." Trela was quickly interrupted.

"That is only a problem in your mind! Nowhere else." Lishean looked almost angry. "Why are you here?"

"What do you mean?" She was not used to him being so short with her.

"Why are you here?" He pointed down at the turret under his feet. "Right now, talking to me, why are you here?"

"To ask advice from my General." It seemed as if her shield kept getting struck so constantly that she was unable to muster a counterattack.

"No. You do not need advice. You want to be absolved." Lishean took a deep breath. "You are here because you already know your answer. You are here because you feel that leaving the realm will make you less of a queen. You feel like you are running away, that you are betraying your subjects." He placed a kindly hand on her shoulder. "But you already know all of this so, here... I absolve you. I permit you to go. Even more, I tell you that you are incapable of betraying your subjects. Or if you are capable, then it is your destiny to do so. I know that there is no meanness to your spirit. I can tell that this decision is eating you up. But I also know that you have already made up your mind. Your decision is made, the die is already cast. Arguing about it now, after the decision is finalized, is childish, Trela. It is beneath the likes of you and me." He let his hand drop. "You will go and do what you need to do. That is all there ever was. And, what's more, that is all there ever needed to be."

"I..." Trela thought that she wanted to thank him for his tirade, but she was not sure. She was still a little off balance.

"You are welcome, my Queen. Now, if you will excuse me, I have warriors who truly need my advice and tutelage." He bowed deeply to her.

"Of course." As he turned to leave, she impulsively placed a hand on his shoulder. "And thank you, Lishean. You always know just what I need. Even if I don't."

"That is why I am your General, is it not?" He smiled sweetly and disappeared down the trapdoor.

Trela stood on top of the turret, staring warmly at the city below her. Her mind softened as she thought about Lishean. He was completely correct. As always. About everything. Especially about being her General.

✳✳✳

It was while Trela was alone in her throne room that she found it. She had gone there to think, to be alone without an agenda. With a clear room and a clear mind. She knew that she would have to set up a meeting soon. A meeting with all of them. Clerin and Taglo were inseparable since the summoning and would surely arrive together. There was Knill and Croy, and both Gaens appeared eager. She would have to get Feyazki to promise to show up; he had been notoriously difficult to get to do anything lately. Then there were the warriors. Trela wanted to bring any of the Luftens who wished to join. She wanted those that had helped at Parthia, Dun Oengen, and the Dekhan Plateau. She wanted some from Rewista's warpack and some from Iventorn's. There were so many highly skilled specialists amongst the warpacks of her vast realm. The list in her head grew much too large much too quickly and needed to be pared back. She needed to decide how many to take firstly. Then she could make her list and begin crossing off names. She was in the throne room, trying to think of the perfect number. How many mages would she need? How many warriors? Could she afford to bring any porters or cooks? She did not even want to start thinking about horses versus pack mules.

Trela was frustrated. She felt that once she could decide how many to bring, she could begin the slow process of deciding who to bring. That was much more interesting to her, to weigh each derlian's strength and weaknesses against each other. To find the most balanced fit to the puzzle. That was engaging to her, almost exciting. It would still be grueling and time consuming, but it would be something. She felt like she was just beating her head against a wall about the number, racking her brain with nothing to show for it. A small voice in the back of her mind kept telling her to ask for some help. But she wanted to arrive at the meeting with answers, with a plan. She needed to set the meeting up, to take control from the beginning and bring only those that she trusted on board with her. If the expedition needed to be made, she needed to head it. So, even though she was stumped, she felt that she could not ask for help.

It was this worthless feeling of frustration that had her on her back. She was lying on the plush red carpet that led to the thrones, half on the wide and shallow steps of the dais that the thrones sat upon. She was lying back and lightly beating her thigh with the soft hammer side of her fist, certainly not hard or painful, but in an unconscious rhythm. That was when she saw it. It was just a glimmer at first. Just something out of the corner of her eye. Something under the throne.

Trela rolled over and crawled up to the chairs that served as thrones. There, under the one that she had chosen to use for herself, the one used by Qizern and traditionally thought of as the "male" throne, the one on the right as you faced them, there was a small bronze lock. The chair and cushion portion of the thrones were quite thick, but she had never thought twice about it. As she crawled up the final steps she knew, she *knew*, that there was only one key that could open this lock. How many times had she sat up there and not noticed? How many times had she specifically looked in this room for a lock to fit her key? She would have cursed herself for her stupidity if she had not been so excited. It was with shaking fingers that she produced the key she kept constantly on her person.

It fit perfectly. She crouched like that for a brief moment in time. She was kneeling down and staring upwards, bent sideways and awkwardly, key in lock, ready to turn. She breathed in and out deeply. It was not fear of a trap that made her hesitate, nor was it anticipation of something great; this was a small space hidden under the seat cushion, to be sure. No, it was the trepidation that she had been carrying a useless key around, searching vainly for some secret treasure, that she would turn the key and only dust would fall to the floor, that it would all be for naught, that it would be empty. Why would it not be? If Qizern had hidden some treasure in there, would he not have moved it before confronting her warpack on the Dekhan Plateau? But maybe he had assumed that there was no way for him to lose? Maybe the key was left by a predecessor and never even found by Qizern? Maybe…? She was beginning to cramp up stuck in her uncomfortable position, so she turned the lock.

Trela need not have worried. Four scrolls, a pendant, three rings, a bejeweled dagger, and a pouch full of coins fell out amidst the dust. She unconsciously let out a laugh of relief. She sat on the cushy carpet with her back against her throne, left the bottom of the chair open, and gathered her treasures before her. The dagger was finely wrought but appeared to be ceremonial. There was certainly no edge on the blade, and even the point would not puncture skin when Trela pushed her finger against it. It had a large ruby on its pommel, dark red, almost the color of blood. The hilt itself was a smooth white spiral of something, maybe a tusk or horn of some animal, or maybe some rare and light stone. In the spiral itself were laid gold and silver braided wires. It was these wires that allowed one to grip the hilt. The quillon guard swept up on both sides of the blade and had two small hoops perpendicularly arranged, offering a full degree of protection if the dagger were able to be used. The circular hoops were encrusted with tiny diamonds on all three exterior faces. The quillons swept up to points like a heraldic bird and had medium-sized emeralds adhered to the ends. The blade had a cannelure blood groove down its center and was finely etched with complex and busy filigree that extended all the way to its straight, pointed tip. The rings were similarly encrusted, each with a large stone at its center and surrounded by flowery secondary stones. One had a star sapphire as its central stone that was crowded by tiny diamonds and set in platinum. Another was a diamond itself that had many colored stones spread around a delicate lacework of metal, almost like a wide spider's web. It was sized so large that Trela would not have been able to wear it on her thumb. The third ring was of a stone that she did not recognize. It was alabaster white with shimmers of rainbow flowing around its surface. The pendant held more gems and jewels adhered to it than all of the other items combined. Its central stone, however, was pitch black and gigantic and did not have the raw beauty that the other stones had. It was smooth and glossy and utterly opaque. She left the coins to her side for a moment because what really interested her were the scrolls. They were each individually labeled: "To my Murderer," "To my Faithful Follower," "To my Successor," and "To my Lover." If she was not mistaken, each label appeared to be in Qizern's own hand. They were all certainly written in one hand alone. She opened the one labeled "To my Murderer" first:

"I knew you would open this one first. I knew it because my predecessor left me similar scrolls and this was the first of his that I opened. It has a certain ring of truth to it, does it not? However, I will not harangue you about it like my predecessor did to me. Calling me all sorts of vile names from the grave. I understand that there are some implacable truths to reality. You have murdered me. Another will follow to murder you. And so it goes. I will say that I hope you murdered me in open combat and did not slip behind me like a thief. I would hope that you would be filled with crippling guilt, regret, and embarrassment if that is the way it happened. However, I have known enough assassins in my life to realize that this will not be the case. And, truly, if one is capable of doing a despicable thing, one should be capable of enduring the consequences. If the derlian mind is the master of any one thing, it is this: justifying itself. But I digress.

If you are not my murderer and are something more mundane, like some curious maid, rest assured that I will know that my throne has been tampered with. I will find out who you are and I will torture you until you beg me for the sweet release of death, which will not come quickly. Your only hope is to confess this crime immediately. Now, before you read any further.

This scroll shall be short and simple. I will not attempt to explain my rule here, that will be in the scroll to my successor. I will not attempt to explain my life here, that will be in the scroll to my faithful follower. You will probably skip this scroll. Do not worry, it will not bother me. It will be there if you ever get curious. I hope, with all of my heart, that the scroll to my lover is not for you. It is my last wish that no one read that scroll except for my lover. If you, my murderer, has any iota of honor or respect flowing through your veins, then you will grant this last wish. I ask that you find my latest lover, whomever they may be, and give them the scroll unopened and unread. I am dead now, you can give me this much.

The coins that are in the pouch adjacent to this scroll are ancient. This is one of the traditions that I fully embraced when becoming King. There is one coin for every ruler that this realm has ever known. Each with their head emblazoned on one side of the coin. There are only about eight different tails. The most common, of course, is a mighty spewing volcano. But I shall let you peruse through them. When I became King, one of the first things I did was to mint the new coins. There is little in this world that will make you feel more like royalty than spending monies with your own face on them. It is glorious.

The rings and the dagger are baubles. They were placed there by my predecessor, or his, or so on, and I had little use for them, so I stuffed them back up into the throne and there they stayed during my reign. You may, of course, do with them as you wish. The pendant I had commissioned for my Queen. She was, unfortunately, stolen by another. One of my own Guard, I might add. Be careful of which bodyguards you choose to protect whom. You never know who will wield the knife that buries itself in your back.

I hope that you hold Strife now. I will understand if you are a swordmaster and wish to keep your own mistress, but let me tell you of mine. She was forged by a master Gaen smith who folded the metal over a thousand times. He used the very fires that pulse behind Agoge. She is perfectly balanced and keeps a razor's edge. There are few pieces of steel in this realm that could compare to her naked truth. However, she, like all good mistresses, has a secret. I was not content with having an amazing piece of steel, even as close to perfect as she was when she was finally quenched. I needed an edge over my enemies, double entendre intended. I had heard of an amazing Cabal that could make items eternally magical, the Cabal of Lochom. I will not bore you with the details or the costs, but her edge will never dull, she will never rust or pit, she can bite through steel armor, she can glow at your will to assist you in the dark, and most importantly, she can maim with a scratch. She has a Yaven living within her."

Trela instantly stood upright. She could feel the blood charging through her neck like a panicked herd of wild horses, her pulse made up of deafening hoof beats. She had to consciously stop herself from charging out of the room. She still had scrolls to read; she had not even finished the first one. There was an urgency to her now, however. Something told her that she must find Clerin and Taglo. She must tell them about the scroll. Immediately. And, most of all, she must find Strife. She could not even think of what had happened to the sword. Lishean would probably know. Or maybe Tweltas or Pejal. One of those present when she defeated Qizern, surely. Who had picked it up? When Trela closed her eyes, all she could see was the swarm of Pyrans around her, lifting her on their shoulders and parading her around. There were plenty who stayed stoically still and stared grimly at her with hard eyes and set jaws. One of them had to know.

Trela summoned her Guards. The one outside of her chamber ran to grab the few who were at her antechamber. When they arrived, she told them she needed a meeting with all those who had watched her defeat Qizern.

"No, not a meeting. A triumphant meal celebrating an anniversary of the great event. All those present at the last battle are invited. No, not invited. All those who were present when I defeated Qizern are required to attend in their finest dress uniforms. Military honors will be bestowed!" Trela rattled on to the confused Guards in front of her. The fantastic thing about being Queen, however, was not having to explain yourself. They dutifully bowed and ran off to do her bidding.

How could she have left the sword lying in the dust? Qizern's sword! She should have at least kept it as a souvenir. Or given it to a specific warrior as a reward. She still wore Talon when she needed to have a sword at her hip. She wanted to be annoyed with someone else for not picking up the treasure for her. But in the end, and rightfully so, she only had herself to blame. She gathered up all of the treasures from the throne and left the room in a tizzy. There was much work to do.

Chapter 4

Vrric awoke in a sour mood. It had not happened for a while and it reminded him of when he had first arrived at Agoge. The first week after Trela's victory was fantastic by all accounts. It was a complete city-wide celebration. No, it was the entire plateau's celebration and, for all Vrric knew, it was the entire realm that squealed and cavorted throughout the days and nights. When he was not partaking in the revelry, he would look out his window and watch the fires dance across the plateau. They dotted the landscape like the stars in the sky but much, much brighter. He truly enjoyed that first week. It was the week afterwards that placed a low and hazy malaise about him. He had danced with Clerin, and then with Gyllhelon, and then with the myriad parade of Pyrans that surrounded him. After the week was over, however, he was again alone. But this was not the cause of his malaise. In fact, it was alone that he felt most comfortable the vast majority of the time. Nor was it being a foreigner in a strange land. Nor was it the bored ennui caused by a contentless comfort, though he felt that the lack of challenges did adversely affect his mood. The real problem was that he could not define what was bothering him, only what was not. He would take a viable candidate, examine it, poke it and prod it, and place it back from whence it came. He could say, with complete surety, that this particular candidate was not the cause. But then he ran out of candidates and he was no closer to figuring out the underlying issue. It was a bit maddening in itself, and he would have been more concerned over it but could not muster the interest. Then, just as suddenly, it had vanished. Poof. It vanished near the time he first started going to the mage's guild in Agoge. He knew there was some link there, though it lay just as hidden as his overall aura of malaise had. But this day, after a couple of moons of relative happiness, he awoke feeling out of sorts again.

It was in the middle of the week. He sometimes had difficulty telling what day it was since he had no routine there in Agoge. No job, no schooling, no obligations, no reason to keep track of these things. He knew that it was about the middle of the week, however, by instinct if nothing else. The sounds that came into his window from the outside realm were muted by the heavy velvet of routine. These were not the sounds of suppressed excitement of the approaching days off, nor were they the grumbles that accompanied the beginning of the week. This was somewhere in the long stretch in between. Heads were down, watching their own booted feet shuffle along the same worn path. Quiet pleasantries, though certainly not forced, were doled out with an absentmindedness that bespoke of gray habit. The day should have induced a low melancholic feel to Vrric, but it did not. It was a surly sourness that coursed through him. The numbing melancholy was there, it was an ingredient, a spice, but it did not fully define the taste of his mood. There was a little too much... angst. That might have been too shy of a word, however, plus there was not any fear involved, though maybe some dread. And there was a little too much anger in Vrric to be truly melancholic. There, it was out in the open. The trouble was he did not know why. Like before, there was no concrete reason to be feeling angry, nothing had happened to him at all. He had just awoken with this in him, as a part of him. He could already tell it was going to be a long day.

Vrric tried to hide the day away. He felt that if he quarantined himself from others, his mood could not get any worse. Barricaded in his room, he studied his books and then tried to relax by meditating. He sat on a pillow in the middle of the floor, with each foot resting on an opposite thigh. He straightened his back and began to build a smooth cadence of breathing. It took a while to clear his mind, but with much concentration he was finally able to calm his thoughts. He breathed in deeply through his nose, held the breath for the briefest of moments, and then let it slowly out through loosely pursed lips. He could move the energy above him and out from him quite easily. The branches of his energy tree had always seemed simple to perform, no matter what state he was in, but bringing the energy back into himself seemed difficult that day. It was as if his roots could not penetrate the flagstone floor beneath him. He was unable to complete the loop, which left his energy wafting about himself, unfettered. He squinted his eyes down tight and pushed with all his might, but to no avail. He could not seem to get his roots to burrow down, could not draw energy up into him. He thought about it for a while and decided that he was going about it the wrong way. Typically, he could easily drill down with his roots and lap up all the untapped energy that lay beneath him. Tap into that invisible net that held all the known realms together. Then he could flow the energy out of him through his branches. Eventually the ebb and flow would bring a balance to his chaotic world and he would be left with the perfect amount of energy thrumming through him. But here in the Pyran realm he sometimes had difficulties getting his roots down, especially at Agoge.

It had always seemed so simple for him in the Luften realm and even in the desert. He thought that maybe he should not concern himself with roots here, maybe he did need to drill deep into the well of the world. Maybe he should think of it more like a siphon. Maybe he should just pour all of the energy out of himself through his branches and when he was empty, the energy might just be drawn up into him like water drawn up an empty straw. So he tried. He poured everything out of himself. His branches, the air around him, and even the hairs on his head seemed to have a vibrant tingle about them. It was similar to the odd sensation just before he cast a lightning spell. And then, when he thought he could do no more, that he was just an empty husk, there was a "pop" and he felt energy pouring into him from his roots. It was a delicious feeling after so much frustrating nothingness. It had taken some time, but he finally felt that he was getting his mood under control. Just then, there was a knock at the door. Something told him to ignore it, but he was worried that the sensation was merely a selfish knee-jerk reaction to being interrupted. So he breathed in one more deep breath and forced himself to get up and answer the door.

Vrric inwardly, and hopefully surreptitiously, groaned once the door opened. There were certainly many derlians that he would not be excited about seeing, that he could be said to be quite neutral or ambivalent about, but there were a select few that he just did not like at all. Olsfang was one of those few. Much like the impetus for Vrric's mood, however, he was not quite sure what triggered his distaste for Olsfang. There was an odd combination of long pauses coupled with quick interruptions as they conversed. There was a certain haughtiness to his demeanor. A bit of agonizing self-pity, just hovering under the surface. It seemed that no matter one derlian's problem, there was a similar, worse one that Olsfang was currently going through. To be able to pinpoint an exact issue that was the culprit, however, was impossible.

"I see that I have interrupted you." Olsfang gave an ingratiating smile. The spreading of his face only seemed to increase the thin and sickly nature of his beard.

"No. No, really, come in." Vrric stepped aside for Olsfang to enter.

Olsfang, for his part, merely cocked a shoulder inside the open doorway. He craned his head around briefly and gave another smile. Though this one was still ingratiating, it had a bit of a pained look to it as well.

"Are you sure that I am not interrupting?" His voice shot up an octave at the end of his sentence. "I really do not want to be a bother."

It took all of Vrric's self-control not to yell "Too late!" at that statement. Instead he forced a smile and waved Olsfang in. "You are not a bother at all, please come in." As he smiled though, he had a scary moment where he wondered what his own face looked like during the exchange. Surely his own insincerity was visible.

"Thank you, you are quite generous." Olsfang quickly strode in and flopped down on one end of Vrric's couch. Then he stayed oddly quiet, staring at the empty end of the couch.

Knowing his cue, Vrric quietly shut the door and sat down. He stared at Olsfang. Olsfang stared back. He was about to ask why Olsfang was visiting, attempting to formulate a non-aggressive question with lips barely parting in anticipation, when he was preemptively interrupted.

"I am sure you are wondering why I am here." Where a normal derlian would have continued speaking, Olsfang stopped.

"Yes." Vrric nodded to Oslfang. Who, for his part, kept staring blankly at Vrric. "I certainly am curious as to the reason for your visit."

"You know that I work with Ryshial, correct?" He waited for Vrric's nod before continuing. "Yes, we work together quite often, her and I. We feel you should spend more time at the mage's guild, Feyazki. We feel that your skills, as rough and unhoned as they are, are a good match for the guild. Maybe tempered with some more study, you could find yourself a position there."

Vrric could not tell if he was being complimented or debased. It was an odd feeling. Though he had never met Ryshial, he knew she was a powerful member of the guild. He decided that she had requested his appearance and that Olsfang had argued against it. There were many mages at the guild that Vrric got along with just fine, however. For the life of him, he could not fathom why she would send someone so odious to make the request. Unless she wanted him to refuse. But then why send anyone at all? Unless she wanted to be seen making the gesture. He had been skating by with being part of Trela's inner circle, somewhat halfheartedly thinking he was untouchable. He realized that he would have to start paying more attention.

"Of course, that sounds like a lovely idea." Vrric put as much enthusiasm into it as he could muster. He thought that immediately acquiescing to the invitation would do two things; annoy whomever had sent Olsfang to his door, and have the added benefit of removing Olsfang from his quarters that much sooner.

True to form, Olsfang stared blankly at Vrric until he opened his mouth to speak again. "That is excellent news. I am sure Ryshial will be pleased to hear of your coming." He was quiet for another moment. Instead of opening his mouth and giving Olsfang the satisfaction of interrupting him, Vrric stared back intently. Waiting for the continuation. It finally arrived. "When shall I tell her you will be arriving?"

"Tomorrow. Tell her I shall arrive at the mage's guild tomorrow at noon." Vrric refused to show up the same day that he was asked. That would have made him feel subservient. He could feel another long pause boiling up in Olsfang. Instead of waiting, he charged forth. "That should satisfy both Ryshial and yourself, thank you for stopping by." Vrric stood and swept his hand towards the door. "I look forward to our further discussions." He paused, ever so slightly. "Tomorrow."

Olsfang slowly stood and smiled his sickly, ingratiating smile. With an almost imperceptible nod he turned and shuffled towards the door. At the entrance, or the exit, depending on which way it was thought about, he turned back. His black eyes had an almost sad twinge to them, but with something else behind them as well. Almost… a distaste?

"Ryshial is not one to be trifled with." He then turned and slowly walked out.

Vrric let him leave in silence, let him have the last word. He did not want to give Olsfang any excuses for staying a moment longer. Also, it was a bit of an odd statement and Vrric wanted to mull it over before responding. Was Olsfang annoyed at Vrric's choosing the meeting date and time? Was he warning Vrric to show up with a formal demeanor and dress, or to not be late? Or was he actually warning Vrric that Ryshial had something nefarious in mind? He shut the door behind Olsfang's diminishing figure and sat back down at the couch. Sideways, with his feet up. He pondered the matter for some time, forgetting that he was supposed to be in a foul mood.

Vrric awoke the next morning to the bright and sunny day, listening to the happy chirping birds outside his window. It was almost too beautiful. He lay in bed for some time, just listening and relaxing, before starting his day. After cooking his breakfast, he cast a spell to heat up some water for his bath. While soaking, he tried to decide what to wear. It had been a long time since he had worn his mage's robes, all gray and hemmed in glyphs. Even when he had visited the guild at Agoge in the past, he had worn his typical traveling clothes. He always attended informal gatherings, nothing official. He also had some court attire, hastily bought for Trela's celebration. But that seemed a little much. He could always show up, once again, in his traveling clothes. He would certainly be recognized then. His forehead wrinkled while he thought about it.

Vrric wandered the halls and the courtyards of Agoge, enjoying the simple meander through other derlian's lives. Though he was prone to becoming bored with complacency, there were days when he completely enjoyed doing nothing, watching others and contemplating trivial matters like what to wear. Today was such a day. He could have wasted the entire day wandering around in his robes.

A small courtyard beckoned through an alleyway. He ducked under the stone arch, not that it was very low, and wandered into a lush garden. There was a small stream bed, with only a trickle of water flowing, that appeared from a small hole in a wall. It escaped through another hole on the opposite, downhill side. A smaller, but quite healthy, willow tree stood in the center of the courtyard, with the stream meandering beside and a circle of grass and flowers surrounding the willow like a rapt audience. Each corner of the courtyard, split by the intertwining paths, had a triangular piece of grass with clumps of raucous colorful flowers. It was like a dream world. Vrric walked over to the willow, stepping off the path and onto the surrounding grass, and pressed his hands upon the bark. There was a hum, a whisper. He pressed his face upon the bark. There was the murmur of a caress. Was this the cause of the malaise? There were so few trees there in the Pyran realm. Certainly no living buildings like the helioarcs. Was he just pining for his home? Missing the energy that flowed through life that was condensed and concentrated by trees? Maybe, maybe not. He did not answer anything that morning on his way to the guild, but he felt better for stopping at the little willow. He gave it a light kiss before wandering again on his way.

He finally found himself in the courtyard that contained the entrance to the mage's guild. The gigantic doors, flanked on either side by rounded turrets, always seemed out of place in middle of the Blaze, in the middle of Agoge. And they served little purpose, for almost anyone could come and go as they pleased. Vrric thought they existed to remind the average citizens of what they were about to enter, or walk by. They were a statement of the guild presence.

Vrric strode purposefully towards the doors. There were giant brass lion heads with heavy rings held in their mouths and with balls on the ends for the knockers. Their golden manes shimmered in the morning sun, giving them a slight lifelike regality. He lifted one of the rings and crashed it down on its striker plate in one heavy motion. The brass ball made a satisfying clacking sound that reverberated through the wooden door. He did not have to wait too long until the door swung open.

A young shy neophyte in white robes was waiting on the other side. He had slightly unkempt hair and light brown eyes. He kept his eyes downcast as he introduced himself to Vrric.

"I am Hulind and I will be your guide for this day." Hulind's overarching demeanor was too timid for Vrric to enjoy, but he did like the underlying respect.

"I am Feyazki, personal mage to Queen Trela." It had been over a moon since Vrric had last spoken with Trela, but he did not feel that he needed to tell others that.

"Yes, all of us neophytes have heard of your exploits." He turned on his bare feet and began walking away. Vrric assumed correctly to follow him. "Is it true that you can summon lightning?"

"Yes. Currently that is my only Minora syllable." It felt odd to be speaking to the back of someone's head, but it did not seem to bother Hulind at all.

"And is it true that you defeated a Tlana?" Hulind's voice sounded excited, but his back was stiff and he made no effort to turn.

"That is also true. Or, at least, that I survived a Tlana." Vrric followed Hulind deep into the maze of the guild without much thought. He had been through the bowels of the guild before, but never through this particular area. He wondered, belatedly, if he should have been paying more attention to the path he was on.

"If you are alive, then it was defeated." Vrric though he heard a smile in Hulind's voice. "I have yet to hear of a Tlana showing any mercy, or giving up the hunt, as it were. Not that I have ever come near one, and believe me that is not on my agenda, but their most rumored attributes are tenacity and ruthlessness." Hulind stopped at a door. "We are here."

Hulind knocked a short, five-note rhythm onto the wooden door. A few fleeting moments of silence passed where Vrric wondered if he should continue with his story. It was too quiet to speak, however.

"Enter." The voice was strong and melodic at the same time. It had a bit unconscious power behind it, like someone who was used to having their orders followed promptly.

Hulind promptly opened the door. He bowed to the mage at the interior, swung his bow to encompass Vrric and, somehow, he swept his arm out to encourage Vrric to enter. Vrric wondered if Hulind was at the guild to learn magic or protocol. He wondered briefly where the Pyran's desires lay; his natural abilities were obvious.

Vrric walked wordlessly by Hulind. The room was small and cozy. Certainly not a study, nor a library, it only included two tables and a smattering of chairs. The Pyran at the end of the far table immediately caught Vrric's attention. She had long hair, pulled back by a thong of leather across her forehead. Her brown eyes were a shade lighter than her hair and they seemed to reflect the glow from her smile. She had a tight bodice laced up with a bit of shoulder peeking beyond her overdress. Vrric found his mouth automatically curving into a big grin.

"You must be Feyazki. I am Ryshial." She stood and extended her hand, palm down. Vrric took her long delicate fingers in his hand and lifted her knuckles for a light kiss.

"Pleased to make your acquaintance." She smiled appreciatively at his gesture. They both sat and Hulind brought over some water.

"And I yours. I have heard much about you and your exploits and decided it would be best to hear them from you." Her laugh lit the room.

"He was telling me of his besting the Tlana." Hulind kept his head down but obviously nodded towards Vrric.

"Thank you for your clumsy segue Hulind, however I doubt your services will be needed much further. Please wait elsewhere." There was a small flash of anger that shot from the corner of her eye, but it disappeared as quickly as it had formed. Vrric decided to rethink where he thought Hulind's talents lay.

Ryshial was quiet until the shamed Hulind retreated from the room. Then, suddenly, she brightened back up. She took a deep breath and turned back to Vrric.

"I am studying the desert and all of its denizens. The stories of your confrontation with the Tlana highly interest me and, if I am honest, are the main reason that I asked you here. I am curious about the Vijen and the rumored well, but the Tlana, in specific, hold a great interest for me. If you do not mind continuing with your retelling... I have never heard from any derlian who has survived meeting a Tlana."

"Well, to be honest, I only survived due to two things. One, the Tlana was wildly overconfident. Two, I discovered a Minora syllable just at that crucial moment." Vrric spoke animatedly. He had wanted to be calm and in control, quiet almost. For some reason, however, he felt excited to tell his tale to Ryshial.

"So it is true. You learned how to cast lightning during your fight with the Tlana." She was nodding absently towards him.

"Yes. I would have died without that realization. But, and this is the weird thing, I do not think I would have found the Minora without the Tlana." Vrric took a deep breath. "I had been thinking about it a long time, for sure. I had been wondering if it were its own element. Was it fire, was it air, and the like. There was some serious... not forethought, but maybe pre-thought... that went into the realization. The deepening, if you will, of my understanding of the concept." He took a sip of water, part of him wishing it was the numbing grog that he was used to during these types of conversations. Ryshial stayed silent. "You see, I heard the syllable. I heard it before I saw it, before I felt it tearing through me. That is the only reason why I knew what it was. Why I understood it."

"What do you mean that you heard it?" Ryshial leaned forward expectantly, eyes bright with wonder or excitement, he did not know which.

"I heard it." He racked his brain. "I had thought it was not real at first. A hallucination. You see, the thing, the Tlana, it was hunting. It found me by chance, or maybe it was stalking me. But there was this horrendous thunderstorm all around us. There were flashes of coherence followed by deafening shouts of outrage. It was quite confusing. But there it stood, in front of me, the Tlana. I believe that it wished to give chase but I could not move. Then I heard a small chant in my head as the air grew thick with potential. Then I was struck by the Tlana. It was like a bolt of lightning. For all I know, it was a bolt of lightning. Then we would struggle. I would do my best against it, but nothing seemed to phase it. Nothing. Then I would hear the chant again. Then I was struck again. For the life of me, I do not know how long this repeated itself, but finally, through all that pain, I realized that the chant was the harbinger. It was the syllable. It was the lightning. In that moment, on the verge of capitulation, I equated what I heard with what I had been thinking. The chant became reality and through that equation the syllable became reality. At that moment, the time that I was meant to die, or the time that I could have died, I realized that I needed to strike back with the weapon that was being used against me. I could not use fire. I could not heal myself and retreat. There was only forwards. Into the breach." He squinted at her. "That was when I cast my first lightning spell."

"And you won?" It was a statement posed as a question.

"I passed out. When I awoke, I was covered in leaves. Vijen leaves, I believe." Vrric smiled his response over to her.

Ryshial's eyes widened and she clapped once. It appeared unconscious because she stopped herself quickly and pressed her hands flat together in front of her. They then raised up to almost touch her chin.

"Are you sure? You must be absolutely positive. Were they Vijen leaves?" Though she still looked excited, her eyes had gained some serious levity during her question.

"Yes, I—" He was quickly interrupted.

"Please, think about it." Her hands hand dropped back to their usual position at the edge of the table. "This is important to me."

Vrric took the time to think about it. He tried to imagine them, to see their exact composition, but could not be positive. They had been labeled "Vijen leaves" in his mind when he awoke and saw them and when he first told this story, and every telling afterwards only solidified the label.

"I am as positive as I can be." He spoke the truth.

"Then let me tell you a story. There is legend of a great Pyran king who had a suit of armor made out of leaves. This was eons ago, but a while after the derlian inception, and the king's actual name became lost to oblivion. The armor was said to be impervious to both weapons and magic. During my father's youth, before the reign of Qizern, it became vogue to attempt to replicate some of these types of old legends. Every imaginable leaf was tested. Every imaginable spell was cast upon them. In the end, it was decided that the legend was either false, or that the king was a great magician and was able to cast a protection spell surreptitiously upon himself before each attack. The collective interest, the collective unconscious, let go of this particular legend and let it be itself. A legend. All but my father." Ryshial took a deep drink of water. "There is another legend in the Pyran realms, and this may extend into the Luften, I do not know. This legend states that the Tlana are ethereal. Non-corporeal smoke. Maybe akin to wind." Here she smiled mischievously at Vrric. "They do not exist except in the mind. However, the Vijen are very much rooted to this physical realm. Though there is no Pyran record of it, either written or in legend, it is assumed that the Vijen can be touched and felt. It is assumed that their wooden trunks are covered in bark and their leaves are wrested from their grasp by age and wind like all deciduous trees. This process, abscission, natural or not, means that one could gather Vijen leaves. This legend states that the Tlana wear the leaves to become corporeal. This legend drew my father to the great desert soon after my birth, or so my mother tells me. For he, unlike his contemporaries, thought he had figured the reality behind the great king by combining two separate legends. He has never returned and the little girl inside of me likes to think of him wandering about the desert, still trying to gather enough Vijen leaves to make a suit of armor. The adult in me, however, has been instilled with a passion to understand the desert and all of its denizens. Especially the curious relationship between the Tlana and the Vijen."

"Maybe your father drank from the well. Have you heard about the well in the middle of the desert?" Vrric almost felt bad for leading her away from the leaves, but he was not sure what else about that subject could be discussed. He felt that it would all be mere speculation.

"Did you also see the well? I have been yearning to speak with someone about the well of immortality. Someone who actually knew something, not just stale and regurgitated rumors." Her eyes brightened again with enthusiasm.

"Well of eternity…" Vrric corrected her unconsciously.

"What?" Though he had been quiet, she did not let his statement slip by.

"As far as I understand it, the well does not imbue immortality, but it does extend life for as long as you drink from it." He instantly realized that he had placed himself back into the position of speculating.

"You must tell me everything you know about the well." Though just as cute, Ryshial's grin was less infectious than it had been earlier.

"Well, I do not know much, we were only there briefly and I did not interact with the denizens of that barren village as much as some of the others." He reeled his mind back to begin his spiel.

"I am sure you will be a wealth of information." He could not tell if she was nodding at him or at herself. "Then we can go back to your fight with the Tlana."

Vrric opened his mouth, but then he closed it. His mind furiously wandered to the Tlana and back to the well. All motion with little substance. He squinted at Ryshial.

"You shouldn't interrupt someone who is telling a story about them that you have asked them to tell. They are following their own script and may have difficulty picking up where they have left off. I understand that you want truth, but there is a rhythm to a re-told story that attempts to put the listener in a trance. The trance of experiencing the story. Much of the time, there is also a trance induced, consciously or not, into the speaker. This rhythm brings forth details, chosen during the first telling and refined during subsequent ones, that are essential to the flow of the story. The flow of the story is essential to the recall of the subsequent details, and so on. There will definitely be deceit, unconscious or not, that is woven into their script. This you will surely want to ferret out later. But if you can keep all those questions within you, only to be released after the initial story has been told, you will be able to better hone your questions and, therefore, able to glean a more comprehensive truth." And he stopped himself.

He knew immediately, knew in his very heart, knew beyond any shadow of a doubt, that he had just said exactly the wrong thing. But it was wrong for more than one reason. He thought it was wrong because it would… well, not necessarily hurt Ryshial, but maybe shame her into silence. What was the phrase? "Suck the wind out of her sails." This happened and he immediately felt bad for it. She stayed silent as he fumbled through his memories of the well. But the other reason was a thousand times worse. She let him tell his story, but then drilled him with hundreds of questions afterwards. Some were about things he did not even realize he had thought, let alone spoken aloud. He had never met a derlian with such a memory for minute detail before in his life. Then, just when he felt that he had been through enough, she asked about his fight with the Tlana again. He left feeling sore, physically sore. He vowed to never return to the guild again. He decided he would live out the rest of his time in Agoge as a hermit, hiding alone in his room. Maybe, just maybe, he would come out if Clerin ever deigned to visit him, but that would be it. It was with an air of finality that he collapsed on his semi-comfortable couch. His only consolation was that he had not run into Olsfang while he was at the guild.

Clerin did not visit him, but Gyllhelon did. She showed up with Torpalin and Escha. He could not tell if he was surprised by Torpalin and Escha's budding relationship or not. Neither one could be classified as a genius, but both were incredibly nice, honest, joyful, and hard-working Luftens. While Escha was a bit of a quiet loner, a little awkward around others, especially crowds, Torpalin was gregarious. While Torpalin was a little loud, rambunctious, and could take a joke a little too far, Escha was always earnest. They were both scarily loyal friends once you got to know them. In some ways they were very much like each other, and in others they were exact opposites. Vrric wondered if all complimentary relationships were made up of juxtapositions such as those. Whether or not he was surprised about them, he found himself rooting for their relationship.

"You have got to come out to the Turbinium festival with us. It is supposed to be mystical, the whole town will be there." Torpalin was grinning broadly.

"The whole town always shows up for all of these festivals." Vrric was tired and, for no good reason, a little grumpy. "What is this one for, anyway?"

"Some harvest thing, but not the main harvest festival. Maybe an early harvest festival? A summer harvest?" Escha cocked an inquisitive eyebrow.

"But you are missing the point. The whole town will be *there*. As in out on the plateau. Nobody celebrates within the walls of Agoge." Torpalin was gesticulating with his large fingers. Vrric would have called them stubby, but they were not short.

"Everyone camps out for five nights. Apparently, it is a sea of tents for as far as the eye can see." Gyllhelon smiled at her own simple cleverness. Her smile was infectious, cutting through Vrric's own mood. "Come on, Feyazki. It will be a lot of fun." She had a small lilting laugh. Her long fingers, held loosely in her hand, tried vainly to cover her mouth as she laughed, but he could still glimpse her lips and gleaming white teeth behind. Like joyous prisoners behind the flimsy cage of her strong fingers. Her raven-black hair vibrated with her laughter, framing her high cheekbones and scintillating eyes. His pulse quickened and his mouth got dry for no conscious reason.

"That... that sounds fantastic." He could not say no. "When does the festival start?"

"Tonight!" Torpalin's voice boomed through Vrric's small room.

Vrric had spent the day packing his meager things. He did not need a tent, since Torpalin's would easily fit four. "It will fit six or seven if we are all real cozy with each other," he had quipped. Nor did Vrric need to bring his blackened cooking pots or pans or food. All he really needed were some clothes, coins, bedding, and toiletries. It had been over a week since he had left his quarters for more than small errands. He felt a certain amount of nervousness mixed with a little bit of excitement.

Gyllhelon arrived to walk him down to Torpalin's tent. It was a little odd to see her without her long, thin blade strapped to her left leg. Kind of like she was missing an appendage. She strode in purposefully and glanced at his sparse, well not squalid, but certainly not opulent, residence. He could not tell if her eye was disapproving or not. He briefly wished he had spent more time tidying up before her arrival. He was not one to worry much about the unchangeable past, however.

"I see you are all packed up." Her voice lilted up slightly at the end of her sentence. As if it could be a question if he was not quite finished.

"Waiting as patiently as possible." Vrric found himself in a good mood.

"Well then, we should not keep you waiting any longer, should we?" She smiled and nodded her head towards the door.

Vrric grabbed up his various bags and situated them about his body before stepping towards the door. Though she had nothing with her, Gyllhelon did not offer to carry any of his stuff for him. He would, of course, not have let her burden herself, but he felt a little odd that she had not offered. The thought quickly faded from his mind as they left. He locked his door and then tried to open it several times just to make sure it had locked properly. He smiled weakly at her while she watched his little ritual dispassionately.

They wandered through the Blaze and out into Agoge proper. The sun was low enough to cast long shadows, but still beat down upon the mostly stone city with merciless energy. There were a couple of times during their walk that Vrric swore he could see the heat vapors rising, making hazy waves. They walked side by side, but since he had a bag on each shoulder as well as a central backpack, she was farther away than he would have liked. It made following her sudden turns through the maze of streets that much harder to keep up with. It was nothing, however, compared to the maze of tents that were tightly clustered outside the city's walls. For as far as the eye could see there was varied colored canvas fluttering in the hot and dry wind.

They walked along a wide and open avenue as they left the gate, and off to either side, there were many meandering paths through the tents. Vrric knew that if he wandered off the main thoroughfare he would become instantly lost. He quietly hoped that Gyllhelon did not feel as overwhelmed as he was. After all, if they had set the tent up earlier today, how well could the path back be rooted in her mind?

The main thoroughfare came to a circular plaza of open ground. From there, four large avenues shot off in different cardinal directions. Vrric squinted in one of the directions and could see another open circular plaza off in the distance. The one they were currently in had a large wooden stage in its center. The curtains were down, shrouding the stage in velvety secrecy. As they walked around, he noticed that there were several booths on the back side of the stage, selling various meats on a stick and other Pyran delectables. There was a small group of acrobats off to the side, one balancing on a low tightrope and another juggling knives. There was one standing on another's shoulders, squatting a little for balance, while another was doing a small series of backflips. It appeared more like they were practicing than performing. There were several children surrounding them, but certainly no crowds. Gyllhelon turned right and walked down another avenue towards another circular plaza.

There were two more plazas, or maybe it was three, before she dove into the tight paths amongst the multi-colored tents. It was not until they had reached Torpalin's warpack-issued beige tent that Vrric fully realized how odd the colored tents were. These could not hide amongst the barren rocks, nor the forests, nor anywhere. The sea of tents that he was surrounded by were obviously civilian tents. It was a little bit of a shock to realize this. It had seemed to him that every Pyran served in a warpack at one point in their lives, and should therefore have the same boring type of tent. It made him wonder how many Pyrans actually participated in the warpack lifestyle. It certainly pervaded their culture, but it might not be as ubiquitously prominent as he had once thought.

"You finally brought him!" Escha popped out of the tent. Though the flap was standing wide open, the entrance was turned such that the hole was pitch black. Vrric amused himself with the thought that she had just stepped out of the Void.

"It is amazing how long it takes to wind up to the Blaze and back." Gyllhelon smiled weakly.

"Why didn't Feyazki fly you down?" Escha's eyebrows shot up and she snuck a sidelong glance at Vrric.

"He never offered…" Gyllhelon's voice was a little muted.

"Saving your strength for later?" Escha kept grinning through it all.

"Sure." Vrric was not really sure what she meant. Maybe he could fly Gyllhelon around later tonight? Truthfully, he had just not thought about it when she picked him up. It probably would have taken less effort to cast the spell than it had to walk down.

"Let's get you situated." She extended an arm to take one of his packs.

Vrric stepped inside the tent gingerly. As long as he stayed in the patch of light from the open flap, he was fine. He heard Escha rustling in the corner with his things. He crouched down and shifted into the corner alongside her and it got eerily dark quickly. He had to stop moving for a moment to let his eyes adjust. It seemed like Escha smiled. She clapped his shoulder briefly and headed back out.

It took a few moments for him to spread everything out to his liking. He kept beating his pillow and lying back on it. He had thought the bed in his quarters was uncomfortable, but had apparently forgotten what sleeping on the ground was like. It amazed him just how long he had been in the field, and just how short he had been staying at Agoge. The differences were so stark as to demarcate individual lifetimes. Luckily, the quiet murmur of voices outside the tent kept his mind from wandering too far.

Vrric emerged into blinding light, but since they were already primed it did not take long for his eyes to adjust back. Both Escha and Gyllhelon were sitting on small wooden folding chairs, chatting. Torpalin was nowhere to be seen.

"Why don't the two of you go hit stage number five? I hear they do some hilarious skits over there." Escha looked between them both. "Torpalin is getting another keg of water. Turns out the next couple of days are going to be hotter than we had at first anticipated." She patted Gyllhelon's knee. "Don't worry, we'll catch up."

"What do you think?" Gyllhelon smiled up at Vrric.

"Sounds great, I could use a good laugh." He smiled back at her.

It took them some time to find the correct stage. Vrric was thinking that Escha and Torpalin might have beaten them to it, but they were nowhere to be seen. Gyllhelon turned sideways and wormed her way through the crowd towards the front, with Vrric following haphazardly in her wake.

The sketches were indeed entertaining and Vrric forgot that they were supposed to be waiting for anyone. It was not until the crowd was slowly dispersing and they were walking back towards the tent that he even remembered that some were missing. He followed Gyllhelon's lithe form as she wound through the press of bodies. It took some time until he noticed that they must have passed the turn off to the tent. He did not notice due to distance but due to time, which it was why it took him so long to realize. He was still barely keeping pace, however, and unable to ask where they were going. Then they got there.

The round plaza that they entered was striped with long wooden slat tables with long wooden slab benches. It was teeming with Pyrans. The smell of cooked meats hung heavily in the air, making his face feel slightly greasy just by walking into it. He was incredibly grateful that it was out in the open air where the noise could dissipate upwards. Even a thin fabric ceiling would have echoed back too much rowdy conversation, made all the louder by the drinks crowding each table.

Gyllhelon reached back and grabbed Vrric's hand while diving forwards into the fray. He was not sure how, but she managed to spot and procure the seemingly only two adjacent seats left open in the entire plaza. They sat and yelled their order to a scurrying Pyran. They yelled amongst each other and to the Pyrans sitting across from them. He found himself laughing without knowing why. It seemed that the evening air had something happily contagious floating through it. And Gyllhelon was as intoxicating as the grog.

Vrric was not sure how long they sat there. They ate and drank and laughed and yelled. There was a mass of Pyrans standing at the edges eyeing those sitting, but no longer eating, with a sense of jealously. Gyllhelon turned, smiling, and placed her lips to Vrric's ear and whispered loudly, "Let's get out of here."

They left and wandered, their seats immediately filled by an impatient but grateful couple. Vrric felt deaf as they walked. Not fully deprived of hearing, but muted and distant, as if he had cotton filling each ear. His feet felt slightly wooden, as if being unable to hear his footsteps somehow affected his sense of touch. He had no idea where they were, where they were going, or how to get there. He was just enjoying walking next to Gyllhelon.

"I want to fly." It came out of nowhere and she stopped in her tracks. Vrric could not later recall what they had been talking about before her request. He had to stop and turn to face her. "I want to fly back to the tent, I don't want to walk." Her smile seemed a little nervous, which struck Vrric as odd since she always exuded such confidence. "Besides, it is such a beautiful evening."

It was a nice evening. There were no clouds and the stars had all come out with the top portion of the moon peeking over the horizon. He knew that he should say something poetic, or at least complimentary. There was a certain expectant heaviness in the air. Unfortunately, he could think of nothing.

"Of course, of course." He cursed his feeble mind. To cover up his lack of eloquence he quickly cast his spell. "Narkinderclo!"

He shot them straight up to avoid anything low and hanging. He had a hard time seeing ropes while he was flying, even in the light of day. They were both still standing, facing each other. Gyllhelon's hands raised up in front of her mouth at their rapid ascent and she giggled appreciatively. Once they were well above the festival, he started sliding them sideways.

"You know, I am not sure where we are going." He absentmindedly noticed a slight chill in the air. It always amazed him how quickly the desert could cool off once the sun had departed.

"Oh, I don't care. I love this feeling." She made like she was kneeling and then lay down on her side, facing him. "It's just so… delicious."

Vrric lay down as well, facing her. Her head was held up in her hand as if her elbow were on a pillow. He was always amazed at how derlians postured themselves while flying. They could be in any shape they wanted, but they always seemed to orient themselves towards the ground. If they were going slow enough, the tug of gravity was still noticeable, but even at higher speeds it seemed like everyone wanted to orient to the ground. He wondered what it would be like if it was completely black, if the ground were invisible. Then, he supposed, he would not be able to see what the others were doing anyway. He propped his own head up to mirror her and shifted their motion so that they went exactly head first, sideways.

"You really are an amazing Luften. You know, what you can do with your mind." She smiled sweetly. It was a little odd since he did not think of her as sweet. She was very nice, but he felt there was a certain amount of innocence wrapped up in the word "sweet", and she was much too confident and competent of a warrior to truly be innocent. Not like someone like Clerin. Vrric's mind flashed, suddenly and for no reason, to the day he had spoken with Elange in the Eshram. Elange had allowed the "mice" in—Clerin and Vrric—but had insisted that the "cat" stay outside—Gyllhelon. It struck him so hard that he almost mentioned it. But it seemed like quite an awful lot to explain. And to what purpose?

"I think you're the amazing one." That cringe-worthy response was what he spoke instead.

"Don't be a parrot, Feyazki. I was just handing out a compliment." The top of her nose, between her eyes, wrinkled slightly when she got annoyed. For some reason, Vrric thought it was incredibly cute. "I do enjoy flying so. Look at all those Pyrans down there. They look like insects." Her cute wrinkle disappeared as she stared downwards. Her eyes were wide with peaceful wonder, her hair fluttering back in the wind and her smiling lips were slightly parted. She looked utterly beautiful to Vrric at that moment, staring in rapt attention at the insects crawling along the ground.

Vrric had an incredible time at the Turbinium festival, and he truly enjoyed spending time with Gyllhelon. He enjoyed it so much that he began taking her to the mage's guild meetings. The word meeting was maybe used a little loosely. There were certainly several a year, hovering around ten to fifteen percent, that were always completely serious. But mostly they were excuses for the mages to get together and socialize. In fact, many of the meetings were full-blown parties that lasted well into the night and sometimes into the morning. And Gyllhelon was a natural social butterfly. She had seemed so serious during the campaign. She had always seemed relaxed around the other Luften warriors, but had been quiet during Trela's inner circle meetings. Here, however, she was delightful and fit right in with the mages they chatted with. She could make jokes and crack wise. She could be serious and intensely engaged. She had both a quick smile and a sympathetic ear. It was over a moon that she had been accompanying him, and Vrric was still amazed by her ability to navigate difficult conversations.

Due to the frivolity that accompanied many of the nights, most serious business was actually accomplished the next day in private meetings set up the night before. One such meeting was weaseled out of Vrric after he got cornered by Ryshial while Gyllhelon was getting something, probably more grog. He doubted that it would have helped if Gyllhelon had been there. She got along swimmingly with Ryshial, and at the time it had seemed important even to him. By the time the next morning arrived, however, it no longer seemed as important. He was ruing getting out of bed, let alone attending a meeting. His mind quickly checked to see if there was anything else she could ask about the Tlana or the well. Of course, just because he could think of nothing, did not mean that she didn't want to talk about it some more.

But it was all about Croy. Ryshial felt that she had gotten all of the good information out of Vrric already, with "more painful and exhausting extraction for diminishing gains" on the horizon, or some such reasoning. He did not argue. She wanted to talk with Croy since he had actually traveled with the well and returned to be able to tell the tale. Apparently, that sort of thing did not happen very often, even in the age of legends. Vrric, however, was mindful of the strenuous talks that he had with her about the Tlana and was a little worried that it may tax Croy's delicate constitution. Not that it was typically delicate—he had personally witnessed Croy's indomitability and endurance during particularly trying portions of Trela's campaign—but it did seem to have a certain weakness to overbearing conversation. The word shy was too simple, but there was something a tiny bit unsociable about Croy. So Vrric balked.

"I understand your desire, Ryshial, but I don't think I can force him to do anything. I'll certainly let him know that you wish to speak with him." It was the least he could do.

Ryshial was quiet for some time, staring at the crystal water goblet held delicately in her hand. Her brow was not furrowed, but her eyes did not waver from the clear image before her. They held a quiet energetic intensity. Vrric tried to think of counters to various things she might say, trying to stay a couple of moves ahead of her, but had not expected her actual words.

"You are correct, of course. I did not mean to place myself between you and your friend. Forget I mentioned it." Her smile, though sudden, seemed completely sincere.

Vrric should have sensed it approaching. He should have had some inkling of an idea. It happened so slowly, over a moon it seemed but probably just a fortnight, that he just did not realize he was being set up. It started out innocently, during the nighttime mage's guild meetings. Olsfang bet Vrric that he could lift a larger stone than Vrric. Vrric had been drinking and could not stand the thought of Olsfang gloating, so he agreed to the challenge. The next time it was how quickly they could turn a bucket of water into ice. Then it was calling forth the wind. And so on. Each time, Vrric won. And each bet got more extravagant. He had won money and humiliations (he had gotten Olsfang to bark like a dog one entire evening) and heirlooms (an emerald ring) and promises (he made Olsfang skip one of the guild meetings) and, of course, bragging rights. It felt like he could not lose and, oddly enough, he began to look forward to seeing Olsfang at the meetings.

Then came a sparsely populated meeting. There were only a few random mages beyond Vrric, Ryshial, and Olsfang; maybe three others. For some reason that Vrric could no longer recall, Gyllhelon was unable to make it to the meeting. The drinking started quickly and was monumental. The wager this time was on who could create the largest pillar of flame. Vrric felt a little overdone and had some misgivings about the challenge, but then Olsfang told him what the wager would be.

"I know who Qizern's secret wife is, or was. I know where they used to spend their summers. Where she still lives. I am honor bound to keep the secret, but maybe…" He trailed off.

Vrric's mind reeled. He had heard of such a rumor before, back when Trela was first examining the castle, but nothing had come from it. Surely someone else had already divulged this information to Trela. Surely Olsfang was not the only Pyran to know these things. But maybe he was the only one who had little enough honor to tell. Vrric had some difficulty standing, but eventually found his feet.

"That! That is our wager. And you had better not be making this up." The world felt wobbly.

"But what about you? What prize are you willing to chance?" There was suddenly a shrewd look in Olsfang's eye but Vrric ignored it. Truth be told, he did not think much of his own bet. He had won all of the other contests and was not even sure if he spoke his own bet out loud the last couple of times.

"How about your great-grandfather's emerald ring back?" It was all he could think of.

"No, no. It is already tainted for me. Besides, I do not think those two items are comparable." He tapped a finger on his scraggly chin.

"If you win, Olsfang will break his oath with the dead King and let you be the Queen's hero. If you lose, I get to interview Croy." It was Ryshial. She had walked over as quiet as a thief in the night.

This all should have rung alarm bells in Vrric's mind. Why was he this drunk? Why were there so few Pyrans around? Why had he not heard that Olsfang had these large secrets? And the kicker—

why would Ryshial be involved in making the wager? His mind did not ring with bells, however. To his great shame, he did not even think twice about it.

"You're on! Prepare to be bested once again!" He wobbled while he laughed. Another missed indicator.

He started to move to the center of the room and began to pace his breathing, but Ryshial touched him lightly on the arm. "Not first this time. Let Olsfang go. Then you can see what you have to best." Her wide and beautiful smile did not touch her eyes. He backed up without a word. For some reason he felt thirsty and unconsciously looked around, but knew that he should wait until after the challenge.

Olsfang strode into the center of the room with chest puffed full of air. The other three mages were sitting by one wall, watching. For the life of him, Vrric could not think of their names, or even if he had seen them before. Olsfang shook his arms and each leg in turn, as if he were going to run and jump between two cliffs. He breathed out heavily. Vrric stood directly behind him, staring at his shaggy and somewhat greasy mane. A low drone seemed to emanate from him, then seemed to emanate from the entire room. Vrric glanced over to the three seated mages. They had their eyes closed and made no discernible movements. He was trying to figure out why they were not watching, were they not there to judge the extents of the flame, when Ryshial touched his arm again.

"You should watch. Olsfang is not good for much, but he can throw fire like few others." Her lips breathed warmly into his ear.

Vrric turned his head and watched Olsfang's back. He did not even hear the spell being cast before the entire central third of the room exploded into fire. The noise was deafening, the light blinding, the shame maddening. The fire swirled and danced and spun like a tornado. It roared and crackled and spit and was gone. There was not even a charred mark on the floor. It was huge—Vrric was not sure if he could match it—and then it was over. The three mages against the wall had their eyes open and were smiling widely.

"Even on your best days, I doubt you could match that." Olsfang swaggered past Vrric towards the back wall.

Unfortunately, he was probably correct. Vrric knew how to cast fire that lasted, that produced heat, that burned through flesh and armor. He used fire in combat and with devastating results. At a minimum, he used it to light a candle. He stared hard at the immaculate floor again. There was no indication that anything had happened there at all. But he had seen it with his own eyes and heard it with his own ears. It had been most impressive, as far as "the largest pillar of flame" was concerned.

Vrric walked slowly and quietly to the center of the room. Though he could sense no heat, and that did bother him, he also realized that the three unknown mages against the wall had their eyes closed again. That sapped his attention from his task at hand more than the lack of heat. His mouth was dry. He closed his eyes and clenched his fists and attempted to draw energy. Nothing. He breathed in and out several rhythmic times. Still nothing. He tried to dig his roots down through the stone floor, but it was as if something was blocking them, something more solid than stone. He glanced back at Ryshial, but she was watching the motionless mages against the wall. He hesitated. He wanted to call off the wager. He knew, however, knew in the deepest depths of him that Olsfang would never let that go. Refusing to cast the spell now would doom Vrric to constant jibes for the rest of his time in Agoge.

"Surdepiclo!" But it did not feel like Sur. It felt much less, like maybe Nar. He did not get a headache or feel nauseas. The flame was still impressive, the heat was overpowering, even for its caster, and the scorch mark in the middle of the floor, like a dirty sunburst, was a testament to the size of the spell. But it was not enough and Vrric knew it. He could not imagine how he had been unable to draw more energy, but figured it must have been the alcohol and the late hour. It was not until he was explaining everything to Gyllhelon that it truly dawned on him. He had been duped. He had to have been. The whole thing stunk of Ryshial's manipulations and, worse yet, of Olsfang's acting abilities. He wondered if Qizern even had a secret living mistress. It was shameful, the stupidity that pride had wrought on Vrric. But his word was his word, and honestly, Croy would probably have had to talk to Ryshial anyway. Trela probably would have ordered it if she had been asked. And who was to say that Croy would not mind speaking with her. Maybe his earlier misgivings had been misplaced. Maybe all this had just delayed the inevitable. Maybe. But then there was the feeling of being duped. He had been consciously played and had not realized it while it was happening. And all because the gambit was catered to his ego. Pride went before his fall. He vowed to pay more attention, even when he thought he was amongst friends. Especially when he thought he was amongst friends. And Olsfang. The thought that he, of all the Pyrans in the realm, was the one who had tricked him left a bitter taste in his mouth. Even the thought that it would not have worked without Ryshial, that it was actually her who played him and not necessarily Olsfang, did little to assuage the taste. It was a bitter flavor that lingered on the palate.

Vrric took a couple of days to find Croy. He had heard that Croy was spending his days out on the plateau, but only as far onto the plateau as he could get while still being within walking distance of Agoge. So, after a full day of rest, Vrric took to the skies in an attempt to sense him. He covered a large amount of distance the first day, but it was not until the afternoon of the second day that he made contact.

Vrric landed to find both Croy and Haswyxe waiting for him. He did his best to be upbeat. Since, for some reason, he was in a great mood that day, it was not too difficult. He was doing something he would prefer not to be doing and yesterday he had spent the whole day in the burning sun in a futile search. It was a wonder that his mood was so buoyed. He tried to remind himself to examine the morning to see what, if anything, had affected his mood. Of course, he forgot by the day's end.

Much to Vrric's relief, it did not take any wheedling or cajoling to convince Croy to see Ryshial. He had not been excited, but had not been reluctant either. He insisted on three days' time and gave an ominous "you owe me a favor" line, but that was to be expected. Vrric did owe him for this. Plus, even at his most menacing, Croy was just not very ominous.

The meeting, however, was completely brutal. It was a long and intense trial, an interrogation really. Vrric marveled at the seemingly endless reservoirs of strength Ryshial had to be able to keep up her attention for that long. He also marveled that Croy was capable of sitting there and taking it. Hour after hour she made Croy examine each miniscule detail. Eventually, Vrric tried to intervene. He told Ryshial that Croy could not be expected to recall such things in such great detail. She glared back at him, saying nothing but shooting daggers from her eyes, and continued with her interrogation. He wished there was a way to kick her under the table, but its feet were large wings of wood that did not allow him sufficient open space to reach her. He could feel Croy pleading with him as she pressured him into more complete detail, but there was just not much he could do. He smiled weakly at Croy. It felt a bit hollow and forced, even to him. He could not imagine what Croy thought of it.

When they left and Vrric flew Croy back to his quarters, they did so in silence. He was not sure what to say to Croy, what words could salve the ordeal, so he said nothing. Croy, for his part, appeared to be stunned into silence. There was somewhat of a glazed look in his eye, as if he had just been witness to some horrible murder. It was mildly comforting that he did not look personally damaged. Just the dazed countenance of an observer.

Vrric pulled away from all the others for a while, even Gyllhelon. He folded back unto himself, as he was when he first arrived at Agoge. The odd moods came back as well, the undefined malaise. This was definitely not just homesickness. He was also certain that his self-imposed isolation was not the cause of his moods. He felt bad for Croy in a general sense, but the malaise was more selfish than that. It was as if he felt bad for himself. Attempting to explain it did not get him any closer to getting rid of it. So he ignored it. He poured himself into study. Each day was begun with meditations that would last, sometimes, hours. During the day he would sit in his quarters and cast spells. Little myriad ones to keep himself well rounded. Long, powerful ones to stretch his "muscles." There were some that he needed to cast outside, of course. He would take long, meandering flights away from Agoge and away from any opportunity to see someone he recognized—certainly away from Croy's sheep pasture. He would sit on a cool rock and cast dangerous fire spells directly into a nearby stream, sending steam billowing out in all directions. He would lie back down on the rock and stare at the sky. In the unfettered chaos of magic without spells, of pure energy, he would lazily attempt to cloudburst. He would pick a small cloud and stare at it until it would disappear. He was never really sure if it was him, however. He *was* in a fairly dry climate and the clouds often disintegrated on their own. But it was relaxing, a bit of unstructured meditation maybe.

Other times he would sit in his quarters and close his eyes and toss a candle into the air. "Lodepiarc!" And he would open his eyes to see if the candle was alight before it blew itself out. Maybe the correct end was lit, maybe he had missed and the couch was on fire. Cleaning up after the trick was certainly difficult, but he could not help himself. It was the way that he tried to aim while his eyes were closed that really interested him and kept him coming back to the same test. If he tried to predict where it would be by estimating its current arc, he would miss quite often. If he tried to track it, to visualize it with his mind's eye, he would miss more often than he would hit. If he tried to sense the wax, he would hit about half the time. If he tried to sense the wick, however, he found he had fairly good accuracy. What interested him most was that he was not sure what he was using to sense the wick. He knew that imagining the wick tumbling through the air, embedded in the wax, was important. But even more important was calling up the smell of a candle that had just been snuffed between his fingers. He knew that smell well and could conjure it in his mind easily. Somehow that smell, the imagining of that smell, increased the accuracy of his targeting immensely. The feel of the wick, black and charred to fragility, was important as well. Probably more important than imagining the wick itself, but certainly less important than imagining the smell. For Vrric, it was a great realization that the power of scent had in focusing his mind.

Each night he would study. He studied his books from Revkin and Elange, of course. But he had also borrowed several ancient tomes from the mage's guild library. He poured over them for any different ideas of how to approach the same problem. For any hidden nuances that would help his mind bring forth magic easier, stronger, and for longer. He would make himself stay up if he felt he was close to something, to some new kernel of knowledge, to learning some new trick. Then he would sleep in and meditate upon it in the morning. Each day was an incremental increase. Each day he made himself become more powerful.

Knill had been the one to invite him to the dinner. Vrric was pleasantly surprised to see him when he opened the door. He had been expecting someone from the guild to ask him where he had been. The knot in his stomach at the sound made him think of Olsfang. But it was just kindly Knill. They chatted about nothing. He could tell that Knill was upset about Trela, but did not pry. Knill asked what Clerin was up to, and he stayed silent. It was quick, but comfortable. Each not wanting to bother the other. After Knill left, he wondered why they never really hung out in the warpack. Knill had always seemed to be Croy's friend, he guessed.

The appetizers were tasty and the grog was fine. He tried to apologize to Croy once again for the Ryshial incident but was somewhat rebuffed. He could not tell if Croy did not care and was not worried about it, thus being somewhat cool to the conversation, or if he was still annoyed about it, which could have made him appear cold as well. So Vrric gave up and chatted with Trela. Croy appeared relieved.

Unfortunately, Trela was pressing her own agenda to get Vrric to officially join the mage's guild elite. He was not really sure why. Maybe she thought he would provide her with information about the guild she was not getting elsewhere. Rather than deal with it, he told her that they would not accept him since he was a Luften. He felt that they may have made an exception for him, but he had never asked, so he did not really know. Just then, Clerin arrived.

"Ah, there you are. We were beginning to get worried." Trela smiled at her. "I thought I was going to have to get Feyazki to check up on you."

Vrric stared at the ground with furrowed brow. Could they not tell that Clerin would rather be off with her Pyran acrobat than spend time with him? He would have put his hands in his pockets, but his dress pants did not have any. Luckily Trela, as always, was quick to pick up on an awkward situation and pulled a chair out for Clerin. "You should all relax, we will be enjoying our meal shortly."

Trela sat at the head of the table, of course. Croy moved to sit next to Clerin, so Vrric sat opposite him next to Knill. The dinner conversation was… comfortable. He thought it was like an estranged family that used to be close. Each participant knew how to get a good laugh out of each other, and each awaited their turn to speak with patience. The flow was constant and interesting; he really did enjoy himself. There was no silence, however, since they all knew how uncomfortable it would get if it was too quiet. But there appeared, at least in a vague feeling deep in the middle of Vrric, to be something not being talked about. Something avoided, maybe. It was like an odd version of the children's game "hot potato." They all took their turns to keep the potato up in the air, but no one wanted to hold it for too long.

After their meal was over, Clerin spoke up. It was, apparently, she who had requested they all dine together, for she had a story to tell. She went into great depth about her conversation with Gorbanax at the Temple of Fire and what she thought it meant. It had been some time since he had been around Clerin, had really looked at her. He marveled at her raw beauty. The way her clear blue eyes sparkled. The way her dimples appeared and disappeared while she talked. How she always seemed to be smiling, even when describing painful things. He found himself staring and had to force himself to sit back and sip on some grog to not appear so... eager. Yes, if he were honest with himself, he was eager to hear her voice. To be able to chat with her. Alone. About anything, about nothing. He tried not to admit it to himself, but he found himself missing their time together. Missing her.

Clerin suddenly turned to Croy, sitting next to her, and asked him for his interpretation. Vrric had thought that she would ask each of them what they thought her conversation with Gorbanax meant. He missed Croy's first few sentences while trying to think up how to put his own ideas into words. Then he realized what was happening. Clerin did not need, or want, any other interpretation. She had her own and merely wanted it backed up by Croy. He was able to pull himself out of his own thoughts to get the main gist of Croy's version. He had not realized that this dinner, this story, this interpretation was really just a call to arms. He had not realized they were going to suggest leaving the lazy comforts of Agoge. Not that he wanted to stay, but he did not necessarily wish to leave either. He thought it best if he gave it some time to sink in.

They spoke of Yavens dying as if it were the most abhorrent thing in all the realms, but were quite blasé about their own fellow derlians being tortured to death. It was odd, but what was even more odd was that he was definitely the odd one out. Rather than risk alienation, he quickly backed down. He smiled warmly at Clerin hoping that she would reciprocate. He was rewarded handsomely.

"I do not think that Gorbanax will allow me to commune again until the Cabal is destroyed." She was looking at Vrric when she spoke.

"Then we should all go." Knill interjected

"I cannot go." Trela spoke to her empty dinner plate. "I have just started my reign..."

Knill glared angrily at her and she would not return his gaze. No one spoke and the silence became palatable. The potato lay on the ground, dirty and cooling off. No one reached down to pick it up, certainly not Vrric.

Vrric spent the next few days much like he did the previous moon. In intense study and practice. He was sitting with his feet on his legs, meditating, when he felt a great surge. In less than a second he was completely flooded with energy. It made him open his eyes and stand up. He jittered on one leg then the other. It was not necessarily an eerie feeling, but it was of such an intensity that he could not hold still. Then there was a knock on the door.

He wiped the instant cold sweat that had formed on his brow and walked over to the door. He took a large deep breath before opening it. Clerin was standing there, grinning. He wished, for that quick first moment, that he had bathed recently, that he looked, if not his best, then at least not as bad as he was sure that he did. He reached to wipe another errant bead of sweat from his brow when he noticed the gigantic bonfire just beyond Clerin.

"Taglo would like to speak with you." Clerin strode past Vrric with unconcerned purpose.

Vrric moved out of the way to allow the pillar of fire to enter. Once the Yaven was fully inside, Vrric stuck his head out of the doorway to look both ways for nosy neighbors before closing the door. None were to be found.

"Taglo, this is Feyazki. Feyazki, this is Taglo." Clerin swept her palm in front of each of them. Then, with a girlish giggle, she flung herself onto the couch and curled her feet under her.

"It is a great honor to welcome you into my abode." Vrric bowed deeply.

"I am also honored by your presence. You have been touched." The pillar that was Taglo took on a vaguely derlian form.

"Touched?" Vrric was taken aback.

"Yes, by more than one entity. Most of them are light and somewhat common. But the incredible thing is that you were touched by a Tlana and lived. That is a rare occurrence for a derlian, during any Age. A Tlana's touch is never light. For that, it is an honor to meet with you." Taglo appeared to perform a quick bow.

"Have you… Has any Yaven met with a Tlana, or a Vijen for that matter?" Vrric raised his eyebrow inquisitively.

"Ha! You have much… I am unsure if the correct translation is 'moxie' or 'chutzpah.' Either way, you have much. We may speak of other things later. Now is urgent. Do you know why I am here?"

"I assume it has something to do with our conversation at dinner." Vrric turned towards Clerin, who was only watching Taglo, and rotated his hand uselessly a couple of revolutions. "The Cabal, yes? You are here due to Croy's Cabal."

"I assure you that the one you call Croy does not own this Cabal. He would have already been consumed if he had anything to do with it. But you are correct. The Cabal of Lochom must be destroyed. I have allowed myself to be summoned here to assist but this destruction, like the lamentable creation, must be accomplished by derlians. I am compelled to convince those that are necessary for the success of this mission. You realize that you are necessary, do you not?" The Yaven appeared to be getting brighter, though not necessarily bigger.

"Of course I am." He knew that he would go on this mission, if for no other reason than to travel with Clerin again. And how does one really refuse a Yaven, anyway?

Chapter 5

Clerin and Taglo examined each derlian who had anything at all to do with Trela's inner circle during her ascent and some from the outer circle. They had lists of them. She would speak their names and tell Taglo anything that she might know about the prospect. Taglo would ponder briefly and then state if that derlian was not necessary at all. They would then visit the derlians not immediately dismissed individually. Clerin would speak with them about subjects of little importance at first, chatting nostalgic about Trela's campaign or something similarly benign, while Taglo would "read" them. Eventually it would make its decision. Taglo would either state that it was time to leave, or it would give a little speech that ended with "you realize that you are necessary, do you not?" or some similar version of that. Every once in a while a derlian would turn down the offer/request. Several times Taglo let them refuse, but in an even rarer event, Taglo would turn to Clerin and say, simply, "convince them." The first time this happened was with Malghain, the Luften warrior. She was grateful that Vrric had agreed to join up so quickly, for all she needed to do was mention that he had already agreed and most would instantly change their mind. Malghain certainly did.

They had gathered many, but there was still the first one to refuse Taglo. Clerin set up another meeting with Trela once Taglo was satisfied with the rest of the team. And the rest of the team was quite extensive. She was not sure where she had gotten the idea that it was going to be a small commando team of six or seven, but it was far from that. There was the full contingent of the Luften warriors. There were Pyran warriors adept at close fighting, such as Zira, Estfale, Dartsyle and Yarsurle. There were archers, such as Hygen and Urwst. There were Pyran mages, such as Serghno, Nochiel and Arnasta. There were spies like Jalin. There were other commanders like Rewista and Kryhir. There were some from Qizern's old warpack like Tweltas and Pejal. They had been allowed to scoop up Wesduin as well. There were several that Clerin did not know but others did, like Ryshial and Olsfang. And, of course, there were many that she did not know. Mostly warriors, but several spies and a couple more mages. Croy and Tumu were also coming, but they could not convince Knill without Trela. She hated to admit it, but it seemed strange to her that Taglo was so incredibly insistent about Knill. Taglo did everything short of threatening to burn him to a cinder where he stood. It was as passionate as Clerin had seen from Taglo. Though she could not place the exact emotion, it was not just disappointment. It was something akin to anger. She was not positive why he was so necessary, but she felt sure that he would join immediately after Trela did, and she told Taglo just that. There was just one more, and convincing her would bring the two.

Clerin had not wanted the meeting to occur in the throne room, so she had not explained that Taglo would be coming as well. She had wanted it to seem like an informal meeting, something quick and light between old friends. They were to meet at Trela's secret study. She was not sure if this was really a deception; she had not truly lied, but merely left out some of the, some might say, crucial information. She needn't have worried. She had not fooled Trela for a slight second.

"Welcome, Clerin. Welcome, Taglo." Trela's smiling countenance was a bit of a shock, but a tiny one. Like an extra step on a dark stair. What happened next, however, was like stepping into a dark well. It was falling. It was pure confusion filled adrenalin. It was panic.

"WHERE IS IT?" Taglo grew three times in size and would have swallowed Clerin had it been as ethereal as it seemed. Instead she was tossed aside like a child's doll. It was not hot, she was not burnt, not on fire, but flames were everywhere. They spit from Taglo in every direction. They shot through the hallway and into the study and engulfed the door. The screaming was a deafening roar, like a thousand furnaces churning steel cities into molten slag. Though there was no heat, there were smoke and scorch marks everywhere. Clerin lay on her back in the hallway, an ineffectual arm held defensively in front of her. Stunned. "WHERE IS IT?!?!" Taglo pushed its way into the study. Clerin could not see Trela, but was sure that she was somewhere in front of Taglo. "I WILL DESTROY IT. I WILL DESTROY YOU!" Taglo disappeared into the room, leaving behind a rainbow image burnt into Clerin's retina.

Clerin shook the cotton from her head and stood. Taglo's screams were becoming incoherent. If she had thought about it at all, if she had been capable of thought whatsoever, she would have fled. She would have turned and ran. She would have run all to the way to Tureyn and hidden under the temple waters in the invincible embrace of Lembin. Instead she charged into the study and jumped into the sun.

"She is necessary. She is necessary!" Clerin clung to Taglo's back, her arms embracing what would be its neck, her legs failing to encircle its waist, as if she were clinging to a log. It was all she could say, the only thing she could do. She clung there repeating it, chanting it. In the end, however, if Taglo had wished to destroy Trela at that moment, Trela would have been dead. Clerin was an insect clinging desperately to twig in a mighty river. Heading towards a waterfall.

"Here, here it is. I got it for you. I brought it to you. I did not make it, I did not use it." Trela was half kneeling, half sitting on the stone floor. Her head was down, her face averted to the side, but her arms were held upright above her, stiff at the elbows. There, resting upon her open palms rather than being gripped, was a thick broadsword. Clerin peered over Taglo's shoulder, her chant forgotten. "I knew you would want it."

"I want it destroyed!" Taglo was shrinking slightly. Fire had stopped spitting in all directions.

"Then destroy it!" Trela turned her head and looked up into Taglo. Clerin was astounded that there were no tear tracks in the blackened soot that covered Trela's face. No trace of fear or of trauma, only something akin to anger.

Clerin dropped from Taglo's back and wiped her own tear-stricken face with the back of her sleeve. She took several deep and ragged breaths. She felt like someone who had almost drowned, but now lay on the banks of a river, heaving and coughing. She felt a kind of desperate relief.

Taglo was obviously not going to take the sword from Trela, but it was not moving away either. Trela, for her part, kept still as well. They were at an impasse, at a stalemate. The sword glistened in the firelight and Clerin stared intently at it as the silence grew.

"What is it?" Clerin's voice sounded clear and strong compared to how her throat felt.

"It is Strife." Trela did not take her eyes off of Taglo, but the little laugh and twitch of a smile were clearly meant for Clerin. Unfortunately, she did not understand the joke, if that was what it was. But before she could ask a clarifying question, Trela spoke back up. "It is Qizern's old sword, Strife. There is a Yaven trapped in it."

"So how do we free the Yaven?" Clerin knew it was a question with no answer, but it was one of those things that needed to be expressed, even as useless as it was.

"I know not." Taglo's voice, much like its stature, were again muted.

"So how do we destroy it? The sword, I mean." Another useless question.

"I know not." As impossible as she would have thought, Taglo sounded a little tired.

"So what do we do now?" Clerin could not help herself. It was like a quiet and sad compulsion.

"I will not repeat myself." And so Taglo did not. It turned and left the room in stunned silence.

They were motionless for quite some time. Clerin, not knowing what to do, and Trela in her half kneeling, half sitting pose, still holding the sword up to no one. Clerin wanted to walk over and remove the sword from her, but felt a terrible trepidation about even touching it. As if Taglo would come bursting back into the room if she merely gripped its hilt.

Clang! Bang! Clamor! Trela let the sword clatter unceremoniously to the ground. "Did you think we were all about to die or what?" She gave a throaty laugh.

"No. Just you." Clerin wondered briefly if she should follow Taglo. It was a foolish idea anyway. It was too late now to see where it might have been headed. "You shouldn't just drop that on the stone floor."

"That is probably the nicest thing that has ever happened to that sword." Trela stood and stretched. "Besides, I was half hoping that it would shatter upon impact and free the Yaven."

"Nothing is that simple." Clerin took another deep and ragged breath. "Does this mean you are coming?"

"It is my destiny."

Suddenly Clerin burst out laughing. Luckily, so did Trela. They laughed until their sides hurt.

"Well, you are necessary." Clerin spoke mirthfully into the exhausted silence, but it did not trigger another laughing fit.

"I had spoken with Lishean and decided that I could leave my throne, then I tried to think of all the derlians I should bring. I wanted to choose the group, you see." Trela was still smiling, but her eyes looked more serious. Almost pensive. "Anyway, I found a letter explaining the sword. It took me a little while to find it, and when I finally did, you asked for this meeting. Pretty good timing." It was difficult to tell from Trela's voice if the last sentence was meant to be ironic or not.

The preparations seemed to take forever. Trela and Wesduin, her quartermaster from the campaign, were almost inseparable, arguing, or maybe discussing, about each item to be brought from Agoge. Luckily, they had yet to dictate what Clerin would be carrying herself.

Almost a fortnight ago, when she thought they were about to just pack up and leave, she locked herself into her quarters for a full day making the difficult decisions of what to bring and what to leave behind. She tried to think of each needed item, anything at all that could come in useful. Unfortunately, this split her accumulated belongings approximately in two. A much too cumbersome amount to carry.

Almost all that she now owned was foreign. Some items were of Luften construction, but most were from the Pyrans. She always began her piles with her meager Fluen items still usable. However, the most undamaged of these were the court attire she had thought she would need for the queen and king of the Luften realm, Vanelia and Hulgert. That had seemed so long ago now and these items, barely above useless in the best of times, were completely unnecessary for this next leg of her journey. The words "velvet" and "desert" should never go together. So, from her home of origin, she only packed the travel-stained rags she still had left. Of course she brought her knife, and her boots were, amazingly enough, in good enough shape to keep on abusing. But the amount of nostalgia she could bring with her was depressingly minor.

Her next stage was to identify anything that could do more than one job. If an essential item could be substituted with another item doing double duty, she would toss it into the staying pile, no matter how poor a replacement she would be bringing. This was how she lost all of her dresses and most of her skirts. Pants, though hot and confining, would cover and protect her legs, while being able to be worn on a horse and, at worst case, in battle. Her bedding only consisted of several thin blankets. She could fold them into pillows and layer them for warmth if need be. She did bring a pair of sandals to wear around camp in addition to her boots. And against her better judgment, she brought her flimsier knife from home instead of the stout dagger she had gotten used to carrying during Trela's campaign. To overcompensate, she brought the small short sword with her that she had picked up along the way. She allowed herself a moment of remorse for her unfortunate choice to halt her rudimentary training in that weapon. Agoge was, for better or worse, a complete oasis of respite for Clerin. She had stopped all attempts to better herself and had just relaxed.

She finally separated her piles and made a small one to bring with and a much larger one to leave behind. She felt fairly comfortable with her choices. The pile was efficient but thorough, essential, and lean. It was a good day's work. Then a week passed. Clerin began to have doubts about the wisdom of her decisions. She reexamined the pile thoroughly, but made few changes. Her rationalizations had not yet evolved. Then another week passed. She felt that she should not revisit her decisions for a third time, no matter her continued doubts. Then Trela arrived.

"Show me what you plan on bringing." Trela's smile was in place and her eyes carried a light feeling of mirth, but there was something else there as well, Clerin could just not quite define it. Something a little ominous.

So Clerin showed her. Trela gave each item a discerning glance, a squint, some pursed lips, maybe a finger tap on her chin, then she would nod. To her credit, nothing that Clerin had picked out was rejected.

"This is not enough for you. You are my ambassador and must look the part. Now I understand that to ask you to carry a trunk full of clothing and accoutrements would be cruel. So, I have convinced Wesduin to make a little room on one of his wagons for you. We will go through what you have here to figure what we can add, but I also have several merchants that have royal accounts and will be quite willing to provide us with anything else we need. As for your weapons, definitely bring your dagger as well as your knife. One cannot have too much steel where we are going. In that same vein, you should also bring your sword, as you have planned. Practice often during your down time, of course. But you will be well protected in the center of our pack, and, I hate to say this, if you need to use that sword to protect yourself, we will already be well on our way towards failure as a group." Trela's smile looked less ominous now.

"Would you rather not have a Pyran ambassador? I do not wish to sow the seeds of jealously amongst your subjects." Clerin's lopsided smile gave her only one dimple.

"Do not worry yourself about my subjects. One of my myriad, and more powerful if I may say, gifts is to be able to choose the talents I need from others to accomplish my aims. This I choose from you. You have never failed me before." She paused long enough to leave a slice of silence, but short enough that Clerin was unable to think of an interjection. "Besides, though we are heading specifically towards the Gaen realm, we may get quite close to the Fluen realm as well. At least, that is the rumor. Having a Pyran ambassador will only help me for so long. We would call this direction northwest while sitting at Agoge."

"Are we to travel through the Northern Desert?" This was the first that Clerin had heard of any indication of where they were headed. It was certainly not a destination, but at least it was a direction.

"As little as we can help it. Taglo is quite concerned about the Tlana. As we all are." She let out a small sigh. "We have gained what information from Croy that we could about Aedon Dea'sol and her research into the Cabal, but, unfortunately, he only had so much information to provide. Taglo believes we will need to visit this Aedon, which is why we plan on hugging the Gaen hills at the edge of the desert. Ha, I might even retrace some of my steps I took 'escaping' the Gaen realm." Trela used air quotes during the word escaping. As if making a wry joke. Clerin was not sure that she got it.

"I sometimes forget that you spent time in the Gaen realm. You are such a powerful figure and Croy is so… meek." Clerin cocked an eyebrow towards Trela, to check if she was overstepping any bounds. "I forget that you were his charge for a while. Does that ever sting?"

"No, not that. It's funny, but while it was happening, while I was wandering the underground caverns of Serif, it seemed to take forever. But now that I think about it, it seems like such a brief part of my life. One that was a bit squandered, if I am to be honest with myself. I did not want to be there, learning anything Gaen. Learning another culture, learning about peace. I only wanted to be rushing towards my destiny. It was such a long time ago…" Here she took a deep breath and let it out slowly, waveringly, emotionally. Clerin thought her eyes became misty and moist. An aura of vulnerability settled upon her shoulders. It was notably odd not only in how fast it all appeared, but also because Clerin had rarely seen her appear vulnerable. "The only thing that still stings is the death of Nolt. That is an image the fates will not allow to fade over time." Then just as quickly as it came, the vulnerability disappeared. Trela snapped her fingers. "Get undressed. We have a lot of outfits to choose."

Very few of Clerin's available outfits satisfied Trela. They were soon out of the Blaze and on the streets of Agoge. Trela's Pyran subjects gave way in complete deference, but they did not scrape and bow. Clerin was again reminded at the differences between their two cultures. They visited five different merchants. They had some pre-made clothing, but their best tailors were also on hand. Some things could be fitted, but there were some styles that needed to be made from scratch. Clerin wondered how much time could be spent on such trivial items and said so.

"These are not trivial items, but I suspect that is not your real question. We have run into a snag." One of the tailors stopped pinning the dress that Clerin was wearing and looked up at Trela, who just glared back down at her until she got back to her business. "It will be one more week before we are able to embark." Trela kept her glare on the tailor at Clerin's feet. "Did you hear that? You have four days to finalize everything we have purchased today."

Clerin thought the outburst was a bit out of Trela's character. She wondered what the snag was, but decided to wait until they were alone before asking. By the time the grueling day of shopping had ended, however, she had forgotten. Trela walked her back to her quarters and reminded her to pick up their orders over the next couple of days. She would provide the empty trunk that Wesduin had made room for shortly. Until then, Clerin could do as she pleased. Unfortunately, she was not quite sure what that was. The definition of waiting included an unrealized feeling of anticipation that she typically had difficulty ignoring. This feeling soured most forms of relaxation for her. She had always hated waiting.

Though each day was filled with some boredom, the week passed quickly. Clerin spent a couple hours each day in the saddle with Riverlightning, attempting to re-acclimate her muscles to the rigors of riding. The moons spent at Agoge had softened her considerably, but by the end of the week she felt she would be able to ride the majority of a day without too many additional bruises or blisters.

The first day of travel was almost a complete waste. It took them until after the noon hour to even get moving, and it took another hour for the procession to wind its way through the city. They made it far enough along the Dekhan Plateau to only see the glow from Agoge, not the individual lanterns or fires. It would have been a pleasant ride if it had not been such a warm day.

The first night was subdued. It seemed to Clerin like a shy but earnest first date. There were, of course, the cliques of old as friends reconnected at the beginning of an adventure. But more than that, it was derlians who did not know each other slowly reaching out. The intention was there, the desire was there, but it was a nervous and tentative affair. Torpalin was not loudly boasting, Vrric was not casting entertaining illusions, no one was running or wrestling or chasing. It was quiet and subdued, with everyone attempting to put their best foot forward. The embarrassing and raucous showing off that comes with a familiarity that leans to, well, the familial, would surface later in their travels, she was sure. But tonight she enjoyed the well behaved and well-meaning getting-to-know-you stage. The warm up and stretching that is essential before any successful long endurance race.

There were so many Pyrans that she did not know. Even most of those that she did know would be called acquaintances at best. She knew that if she wandered around she would inevitably end up only chatting with Vrric or Knill, or Torpalin and Escha, so she stayed in one place, sitting by the main fire, and let them come by and introduce themselves. There were several nice and charming youths, warriors all of them, that hung around for much of the night. They told increasingly unbelievable stories of their prowess and boldness. Clerin did enjoy their attentions. But if she was honest with herself, they seemed to be merely boys to her. There was, however, a spy that truly caught her eye—Altrond. There was a certain lithe catlike quality that reminded her of Yirhum. He did not perform any sleight of hand for her, at least not on that first night, but she could tell that he had that same sly quickness. He seemed much more mature than Yirhum. Of course, that was a very low bar, it did not take too much to achieve that. More than anything, he was funny. He spent the little time that he was around her just trying to keep her smiling. Against her better judgement, she found herself thinking about him before sleep overtook her.

The next day they all awoke with the sun. Trela was loud and energetic, rousing them with laughter and bawdy jokes amidst the clanging of steel pots. She loudly claimed that they were her "coterie." Her small coterie against the entire Cabal of Lochom. Everyone seemed to take her in stride, and they were quickly fed and on the road. That day was prodigious in the amount of distance covered. In fact, so was the next and the next. A full week of quiet nights and hard days. They were off the plateau, but still not to the desert proper. Almost imperceptibly at first, they began to veer towards the Gaen realm. They pushed themselves a little less the second week. Or more accurately, Trela pushed them a little less. She kept saying that they were not on a stealth mission, but she managed to avoid almost every settlement of any size along the way. Clerin was sure that it was on purpose. But the end of the third week brought them to Wazschial. It was, by all accounts, the last town of any size before either the desert or the Gaen realm.

They arrived near dusk, but Trela made them camp well outside of the town. There were some minor grumbles, but nothing loud enough to reach her ears. No fires were lit, so it was simple iron rations for the lot of them.

The next morning, however, Trela lined them all up in the direction of the town. As each passed by, she pressed a few silver coins into their palm. They were given a full day to enjoy their last Pyran town.

"Anyone not back here by sunup has deserted the mission. They will be dealt with in the harshest terms. Understood?" They all understood. "And a warning to you all, we are going to travel hard tomorrow, so stay in shape. Understood?" They all understood.

The town was not visited, it was invaded. It had two pubs and one tavern. Each time Clerin would enter one she would see someone from the mission who would invariably want to buy her a drink. She soon avoided those establishments. The inn served food as well and she attempted to find some refuge in their common room, but much like the more targeted establishments she first visited, she ran into a group of compatriots who loudly hailed her from across the room. It was quicker to share a drink than it would have been to share a meal. She left sooner, but was beginning to feel the cumulative effects of the grog. She staggered across the main thoroughfare and rested amongst the ash trees and some undergrowth.

That was what she truly wanted. She enjoyed all of those that she traveled with, but this might have been the last time that she could be amongst strangers. The last time that she could be alone. She rested for a little while, enjoying the birds in the trees. The ash trees were gloriously tall and wide, with a lush green foliage. Eventually, however, as she was wont to do, she got bored. As much as she was concerned about this being the last stop before being surrounded by the same derlians every day for the foreseeable future, she did get a certain jolt by being around others and was naturally gregarious.

She found a pleasant place full of quiet strangers. Wazschial was one of the few Pyran towns of that intermediate size that could boast of a library. Clerin thought back to her father's small library fondly. She had whiled away many hours perusing his books on history and politics. She thought back to the cavernous library of Tureyn. Books lining the walls as far as the eye could see, levels of mezzanines ringing the exterior walls, large rooms full of others all reading at wooden tables, cozy corners with large chairs and the occasional tiny room hidden away for examining the ancient manuscripts too delicate for the commons. The thick and tall columns branched at the top, supporting a web of girders, purlins, and sub purlins. They had always reminded her of trees. That is, until she saw the gigantic helioarc trees that the Luftens made their cities in. Then they just seemed too delicate.

The library in Wazschial was somewhere in between her two remembered Fluen libraries. It was, of course, much larger than her father's personal collection. It was completely dwarfed by the memory of Tureyn's library which, in Wazchial's defense, probably dwarfed the library in Agoge as well. It was a completely comfortable size. It was not daunting, not intimidating, but it had enough different books in it that she could just spend time browsing. She loved browsing through the selections, to get a feel for what the library held as a whole. Not surprisingly, this one held a cornucopia of books on military strategy. She pulled a random one off the shelf and let it open at its worn spot, at the break in its spine, to see what the popular passage was. There was a map on the right-hand side, highly detailed with little trees and the contours of hills, with horizontal bars stacked against little arrowheads, like a capital "A" without the cross-bar in the center. The bars were grouped together, at the bottom of the hill, while the multitudinous arrowheads were scattered loosely all around them.

The left side of the page was dense with cursive words. A passage was circled. "When attacking, terrain is the most important strategy around which to plan your tactics. It is always there, it is always different, it is the piece of static chaos with which you can swivel momentum. You must train your mind to read the land from any angle. Is that a hill or an escarpment? Is that a valley or a dell? How deep is the river, how fast does it flow? When attacking, the terrain is usually chosen by the defender. This should not be so, not if you wish victory. Most successful assaults were achieved by the attacker forcing the defender out of their chosen terrain. Take the Battle of Railqorg. Hewoll had his warpack in retreat. He kept his harassments up, but was unable to push back the warpack of Lipnuel. To avoid a total rout, he tried to regroup at the hilltop known as Railqorg. This would have provided his warpack no end of tactical advantage. If he could have gained the hill, the story may have ended differently. Lipnuel recognized immediately what Hewoll's aim was. He recognized and understood terrain. Against all better judgment, he scattered his warpack. The scattered warpack is, eight times out of ten, the loser of the battle. But even worse odds involve running up a well defended hill. The choice was made. The bulk chased Hewoll, but not too hard, not too fast. Lightly. Small groups were sent to each side. Why? They did no damage and they decreased the main warpack's power and punch. They were sent to hide the real warriors and to provide the psychological buffer that Hewoll was surrounded. The real warriors, those handpicked by Lipnuel as the fastest, not the bravest or the most skilled, raced around those groups on the side. They raced all the way to the back of the hill. Not the side of the hill. Why? If they were seen anywhere along the slope of the hill, the illusion would have been shattered. No, the important thing, the essential thing, was for Hewoll to arrive at the bottom of the hill, followed close behind by Lipnuel, surrounded without escape, and to look up at the top of the hill. At his aim, at the destination. And see another warpack at the top. That is what broke Hewoll and gave Lipnuel the victory. Hewoll could have rushed up the hill and slaughtered the few tired, winded, and weak warriors at the top. No historian argues that Hewoll would have had much difficulty in killing them. Then he would have had his defensible position, and even without the respite he desperately needed, might have been able hold the hill. But he did not make that decision. He turned, he fought valiantly, and he died nobly. He did so because he thought he had lost the terrain. Lipnuel's illusion, as all great battlefield illusions are, was completely thorough. When twenty warriors appear to number in the hundreds, through constant motion and cacophonous sound, the confusion becomes thick as fog. When it appears that you are surrounded, when your goal has been taken from you, used against you, when the wolves are baying all around you, the illusion is complete. Two choices are left. Fight or flight. When this is an illusion, neither of those choices will lead to survival. This is your enemy defeating you. When you are faced with these choices and only these choices, when you are being relieved of rational thought, you must realize that you are in the midst of an illusion. You must read your immediate terrain. You must swivel any momentum you have towards the terrain of greatest tactical advantage. You must be savage and ruthless, you MUST gain that terrain. Only then can you turn back and face your enemy. Only then can you see through their illusion."

Clerin smiled to herself and closed the book. She wondered if she could buy it from the library, Trela would certainly enjoy it. She turned it over to read the title. "The Consequences of a Life in Battle" was embossed boldly across the front, "by Anonymous." Then she wondered about each of these books. What if one were to enter the library, pick each individual book from its shelf, open it to the most worn location and read the associated passage, put it back and move on to the next one? Would you gain more knowledge than if you read ten of the books thoroughly? Was popularity, in any way, more important than depth? Well, she surely could not purchase every book, nor could they carry them all, so maybe she would just assume that this anonymous book was the best book in the library for Trela to read. The randomness of it all had an air of destiny. Trela would love it.

Clerin turned with a smile on her lips, and who was at the end of the aisle? It was Altrond and he was also smiling. He walked straight over to her.

"I knew I would find you here." He smelled faintly of grog, which made her wonder how many different places he had checked before arriving at the library. However, she probably also had an air around her, and he did not stagger or sway or show any signs of excessiveness.

"Took you long enough." She could not resist the jab.

"Fair enough, but surely you must know how difficult it is to break away from the group." His smile got bigger, not smaller.

"Of course. Honestly, I just barely got here myself." Clerin laughed lightly and placed her palm on the confluence of his arm and shoulder, just above his heart. It was a quick gesture, a split second, but she had felt an unexpected ripple of muscle under the tips of her fingers. Her laugh unconsciously dropped an octave. "I was just about to try to purchase one of their titles." She held up the strategy book.

"Actually, there should be something here I'm looking for as well. Are they in order by author or title?" His hand twitched slightly but he did not attempt to reciprocate her touch.

"Well, I think they are grouped by subject. It's hard to tell since there seems to be only one subject of interest here. From there it appears to be ordered by title." She squinted around to find a sign sticking out from an aisle edge. "You would be amazed at how many of the books here are by anonymous authors."

"That is not uncommon in the Pyran realm. However, the author of a popular book is usually a well-known secret amongst the lettered. Often a library will file the anonymous books with that author." He glanced at the small book in her hand.

"That is odd. A Fluen would never allow a work of art to go unsigned. How do artists get paid?" She raised an eyebrow.

"Art is not a vocation. Art is something done while not working so that you don't go crazy while you are working. Besides, I think getting a book so widely read that the lettered take the time and effort to track you down and attribute your anonymous book to you is quite an accomplishment. It is surely a form of payment and one highly prized by our anonymous authors. Let us see what you have there." He held out a hand to receive her book. She handed it over to him with a small flourish. "This book is by…" He squinted hard at the title. "…I have no idea."

"Really? Does that author write a lot of books?" She took her book back with a mischievous grin.

"More than you might imagine. Let's look for what I came here to find before I embarrass myself anymore." He laughed a small but bright laugh and started to walk the aisles.

She probably should have been helping him look, but since she had no idea which book he was looking for, she just watched him move. She had to admit it was a bit mesmerizing. They wandered most of the library like this, him seeking and her appreciating. Suddenly he stopped and immediately flowed into a crouch, peering at the book spines in front of him.

"What exactly are you looking for anyway?" She leaned back against the sturdy shelving.

"Aha! This. This, is what I am looking for." He handed her a ratty book, smaller than the one that she was holding. "I was worried that they would not have it. I was unable to find a copy in Agoge before we left."

The cover was faded, but the words "Of Tlana and Vijen" were still visible. As was the author. It made her giggle a little.

"So, who is this anonymous author?" He gingerly took the book back from her.

"This book is also unknown." He held up a hand before she could interrupt him. "But this is due to the age of the book. This was written so long ago that the author has been forgotten."

"You have every word that the author wrote, but not the one or two that would identify that author?" Clerin realized that she was nearing being insulting to his culture, so she veered away. "What secrets does it contain?"

"I don't know yet, but I am going to find out." He swept his arm to indicate for her to lead.

They walked towards the massive checkout counter. The polished oak surface spanned almost the entire width of the common room before turning and sealing off a large corner of the building for the exclusive use of the librarians.

"May I help you?" The librarian was an ancient Pyran, wrinkled and shrunken.

"We are travelers passing through and wish to make a couple of purchases. If we come back through Wazschial on our way back, we will return the books." Altrond had on a disarming smile.

"And which books do you wish to purchase?" The old librarian's hands shook slightly, held up as they were to receive the books. He peered at each one individually, bringing them close to his face. "This one is a silver coin. The other is not for purchase."

It seemed expensive for a random book purchase, but it was not even her money, really. Clerin handed over the coin and picked up her book. One thing was nagging at her, though.

"Do you know who the author of this book is?" She smiled at the librarian.

"Nope." That was it. She had kind of been hoping for a little more conversation if not for more information.

"I'll just go put this book back, I'll meet you outside." Altrond turned and walked back into the confines of the library.

Clerin walked outside, clutching her book, and the sun beamed warmly, but comfortably, down upon her. She squinted up at the burning ball of fire in the sky. When she was in the Fluen realm she had always looked forwards to the few sunny days during the summer that could dry out the soil. But here, it was opposite. Here she looked forwards to cloudy days, with or without any rain. Apparently, all she was really looking for was a break from monotony. Something to dull the edge. She wondered what she would look forward to if each day were "perfect."

They wandered the entire town. They entered each shop, wandered through the market, checked in on the empty amphitheater and the large public gymnasium. There were supposedly some geothermal baths by the river that they did not get to. They had turned back after watching the mesmerizing waterwheel at the mill. They were close enough to the Gaen realm that, despite the continued hot air, there were many streams and trees and brush. Clerin truly enjoyed Wazschial, it seemed to have everything without the incredible sprawl and press of bodies that encompassed Agoge. She thought to herself that if she was required to make a home in the Pyran lands, she would prefer Wazschial out of all the towns she had visited to date. Not that she had visited many different towns, and Agoge was the only one she had spent more than a few days in.

The sun dipped behind the horizon, briefly splashing reds and oranges across the sky. There were some hills that raised the small forest visible to the west, but the tall snowcapped mountains that she had heard peppered the Gaen realm were still too far away to be sensed by anything besides imagination.

They were standing in the middle of the hard packed road. Everything had been glanced over and most of it was now shuttered. The market square was empty, the shops were all locked up tight. The darkness began to settle upon the little town like a crouching cat.

They moseyed over to the tavern, taking their time. Clerin knew this would be the last stop before heading back to Trela's camp outside the town, so she was not in a hurry to arrive. They had chosen the tavern in lieu of either of the small pubs to get a taste of the raucous night life there in Wazschial. If you are going to see a thing, may as well see it at its grandest. At least that was what Altrond told Clerin.

Clerin squinted as they walked into the brightly lit common room. There were some musicians in the corner playing something slow and soft. There was a mandolin, a lute, a bodhran, and a fiddle. A young and waifish Pyran was singing a wordless lilting tune. There were many long tables and benches that took up the central portion of the room, with a hanging lantern shining down over each one. There were benches against the wall and nicely wrought sconces that carried dim candles, adding minimally to the ambiance. A long bar was at the far end of the room, corralling two bartenders. They were both muscular, but the male was quite bulky, verging on Torpalin's size, while the female was more toned. And they both had long hair and quick smiles. Altrond ordered some grog for the two of them.

Many of Trela's warriors were already there at the tavern and more arrived by the minute. By midnight, almost the entire pack was there. Trela's coterie, as she called it. Conspicuously absent was Trela herself. Clerin also noticed that Knill, Vrric, and Gyllhelon were missing as well. She wondered if anyone else noticed them missing. Of course, there were probably others missing that she had had not noticed. She only realized that Knill was missing because she assumed he was with Trela. She only realized that Gyllhelon was missing for a similar, though slightly more twisted, reason. Instead of thinking about it, she ordered some more grog.

It was not until the first wave left, somewhere around two in the morning, that Clerin realized that Altrond was a thief. She knew he was a spy, one adept at picking locks and silently scurrying through third floor windows, but had somehow not equated those types of skills with thievery. She had casually asked what he was to do without the book on Tlana, since the librarian would not sell it to him. He had merely smiled and produced the ancient tome from somewhere amongst his clothing.

"The book is too important to leave behind." He smiled rather warmly at her, but she thought it was the grog inducing the soft smile. "Besides, it has not been checked out even once over the last sun cycle. They will not even miss it." She opened her mouth to protest. "Double besides, I left two silver crowns in its place on the shelf. That is twice as much as you paid for your book."

"But… you stole the book." She tried to furrow her brow in seriousness, but his immediate laughter meant she had missed the mark.

"No, no. You see, I paid for the book." He held his hands in front of him to assist in professing his innocence.

"But… they did not want to sell it to you." She knew she had a point there somewhere and was not about to let him shrug it off.

"No one was reading it there. It could be incredibly important for us, for Trela's mission. Is the value of an object not tied with its usefulness? Its usedness?"

"Its usedness?" It threw Clerin for a small loop, the absurdity of the word.

"Don't objects cry out for use? A tool is not really a tool until it is used. Would you force a warrior to fight without a sword, if that was their chosen weapon? Of course not, because it would insult the sword just as much as it upsets the warrior." He leaned back and straightened his spine. There was something smug about his posture.

"Fine. You know, I am not even going to argue with you." Clerin paused with a mischievous smile. "Because we both know you stole it."

"Can't we agree that providing a good use to a lonely tool trumps the staid laws of derlians? Am I just to ignore the laws of nature?" Altrond had lost any vestige of being smug. It was almost as if he was asking her for a favor.

Clerin had stood up while he was speaking. She thought about chiding him some more, but he was pleading with his eyes. She found herself smiling.

"I suppose I can say that every single thing desires usefulness." He smiled back at her. "Come on, get up. The time to leave has come upon us."

Clerin found herself spending a fair amount of time with Altrond. Most of it was just because he was fun to be around. He was always entertained by something, even if he was not always entertaining. However, some of it was because she was not spending much time with others.

It was not like she was avoiding Trela, but she always seemed to have some task to hand out. It was never boring around her, but it was also never relaxing. That removed Knill from Clerin's circle as well, though she probably could have sought him out when he was in the company of Croy fairly easily. Through no conscious fault of theirs, she often felt that she was interrupting them. Those two, along with Tumu, almost seemed to speak their own language. They would finish each other's sentences and laugh at the oddest moments. She certainly enjoyed their company, but no, she did not seek them out very often.

It was not like she was avoiding Vrric. In fact, she had tried to get him alone a couple of times, but it never seemed to work out. He always seemed to be surrounded by a group of others. Either the other mages, or some of the younger Pyrans eager for stories of glory, or Gyllhelon. She liked Gyllhelon as a derlian, she truly did. They had hung out and laughed uproariously on occasion during Trela's campaign. For some reason, however, she seemed to have an excessive interest in Vrric. And, for an even cloudier reason, that seemed to inordinately bother Clerin.

It was not like she was avoiding the full contingent of Luften warriors, but they seemed to always be around Gyllhelon. At least it seemed like they were whenever she felt like chatting with one of them. Except for Haswyxe, who had started to travel with Croy whenever Croy was not with Knill.

It was not like she was avoiding the Pyran warriors, but she did not always know what to talk about with them. She could shoot a bow decently, but she was not very skilled with knives, let alone swords. And though she was quite fit, she did not have the focused devotion to exercise that most of them had. Their drills and practice bordered on the fanatical. She was just not a warrior.

It was a similar situation with the mages. Sure she could cast spells, but it was not her specialty. She could not cast a huge amount of different ones, nor could she cast particularly powerful ones. If, perchance, she had a strong desire to become a greater mage, she was sure that they would take all the time she needed to help her. But it was similar to the fanatical workouts amongst the warriors. She just did not have the burning desire that she needed to put in the hefty effort. The one part of magic that she had shown promise in, the art of healing, was somewhat tainted by the fact that the greatest healer amongst the group was Nochiel. Clerin felt that Nochiel still held a grudge against her for sending Haswyxe back to Croy for healing. It was interesting that Nochiel had even agreed to join the coterie.

There were certainly Pyrans who wanted to ride alongside her, but she was never quite sure of their ultimate intent. Most were the younger warriors with wide eyes and quick smiles. They reminded her a bit of excited puppies. Fun, but... fluffy?

So, instead, she spent much of her time with Altrond. He was smart and studious in many aspects, but was also quick with a joke. There was an interesting mix of quiet and loud in him. And, though she had given him a hard time about it in Wazschial, she enjoyed to hear him read from the book that he stole from the library:

"There are many differing theories of the Vijen and Tlana. The simplest is that they are Yavens. But which element are they? There has been mention that there are at least one for each element. A more fringe theory is that they are two different unknown elements. Many do think that a fifth element exists that is called spirit or sapience or consciousness. It is posited that this element is in all living creatures and absent in all dead objects. This does little to assist us in understanding the Vijen and Tlana, however. We will examine this theory in more depth later on in the book since this brings up some different conjectures and assumptions.

"If they are not Yavens, of the known or unknown elements, they could be some creature of the Void, trapped here in this world during its creation. This would make them very similar to Yavens, but without a home realm to return to. Or maybe they wish to merely return to the emptiness of the Void itself.

"Another theory, and quite a popular one at that, is that they are some force or idea that has become incarnate. Many feel that they are the embodiment of good and evil. The Tlana are easily thought of as the incarnation of evil, but are the Vijen truly the best that 'good' could come up with? Others think they represent order and chaos, though that is a bit of a stretch of the imagination. By all accounts, both are fairly chaotic and, as is well known, chaos is ephemeral.

"There have been some that say they are the manifestations of the Belegs arguing. That the ebb and flow of their sightings and, indeed, their very existence is due to one Beleg confronting another. This has several flaws, the least of which is that none of the Belegs are known to have confessed to this. The other issues are that there are two of their kind and four of the Belegs. And which Beleg controls the evil Tlana? Some would say that the Vijen and Tlana merely represent winning and losing points of the argument and do not directly represent any individual Beleg.

"They do not have to be real. Many question their existence as a whole. This is a foolish wish to deny life to anything out of our direct senses. They could be illusions, but the question then turns, or returns, to how they were created. Would the Belegs create such bizarre illusions just to confound their derlian children? Maybe they are a mere reflection of the unconscious will of the derlian sensing them and communicating with them?

"They could be just a manifestation of communication. Perhaps they are the image created in the derlian mind as we speak across realms through wormholes or punctures and ruptures of our own reality. Or that they are portals themselves to another realm, a rift between realms created when the world came into being. Or, even more fanciful, there is an ancient derlian who is told to accompany a well of immortality whose home is made in the same desert. Maybe it is that being that communicates through the Vijen and Tlana. Maybe it is the whole village that communicates through them.

"Speaking of the fabled well, there are those who assume that there were several of the first derlians who did not wish to feel the ravages of chaos, of old age and death, and that they petitioned the Belegs for the well. Since they were still a heartbeat away from being eternal, the story says that when they drank the immortal waters, it affected them differently than it does the typical derlians who drink from it. It is this volatile mixture that turned them into Vijen and Tlana.

"Maybe they are not individually conscious? There are those who say they are a form of backwash or a riptide of derlian magic, that they coalesced from the magic, chaos, and pure energy that abounds here, and that they merely pooled into sentience. Or that they were mere 'animals' from the beginning of the world that have mutated and evolved due to the pooled chaos. Or that they are the spirits of the dead, original Yavens that begat our derlian race. Or that they are merely the collective unconscious of the entire derlian race.

"No matter the truth, there is, of course, the question of when they came into being. Where they created with the world? Maybe when the well was created, or the Temples that house the Belegs, or when derlians discovered how to summon the Yavens? Or if we cast our imagination further back, maybe they are older than the world, than the Belegs, or older than the Yavens themselves?

"Even if we knew what they were, how and when they were created, there would still be questions. Are they two halves of the same species? Are they symbiotic? Are the Tlana merely parasitic? Maybe there is only one Tlana and one Vijen since there are no accounts of seeing more than one of them at a time.

"All of these questions, and many more, will be explored in this book. These are creatures of legends that have few reliable reports about them. But I tell you, dear reader, that these creatures are as real as you or I. I am one of the few derlians to have ever been able to witness both a Tlana and a Vijen, though at different times. It is these two experiences that gave me the impulse to write this book, to explore the unthinkable. It is these experiences that I will tell first."

"That is the most chaotic beginning I could have ever imagined. It did not answer anything." Altrond laughed and closed up the book.

"I think it is like a table of contents that has a description of each chapter included." Clerin looked up at the roof of the small tent. "Setting up the arguments, as it were."

"Well, I was hoping the author would just tell me what they believed to be the truth, rather than filling the table of contents with a thousand conjectures." He waved his hand in the air as he spoke.

"I don't think the author knows what the truth is." Clerin laughed a little. "If they knew, they would have written a tiny manifesto and we would all know by now. Then you wouldn't need a book built on conjectures." Altrond did not respond and they left it at that. The tent was hot and stuffy. It was the perfect time to give the book a break and take a nice walk in the fresh outside air.

They soon slipped into the fringes of the Gaen realm. Not very quietly, but certainly without any fanfare. Trela had not wanted to turn their mission into a diplomatic one. She said she needed to pass through the realm as unnoticed and invisible as possible. But she also needed to gain any information she could gather along the way. She desperately wanted to speak with Aedon, that was for sure. Clerin had suggested that Trela contact the Gaens directly, immediately after crossing into their realm, but her advice had been outvoted. She was not positive they were making a mistake, certainly not enough for her to argue more heatedly, but it just seemed like a given courtesy. *You should always announce a friendly visit out of common respect*, she thought. In her mind it held true for old friends or family, let alone foreign sovereigns.

In Trela's defense, neither of the Gaens spoke up about the plan either, giving it their tacit support by default. In fact, the silence lately seemed to be a little contagious, though Clerin could not pinpoint why. Unfortunately, many problems could be solved in just such a way, and success would often be confused with being correct. The consequences of these choices would not be known for some time.

In the meantime, Clerin was with Taglo as often as possible. The official excuse was to discuss the mission. And that did happen, certainly. But she found herself mesmerized by the thought of the other realms and their discussions about the actual mission were less frequent. Taglo, for its part, appeared to enjoy their idle chats as much as she did.

"But you have parents, do you not?" It was early morning and the coterie was keeping camp on the side of an advantageous stream for a couple of days. There was no one else in the tent.

"I have those that created me, certainly. But you live, what, two hundred sun cycles? And you are completely dependent on your parents for, what, twenty cycles? That leaves you under them for ten percent of your life. That is a decent amount, don't you think?" Clerin agreed. "It is impossible for me to fully reconcile how time passes without your sun. Before you were created, we did not reckon time like you do. Even since your realm burst into existence, we do not always pay attention to how many of your cycles pass with each passing moment of ours. It is difficult to keep that much intense focus on something so distant. As if you were trying to listen to a conversation over by that stream sitting where you are now. It may be audible enough to become words, but those words are unintelligible without great concentration. And we are close to the stream!" Taglo had a habit of saying something almost nonsensical, with a pause and an emphasis, at the end of some of their more banal talks. She thought it was its way of showing humor in conversation. Some of them made more sense than others. "But I would say that I am about twelve thousand of your cycles old. My parents, as you would call them, had me under them for, maybe, sixty or seventy cycles. That is a fraction of a percent. And I am young compared to some. Think of those Yavens who are many cycles older than I. Their percentage of supervision is even less. There is great respect amongst us and I am grateful that they decided to create me, but we are also mutual friends. We are judged by different rules than you derlians are. I am who I am. If my parents enjoy what that is, then we may mingle, as it were. However, if they do not, then they do not. If I do not enjoy what they are, I may choose to not mingle with them, as it were. There are so many enclaves in my realm, they... they appear infinite." Taglo paused for a moment. Clerin did not dare to interrupt. "If I had an eternity explore an infinite amount of space... could I?"

"You can't. You've started too late." Clerin thought about her words after she said them.

"Are you serious?" Taglo's pulsating flame paused for a moment.

"Even if I'm joking... Well, that still doesn't mean it's not true." She laughed at herself.

Some of the conversations, however, actually were about the mission. Clerin learned quickly to avoid any mention of trapping Yavens and to instead discuss how to infiltrate the secret society. To avoid the impetus, the reasoning, the why, behind the mission and to stick to the how of the mission. The how of the mission seemed like a safe subject.

In general, they agreed on the direction of the mission. In the beginning, there was only so much that could be done. They had to travel out of the Pyran realm. They had to pass through the Gaen realm to get to the supposed location of the Cabal headquarters. Which, according to Taglo's own accounts, lay somewhere on the foggy border between the Gaen and Fluen realms. It was, of course, in the mission's best interests to stop along the way to gather what information they could. On the subjects of the summoning of Yavens, of Tlana and Vijens, of the Cabal itself... There was not really a way to disagree when the conversations were held at such a high level, especially since they had no real information to digest and interpret yet. After some distance and time had passed, however, they began to venture into the specifics of how to infiltrate the Cabal of Lochom. One particular morning's conversation on the subject opened Clerin's eyes to what the mission really meant. At least, what it meant to Taglo.

It was of the opinion that they should have their mages infiltrate the Cabal first and foremost, leaving all of the warriors behind to rush in at the last possible moment and destroy everything.

"Won't that leave the mages in the heart of the serpents' nest, in great danger? What are the odds of survival in that scenario?" Clerin told herself she was concerned with each of the mages in the coterie, but it was the thought of Vrric's lifeless body draped over a cold boulder that made her speak up.

"I do not consider odds of survival. I only consider the odds that the mission succeeds." Taglo sounded more stoic than typical.

"But if all of our mages die immediately, won't that lower the odds of the overall mission succeeding?" She sort of wanted to ask Taglo what amount of casualties would be acceptable. She was afraid of the answer, however.

"Let me be clear. I will let you die." Clerin felt the blood draining from her face. "Only if it furthers the mission, of course. If there is a way to save you without endangering the mission, I surely will. In fact, I would probably save you before any of these others. If it does not endanger the mission. These mages that you speak of, if they are able to bring each individual with the knowledge of the Cabal into one room and they all die, I will slaughter each member of the Cabal myself. Their deaths will not be in vain."

"I am not sure how privy you are to the derlian mind and its motivations, but I would keep your willingness to lead us all to certain slaughter to yourself. Aversion to self-destruction runs deep." Clerin raised an eyebrow at Taglo.

"But this is a matter most abhorrent. I am willing to cease to exist. I! One who has survived longer than your entire race. I saw the birth of your kind. And, if I am able, I will survive long enough see it destroy itself. The destruction of this Cabal, the destruction of this abhorrent knowledge, is worth a thousand lives. It is worth a million lives. It is worth all life, do you understand?" Taglo had increased in size such that its head was touching the ceiling of the tent.

"You cannot expect us derlians to have the same passion for this. We are willing to die on this mission, but there should be an option out. We need a hope that we will survive. We need a hope that a majority of us will survive. Even if it is a false hope." Clerin was about to continue, but was interrupted.

"Do you know what I told to Gorbanax when I heard of this? Can you imagine our conversation?" The flames that made up Taglo were pulsating in a controlled, almost slow, pattern.

"I… I cannot imagine." Clerin was not sure if Taglo actually wanted her to guess at what was communicated. Since it was already agitated, she decided against it.

"I told Gorbanax. No wait… I begged Gorbanax. No wait… I commanded? I beseeched? I do not know the word. I told Gorbanax to destroy this realm and everything in it. Everything. Extinguish all of its life." The pulsating became faster and more erratic. "We do not need you. Your entire existence does not sway the Yavens one iota. You were toys created by the Belegs in a fit of jealous rage. No wait… In a fit of self-pity? In a fit of madness? They were racked with something. Something they did to themselves. Something they refused others to experience. We tried to make the best of the situation. We played along with their madness because we felt love for them. But then this. This…"

"Why was your suggestion not chosen?" Clerin was a little shocked by Taglo's vehement honesty.

"It is not just my suggestion, little one. It is the suggestion of the vast majority of Yavens. It is the only real solution. What if we root this evil out? Will it never return? If we kill every evil derlian that currently walks this realm, will it never return? Can you guarantee that this mission, even if it succeeds beyond all wild expectations and no 'good' derlians die, can you guarantee that this will not return? No, of course not. The only guarantee is if there are no more derlians." The pulsating was wildly chaotic by now. "Know that it is only the Belegs that keep you and all of your kind safe. They have an overdeveloped sense of responsibility for your welfare. The Yavens would not be so kind. They will not be so kind. If this mission fails, if we are unsuccessful due to any one derlian's foolish wish to survive, it will mean the destruction of everything you have ever experienced. We will make this place back into the Void from whence it was born. If this mission fails, the Belegs will be unable to save you from us. We will eradicate you. Is that a sufficient purpose for you? Is your aversion for self-destruction kicking in?"

Clerin was taken aback by Taglo's speech. By the intent and by the words themselves. The frustration and anger that emanated from the Yaven was palpable. But what really stuck in her mind, what really shook her beliefs, was the fact that Belegs and Yavens disagreed. They were not of one mind, not even close. She was always under the impression that the Belegs still ran the Yaven realms. She knew they were no longer the rulers in truth, but in practice… She had thought they were considered the wise old advisors that the new rulers went to with their questions. Though she knew it was true, she did not really think that there were many Yavens older than the Belegs. That there were those that looked down upon the Belegs. She had been told of their persecutions, but it was always stated as if they were persecuted for being different. As if there was some petty jealousy involved. That it was some Yaven's failing to be compassionate or to fully understand the difficulties of being a Beleg. Not that there were some Yavens who merely thought the Belegs were fools. Thought they were like children playing with fire inside the house. Somehow, in some major but invisible way, Clerin's view of the Belegs changed forever. There was some unseen schism between eternal powers. And, worst of all, that the Belegs may not always be on the correct side of that schism. The Belegs were not infallible. And the idea that the Belegs might be the last argument for the derlians' survival only made the schism more tactile.

Maybe this was more of a Pyran issue, she thought. It was a desperate attempt, she knew. But maybe the Fluen Yavens and Lembin got along much better. Maybe they had a deep and undivided respect for each other, one that transcended the mistakes in each of their paths. But then she wondered why she was trying to justify her preconceived notions. Those were merely hand-me-downs in her head, stuffed in there by her mother when she was young and still thought she could buy her mother's love with accolades from her teachers. So she took a deep breath and did what many Toswins were known for—she ignored the mind-shattering revelation until she could, at some later date, properly examine it and all of its ramifications. Or not.

"Still, I think it will be prudent if you leave such talk off the table. At least until we are at the point in the journey that we cannot turn back. You will get much better results from the derlians and it will improve the odds of the mission working the way you want it to. Just… trust me on this one." Clerin had a hard time focusing her mind on making her words fully match her meaning. It was like spear fishing along a riverbank. Every time you threw your spear at the image of the fish, the spear would reach out too far and break its tip on the round rocks lining the riverbed. You could compensate through experience, but your sight was still mistaken.

"That is your honest opinion?" Taglo had stopped pulsating and had shrunk back to normal size.

"Yes. I feel they will need something to believe in. Some hope that they will all make it back to their families once this is all over, no matter how tenuous the belief. Especially at the beginning of the mission." She was not positive if it was correct, but it was certainly her honest opinion.

"Then I will consider the wisdom of your deceit." Taglo paused for a moment. "To increase the odds of a successful mission."

Clerin still enjoyed their talks, especially when they spoke of the Pyran Yaven realm. She could listen to Taglo speak about the foreign landscape, or firescape, for hours, for days. Trying, oftentimes vainly, to comprehend the descriptions that Taglo struggled to bring into words. It was completely fascinating to Clerin. Her favorite was lying down with her eyes closed as it spoke of wandering through misshapen castles. The fact that all of the building materials were essentially the same substance as the inhabitants was especially mind boggling. That items and buildings and beings and the road between them and the air around them were all fire—Taglo had taken to calling them live-fire and dead-fire in an attempt to differentiate between them. That there was little difference between background and foreground. That sky and ground met in a horizon of flames. And that the realm's natural denizens were not confused by such similitude.

"How can you see that far peak from here?" They had been chatting outside one morning.

"Well, with my eyes." Clerin tried to discern the deeper question but was unable to.

"But there is air between you and it. How can you see through the air?" Taglo appeared to keep staring at the distant peak.

"Because air is invisible?" It was no answer, but it was all she could do at the early hour.

"Why is it invisible?" Taglo, thankfully, did not wait for her to attempt an answer. "Because it is much, much less dense than the rock that the peak is comprised of. That is the way we sense in my realm as well. We see through the non-dense at the denser objects beyond. Our realm is… discernable to us. Just as yours is to you."

"And what about here, in my realm? Can you discern fire more readily than air, or is air still less dense?" Clerin had a real curiosity.

"There is nothing less dense than fire. Fire is the purest form of energy." Taglo sounded somewhat smug to Clerin.

"But I can see through air, but not through fire." Her eyebrows unconsciously furrowed together.

"That is only because fire produces light. It obscures by oversaturating, not because of its density." Taglo's pause was too short for Clerin to interject. "But, to answer your question, I am able to discern fire, both live-fire and dead-fire, from a much greater distance than a derlian. And through the densest of materials, no less."

Yes, she certainly still enjoyed speaking with Taglo. But something was a little different, a little off. Something was quieter. Not the words, not the foreground, but something unspoken in the background. And the soundscape that used to be full of silent chatter was now completely and discernibly empty.

Chapter 6

They were still in the interstitial fringe between the two realms, but Croy thought he recognized a familiar smell. It was a little more wet than the Pyran realm, twinged with a hint of mold. The air may have been a little thinner, a little more chilled. But it was the faint smell of soil, of dirt, of rich loam that really triggered his memory. He stopped his horse, Buttercup, as they were winding up a narrow trail. He led her off to the side to allow the others to pass him by. Smiling to himself, he knelt down and pressed his face close to the short grass, inhaling deeply. Yes, it was the smell of soil. The scent lifted his heart and cleared his mind. It was a heady aroma. He rolled to his side, then to his back. The soft ground contoured itself to his body. He grinned like a fool and imagined the sky through his closed eyelids and breathed. Full deep breaths. It was an ecstatic feeling. It was the feeling of coming home after a long journey.

Eventually the sound of hooves began to fade. He realized that the coterie had passed him by. He opened his eyes, wet but not teary, and stared at the clear blue sky framed by a couple of trees stretching themselves away from him towards the sun. From this perspective, they took on an elongated, dreamy quality. He watched them sway for a moment. He thought of Ilana and wondered if she was looking up at the same sky, eternally lost in the middle of the Northern Desert. He supposed she would have little reason to stare upwards towards the baking sun. He wished that she was with him now, that she could also feel the ecstasy of coming home. The realization of that impossibility got him to stand back up and gather up Buttercup's reins. Though dampened a little, his spirits were still high as he made her trot uphill to catch up with the others. He was quite used to being the straggler.

They had left the wide, hardpacked roads behind in the Pyran realm. They were certainly not on narrow trails winding through the forests and foothills—they had several large wagons in their train, after all—but the path felt quite hidden comparatively. And though he was not walking himself, Croy could feel the effort of the gentle rise. He wondered how far into the distant mountain range they would travel, how close to Serif Trela would take their little team. She had said she wanted to travel invisibly through the realm. Croy had tried to explain to her how impossible that was, how watchful the Gaens were of their border, especially of their foothills.

In fact, Croy was quite hesitant about running into any other Gaens. Even the lowliest farmer would immediately alert the 'jin class to their presence. And Croy was unsure of what they would think of him. He was sure that Knill would be forgiven and might even be allowed to freely travel in and out of Serif. He was much less positive about his own reception. Swaying lazily in his saddle gave him plenty of time to wonder what Aedon had told the Blind One when she had finally returned. Assuming that she had returned. For all he knew, they could have all perished in the desert as he and Ilana were swallowed into the village around the well. The idea of being trapped alone, surrounded by 'jin, being questioned by the Blind One about the failed mission, sent shivers down his spine. It made him hesitant about advising Trela to make contact with anyone from Serif. The mere thought of it made him bite his tongue and bide his time. He knew, somewhere in the back of his mind, that it was a foolish action. Or to be more precise, a foolish inaction. But he could not seem to help it. It belatedly reminded him of hiding under the covers as a child. He knew it did not make sense. He even knew it at the time, that the thin fabric offered no real protection, but it would make him feel so much better that he would almost suffocate himself on the stale air trapped under the blankets with him rather than risk any small part of his flesh to the dangers roaming around outside. As time passed, as they wandered deeper into the Gaen realm, Croy's unease increased. It was horribly stifling, as if he could hear something quietly rummaging through his room while he was sweating under the oppressive weight of his bedsheets.

So he decided to take his mind off of the oppressive feeling by keeping himself busy. He usually spent his spare time talking with Knill and Tumu, but they were not distracting enough this time. He tried to lose himself amongst the Luften warriors, and there were certainly times that he and Haswyxe would while away a few hours. But there was always a nervousness in the back of his mind. It could not be fully quenched.

Croy began to wander the coterie, finding strangers to speak with. He found that took more effort, more conscious energy, and was, therefore, more distracting. He had to remember their names and faces, for sure, but he also tried hard to memorize the tidbits he heard about their families, about their loved ones left behind in Agoge, about their likes and dislikes, their fears and dreams. He tried to keep a catalog in his mind of all the different Pyrans in their group.

And that helped for a while. But what really took his mind off the thought of the Blind One was Nochiel. Of course, that had a lot to do with the nervousness that she instilled in him. The mild unease and discomfort that he felt while just being around her drowned out everything else. It was a trade-off that he was willing to endure.

They mainly spoke of nothing. Sometimes of magic, usually about healing, and sometimes about Agoge or the more benign portions of Trela's campaign. Eventually, however, she broached the subject that was the source of the unease.

"Why did you ignore my request?" She did not name the problem, but strode around the subject like a large, predatory cat. He thought about feigning ignorance of her subject but quickly disregarded that idea.

"You know why. He was a friend." Croy audibly sighed.

"You know, it was not even a request. You disobeyed a direct order." Her brown eyes flashed angrily.

"I could not just stand by and watch a friend die." Unconsciously, he let a little exasperation creep into his voice.

"You know that at least two others died later that day that you could have saved. Maybe three, but I will give you the benefit of the doubt. Two needless deaths." Nochiel raised two stubby, somewhat Gaen-like fingers in front of his face. "You are going to tell me that your Luften friend is worth two Pyrans?"

"I kept up as best as I could." He looked down at his travel-stained boots. It was not an answer, he knew that. But to his everlasting shame, the first answer that popped into his head was simply, *Yes.* He surely could not have spoken it, however. His second thought was that he had not realized that others had died that day, after he had healed Haswyxe. He had, essentially, not wanted to know. His third thought was one of amazement. Considering how much Nochiel had been angered by his actions, he was shocked that she had not mentioned the deaths before. He was not quite sure if that made him feel better about her, or worse. Finally, just because two warriors had died, did that make it his fault? Was he, alone, responsible for that? But he could not have spoken that last thought either.

"Yes, you did. And you failed at least two Pyrans. I watched it with my own eyes and sinking heart. You took too much time. You dawdled. You sent others on to the physicians too quickly. You were a mess." Her chest heaved while she spoke.

"I gave my full effort the entire day, I did not shirk. If I do my best and some still die, how is that shameful? I am not perfect. I am not as strong as you." He kept his eyes down.

"Strength is about pacing, Croy. Healing is a cross-country run, up hills and down valleys. It is not a mere sprint, flying across flat ground as fast as you can move." She took a deep, calming, breath. "I warned you of that. I begged you not to disobey me." Her voice got quiet. "You ignored me."

"Let me say again how sorry I am. I apologize. Fully, humbly, and sincerely. I have done so, repeatedly. Over and over. We always end up back here." He took his own deep calming breath. "I cannot watch a friend die. Not if I am able to do something. Not if there are a hundred others behind them, not even if there are a thousand. It is my nature." His voice got quiet. "I did the best I could."

"That is an excuse, not an apology. It is always an excuse." Her eyes flashed once more. "You know what? There is something you can do."

"Of course. Anything." An eyebrow popped up in a small reaction to hope.

"Have you met Trasdou yet?" There was almost something akin to muted glee in her voice.

"Yes, yes I have. He is one of the younger Pyran warriors. A swordmaster, I believe." Croy cast his mind back. "I think… I think his sword's name is Cobra." Croy felt a little twinge of joy at his memory.

"Get up, come along." Croy stood and followed without questioning.

They wandered amongst the small, coalesced groups of warriors. Nochiel held her head high, spying around in all directions. Finally, finding what she was after, she hustled towards a small group of four young Pyrans. They were standing next to a dangerous looking hawthorn tree.

"Trasdou!" She flung her arms open.

"Nochiel!" He patted her on the back as they briefly embraced.

"Trasdou, you know Croy, do you not?" She pulled back and waved an arm towards him.

"Yes, yes, of course." He moved towards Croy to embrace him. Croy felt himself grinning.

158

"It is because of Croy that your brother died at the battle of Geltroin." Trasdou froze. Croy froze. Trasdou's companions froze. Nochiel continued. "Your brother had the misfortune of being placed in front of Croy as the afternoon waned. He had spent all of his energy on a friend of his, a friend doomed to die I might add, and was unable to properly attend to your brother. He sent Lapallc to a physician without casting enough healing spells. He was too tired." They all stood there, staring at each other. Frozen. "I warned him when his friend was placed in front of him that he would weaken himself too much. I promised him that I would put him in front of the family and friends of those who died so that they would know why their loved ones were no more. I have fulfilled my promise." Nochiel turned to go but paused briefly and looked hard at Croy. "Now I forgive you." She walked away in silence.

Croy turned from her and looked at Trasdou. The blood drained from his head and he felt weak. He did not know what to say. He opened his mouth but could bring forth only pained silence.

"Is this true?" Trasdou broke the silence. He stared hard at Croy and absently pointed to the ground between them as he spoke.

"True enough." Croy's throat felt tight.

"Why did you not speak of this earlier?" There was a mist in his eyes.

"I... I did not know." Croy watched Trasdou's jaw tighten. "I knew that something had happened. I knew that I had defied Nochiel to save my friend, but did not realize that any had died, let alone who they were. We spoke little afterwards and I had always attributed her coldness to my defiance. Not to any particular death."

"Would you have told me had you known?" It was like all of his muscles were clenched. Like his body would crush inward into a sphere at any moment.

"Yes. Of course." Croy was less positive than he hoped his voice sounded. He *was* positive that Trasdou would have known earlier had Croy known.

"You know I blamed myself for his death." Croy could not tell if it was a question or a statement. "I was there at Geltroin. We fought shoulder to shoulder. A group of five loyalists charged our line, screaming at the top of their lungs." Croy thought it was odd that Qizern's warriors were only called loyalists after he was defeated. "We had several warriors behind us, so I was not too concerned. I lunged forwards with Cobra and struck one of them in the side, just up under his shield. I pulled back mightily to add a slice and elbowed a young warrior behind me." He gave a bark of a laugh. "It was stupid, really. Why was he that close? Anyway, I felt his nose give way and I naturally turned to see if he was okay. There was blood all over his face and into his failed attempt at a beard, but it was not even a wound, really. His eyes, however, were huge with shock. I thought maybe I had shifted a bone backwards, or something. Maybe that I had done some real damage. But then I noticed it." Another short bark emitted from him. "He wasn't looking at me at all. He was looking in front of me or, I guess, behind me since I was half twisted. He probably didn't even know he had gotten tagged in the face, he was so far in shock. Well, once I realized that, I turned back around as fast as my muscles allowed. There was Lapallc, stuck with two swords at once." Each muscle in Tradou's body seemed to be clenched. "I went crazy with rage, Lapallc had taught me everything I knew about sword fighting. He was more than a brother to me. I killed the other four loyalists in front of me much too quickly to transfer the amount of pain that I wished, but it could not be helped. I'm... I'm actually glad that I no longer have to blame his death on myself. His father will be pleased as well."

"Please, I... I am so sorry for your loss." Croy had no idea of what to say.

"That is not an apology." He raised his hand just as Croy opened his mouth to offer up something more longwinded and heartfelt. "If I had a friend in front of me and a stranger behind, you bet I would waste my energy on my friend. That is how these things go."

"Well, I—" Croy was again interrupted.

"Who was your friend, did they survive?" Each muscle had stayed taut. "Nochiel had said your friend was doomed to die, did she not?"

"Actually yes, he lived. It was Haswyxe, the Luften." Croy half turned to point towards the main camp.

"Then that is where the recompense must come from. Thank you, Croy." Trasdou started to walk past Croy and his three friends quickly followed.

"Wait, what? What do you mean by recompense?" Croy struggled to catch back up.

"For the loss of my brother's life. I cannot thank you enough, truly." His long legs kept their grueling pace. "Haswyxe!

Luften, come here! Haswyxe!" They were all walking so fast that they were almost running. Everyone they passed stared in quiet astonishment at the commotion.

It was not Haswyxe who first appeared, however. It was Malghain. His stride, his smile, his body—it was all completely relaxed. He was hurrying towards them, for sure, but the leisure that seemed to flow through him was the complete opposite of the clenched body of Trasdou.

"May I help you, Pyran?" Malghain planted himself in front of Trasdou and kept an arm out with open fingers to keep some distance between them.

"You are not Haswyxe." Amazingly enough, Trasdou did stop.

"No, but when you start yelling across the entire valley for a Luften, you get me." His smile appeared relaxed and genuine, but for no conscious reason, Croy felt danger emanating from him. Malghain was not going to let the confrontation go by.

"Haswyxe has something of mine." Neither derlian had their hands on their weapons, but Croy could not get the image of battle out of his mind.

"And what would that be?" His hand fell to his side.

"My brother's life!" Croy could see the veins in Trasdou's neck. He glanced at the other three Pyrans, but they were as calm as Malghain was. "This healer chose Haswyxe over my brother."

"Then your issue is with Croy. You cannot blame an unconscious warrior for the help they received." Croy felt the blood drain from his face once more.

"No, it is a life for a life. I cannot blame a healer for choosing a friend over a stranger." Trasdou's brow clenched.

"Of course you can! That is the only logical conclusion!" Croy turned to find Nochiel striding up to them. "The decision that was made was Croy's, not Haswyxe's.

"No, he is correct. It was my life that was spared. If there is to be any trade, it should be me that pays the price." Haswyxe appeared out of nowhere. "You will have to work for it, however."

"Of course, I never thought otherwise." Trasdou raised both of his arms straight out from his sides. His three friends backed away.

"Stay out of this one Malghain, no matter what happens." Haswyxe gently pushed on Malghain's chest. It was the first time that evening that Croy saw Malghain not looking relaxed.

Both swords flashed from their scabbards at the same time. They began a slow circle. Trasdou was half crouched and still looked clenched up. Haswyxe was standing, facing Trasdou with his back straight. Croy knew that he did not know much about sword fighting, but most of the time a warrior kept their legs in a line, not side by side. He wondered what Haswyxe's aim was.

"Stop this stupidity!" Trela finally arrived. "What is this?"

"It is an honor duel, my Queen." Trasdou kept his eyes fixated on Haswyxe while he talked.

"You do *not* speak to your Queen with live steel in your hand!" Trela walked herself to the edge of them. "Sheath your weapons! Both of you!"

To Croy's great astonishment, neither derlian moved. They stared at each other with intense eyes, Trasdou's were squinting while Haswyxe's were wide and black. Trela looked back and forth at each of them, then she stepped in between them. Haswyxe twitched the tip of his blade up, to the vertical position, so that she would not run into it. For her part, Trela turned her back on Haswyxe and stared hard at Trasdou.

"Are you deaf or are you daft?" There was a low, hard steel in her voice.

Trela usually sounded so positive to Croy, so sure and upbeat. But here and now, she sounded truly dangerous, with Trasdou's blade a mere fist away from her face and her smoldering yellow eyes. He knew that she had killed many during her campaign, she had led thousands to battle, she had defeated many talented killers in single combat, but in the back hidden part of his mind, a small part of him had always thought of her as his charge. There was this illusion, given to him by Synde, that she was someone to be protected. He had long known that it was a mere illusion, that she had taken care of him for far longer than he had ever taken care of her, but... More than the image of her covered in blood at Dun Oengen, matted hair framing her wild grin as she circled the poor befuddled Lieutenant Uriels; more than her leading the cavalry charge at Eltrond, standing up in her stirrups and screaming like one of the deranged; more even than her steely resolve in the face of Qizern's massively overwhelming forces at the Dekhan Plateau; this image finally destroyed all remnants of that foolish illusion. There seemed to be a deep anger in her. Not necessarily a rage, nothing uncontrollable, certainly not hate, and it was not fully directed at anyone, but it was a slow burn of churning anger that made Croy think of rivers of magma flowing in the ground under unsuspecting feet. She held her right hand up, palm towards Trasdou, but he said nothing, did nothing, did not even blink. She placed her hand against his sword, against the sharp edge of Cobra. Her lips pulled back into a grin and her head tilted forwards. Still, no one spoke. No one moved. Trasdou would not move his sword out of her way, so she pressed. The sword slowly moved backwards, towards its master, as slowly as the rivulet of blood that crawled down her forearm. Still the entire world was silent. Croy began to wonder if Trasdou was in a trance. His eyes became crossed as he watched his sword move ever so slowly towards him. The blood was dripping down her arm and falling onto the ground between them. Eventually the sword was pushed back such that it touched his forehead. Somehow that reached him and he was able to move. He stepped back and lowered his sword. His face was slack as if he was in a daze.

"I have given full amnesty. To everyone. I have given it to Qizern's most loyal servants. I have given it to those who tried to kill me, to those who tried to kill you. To those who have killed so many of our brother and sister warriors." Her grin was still in place. Her eyes stayed steady and her hand did not waver from where it was held, though the sword was no longer there. The stripe of red down her arm looked to be getting wider. "Who do you think you are to question my amnesty? What audacity hides in your heart that you can ignore my commands? How dare you attack a fellow warrior on a communal quest? How dare you to speak to your Queen with live steel in your hands? To refuse her simple request of peace, to refuse to lay down arms long enough to speak. What hateful pride stuck in your craw makes you think your pain transcends everyone else's pain?" She lowered her arm and raised her head to scan the gathered crowd. "Zira, you lost your husband, did you not?"

"Yes, my Queen." Zira stepped forward as she spoke.

"Arnasta, you lost a sister?"

"Yes, my Queen." Arnasta stood forward as well.

"And you, Grungle, you lost your father, correct?"

"Yes, my Queen." One of the warriors who had followed Trasdou spoke up.

"Do you know what happens during battle? During revolution?" Trasdou did not speak, but lowered his eyes towards the ground. "Derlians die. It is horrible and painful and regrettable." Trela kept pressing her point. "After amnesty was given, did any of you still seek vengeance?" No one spoke. "Truly, I am full of forgiveness on this day. If anyone secretly sought vengeance after amnesty, speak now. There will be no reprisals." Still, no one spoke. A heavy silence hung over the camp.

"No, my Queen." Grungle finally broke the silence. His deep voice was soft and quiet, almost sad.

Then a chorus of quiet, sad voices joined in. "No, my Queen." They all spoke the same refrain. The crowd sounded like a slow wind rustling through dry leaves.

"So, what is it about you, Trasdou? What is in you that is so different from all these others? Why is your pain more deserving than theirs?" Trela clenched her fist in front of his face, which only reopened her fresh wound. The blood began to drip from her closed fist while she shook it in front of him. It seemed as if she were, indeed, squeezing blood from a stone. "What hubris in you gives you the right to cut your Queen? How can you live with yourself?"

"I can't?" It was a question. Trasdou's eyes began to mist even as his face stayed slack.

"That is correct." Trela's eyes were hard as stone and focused intently on Trasdou's. It seemed that she was slightly nodding.

Trasdou looked around. There was not one amongst the crowd that would meet his gaze, not even Croy. There was a small quaver to his lip. The silence was deafening. He dropped to his knees and looked up at Trela. She stared mercilessly back at him. He scraped his sword around so that the hilt was against a rock and the tip was held in his hands against his soft belly, just under his ribs. He closed his eyes. Croy, no matter how much he wanted to, could not look away. No one spoke as Trasdou drew in a deep, long breath. Then, at the last moment, as he knelt there holding his breath, Trela leaned down and kissed him on his dry, cracked lips.

"I forgive you." It was a whisper, but it carried throughout the crowd. His eyes, heavy with unshed tears, opened and looked into hers. She pulled his hands into hers, letting Cobra fall to the ground without striking. "I forgive you." She pulled him upwards and made him stand. "You are lucky I do not take ghulzans." It was a whisper that was much harder to hear. Then, still staring into Trasdou's eyes, holding his hands in front of her, she spoke loudly and confidently. "I forgive you all. You all have my amnesty. We are of one mission, one mind. We must be strong together if we are to defeat the evil Cabal of Lochom. We are all brothers and sisters here. We are a family. We cannot bicker and squabble about the past. We must gather our collective strength and stride forth together towards triumph."

Trasdou hugged Trela like a drowning derlian clings to a floating log. The crowd let out a collective sigh of relief, as if every single one of them had been holding their breath. Croy started to laugh for no reason.

There was a sound of clapping. It seemed to fit the mood of the moment, so Croy ignored it at first, but it kept insisting itself. He realized that no one in the crowd was clapping. He shook his head to clear it. There, all around them, were at least one hundred Gaen 'jin. Croy's heart sank to the soles of his feet.

"That was indeed moving, Pyran. Your kind are endlessly entertaining. I could normally listen to such antics for hours but, you see, I am on a timeline. And you… you have something of mine that I wish back." It was the Blind One. And his solid white cataracts were pointed directly at Croy.

Croy wished that he had been able to take this scene, this realization, this confrontation, with dignity. With quiet acceptance as Trasdou had just done. He was unable to keep calm, however. He vomited a tiny amount in his mouth and felt his eyes fill with frustrated tears.

"And what would that be?" Trela turned away from Trasdou and walked over to place herself between the Blind One and Croy.

"Well, let us see. First and foremost is my apprentice, Croy Sie'tin. Then there is the matter of the runaway, Knill. Note that he has yet to earn a surname. And then there is the case of a young Pyran girl wanted for the murder of one Nolt Sie'tin. Have I missed anyone?" The Blind One smiled wide.

"Your guards are who murdered Nolt, not I." Trela's clenched fist continued to bleed.

"We both know that you put him in that circumstance. We both know he would be alive if you had not fled Serif." He swiveled his head around the camp. "But no, I am not concerned with the law.

And besides, I am not here for a fight. I know that snatching you to face a just trial for your crimes would lead to much bloodshed. And, no offence, but I am not concerned about Knill either. You will be happy to know that your father has already replaced you with an eager orphan. Twice as smart as you ever were and much, much more loyal, I hear. It is amazing at how quickly some Gaens can overcome tragedy. No, I really have only one interest here. Only one that I am willing to risk bloodshed for."

"Croy is my apprentice now." Feyazki stepped forward. That took Croy completely by surprise. He had not even spoken to Feyazki for at least a week.

"You have an interesting… scent. And though I have met very few Luftens, that is not what I am referring to. You have a …foreign… smell of magic. Like a rare spice. Show me what you can do." The Blind One walked down to where Trela and Feyazki were standing. "Please. Give me a small taste."

"Eqedeelearc!" Feyazki shot a gigantic branch from a nearby tree clean off with a bolt of lightning. He did not even look tired.

"Impressive. Quite impressive, indeed. Delicious." The Blind One had kept his face towards Feyazki the entire time. "Now I want you to hold onto Croy's right arm. Croy, my boy, come over here."

Croy knew something was wrong. He did not want to walk over there. He did not want to get any closer to the Blind One than he had to. He looked around for Taglo, but it was nowhere in sight.

"Everyone is waiting, Croy. Do not worry, I will not lay a hand on you." The Blind One was nodding, but he kept his face towards Feyazki, not Croy.

Croy walked over and stood next to Feyazki. He was exceedingly nervous. Something seemed odd, but he could not place his finger on it.

"Good. Now you, young Luften magician, you grab his right arm with both your hands. That's right, good and tight." The Blind One was nodding to himself. Croy looked around like a caged animal. He tried to peer at the Gaen 'jin surrounding the camp. They hadn't moved at all, he was certain of it. "Now I'll show you what I can do." The 'jin flickered—as if Croy were looking at a reflection on a placid lake and someone threw in a stone. *It's an illusion*, he thought. They aren't really surrounded. He opened his mouth to scream to Feyazki, to scream to Trela, to scream. He was screaming as the Blind One cast his spell, so he did not hear the word used, but it would not have mattered even if he had heard it. Because suddenly, in an instant that was a fraction of a heartbeat, he found himself surrounded by stone. He was underground. He was alone with the Blind One. He was screaming.

Croy awoke surrounded by trees. He was in forest of evergreens, which made him think he must be high up in the mountains. He gave a small start and then quickly stood. He almost laughed with relief that the Blind One was not around, but he felt far from his friends and he worried that the Blind One would be somewhere nearby. Maybe even watching him. He brushed the dust off himself as he looked around the quiet trees for any signs of life. It was silent and still, like the calm before a large storm. He searched for the sky, maybe there *was* a large storm coming. The few patches that he could see through the branches, however, were a placid blue. He shook his head, attempting to shake the feeling.

He decided to investigate his surroundings more thoroughly, he could only stand still or turn in a slow circle for so long. He remembered something vaguely about flying with the Blind One. There had been a great struggle and he had been dropped or something. He certainly remembered a sensation of falling. Of barely being able to think of the words to save himself in time. He had somehow won his freedom, now he just needed to figure out where that escape had left him. He shook his head again.

There was an intense green glow around everything up above, while everything head height and down felt brown, dried, and drab. The lower branches seemed skeletal, the uppers slowly tapering into an elongated green pyramid. There were large gray boulders scattered about, half covered under dried pine needles. There were partial paths and animal trails emanating from this central area. He was in a small depression, the bottom of a rounded bowl, and the choices were splayed out in front of him in any direction he might want to go.

So he picked one at random and began walking. Though he did not recognize the land at all, it did appear to be in the Gaen realm. He felt *comfortable* there. There was a smell in the air, or a vibration too subtle to be consciously noticed, that made him think of walking his sheep alone along a mountainside outside the hidden underground of Serif. It brought a warm, heavy feeling. A cozy feeling. A protected feeling. And yet…

As he was walking along, he stumbled across a huckleberry bush. He could not believe his luck. First, he planned on eating his fill which might take a while considering his state of hunger. Then he figured he would load up every pouch and pocket with them, so he could continue on his way, sated and still harboring a precious burden. It was while he was sitting there, eating and looking up at the sky, wondering how he had escaped, that he met the crow.

The crow was timid but insistent. It would hop back and forth in front of him, training his black, beady eye upon him. Most of the examination came from the bird's right eye. *Maybe that's his good eye*, Croy laughed to himself. For the want of anything else to do, he began talking to the bird.

"I'll bet you know where we are." They started out as statements, but they morphed quickly into questions. "I wonder where my friends are?" He shook his head, exasperated at this own foolishness.

Throughout it all, the bird hopped around, staring at him. It took him a while, but he finally realized that the crow was not so much interested in him, but in the huckleberries he was in front of. Smiling to himself, he took three juicy berries and scattered them in front of the crow. The crow quickly picked one up delicately with its beak, still eyeballing Croy. It tossed its beak back and swallowed the berry whole.

"You're not worried about being lost at all, are you my little friend?" The crow grabbed up another berry. "Just worried about me stealing all your food, huh?" It peered at him with staccato twitches. He tossed a couple of more huckleberries from his pocket in front of the crow. The bird happily hopped back and forth as he prattled on. "You must enjoy the simplicity of it all. Not having to worry about old vindictive mentors attempting to seal you away in a jail." But then he thought of song birds trapped in a cage. In response to the unbidden image of imprisoned birds, he tossed some more berries for the bird. "I guess that even the simple life is not very simple." His voice dropped to a low whisper. "Not while there are derlians around."

The bird seemed to be getting bored with his ramblings and even the berries. It hopped a little ways away from him and fluttered up onto a low tree branch. It eyeballed him from its good eye. It ruffled its wings. Croy leaned his head back and stared up into the blue sky. If the bird could ignore him, he could ignore the bird. He ate a couple more huckleberries. They were succulent and sweet. He smiled to himself. He could stay lost for all he cared, just as long as he was not found by the Blind One.

"Cah, cah, cah." Three small, rough, and gravelly notes emanated from the crow. He straightened his head to look at the bird. The way it moved made it seem agitated. It hopped sideways on the branch. "Cah." It peered at him with its left eye, then its right. "Cah!"

Without really understanding what he was doing, he stood. The bird took flight straight at him. He ducked as it flew past his head. "Cah!" It swooped past him once more, flying in the direction of the tree that it had been perched upon, then it flew past that and into the distance. Croy was in no hurry, but felt compelled to follow after the fleeting bird. His pockets still heavy with huckleberries, he meandered down the trail a ways. Just when he thought the trail vanished into brush, the crow, or maybe one that looked and sounded like the other, flew past and shot in another direction. He started to jog along the trail, trying to keep up. The bird would sit in a tree ahead of him, cawing if he walked in the wrong direction or even if he stood in one place for too long. It was an odd sensation, being harassed by birds. Being... herded.

Soon, however, he reached the edge of a tall cliff and could follow the crow no farther. He stood at the edge of the trees and looked out over the valley below him. His hand naturally, but blindly, reached for a nearby branch. There was a forest below him, lush as anything he had ever heard of, with low clouds misting the deciduous treetops. It was breathtaking. He had an unconscious and slightly vacant smile on his lips. There was a small wind that flowed over the treetops below him, making them bow and sway together. They ebbed and flowed so slowly and seamlessly, it made him feel as if he were seeing things underwater.

Then he saw it approaching. It seemed small at first, like a crow in the distance. That was just because it started out so far away, however. It appeared to gain in size as it approached. It was the size of an eagle, flapping slowly but moving swiftly towards him. Then it was the size of a condor, of an albatross, still flapping its way over to Croy. It soon surpassed any bird that he had ever seen. It surpassed any bird that he had heard of, it was truly gigantic. Still it slowly beat its wings towards him, still it grew in size. It was black, like a raven or crow, with a slight inky sheen to its feathers. It appeared larger than the great hall of Serif. It appeared larger than Agoge. It filled the entire valley. And then he noticed what it really was. It was not one gigantic bird that slowly flapped its wings. No, it was thousands and thousands of tiny birds that flew as one. They ducked and dived so quickly that the overall shape barely seemed to shift. They were so dense that he could not see through them. They surged to and fro madly as the gigantic bird they constituted reared up in front of him. It flapped its wings once, then twice, as if were about to land at a nest. Then, all at once, as if from some invisible cue, they burst apart from their grander image. It was as if the gigantic bird in front of him exploded into thousands of shards. They screamed in unison. It was a deafening cacophony. Without really understanding what he was doing, Croy screamed with them. The whole world screamed. Then they swooped at him and attacked. Pounding wings and feathers surrounding him, blinding him with their density. Cold, hard talons shredding the skin from his face. Then his screams came for real. They were filled with pain, they were filled with terror. He screamed as if his life depended upon it.

He awoke screaming. He was drenched in sweat and had already thrown the thin blanket that had covered him onto the stone floor. It took him the briefest of moments to realize where he was. He had been captured by the Blind One. He was on a hard cot in a cell in Rycher. His first thought was that he would rather be torn apart by birds.

Croy was not sure how much time he spent in Rycher before the Blind One visited. There was the unknown amount of time he spent unconscious since he could not remember arriving. He did not feel that the blankness lasted very long, at least he certainly hoped it had not. Once he woke from his dream, he assumed that about three days had passed, judging from the amount of meals he received. So... maybe four days total. He was wondering what had happened to the coterie after he had been abducted when he heard the jingling rustle of keys. Then came the rusty scrape of the cell door being unlocked.

The Blind One entered and the cell door closed behind him. He had on a loose leather jerkin and carried his gnarled wooden staff with him. But, as usual, Croy could look at little beyond the milky white cataracts that sealed the Blind One's eyes as surely as Croy's cell door sealed him in.

"I trust you have found your accommodations comfortable." The Blind One smiled at his own joke. It rubbed Croy the wrong way, however.

"You have never spent the night here, have you? This is just a place you dump others to soften them. A place to visit." The door clanged behind the Blind One and the noise made Croy hop a little. He almost regretted what he said. Almost.

"If I were to be honest with you Croy, I would tell you that I do not even like visiting this place." His smile did not slip. "I believe it is the smell that annoys me most. It reeks of sweat, urine, and desperation. It is an unhappy aroma that wants to linger in my nostrils long after I have bathed."

"Good." It was all he could think of. And that depressed him more than his cell did.

"I take it you are unhappy with our reacquaintance." There was a touch of something in his voice. Maybe... compassion?

"Look where I am! Are you serious? Do you really think I would welcome you with open arms? I have been down here for days!" Croy could feel real anger bubbling up in him. Giving in to such emotions was rare for him, so he was not quite sure how dangerous it was getting, but his usual nervousness was being overshadowed.

"Hmmm. Your time away has toughened you up a bit. I am not sure how much I like that, but I suppose it cannot be helped." The Blind One tapped his staff on the ground three times. "You are correct about the surroundings, however. If we are to speak to each other as if we are equals, we should do it on neutral territory."

The door reopened with a rusty scrape. The Blind One stood back and opened his arms for Croy to leave first. It seemed to be a gesture of the sighted and brought up an issue that he had pondered earlier. Was the Blind One truly blind? Physically, he certainly looked it. When Croy silently moved, his eyes did not twitch, his head did not turn. There was no real reason to think he was sighted, that he had been faking it for his entire life. But there were times when he appeared to know what Croy was doing, some gestures that he made, the oddly eerie fact that he never ran into anything, that gave Croy the seed of doubt. He promised himself that if he kept his angry edge through the night, he would voice this question directly.

They left the underground prison for a section of the underground city that he had never seen before. It was a long walk to get back to what felt like Serif. Though there were two guards with them, one in front of him and one behind, with the Blind One taking up the rear, he had some fleeting images of himself escaping through the tunnels. Of running all the way to the great hall of Serif, or the lake, or even back above ground. He knew deep down that those images were worse than useless. So he plodded along in silence until they reached their destination.

It was a nicely sized room with a large dining table centered in it. Not nearly as echoingly large as Trela's dining hall in Agoge, not even close, but it seemed large and opulent compared to the cramped cell he had just been inhabiting. The table was set and there was steaming food resting on silver plates. Croy's mouth unconsciously watered at the delicious smells after being stuck the last few days with unappetizing gruel for all of his meals.

"Please sit. Eat." The two guards faded out of mind, but not quite out of sight. The Blind One took his time getting to his chair while Croy sat down. He told himself he would not just tear into his food, would not begin shoveling nourishment into his body. It had only been three or four days, he reminded himself, he could not actually be that hungry. It took some willpower, but he forced himself to wait until the Blind One had started eating before he did.

"So, how long were you following us?" Croy thought that if he talked during their meal it would distract him a little.

"The Pyrans were spotted as soon as they entered the Gaen realm. They can be stealthy when they wish, but their natural state is to be as subtle as a herd of elephants." A small laugh escaped his lips. "The 'jin were just keeping an eye on them, nothing too in depth, mind you. We had heard of the revolution and the deposing of the king. What was his name?"

"Qizern." It slipped from Croy's lips.

"Yes. Qizern. A nasty fellow by all accounts. We were mildly interested since there were Pyrans tromping through our realm, but we assumed they were refugees fleeing the violence. Then we realized that the new ruler was amongst the party. Leading it, as queens are wont to do. That piqued my curiosity. Why would a new queen be wandering a foreign realm?" The Blind One was not eating much, but that did not slow Croy down. "Then we found out who the queen was. We realized that she had been one of the few Pyrans to ever live in Serif. But that was a little less shocking than what our spies found in their midst. There were Gaens traveling with them. Fugitives."

"I was never a fugitive. You arrested me for the deeds of others. I was nowhere near any part of that fiasco." Croy pushed his plate away, though not too far away. "But that was all pretense, wasn't it? The real reason you arrested me was to force me into being your apprentice. And why is that? Why are there not Gaens lining up to sit at the feet of the master?"

"I am enjoying your new boldness, Croy, truly I am, but you are beginning to lash out haphazardly. I chose you for my apprentice because of what I saw in you, not for the lack of other willing students. And, if I were truly honest, it was not merely a knack for magic that I saw in you, that I see in you, but something more. Something I am unable to put my finger on. You may be a pawn, Croy, but whoever is moving you across the board is a master of the game." He leaned back in his chair.

"Why did you abduct me? Why did you bring me back to Serif? And why, of all places, did you intern me back in Rycher?" Croy's anger began to well back up in him.

"I needed to monitor your dreams. Rycher is the simplest way of doing that. We have several adepts from the school of Larelt permanently employed there." The Blind One's mentioning of Larelt immediately made Croy think of Ilana. He shook his head to clear it.

"You spied on me while I was unconscious? You kept me imprisoned to spy on me?" All thoughts of Ilana were pushed from his mind by his rising anger.

"Your dreams do not always come from within, Croy. Most sleeping Gaens are like... the inside of an egg. They are sealed off from everything. Their brains fire a chaotic pattern that their minds attempt to interpret. But you... there are small parcels moving about you. Into you and yes, even out of you. They are tiny and fast, almost imperceptible. But there is... something." The Blind One seemed a little deflated.

"You spy on prisoners' dreams?" Croy was annoyed that he had been spied upon. He was intrigued about the Blind One's opinions of his own dreams. But more than anything, he was shocked and dismayed that such a fundamentally personal thing as a dream was being monitored by the 'jin.

"Of course. What better way to determine a prisoner's deeper problems? What better way to find the most effective way to modify their behavior? What better way to assess their risk of recidivism?" The Blind One looked genuinely shocked at Croy's response.

"Ilana went to Larelt. She took oaths. To see into another's dreams, to DreamWatch, was supposed to be done at the patient's request, to help them, to aid them. At least, at the very tiniest minimum, they should know that they are being spied upon. You are only helping yourself." He pushed his plate of food a little bit farther away from him. He was not really sure why.

"These are prisoners, Croy. You speak as if they are equal to a citizen." Oddly, his eyes narrowed slightly while speaking.

"They are still Gaens, are they not?" Croy could feel his nostrils flare slightly.

"They gave that up when they broke the law. A prisoner has some rights, since they are, as you say, still a Gaen. We feed them, we clothe them, we provide them with shelter. A prisoner also has privileges. Privileges are not necessities, but are... extras. The removal of privileges for bad behavior, the reinstating of privileges for good behavior, these are our main tools to modify said behavior. The monitoring of dreams allows us to find which privileges are most prized, which will modify behavior the quickest and the surest. There is no maliciousness in it, it is merely a tool. And a very effective one at that. You don't understand what some of these prisoners are like. Many are barely animals..." He may have been about to say more but Croy interrupted.

"*I* was a prisoner!" He could not believe the conversation he was in. "I did nothing wrong. I was stripped of my freedom, stripped of my privileges as you call them, and no matter what you say about it, I was stripped of my rights. Keeping my own dreams private is a right, not a privilege." He felt his eyes begin to water. "You have no right... no right..."

"I have every right, Croy. I am of the 'jin. I am the law. But I am not here to argue policy with you. Let me apologize for my treatment of you. I should not have imprisoned you." The Blind One did look contrite.

"You could have spied on me anywhere." Croy audibly sighed. "It did not have to be Rycher."

"Something is happening, Croy. I am not sure what, or why, but I can sense the movement. It is in my nature to keep things hidden until I know what game is being played. There are only so many places I can hide you." The wondrous meal in front of them was cooling. "Did you know that Aedon Dea'sol made it back? Verin, Nyhan and Tesjuk as well. They thought that you and Ilana had perished. They said you snuck away in middle of the night, that Ilana was sick and you went in search of a well. I did not think I would converse with you again. Then, when I had resigned myself to that, you show up at my doorstep with a Pyran queen."

"I am glad they all made it back." Croy felt tired.

"Why did she come back, Croy? Why is Trela walking in our realm once again?" The Blind One leaned back in his chair until it quietly creaked. "I have racked my brain, but there does not seem to be any logical reason. The most important time to shape the path of one's reign is at the beginning. What if another attempts to seize control while she is gone? No, no, it just does not make any sense."

"She is here for the same reason that Aedon wanted to find the Vijen. She is here at the request, nay the command, of Gorbanax. She is here to keep the Yavens safe from us, which is the only way to keep us safe from the Yavens. She is here on her way to destroy the Cabal of Lochom." Croy knew that it was not really his story to tell, but he also knew that the Blind One could easily find the information himself. Or throw Croy back into Rycher for a hundred cycles. "In fact, I know she would be quite grateful if she could speak with Aedon before moving on."

"Interesting. Very interesting. I had heard her mention the Cabal during her little speech, but had no idea Gorbanax was directing her." Then... nothing. They sat in silence for some time. Croy began to feel peckish again but decided against eating any more. "I will grant the meeting. We will need to meet them in the forest, away from Serif. There are already too many that know of your return. But, sadly, that could not be helped." He abruptly stood. "I will need some time to prepare Aedon. I understand that you will not wish to return to Rycher and, you must understand, I cannot allow you to return to Serif. Therefore, you will have to stay here. Vulthrim!" One of the not-quite-hidden guards trotted over. "Gather some bedding for our guest." The Blind One paused for a brief moment. "Make it as luxurious as you are able, I want my friend to be comfortable." Croy stood because he was not sure what else to do.

"Of course, Dea'jin." The guard used the Blind One's last name as a title of station. He bowed twice, once to the Blind One and once to Croy, then turned and trotted out the same way they had entered.

"Hopefully the food has not cooled too much. Ureyast!" The other guard trotted over. "Come with me, we have much to do. I will be as quick as I can, Croy, but it may take a day or two to gather the required resources. Vulthrim will attend to any need of yours."

Then they walked away. Croy stood there, listening to their footsteps fade until he could hear them no more. Then it was just quiet. He was utterly alone with his thoughts. Instead of listening to them, he sat back down and worked on his tepid meal. It was still quite delicious.

Two days passed with only Vulthrim to keep Croy company, and he was rarely around. Croy did not dream again. While the lack of another dream did not distress him, it kept him thinking about his last one. There was a main question about it that bothered him, that he had been unable to figure out. Was it one giant bird made up of thousands of smaller birds, or was it a large group of smaller birds that made up one giant bird? Was there one mind or many constantly communicating smaller ones? When ants or bees act as one creature, is it because they are being controlled by one creature, one spirit? Or is it the small, random actions that inform the whole? Insects, as simple as they are, were surely still individuals, weren't they? Croy wondered about how his own mind worked. He wondered if a small, somewhat independent part of his brain could have an impulse and if that impulse would creep through his brain, affecting more and more parts, rippling like a pulse of waves, spreading throughout until his eyes snapped up and he decided, "I am hungry." He wondered what the difference would be if his mind, as a whole, decided that he was hungry and then informed the small section that it needed to send an impulse. Or like most derlians believed, did his stomach decide for his brain? As if there was a kind of small brain inside his stomach that could communicate with his mind. He knew from experience that he could keep hunger at bay by forgetting. He would be caught up in some small task, something completely engaging but otherwise meaningless, and would suddenly realize that he had been hungry for hours. Would that indicate that the small portion of his brain in charge of announcing hunger was merely overridden by concentration? Did that indicate the wave pulse was too small to propagate? Or was that sensation pointing in a different direction, that the whole is greater than the sum of the parts, that there is only one overriding mind, and that the myriad parts merely take directions from the master. Was it one bird, or many?

Then his thoughts turned to other dreams, those he could not remember. He closed his eyes and tried to cast his mind back. The Blind One had mentioned that he had watched Croy's dreams—plural. There had to be something. He fished around in his mind for a while, wandering in the darkness, doing his best not to think of the birds. All he could get was a vague image. A warning of some kind. A warning about someone. A Fluen. A warning about Clerin? That she was somehow a threat to something? It did not make any sense. He almost felt something else, something in the future. A tall narrow wall full of long names.

Then Vulthrim arrived and interrupted his thoughts. And ironically reminded him that he was hungry. Croy would try to get information out of Vulthrim, any insight, no matter how slight, into the goings-on of the Blind One. But he never got anything. Vulthrim was either completely ignorant of anything the Blind One was doing or he was a skilled liar. Since Croy understood that he was not the best at exposing skilled liars, he put the odds of either being true at fifty-fifty. It was as useless as his earlier mental exercise.

They did chat at length about all manner of trivial items. Croy did his best to learn about any changes in Serif during his absence, but of course, nothing major ever changed, and any of the minor things that might have changed, he did not have in common with Vulthrim. They realized quickly that all the shops and restaurants that he used to haunt were not known to Vulthrim. And vice versa. Though it was as useless as trying to get information about the Blind One out of him, it did pleasantly pass the time they had together.

Then, while alone and isolated with his thoughts, the door flew open and a clamor burst in. It was led by the Blind One and Ureyast, but was quickly followed by Aedon, Tesjuk, and Nyhan. The chatter that accompanied them was cheery and light. It overrode both the nervousness he typically felt around the Blind One and the frustration he currently felt, immediately lifting his heart and making him smile.

"Croy Sie'tin, may I reintroduce you to Aedon Dea'sol, Nyhan Cru'wir and Tesjuk Fyr'jin." The Blind One seemed to be enjoying himself.

Aedon was just as he remembered her. Her long, jet black hair was unfettered but tamed. She smiled warmly at Croy, her brown eyes soft and expressive. Nyhan appeared to have put on a little weight but was still lighter than Croy. Tesjuk appeared a little smaller than Croy remembered, but maybe that was because his mind now compared Tesjuk to Torpalin. He gladly shook all of their hands in turn.

"So, no one got a promotion?" Croy had expected at least one of their last names to have changed. They all laughed heartily.

"Well, it's a sight better than Sie'tin." Tesjuk laughed briefly by himself while the others looked a little nervous. This type of thing never bothered Croy, however, so he quickly burst out laughing. Then the others added some chuckles.

"I was thinking of petitioning for Beo'rem. How does that sound, Croy Beo'rem?" He smiled broadly at them.

"I did not know you were interested in the healing arts." Nyhan's mouth crooked into a lopsided smile.

"Neither did I, but it was better than learning how to swing a sword. And when you are trapped in the Pyran realm in the midst of a revolution, well… Let us just say I did not have time to show off the skills I brought with me from my life in Serif." They all chuckled again.

Croy then did what he had not done with the Blind One. He told his story. He started at the village that followed the well. He quickly moved on to reuniting with Trela, the Luften Temple, and the long campaign through the Pyran realm. He spoke of how he felt leaving Ilana behind, of learning healing from Nochiel, of Trela's conquering of Qizern. He spoke during the steins of beer that made up the aperitif, during their meal, *and* while they sat around the table afterwards. They rarely interrupted, and when they did it was with a question that was intelligent and poignant. It made him feel great to talk to Gaens who appeared to listen. At first he was hesitant to tell his story, worried that they would become bored with his ramblings, but then he realized just how much adventure he had been through. More had happened to him in the cycle he had wandered outside of the Gaen realm than had happened for all of his cycles before added together. And that could include his internment in Rycher and his apprenticeship with the Blind One. But more than anything he felt inside, it seemed they were genuinely interested in his stories. All of them. Eventually, he got to the part about the Cabal. The air in the room seemed to shift and all of them, but Aedon in particular, perked up a bit. That was when he realized he had no clue what had happened to any of them after he and Ilana had left the group and found the well.

"But I have been talking for much too long, you are all too kind." Croy nodded to himself, and by habit more than anything else, looked down at his fidgety hands. "What I really want to know is how you all made it out of the desert."

"But you stopped at the most interesting part." Aedon smiled kindly at him. "As you know, we entered the desert to speak with a Vijen, to find the reason for the increase in Tlana attacks of our outpost villages at the northwestern edge of the Gaen realm. As you may recall, the Vijen alluded to the Tlana responding to an evil begun by derlians. It is my opinion that the Cabal of Lochom, those that practice Yavencide, are the direct cause of the more numerous and aggressive Tlana."

"But that is not how you escaped the desert." Croy pressed her because he wanted her to continue talking.

"True, but that is a boring story." Aedon was quickly interrupted.

"She's right, absolutely nothing happened. We didn't see another Vijen or, thankfully, a Tlana." Tesjuk grinned at Croy. "I don't think we even saw another animal. Not even a soaring vulture."

"Well, it was not that bad, but nothing of note happened. At least not until we returned to Serif. I will not speak for the others, but the 'sol guild considered the expedition a complete failure. Try as I might, I could not get them to see my interpretation of the Vijen's speech. They complained heavily of the amount of treasure my expedition had cost and wondered openly if I should keep my rank. You joke that none of us got promoted, but in truth, I am quite lucky to have not been demoted. It was quite… ugly at times." She sighed and leaned back. "I was almost kicked out of the Assembly. There was even talk of a trial."

"The 'wir guild was not that negative, not in the least. If you recall, Croy, I was able to gather up one of the Vijen's leaves. The fact that I was able to bring that back to Serif, to the guild, assuaged any anger about their portion of the expedition's cost. They did not attempt to censure me, even though the leaf rotted soon after I handed it over. However, they were also deaf to any interpretation I tried to attribute to the Vijen's speech." Nyhan did not sigh, but he also leaned back at the end of his brief speech.

All eyes then turned to Tesjuk. He was intent on picking the last vestige of meat off of a bone. He raised his head when he felt their gazes upon him. Or maybe he noticed the silence. He blinked once, then twice.

"The 'jin guild doesn't care about anything." He glanced at the Blind One out of the corner of his eye. "Or, well, they got paid for their services. Verin and I were probably the reason the expedition cost so much." He laughed heartily.

"So you see, the Assembly leaders are not interested in the Vijen. They are not interested in the Cabal. They are barely interested in the Tlana." Aedon leaned forward again. "In fact, they would not even be interested in them if Gaens were not dying in droves. Just a week ago, a whole village disappeared."

"We have lost contact with them." The Blind One had been frowning ever since Tesjuk started talking. "We do not know if the village disappeared."

"Have you heard back from the 'jin who went to investigate?" Aedon's brown eyes flashed with a touch of steel behind them.

"There has not been enough time Aedon." The Blind One looked weary.

"Only one 'jin with any power will listen to me, and he hides behind a cloak of bureaucracy." She was definitely glaring at him.

"I am here, am I not? I performed the tasks you asked of me, did I not?" It was the first time Croy had seen the Blind One get that defensive. "If you keep pushing the Assembly they will do more than just kick you out, as you so poetically put it."

"You've just mentioned that the Pyran queen is in the Gaen realm and that you were traveling with her. Is it true that she is attempting to find the Cabal?" She turned away from the Blind One to stare hard at Croy. He merely nodded in response. "Does she trust you? Can you get me an audience with her?"

"I told her of the expedition you led, that led us to the Vijen, that led Ilana and I to the well, and I can tell you that she already wishes to speak with you." Croy nodded to her again. "It would not matter if she trusted me, though I believe she does. It would not even matter if she thought you were lying in ambush to assassinate her. You have information that she wants to glean." Croy thought for a second. "The Pyrans are different from us in many aspects, but few so glaring as our myopic and tenacious habit to cling to safety. And even compared with other Pyrans, Trela's lack of concern about her own safety borders on the suicidal. Oddly enough, however, she is quite protective of her companions."

"Then set up the meeting." Aedon's eyes were still glaring. But though she was looking at Croy, he felt that she looked like that due to the Blind One. He could not put his finger on it, but there was certainly a long argument between them.

"So… why was I kidnapped? If this was the point, then all you had to do was walk up to Trela's coterie and ask for the meeting yourself." Croy started to wonder what was really going on. It did not immediately make sense.

"Coterie?" The interjection came from Tesjuk.

"It's a small warpack." If he were honest with himself, he was not positive about the exact definition of the word. It was what all the Pyrans were calling it, so that was how Croy referred to it as well.

"You should not question our plans or our motives, Croy. We have much to consider and account for." The Blind One's chest inflated slightly.

"Don't be dodgy, Narst. He wanted to watch your dreams, Croy." Aedon interrupted the Blind One almost absentmindedly. "Larelt would be spinning in her grave if she knew how many of her students work for the 'jin. She wanted her own guild, or at least to be absorbed by the 'rem."

"Larelt is dead?" It was Croy's turn to interrupt. There was an awkward pause before Aedon spoke again.

"Yes… she died while we were in the desert." Aedon kept her eyes on the table as she spoke in a quiet tone.

"There. You have all the answers you will receive. We should prepare ourselves." The Blind One stood abruptly. "We will leave in the morning." He left his chair scooched away from the table and began walking towards the exit. Croy had almost forgotten about Ureyast until he escorted the Blind One out. "Come along!"

Tesjuk and Nyhan immediately stood and began following him down the long hallway. There was movement on the opposite side of Croy, which made him start slightly. It was just Vulthrim coming over to clear the table.

"So tell me, how is Ilana? When you left, did she beg you to stay?" Aedon was staring hard at him again. It was odd, but she had seemed nice while sparring with the Blind One. Now that they were alone, however, she asked questions like that. There was something enigmatic about her.

"The villagers there often appear dazed. There were plenty of tears shed by both of us, but I am sure she is doing well." He had not intended to answer her, but he liked the silence even less.

"It's not her that I am worried about." Aedon slowly stood, paused, and put her chair back into position with its seat under the table. "I think you will find life easier if you stay busy, Croy. Peace and quiet do not always equal solace. Take it from someone who knows."

The Blind One teleported them close to where his spies had kept watch on Trela's coterie. Croy did not, of course, realize it at the time, but she had set out straight for Serif after he had been taken. She had no real way of telling where Serif lay, but Knill did his best to point them in the right direction even though he had only been that far outside of Serif the one time they had escaped from there. They were not completely lost.

All of those from the meeting the evening before were traveling together, plus Verin Mur'jin had joined them. The Blind One flew them for the last half-league or so. They hovered over the moving column of warriors for a few moments before slowly, and obviously, descending down in a clearing a little ways in front of the plodding coterie. It did not take too long before the warriors arrived, with Trela at their head.

"So. You have returned with Croy. To what may I assign this pleasure?" Trela swung her leg over her horse and slid to the ground in one smooth motion. She was smiling warmly as she walked towards them. About a third of her warriors dismounted when they reached the clearing. Few of them, however, were smiling.

"We wish to offer our services." Aedon strode forwards and held her hand out in front of her. "I am Aedon Dea'sol, and you are?"

"You may call me Trela." She shook Aedon's hand heartily.

"You are the Queen of the Pyrans, are you not? The first in a long dynasty, I hope." Their hands parted, but they did not move away from each other. Nor did they move towards each other.

"Pyrans do not have dynasties. You are thinking of Fluens." Trela's right hand hovered near her long dagger's hilt. Not menacingly, quite naturally in fact, but it gave off a whiff of distrust. "If I recall, you were with Croy when he entered the Northern Desert from the Gaen side."

"Quite correct." Aedon's hands moved around a little as she talked. "I hear we have similar interests."

"I certainly hope so. I know where I am headed, but not how to get there. Any help would be greatly appreciated." Trela seemed to relax by the moment. "But to be honest, I am having a difficult time trusting you due to the company you choose to keep."

"Narst! Apologize to the young Queen." Aedon barely turned her head as she spoke behind herself.

For his part, Croy took this opportunity to walk over towards them. He stopped before he reached them, not wanting to adversely affect the parley. He wanted to show that he was free, but did not want to go cower amongst the Pyran warriors. The situation seemed oddly delicate. There was a rustling behind Croy as the Blind One took a few steps forward.

"I promise you that I will not do that again. I promise that I had no nefarious intentions for Croy. He used to be my apprentice. I promise to respect your authority for as long as I am with your coterie. I promise to do my utmost to assist this mission, if you will have us." Croy did not turn around, but kept his eyes on Trela during the Blind One's speech. One corner of her mouth was raised, reminding Croy of a crescent moon, in a kind of wry smile.

"That was not an apology." Trela was looking past Croy towards the Blind One, but it was Aedon who replied.

"It is better than I have ever gotten." She did not turn either.

"I can see we are going to be friends." Trela laughed. Aedon laughed. It seemed like everyone exhaled at the same time. The Gaens walked over to the Pyrans and began introducing themselves. Suddenly the clearing was full of conversation.

Chapter 7

"We will make camp here today. We have been pushing our marches to reach the Gaen city of Serif but we are no longer headed there. I appreciate your efforts to retrieve Croy from... well from him." Trela pointed at the Blind One. She knew it was a cheap shot, but she was still angry and could not help it. Or did not want to. How could he be incapable of apologizing? "That is why I am allowing a cask of grog to be opened tonight!" She knew she should have checked with Wesduin first, but she wanted to speak with Aedon and the others on their first night with the coterie while the unspoken conversations were still fresh. She wanted to know everything they knew about the desert, about the attacks on the Gaen villages, about the Vijen and Tlana, and most importantly, about the Cabal. A small cheer arose all around her.

The camp was finalized around noon. It was the earliest that she had made camp so far and it gave her a brief pause. She spent some time second guessing her decision but it was too late to turn back. Never straight, but always forwards.

Escha had taken down a deer, so they would feast tonight. While the others were getting acquainted, all except for the Blind One who sat with two Gaen guards off a ways from the rest of the camp, Trela took Aedon aside. She wanted to be able to converse with her, one-on-one, so there would be no reason for self-censure.

"We must talk." It was a simple imperative and one that Aedon obeyed without question. They ducked into Trela's tent. She had thought about trying to wander off, to be farther away from the crowd, but thought that would actually attract more attention. She did not want anyone looking for them.

They sat and were quiet for a brief, but awkward, moment. Trela poured them each a goblet of grog. She held up her drink. "To Croy's health." Aedon cocked her head to one side quizzically but smiled immediately. They both drank heartily.

"I do not know how much Croy has told you about our mission." Trela paused.

"Nothing beyond the Cabal." Aedon leaned back into the pile of pillows that Trela used for furniture during her campaigns. Aedon's left arm was slung lazily across one of them, while her right was half raised, holding her goblet. Waiting to take a drink once Trela had started talking. Eyes sparkling and lips curved into an unconscious smile. Waiting. Anticipating.

Trela had wanted Aedon to talk. It was information from her that she wanted, that she needed. She realized, however, that she would have to go first. She would have to entrust this stranger before she, herself, was trusted. It was an uneasy position that she was not used to being in. At least not since she had taken the throne. It was almost scary, how quickly she had gotten used to the small unknown comforts of royalty. But metaphorically speaking, they were already in bed together. If she could not trust Aedon, it would be better to learn that sooner rather than later. So she began.

"Well, that is the gist of it. I have entered the Gaen realm to destroy the Cabal of Lochom. But why me, why now?" Aedon took the drink she was waiting for when Trela started speaking. "My coronation happened several moons ago and I was happily ruling my realm in peace when I received a message from Gorbanax. You see, I have a traveling dignitary with me, one who communes with Belegs. Can you keep a secret?" Trela thought if she gave up something specific, something interesting but not dangerously secret, she could then find out if Aedon would or would not blab to her Gaen compatriots.

"Of course, I am a member of the Assembly. The Assembly is full of secrets, some open and some closed." Aedon placed her goblet precariously on the rug next to her. "In either case, not speaking about them to other members, even if they are privy, is a matter of respect and honor to the one who confessed the secret to you."

The logic placed before her made her mind swim a little. If it was honorable to keep the secret you heard, then what about the honor of the one who confessed the secret to you? Maybe it was that Gaen's own secret, theirs to hand out as they wished. Maybe they were not real secrets, just tests of another's ability to keep quiet, as she was currently devising for Aedon. Maybe the real information was kept back, as when she might pose a question about a warrior's behavior to Lishean, but keep the names, the specifics, to herself. Looking only for generic advice from a wise and trusted advisor. In the end, that was the way the world worked. Secrets were spread like communicable diseases, from friend to friend, from close associates, from trusted advisors. One derlian coughs and soon they all have the sniffles. Trela realized she was being quiet for much too long while her mind wandered amongst her inconsequential musings.

"Clerin, my Fluen princess, communes with Belegs. She has spoken to all besides Gunzgak, as far as I know." Trela paused for a brief moment, but could not read a reaction on Aedon's face. "It was while she was communing with Gorbanax that it impressed upon her the Belegs' desire to permanently remove those who committed Yavencide from all of the realms. It was only after discussing this imperative amongst my privy council that Croy mentioned that you had spoken of the Cabal. I had not even heard of it until that moment." Trela paused briefly, allowing Aedon to interrupt with all the information about the Cabal that she was looking for, but that did not happen. "So I did what any sane ruler would do. I decided to delegate the issue." At this, Aedon laughed heartily. Trela smiled at her over her goblet. "I was certainly going to send my most trusted advisors, warriors, mages, and spies. I was certainly going to make sure they were well equipped, that they were well provided for. I was going to provide everything they needed for a successful mission. But I am not too ashamed to admit, I was not planning on going myself."

"So, what changed your mind?" Aedon's eyes sparkled. "I know nothing about you whatsoever and have only spoken with you for a couple of moments, but it seems that you, like myself, are most comfortable when you are in control. Were you concerned that the mission would fail without your guiding hand?"

"Ha! You are correct about my comfort, but no, that was not the reason." She took a deep breath. "Clerin summoned a Yaven to convince me. A Pyran Yaven, of course." Aedon seemed to perk up at the mention of a Yaven. "It appears that it is quite impossible for me to refuse the request of a Beleg sent through a Yaven."

"You are saying there is a Pyran Yaven with you? Here in this camp?" Her eyes were wide with excitement.

"Yes, yes, and there are plans to bring more Yavens into our coterie before we reach the Cabal." Trela patted the air with her right hand, in what she assumed was a calming gesture. "We do not wish to alert the Cabal, however, so we are keeping this information as tightly controlled as possible. This is another secret."

"Will I be able to see this Yaven, to communicate with it?" Her spine relaxed and she settled again into the pillows.

"Eventually, maybe even tonight once the others have taken to their tents. But now... Now I need you to tell me all you know of the Cabal." She did not feel Taglo would be too vexed about speaking with Aedon, so it was a simple promise to make.

"Well, I wish I knew more. I will start with what I know about *birds*. Do you know what I mean about birds?" The way she emphasized the word, it could only mean Tlana. Trela knew there were some who refused to speak to the word out loud, at least anywhere near the Northern Desert. Though she was not one of them, she understood the fear of being overheard. "It began over a cycle ago, or at least we realized something happening over a cycle ago, it could have been going on unnoticed for far longer. We have several villages in the northwestern border of the Gaen realm, near the Yulhpin and Black Bear rivers. These are peaceful fishing villages under the auspice of Hifrim, the large western underground Gaen city, comparable to Serif here in the east. The largest of these villages was called Lethos and was of a fair size for a small village, maybe one thousand Gaens strong." Aedon finished her goblet and set it back on the rug.

"Suddenly, a villager would disappear without a trace. Life would go on. Another villager would disappear. This happened slowly enough at first that it was assumed they had left for another village without telling anyone, which, though rare, happens more often than you might think; or maybe that they had drowned, with their body jammed under a log or something so that it did not float. Eventually though, enough had disappeared that they assumed they had a murderer in their midst. The local 'jin could not find a murderer, so they requested a small contingent from Hifrim. Before they arrived, two more villagers had been killed. This time, however, they did not disappear, no. Their bodies were left in the middle of the road in the middle of the night. They were frightfully mutilated, their guts splayed out in bizarre patterns. The villagers left the bodies there for another two days before the 'jin arrived, baking in the sun, so they could be examined by the experts.

"So they locked down the village and they found the murderer. A youth who they claimed was completely insane with his ranting and ravings. No one of note, really, just a poor carpenter. They gave him a quick trial and hung him by the neck until he was dead. It was the various wood carving tools that he used in his profession that the 'jin said he used on the two murdered Gaens in the road. The 'jin congratulated themselves and headed back to Hifrim. Before they were two days' ride away, however, another body was found in the road. By this time, the village took to keeping torches lit all night long and had trebled their night watch. But no one saw anything that night. Nothing untoward or suspicious.

"So the 'jin came back. They said it had to be a member of the night watch. That was the only way it would make sense. So they picked a poor watcher whose duty it was to walk that stretch of road and they found him guilty. He was not mad, did not rave or show erratic behavior at all. Oh, they tortured confessions out of him, but the village did not trust that the 'jin had the correct killer.

"So they made the 'jin stay. At least for another week. It only took three more days for another disfigured body to arrive, this time near the small river docks. When they investigated that, they found three more bodies hidden in barrels in one of the warehouses. They arrested the warehouse owner, who was a fine and respected Gaen in the village, and put him on trial. He was found guilty, as the others were, but the villagers stood behind him and told the 'jin to put him in jail rather than on the gallows. If no other murders took place, then they would allow the 'jin to execute him.

"The very next night, while he was safely locked away, two more villagers were murdered. They were found in their beds by their families. I hear that the screams could be heard throughout the village that dawn. The 'jin ordered another contingent from Hifrim and began patrolling the nights along with the watch. It took almost a week for the next one, a day before the other 'jin arrived. A curfew was put in place but it was not needed. No one so much as stuck their little toe outside their homes at night. But that did not help them. Whole families began to be slaughtered in their sleep. Everyone in the house, even the pets. Never a sound was made, nothing could be heard by the watch outside, wandering the brightly lit streets in large groups of frightened and paranoid warriors."

Aedon took a pause and picked up her empty goblet. She smiled and shook it lightly back and forth for Trela to refill. Quietly, so as not to be interrupting, she filled it as much as she dared, then refilled her own.

"Then, one night, several of the watch swore that they saw a black flash of smoke exit a chimney and take to the sky. They ran into the home and immediately found the fresh horror. There was blood all over each of the previously occupied bedrooms and the bodies were still warm. There were no survivors to gain evidence from, but the image of the black smoke that was imprinted on the 'jins' minds, accompanied with the silence and gore of the murders, made it obvious that birds were involved. The village was abandoned. Normally I would think the 'jin might have just been lazy or superstitious, for them to just pack up the entire village and leave like that. But Hifrim was worried enough that they requested a full investigation, made up of both their own 'jin and those from Serif. I was one of those sent from Serif and I can still recall the eerie emptiness of the village. I can feel it even now when I talk about it. The roads and buildings were empty, there was an uncomfortable silence, and yet there was the unmistakable feeling of being watched. Not just of being watched, but of being examined. As if you were surrounded by crowds of onlookers, but every time you looked up into the windows there was nothing there. There almost was, you could almost catch a shadow of movement, but no. The hairs on the back of my neck were standing up the entire time I was at Lethos. It was the creepiest... I just... I don't even know what to say about it. I don't know how to explain it." And then she shivered uncontrollably in the warm tent. The creepy feeling of being watched was infectious and Trela had to exert an incredible amount of willpower to keep herself from twisting her head around to look for someone, or something, hiding behind her, just out of reach of her senses.

"So you entered the desert with Croy after this experience." It was a statement, but it was stated like a question.

"Yes, I convinced my guild and the Assembly in general to fund the expedition. I purposely made it inexpensive to make it more palatable for the benefactors, or so I had thought. Apparently any amount of money spent on something that does not produce more money is a waste of... well... money." They both laughed for a moment at her loop.

"We had entered the desert because I believe there is a link between the Vijen and the birds. If the birds were visiting evil upon derlians, I had assumed that the Vijen would provide some assistance to us. My hypothesis was that they were opposites, that they were enemies. Unfortunately, it seems that the Vijen are more neutral than positive and did not offer any assistance whatsoever, even though the birds are definitely evil and I am pretty sure they are enemies. I did, however, get several pieces of good information from that trip to the desert. Mainly I believe deeply and thoroughly that the Yavencide is directly linked to the increased bird activity. The Vijen I spoke with as much as stated that, or at least as close to stating something as a Vijen can get. Have you ever seen a Vijen?"

"Yes, I have spoken with one." Trela immediately grinned from ear to ear. "I think I was given some good advice, from what I could make myself understand of the conversation. I do know what you mean about their inability to make understandable statements. However, I would be dead without its interference. You speak of them being neutral, but I was attacked by a… bird… in the desert. I had no mage with me, and I do not cast spells myself. I fought my hardest, and when I had bested the bird, a Vijen appeared. It told me that it had stopped the bird from using its lightning. And it stated, in no uncertain terms, that I would have been destroyed without its assistance. Having lived through that and later having heard about a mage named Feyazki fighting with a bird, I fully believe I would have been destroyed if I had been alone."

"Who was this Feyazki?" Aedon leaned back again.

"Not was. Is. Feyazki beat the bird with its own lightning." Trela unconsciously nodded her head towards the tent's exit. "He is a Luften mage and helped secure my overthrow of Qizern. I have yet to see his equal, and you will be amazed at how young he is. He will only grow more powerful."

"You have a mage who defeated a bird in your… coterie?" Aedon's eyes squinted a little as she spoke the last word, as if trying to recall it or, maybe, to further commit it to memory.

"Yes. We have quite the menagerie gathered. And now you have joined us." Trela lifted her goblet. "To your health." With barely a pause, Aedon raised her goblet in a loose salute. "But now… Now I need you to tell me all you know of the Cabal."

"That *was* what I was supposed to be talking about, wasn't it?" Her laugh had a musical quality to it. "Well, you know we left Croy and Ilana in the desert. We found our way back to Serif with nothing but one golden leaf and a fanciful tale. The Assembly was not impressed, to say the least. Also, for some unknown reason, the leaf rotted and turned a useless pulpy black about a week after we returned, angering them even more. We were told to forget our conversation with the Vijen, supposed to forget about Yavencide, supposed to forget about the Cabal. We were supposed to go about our daily lives without a care left for the outside realms, as if all that mattered were held within the rocky confines of Serif. I do not know how the others felt about it, or how they dealt with it, but for me it was like living in darkness your whole life, then for a brief moment, getting shown the sun and color, then being put back into darkness and told to forget everything you had just been shown. I was unable to forget it, unable to put it from my mind for very long. It was burned into my retina. I knew the Cabal existed, I knew they committed great evil, I knew that the evil was causing more bird attacks upon other Gaens. I… did not easily take to my daily life again. It seemed empty. So I found a 'jin mage who would at least listen to me. I researched what I could about the Cabal and, most dangerously, I did my best to find its members and join its ranks."

"What did you find?" Trela was filled with a nervous excitement.

"Unfortunately, not much at all. Those that I had thought might have an inkling about the membership either realized I did not have their best interests at heart or they were ignorant of any other members. I tried to pretend sympathy to their cause, to find a way to join, even at the lowest levels. I even tried to start my own meetings, but all to no avail. Eventually, stymied at every turn, I decided to try to purchase an item. I pooled all of my funds and I begged and borrowed from friends. My guild and the Assembly would not provide me with one pebble, but I scraped enough together to try to purchase something small. So I let it be known that I would pay handsomely for a Stone Shield. I had heard of the Cabal trapping a Gaen Yaven into a piece of armor to make it impenetrable. Not being a warrior, I tried to allude that I was purchasing this for an unnamed friend. Kept anonymous to be able to protect the honor and good name of the final recipient. And finally, after moons of sending feelers out into the realm of my sympathies to the Cabal, I got an offer.

"The Gaen who approached me only gave their first name, Jeschet, and would only meet with me under full masked disguise. The price was higher than I had anticipated and Jeschet wanted half up front, so I gave most of what I had. With the rest I hired a spy, Gyaer Cru'jin, to follow whomever I met with that day. Gyaer came back over a moon later, saying that Jeschet had gone to the border village of Pulthrim. This village is near the Yulhpin river and somewhat close to the doomed Lethos. Gyaer said he lost track of Jeschet in that village. While I did not necessarily believe him, I paid him the rest of what I owed.

"Then, a week ago, we received a distress *whisper* from Pulthrim. We assume they also contacted Hifrim, since that city is so much closer. The *whisper* contained concerning information about strange fires and murders, about growing fear and paranoia, about mass hysteria. It all pointed to another bird attack. I convinced Narst Dea'jin, the Blind One, to send a small contingent of 'jin to the village to investigate. I sent Gyaer with them since he knew the village. Narst sent a mage, one Vuildan Fyr'jin, with them to speed up their travel." Aedon paused for a moment to draw in a long breath. "We have not heard from them since. None of them. So you see, I am unable to offer you any real information about the Cabal or its members. All I can provide is the most tenuous of links to their location. And that only involves entire villages being wiped out or abandoned due to bird activity. I don't really know if that has anything to do with the actual location of the Cabal."

"Well, it seems to be all we have to go on, and it is certainly better information than what I was working with earlier today." Trela smiled warmly at Aedon. She smiled back. "I have enjoyed our talk and truly appreciate your time, but we should probably join the others."

It was with a heavy heart that Trela followed Aedon out of the tent. When the Gaens had all arrived, she had high hopes for the information they might have brought with them. While it was certainly interesting and gave them a direction to aim for, it was certainly not full of insight and knowledge. The only name they had was Jeschet, and that was probably fake anyway.

It was almost midnight and Trela knew she should sleep soon, but she was enjoying herself too much. The Gaens seemed to fit right in with her coterie. All except for the Blind One, maybe. She knew that opinion hinged on two emotional triggers, however, and it was probably unfair of her to judge him solely on them. The first was, of course, her feelings for Croy and what she imagined the Blind One had done to him. If only facts were examined, she really did not know everything that had happened between them, or even anything that had happened, or to be as fair as possible, if anything had happened besides the imprisonment. It was more of the aura of mood around Croy when he spoke of the Blind One; the aura spoke volumes of minor tortures. The second was his constant uptight attitude. He did not appear to be able to relax and just trade stories with strangers. There always seemed to be a frown on his face, a scowl with a furrowed brow for an awning. She had known several Pyrans who were very businesslike when she first met them, but they eventually loosened up and became quite friendly and jocular around her. And there was the fact that he was blind. Maybe facial expressions did not come naturally to him, especially if he had never seen any, had never seen his own. So part of her wanted to entirely discount his presence, but the other, more fair and maybe wise part, wanted to give him the benefit of the doubt. It was a bit of a moot point, however, since he and his two guards stayed in their own tent during the hours between evening and night.

The others, however—Nyhan, Tesjuk, Verin, and of course Aedon—were all a delight to be around. Tesjuk and Torpalin became instant friends, for which Trela was glad. Sometimes when two similar personalities met, they could clash, but they merely compared muscles and arm wrestled with big stupid grins on their faces. Verin was incredibly gregarious with all of Trela's warriors, but not with any of the mages. She quickly traded war stories and started knife throwing competitions and argued about the benefits of holding a sword in your left hand instead of a shield. She was in constant motion and quite small, but she moved with the same warrior's grace as Gyllhelon. Trela could tell that she could be quite dangerous if she had a mind to. Nyhan was also friendly, but much quieter and more inclusive. He was short and wiry, much like Verin but a little bigger. He had reddish hair that was held close to his head in tight curls. He was able to speak to anyone in front of him about just about anything. He seemed to know a little about everything, which made Trela a little unsure of what his specialty was. He seemed to be a master of the trivial. It was not until later on in their travels that she realized he was a master horticulturalist with an amazing knowledge of different trees and plants. That first night did not provide him with an adequate opportunity to showcase his skills.

It was really Aedon that Trela was drawn to, however. Even though they had spoken at length earlier, even though they had spoken during the evening, she found herself enjoying Aedon's company during the night as well. She found herself with Aedon and Clerin by the time she was well into her cups. They were laughing about something inconsequential when Aedon interrupted.

"I want to see the Yaven, I want to speak with it." Her dark eyes were wide with enthusiasm. "Please!"

"What do you think?" Trela asked Clerin. She was the queen, she ruled the coterie and all of her decisions were final. But ever since the incident with Qizern's sword had happened she had let Clerin handle all of the decisions concerning Taglo. It was in Clerin's tent that Taglo stayed hidden.

"I don't know why not." Clerin's clear blue eyes sparkled and her dimples deepened into her smiling cheeks. Trela hoped that it was not a sign of mischievousness. She sometimes had a hard time reading that correctly when they had both been drinking. They stole away quietly to Clerin's tent, careful not to call attention to themselves. Taglo might not mind talking to one stranger, but the entire coterie would have been a bit much.

Clerin held the flap to her tent open for them. Trela ducked in and stepped gingerly aside to leave room for Aedon while her eyes adjusted. There was a small hurricane lamp at the back of the tent with a small flame flickering in the center of it. She was staring into a dark corner to get her eyes to adjust faster. Though she was not sure how much that sped up the process, if at all. The tent flap silently closed behind them, cutting out the moonlight.

"Where is it?" Aedon's whisper was a little loud and a little slurred.

"Sshhh." Clerin was almost as loud as Aedon. A long finger was placed comically against her grinning lips. She slipped further into the tent and deftly around the half-rolled blankets that made up her bedding. "We have to find it." She took the small hurricane lamp from the peg at the back of the tent and held it high, her eyes casting around on the ground.

Both Trela and Aedon had their eyes down when Clerin opened the tiny door on the hurricane lamp and the flame leapt out. It immediately grew into the form that Trela was accustomed to, though a little smaller and much dimmer. The outline shimmered and shook.

"Greetings, Gaen. I was hoping to be able to speak with you." Taglo appeared to ignore both Clerin and Trela. It stood before Aedon, facing her alone.

"How do you know of me?" Aedon sounded more sober, demure even.

"Several ways you are known to me. The simplest is the common bonds of these derlians. These and the one called Croy. From them comes the acknowledgement that you sought to root out the Cabal first. You began so early that you turned to the Vijen for advice. Which brings me to another. That I will skip. I have heard about you through the stones as well, yes. You are quite popular there. Fire used to avoid the stone, only magma was made. But now, I can state with pride that Gorbanax has come to realize Gunzgak's wisdom. Earlier times were engulfed in wondering and yes, maybe, some scheming. Gorbanax's natural ally was Linchon. But Linchon walled itself away and the schism caught it unawares. Now. Now time is in flux. Now comes important choices. These times ahead, short decisions to be made in the blink of a derlian eye, will solidify the magma into basalt by removing the fire. Hard choices will be quickly hardened to permanence. Now. Now you realize that you are necessary, do you not?" Trela was taken aback from Taglo's speech patterns. They seemed a little different than any other time she had spoken with it. She briefly wondered why.

"That is why I am here." Aedon's dark eyes stared widely straight into Taglo. They seemed to swallow the dim light that emanated from it.

"Ha! This is why your reputation precedes you. Excellent. You... Have you ever summoned a Yaven?" Taglo pulsated softly.

"No, never. Narst Dea'jin would be a better candidate..." Aedon sounded like she would have continued, but Taglo shrank at the name which slowed her speech such that it trailed off.

"That is another preceding reputation. That is a great help and a great mage, and we are gladdened to have such skill and determination assisting us. But, no. The summoning for this mission is different from other missions. The emphasis is not required to be on skill or power. It is a... differing emphasis that we seek. Those stones that speak with me wish you or the one called Croy to perform the call. There is still much discussion concerning this decision. So, if you happen to be chosen, you are willing, yes?" Taglo had shrunk to almost half of its original size and had dimmed so much that it was almost as dark as Clerin or Trela.

"If I am needed, I will do what you ask." Aedon's face was covered in shadows.

"Excellent. Truly. We will talk again soon. But now... now I must camouflage myself once more. I have been too obvious for too long. I am leaving too much spoor. Thank you, communicator and ruler, for bringing the Gaen to me. This was a beneficial conversation. However, we need to be more cognizant of the traces we are leaving behind. We must be quieter. We must learn to whisper." Taglo then shrank to a tiny flame and flew back into the hurricane lamp. Clerin closed it up and hung it back on the peg.

Trela left the tent and held the flap open for Aedon. When she emerged, her face seemed to have small beads of sweat condensed on it. As if she had just run uphill for a while. Clerin came out right behind her.

"I have not spoken to many Yavens, but I must say that one sounded like a Vijen." Aedon wiped her face with the back of her sleeve. "Not exactly, for sure, but… it made me think of that. Not the voice at all, just a bit of the speech pattern."

"Well, Taglo did sound a little odd, but… I've never spoken to a Vijen, so I wouldn't know. I had just chalked it up to being nervous about leaving too much spoor." Clerin's smile was disarming. They moved away from the tent and talked of other things.

They did not get the camp put away until noon the next day. Trela pushed them hard into the evening in an attempt to make up for some of the lost time. It was dark by the time they stopped, but luckily the weather allowed for open-air sleeping for most. That morning they awoke with the sun, and having little camp to put away, they left within an hour. They swung a little north, towards the desert, to find a road. Trela had pondered staying on trails for a while, zigzagging across the Gaen foothills, to stay more hidden. But she was concerned that a group of derlians as large as her coterie would not go unnoticed no matter how obscure of a path they took. And, therefore, the amount of time saved by traveling upon a real road was deemed worth the risk.

The next week was spent pushing the coterie as fast and hard as she felt they could go. Due to Wesduin's wagons they could only move so fast. A pleasant rhythm was quickly created amongst the travelers. The road wound near the wooded foothills, so there was still decent hunting to be taken advantage of. Nyhan and Ureyast both seemed to know the road fairly well, which made travel that much easier. Plus, the road was well marked. Each crossroads or split in the path had a waist high stone marker made up of piled stones and a wooden sign with the names of villages pointing in different directions. It was a Gaen tradition for those passing the marker to toss on another stone, to slowly increase the size of the pile. Several of the Pyrans and Luftens took up the habit as well. It made for an interesting sight as they neared another marker, as warriors would scour the roadside for the largest or most interesting rocks to carry the rest of the way to the marker. A little harmless competition to ease the tedium.

In the early morning Trela was quietly told of a large upcoming inn along the road. Nyhan's bright eyes filled with a silent hope. He was ready, if Trela made him, to find a way around the inn, ready to take a trail that bypassed it and met back up with road a little further on. But she felt they had been making some good time lately. Much of leading was deciding when to push your subjects and when to give them some slack.

"There is not another inn of this size until we reach Pulthrim." His smile was a little lopsided and a sincere warmth radiated out of it.

"We can reach it tonight?" Trela had just mounted her horse.

"Yes, easily. In fact, we should not push too hard or else we will arrive in the afternoon. Unless you want to arrive a little early?" It was a question, but there was a small hint hidden in there as well.

"Go ahead and tell the others." Trela held back an automatic sigh. In truth, she would enjoy the room as much as her coterie, but it was her nature to feel put out by comfort. The sight of Nyhan scampering off to dole out the good news put a smile on her lips. They rode hard that day and arrived at the inn in the middle of the afternoon, with several hours of daylight left.

The inn was a massive structure, built of red fired brick instead of the typical gray stone walls the Gaens were so fond of. It was three stories tall in places and had five chimneys poking through the low sloped slate roof at various locations. There was a stable off to the side, with three solid brick sides and one long side open to the elements. The warriors let out a small cheer when the inn came into sight.

Trela, Knill, Croy, and Aedon rode the last league to the inn while the rest of the coterie waited behind. Trela was worried there would not be enough available beds and that some would have to make camp outside. She wanted everyone to be comfortable. If not, she was prepared to make them skirt the inn, even after she had made her promise. If she ruined it for everyone, at least she would be hated equally by all. She did not like to play favorites, for that was a fast way to make her warriors begrudge each other. Warriors will forgive a leader a difficult decision a thousand times faster than they will forgive a fellow for getting the tiniest, maybe even imaginary, preferential treatment from that same leader. Leading did not always make sense.

The inn had a large, wordless sign hanging from a tall post showing riderless horses milling about in a field. The inn itself was called The Forgotten Junction, as spelled by brightly colored slate tiles above the large front entrance. Trela's eyes rolled down from the roof to the three sets of large wooden double doors. They had rounded tops that hugged the brick arches and were held together by fat iron straps. There were five roads that met in front of the inn. Trela doubted a junction as large as this one was ever forgotten. They sat there atop their horses for a quick moment before one of the doors opened and a young Gaen scampered out.

"Welcome. Welcome to the Forgotten Junction, the inn equidistant from both Serif and Hifrim. You have truly reached the middle of nowhere. May I stable your horses?" Though the speech was obviously memorized it made Trela smile. There was nothing wrong with a little gimmick.

"We will need to speak with the inn's owner." Trela swung down from her horse and tossed the boy a small coin. She was unsure of what the Gaen custom was for how much to give a stablehand, but she figured she could start small and move upwards once the others arrived, if taste dictated.

"Of course, mistress. My father, Tyraulk Cru'lak, will be waiting just inside." He was smiling at her with his right hand loosely gripping the reins. She assumed the copper was appropriate.

Trela walked in through the open door without looking back at her companions. The lobby area was large with a vaulted ceiling. The opposite wall did not exist and was defined by a colonnade with repeating arches, completely open to the green courtyard beyond. The small courtyard had a giant oak tree centered in it. Its boughs majestically covered about a third of the area, casting shade on almost a third of the grassy area. The sound of fountains and low waterfalls was a bit mesmerizing, and Trela had to exert some willpower to turn towards the large reception counter to her right. There was a middle-aged Gaen standing behind the counter, grinning like a cat.

"Greetings and welcome to the Forgotten Junction." He appeared to be itching to continue with a similar speech to the one the boy had given, but he held himself in check.

"Greetings, you must be the honorable Tyraulk Cru'lak. I have heard that this is the greatest inn in all of the Gaen realm." Trela strode up to the counter with a warm smile on her face.

"You flatter me, truly. We are an oasis in the middle of nowhere, that is true. Sometimes this isolation enhances the experience beyond the real sensation." He laughed warmly.

"Believe me, this is a sight for sore eyes." Trela looked appreciatively about the lobby and smiled when her eyes reached the courtyard and the giant oak. She turned back towards Tyraulk. "This inn seems massive. How many rooms do you have?"

"Well, some of what you see from the outside is the stables, some are the common eating hall and kitchens, and some of it is my family's residence, but we surely have enough room for you and your companions." He nodded to himself as he talked.

"But how many rooms do you have right now? How many are empty?" She stared at him without blinking.

"It has been a busy couple of days. There is a group of warriors heading back to Serif who have been enjoying our hospitality here." He smiled and lightly held one hand in his other. "We have about thirty open rooms, mistress."

"Hmmm. And how many beds per room?" She was doing some quick math in her head.

"Our typical room has two beds, but we have several with only one. They are quite nice, I must say." He glanced to her companions before settling back on her. "I could certainly place you away from the warriors. We do not get many Pyrans out here in the middle of nowhere."

"How much for the rest of your rooms?" Trela ignored the Pyran's comment.

"Well, I..." And here he paused. He had been about to question her needs, she was sure of that. His business sense quickly took over and he began nodding again. "That would be thirty gold pebbles, mistress. That will include breakfast in the morn, but not dinner tonight." He again glanced at her companions.

"Great. Knill, get the others." She was sure she could force many of her warriors to share a room, but she wanted to give them as much space as possible.

Trela did not think that the innkeeper would care that his new lodgers would be mostly Pyran, but she did not want to give him a chance to show any prejudices either. Some innkeepers would be worried about two groups of warriors that were the same race sharing the same common room, let alone a mixture. Her mind wandered briefly to what the Gaen warriors were doing there while she was counting out her heavy coin, but figured that this was a large enough junction that they could be just randomly passing through to just about anywhere. She would have to send some of the Gaen warriors down to the dining hall to do some investigating, just to satisfy her curiosity.

They inundated the inn as if they were storming a castle. Tyraulk was valiant in his efforts to take care of each of them, or at least to disperse them all into their rooms. His two sons, Bolgiene, whom Trela had met outside earlier, and Gelday, were doing their best to stable all of the horses. Wesduin refused to enter the inn until he felt comfortable about how his wagons were situated, so he was out there assisting them. There were a few others out there. Trela was not sure, but knew that at least Zira, Pejal, and Vulthrim were out there. She did not really know Vulthrim, but he seemed to be the type of derlian who preferred to be constantly doing something, somewhat like Knill. It was a true asset at times like these.

Trela shared a room with Knill, as they always shared a tent. It was the largest one available and she almost felt guilty that only two of them were sharing such a large space. Almost. There were quite a few who were doubled up, but that was mainly up to the warriors themselves. Friends, and more than friends, were able to room together at their leisure. It was those who wished to room next to someone in particular, but did not want to share the same space, that gave Tyraulk the most difficulties. His efforts were truly heroic. He seemed to have a detailed map of his entire inn stored in his brain. He would listen to someone's request to be next to a specific friend, but kept away from another, but be near an exit hall or the communal bath stashed on each floor or away from the smells of the kitchen's compost pile, and he would switch keys amongst the others milling about the lobby with the grace of a dancer. She had let Knill take their things up to their room while she stayed near Tyraulk in case there were any arguments that she needed to step into. But there were none. In an amazingly short time, considering the buzzing chaos that her coterie made, the lobby was cleared.

"Very impressive." Trela pressed another gold coin into the innkeeper's hand. There was a small bead of perspiration at his temple.

"We aim to please, mistress." His smile was genuine, as if he enjoyed the chaos. Thrived on it, even. She wondered if that was more of a Gaen trait than a Pyran one. Pyrans usually got their dose of chaos through battle, not vocation.

"And at what time does the common room open?" Trela was not even sure where the common room was. She assumed it was across the courtyard.

"It has just opened." He nodded towards where she was looking. She was not quite sure if he was opening it just for her, or it really was just opening as they spoke. It did not really matter.

"Perfect, thanks again." Trela and Tyraulk gave small bows to each other at almost the exact same time.

Trela joined Knill in their large room. It was at the top floor of the inn, which was nice not to have anyone above them, but it meant that she had to climb several different stairs to get there. By the time she arrived Knill had already scattered their belongings about the room.

"You know we will just have to repack all those things." She was not sure why this type of thing bothered her. He was just such a nester. Every time they stopped anywhere for any length of time, he had to unpack everything. It reminded her of a dog marking its territory. Though he unpacked everything, he was also the one who did most of the repacking as well. Truly, it should not have bothered her.

"Do you know what Delubayn is?" He stood there, motionless in the middle of the room, staring straight at her.

"Of course I do. I'm a Pyran." She stopped moving as well and hung her arms lightly at her sides, as if preparing to pull a weapon. As if preparing for a fight.

"Is that what this is? Is this unrequited?" He took a deep breath. "You know how I feel about you. How do you feel?"

"I don't feel like having this conversation with you. That's how I feel." Trela could imagine some conversations as battles. She could see how words could cut like knives, how looks could crash into faces like hammers; how to dodge, how to block, and how to counterstrike. In this imagining of verbal combat, most derlians appear to want to win. Not always at the expense of others, but the desire is still there. They wear their armor to protect themselves from the sharp words of their opponents. Knill, however, fought unlike anyone she had met before and it drove her mad. It was as if he enjoyed losing. No, that was not quite it, that was not the maddening part. It was as if he thought losing would bring him victory. At first Trela imagined him walking into combat naked. Weaponless and armorless, he would bait her by throwing sand and mud, then stand there motionless, waiting for the strike. He seemed to wear the scars she gave him with pride. But that was not quite it either, that was not the maddening part. It was as if he had somehow found armor that, when struck, would damage its wearer more than if they were merely naked. Like armor that had spikes on the inside, and anytime she struck him, the spikes were driven into his flesh. It was this image that annoyed her most about Knill. Of him looking plaintively at her, slowly donning his reverse spike armor. That was what drove her mad, this plaintive ritual. It was her turn to take a deep breath.

"Listen, I am sorry I said anything about the room. I was worried that we would not be staying here as much as you would desire, that is all." She quickly held up her hand, realizing her mistake. "As much as we both would desire."

"I'm... I'm sorry. I had just imagined our time together up here differently." He looked down, his quick voice flattened a little.

"Me too. And don't apologize." Trela felt herself getting worked up again. "I need to change. Why don't you head down to the common room? I'll catch up with you soon."

Trela went downstairs and into the cavernous common room with Clerin, Aedon, Tesjuk, and Nyhan. She wanted to be surrounded by Gaens she knew. She knew that Knill was already down there, but she had not realized just how many of her Pyran warriors were packed into the hall as well. The room thrummed with vibrant and varied life. There were conversations in every corner, which made hearing any individual out of arm's reach almost impossible. Trela stood there in the middle of the entryway for a moment, soaking it all in.

The common room was one long hall with a pair of tall wooden doors to match the style of the inn's main doors, with rounded tops and black iron straps. They stood wide open, allowing the raucous laughter to spill out through the courtyard and into the lobby. There was smoke in the air, but Trela could not place the scent. There was a bar at the far end, with several Gaens in aprons hastily pouring beer and taking coin. Sharing the far end of the hall, tucked into a corner, was a tiny stage, devoid of musicians. The layout of the room, if not the decor, reminded her a little of the tavern in Wazschial. Her warriors occupied all of the tables in the right half of the hall and even spilled across the meridian a little. There was a small buffer of empty tables and then, against the left wall, about eight tables that were filled with Gaen warriors. She thought they had to be warriors from their gruff countenances and stout frames, their visible scars and travel-stained clothes. But they were quiet, huddled amongst themselves and casting periodic glances over at the loud Pyrans.

Her warriors began to shift around to make room for her in their midst. Instead, she turned to her left and took up the closest empty table next to the Gaen warriors. She gave Nyhan a silver coin and bade him to return with a couple flagons of beer and some mugs. They spoke quietly until Nyhan returned, exchanging quick glances with the Gaens right next to them. Trela poured herself a full mug and took a large drink. She was trying to decide which one of them to offer a drink to when one of them stood up. Gaens were definitely the shortest of the four races, with Pyrans at least a head taller. This Gaen, however, was almost as tall as Clerin, with a long, thick beard. He grinned a smile with more missing teeth than he had remaining. He was still as stout as most Gaens and had a large double-bitted battle axe strapped to his belt. He glared at their table for a second in silence, his eyes roving over each of them in turn, until he reached Tesjuk. He then turned to Trela.

"Why would you want to share a table with one who sleeps with goats?" He nodded slightly towards Tesjuk.

"Better than one who lies with dogs!" Tesjuk stood so quickly that his chair toppled behind him. Then they laughed together. Tesjuk walked around the table so they could clasp hands. "Trela, this is Roqural Mur'jin, a completely amoral and ruthless killer.

Roqural, this is Trela, Queen of the Pyran realm." He wandered back to his chair and picked it up off the floor.

Roqural sat down next to Trela and grabbed the flagon sitting on the table to pour himself some of their beer. He glanced at the others while doing that, lingering a little on Clerin. Then his eyes reached Aedon. Though it was subtle, Trela thought that his eyes widened for a second upon seeing her.

"My lady." The words were quiet, but audible. He barely nodded towards her when he spoke. Aedon did not twitch one facial muscle but she was certainly staring hard at him. He then turned towards Trela. "A real queen, eh? I've never met a queen before." Before Trela could respond, he turned towards Tesjuk again. "And what would you be doing in the company of your betters?"

"The same thing you are doing." Tesjuk looked completely relaxed and at ease; he looked like he was enjoying himself.

"Oh, I doubt that." Roqural, almost imperceptibly, glanced at Aedon once again.

Trela was not positive what was going on, so she continued to sip her beer. It had a bitter flavor and the bubbles filled her stomach too quickly, but as Torpalin had said while first tasting grog, "it did the trick." She quickly became bored with the vague and nondescript banter, however. If she wanted to listen to poor quips traded back and forth, she could have sat down in the midst of her own warriors. She leaned over and topped off Roqural's mug.

"So, what *are* you doing here?" Trela set the flagon down on the opposite side of her, so that he would have to reach over her to refill his own drink.

"Well, a caravan of Gaen 'jin are quite a common sight around here. We are just passing through from one part of the realm to the other. It is you that is out of place, queen. What are *you* doing here?" He leaned back and gave her his gap-tooth grin.

"I am hunting Tlana." Normally she had more patience for this sort of game, but she was feeling a little on edge. "I heard that the Gaens were incapable of protecting their own citizens, so in my own grandiose humility, I've decided to travel from one edge of the world to the other in order to do your duty for you."

"You take that back!" His axe was in his hands quite quickly, but not faster than Trela's long dagger was at the top of its hilt, just under the blade, as if caressing a naked neck. A little warning tap.

They were both mostly standing, but partly crouched. Their chairs had toppled like Tesjuk's.

"A sore spot?" They were all frozen. Everyone. The entire room. "Your dodges, your quick anger, your… frustration. Yes, your frustration is palpable. This room reeks of it. It all speaks to me plainly. Since you will not tell me, let me guess." Trela was unsure of how to move her dagger without causing the room to thaw, so she kept it held high with her muscles taught. "You were charged to investigate the attacks, correct?" She watched his face intently as she talked. Searching for any clue that she was walking on the correct path. His eyelids got a little soft, just a little droopy. His breath slowly left his barrel chest through his nose. "But you didn't find anything, did you? Just emptied buildings? Maybe some signs of struggle, maybe some fleeting glimpses into the horror, but nothing definitive, no one left to tell you their tale of woe. You took longer than you were supposed to, hoping to find some sort of evidence to bring back. Something tangible for your superiors to mull over. I'll bet you didn't even camp in the village but on the outskirts." An eyebrow twitched. "Villages?" Roqural glanced at Tesjuk and then back at her. "You were supposed to report back already, weren't you? You have been dragging your feet on the way back because…" Trela was going to continue but Roqural took a short step back and lowered his axe around her dagger.

"Close. You're close, but… We were not dragging our feet because we found nothing. We found… everything. It's all with us. Our wagons are laden with the dead. With the evidence. We left them hidden in the forest a ways off, so as to not alarm the innkeeper." He snorted quietly, as if at his own joke. "We drew lots to see had to stay behind and guard them while the rest of us had a night—one night! —of rest before continuing. But we couldn't do it, you see. We couldn't leave just a few warriors out there. Alone with the wagons while the rest of us enjoyed the warm hearth, cold beer, and soft beds. So we split up into thirds. One third sleeps outside, two thirds sleep at the inn. We are on our third night." He spoke quietly, without the brusque and boisterous attitude he had so shortly before shown.

"All Gaens drink free tonight!" Trela knew that she could not keep spending money like this, but she could think of nothing else to say, and besides, it was the least she could do.

The room unthawed, but it was the most unenthusiastic response to free alcohol that Trela had ever witnessed. That was, however, understandable. No one stood or cheered. The two groups of warriors did not suddenly mix and begin conversing. It was all very subdued. The Gaens wearing the aprons were the only burst of activity and they quickly distributed a flagon to every table. Even the ones that only had Pyrans.

Roqural secured his axe, picked up his chair, and sat back down. Trela sheathed her dagger, righted hers as well, and sat back down. She topped off his mug and left the half-empty flagon in the middle of the table, within reach by all.

"I apologize for goading you callously. I didn't realize how traumatic it must have been." She now had to figure out how to get Roqural to talk for the rest of the evening.

"Are you really here to hunt Tlana?" He looked tired.

"Our mission is to reduce the Tlana by any means at our disposal. This means that we may have to hunt some of them, yes." She was unsure of how much to reveal.

He glanced at Aedon again. He took a drink. Trela followed him and drank heartily. She also glanced at Aedon but there was nothing to be read there. She wished she had time to speak with Aedon alone, even if just for a few moments, before continuing to speak with Roqural. She glanced at Tesjuk as well, but he did not appear to be hiding anything. There did seem to be a quiet look of concern in his eyes, behind his jovial smile. She wondered how long Tesjuk and Roqural had known each other.

"How about an ambush?" He tilted his head back and finished his mug. He wiped his mouth with the back of his hand and grinned at her.

"I would give anything for the opportunity. I would kill for the opportunity." Trela felt her face quickly warm with a flush of blood. She leaned forwards, studying Roqural's face. Was he serious?

"Perfect, because that is all I want. Something must pay for what is waiting out there in the forest for me. There's a whole village out there." He was looking down at his own belly as he hiccoughed. "Well, I should probably say 'in pieces' rather than 'whole,' ha!"

"How do you know? How can I trust that you know where they will attack next?" She was intrigued. Skeptical but hopeful.

Roqural appeared to be getting more and more drunk by the moment. She did not want him to lose his train of thought. She felt close to something. There was an air of anticipation around them, thick as fog.

"Well, think about it. That is what they would do if they knew you were hunting them, isn't it? How best to fight something like that, but to use its own tactics against it, yes?" His head lolled slightly while he was talking. He had appeared tired at first and the drink was just compounding the image. She needed him to stay coherent.

"Of course it is a great idea. Of course both sides would like to lure the enemy into a trap, into an ambush. The issue is how to anticipate them. How do you set up a location and lure them in and ensure that they do not know what is happening until it is too late? Do you know which village they are going attack next?" That was what she was really hoping for. The name of the village to be attacked next. Especially if she had any time to position her coterie.

"It's here." He placed his finger over his wet lips. "They are following us, you see. They got our scent in the last village. They hang back, thinking they are invisible to us. But we know, we can feel them… we know." His head began drooping again.

It was maddening to Trela. She wanted to know so much information, and he was lolling around like the town drunk finding a place to pass out. When? When?! It was a question she wanted to shout. She wanted to grab him by the shoulders and shake him until he became coherent. She thought about slapping him but knew she was just being impatient. Maybe they should continue their conversation tomorrow.

"Trela. Trela, something's not right." Aedon slowly stood and reached a hand out towards Trela's shoulder. "I know Roqural, I hired him… He is not usually—"

Aedon stopped in mid-sentence. The hair on back of Trela's neck stood up. A shiver shot down through her spine. The room seemed to suddenly get freezing cold. A blood-curdling scream shattered the sudden quiet. There was a high wail to it, like a frightened girl. There was a low growl to it, like a bear and a giant cat mixed. There was a rough tearing sound, a howling wolf, falling gravel, a dying warrior, and a bit of thunder. It was all these audible things. But it was the inaudible portion that seared through Trela's skull like an icy claw.

Roqural's head snapped up. His eyes glowed eerily in the firelight as he stared straight into Trela. His nostrils flared widely. He seemed more animal than derlian. For some reason her mind thought of Qizern, that night in his parley tent. "You are known to us." His voice was not his own. It was deeper and yet… more hollow?

All of the fires in the room were snuffed at once. All the light fled. They were in complete darkness. Then the scream came once more, but closer. Much closer. It sounded as if it were just outside the entrance of the hall. Then pandemonium broke loose.

As quickly as she was able, Trela pulled her long dagger out and held it in front of herself in the darkness. She held it as tight as she could, with both wrists stiff in anticipation. Clang! The strike came from her left. She pressed against it but also took a small step back and to her right to steady herself. Then she kicked out with her left foot and felt it strike flesh, eliciting a quiet groan from Roqural.

The darkness was briefly shattered by a sheet of flame. Serghno was sweeping the entrance to the hall but there did not appear to be anything there. Trela only had enough time to glance before she turned back towards Roqural. He was on the ground, trying to get up, but it was the other Gaens that caught her attention. They all had their weapons out and were screaming wildly. Trela grabbed Aedon and rushed back over to her coterie's side of the hall. Somewhere in the back of her mind was the thought to look for Clerin, but Serghno's fire had stopped and the room was plunged once more into darkness.

There was an expectant hum somewhere behind the screaming. Trela crouched and held her dagger stiff in front of her in anticipation. But a strike never came. The room lit up again, not with fire this time, but with lightning. It came from something at the entrance, something derlian shaped, but somewhat tall and skinny. Something gaunt. The lightning shot through her own coterie, bouncing from one warrior to the next. Then the Gaens arrived and the clamor of steel striking steel was deafening.

The figure at the entrance was certainly a Tlana. That was what she needed to focus on, that was what she needed to destroy, what she needed Feyazki to destroy. She started fighting her way over towards where she last saw him, but she was lost amongst the flashes of light and dark. Serghno and Ryshial were taking turns shooting fire through the horde of Gaens while lighting bloomed around the room in short, bright bursts. It was all she could do to keep moving while blocking and striking, to keep a general flow of direction in the midst of the turbulence. It was maddeningly slow.

The closer she got to the front of the hall, the more she realized she would never reach Feyazki. He was, for better or worse, in the middle of a tight pack of her warriors. She had to change her plan, to shift her trajectory. In her mind she knew what needed to happen. She needed to distract the Tlana enough for Feyazki to strike a powerful enough spell, one that could slide past the Tlana's defenses. Not only was she unsure of how to accomplish that feat, she was unsure of how to let Feyazki in on her plan. Would he be paying attention when she was in position? Another Gaen placed himself in front of her long dagger, screaming wordlessly with a wide, bearded mouth and swinging a half-moon axe in a wide arc. It was coming towards her from the right and he had both burly hands swinging the axe, twisting mightily from the waist. Rather than bracing herself and blocking, she tilted her dagger and thrust it, just above his wrist, between the two bones of his lower arm. She had not thought it possible, but he somehow screamed louder. He dropped his axe, but still moved his head towards her, trying to bite her. She swung him around to her right with the dagger skewered through his right wrist. He slid, or maybe flung, off her dagger and staggered into some warriors behind her. She could have no hesitation, no worry, no doubt in her mind. There was no time, the whole fight would only last minutes. If that. She had to trust that Feyazki would be prepared when she needed him to be. It was out of her hands.

Trela struck out straight towards entrance to the hall, towards the gaunt figure. She could feel that she was the tip of the spear, that her warriors, some of them at least, were following in her wake. It helped her to keep her momentum up. Then, as she neared the figure at the entrance, she slipped on a pool of blood. Her right knee hit a wooden plank that was the floor and she almost flung her dagger as her arms whirled trying to unconsciously keep her balance. It was a fortuitous fall. A giant war hammer swung over her lowered head, crushing a Gaen's face above her. While crouched on the floor, she reached around and hamstrung the hammer-swinging Gaen. She then gathered her feet underneath herself and lunged upwards, using her thigh muscles to help drive her dagger into the chest of yet another Gaen. She spun away from his open mouth and tugged at her dagger. And tugged. But it was stuck fast, and he was falling backwards, away from her. She stood there for a split second, weaponless and stunned.

"Trela! Trela, you must save Clerin. Now!" There was no way to hear anything in the hall, no way that a voice could carry intelligibly amongst the clamor. But there it was, placed wholly into her mind—Feyazki's panicked voice. She looked over at the entrance and there was Clerin, held high by her throat. The gaunt figure held her with its left hand, its right was loose at its side. Both of Clerin's hands were gripping the wrist of the hand that was choking her. Her left leg was swinging valiantly towards the gaunt figure's torso.

Time slowed. Stopped. All thoughts left Trela's mind. She could not hear the clanging noise around her. She could not hear Feyazki's panicked voice screaming in her skull. Oddly, the only thing she could feel was her hair stuck against her forehead with sweat. Then there was only her own motion. She pushed off the floor with her right foot. Her leap made her feel as if she were flying. The air was soft as it kissed her cheek. Her left foot then pushed off on a Gaen half-kneeling below her. In those two tall steps she reached the height that Clerin was being held at. In that split second Clerin's foot struck the Tlana, to no visible effect. In that split second the Tlana pulled its right hand up and back, near its ear, fingers half-curled into a claw. Trela tilted her body back so that both of her feet were in front of her. She was almost horizontal.

Crash. Time resumed its normal pace. Both of her feet slammed into the Tlana's face. It fell back and it let Clerin slip from its grasp. From its right hand, from its clawed fingers, lightning burst forth and flung Trela across the room, into the opposite wall. The blue-white lightning was a pure and blindingly hot pain. That was the last thing she could remember before the cool darkness gratefully enveloped her in its velvety arms.

Trela awoke to two figures leering over her. No, they were not truly leering, it was only her vantage point that made it seem so. She could still feel her wet hair plastered against her forehead. It made her smile for it meant she was not dead. Such mundane and banal feelings should not follow you unto death. She felt that to be true. The face to her right she recognized. It was an older Gaen face, eyes scrunched up in worry. His face always seemed to be scrunched up in worry. She knew that she knew his name, but could not think of it. There was no pain in her body, but there was no numbness either. It was a curious case of floating, or maybe of being wrapped in layers of billowy cotton. There was a feeling of tightness around her. Of being cocooned. The face to her left was an older Pyran, her brown eyes were soft with concern. Like a doe's. Her face was recognizable. Trela felt that she should know her, but it was less familiar than the other face. The knowledge of knowing was much weaker. And when Trela thought older, she did not think old, but just older than herself. Which made her wonder, how old was she? And that made her wonder where she was. And... why she was?

"Synde?" Her voice sounded weird coming from her throat. She knew something was amiss but could not place what it was. Maybe it was the wrong name? She tried to think of another. Maybe... Knill? But she did not speak it. She was just so tired. She felt like resting. Maybe death was preferable to the mundane and banal world that she knew awaited her. Trying to think of names was just too tiring.

Trela woke again but no one was leering this time. It was dark. As before, there was no numbness, but there was also no sensation of floating. The pain was there, but it played quietly in the background and did not really bother her. Her skin felt tight and warm, like a sunburn, but the dark air was nicely cool against her cheeks. There were several beautifully peaceful moments there in the cool darkness before she was racked with a coughing fit. She could not stop, could not breathe. Her body curled and convulsed. Her eyes involuntarily filled with tears. Her face felt even hotter against the cool, dark air. She wanted to cry out, to scream, to plead for help, but could not breathe in enough to exhale anything beyond the coughing.

"Mekliderto!" A soothing voice pulled the hateful liquid from her lungs. It was a voice that she knew she should know. She stopped convulsing and breathed. Her skin felt less tight and the quiet pain subsided. She stayed curled up on her side and did not want to open her eyes. It was as if opening her eyes admitted that she was still alive. She was not quite ready to admit that yet. It felt a little like... defeat?

Trela awoke again. No one was leering. It was light outside, somewhere. The air smelled crisp and she felt that there was birdsong just outside of her hearing. She did not feel like coughing, but her skin still felt tight and warm.

"Water." She thought speaking it would bring it to her. Nothing stirred outside of her closed eyelids. She did not want to open them. She did not want to admit anything, but she was quite thirsty.

She opened her eyes and saw that she was in a hall full of cots. About half of the cots were full of various wounded derlians. There was a younger Gaen sitting next to her in an uncomfortable looking wooden slat chair, sleeping. No, not just a Gaen, but Knill. She slowly lifted herself into a sitting position, which was not easy on the cot. She coughed once, but it was a hollow barking sound, not the fluid-filled fits from before. Knill shook himself awake.

"Trela, you're awake! How do you feel?" She could tell that Knill wanted to grab her up, his hands twitched with barely controlled emotion, but he contained himself.

"Water." It came out like the croak of a frog. The notion was all she could really cling to. Her only desire was so great that it woke her up. She could tell Knill wanted to talk with her about things, always so many things. But she was still unsure of how capable she was of complicated speech. She barely felt derlian.

"Of course, of course." In a burst of motion, he flew to a corner of the room to gather her request. She imagined him talking to himself while he worked. She could not exactly hear it, but she could almost feel it happening.

He came back with a tavern mug full of water and held it out to her with both of his small hands. His eyes were bright and his smile was sincere. She could tell that he wanted to speak but he kept himself in check. She knew it must have been difficult for him. He was always a slave to such urges, speaking out of turn with odd sayings that only made sense if you thought about them for too long. He had always been like that. Too eager. She imagined him sitting by her cot for… well, for however long she had been resting. It made her wonder if she was too hard on him. All he had ever done was try to be as helpful as possible. And she had let it annoy her. His only real trait was loyalty. How could that be so obnoxious? How could he rub her the wrong way when all he ever did was what she told him to do? It made her think of the cruelties of Delubayn. She vowed not to continually take him for granted. She vowed to listen to him the next time he wanted to talk to her. But now... She drank the entire glass of water, handed it back, and then she lay back down.

"Thank you. You're sweet." She breathed the words heavily but through soft, parted lips. The world slipped comfortably away from her.

Trela finally awoke feeling fresh and invigorated. Knill was standing there, smiling down upon her. But there were many more faces around her as well. Nochiel took her cool hand from Trela's forehead. Croy was standing near her feet. She recognized both of them from the first time she was being healed. There were Feyazki and Clerin, both unhurt, or at least already healed. There was Aedon and Estfale and Rewista and, off to the side, almost out of view, was a vigilant looking Malghain.

"I'm up, I'm up. You can all stop standing around." She rose from her cot and quickly felt weak. Knill ducked under her arm masterfully and put an arm around her waist. She did not like feeling that she was on display. All those scrunched, concerned faces. "I need a bath, I need a meal, and then I need the debriefing."

"Trela..." It was Estfale.

"In that order." She did her best to glare at them all. When they did not move, she became worried. "Are we under siege?" They shook their heads. "Does anything need my immediate attention?" They shook their heads. "Then what is it?"

"Nothing. We will debrief you after your meal." Estfale turned and walked away.

She ignored them all. She had a wondrous bath. She did not take too long but gave herself a serious scrubbing. She ate ravenously while wrapped in a towel. She tried to be as quick as she could with everything. She did not want to be accused of dilly-dallying. She was finally ready for an audience and had Knill gather those who wished to speak with her.

They met in one of the inn's suites. Someone was thoughtful enough to bring beer. She looked at the somber faces and made her guess.

"Who died in the fight?" She was looking at Estfale when she spoke.

"Yarsurle." He looked her in the eye. It did not seem to be an accusatory look, for which she was grateful. "He was like a brother to me." He inhaled a slightly ragged breath. "You cannot imagine how Dartsyle is taking it."

"Lotuchkin and Raif. Urwst and Elhume. Valgo and Puche." Rewista listed the dead Pyran warriors.

"Ureyast." Aedon raised her mug and drank a drought.

"Then there were those Gaens who were under the Tlana's sway. We killed at least half of them before Feyazki blasted the Tlana into a pile of leaves. We didn't... or I should say that I didn't realize that they would stop fighting once the Tlana was defeated. They all just suddenly dropped their weapons. Some cried, some vomited... You will have to speak with them to understand their experience. I don't..." It was Ryshial who had spoken up and then trailed off. Trela made a mental note to herself to get to know Ryshial more. She was a powerful mage and seemed to have more hidden knowledge about their enemies than most.

"And what of Taglo?" Trela hated herself for it, but her first thought was that the outcome was not as bad as she had feared. They had been ambushed by a Tlana and the Gaen warriors under its sway. That was the truth of it, the hard facts. She would certainly miss those who had sacrificed themselves during the fight, but she knew that many more would die before she got to her goal. To Taglo's goal. She would especially miss Yarsurle if she were honest with herself, if she even allowed herself to rank those who were gone. He was one of the first she had gotten to know in Iventorn's warpack. He was one of the few who she had snuck into Parthia with. He had been waiting for her at the edge of the desert with Lishean, and he had been a constant presence in her inner circle during her campaign against Qizern. In fact, other than Lishean, Estfale, and Dartsyle, she could not think of another warrior from Iventorn's warpack that she had been closer to. Plus, he was an amazing warrior. His skills would be missed almost as much as he himself would be. They were hard losses. The Tlana were onto them, and she could ill afford to make any mistakes, to take any losses at all. But it could have certainly been worse. Much, much worse.

"Taglo was in my chambers during the entire fight." Clerin looked up as she started to speak.

"Well, that's not very helpful." Trela answered without really thinking.

"To its credit, the fight was quite short, but…" Clerin trailed off a little. She glanced around as if noticing the room full of derlians for the first time. "There were other reasons as well."

Trela's immediate desire was to go to Clerin's room and speak with Taglo. She realized, however, that there were too many others present for her to be able to leave. They had all just survived combat and many there had lost some dear friends. Dartsyle had lost his lover. There were many feelings to assuage, nerves to calm, and spirits to lift. She was not even sure how long she had been unconscious. There was so much to do before she could even think of speaking with the Yaven. She needed to keep focused on logistics. She needed to heal her coterie before they could continue. Before the wounds went septic. She remembered a quote from Synde that had flashed through her mind during the fight. "We drop everything when we fall. It is natural. It is instinct. A good warrior is in control of their instincts. A good warrior drops nothing as they fall." She had been unable to pay it any heed during the chaos of the short battle. She had been able to keep hold of her dagger when she fell, but it had still been torn from her grip shortly afterwards. She would not drop anything here, however. She took in a deep breath. She needed to stay focused. She gave everyone in the room her largest and warmest smile. Then she began to give out her orders. She wanted a large dinner that night, with everyone in the same room. She needed to be able to give each of her warriors her time and attention.

Chapter 8

The fight had been horribly intense for Vrric. The image of the Tlana holding Clerin aloft was burned into his nightmares. His frantic *whispering* to Trela which, at the time, had seemed a completely futile gesture. And then, to his complete amazement, she had been able to burst forth from the melee. As she started to rise out of the crowd he knew he only had the one chance. It had been what he had been hoping for, a full head-on frontal assault of the Tlana to take its mind away from shielding itself in all directions. To distract it enough so that he could get his strike in. So, with no thought to her safety and barely any for Clerin's, he let loose with a Sur level lightning strike. It was at that same moment that the Tlana had started blasting Trela across the room with its own strike, luckily cut short when it exploded into a forest of leaves with a deafening scream. The room had gone quiet and black. When Vrric had finally come to it was on one of the myriad of cots dotting the inn's common room. He had only been out for a couple hours and the room was still quite full. He woke with a start to the image of the Tlana holding Clerin. For each of the nights that Trela was still out, he woke the same way, with the same image. It made him realize how much he truly cared for her. But while Nochiel and Croy had saved Trela, and Knill had refused to leave her side, it was Altrond that Clerin seemed to attach herself to after the fight. He did not save her. He did not heal her. Vrric was not sure what his skills were or why he was even a member of the coterie. It was an oddly frustrating experience, one not easily defined.

The warriors certainly showered Vrric with praise and respect even if Clerin ignored him. They smiled each time he entered the room and every time he set his mug down it was filled before he could lift it again. Even the mages were more engaging and respectful. He had always gotten along with Serghno and Ryshial, but Nochiel had barely given him the time of day before, and even Olsfang appeared to be making an effort to be less obnoxious.

The days without Trela dragged slowly on. Vrric had not realized how much she had kept things moving, how much she stirred the pot. Everyone should have known what they needed to be doing. Each warrior had their typical daily tasks and periodic additional chores when things got slow. While Trela was around, he rarely saw her specifically tell anyone to do anything. She just wandered through the encampment and nodded, winked, laughed, slapped shoulders, or, much less often, she would frown or ask a warrior why they were doing something a particular way. It was more like she was the grease on the axle keeping things running smoothly than she was directly giving needed orders. It was like she was superfluous, almost a wandering ghost. When she was out of commission, however, it became painfully obvious how much she was truly required for the smooth operation of the coterie. Derlians wandered listlessly about and shirked their simple chores. They gathered in groups, slothed together with their combined inertia. They would wander to the inn's common room, glance at the ever watchful Knill, and wander back out. Everything was waiting for her to recover. They were at a standstill, a cessation of events. They were in remission.

Still, there were plenty of things to do and most of it got done somehow. For one thing, the burials could not wait. The remaining Gaens showed the coterie where they had hidden the wagons in the forest. The Tlana appeared to have attacked them first, for none of those left guarding the wagons were found alive. The wagons had been torn apart and scattered as if by a tornado, but the surrounding trees were fully intact. The entire scene was eerie. To avoid helping find all the splinters and bits of cloth and pieces of iron and shards of steel, Vrric helped to create the mass grave. It was a long and somber day.

Tyraulk Cru'lak and his entire family had died at sometime during the melee. It was odd, since they were found scattered throughout the inn. In particular, his wife, Poilanh, who had no visible wounds or scars and appeared to have died a while ago, was quite far away from the fighting. There was also an odd reaction amongst some of the Gaen warriors. The common room had been filled with bodies that had been struck down with sharpened steel. But it also had some bodies in it that had no visible wounds. It was only a few bodies when compared with the overall carnage, but they were bizarrely placed about the room. As if hiding in corners and under tables and chairs. There was even one body found crouched in a cupboard. And, though Vrric did not personally verify this, it was said that many of their tongues were swollen and black. There was also a rash of what appeared to be suicides. About ten to fifteen percent of the dead Gaen warriors seemed to have had self-inflicted wounds. One of those was Roqural Mur'jin. They had put off burying his body to allow Trela to examine it. Nochiel placed the body under stasis to ward off the natural rot. Vrric was not sure what good it would do to have Trela examine the body, especially considering the amount of meticulous notes that Ryshial was making, but he did not argue. For his own curiosity, he peeked at the swollen black tongue that filled the corpse's mouth.

He was hoping to speak with Trela soon after she finally woke, but he would have to be patient. She had ordered a large dinner to be attended by everyone. Slowly her coterie came out of their fog. The inn was soon a bustling hive of activity once more. Even the surviving Gaens seemed to be more energized with her awakening.

Vrric also attempted to speak with Clerin before the dinner, but she was constantly being shadowed by Altrond. It seemed he could not muster enough energy to think up some logical reason to pry them apart and get her alone. If he had thought about it for long enough, he would have realized it was not really a question of energy. Maybe a question of will? The will to impose upon another's will. Instead of worrying about it, he wandered the inn and assisted with the preparations where he could.

The day sped by. Relatively. Soon the bells were ringing, signaling them to gather for the dinner. It was a slow procession to the courtyard. The common room was still being utilized as a makeshift medic hall, so they had decided to serve the dinner under the open sky. Unfortunately, once the sky darkened, the fires and torches and candles were all lit and Vrric was unable to see many of the stars.

They all shuffled in and got seated. Water was poured. Food was served. The beer began to flow. Though she did not wait until the second course was served, Trela let them take any edge off their appetite before standing. A hush cut through the dining clatter.

"We have encountered a great evil here. We were taken unawares, we were ambushed. Though not outnumbered, we fought something that is, as far as the miniscule derlian mind can comprehend, as ancient as this entire world. And we survived. We won. We have conquered a great evil here!" She raised her goblet high. "Applaud yourselves, my warriors! Drink to yourselves!" They each followed her lead and took a deep draught. A forest of goblets were upended towards the sky. They cheered and clapped and patted each other's backs a little too heartily. "We have just begun, do not forget. We only fought one Tlana, do not forget. There are many leagues to travel ahead of us, many fights, many struggles, do not forget. But this battle was ours, my friends. Do not forget that, either. Never forget that." The cheering began again. Trela stood there smiling, drinking in the exaltation. She finally raised her empty hand to quiet them. "I have ultimate faith in you, in all of you. Many of you have admirably accompanied me through many battles in the Pyran realm. I am not sure if I should admit this, but I had been concerned that a Tlana would be too much. I had been unsure if our morale would hold under such a fierce assault, unsure if our capabilities would be able to hold. I do not have to worry anymore. They have loosed their one arrow of surprise and it did not shake us, it did not break us. You have proven yourselves admirably. Tonight we dine. Tomorrow we rest. But soon… Soon, we shall be hunting again!" The cheering began again.

The dinner was entertaining and joyful for Vrric. Warriors and mages alike raised their glasses to Trela, the coterie, themselves, and him. There were times that he felt his cheeks warm during their praises and he wore the hot flush as a badge of honor. He was truly enjoying it, but eventually realized that they were crediting him with the full victory. It made him think about it for a minute. He did strike down the Tlana, that much was true, but even if he was the only derlian in the room, even if the victory was purely his, this was not truly healthy for the group. The coterie had a mission that he was unable to achieve alone. No matter how wildly he daydreamed, it could not be done. This needed to be a group effort. Even more than that, however, was the fact that it already was a group effort. He would have died if he had not had a contingent of warriors around him, protecting him. The Tlana would have gained entrance into the room if not for Serghno and Ryshial throwing fire about. The Tlana would not have been distracted enough to allow Trela to strike if it had not been for Clerin. The Tlana would not have been distracted enough to allow him to strike it down if it had not been for Trela. So many things needed to fall into place in the short amount of time they had had, so many little details. These things could not have happened without the entire coterie. The warmth in his cheeks faded as he stood.

"Thank you. Thank you all for your kind words." He took a deep breath. How to explain?

"Thank you for saving us." This came from a Gaen that Vrric did not recognize. He was sitting at the other end of the row of tables lined up in the courtyard. Others chimed in and raised their goblets.

"Again, thank you." Vrric raised his empty hand in the universal gesture of stop. "I would like to thank all of you for saving me." He took a deep breath. How to explain? "There was a warrior who charged at me just when the room went dark. When next I could see, Malghain's sword was stuck in his head. Thank you, Malghain." He raised his goblet to his fellow Luften. The others, not really needing an excuse, raised their goblets as well. "Another warrior attempted to bound past Yarsurle but was cut down in midair. I would like to thank you, Yarsurle, may you rest in peace. Another warrior thrust a spear at me just before I was able to cast a spell and…" Vrric looked around frantically. "You… you struck the spear with your sword before it could find its mark. I would like to thank…"

"Pejal. My name is Pejal." The young Pyran spoke up. Vrric smiled warmly at him. "I was just doing my duty. And to be honest, I am glad to have had the opportunity."

"Yes, just like me. We were only doing our duty." Vrric drank to Pejal. "All of us, in full cooperation and pride and capability, were doing our duty." Pejal had handed him the ending to his speech too soon. There was nothing to be done about it now, however. All he could do was try to bend it back towards Trela. "More than anyone here, I need to thank Trela. I was unable to break through the Tlana's defenses. I had tried several frustratingly futile times. It was too strong for me to strike head-on. As it was striding into the room, as it was cutting through our brave coterie, Trela leapt up from the crowd, from out of nowhere. She charged a Tlana without any weapons, with only her feet and her fists. I am not sure if that is brave or just completely idiotic." Many of the derlians laughed heartily at that. "In fact, I almost missed it. I almost missed my one opportunity to strike. But there she was, flying towards the lightning strike awaiting her. The Tlana was completely bent upon destroying her and it let down all of its magical guard. Not only did Trela provide me with the means to attack with all my concentrated might, but she took a blast from that Tlana and lived to tell the tale. Thank you, Trela." He turned towards her, sitting at the head of the long run of tables, and raised his glass high. "To Trela!" The others shouted along right after him. "To the Queen!" And they drank. Oh, how they drank.

The next morning Vrric slept in well past dawn. He slowly got cleaned up and dressed. He moseyed down to breakfast. He wandered listlessly about the inn for some time before he ran into Trela and Aedon. They were whispering amongst each other as they approached him. Trela had her arm in Aedon's.

"You both appear to be what my old mentor would call 'thick as thieves.'" Vrric was not sure why the phrase popped into his head, but they both smiled mischievously at him when he spoke it. Yes, even their smiles were in sync.

"It has been a while since you have spoken of Revkin." Trela unhooked herself from Aedon, stopped and crossed her arms. "It's sweet."

"Oh no, not Revkin. My first mentor, Kaihlu." He nodded absently to Trela. "The smith." He was not really sure why he tacked on Kaihlu's vocation. Must have been for Aedon's benefit.

"You were a blacksmith?" Aedon's eyebrows raised inquisitively, but her mouth kept its earlier mirth. "You grow more intriguing every day."

"Yes, that was what I was apprenticed to do when I was young. It was not until the Trivaste tests…" Vrric thought for a brief moment on how to explain that phrase. He sometimes forgot how few Luftens there were in the coterie. He wondered how Clerin fared, being the only Fluen. "…vocation tests when a Luften reaches the pre-age of adulthood. During the tests I found that I had a disposition and even, if I may be so bold, a hidden talent for magic."

"If anyone here could be that bold…" But Trela was swiftly interrupted.

"So, you left what you spent your life learning and flung yourself into what felt natural to you?" Aedon crossed her arms in an odd mirror of Trela.

"Well… yes." He was not really sure if he was being complimented or chastised.

"Then why do you still consider this Kaihlu a mentor? Did he teach you any magic? Do you ever use your smithing skills?" Her brows had fallen back down, but her right one shot back up at her last question.

"Well… no." Vrric cast his mind back and could find nothing but the feeling of truth. Kaihlu was definitely his first mentor. "It is true that Revkin showed me the ways of magic, but it was Kaihlu who taught me who to be. I believe I learned more about life, in general, from the smith than I did from the mage. I learned more about myself, in specific, during my cycles as a mage, but I do not think that it was necessarily due to Revkin. I mean the process was due to Revkin, but I feel that the way I conquered the process was due to my earlier teachings from Kaihlu."

"So… Do you ever feel bad for turning your back on smithing?" Aedon was relentless.

"No. I am, fully and completely, a mage. There is nothing more exhilarating than flowing, funneling, and shaping chaos as it pours through you. I feel I would wither away if I was unable to touch that pure energy anymore." Vrric looked upwards to regroup his thoughts. "I do feel bad for not being able to assist Kaihlu after all of the energy that he poured into me. But I am not sure if I had much of a choice. Is the horse that plows the field happier than the one who carries its master into battle? Does the horse even have a choice? Or, like me, does the horse just happen to have certain skills? I think I would feel worse if my skills went unutilized. And even worse, somehow, someway, if they went unbeknownst to me. Perhaps, when I return to my own realm, I will shower both of my mentors with all of the riches that Trela has promised me. But until then I will be happy that I am a horse who is being utilized how my skills and talents have prepared me to be used."

"And right now, I need your skills and talents to accompany us to Clerin's room." Trela jumped into the moment of silence before Aedon could. Vrric was certainly ready to leave it at that.

They arrived at Clerin's and Trela knocked lightly on the door. They waited for a quick moment. Trela tilted her head and pressed her ear close to the door. Her brow furrowed. Vrric wondered if that was reflexive or due to something she heard. He, for one, could hear nothing, try as he might. Trela knocked again, this time with more force. Rap, rap, rap. The noise of muffled shuffling filtered through the wooden door.

Clerin opened it quickly and smiled warmly at them all as they entered. Vrric entered last and his eyes lingered on her dimples so that he did not realize she had not been alone until he was in the middle of the room. Altrond was lounging comfortably on the red velvet couch that rested against a side wall.

Clerin shut the door softly behind them all. It seemed to Vrric that Altrond should have stood as Trela entered. She was his queen, was she not? Altrond's gaze quickly passed by Aedon and then stopped on Vrric. Vrric had not realized, but he felt that his brow was furrowed. Altrond grinned and nodded at him just as he had done to his queen. Stubbornly, Vrric did not want to relax and smile back. He kept his unconscious frown and turned towards Trela so that he would not just be glaring at Altrond. Her eyebrow twitched and she glanced quickly to Altrond and back again to Vrric. Then, suddenly, her face broke into a wide smile.

"Please, everyone, sit." Trela, herself, took the end of the bed near the middle of the room. Clerin moved towards the end of the bed and Aedon, thankfully, moved to the red velvet couch. Vrric grabbed a wooden chair from the table opposite of the couch. He brought it closer to the group and found himself next to Clerin. He finally smiled across the small room.

"Where is Taglo?" This came from Aedon.

"Here, derlian." Vrric had not even noticed the lit candle in the corner until its flame left the wick and began to grow. Soon the blaze grew to a muted stature, about half its typical size. He was always amazed at the lack of heat emanating from the Yaven. He knew it could make itself hot if it wanted, but he wondered if it could happen accidentally. Maybe while it was angry.

"Good, we are all here." Trela nodded to no one in particular while looking around. "I feel we should discuss the Tlana. I need to have a better understanding of what we are up against."

There were times when Vrric had heard others use the word "bird" for "Tlana", not that he was a specific adherent of that. Everyone had forgone that at the Forgotten Junction, however. The Tlana already knew where they were, there was no need for secrecy.

"Then Ryshial should be here." Vrric looked around at everyone looking back at him. "And maybe that Gaen that stole Croy…"

"Well, I was trying to keep this as small of a group as possible, but if you think it is wise." Trela looked around as well.

"Well, I did see the Pyran mage taking extensive notes while you were incapacitated. And though I begrudge his personality, Narst Dea'jin has a large body of knowledge." Aedon looked as if she were ready to jump up and grab them both.

"Not the Blind One." It was Clerin. There was an odd, barely concealed vehemence in her voice as she spoke about him. "I still cannot believe he stole Croy." She slightly turned her head towards Vrric. "Right from under our noses."

"Well, I do not see a reason to bring anyone else into this conversation anyway." Altrond added his opinion. Vrric still did not know why he was even there. Why was *he* involved in "this conversation?"

"Ryshial's life work concerns the Northern Desert, you can even ask Croy. That includes both the Tlana and the Vijen." Vrric took a breath. "I think it would be foolish to not be able to ask her questions, at the very least. Even if you did not want her privy to this conversation."

Trela raised her hands. "Yes to Ryshial. No to the Blind One." She turned towards Aedon. "Would you mind?"

Altrond quickly stood. "I believe I can find her quickly." He smiled his relaxed smile and nodded shallowly to Trela, turned, and left.

He was gone for several moments while they all sat in silence. "So, if I may ask, why is he pertinent to this conversation?" Vrric could not help himself.

"He has an odd collection of books." Clerin glared, a little, at Vrric. "What is your problem with Altrond anyway? What has he done to you?"

"Yeah, Feyazki, what has he done?" Trela looked like she was completely enjoying herself.

"Nothing. It's just... As far as I can tell, he's done nothing. I am not even sure what his skills are." He knew they were just egging him on, but it slipped out anyway.

"He's a spy, Feyazki." Clerin exhaled audibly. "Like Jalin."

"Yeah, you don't have a problem with Jalin, do you?" Trela was still grinning.

"I don't have a problem with anyone. I just wasn't sure why he was so exalted. Jalin was certainly not invited to this conversation." He just wanted this portion of the conversation to stop. He almost admitted he was wrong, almost apologized, just to end it. But he stopped short. Why should he have to apologize?

"This is frivolous. Are we waiting for more participants before we can begin?" Taglo's voice rumbled from somewhere deep inside.

"Yes, we are waiting so we don't have to repeat ourselves." Trela turned on the bed to look at Taglo as she spoke.

"Then I have a request for the communicator that does not preclude our future conversation." Taglo flowed to the center of the room and sort of turned towards Clerin. "We will need more Yavens for this journey. I wish you to summon the one you spoke of earlier. The one you called Wil."

"I... I do not know the entire name." Clerin looked suddenly nervous.

"How would you retrieve it?" Taglo paused briefly. "Let me re-phrase that. How could you retrieve it?"

"The only one I know who knows Wil's full name is Olwinn. And I... I am not sure where he is, or how to speak with him." She furrowed her brow and turned to Vrric. "Could you *whisper* to him?"

"I doubt it. Maybe if I knew enough about him, and he happened to be in the Gaen realm. Or maybe in the Northern Desert, somewhat close to us." Vrric did not know how far he could whisper. Even when trying with Croy, they had to be within several leagues of each other. This mage may have been more powerful than Croy, but he would not be listening for a *whisper*. And from a complete stranger, no less.

"You said you heard the name?" The question came from Taglo. "You had heard it but could not remember it due to its length and complexity?"

"Yes. But really, I have tried my best to recall the full name. It has slipped from my mind." Clerin bit her lip unconsciously.

"Let the mage sift through your mind." Taglo turned towards Vrric. "If she were willing, would you be able to find the forgotten sensora?"

"Probably. I have never performed that spell before. I would have to think about what to cast." Vrric turned towards Clerin and realized her eyes held a small panicked look in them. "You would have to trust me enough to let go of your unconscious defenses."

"The Blind One knows the secrets of the school of Larelt." As Aedon spoke, the panicked look in Clerin's eyes became even more pronounced.

"No. Not him. I can't have him sifting through my mind." Clerin broke her slightly pleading gaze from Vrric and shifted to Aedon.

"No, of course not. But he may have some suggestions of how to best set everything up, what specific spell or spells to cast and the like." Aedon immediately backpedaled after seeing Clerin's reaction. "Just as an advisor. He would not even have to know the who or what of the search if Feyazki can propose his inquiry vaguely enough."

Clerin opened her mouth to speak again, Vrric was sure it was to voice more protestations, but just then a knock reverberated through the wooden door. Clerin started a little at the noise. Trela quickly stood and walked over to the door. She held her hand on the handle and turned back towards Taglo, who was slowly floating back to its corner, still facing Clerin.

"I do not ask this lightly. I do recognize the discomfort you are displaying due to this conversation… this request." Taglo positioned itself in the corner. "Please, communicator, I would not press you if this was not important. Let the mage sift through your mind for the Yaven's name."

Clerin did not speak, but barely nodded to Taglo. Her eyes appeared wet to Vrric. He was not sure why she seemed so vulnerable at this moment, but thinking over the request, he wondered if he would let another derlian wander the forest of his own mind. His mind had settled on the word "no" when Trela opened the door. In walked Altrond, wearing his easy smile, and Ryshial followed closely behind. The door was shut quickly behind them.

They both sat on the couch, Altrond nearest the door, then Ryshial, then Aedon. Trela sat back on the edge of the bed, near Aedon and next to Clerin. Vrric was opposite the couch on his chair again while Taglo slowly repositioned itself near the center of the room. It was quiet while most of them stared at Trela.

"I have gathered you all here to listen to a passage from Altrond's book. The book is called 'Of Vijen and Tlana,' right?" Trela turned her head towards the couch.

"The other way around—the Tlana are listed first." Altrond smiled lazily at her. "First, let me say that this ancient book appears to be a list of possibilities more than pointing to any one answer. It is set up as a series of questions almost. I want to say that this is because there are many authors, or at least many voices, that it is narrated through. Maybe a compilation of theories?" His voice lilted upwards at his last sentence, turning it into a question.

"Where did you find that book?" Ryshial turned to Altrond such that her back was almost pushing on Aedon.

"The library in Wazschial is known to have far fewer books than the libraries in Agoge, but it does have some rare gems." Altrond scooched against the arm of the couch, giving some extra space between the both of them.

"But… With such a rare book, I doubt they would let you check it out. How much did they charge you? It must have been extravagant." Ryshial glanced around a little, looking for agreement.

"He stole it." Clerin spoke with a twinge of mirth in her voice.

"Well, that's…" Ryshial trailed off. Vrric could almost see the gears in her mind churning slowly. She was usually quite insistent on rules being followed. However, she also had an insatiable thirst for knowledge. Especially knowledge about the Northern Desert.

"That is fortunate for us that Altrond is such an accomplished spy." Trela held her chin up while looking at Ryshial. Almost daring her to look down upon Altrond. Ryshial sat back against the couch, allowing Aedon to see Altrond again.

"I swear to everyone here that I will return this book to the Wazschial library when our mission has been accomplished." Altrond nodded slowly to everyone. Vrric, for his part, could not care less that the book had been stolen. They needed it a thousand times more than anyone living near that village would have need of it. Altrond still rubbed him the wrong way, however.

No one moved or spoke. Vrric stared at Taglo since there was nothing else to do in the silence. For some reason, Taglo looked like it was slowly getting smaller, slowly deflating. It made him wonder if it took energy to keep a Yaven in the shape of a derlian. He wondered if the tiny candle flame that hid in the hurricane lamp was the shape with the lowest energy state, or if it took more energy to become tiny. Or, maybe, no energy needed to be expended for any shape. Maybe it would slowly shrink and slowly grow like Vrric's own chest during breathing. Finally, Trela waved her hand for Altrond to continue and took Vrric out of his useless reverie.

"This section is called 'The Dance for Leaves.' " He coughed and reopened the book. "Leaves and skin: A leaf performs some of the simple tasks that skin does, but less than bark does. It provides protection from the sun by absorption, not by blocking the warm light like bark does; sunlight is the magical energy of chaos to a tree. It funnels water like a skin that sheds it. This is less of a passive collection than sunlight, but still saps no energy from the host. It is also the aesthetic clothing worn by the tree. The rustling of the leaves provides the emotive response of the tree as represented to the world. It is in the wind that the tree appears to become animate, to become sapient. But does it offer protection from the wind? No, it does not. In fact, it is just the opposite. It is because of its leaves that a mighty oak may be blown over during the spring or autumnal storms but remain unhurt during the deadly winter. The leaf has a special relationship with the wind, for it is with the wind that the leaf reacts most like skin. Is this symbiotic? Is this parasitic? No, it just is." Altrond, not taking his eyes from the page, took a small pause and a deep breath.

"But what about a tree that contains spirit, that non-corporeal element born of chaos, but older than law? What about a wind that contains spirit? Is this not a different relationship to each other than the simple oak swaying in the breeze? Yes, it is. It is vastly different. The spirited wind wishes to tear the leaves from the branches. This is its dance. The tree becomes more spirited with each gust. There is a tear and pull on the roots. It is much easier to lose a leaf than to topple. This is what the wind truly wants. It wants to pull, piece by piece. It wants to continue its dance. A toppled tree produces only dead leaves, its nourishment forgotten once its roots leave the soil for the air. But a live tree, a tree imbued with spirit, this is an eternal supply of leaves. The imbued wind dances through the limbs, singing and cavorting, begging and cajoling, 'just one leaf,' it says, 'just one more leaf,' it repeats. Is this symbiotic or parasitic? Is this accidental assistance from the tree? Is this a form of persistent, and dare I say, intentional ignorance from the tree? Does that spirit not sense the evil in the other? Could the leaves be held fast if convinced of the dangers of letting them go? Or is it, as my predecessor has posited, that the leaves must fall from the imbued tree as much as the lesser spirited tree? That the wind just happens to be there when the leaf falls? I believe that something more bizarre is at work here. I believe this is the rarest type of symbiosis, that of the double parasite. I believe there is a balance between the two spirits that is self-leveling. The leaves of the Vijen are the skins of the Tlana. This is known. At least to me. The smoke of the Tlana is the wind in the branches. This dance is also known. We know that the Tlana need the Vijen leaves to become corporeal. The wind is a necessity for the tree, however, and this is what is not known. The Vijen need to be pruned, they need to lose their old leaves to produce new ones. Like the pulling of a string through a straw, as if you could produce fingernails faster under the duress of tension. The trees become more spirited with each gust, with each sigh, with each dance. This is what produces the willful ignorance. This is what turns the blind eye. The evil smoke breathes spirit into the neutral tree which, in turn, allows it to shed its own skin and grow which, in turn, provides the smoke with the scaffolding to make the body that affects the physical world. This is the cycle. Without a way out of this cycle, there will never be any assistance from the Vijen to remove the Tlana from our realm. This is my belief."

It was quiet for a moment. Vrric half expected Altrond to continue reading; the book lay open on his lap even though his head was up and his gaze wandered to the others in the room. It did not seem like he had truly stopped. It felt like a pause.

"The Vijen I spoke with said that their leaves just fall off. That they hold onto them for as long as they can, but when a leaf finally sheds, any nearby Tlana thinks that it was their dance that caused it." Trela broke the silence. "It seemed quite amused at the Tlana's confusion."

"The Vijen I spoke with said that there was an increase in Tlana that was directly related to the increase in evil amongst derlians. I tried to pin it down but could not. It is my opinion that the increase in evil is Yavencide." Aedon spoke up after Trela. Taglo shivered and grew a little at the mention of Yavencide. "It did not seem to consider there to be an increase in Vijen, however. You would think that more Tlana means more leaves are required."

"Is there one amongst you who has seen two Vijen at the same time?" Taglo's voice filled the small room. They all shook their heads.

"Has anyone seen more than one Tlana at the same time?" The question was posed by Ryshial. Everyone shook their heads again, but it was a slower and more thoughtful pause than for Taglo's question.

"I could conceive that there might be only one Vijen, not that I agree with that idea, at least not yet, but it seems foolish to think there is only one Tlana." Vrric was not exactly sure why he felt that way, but he did.

"Why do you think that?" Ryshial pressed Vrric lightly.

"Everyone is always talking about the increase in Tlana, right? That is the whole concern. That is why we are here, is it not? The Tlana are increasing, and we wish to put a stop to it." It just made sense.

"Why would they have different populations?" Clerin spoke up while staring at the floor.

"Well, why not?" Altrond closed his book with a finger stuck between the pages to keep his place.

"If they feed off of each other... if the relationship is mutually parasitic as the book states, their populations would need to rise and fall together, don't you think?" Clerin looked around the room for supporters.

"But should we take that story at face value?" Trela turned on the bed to better look at Clerin while she spoke. "I really think that dance the Tlana do is useless. The leaves just fall."

"And why..." Altrond was quickly interrupted by Trela's retort.

"Because I was told that, by a Vijen." Trela took a deep breath. "Didn't I just say that?"

"And you just immediately trust the Vijen?" It was Altrond again.

"What other being would have a better idea of what is going on?" Trela grew a little tense around her eyes.

"That's not what I asked." Before he could continue, however, he was interrupted.

"Does anyone know if they have been lied to by a Vijen?" Taglo broke through the back-and-forth.

This time they all stared at each other. Thoughtful faces staring into space. Thinking, wondering.

"That is difficult to ascertain, as they speak in riddles." This came from Ryshial, but both Trela and Aedon were nodding in agreement.

"Wait, wait. Who here has seen, or communicated with, a Vijen?" Vrric was getting confused, he had not realized that Ryshial had spoken with one.

Aedon, Trela, Altrond, and Ryshial all raised their hands. Vrric looked over at Clerin sheepishly. They seemed the odd ones out.

"And Croy, Tesjuk, Nyhan, Verin." Aedon piped up. "We all communicated with the same Vijen."

"And Knill." Trela spoke softly, looking downwards.

"Why are these other derlians not here?" Taglo got a little brighter as it spoke.

"At least one member from each conversation is represented here." Trela again sounded demure.

"We did want to keep the number of participants low." Altrond leaned back on the couch, half-smiling at Taglo.

"I wish to hear all of your stories. Any contact with the Vijen you have had." Taglo grew a little larger.

They all stopped for a moment. Who first? Trela told her story in great detail. About the Tlana pretending to be Synde, about their fight, and about her conversation with the Vijen afterwards. She ended with the Vijen telling her which direction the well was in and that there were companions waiting for her there. Vrric had heard the story before, or at least bits and pieces of it, but never in so much detail. He was glad he was one of the few participants picked to take part in the conversation. Then Aedon told her story. This one Vrric had heard more about, having picked Croy's brain about it himself and then listening to Croy cover it in great detail with Ryshial back in Agoge. It was Ryshial's and Altrond's stories that were completely new to Vrric. Ryshial had grilled him about his encounter with the Tlana so much that he would have thought she would have mentioned her encounter. But no, she was the type of derlian who felt compelled to keep her own experiences secret, even while digging hard into other's.

"First let me ask a question. Have any of us touched a Vijen? Did any of you see one of your companions touch the Vijen you communicated with?" Ryshial looked around the room.

"Only a leaf. And only after it had fallen. It was given to Nyhan after he asked for it, or at least that is how Nyhan tells it." Aedon looked around for others to interject, but everyone else was silent.

"No, I never touched the Vijen, nor did Knill. In fact, we did not even get a leaf." Trela smiled over to Ryshial. "Of course, we did not think to ask for one."

"Just checking." Ryshial nodded to herself. Her long delicate fingers twitched slightly. Vrric had not seen her of late without her notes and he wondered if she was itching to write stuff down. "There are many questions about these things—the Tlana, the Vijen, the Northern Desert in general—that only become apparent if we all have the same answer. But that is for later." Ryshial shifted to make herself more comfortable. She ended up sitting back against the couch, almost hidden between Altrond and Aedon. "Many cycles ago, when I was a young apprentice mage, I went looking for my missing father. I was not alone, but my companion at the time, another apprentice named Istlona, has since met her demise."

"Nothing to do with the Vijen? Nothing to do with the Tlana?" Taglo had positioned itself near the door. This allowed it a bit of centrality but did not place it in the center of the circle of derlians.

"No. And her death had nothing to do with the Northern Desert either. It was many cycles after our journey. She was almost exclusively concerned with throwing fire, a pure warpack mage if I ever saw one." Ryshial smiled to herself while speaking of her friend. Then her face took on a more serious look. "She died while in the service of Hoplung. It was a simple siege, I think. Nothing she hadn't been through a hundred times."

"You may continue with your story." Taglo interrupted her reverie.

"Of course. Sorry." Her head straightened itself on her long neck. "We had been traveling for quite a while, at least a fortnight, by the time we reached the edge of the Northern Desert, so we were quite concerned about our diminishing supplies. We stayed at the edge of the desert for a few days, gathering as much water and meat as we could. We used the last of our salt and buried everything we couldn't carry into the desert. We thought we would be able to find it again after returning. Ha!" She laughed a little.

"Anyway, we finally got into the desert and made it about four days before deciding we should head back. We had wanted to head back while we still had a fair amount of provisions. We instantly became lost. I have an inkling that our compasses were not working correctly, as is wont to happen in the Northern Desert. We wandered for another couple of days before we started to worry. Another couple before we felt panicked. It was during this stage that we began to feel like we were being watched. It was just an air of paranoia at first. That's what we told ourselves. But it soon became overpowering, oppressive. I remember Istlona screaming at the sky one morning. Begging whoever it was to just come and kill us. She was always a little dramatic." Ryshial laughed again. It was quick and quiet, but Vrric could still detect a tiny bit of ironic self-deprecation in it.

"The next day we woke with the sun and crawled out of our tent, and there was the largest shade tree we had ever seen a little ways off. We did not even notice the golden leaves at first, we just noticed the shade. It was such a blessing. We laughed and pushed each other out of the way, racing towards it, wondering aloud how we had missed such a large tree so close to our tent. We had traveled into the night, but still… it was just so massive. Anyway, we rushed over to it. I don't know about Istlona, but I planned on parking myself at its roots for the entire day. We could travel at night, which is what we should have been doing anyway.

"Well, we got to within spitting distance and we heard this booming voice, 'Stop! Come no farther!' so we stopped. We looked around, not understanding where the voice was coming from. 'It is I, that which you are searching for. And you are trespassing.' I was still looking for the voice, but Istlona understood it was the tree quite quickly. She knelt down in front of it, resting on one knee like a warrior pledging loyalty to a liege lord. I quickly followed her motion. 'We were not searching for you, we are searching for my father, Wopschole. He entered this desert many cycles ago, when I was but a babe.' I was going to speak more, to provide the description of him I had memorized from my mother. To speak of his quest. To ask for assistance. But the Vijen did not want to hear any of that.

"Again the voice boomed from somewhere partially up the tree. 'You may not understand what you seek, you may think you seek what you desire. I am here to tell you that you do not. You are too early, much too early. There is one hope. One hope only to learn the truth of what you seek. Learn to learn, yes, that is your only hope. You are destined for greater things than to die of thirst in a desert. Or worse, yes worse. You are being followed. Being tracked before the hunt begins in earnest. Your plight has called to us through our roots and we have responded. Leave this place. Escape and do not look back.' But I could not just stand up and run, if that was what it truly wanted. I needed to know about my father, just something, anything.

"I begged the Vijen for more information. 'The one you call your father found what he was seeking. Was that a comfort as he lay dying? No, I think not.' So I asked what he was seeking. I just wanted some form of closure, something beyond 'he's dead, move on' or whatever the Vijen was trying to tell me. 'He knew more of what he was seeking than you do now. Even though he was only a little older than you are now. Very knowledgeable, very tenacious.' I was getting angry now. I couldn't understand how it could not just tell me what I wanted to know. It knew, I know that it knew what had happened. I asked it once more what my father was seeking. Who am I kidding? I yelled once more. 'Eternity. Your father sought ancient knowledge of eternity. But he looked in the wrong places.' Then I was even angrier. Here the Vijen was telling me that my father had found what he was seeking, but that he was looking in the wrong places? It didn't make sense. I threw myself at the Vijen. I don't know what I was going to do, maybe climb it? Ha! It disappeared, however. I flung myself onto the sand-filled desert floor. I never even touched it."

"Did you see it disappear? Were your eyes open? Was Istlona watching it when it vanished?" Aedon's voice went up in pitch slightly as she asked her questions.

"I... I don't know. I had thought my eyes were open at the time, but I suppose I do not recall actually seeing it disappear. As for Istlona... She did not explicitly tell me one way or the other." Ryshial looked wary, almost. "Why?"

"I had heard that you could keep a Vijen still by keeping it fully in sight. By never blinking. When my group spoke with a Vijen, we tried to keep it on a hilltop by taking shifts staring at it as we approached. It... it even acted like we had been keeping it in one place when we spoke with it." Aedon looked around the room a little, as if asking for corroboration. The room was silent on this topic, however. "I was just checking. Like when you asked if anyone had actually touched or felt a Vijen."

"I am unable to answer your question satisfactorily." Ryshial sounded more crisp, more businesslike, more how Vrric thought she naturally was. But was that really correct? Or, maybe, did he just witness her speaking naturally and every other time he spoke with her, when she had seemed more detached, that was less natural? He could not be sure either way.

"Now it's Altrond's turn." This came from a smiling Clerin. It made Vrric wonder if she had already heard his story. Not that it mattered.

"Ah, yes. Mine was an accident." Altrond looked a little smug to Vrric.

"I do not think meeting a Vijen could be accidental." This was from Trela, but Vrric was thinking the same thing. He exhaled through his nose and made a small nodding motion to show his support for her statement.

"Well, certainly not for the Vijen. But for me... it was definitely accidental." Altrond paused for a moment to allow any others to interject. No one else did, so he continued. "I was with a friend who has also, unfortunately, already passed on. His name was Baventian, and he was a spectacular spy. He specialized in climbing and acrobatics. He could sneak through any upper-story window, no matter how difficult to get to or get through." He paused and had a wistful smile similar to Ryshial's. Vrric wondered briefly if everyone viewed their young friends who'd died in the same glorified nostalgic light. He did not have that dilemma, though that was probably more due to his dearth of close childhood friends rather than all of his acquaintances being alive and well.

"Bavey was obsessed with the Northern Desert ever since we were children. He read all he could about it. In fact, it was he who first showed me this book." Altrond lightly waved the book he was holding, his finger still holding a place between the pages. "Now before you say that our meeting could not have been accidental, I am just mentioning this because he loved to camp out at the edge of the desert. We grew up in the village of Salcrom, just at the edge of the desert, and whenever we had a week to spare we would head out with as many provisions we could carry and build a canvas shade bivouac. We were always careful to stay at the edge, to avoid the shifting dunes. Bavey's mother was particularly adamant about that, and there were always stories of children getting lost and dying of thirst out amongst the dunes. Of course, their bodies were never found, so the stories always had an air of speculation about them as well. But I was young, and I believed, rightly so, that the desert was dangerous.

"So there we were, children on the edge, sipping safely from the cup of danger, when Bavey suggested we take a quick day hike. 'We'll keep the bivouac in view the entire time,' he says to me. Luckily, we still carried a fair amount of water with us, just in case. I kept glancing back and saw the canvas flapping in the breeze. It seemed so close every time, even though we had been walking for a while. It was comforting. Then, even though I glanced back on the same interval as before, when I turned back there was just nothing there. We stopped and stared. We could see our footsteps stretching out in the direction we had come from, so we headed back with the small haste that worry brings. Then, even though the entire day had been as calm as could be, a gust of wind picked up and did not die back down for an incredibly long time. I would like to say the windstorm lasted for an entire hour, but my sense of time at that moment was admittedly askew. At first we tried to run back towards our camp, to follow what was left of our footprints, but it was incredibly disorienting to move at all. So we made the choice to hunker down and wait the storm out as best we could. When it finally ended, we could see nothing but dunes. We were completely lost. We had placed our legs facing where are tracks were headed, so we went in that direction, but we just never ended up anywhere. I kept expecting that at the top of the next rise we would see our bivouac. But… nothing. As the sun was hanging low in the sky, our panic began to set in. We had brought plenty of water but no food. Not that we would have died of hunger before succumbing to thirst, but our bellies were rumbling, which made the panic that much more pronounced.

"It was then that we saw a tree in a valley of dunes. We ran from the ridge we were traversing, half sliding down the slope, to get to the tree. There was no reason to it, but in my mind I kept imagining another windstorm rising up and obscuring our vision of something other than sand. When we reached the bottom, we heard the overly loud voice. It flowed along the valley floor like a river of sound. 'You have finally arrived. We have been waiting for you both, yes. We have tugged at you for some time now, but you have been adept at avoiding us. No more.' It was the oddest greeting, chastising us for something we were not conscious of. As if we would have even known what to avoid." Altrond smiled for a moment and looked around the room, as if seeking commiseration. Everyone was quietly waiting for him to continue, however. "The Vijen shook itself for a brief moment, but no leaves fell. 'There is a riddle in the desert and one of you should glean the answer.' Bavey was quick to respond. 'What is this riddle?' The Vijen would not readily answer but dodged the question with one of its own."

"That does sound like a Vijen." Clerin broke in. She was a little late for the commiseration, but Altrond smiled warmly at her for her efforts just the same.

"The Vijen shook itself again and asked, 'Which of you desires the knowledge the most? That is one part of the riddle.

Another part is to deny desire and reward patience. But then, you ask, what is the reward? Some rewards are so difficult to ascertain, so miniscule to the impatient eye, as to not be desirable. Some quests should be forgotten, and some cannot be. You will not know the latter until you attempt the former. Listen to your own voices, hear yourself speak. Desire is made, it is not born, it does not burst from nothingness like the last element. Your search for the riddle will bring you to questions, questions that will be answered by knowledge gained, that knowledge will bring you desire, that desire will rob you of your patience, and you will be unable to answer the riddle with the knowledge you finally hold. But how else to find the riddle?' And here it stopped. We waited for it to continue without any prodding, but the silence just kept stretching. I could think of nothing to say, nothing to contribute.

"Finally, Bavey spoke. 'You are the riddle and we have just found you.' At this, the Vijen roared and laughed and shook itself mightily. 'You are close, young derlian. Much closer than many who are older and should be wiser. There is more to the riddle than just I, however, and that is your first error.' It went silent once more.

" 'What is the next error?' That was my one contribution to the entire conversation.

" 'So many to choose from, how does one put them in order?' It was quiet for a short moment while it shook some more. 'Your point is taken, however. We may not lead your questions and then mock them because they are too broad. Though they definitely are too broad. Back to the question. Another mistake in your assumption, hmmm… We will state this: you have been seeking the past as if time flowed for us. It does not. It is in total, even though we have chosen to desire to speak with you now. Beyond us, however, the past is dead to all derlians. It is the future you may mold and shape only. You should focus all of your seeking to your future.' The silence grew once more until Bavey spoke up once more.

" 'Which one of us shall glean the answer?' The tree shook and bellowed with mirth for another brief while.

" 'Too poignant. How to answer such a thing? We will state this: the one who realizes what the riddle is will not be the one who gleans the answer.' Then Bavey became angry, his hands became fists, and he shouted wordlessly to the sky.

" 'How can you tell us to find a riddle without any directions? That is like saying there is a specific grain of sand here amongst the dunes. Every grain of sand is specific! There are riddles everywhere! We need some differentiating characteristic if we are to even attempt a search. Or else there is no search, just a perusal of various grains of sand.'

"The Vijen stopped shaking. I thought Bavey had angered it with his outburst, but it did not retort with any emotion. It simply said, 'Turn around and look at the horizon. There you will see what you are to seek.' So we did. And you know what, there was nothing there. Just dunes fading into the distance. I did not want to seem like I didn't know what I was looking for, so I stood there staring for quite some time, squinting with my hand held flat over my eyes for some shade.

"Bavey broke first and turned back around. I was waiting to hear him yell at the Vijen again, but when he spoke it was in a quiet and defeated voice. 'It's gone, Altrond. You don't have to keep staring at nothing.' But then I looked down and to the side, rather than turning back with the bleak Bavey, and there was our bivouac flapping in the distance.

" 'I found the way back.' I know there was too much joy in my voice, but I was just happy to have a direction to head. More than talking with Vijens, more than solving riddles or figuring out what they were, I didn't want to be lost in the desert anymore. At that point I figured any one path was as good as any other. Before I could start walking, however, Bavey interrupted my thoughts.

" 'Look, a leaf!' I turned and walked over to where he was standing and there it was just lying in the sand, a golden leaf. We looked at each other, wondering to each other in unspoken glances. I shrugged my shoulders to him, hoping he would pick it up. His lips curled into a small smile. He took two steps and bent over, his hand extended out towards the leaf. Just then a huge gust of wind picked up. It tore the leaf from the sand and sent it tumbling through the air. Unconsciously, I lunged for it, but it was moving too fast and too erratically for me to catch. We watched it sail up and away for a moment, not really understanding the significance of it, when the wind shifted directions and began to blind us with a stinging wall of sand. That's when I grabbed Bavey's hand and ran flat out towards where I last saw the bivouac. Typically, Bavey was the type of Pyran to immediately resist when you tugged on him, but this time he was completely compliant. We ran together at the leading edge of the dust storm. There was the sound of the wind, of course, but there was a low growl, a grinding noise, along with the higher-pitched howling of the wind. We half ran, half slid down the hill we had been standing on. Finally, before the storm really hit, we made it back to our bivouac. This storm lasted longer than the previous one, but it was easier to weather since we had some shelter."

Altrond sat back and looked around until his eyes settled on a glass of water. His lips looked dry as he reached over to the little table. It was silent while he drank half the glass in a single motion.

"You have an amazing memory." It just popped out of Vrric's mouth. Drawn upwards by the vacuum of the silence.

"Yes, I'm eidetic." He smiled lazily back at Vrric.

Vrric was not sure if that was the proper way to say that. It was odd, he had almost warmed up to Altrond during the story. Well, to be perfectly honest, he had warmed up to him, but now he remembered what annoyed him about Altrond. There seemed to be a certain air of smugness that clung thickly around him like a fog.

"So a Tlana is non-corporeal, just smoke, without the Vijen leaves, yes?" Trela dove into the conversation and began to steer it. Everyone nodded quietly, but thoughtfully, at her question. "But this smoke form can still affect the minds of derlians, even if it is unable to affect their bodies, yes?"

"Wait, wait." This was Ryshial. "I agree with your statement, but I am not sure if it runs in both directions." No one interrupted her as she gathered her thoughts. "Tlana can certainly affect a derlian's mind whether they are corporeal or not. I also think, but I am not sure, that they are unable to affect the physical world while they are non-corporeal. Opening doors, swinging swords, stealing books, or whatever. But what about casting lightning? Has anyone heard of them doing that while they were merely smoke? And at what level is the mind control in their different phases? When the Tlana that attacked us controlled the Gaen warriors, it was definitely encased in leaves."

"I have never heard of a Tlana using lightning while they were in their smoke form." Aedon joined in. All the others agreed. "As for their mind control, I believe you are onto something there. The Gaen city of Lethos was attacked by… well, by at least one Tlana. We do not really know how many there were, but I do not believe anyone stated they ever saw a corporeal Tlana. The murders there were very curious. At first, and up until the villagers fled, it seemed like they were performed by a single Gaen. Towards the end, there were maybe two or, on an off chance, maybe three attackers. But certainly no one was ever attacked by lightning." She gathered her thoughts while the others waited. "I am thinking that a Tlana, in smoke form, can infiltrate at least one derlian at a time and control their minds. They can make them do things that are completely antithetical to the host's normal character. Murder, rape, theft, arson—the host may not even recall doing these things, though I am not positive about that. I think the Tlana can kill the host at their leisure, but then must escape as smoke. I think they thrive on that mischief. But to truly do some damage, to be able to shoot lightning and control entire swaths of derlians, they need to be wearing the Vijen leaves. I believe they are much, much, more powerful in their corporeal form."

They all agreed. They all nodded together and smiled at each other. Yes, progress. Then Clerin spoke up.

"What would really be scary is if they could become corporeal by killing enough derlians, rather than just by being encased in leaves. If they could somehow slowly coalesce into a corporeal form with enough misery and bloodshed." She was squinting at something on the floor in front of her. Or at least that was what she appeared to be doing.

"No, we cannot not think that." Altrond looked serious for once. "The Vijen are the key. They have always been the key. They have always been linked with the Tlana. The two cannot be fully teased apart. We need to enlist their aid if we are to hope to accomplish anything."

"So if we destroy every last Tlana, do we also kill the Vijen?" Ryshial had a wry smile on her face. It made it difficult to tell if she was being serious about her question or not.

"What? Well, I don't…" Altrond attempted to defend his theory halfheartedly but was immediately interrupted.

"The Vijen are neutral and do not need to be destroyed. If honesty were of the highest value, I would admit that even the destruction of the Tlana is out of our scope." Taglo had been silent for so long, tucked away out of view, that Vrric had almost forgotten it was still in the room. "Our mission is narrowly defined; it is deliberate and imbued with intent. We are here to destroy the Cabal of Lochom. We are here to stop the Yavencide. That must be accomplished at all costs. Everything else is a purely academic exercise."

"If you recall, we were recently attacked by a fully corporeal Tlana with a horde of Gaen warriors under its control. I hardly think this is an academic discussion." Altrond glared at the Yaven. The quick image begrudgingly increased Vrric's respect for the Pyran spy.

"The Cabal is made up of derlians and its destruction is paramount. We need more Yavens on this mission. You!" Taglo suddenly turned towards Vrric. "Search through the communicator's mind. Sift through every corner if you have to. I shall have a Fluen Yaven join us before we leave this decrepit inn." The Yaven then flowed towards its empty candle in the corner and dissolved into a tiny flame.

The room was quiet for a while as they all looked at each other. Was that a dismissal? Had Taglo "turned off" for the night? Was it still listening, waiting?

"So what happened to the pile of leaves here? I was out for quite a while." Trela broke the silence before anyone stood to leave.

"All rotted. Almost immediately." Aedon looked a little downtrodden, as if the leaves rotted just to spite her.

"Didn't you have a leaf separated from a Vijen for quite some time?" Trela was looking impassively at Aedon as she spoke. "How long did that leaf take to rot?"

"A fortnight. No, wait. It was closer to a moon." Aedon looked at Trela for a moment, as if she were waiting for a reply. When none was forthcoming, she spoke again. "I figure the time difference is due to the leaf coming straight from a Vijen as opposed to being worn by a Tlana for who knows how long."

"Hmm. I wonder if the leaves rot while the Tlana are wearing them. I had never really thought about that." Trela scrunched her forehead in thought. "How fast did the leaves rot when you destroyed the Tlana in the desert?" She stared straight into Vrric.

"I... I don't know. I am not even sure how long I was unconscious for." It was Vrric's turn to scrunch his forehead.

"Almost a full day. It took us a while to find him and a little longer to rouse him." Clerin turned towards Trela. "We left what was left of them in the sand as we entered the shantytown that follows the well. They had not rotted yet; we had just gotten distracted so quickly."

Trela nodded to herself. They smiled and talked a little more, but about nothing of consequence. The energy in the room was subdued. It seemed to have been sucked out of the room by Taglo. Eventually they all dispersed. Well, not all of them, of course. It was, after all, Clerin's room, and Altrond stayed sitting and smiling lazily. Vrric did not feel like trying to wait him out, so he left with the main group. Others peeled away as they walked down the hallway. He almost followed Ryshial, but his room was on the other side of the inn, and it seemed presumptuous of him to just invite himself over. So he found himself walking with Trela and Aedon. Trela stopped in the middle of a hall and glanced around briefly.

"You must find out the spell you'll need from the Blind One. Taglo is right, we will need more Yavens on this mission." She turned to Aedon. "You should go with him. If all else fails, tell the Blind One you need Feyazki to look for something in yourself."

"He will volunteer to perform that service himself." Aedon had her arms crossed, but Vrric did not think it had anything to do with their conversation. "He knows me."

"Then that is the perfect excuse to not to want him to do it." Aedon did not move. "Or tell him it is for another, but do not mention Clerin. Do not mention me either."

"We could say it was for one of the Luften warriors. They would trust me, but not necessarily trust a Gaen." Vrric was starting to wonder if he could just figure out the spell on his own. He thought that if Clerin was willing, it should not be too difficult.

"Perfect, yes. Tell him it is for a Luften. You should not even have to name one of them." Trela brightened. She raised her shoulders and then dropped them and smiled. "Now, I must really be going. I promised Knill that I would not be very long this time." She laughed a little, hugged Aedon, turned and strode down the hallway.

"Well, no time like the present. Follow me." Aedon began to wind her way expertly through the inn. Vrric dutifully followed.

It did not take long to get to the Blind One's room. Somehow, he had inherited the robust innkeeper's quarters. Knock, knock, knock, went Aedon on the stout wooden door.

"It is open." The voice sounded faint through the door.

Aedon swung the door wide and walked slowly in. Vrric peered around her small frame more out of habit than any sense of danger. He only saw one derlian towards the back of the front room. The Blind One was sitting in a large chair that was diagonally situated, staring at nothing.

"You bring a friend, how nice. Please, come, sit." He waived his hand in a vague direction. "Since you have not brought a friend before, may I assume this is not just a social visit?"

"I come seeking advice." Vrric let Aedon sit on the nearby couch and get comfortable before he sat himself down beside her.

"You? You are the destroyer of Tlana. What advice could a humble dirt-dweller like myself offer up to one such as you?" The Blind One's smile was at odds with his words. It seemed sincere and jovial. The self-deprecating statement made Vrric think of the name his old mentor had called him, the hated "Mudfoot." It seemed oddly nostalgic now to think of it. So much so that he almost mentioned it, but Aedon spoke before he could gather his thoughts.

"We have some questions about the skills learned at the school of Larelt. You are the local expert on these matters." The Blind One's smile grew even larger as Aedon spoke. It took on a twinge of… well, it was certainly not sinister, but maybe just a tiny bit of conscious mischievousness.

"And here I had assumed those skills were supposed to be shameful." He swiveled his head from Aedon to Vrric. "Is that not Croy's opinion? He is your apprentice now, is he not? You should hear what he learned from Ilana. She actually graduated from that school, you know. She knew Larelt herself."

"No, unfortunately, Croy is not my apprentice." Vrric was slightly surprised to feel that way. He almost paused to mull it over but he did not have the luxury of time to contemplate. "And from what I understand, Ilana only learned how to work on willing subjects. She did not need to keep them in a jail cell to work with them." The words just kind of popped out.

"If you knew what that Gaen's dreams consisted of, you might have a different opinion. But no matter, you did not come here to discuss my old apprentice." The Blind One's smile grew just a shade tighter and darker. "I assume you wish to peer into someone who is not willing? Or maybe just to do it surreptitiously?"

"Is there a difference in the spells?" Aedon broke in again.

"Is the world different during the night than during the day? If nothing has moved, if every object is exactly the same, is there a difference?" He let out a small chuckle. "If the world is made up of reality, then there is nothing that affects the world like intent. And intent can make as much difference as night and day."

"So much so that the syllables are different, or is it just the guiding will that is different?" Vrric took back over. He did not wish to argue with the Gaen mage, he just wanted an understanding of the word, the somatic element of the spell to be used.

"Ha! You are quick, yes. Croy could learn a lot from you. It's a pity, really." The Blind One leaned back in his chair. "Yes, the difference is great enough to be felt through the syllables. They both use Tot, of course. But you would use Sid on someone who was willing, while you would use Fin... in the other circumstances." The Blind One was nodding to himself.

"It seems odd to use Sid when communing with a live derlian." Vrric squinted a little.

"But you are not communing, are you? No, you are investigating a mind. Try not to think of it as a Majora syllable, but a Minora one that has a specific use." There was a pause after his words that stretched into a large gap. "That is the advice you seek, is it not? Or would you like a demonstration?"

"No, no demonstrations." Aedon waved her hands in front of herself like horizontal knives.

"And what if I cast it before you walked through that door? What if this entire conversation were a demonstration?" The Blind One's smile looked positively evil. "What if every time we have had a private conversation, I have been sifting through that beautiful mind of yours?"

"You wouldn't..." Vrric believed that Aedon meant it as a statement, but due to the up tonal inflection in her voice, it could have been thought of as a question.

"Of course not, Aedon Dea'sol. I have too much respect for you. But... that is why I am distrusted, yes? This is why I do not have any visitors." The smile slipped into a flat line. "You. You shoot lightning from your fingers. Powerful. Yes. Rare, yes. Strange, yes? But what ill effects do you suffer? Do others avoid you? Do they whisper behind your back? My talents are teleporting and looking into others' minds. I am trusted by no one."

"It is not just your talents that put others ill at ease, Narst Dea'jin." Aedon stood but did not move to leave. "It is not even your little taunts, though they do not help at all. It is not necessarily the odd way your compliments are coated in condescension. It is your actions, plain and simple." He seemed to be staring at her while she berated him. "You stole Croy, Narst. What was that? How did that help anyone? While we are sitting here, having a friendly conversation, you tell me you look through my mind when I stop by in an attempt to give you some company. How am I supposed to take that? How would you like me to react?"

"I was joking." His eyes were scrunched at the middle, erasing lines from one part of his face only to make them more deeply furrowed in the front. But it also seemed like he was concentrating. Vrric tried as hard as he could without giving voice to a Word to sense any magic. He could not sense anything.

"You may have been fibbing about violating my private thoughts, but that is no joke. The idea of it is no joke. And you know that it is not. You know the idea of it is disturbing." She started to leave and talked over her shoulder as she walked over to the door. "The worst part is that you want me to feel bad for you. As if your isolation were induced by ignorance, by the ignorance of others. You are right about one thing, however. You are not trusted."

Vrric was still sitting as she left. He knew he should follow her but was somewhat fascinated by the look on the Blind One's face. There was some dejection in there, a little sadness, even some shock, as if he were caught off guard by Aedon's reaction. But also, barely perceptible, so hard to discern that Vrric wondered if he was imagining it, there seemed to be a little satisfaction.

"If you wish to be left alone, you could just ask us to leave. Or better yet, you could have not answered the door." Vrric looked at the Blind One for a moment before standing. He had taken a wild guess and was still not sure if he was at all close to the mark.

"You are aware of much that is going on. You have a keen sense of insight and a powerful mind." Somehow the Blind One's brow furrowed even more. "But do not think you understand my motivations. We are playing two different games, you and I. They are not compatible, even though they use the same board. But you are right about one thing. I wish to be left alone this day." He made a shooing motion with his hand. It then flopped down on the arm of the chair with a leaden thud.

Vrric thought about staying and arguing. He thought about staying and trying to comfort the ancient Gaen sitting in front of him. He thought about chiding him, about getting in one more swipe. Instead, he turned on his heel and walked silently out of the room. In the forefront of his mind, however, he was worried that he would be followed. He worried that if he went straight to Clerin's and cast a spell to look into her mind for the Fluen Yaven's name, he would not be alone in there. The Blind One would follow him in, maybe even invisibly, just to satisfy some… well, to satisfy something. He was right about at least one thing: Vrric should not attempt to understand his motivations. He left the room wondering what the Blind One had seen in Croy's dreams. He was sure he would not get a straight answer if he asked, though. Aedon was nowhere to be seen. She must have gone back to her own room. As he walked away from the Blind One's quarters, Vrric kept his mind on other things. On random things. Unbidden came the image of Gyllhelon. Therefore, with no other thought than to place more distance physically, mentally, and magically between himself and the Blind One, he walked over to the small enclave that the Luftens had made for themselves. He refused to think of Clerin the entire way there.

Gyllhelon was rolling knucklebones with Malghain and Haswyxe. He joined in the drinking and in the game. He spent a couple of hours there, not paying any attention to time, before he remembered that he was on an errand. It was well into the evening by the time he made it back to Clerin's. He had made sure he was not followed, both physically and magically. Or at least, he was fairly sure he had not been followed. It was hard to be one hundred percent certain of anything.

He knocked lightly on the door. There was some minor commotion and Vrric stood there, waiting for the shuffling to die down. Finally, the door was swung open. Clerin stood there, beaming her disarming smile at him. Somehow it washed away any lingering feelings from his meeting with the Blind One, as well as the fog of drink that he was under. She had a light blue dress on with white piping and lace.

"I was wondering when you would be stopping by." She held the door open for him to enter. He strode in and passed Altrond on his way.

"I was just leaving." Altrond nodded at him as he ducked out the door.

Good, was Vrric's unspoken reply. Even though it went unvoiced, it rang back and forth in his own head. The door was shut softly, darkening the room a little.

"So… I guess there is no time like the present." Her dimples deepened slightly. It was odd. He knew she was nervous, but she appeared to be in full composure. Almost relaxed even.

"Would you like to lay down?" He wanted to make her comfortable but wasn't really sure what would help.

"Yes, yes." She climbed onto the bed, straightening her dress as she did so. She had plenty of pillows at the head of the bed, more than enough. She did not arrange them very much, but placed her hands folded over her torso, above her stomach but below her breasts. Like the classic Luften death pose the corpse is placed in during a viewing. He forced the thought from his mind. "Don't wander or dilly-dally or go fishing for other information. Okay?"

"Okay. Just in and out." Vrric took a deep breath. "Relax and take a deep breath." She did so, heaving her chest upwards and then slowly letting her breath out through pursed lips. "Take several slow, deep breaths." He looked around for the small wooden chair he had been sitting in earlier in the day. He found it and quietly set it next to the bed. He did not think he could cast anything sitting on the bed with her. He took several deep breaths himself as a calming measure. He had thought they would sit and chat for a while before delving in.

"Wait, derlian. There is a small disturbance. Everything must be cleared and sealed before you begin." Taglo's voice was not overly loud, but it carried throughout the room. Vrric had not even noticed the candle sitting on the table.

"Thank you." Both Vrric and Clerin spoke the same words at the same time. Then they laughed together. It took a couple of moments, but she brought herself back under control and in a relaxed state.

"I have done what I can. Now you." Taglo stayed the tiny candle flame. Vrric was not used to communicating to it while it was so small, it usually took on a much larger derlian shape. He was not going to comment on that, however. Taglo could obviously do what it needed to do at any size. Not that Vrric understood what it was doing. Yavens were unable to cast magic, so how was it sealing anything?

Vrric could sense nothing. Not the first small disturbance, nor whatever Taglo had done.

"Mekfintotclo!" He cast a sensory spell, but he was still unable to sense anything. Maybe he had cast it at too low of a power level? He glanced over at the tiny candle flame, but it barely even flickered. "Eqetectotclo!" He decided to cast a large protection spell, just in case. Still there was no response from the candle. So he decided to proceed. He glanced once more at Clerin's prone form to make sure she was fully relaxed. "Narsidtotto!" He was not sure how powerful of a spell he really needed for a willing participant, so he overshot a little, just in case. He lightly touched Clerin's limp arm and felt as if he were transported.

It was as if he were in a well-kept garden, but full of tall hedgerows. It was not quite a maze, but he could see the tops of marble statues half hidden behind the landscaped bushes. He had no clue what he was doing. He wished that the Blind One had been easier to speak with. He wished he had been able to garner some more advice. He had hoped he would just have to speak the question and the answer would appear. That made him pause. Why not? "What is the full name of the Fluen Yaven that you traveled with, the one you call Wil?" He spoke it forcefully, but quietly, just in case he was also speaking aloud inside Clerin's room. He waited for several moments, but the answer did not appear before him. He turned and started walking between two large hedgerows. Around the corner stepped Clerin.

"I heard you needed a guide." Her blue eyes sparkled. "I'll show you where it is, but you may have the same problem I'm having."

Without waiting for a reply, Clerin turned and started wending her way amongst the greenery. Vrric followed quietly. It took some time, but he finally found himself at one of the statues. It was an angry looking Fluen holding a trident. The bottom half of her was a large scaly fish tail. She was on a small pedestal that rose up out of a large fountain. The fountain was surrounded on three sides by holly bushes, their sharp leaves creating an impenetrable barrier. He stopped at the open side of the fountain and stared at his own image in the rippling water.

"It's in there." Clerin pointed to the fountain. He turned to look at her. She just grinned and pushed him in.

He tried to hold his breath but he yelped when he hit the water. He was fully submerged, swallowed hole. His legs kicked in wide random circles, trying to find the marble edges that had seemed so close just a moment ago. He was finally able to tread water and push his head above the surface, which seemed in the opposite direction from where he fell in. He was at the edge of a small river and struggled to pull himself up on the bank. There was a copse of trees nearby and a small horse path that ran along the riverbank. He coughed and sputtered for a moment but was easily able to stand up. The sun was high and was attempting to dry him out. He looked to his left. Nothing. He looked to his right. There was Clerin and two other Fluens. As he walked over to them, Clerin brightened.

"This is my mother, Midinarre, and my old magic tutor, Olwinn." Clerin swept her arm towards each as she spoke. They completely ignored him, as if he were not there at all. He walked over to them and studied them. Their features were fuzzy and out of focus, like looking through a reflection, or if you squinted so hard that only rough outlines reached your eyes. Midinarre was more in focus than Olwinn, but what was odd was that there were a couple of items that were stark and vibrant. A brooch, a dagger hilt, her mother's boots, one of the horses, and in vivid imagery so sharp that it appeared to move in slow motion, a geyser erupted from the river they were next to. As it boiled and bubbled, everything else became fuzzier and out of focus. Waves crashed over waves as it moved itself onto the land. Olwinn began speaking to Midinarre, but it was impossible to decipher. There were words, but it was as if they were not fully spoken, as if there was a buzzing hive of bees in the background, making comprehension impossible.

"Midinarre! You... zzzz... possible... zzzz... amaze... see... zzzz... brought Wilshengar... zzzz." The scene stopped and Clerin walked back over to Vrric.

"I have played the scene hundreds of times in my head, but most of the details are just not there." There was a look of frustration on her face. Worried frustration.

"Try again." Vrric was wondering what he could do to help. But nothing came to mind.

The amazingly scintillating scene of the Yaven raising itself from the river replayed out again in perfect detail. Olwinn started to speak. Vrric let it run through. "amaze... zzzz... see... zzzz brought Wilthenzar..."

"It was different this time." Vrric spoke up once she had paused the scene once more.

"What?" Clerin looked quizzically at him.

"The beginning of the name, it's a little different this time." Vrric crossed his arms and started to pace. "This isn't going to work. Your memory is warping it each time you replay it." His mind was working furiously but not getting anywhere. He needed deeper. He needed to be able to see the scene, but not from Clerin's memory.

He needed to see what she actually saw, to hear what she actually heard. He knelt by the edge of the river, staring down into its shallow but invisible depths. He waved over to her. "Come here, you have to see this." He saw her approach in the warped reflection. She knelt next to him. He turned to her and smiled. Then, with as little warning as possible, he grabbed her and threw her into the river. He jumped in after her and dragged her down towards the riverbed. The current was strong and she struggled in her panic, beating him with slow-motion fists. She spun him around, he spun her around. He lost track of where the surface was. Then he found the bank. He struggled to drag himself out. He wasted no time but stood, looked left, then looked right.

All three Fluens were standing there as bright and vibrant as if they were standing before him in broad daylight. Clerin did not look over or acknowledge him whatsoever. He jogged over to where they were to be able to hear them better. Just then the river began to boil and the Yaven coalesced into being. Olwinn began to speak again: "…brought Wilthenharkenopnorang." Vrric replayed the scene several times to ensure he had it memorized. Then he pulled himself out of Clerin's mind. He did not wander or dally or fish.

As soon as he snapped back, away from Clerin, he felt the nauseous vertigo of casting a spell above his skill level. It was a little odd, since he only cast at the Nar power syllable. Maybe it was due to the other spells he cast before that one… He was unable to ponder it, however, since Clerin began screaming almost immediately.

Taglo grew as it leapt from the candle to the table to the floor. It was roaring as loud as Clerin was screaming. Her eyes were squeezed tight shut but her mouth was wide open. Suddenly she began coughing and sputtering, her whole body racking with the effort. Water shot from her mouth as she coughed. It soaked the bed sheets in front of her.

"What did you do to her?" Taglo was a gigantic inferno at the side of the bed. The flames flickered and seethed. "Her importance is greater than yours!"

Vrric did not know what he had done. It must have had something to do with pulling her into the river in her mind. While his body moved and reacted, his mind wondered how real water had gotten into her lungs. He curled behind her on the bed and held her torso upright as she coughed up more water. Her bones felt thin and hollow as he gripped her, as if he could snap her in half if he held her too hard. She coughed for some time while Taglo made its vague threats.

"Mekliderto!" She coughed again after he cast his healing spell. "Mekliderto!" He cast it again and she vomited up more water. Her body was held tight, but she stopped coughing. She took a few ragged breaths. She tucked her arms in against her chest and then suddenly, without warning, she shoved him off the bed.

"How dare you leave me in there to drown!" Her icy blue eyes flashed with a quick rage. He just lay there on the wooden floor, trying to collect his thoughts.

"I'm sorry, I had no idea…" He tried to apologize, but she threw a pillow at him.

"Get out!" She grasped at a small dagger on her nightstand. Luckily it was still sheathed as it struck him. "Leave! Don't you hear me? Leave!"

Vrric stood while she franticly searched around for something else to throw at him. "Wilthenharkenopnorang. The Fluen Yaven's name is Wilthenharkenopnorang." He turned and left, not knowing what else to do. His apologies could not do any good at that moment. He would have to try again later.

Chapter 9

Author's note:

Conversation between Yavens does not occur in simple words. However, due to the difficulties in translating non-verbal communication, that is how the conversations are represented here. The author regrets any errors or omissions due to this inferior attempt at conveying this type of communication.

Wilthenharkenopnorang pondered the meaning of identity. Each thing was unique in the Yaven realms, and each unique thing was named. There was, of course, the constant surrounding water. That was not unique, not named, not specifically at least. But the water that coalesced into a being, the water that could think of itself as a Fluen, well that was certainly unique. The naming of a thing was rooted in language. Truly, in the beginning, that was the only reason for language—to name things. Language was a tool of separation and not, as Wil had heard some derlians posit, a tool that brought things together. Of cooperation maybe, but certainly not of melding or even congealing. No, a name was a designation of separate uniqueness. "I am me. You are you. We may agree, but we do not think the same." To a Yaven, the length of a name did not matter. Before derlians, names would take time to speak. Real time. Yaven time. It was a form of entertainment, really. Instead of a word at the beginning of a sentence, it was a paragraph at the beginning of a chapter, a chapter at the beginning of a novel. The first book of a series. It spoke volumes. It held nuance. It was a description of the creativity of the owner. It was the first type of Menel. Before the Belegs created the derlians, before the derlians found magic, before they found the Yavens. After that, names were shortened immensely.

Wil pondered the meaning of magic. It was understood to be spawned from the inexorable chaos that emanated from the mixture of the elements. It was understood that derlian mages could sift through chaos and bend the immediate future to their will. It was understood, but it did not make sense to Wil. Just because anything could happen did not mean that everything did happen. That was self-evident. And how did the first derlian mage to make contact with a Yaven even think of such a thing? Were the legends of the derlian homeland that strong as to tug at such a chaotic thing as derlian imagination? Was it the remembrance, in their blood, in their essence, of whence they came? It made no sense. It made nonsense. It was not more improbable than the existence of magic—nothing made less sense than that fundamental derlian experience to Wil than that—but it was highly improbably just the same. It made Wil wonder how much help the derlian children were given by the Belegs. Why would a creature create a caricature of themselves, an imperfect and fragile caricature, rather than stay with their fellows? Why would a Beleg help a derlian instead of assisting a Yaven? What fundamental change made them turn their backs on what they were, on their very reality? Why would an imperfect fiction be preferred over the truth?

Wil pondered the minds of the Belegs. This was where chaos must have begun. This was where magic must have first been imagined. Wil pondered their meetings in the Void, before the creation of the derlian realm. Before the transformation of Yavens into derlians. Back in the darkness, back in the emptiness. Before they even became Belegs, back when they were still Yavens. Staring at each other across the vast nothing. Did they think of chaos at that point? Was it a tiny glimmer? Was it discussed? Was it desired? Or did it not come into being until they became Belegs? Did chaos spring into being at the first realm they immersed themselves in, unknown and unknowable, or did it spring into being only after they had visited all the realms? Did they notice it in that brief in-between time? Tiny, but growing. No, not quite growing, but consuming. That was how Wil thought of chaos, as an inexorable hunger, an eternal consumption. Did that mean that the Belegs were more than other Yavens, as was generally supposed, or did it mean that they were less? If they were partially consumed, even if they were infinite, would they be less? Is half of infinity less than the whole of infinity?

Wil wandered while pondering. It was a common Fluen Yaven trait, traveling and thinking. Shifting slowly through the realm of water, not having to pay attention to obstacles, floating. The mind wandered as much as the body did, or the body wandered as much as the mind. Wil often thought that the mind and body of a Yaven were symbiotic. They worked well together. It could be conceived that the body was under complete control of the mind. That the one precluded the other. And it was certainly true that the Yaven body could immediately take on any shape that the mind could think of. But Wil liked to think of them working together in concert. This was in contrast to the derlian dichotomy. It seemed to Wil that the derlian mind was in constant battle with its body. And, more than not, it was losing. The derlian body felt such urges unknown to the Yaven body. It could not change shape without damaging itself, it grew fatigued, it grew old, it grew hungry. Hungry!?! The concept was completely foreign to the Yavens. Wil pondered and wandered. It must be that chaos was constantly consuming them, nibbling and gnawing, diminishing them, that they must then be constantly consuming everything surrounding them. Maybe it was a subtle form of aging, a constant reminder of chaos's cadence of decay. It seemed strange that a mind powerful enough to utilize chaos to reach across the Void to communicate, to compel, to summon a Yaven armed with only its unique identifier, its own truncated name, was so weak as to be unable to control its own vessel. Hunger was one thing, strange and horrible but at least understandable if framed within the essence of chaos, but the strange desires embedded within the derlian body were often unfathomable. The uncontrollable passions that led to murder, to rape, to torture, made little sense. Yavens did pair-bond, though rarely for life since life could be an eternity. Therefore, the idea of betrayal was understood by the Yaven mind. In fact, it was one of the few instigators of the rare murders that happen amongst Wil's kind. But torture was unheard of. That was purely a derlian invention. And the rate at which the derlians slaughtered each other boggled the mind. Or, at least, boggled the Yaven mind. It must be the body, thought Wil, that pushed the mind beyond such limits so quickly and easily in derlians. The derlian body seemed to override its own mind so easily. How could such a weak organ control such a powerful force like chaos? Wil did not have an answer.

As Wil wandered, it began to veer towards a friend's home. Though the Fluen realm was made purely of water, there were different densities. The least dense was invisible to the general passerby, much like air was in the derlian realm. There were permanent structures that were opaque, and there was every shade of density in between. This should not be confused with buoyancy, however. There was no gravity, so the Fluen realm knew no up or down, or at least not separate from left and right, forward and backward. There were just open fields and enclosed spaces in any direction. The realm allowed three true dimensions of movement. There was still friction and inertia, things slowed and stopped eventually, but they mainly moved in straight lines through the least dense portions of the water, curving only due to the thickness in their path. Fluen Yavens easily flowed where they wanted to go. Thinking with their mind meant moving with their bodies. The density of their bodies were fluid as well. The least dense water flowed around them as they moved, imparting little drag. The most dense water was impossible to move through, like stone to a derlian. But there was a range of density in the middle that, if a Fluen Yaven was adept, they could loosen their own density and *push* themselves through. That was something that Wil had yet to see a derlian do, even with magic, but with that it certainly seemed possible.

Wil was on its way to visit to its old friend, Glufchentsdonclory. As it got close to Gluf's densely walled home, its mind wandered over to the derlian that had spoken with Lembin. Wil somewhat regretted not gaining more information, more description, of their conversation. There were few derlians, and even fewer Yavens, who had spoken with a Beleg (after the Turning) who would freely discuss their conversations. The Belegs were an addictive curiosity for Wil and now, in the full comforts of the Fluen realm, it felt that it had squandered that rare opportunity. A mistake that it did not plan on repeating if given the chance again.

Wil was traveling diagonally, floating towards Gluf's home, when it thought of how much the derlians appeared to enjoy straight lines. It was true that the derlian realm had constantly varying topography, which made truly straight lines impossible. But they always seemed rooted to the ground, stuck on paths made up of ruts. And how they loved their roads! Each city made up of lanes and avenues lined with dense buildings, each forest made up of trails lined with thick trees. As Wil shifted angles to avoid another dense home, it wondered about what the Gaen realm consisted of. Was that filled with different densities of soil and stone like the Fluen realm? Or was it solid and implacable with only trails cut through the stone for the Gaens to travel along? Was it like what Wil assumed the other three Yaven realms were, or was it like the derlian realm? Wil's only experience with sand and gravel was in the derlian realm. The same as with wind and fire, but they seemed as fluid as water to Wil. Wil examined its own Menel as it traveled. There was a tiny piece of stone at the surface, a hardened slice of elemental gel adjacent to a piece of fire and one of air. Wil had to keep the Menel surrounded by itself since the Fluen realm wished to dissolve the tiny stone, to absorb the tiny air, to extinguish the tiny flame, and was only kept at bay by the eternal vigilance of its owner.

Wil traveled diagonally, sensing the way ahead to avoid any obstacles that might occur, sensing the direction towards Gluf's home, sensing the Menel in the middle of itself, wandering and wondering. The tiny piece of stone was hard and implacable, but so was the piece of air. Why would the essence of stone, as it was represented in the derlian realm, dictate its essence in the Yaven realm? Not counting ice, there was no dense water, no solid water, to be found anywhere in the derlian realm. Nothing like the water that was used as the opaque building blocks in the Yaven realm. So, if stone was only represented as the opaque building blocks of mountains and castles in the derlian realm, why would there not be fluid stone in the Yaven realm? Wil decided that it would like to meet a Gaen Yaven in the derlian realm at some time and discuss this. It was always difficult to meet other Yavens after being summoned, and even harder to speak your fancy. Wil decided that it would refuse to go to the derlian realm for some small errand. It would bide its time until the right summoning happened. Something greater than just a little elemental gel to harden into its Menel.

Wil reached Gluf's home before it was done wondering, but that could not be helped. It was rare that Wil finished wondering. The home was quite spacious, space meaning little in the boundless expanse of the Yaven realm. Its front facade, that which was meant to greet all visitors, was quite pleasing to Wil's senses, which was part of what attracted Wil to Gluf. Like many Fluen buildings, the home's exterior form was a flowing extension of protruding spirals, inverted whirlpools, jutting wavelike curls and wild splashing spray. And the movement! Unlike the dead solid of the derlian realm, the solid of the Fluen realm rotated, spun, ebbed, and flowed. If the home were described musically, it would have been a fugue. A simple pattern repeated upon itself. Now an octave higher, now one lower. Now twice as fast, now four times slower. The pattern might start with a certain instrument, and before it finished, another instrument chimed in, then another instrument and another until, by the time the pattern from the first instrument finally ended, there were too many instruments to count. And then it began again at a different tempo. This was how Gluf's home always appeared to Wil's senses. And what was that simple pattern? What was the base that each curled tip of filigree repeated if you zoomed in close enough? What was the beginning/end of the fractal? A simple splayed cone that spiraled along its longitudinal axis, the base curled upwards in an image that brought a derlian flower to mind, though Wil could not name the flower, the tip split into three and then twisted into thin smoky tendrils. The twisted stem, the ropy spiral, was made of pulsating cords wrapped across each other, rolling with an odd upward flow. These patterns were stacked and fitted together in such a way that their spinning drew the eye upward, to encompass the entire facade. It was an illusion of linear movement produced by an ingenious rotational movement. Wil waited outside for some moments, appreciating the sensory symphony. It was quite pleasing.

Finally, Wil spun through the main entrance. Since Wil already knew the entrance maze, it was able to flow to the foyer quite easily. Gluf's maze was less intricate than most Fluens that Wil knew. Some mazes were so complex that it could take a derlian century to enter into a home if you were unwanted. Gluf was quite gregarious and did not mind uninvited visitors. Wil did not mind visitors either, but even Wil's own entrance maze was more intricate than Gluf's. The foyer was a vast open area. It created an odd effect of widening in the distance, as if the vanishing point were opening up, rather than narrowing down. It always made the interior of the building seem more vast than the exterior. The first time that Wil experienced the foyer, it had been a little disconcerting; now it barely gave it a passing thought. Wil began to flow towards one of the spiraling turrets when Gluf's voice entered Wil's mind.

"I will be there shortly, wait there." The voice sounded light in Wil's head, giving the impression that Gluf was in a good mood. Wil pondered whether or not the voice sounded playful.

The wait took longer than Wil would have liked, but it was not too long. Wil spun in a circle to alleviate the boredom, making little whirlpools that would lift off on their own. It was a habit from youth.

"You arrived sooner than I would have guessed." The voice was in Wil's head before the vision of Gluf floated diagonally into view.

"I had not much else to do." Wil shot several appendages out flat and then slowly curled them back inwards to make an oblate sphere. It was the Fluen Yaven version of a derlian bow. Gluf reciprocated.

"Come with me, there is something interesting I should show you." For all of Gluf's gregariousness, it always enjoyed an air of tantalizing mystery.

Gluf flowed out of the foyer in the opposite direction than it had entered. Wil quickly followed. The way was warped and convoluted. Several times Wil had to thin itself to the size of a wire to follow through the tiny holes in the building that were considered hallways. Wil had never gone this far into the bowels of Gluf's home before. It was intriguing and added to the sense of mystery.

"I know that I was vague when requesting your audience, I hope you do not mind. I had to send the message across too much distance to be more specific." Gluf's voice kept the lightness that it had started with.

"I had no plans, there were no interruptions." Wil finally filtered into the last room. "Besides, I am always interested when you say that you *must* see me." The emphasis was added by Wil, but the word alone was emphatic enough in the original message.

They were in a small room. Though it was mainly trapezoidal in shape, the shorter straight edge had a half circle notched into it. In the middle of the half circle was a small floating sphere. The sphere attracted all attention from Wil. It demanded it. The sphere itself was a darker hue, but it had lighter spots swirling on its surface. The swirling looked somewhat like thin derlian clouds. The darker base material, that of the core, slowly faded a little lighter, then dropped back to dark. The overall effect made it appear to be pulsating deeply while its surface swirled lightly. It was mesmerizing.

"What is it?" Wil was unable to tear its gaze away. There were rough patterns that emerged from time to time, but not long enough for them to become recognizable.

"Guess." Gluf was being terse, but Wil could tell it was proud of... whatever the sphere was.

"It does appear to be water." Wil got closer to inspect it. "May I touch it?"

"It is water. Pure water." Gluf sounded amused. "This is the Fluen realm, what else could it be?"

"Well, it swirls and pulsates as if chaos was embedded into it." Since Gluf did not say Wil could touch the sphere, it kept a small but safe distance.

"It does, doesn't it?" Gluf was definitely amused. "Where would I have gotten some chaos?"

Wil thought for a moment. At first, it thought that Gluf was just going to explain. That they were waiting for a long enough time elapse for Gluf to feel that Wil was properly awed. But as Wil peered into the opaque sphere, it realized that was not going to happen. They could wait an eternity and Gluf would not divulge the secret. So Wil thought. And thought. The only thing that kept coming to mind was too simple. But it was the only answer that came to mind.

"You brought it from the derlian realm." Where else?

"Of course." Gluf was still not forthcoming.

"You placed it here instead of in your Menel... you made a one-dimensional Menel. Of your own element. But how did the gel not harden?" Wil was somewhat shocked. There was never a hint from Gluf that this was going on. It must have taken eons.

"This is my crowning opus. I do not have a Menel, you see. I have never taken a piece of fire, nor stone, nor even air. Only water. Only what you see here." Gluf was almost bursting with pride.

Wil was slightly stunned to think that Gluf did not have a Menel, had never had one. Never showed it to Wil even though they had shared communications of their adventures in the derlian realm. Now that Wil was thinking of it, Wil realized that Gluf had never seen Wil's Menel. They had just never... shared. It was a deception hidden so close to the surface that Wil had never noticed. No, not really a deception. Just an omission. Wil wanted to rerun their entire relationship over in its mind, to examine it at all angles to see if any signs were missed, but there were much more important things to discuss.

"To answer your question, I made the mages that summoned me let me gather the water just before they sent me back, the instant before. I set it up to return here, to this room, to be able to place the chaos-laden water in the collection before it could harden. You see, it takes the other elements to set the gel and since we are surrounded by water at all times... it just never hardened." Gluf had continued their conversation since Wil had paused for too long.

"I have just never heard of a one-dimensional Menel... and the fact that it is still malleable... it is all quite stunning." Wil had a powerful urge to feel it, to taste it, to sense all that it encompassed. With a great effort it was able to resist the desire, however. "Wherever did you get the idea?"

"I was intrigued by magic; I always have been. But I could not understand it, could not cast it. The concept of chaos has no place confined in eternity, has no place in our realm of singular element, even with all its varying densities. So I thought, 'what if I could study it? What if I could examine it completely and thoroughly, for as long as I wished?' It was merely the idea of how I could trap it. How could I bring it here in its dynamic form, not just in a static hardened gel? I thought, 'what is water in the derlian realm? Is it the same as water in the Yaven realm?' It cannot be the same, but it was made from Yaven water, it began as Yaven water. So what was the difference? Why could derlian water be made into a Menel, but then had to be eternally protected inside its owner in the Yaven realms? It had to be the addition of chaos. That puzzle led me to experiment. The first few specimens I brought back failed utterly. The first mistake was letting it sit around, separated, in the derlian realm. That does not work at all. I have to grab it and be instantly transported back for it to retain any elastic resiliency at all. Then I had to learn how to carry it back through the void. How do you think it should be carried?"

"I doubt this is correct, since you asked your question like that, but I would assume it is carried like a typical Menel. In your center, surrounded equally on all sides by your own power, your own protective element, your own self." As Wil spoke, it wondered what the real answer would be. It only proffered this answer to gain the response.

"That is what I had thought at first as well. But something happens under that protection. I do not exactly know how, but the gel would always harden when transported in me. I tried making myself as dense as possible, as protective as possible. I had heard that was just how it was, that the gel always hardens no matter what you do. I had never heard otherwise." Gluf paused for a moment. Wil was mesmerized by the movement of the sphere, such that it understood what was being said, but was not paying full attention. The pattern that constantly swirled was non-repeating. It was not really a pattern, but yet had a vague feeling of similitude, much like the visual fugue that made up Gluf's home. "I was becoming depressed since all my friends were collecting beautiful and powerful Menels and I had nothing to show for my servitude in the derlian realm. With no reason why, I started to wonder how I survived the journey. How were Yavens transferred through the Void, how did they survive the dangerous realm of the derlians?" It took a moment for the mesmerized Wil to realize that this question was not rhetorical.

"Well, as far as I understand it, the Void does not hurt us because we are eternal and the Void attacks through decay. As for the derlian realm, I believe we bring a little Void with us. Like it is somewhat sticky as we travel through it, and it coats us before we arrive." Wil had not done any research into the system for itself but was regurgitating "common knowledge."

"Correct. And what are we? We are the same as the derlian water. And what is chaos? Chaos is a similarly fragile force as our spirit, our own unfathomable animation. So, depressed by constant failure and purely on a whim, I let the gel get pushed along in front of me, such that it was completely surrounded by the Void; but I could, only somewhat mind you, steer it enough that it would not get lost along the way." Gluf laughed with the relief of relived and relieved frustration. "The first few times were only partially successful. It took a lot of practice before I could steer it correctly, 'til I could bring it here, until I could begin to build the actual sphere."

"Then the derlian water does not decay while in contact with the Void." Wil was not really intending to communicate and had, therefore, not expected a response.

"I suppose not. I had not fully thought that through, but that must invalidate the first part of your proposal." Gluf had floated over to the sphere, to watch it with Wil. It took Wil a quick second to remember that the proposal was the regurgitated common knowledge.

"Then I wonder if the Void destroys anything?" Wil could not think of a real reason that is should, but that had always been the consensus. That Yavens were unique to being able to survive the Void. "So… could a derlian travel through the Void?"

"They would still need to be able to breath, yes?" Gluf was thinking aloud, but it had a point. It had *the* point. Yavens did not need anything to survive and that was their main difference. "Even if they somehow survived the journey, for in truth it does not take too long, they would drown upon arrival."

"What if they cast a spell? Not here, of course, and certainly not in the Void, but what if they cast a spell before they left the derlian realm?" Wil was not sure how long derlian spells could last. Most of what Wil had seen disappeared quite rapidly and would not allow for much exploration. Certainly nowhere as long as Yavens could travel about the derlian realm. Not even close.

"That is why I enjoy your company, Wilthenharken-opnorang. You are always thinking, you always come up with something." Gluf turned its gaze away from the sphere to look at

Wil. "Maybe, just maybe, the derlian would survive the Void, would survive the travel. I would guess, however, that the magic stops once they reach the Yaven realm. Chaos does not reign here."

Wil just gestured to the sphere. "Earlier today I would have agreed with you. But now I am not so sure."

Gluf made an indecipherable noise. "Whether or not a tiny amount of controlled chaos, made up entirely of water mind you, has been surreptitiously slipped into this realm makes little difference on what they say their magic is based upon. I doubt, for this complicated scenario, that chaos is the same as possibility. There is simply no future that they could bend into being that would allow them to breathe here."

"They breathe water in the derlian realm. I have witnessed such a thing." Wil wondered if it was just being contrary with its argument. Upon brief reflection, however, it decided it was not. It was merely exploring... possibilities. "In what future even in their own realm are they allowed to breath water?"

"Maybe the possibility they seek is not that they can breathe water, but that the water decays into the constituent building blocks it is made of. And from those blocks, air is extracted." Gluf made a gesture. Wil supposed it was meant to be a flippant gesture. "Like the derlian fishes."

"And that is why I enjoy your company, Glufchentsdonclory. You always come up with something to counter me with." Wil did not think that Gluf was arguing either. They were both merely exploring. "There is a simple way to find out if it will work. Are there any derlians that you are not fond of?"

"I destroyed many elemental gels before I found a way to bring a tiny amount of water to a realm filled eternally with water." Gluf seemed very serious.

"Maybe I have been spending too much time in the derlian realm. That was meant to be humorous." Wil turned back towards the amazing sphere.

"Humorous or not, you are correct about the experiment." Gluf also turned its attention back to the sphere.

They each watched the pulsating, swirling sphere in silence for some time. Wil was not sure what Gluf was thinking, since it had had the opportunity to ponder the sphere for the last... well, how long? Most of its entire life? Most of the derlian realm's entire life? Certainly over a thousand derlian sun cycles. Wil, however, was just now attempting to wrap its mind around the implications. Here it was, Chaos in the Yaven realm. Though it was pure water, which was all that the realm consisted of, Wil somehow expected it to explode at any moment. To rend them asunder, to demolish Gluf's home, to tear a wormhole into the realm and suck all the water out to be dispersed amongst the infinitely vast Void. To do something. But it just sat there, pulsating and swirling. And according to Gluf, it had safely done so for quite some time. Maybe it was not true chaos? Would water, pure water, that had come from the derlian realm need to be filled with chaos? Maybe, even if there was some chaos in it originally, it had been drained during its brief flight through the Void. But there it was, swirling and pulsating, in constant movement. Wil watched intently for a while, clearing its mind, attempting to catch a pattern, or a repetition even, no matter how brief. Eventually Wil decided to give that up.

"So, you have been studying this for some time now, correct?" Gluf made a noise that sounded like a distracted affirmation. "Do you have any insights into chaos or magic?"

Gluf stopped staring at the sphere and turned towards Wil. Well, not really. The face that was staring at the sphere sank into the main mass that was currently Gluf's body and then pushed back out on the side of Gluf's head that faced Wil. It was a Yaven turning, not a derlian turning.

"That is not a very fair question." Gluf seemed slightly agitated. "Is this more humor?"

"No, no. I was not trying to be unfair." Wil had forgotten how sensitive Gluf could seem to be at times. "I was not sure if you had invited me down here to let me in on a secret. You are one of the smartest Yavens I have known, and I figured if there was any Yaven in any of the realms that could come close to deciphering anything about chaos, it would be you." Even after Wil spoke, it regretted it. It was too much. The word "any" was repeated too many times.

"Yes." Gluf appeared to be satiated.

"After all, this is a unique achievement. I would never have thought of a way to bring chaos into a Yaven realm." Wil did not want to leave its last sentence hanging in memory, but wished to replace it with something more akin to truth.

"I have examined and meditated upon it at great lengths. I am unable to make the leap of understanding, however. It is unpredictable, truly. I am unable to find any patterns at all, no matter how long I memorize its movements. Something unpredictable does not dictate the impossible into being, however. It just… does… not. My mind is unable imagine that it does." Gluf's frustration was clearly conveyed. "That is why I thought of you. You have spent more time in the derlian realm than most Yavens I know. You have spoken with derlian mages at great length, have you not?"

"I have." But Wil had to admit that Gluf made sense. Magic just… did… not.

"Then I ask that you examine my prize. That you inspect it and meditate on it. That you provide me with an insight into chaos or magic. I have done all I am able to do with it." The frustration in Gluf's voice gave way to defeat.

Wil stayed at Gluf's home for some time. Gluf did not want the sphere to be taken from its resting place, understandably so. That was an enjoyable time for Wil, for they both enjoyed each other's company. Long ago they had been pair-bonded and they fell quickly into old habits. Much time was spent in leisure. They frolicked and played. They went out and floated amongst the small city of Yavens that Gluf lived near. They stayed in and had conversations that lasted for derlian days. Wil also spent time alone with the sphere, meditating upon its implications.

The largest implication was its mere existence. How was anything that came from Chaos able to survive the eternal Law that was the Yaven realm? Wil truly thought it should be slowing down. It seemed the natural order of things. That chaos could survive there… for a while. That there should be a small drag on it, some sort of friction. Wil thought that maybe it was replenished every time that Gluf brought a new, tiny piece. So, if it were not being reenergized, would it perceptibly slow down? Not that Wil could tell, but it had only been examining the sphere for a tiny amount of time. And since it was chaotic, it would sometimes slow down for a while, only to speed back up. Sometimes the pulsating would slow while the swirling would speed up. Sometimes vice versa. Wil decided that it would need an eon of study to determine if the sphere was losing any energy. And that eon would have to pass without Gluf adding anymore derlian water to it.

The other large implication was magic, of course. That was the whole reason that Gluf had begun this experiment. It was understood by all that Yavens were unable to cast magic, unable to understand it. It was understood that only a creature born of chaos could shape chaos. But that still left a link. The Belegs were creatures of law and eternity, but they were also creatures of chaos. They were, as far as Wil knew, the only four beings who straddled both worlds. That made Wil ponder the essence of the derlian realm. What was the creation method? It was generally thought amongst the Yavens that the realm was created by pouring equal amounts of pure element, of each Yaven realm, directly into a singularity spot in the Void. That the Belegs were merely gatekeepers that turned on and off the spigot that linked each realm to the Void. That what happened during and afterwards were merely natural processes that stemmed from the mixing of those elements. But Wil had heard of a slightly different telling from a derlian. From what Wil could gather, the derlians believed that the Belegs poured the elements through them, that they were the spigots themselves. Would that be a natural process governed by law? Would that be magic? What if the Belegs were the first magicians and the creation of the derlian realm was the first spell? That had a whole host of implications, not the least of which was that the realm would eventually disintegrate. Magic was, after all, the very definition of ephemeral. But it had another implication, a quieter one. It kept dancing at the edge of Wil's mind. Wil could sense its existence but could not quite *realize* it. Could not bring it forth into consciousness. It was a frustrating sensation.

Wil wished it had spoken with Lembin's derlian messenger at greater length. The Belegs were somewhat of a mystery to the Yavens at this point since they refused to communicate anymore. In the Yaven point of view, the Belegs had abandoned them in favor of the derlians. "Why" was a mystery, though it was one that could be guessed at. There were many Yavens who were angered by the hubris of the Belegs. The audacity to create a shadow world full of shadow beings that in some way resembled the monsters that they themselves had become. They were no longer pure, as every other Yaven, as every other known being was. At least all the known beings that were not directly created by the Belegs themselves. Yet there were many Yavens, Wil included, who wished the Belegs well. Who only wished to communicate with them as they had in the past. Wil quite enjoyed the derlian realm, was glad of its creation. It was a nice place to visit that was constantly shifting and changing, constantly full of surprises and entertainments. There were even some Yavens, though fewer in number, who believed the Belegs were the greatest beings in existence. They would give most anything to be able to communicate with them, even if it was just to heap praise upon their chosen heroes. But no, nothing. Not that Wil was aware of anyway. The Belegs had walled themselves off from their brethren and only spoke to derlians now.

Clerin Toswin. That was the name of the derlian messenger. They had spoken of many things, but Wil did not press her for her direct knowledge of Lembin. In Wil's respect for the privacy of the message, it had squandered a rare opportunity. Wil had previous chances to speak with the mother, Midinarre, about Lembin as well, but had missed those opportunities also. Truth be told, that had been much less of a chance than the daughter. The mother was always surrounded by others, always had tasks for Wil, always kept tight control of their conversations. Conversely, the daughter and Wil had traveled quietly through the woods, alone and uninterrupted. Truly, a wasted opportunity.

Then, as if by... well, as if by magic... Wil heard a faint *whisper.* Wilthenharkenopnorang... Wilthenharkenopnorang... The name repeated several times, but the voice was so quiet that Wil almost missed it completely. Wil thought of ignoring the voice, after all, there was so much to do where it was, with Gluf and the sphere. But there was something hidden in it, something slightly familiar, something insistent. So, against Wil's first instincts but more aligned with its second, Wil decided to answer the call.

The feeling of traveling through the Void was a little different each time that Wil experienced it. Most of the time, the overall feeling was of being pulled through the emptiness. Thinned and stretched in front of itself, like being sucked through a straw. Wil usually equated the speed and the (inverse) pressure of the trip with the willpower of the mage casting the summons. There were some that pulled so hard that even if Wil had not wished to answer, it would have been compelled. Some were little tugs, some were neutral questions. This one, however, was barely a thread showing the way to go. There was no pull whatsoever and Wil had to force itself through the Void on its own. Pure push. It flavored the feeling of travel differently. Wil felt like a squished blob. And the effort! It was a monumental task to follow the thread but not pull on it for fear of breaking it. It took all of Wil's energy to keep movement, to keep momentum. The length of time it all took seemed much longer as well. And there was a growing warmth during the travel that somewhat bothered Wil. It was as if the Void had become... thicker, more viscous, more frictious. Wil would have pondered it in more depth if it did not take every iota of effort to stay in motion. Finally, when the heat had almost become too much, when the effort had almost become unsustainable, Wil crashed into the derlian realm.

They were in a wooden building with a stone floor which Wil shattered against. It only took a moment to recoalesce. There were wooden tables and chairs scattered about. Without wishing to, Wil's mind briefly touched on the fact that wood was so prevalent there and that maybe, against all current knowledge, there was a Yaven realm hidden somewhere in the Void that was filled with wood. It was a silly and useless notion that Wil quickly abandoned.

There was a strong lifeforce in the wooden and stone room that immediately caught Wil's attention. It was a Pyran Yaven, burning bright with glory. It seethed and sizzled. Its power radiated from it aggressively. It seemed almost combative. But maybe those connotations were only in Wil's mind. It was difficult to say without any communication.

There were also several derlians in attendance. There was a sinewy but muscular female with odd yellowish eyes that held an unnerving intensity. There was a short derlian with chestnut hair and a short beard. His pale gray eyes were not necessarily staring at the ground, but they were definitely avoiding Wil. There was something odd about the Gaen. It was like a faint scent or spoor that made Wil think of the Belegs for no reason. Then there was the mage who'd summoned Wil. This was what was insistent, what was too intriguing to be ignored. Her large pale blue eyes filled her face with a soft luminosity. It was the messenger!

Clerin was astounded that she had been able to summon Wil. When she had been told of Croy's dream and had summoned Taglo, it had seemed natural and effortless, almost as if Taglo were summoning itself. She was a mere vessel, a conduit, a dry riverbed just waiting to be filled with rushing water. But this... this was a true summoning. Wil had not known what was going to happen, had not already agreed to appear, had not requested the summoning. She had cast her mind beyond the derlian realm and been heard. And had been obeyed!

"Why have you summoned me?" Wil's voice sounded deeper and more aggressive than she had remembered it.

"You are needed to fight the most evil scourge to ever confront the Yavens." Taglo spoke up before Clerin could gather herself, even though the question was quite obviously directed at her.

"And what is this scourge?" Wil turned towards Taglo, keeping the edge of aggression in its voice that it began with.

"There is a group of derlian mages, the Cabal of Lochom, that is destroying Yavens." Taglo swelled as it spoke, gaining in height and in girth.

"That is horrible, but though typically rare, many Yavens have died in the derlian realm. That is one of the risks taken by answering a summons." Wil turned back towards Clerin.

"You misunderstand me, Fluen." There was a condescending sound in Taglo's voice that grated on Clerin. She wondered what it did to Wil. "I did not say killing, I said destroying."

"And… so what is the difference?" Wil spoke in measured tones.

"They trap the Yavens into an item, slowly draining their consciousness until they lose sapience and turn into a mere tool." Taglo explained emphatically.

"Does this lead to death? Is this worse than death?" Wil asked quizzically.

"They are pushed into a coma." Clerin spoke up, trying to clarify. She had heard this explained several times, and at least according to Taglo, it was certainly a fate worse than death. That Wil was not immediately enraged gave Clerin pause. Was this not inherently abhorrent? Clerin's words, however, seemed to anger Taglo even more.

"Their minds are eaten!" The Pyran turned towards her.

"So you have summoned me to help you save these Yavens from these items?" Wil still appeared confused.

"There is no saving them once they have been trapped." Taglo turned back to Wil.

"Then how do you know their minds have been eaten?" It was as if Wil were trying to solve a riddle rather than reacting to the horror of the act. Clerin would have expected that more from a Luften Yaven than a Fluen Yaven.

"They are turned from beings into items." Taglo seemed to sense that its frenetic energy was not assisting Wil to assimilate the issues. It shrunk slightly and moved back a little.

"You are lucky that I wished to speak with you. You were so quiet that I would have missed your invitation if I had not been paying attention." Wil turned towards Clerin. It seemed to be an attempt to close the conversation with Taglo.

"And what do you wish to speak with her about?" It appeared that Taglo could not keep itself under control. It swelled again slightly.

"That is between the two of us." Wil kept itself positioned to converse directly to Clerin, not Taglo. "I am just explaining your good fortune. She is a poor summoner."

"Ha! Yes, I was worried about using someone more skilled but unknown to you." Taglo appeared to be shrinking a little without the direct conflict. Wil did not seem to shrink and swell with the conversation as much as Taglo did.

"I am at a disadvantage. You all know my name, but I do not know all of yours." Wil seemed to be ignoring Taglo. Clerin felt that it was quite an odd meeting. She was not sure what she had expected, but certainly not this.

"I am Clerin Toswin, daughter of Midinarre and friend of Olwinn." Clerin spoke all the names that Wil should know. Everything that she could think of that might have tied them together at one time. "Trela here is the derlian Pyran queen. She rules the warpack we are traveling with. This is Croy Sie'tin, a trusted advisor. And this is Taglo, our… Well, Taglo is the reason we are on this mission to destroy the Cabal."

"My only requirement is to be able to speak with any derlian I wish to, about whatever I wish, whenever I wish, and completely alone. Unlistened to." Will turned towards Taglo. "For that privilege, I will follow you to this Cabal and provide all the power I can bring to bear to destroy them. Agreed?"

"Agreed. I accept your allegiance." Taglo made a small motion with its trunk. A slightly stiff version of a bow.

"Now, I wish to speak with each of these derlians." When no protestations were offered, Wil continued. "Starting with the queen."

Taglo did not speak another word but shrank down to a tiny flame and hopped onto a candle that stood on a brass chamber holder. Croy picked up the chamber holder and walked silently out, eyes dutifully examining the floor. Clerin turned to leave as well, but Wil motioned to her. She stood there for a moment, both of them in silence, trying to understand what it was trying to convey to her. She wanted to ask if it wanted her to stay, to make sure of what she felt the gesture conveyed. But more than anything, she felt that it wanted her silence. In the simplest of terms, she felt that Wil wanted Taglo taken out of the room, to have the presence removed in the most efficient manner. Clerin, and all of the others, let Croy quietly provide this service. It was quiet until door closed and the footsteps faded away.

"Can you sense if we are being listened to?" Wil appeared to be talking to Clerin.

"I'm not sure, but I will try." Clerin thought back to her training with Olwinn. Normally she would cast ---finderclo, or something similar. She assumed that Wil was more worried about Taglo listening in, not just a derlian. Would the Pi syllable work for a Yaven? She had never considered anything like it before. "Nufinpiclo!" Then, because it was a low enough power spell, she added, "Nufinderclo!" She waited and listened while Wil stared at her intently. She could sense nothing. Whether or not that meant that nobody was listing or that she had cast the wrong spells, she could not be sure. "I am not sensing any eavesdropping."

"Good, good." Not that she had found a way to really sense emotions from a Yaven's voice, but she thought she detected a little skepticism in its voice. If so, it would have been well founded. "How about you? Can you sense if we are being listened to?" Wil turned towards Trela.

"No." Trela looked tense, like she was ready to pounce in any direction.

"You are a creature of action, are you not?" Wil spoke in quiet and measured tones.

"Yes. Are you?" Trela stared straight into Wil with her intense yellow eyes.

"No, no I am not. I am a slow creature of patience. I wish to understand things fully before responding, before acting." Wil paused for a brief moment. "I have been asked to make a decision and a promise too quickly for my tastes. I have already responded to these things, so I will not boor you with my lament. I do ask, however—do you trust the Pyran Yaven?"

"Yes and no. I have complete trust in Taglo's dedication to the mission. There is no doubt in that. It truly believes that the Cabal is the greatest scourge the Yavens have ever faced. It truly believes that all of the members of the Cabal must be destroyed. It has true empathy for those Yavens who are trapped and wishes that no others share their fate." Trela took a deep breath. "But I also believe that, like many I have known with an overriding cause, Taglo is completely obsessed. Taglo will stop at nothing. It will sacrifice anything and everything to gain its goal. This is where my trust breaks down. I know, in my heart, that Taglo will stand by and watch me die, watch my entire warpack die, if that gets it any closer to its goal. In that sense, I do not trust Taglo at all."

"Well said. It appears that you, like many creatures of action, are honest and earnest. It is hard to know for sure, since we have just met, but I have little choice but to continue my inquiries. Is there a powerful mage within your warpack that you trust?" Wil continued.

"I know a mage whose only ambition is to gain strength every day. I have found that those with the fewest ambitions are the easiest to trust. Besides, he has had ample opportunity to betray me, in both grand and in menial situations, and never has. At least that I know of." Her laugh appeared to hold real mirth.

"Then I would be grateful if you could put me in touch with this mage." Wil paused again. "You do not mind not knowing the nature of my needs?"

"Of course, not. There are a great many things I do not know, nor need to know. As for setting up a meeting between the two of you, we are preparing a grand banquet tonight, so it would have to be after that." Trela smiled warmly.

"It is not so time sensitive that a day would make a difference." Wil made a small and flippant motion of diffidence. Clerin was not expecting the attempt at body language. "I would like to talk with you at some future date. It appears as if we might get along nicely."

"Yes, I agree. I suppose that is your way of saying you are done talking with me right now." Her smile was reflected in her eyes.

"I do not wish to keep you from your banquet preparation." Wil turned between Trela and Clerin. "The traveling took much more energy than it usually does."

"It has been a pleasure to meet you. I look forward to speaking with you further." She made a small bow.

"Likewise." Wil did a rough replication of the gesture of respect.

Trela opened, slipped out, and closed the door all in one swift, circular motion. Clerin did her best to peek through the gap in the door while it was open. Try as she might, she was unable to glimpse any others outside. Either waiting or listening.

"It has been some time since we saw each other last, has it not?" She stood squarely in front of Wil.

"For you. For me, it has been the blink of an eye." There was a small dent in Clerin's joy at Wil's comment. She tried to recover quickly and was, at first, unsure if Wil had noticed. "I must admit that derlians change quite quickly. Most of the time, I will only serve a derlian once. Sometimes I will only be summoned once in an entire derlian generation, and sometimes even longer spaces of time pass. Of course, there were a few mages that I had gotten to know over several visits. These were usually powerful mages or, at least, they ended up as powerful mages. Sometimes they would start out meekly. I would be summoned by a master or mentor of theirs and shown to the young derlian. Soon, after accomplishing my mission, we would part. The next time I would meet the mage, it would be on their own terms, from their own summoning powers. The mage would exude energy and vitality. After another quick task was completed, I would return to the Yaven realm. Then, almost immediately it would seem to myself and my own sense of time, I would be summoned again. This time the mage would exude confidence and power. The task was almost always more involved this time around, more difficult and more dangerous. Another completed task and another summoning. The mage would now have gray streaks in their hair and some wrinkles. The confidence was still there, but the raw power would be waning. If another summoning were to happen, for four was rare and five has only happened a few times in the entirety of my limited experience, the mage would be a wizened shell of their former glory. Each space in between would leave me with little time to ponder the experience on my own, back in my own realm. Pondering takes so much time when compared to a derlian lifespan, it is unfortunate.

"There were some derlians that each time I was around them, they seemed to be completely different beings. In fact, I would say that many were that way, that they were in the majority. Sometimes I would even treat them as a different being. It was sometimes easier that way, to start over each time. Recently, however, I have thought that thinking of derlians in that way was unfair to them. So I have been trying to keep continuity between summonings which, unfortunately, takes time and effort back in my own realm. It takes pondering on the derlian realm while living in the Yaven realm, keeping some part of my mind on the mage while navigating my homeworld, in the blind assumption that I will be summoned by that same mage again. But sometimes this does not happen. That particular derlian may never summon me again. And this time, even when thinking about you and Midinarre and Olwinn, there was just too much distraction in my own realm. Too many other exciting things to ponder. I was engulfed too entirely to be able to keep a cohesive thought even on a derlian as compelling as you are. So do not feel bad if I say it has been a blink of your eye to me, that our time apart passed so quickly. Do not think that this statement has a disparaging connotation, for it was not meant in that way."

"You are very astute. I had only the most fleeting emotion. I barely had enough time to realize its existence before you reacted." Clerin would have to be more attentive around Wil. She had gotten used to the notion that most Yavens, and most derlians for that matter, did not pay attention to fleeting emotions in others. Clerin found it hard enough catch her own emotions, let alone those of others. "In fact, I do not think that the emotion even lasted long enough for me to have been bothered by it." Her smile felt a little lopsided, it lifted up on her left side. "It would have been forgotten in a moment if you had not picked up on it and explained yourself so thoroughly."

"Truly?" The "face" that Wil kept within the flowing cataract of a veil that was its outer surface squinted its eyelids over its iris-less eyes in a show of the facial expression that was commonly known to be disbelief. Clerin, more than anything, wanted to ask Wil if the "facial" expressions were unconscious. Especially since she did not think that the face was unconscious. The face of a Yaven was malleable and could change at will, so how could the expressions upon it be unconscious? But would that be rude? It certainly would be to a derlian. "How could that emotion be so fleeting as to disappear before being able to be contemplated?"

Clerin thought for a moment. She wanted to shrug and say the word "chaos" and be done with the conversation. That would not be fair to Wil, however. So she searched inside herself for the actual reason. It was a little frustrating since she did not really know the answer, she just knew her statement to be true.

"Well, I think it is a little like your summoning mage. Emotions are so quick to arrive, but they are often difficult to know and understand. Some emotions will only call upon you once in a generation. Or, when they do call upon you again, they do so as different beings. So different as to be unrecognizable. Sometimes, the first time they come, they appear with energy and vitality. Other times they appear as wizened shells." Clerin looked deeply into Wil's veiled face. She wanted to know, more than any other thing at that moment, if the expression shown there while listening to her was *real*. "The effort taken to analyze them, to fully… what did you say? …to fully ponder them is often more taxing than it is worth. Especially if it is fleeting. I do not think you can have a full appreciation for the speed at which a derlian mind can erase, can forget, a complicated and fleeting puzzle. Even one that originates in themselves." Clerin laughed lyrically. It felt great to laugh at that moment, at the absurdity of it all, and she thoroughly enjoyed it.

"Hmmm. I would say 'well put,' but am not yet sure. You have given me much to think about." The Yaven grew taller as it spoke.

"You noticed the emotion by studying my facial expression. My unconscious movements." Clerin paused a moment. She wanted to reconsider but had already begun. "When you speak words, when Yavens talk, are there any unconscious expressions? Or since you have such complete control over your bodies, are there only conscious movements?"

"If they were unconscious, would I know that they happened?" Wil appeared stiff, almost. Like there was less overall movement in the constant shifting veil.

"Well, no. But if they were conscious, you would." She thought for a moment. She did not want to appear to be disrespectful. "Do you have a face in the Yaven realm? Do you need eyes to see, ears to hear? It just seems that Yavens, in general, take on a derlian form just to put derlians at ease. If that was true, then the expressions could also be taken on to put us at ease. And if that was true, they would have to be conscious, would they not?"

"Hmmm. I will say 'well put.' You are correct that my outer perimeter, my shell, my face, whether or not I appear to have arms or legs, are pure conscious constructs. I do not have to look like this.

In fact, I have particular difficulty with legs. They are so spindly and off-kilter, it is like falling and catching oneself, and I have never gotten the true feel for it. It is much simpler for me to grip the ground with a solid base and move as a wave moves across the ocean's surface." Wil gained a little in height while speaking. "However, the face that I have chosen, the way the arms appear, the way my solid base moves, these were all chosen long ago. So long ago that I have forgotten why I chose them to look like they do. Why did I not give myself gigantic, bulbous muscles for my arms? These things are, now, somewhat unconscious to me. When I arrive in your realm, I do not think of how to make my eyes appear, what size of ear lobes to use, or any of that. I think I should put on my derlian mask and converse with the mage that summoned me. In that way, if you knew me well, you might be able to see some unconscious movements throughout my chosen body." Wil shrank ever so slightly when it stopped speaking. Clerin decided to make one more prod.

"I would say one more thing. I think Yavens shrink and swell with emotion more than they change their facial expressions. Even more than their gross body postures." She nodded to herself as she spoke. "At least for unconscious reactions, that is what I look for." She had not fully realized it until she spoke it. But after she heard it aloud, she knew it to be true.

"Hmmm, I did notice that with the Pyran." Wil's size stayed perfectly static. "Thank you for that observation. I will monitor that in myself."

They were silent for an uncomfortable amount of time. Clerin wondered if she should be giving a Yaven any advice. Not just due to the hubris that it implied, that she thought herself intelligent enough to even give such an ancient mind any advice at all, but that it might give unfair advantage to a being already laden with advantage. She did not often think in terms of us versus them, but Yavens were clearly different from derlians. Did Clerin not have some automatic loyalty to her own kind? She decided, quite quickly really, that there was a difference between Taglo and Wil. That speaking freely to Wil was more like speaking to Vrric or Trela. She should certainly keep a tight rein on her speech while conversing with Taglo. For Taglo had told her that it would have no remorse if she died through its inaction, or even its action, if it furthered the cause.

"Is there a scenario in your imagination that involves you killing me?" It just sort of popped out of Clerin's mouth.

"The word scenario is too large. Of course, there is one that might involve your death by my actions. I can honestly tell you, however, that currently there is zero chance of that happening. You are the Communicator. You speak to Belegs. There is so much that I wish to glean from you." It paused for a moment, and almost imperceptibly, got a little bigger. "More than that, however, I do not kill derlians for sport. I need strong reason, almost full nemesis, to kill the mage who summons me. And even more than that, I have traveled with you before. I have enjoyed your company in the past and I look forward to spending more time with you. Though it may mean different things in different realms, here and now, I consider you to be a friend."

"Good. Because I consider you a friend also." And Clerin fully meant it. And though she had no reason to doubt it, she fully hoped that Wil meant it as well. Friendship should be mutually based.

They spoke for a while longer, but of little consequence. Clerin kept steeling herself for Wil to begin prying her for information about the Belegs, about whatever messages that she might be carrying. She did not really know how she would react, how she would respond to such inquiries, and she was afraid of being caught unawares. To her relief, Wil did not bring the subject up. She tried to make a mental note to herself to think of what questions might be asked and how she might respond. To take this reprieve seriously, to use it wisely. To prepare herself for what she knew was coming. Life can have a way of leaving little time for reflection, however. Even when that was what was consciously sought after. The next day they would leave the Forgotten Junction and that evening still held the banquet in front of it. And unbeknownst to Clerin at the time, it would also her first meeting with Vrric since he had left her to drown in her own dream. She had been consciously avoiding him because she was still angry. She was not positive if she should be—could she really die in a dream?—but it was how she felt, and it was easier just to avoid him than to ponder her own emotions.

The banquet was a blandly decadent affair. Much like the rich food, the time entered her with a grand taste but was quickly digested and absorbed and soon left her hungry for more. The only thing that kept Clerin from letting her mind wander too much was the pesky arm of a hazel tree near her chair. Though the tree was quite young and small, the limb curled and curved away from the lower trunk with the seemingly express purpose of tickling her back and arms if she shifted too much. It kept her spine straight and her smile outward.

Trela had decided to not introduce Wil to the coterie. For that matter, Taglo was also absent from the banquet, which was typical. It was only at the end of the meal that she even mentioned her plans to move the next morning. Though she had been hinting for a while that this was coming and Wesduin, the quartermaster, had been in a flurry of activity the last couple of days, it still seemed to take many by surprise. It would certainly be a long night of packing for some. Clerin had already prepared most of her belongings, not that she had much of her own.

She wandered the halls for a little while. There was a restlessness in the air that gave her a quiet feeling of unease. As she finally came to the conclusion that she could not waste any more time, she ran into Trela.

"I have been looking all over for you." The tone was slightly accusatory. "I need you to introduce Feyazki to Wil."

"Why me?" As soon as she said it, she heard how it sounded and she inwardly winced. Of course it had to be her, Wil was in her room. With Taglo? The realization just dawned on her and she wondered if she should be worried. Why would she have left Wil with the Pyran? Maybe, she vaguely hoped, Taglo was still off on its own and had yet to return to the room.

"You know why. And besides, you two cannot avoid each other forever." Trela smiled knowingly. Which was odd, since Clerin had not told her anything about him leaving her to drown in her dream. Maybe Vrric had explained, or maybe even Taglo? Or maybe that was just how Trela smiled and Clerin was reading something into it that was not there? In any case, she felt oddly drained and could not drum up enough energy to overcome her inertia of indifference. Trela had an uncanny way of finding out about everything anyway; resistance was typically futile.

"Fine." Clerin realized that the easiest way to avoid discussing the subject further was complete and total capitulation. "Do you know where he is?"

"I am almost certain that he is in his room. If not, I will put him there before you arrive." Trela nodded harshly and turned to leave. Then, before taking a step, as if she were still thinking it over in her mind, she turned back towards Clerin and grew a wide grin. "Thank you for doing this. It really does mean a lot to me. And to Wil." With that she turned around and left.

Clerin was oddly comforted by Trela's brief statement of gratitude. She turned and headed towards her own room to fetch Wil. It was a gut instinct that Vrric's room would be more secure than her own. She was not convinced that the instinct was correct, but there was certainly no evidence to the contrary either, so she charged ahead with her original thought.

Wil appeared to be alone when she arrived and it quickly agreed to accompany her. Hidden in a waterskin, Wil was quietly conveyed across the ill-fated inn to Vrric's door. They were soon in front of a skeptical looking Vrric.

"And to what do I owe this pleasure?" His smile conveyed a bit of reserved defensiveness, as if he were bracing for a violent blow.

"I need to speak with you." Clerin did not like talking details out in an open hallway. "It's important." She waved her hand towards the open door and stared hard into Vrric's eyes.

"Of course, I do not wish to keep you waiting." Vrric stood back, out of the way, and she flowed right past him.

The reception room of the suite was quite large with several sofas. He motioned towards one of them and she sat down. She felt a small unease at the emptiness of the room, as if all the previous guests had hidden themselves when she came in and were still there, somehow invisible, to listen to her fumble with her words. She shook off the sensation.

"Are we alone?" Just to relieve the last vestiges of worry.

"Yes. Quite." His voice sounded clipped.

"Good, I have someone I would like you to meet." Clerin produced the waterskin, and with a small flourish she removed the stopper.

The roaring rush of sound that came first was of ocean waves crashing upon themselves. Then came an arc of shimmering water. The arc pooled and piled and grew quickly into the shape of Wil.

"Is this the mage that Trela spoke of?" It was said very faintly, as if it did not want to be overheard. Clerin gave a shallow and quick nod. "Allow me to introduce myself. I am Wilthenharkenopnorang, known amongst your kind as Wil, and I... I must immediately ask a favor of you."

"I would perform any service asked by a friend of Clerin's." Then, it was almost invisible as it happened so fast, she thought that he winked at her.

"You do not know the request, so how can you be so sure you will perform it?" Wil finally finished coalescing. Oddly enough, there still felt like there was some water left in the skin, as if Wil took up no extra volume and barely any extra weight. It was quiet for a long moment.

"Then what is the request?" Vrric was brusque after the pause.

"I need to communicate with a friend back in the Yaven realm." Wil appeared to sneak a glance at Clerin. "I was taken so quickly, I was unable to say any goodbyes."

"You see, that is a request that I would gladly perform." Vrric grinned back and forth and then a small startle overcame him. "Do you mean now? In front of everyone?"

Clerin was a little annoyed at the statement. *Everyone?* She was the only other being in the room. As if Wil would even care...

"You are correct, Luften. The less that know, the better." Wil turned towards Clerin. "Would you mind if I spoke alone with the mage?"

"No, of course not. I'll be in my room." She left quickly. She did not want to stand there with their stares locked silently on her.

Did she want to stay and listen? Of course! But it was not the empty snack of gossip that she was craving, it was so that she could provide a more thorough assistance. How could she help if she did not know what the problems were? Or at least that is what she told herself.

Clerin wandered the halls for a while longer. She wondered briefly how Trela had found her earlier. The inn could be a bit of a maze. Or at least it was when they had first arrived. It had been over a fortnight now and winding her way through the crisscrossing hallways felt more intuitive than it had at the beginning. Finally, she looked up and found herself at her own front door.

She walked into the darkness of her antechamber. She walked by a small candle on her table. "Lodepiarc!" The candle lit up and began to flicker with life. She grabbed the brass handle at the base of the candle and held it aloft. She headed to her bedroom, suddenly exhausted from a long day.

As she entered her bedroom, the flame that was on a candle on her mantle leapt off and began to grow at an alarming rate. It was not long before Taglo reached full height. Though Clerin no longer needed her own meager candle, she still clutched the brass base as if it imbued some sort of protection.

"You have spoken with the Fluen? You are prepared to assist me again?" Taglo swelled as it spoke. It made Clerin wonder if that was a defensive or an offensive gesture. The question itself was a bit passive/aggressive, so maybe it was both.

"Of course, what do you need help with?" She decided to ignore it.

"I need a Gaen, another Yaven. I need a Gaen mage skilled with summoning, or at least one who knows the names of some willing Yavens… Can you do that for me?" Taglo's demeanor was exceedingly off-putting and it grated on Clerin's nerves.

"All I can really do is try the Blind One. Do you trust him enough to…?" Clerin was going to continue but was interrupted.

"We have little choice at this moment. Do what you need to but involve that one as little as possible. Either Croy or Aedon is acceptable." Taglo kept increasing in size, but slowly. "Why are we still camped here? When is that queen going to move her troops? We are losing whatever tiny advantage we had after destroying that Tlana."

"We will be leaving shortly, I am sure." She should have stated that they were definitely leaving tomorrow, that Trela had mentioned that at the banquet, but that was not what came out of her mouth.

"We will be leaving tomorrow." Taglo was quite large now. Imposing, but Clerin refused to let it be an imposition.

"That is not your decision. I am sure that Trela…" She was interrupted yet again.

"This is not a request." Taglo half-filled the room. "I need to speak with the queen." Clerin held her tiny candle aloft, ready to carry Taglo to Trela's room. "No! You need to speak with the Gaen. I will speak with the queen. Now!"

Poof! Taglo shrank to the size of a candle flame and slowly dropped to the wooden floor. It then sped off towards the front door. Clerin had always marveled at how the Yavens could choose to affect their environment. There was not a scorch mark on the floor following the tiny flame on its way out. There was not a scorch mark denoting where the inferno had stood. And yet, if it wanted to, Taglo could engulf much of the inn in flames, killing all those trapped inside.

Clerin stood there for a moment, tiny flickering candle held in front of her, and breathed. Just breathed. She wondered briefly if the addition of more Yavens in general, and of Wil in specific, was aggravating Taglo's mood. No, she thought, it really was just the feeling of being trapped by inertia. Of course, her speculation did little for her peace of mind and did nothing for Taglo. She shook her head at herself and turned to leave the room. She placed the candle back on the table and snuffed it between thumb and forefinger. She could not believe she did not tell Taglo that they were already planning on leaving. She wondered what Trela would say. She should have at least warned her.

Clerin decided to visit Croy before trying to find the Blind One to get a name. At a minimum he should know that the Blind One's assistance was needed. She knew that he was uncomfortable around the Blind One, and who could blame him? She felt that, like her, he would rather ignore uncomfortable things. Therefore, she felt that a small friendly nudge was warranted. If he shut the door in her face, she would not begrudge him in the slightest. But he did not.

"I know where he is, I'll take you to him." Croy's head bobbed slightly as he nodded to her, or maybe to himself.

They trod the halls of the inn in silence. She wanted to thank him but was not exactly sure why. She was also not sure if it was the best idea. Would bringing attention to it through gratitude just make the situation more uncomfortable, or would it relieve some tension? A good time never presented itself and so she just walked behind him, thinking that she should thank him later.

The Blind One was not alone. Tesjuk and Nyhan were there sitting comfortably on a large couch against a long wall while Vulthrim opened the door for them. They stood there, in that front room, while Vulthrim fetched the Blind One.

"Have you seen Aedon lately?" The question was innocently posed by Nyhan.

Clerin had thought, at first, that he was directing his question to Croy. It was only after a moment of silence that she realized he was asking her. She smiled at him while trying to think of the last time she had spoken with Aedon. Then she wondered why she had not gone to get Aedon first. She knew the Blind One as well, much better than Croy in fact. He had popped into her head immediately, however, and she had not. Before she could come up with a real answer to Nyhan, the Blind One entered the room.

"Not recently." It was all she could get out before the attention in the room shifted.

"Croy, this is an unexpected visit. We have barely spoken since you have rejoined your foreign friends, and you have not visited my quarters the entire time we have been at this Forgotten Junction. And the Fluen girl. I have spoken with you less than my dear old friend Croy here." The Blind One had his face fixated on the empty spot between Clerin and Croy. "To what do I owe this pleasure?"

"You know why I do not visit. You imprisoned…" The outburst from Croy caught Clerin off guard or else she would have interrupted him sooner.

"We have a request from the Yaven." Croy glared at Clerin before turning to glare at Nyhan and Tesjuk.

"And which Yaven would that be? The Pyran or the Fluen?" The Blind One smiled directly at Clerin, his cold milky cataracts barely veiling the mirth in his voice.

"The Pyran, of course. I had no idea you knew about the Fluen." Clerin quickly realized that there was no use being coy around the Blind One.

"I often know more than those who are told what is going on. Since I must find things out on my own, they are not colored by others' interpretations." He nodded once. "The Fluen is currently with your Luften mentor, correct?"

"Feyazki is not much of a mentor, if you must know, but at least he never imprisoned me." Croy was now glaring at the floor in front of his feet.

"Please, both of you." Clerin was beginning to regret bringing Croy along with her.

"Of course. What is this request?" The Blind One straightened his spine and turned more fully towards Clerin.

"Taglo would like another Yaven summoned, a Gaen." Clerin had not wanted to broach the subject in front of everyone but there seemed little she could do. The Blind One would probably just tell them all anyway, just to spite… someone. At this point she just wanted to get the information and be done with the whole situation. "Taglo would like the name of a Gaen Yaven to summon."

"Oh! Oh, that is quite different than your first statement. Did you not think I would notice?" The smile seemed to be fading from the Blind One's face. "First you say my aid is wanted, my skills needed, my abilities requested. This makes me happy; this makes my heart sing. But then what do you do? You crush everything you laid before me by telling me that all you really want is a name. A name?! Then you can push me back into my hole and go back to ignoring me. This makes my heart ache."

"Well... I think that Taglo is concerned about where the Yaven's loyalties will lie. We are looking for the roots of the Cabal in the Gaen realm." The Blind One should not be the summoner, but Clerin did not how to make that happen tactfully.

"What if I summon the Yaven under your tutelage?" Croy was still glaring at the floor in front of him.

"That would be splendid." The Blind One's smile returned.

"Yes, splendid." And Clerin meant it, even though she knew it pained Croy to even suggest it. It just resolved so many different issues. At least for her.

Chapter 10

Phynalloinchtaghoureack rolled down the tunnel until it was able to rotate the adjacent passageway into perpendicular alignment. Dropping along the chute, Phyna reached out to find the next passageway. It was somewhere close by. Phyna fell for longer than it recalled it needed to. Maybe another Gaen was trying to rotate the top passageway in a different direction. Or maybe someone was using the lower one, the middle linkage, to shift a different tunnel. In any case, Phyna was finally able to connect to it and bend it so that they merged for a split second and then …woosh… Phyna was rolling sideways for a while. It rolled upwards for a bit and then shifted sideways again. Soon Phyna had switched from the middle linkage back to a main tunnel. It rolled along, thinking of nothing, for quite some time. Then another linkage, then another chute, then another passageway, until, finally, the destination was near. Home.

Phyna dropped through a small chute as it passed over its home. Falling, not through air, but through downy silt, or maybe a thin mud, if there had been any water available. And then crashing. Another crack in the stone floor to be healed by time. In other realms, those created by the Belegs, stone began as whole and, once cracked, could never be made seamless again. Unless it was melted by the great underground fires and re-solidified. But there in the Yaven realm, when stone became fragmented, the healing passage of time congealed that fracture until there was nary a scar left. Things wish to be healed, to be whole, and the Gaen realm accommodated.

In truth, that was what the legends stated about the beginning of the Gaen realm. That there was stone in the Void. That there was one mind amongst the stone. That all thought was coherent. There may have been wonder and confusion, but no disagreement, no argument. No discontent. That was aeons and aeons ago. Phyna was young comparatively, and eternity was such a long time ago that only hearsay remained. *This*, thought Phyna, *was why they called them legends.*

It was an interesting concept, that of complete oneness, that of full commiseration. Phyna wondered if the one mind had been lonely. Then Phyna wondered if the one mind could have gotten lonely. If you have never experienced being with another, could you miss them? Words, to Phyna, encompassed thoughts. How could a word for loneliness even exist if it was unknown, unexperienced?

Yet, how could the one mind not be lonely? Even if the word did not exist, even if the thought did not exist, the feeling could still certainly exist. Certainly?

Even more interesting than the legend of the beginning, thought Phyna, was the legend of the end of the beginning. How did the one mind shatter into individual pieces, into individual Yavens? How could discord amongst the living shards lead to a healing of the unknown feeling of loneliness? Was the great fissure planned, an accident, unavoidable, chosen from within or without, agreed upon or argued against? If the only exterior influence was the Void, which according to all sources known to Phyna was no influence at all, the absence of influence incarnate, then how could anything come from without? Phyna stared at the crack in the floor of its home and wondered about the great fissure. It had not planned on those thoughts, which was slightly unnerving for a Gaen, and yet, with no other plans or obligations, it indulged them.

There were three main theories about the great fissure known to Phyna. There were many more smaller ones and many variations of each. The first was that the one mind grew tired of itself. That was the simplest of the theories. That of conscious choice. That of internal forces deciding to release the bonds that formed its own existence. A release. The surrender of simplicity to the desire of complexity. Phyna enjoyed that theory immensely, but like the other two, it left many unanswered questions. Mainly, how were more Yavens created? If the one mind splintered itself into the original individuals, then one would have to conclude that no new minds could be created. If they were, would they not be split from their parents? Would not each generation be split from the previous? That in itself was not difficult to imagine and would be the logical conclusion if the progeny directly drew their existence from those before. But the parents did not die, did not split, did not diminish. Still, that was Phyna's favorite theory. A long time ago Phyna felt that it answered the main flaw in the theory: Progeny could draw existence without diminishment if they were splitting infinities. That answer begot other questions, but it satisfied much of Phyna's doubts.

The second theory was that of natural decay. That the one mind grew constantly larger. That it gained in knowledge and wonderment. That it became so gigantic as to become unwieldy, that it outgrew its confines. It grew and swelled until it reached the edges of the realm. It then built up pressure, swelling without growth, until it all became too much and something had to give. The realm did not, so the swollen mind shattered like an egg scrambled within its own shell. Though this was not the only natural decay theory, Phyna thought it encompassed the idea thoroughly enough to represent the others.

The third theory was that of an external force. There were a couple of differing accounts as to what the external force encompassed and where it came from, but Phyna disliked them all for the same reason. There should have been some evidence. If it was another realm, that of the Pyran, Luften, or Fluen, there should have been some residue or spore. At the very least, there should have been some recollection from either end, but each realm operated for aeons as if they were the only realm in existence. When the first contact happened, after the creation of language and the discovery of the wormholes, it was a complete surprise to all according to everyone's accounts. So, if it were external and it left no trace, that only left two choices. The Void, or some other realm that had yet to be discovered by the Gaens. The Void was pure emptiness. If there was something in the Void that could have caused a fracture of the one mind, then the current Gaen understanding of the Void was completely incorrect and bigger concerns were implicated. The second choice, to Phyna, was absurd and only existed because it could not be disproved.

So Phyna was passively immobile for some time, thinking about the implications of a mostly unknown ancient history, staring at the slowly healing crack in the floor of its home. Wondering about these legends provided little new insight, and part of Phyna's mind reached out to remember why it had begun down the path to begin with. Nothing immediately came to mind except for the statement that, in the Gaen realm at least, things wish to be healed, to be whole. Yes, that was it. All the healing tunnels, all the melding cracks, all of that had to begin somewhere and, to Phyna at least, that had to have begun back when the one mind was whole.

Part of Phyna's mind reached out to an earlier time, before it started to head home, to recall the meaning of why it had left for home in the first place. It was something incredibly important that Alopnoughnreashunglyn had wanted. Phyna, almost unique to its kind, was trying to keep a written record. Alop, an old, if not entirely trusted, friend wished to read part of that library. There had been an argument amongst others and Alop thought it could resolve that argument with history. The rarity of the request imbued Phyna with a certain amount of excitement.

Phyna rolled towards the back of its home. It wished it had come up with the idea for the library itself, but the thought had been initiated by a parent of Phyna's. Most knowledge was known by the Yaven that experienced it. If you wished to know something that had happened before your corporeal existence began, you asked a Yaven that was older. But Hintorsclaernthuflaugrahtoa was an argumentative Gaen. It did not always trust those older beings to speak the truth. It found that, at times, two Gaens of the same age gave a different answer to the same question. That may not have been on purpose, though it may have. Hinto was well traveled and had experienced the derlian realm many times. It was there that Hinto found the idea of writing from the short-lived derlians. Unfortunately, the Yaven language had as many words as it had ideas. It was transferred by thought rather than sound. The walls of the library that Hinto chose to write on kept healing themselves and erasing the meticulous etchings. Many things were against the idea, but Hinto persevered. After an incredibly long time and effort, a room full of writing was etched. What was etched? Hinto's own life. The only thing that it knew for sure, that it knew the truth of; the only thing that could not be argued. Then, once Phyna came into being, the teaching of the symbols began. It was long after the teaching was over, after Phyna had started its own wall of the library, that Hinto had been destroyed in the derlian realm.

To keep the writings legible, Phyna had to periodically re-etch them. From what Phyna could gather, it was almost a form of reading. The deepening of the healing grooves into the library walls. In fact, Phyna had read Hinto's histories so many times that they were memorized, but that was not the point. Phyna had its own life memorized as well, but that was well off the point. The written symbols could settle arguments from outside forces. It was not just as Phyna remembered it—it was as Hinto had written it. Unfortunately, due in part to the constant vigil that was required to keep the writings within the self-healing walls of the library, the idea of writing had not spread amongst the Gaen Yavens as Hinto had hoped. So, the only one who could currently read Hinto's, or Phyna's, writings was Phyna itself. The amount of trust in the writings was about the same as asking an older Yaven. As a tool of settling arguments, therefore, it only worked within Phyna's circle of personal friends. Which meant that it had only been used, as it was intended to have been used, a few distinct times.

After some time had passed Phyna arrived at the library room. It had been so long since it had upkept its vigil that some of the symbols were becoming faint. Not knowing how long it would take before Alop decided to arrive, Phyna began the tedious work of deepening the faintest of the etchings. One of the main problems with the library was that it was impossible to predict which passages would be required in the future. Therefore, all the passages had a similar magnitude of importance. Phyna had wanted Alop to let it know which passage was desired but Alop had refused. It was explained that the trust could only be maintained if Alop could ask about many random passages. The passage that Alop wanted would be somewhere in the middle and each would be weighed. As long as no discrepancy was thought to exist in the random passages, the desired passage would be considered as truth in the midst of the aggregate. It certainly made sense to Phyna.

Phyna lost track of time while deepening the etches. It must have been quite a while since so many lines had been worked over before a gigantic crash echoed throughout the home. Phyna morphed back into a sphere and rolled up the various hallways and tunnels that made up the back portion of its house. It arrived at the great hall to see the large sphere that was Alop slowly rolling away from a large crack in the floor. That fracture had only compounded the earlier one caused by Phyna, deepening and lengthening it.

Alop unfolded itself such that it had a roughly derlian shape to its top half but kept a smaller sphere for its lower half. It was a popular form for in-home travel to take at the time. The arms extending from the trunk could be used to easily affect the physical world around them. In fact, many Gaens enjoyed them so much that they used several of them. Four, five, or six arms were not uncommon to see. There was a head on top of the trunk with vague features. Since that was not how Yavens sensed the physical realities around them, Phyna had always thought it was purely a copy of the ungainly derlian shape. The trunk was placed atop the rolling sphere, being much more stable and versatile than legs, which included the nostalgia that stemmed from the original shape of movement for Gaens. So much so that the full sphere was still, by far, the most popular form to use while traveling any distance whatsoever. Phyna still used it when it was alone. It was the simply most natural and comfortable shape for any movement in its opinion.

Phyna decided it would be best to roughly copy Alop's form. In the Gaen realm there was a strong tradition of copying a guest in your home to make them feel more at ease. Phyna unfolded itself and used an expressive visage. That took more energy, but the amount of energy spent was often used as a gauge of how much respect you had for your guest. Phyna wished Alop to enjoy itself during the visit and to enjoy the library in particular.

Alop reached one of its three arms towards Phyna. Remembering at the last moment to add fingers, Phyna grasped it with one of its two arms. It was a completely derlian gesture and had not been entirely expected. Phyna often kept its own Menel out of view. It was not tiny by any means, but it was nowhere near the size of Alop's proudly displayed one. The cooption of derlian ways by the Yavens was not something that Phyna was excited about, but it could certainly emulate those ways if needed. Their linked arms moved up and then down once.

"Many greetings to you from my friends, my family, and from myself. You are well known for your own efforts and I commend you for them." Phyna waved its arm in the very derlian gesture to skip the traditional listing of accomplishments. Though it had not spent too much time amongst the derlians, it had certainly picked up some of their impatience for certain traditions. Oddly enough, if they were at Alop's home and Phyna was the Gaen who had to list the host's accomplishments, it would have gladly done so. It was more that Phyna did not want to listen to its own list. And it was not only humility that caused this reaction. Alop, for its part, appeared to be completely willing to forgo the tradition. "At this time, I wish to examine the accomplishments of Hinto. You are the most honored of Hinto's progeny, tasked to continue the great work of the library."

Alop also forwent the tradition of using a deceased Yaven's full name. Phyna told itself that it could not pick and choose which traditions others followed, especially after it had instigated the first lapse. Phyna's mind wished to occupy itself with thoughts about the effects of repeated immersion in the derlian realm and the subsequent loosening of traditions back in the Yaven realm, but Alop had continued communicating. Paying attention to an invited guest was certainly a time-honored Gaen tradition.

"...however many there were. Clearly Hinto was a meticulous observer of history." Alop would have continued unabated.

"We should travel to the library and continue our discussion there." Phyna decided to change location and begin any pertinent discussion again. Alop was in full agreement, and they both rolled along the tunnels, delving deeper into the back of the home.

They arrived in front of the etched walls of the library and Alop rolled slowly, deliberately, along the entire perimeter. It took a while to make the circuit at that pace. Phyna did not know what to do with itself as Alop examined the walls, scooting into the many small alcoves that Hinto had created for specific side-stories, to keep the main timeline as the perimeter in the main history. So Phyna situated itself in the center and just turned as Alop circled. Alop did not escape into the adjacent room, the room still under construction, Phyna's room, but returned to the beginning. There was a sense of wonder that emanated from Alop as it marveled at the expanse of the project. That increased Phyna's appreciation, it rarely had visitors and certainly none that spent so much time, with such an aura of dignified curiosity, just drinking in the room.

"This is magnificent. Truly. The vastness of it all." Alop rolled over to Phyna. "This is Hinto's entire life?"

"There are two main sections. From here... to here"—Phyna's outstretched arms encompassed a little over half the perimeter—"...is Hinto's memories of its youth. All that happened before the writing began, before the library began. There are often asides of thoughts or guesses, of philosophical ramblings, of overheard legends of others. It is non-linear at times, almost... chaotic. But here..." Phyna brought its arms together to point to a corner at the edge of a deep alcove. "That is when Hinto began to write everything that happened to it, as it happened. That is when the writing truly becomes a history and not a series of stories." Phyna kept with Alop's dropping of tradition with using the shortened name.

"Which part do you like best?" Alop glanced from one side of the room to the other. "Which part do you read when you are thinking fondly of Hinto?"

"Those are two different questions." Phyna paused, waiting for Alop to clarify which answer it wanted. It did not take too long for Phyna to realize it wanted each answer. "I think of Hinto fondly under different emotional states. So, it depends upon which state I am in as to which portion I enjoy more. The main sections read as two different voices, but both voices are Hinto's." Phyna paused once more. The words "like best" were laden with various connotations and, most unfortunate, those connotations were unspoken and unknown, lying in ambush. No matter what Phyna said, it would permanently affect how Alop thought of Phyna. At a minimum, it would color the rest of their conversation. Instead of attempting to tailor its answer, it chose to keep it as simple as possible. "I like the beginning portion the best."

"Why?" Alop would not let the simplicity stand.

"It is easier to get lost in the digressions." Phyna thought harder. "There is more truth hidden in the digressions than there is amongst the truth. At least for my understanding of Hinto."

"You are remarkable. Especially for one who is so disdainful of the chaos of the derlian realm." Alop's head was nodding absentmindedly. Another derlian habit. "Yes, I have come to the right place. I have come to the right Yaven."

"You have come to the only Yaven who can help you with this library." Phyna felt a twinge of wariness at Alop's last statement. It was not the wariness itself that bothered Phyna, it was not understanding why the feeling came into existence. What had triggered it?

"That is true as well. Yes." Alop rolled over to one of the beginning alcoves, the fourth one from the library's entrance. "Why are there more alcoves in the first half of the library? What are the alcoves for?"

"They are asides. The digressions." Phyna rolled over to be next to Alop. "Here is the remembered past of Hinto." Phyna outstretched an arm to the left side of the alcove's opening. "This particular digression is wondering about the true essence of the Void. It was triggered by Hinto recalling its first summoning to the derlian realm, its first passage through emptiness. You can see by the shallowness of the alcove that there is only so much rumination that can be performed about emptiness." Phyna pointed to the right side of the alcove's opening. "Here the remembered story discusses Hinto's first mission amongst the derlians. The next alcove, much deeper than this one, is Hinto's generalized thoughts on the derlian realm. If they are specific, if they were thought of during a specific visit, they are written in the main library room. Hinto's main library room." Phyna thought of a brief question about its own main library room. Would there be some Yavens, at some future aeon, standing in that room, staring and deciphering the etchings, or would they have faded to nothingness due to neglect? There were certainly no Yavens currently interested in that room. At this point, there were very few even remotely interested in Hinto's room. "If you wish to read the actual history of Hinto, you read to the edge of the alcove and then skip to the other side. There is no pause, no interruption from the digression. You simply continue down the room. The alcoves themselves are written in order on both sides of the wall. It is my opinion that Hinto did this so that it could dig deeper into the alcove if it recalled more regression later in life."

"Why are there alcoves in the latter half of the library?" Alop spun around to face the other side of the room. "Surely, all of the digressions happened earlier."

"Most of them, yes. There were, however, thoughts that came upon Hinto late in life that had to be explored." Phyna turned and pointed to the last alcove. "That alcove ruminates upon the legend of a well in the derlian realm. It supposedly halts the deleterious effects of aging, the physical manifestations of being immersed in chaos, from any derlian who drinks from it." They were quiet for a moment. "Though it is hard to say when a particular alcove is finished, if that could be said at all, I feel that the last alcove is not even halfway completed."

"And which is the deepest alcove?" Alop spun in a small circle and stopped facing the entrance of the deepest one. The third one from the entrance. It had a good memory of their sizes from its earlier examination. Phyna was impressed.

"The Beleg digression is the largest. Larger even than the one covering most of the derlian realm." Phyna might not have been able to say what the seventh or eighth largest alcove contained, but it felt comfortable stating what was in the deepest one.

"Then that is where I wish to begin." Alop rolled into the Beleg alcove.

"The difficulty with the alcoves will be that there is not really a timeline. You won't be able tell me which part you wish me to read." Phyna followed closely behind as Alop rolled deep into the alcove.

"I want you to read this part." Alop stopped and turned towards the wall on the left. "Here." Alop pointed to a specific passage.

"Well… that is in the middle. How about I begin a little earlier?" Phyna knew that Alop had wanted to choose the passages completely on its own but figured that it was being random on purpose and would not mind, or even notice if it was not told, if the start location was shifted slightly.

"By all means, it is your library." Alop stopped oddly for a brief moment. "But let me know when we get to this passage."

"We'll begin here." Phyna showed Alop which symbol was the opening of the paragraph. " 'The mind of the Belegs, or at least the mind of the Beleg that I met, was amalgamated of each realm. It makes me wonder at the beginning of our realm, when there was only the one mind in the Gaen realm. There is an all-encompassing nature of the Beleg mind that makes me think back to the beginning of time, not that I was alive at that moment. But the one mind was created that way. It was naturally that way until it was, for some unknown reason, shattered. The Beleg mind was molded, through conscious choices, to become a larger singularity than any individual Yaven. This gigantic, singular, amalgamated mind could not have been as complex as the one mind. Surely? But the one mind, being full and complete, still only had the experience of one element. One sliver of reality that, no matter how complete, could never match a mind that understood other elements. This is where I am stuck.' We are coming upon the passage that you pointed out. 'Every piece of me, each tiny section of reality that calls itself me, cries out against this premise. Can it be that Gunzgak, the Yaven who became a Beleg, has a greater mind than the one mind that spawned us all? The thought is abhorrent to me. But it can only be argued amongst eternities. How much could a mind learn in an eternity? What if it encompassed all minds? Would that knowledge not approach infinity?' Here is your passage. 'What about one little mind? One sliver of the original mind. This mind also lives into eternity, but it is much younger and, therefore, starts out with much less knowledge. But this mind is given three other realms, three other elements, three other sets of knowledge that approach infinity. Each element completely distinct and unknowable to each other. Could not this second mind, though younger and smaller, hold more knowledge than the original? Would it not have to? It does not bother me that the Belegs are greater than the Yavens. That feels almost natural, even if it is ultimately unfair. So be it. But to think that each of the Belegs are greater than the one original Gaen mind, the one mind, that is impossible for me. It is cruel. It is untenable. It is a defiant slap in the face of reality. More than at any earlier time in my life, I hope that I am wrong. But in whom, or in what, do I place my hopes? From what can I beg truth from?' "

"I see what you mean." Alop waved an arm vaguely. "This is digression. Are there locations where Hinto describes meeting Gunzgak? In a true historical sense."

"Ah. That passage is what leads to this digression." Phyna turned and rolled out of the alcove. It slowly shifted sideways, examining the etches, looking for the best spot to begin. "Let me see… Ah, here it is. 'I had met Gunzgak once before…' Hinto then describes where to find the earlier description of Gunzgak. 'We all gathered in the Great Hall, waiting to hear why our ruler had been in absentia for so long. Why it had spent all that time with the other rulers and not with us. There were, of course, rumors and wild guesses as to the cause, but those of us who waited wanted some truth. Any truth. When Gunzgak finally arrived, it was unrecognizable. The stone may have still been there, hidden in its midst like derlian bones, but it was covered by a constant shivering and shimmering skin. The molten rock roiled and smoldered, casting a smoke and steam veil in front of it all. It was the constant movement that bothered me the most. It induced a sickening sense of vertigo in me that then induced a great sense of panic. It was only with utmost self-control that I was able to stay in the room. Many of my compatriots failed this simple but overwhelming test and fled from the Hall.

"Then Gunzgak spoke to us, 'I have escaped this realm. We, the Belegs, the four of us, we have escaped our realms. We have visited the others and taken them within us. I am no longer merely stone for I have been immersed in air, water, and in fire. The possibilities presented to me appear to be infinite. They are so much greater than just stone. So much greater than just Gaen. So much greater than just Yaven. We, the Belegs, have outgrown you. We no longer need you. You can only hold us back with your one-dimensional thinking. We have decided to transcend you and this realm. I am here to say goodbye and that is all.' It was a quick and remorseless speech. It was pure hubris. And the whole time I stared at the constantly shifting form that was Gunzgak and tried not to panic, not to flee. The conflicting urges of striking out in anger and of retreating in fear made me feel how a derlian must feel all of the time, not that they had existed yet. It was then that a cobble-sized dense stone was hurled at Gunzgak. It was melted and absorbed into Gunzgak's body, causing no noticeable damage or discomfort. Then the crowd went mad with rage. Stones were hurled from all directions, though not from mine. None of them appeared to do anything to Gunzgak but anger it. 'You dare strike at me?' Or some such tripe was retorted. Gunzgak's body flared and sputtered, but nothing came out. Nothing attacked us. There was no retribution. I do not know if Gunzgak was trying to do anything to us, but certainly nothing happened. Then, almost unimaginably, Gunzgak appeared to panic. It began to retreat under the hail of cobbles, though it still did not look to be wounded. As quickly as it had appeared, Gunzgak left for the Void.' "

"Hmm. A little more interesting, but I have heard that story before. You would be amazed at how many Gaens have told me that they were the ones that threw that first stone. Ha!" Alop started to roll towards the entrance. "Did you say that Hinto knew Gunzgak before it became a Beleg? Even before it became a ruler?"

"I do not think I mentioned that..." Phyna cast its mind back to their earlier conversations, before Alop arrived, but was interrupted before it could take full inventory of the past.

"But it is true, is it not?" Alop was still slowly rolling towards the front of the library. "I wish you to read me an earlier passage."

"Well, yes..." Phyna followed Alop over to where it had stopped. Amazingly enough, they were very close to Hinto's first description of Gunzgak, long before it had become a ruler. Long before it had become a Beleg. It was somewhat eerie.

"Please." It was a simple, plaintive request.

Phyna rolled a little to the right, to find the actual passage. Alop rolled just in front, staying out of the way, but staying close. Phyna found what it was looking for.

" 'The first time I met Gunzgakaphunchistiolanwendug we were...' " Phyna started at the beginning. It was not sure for how long it should read but was quickly interrupted.

"I am sorry, what was that?" Alop's body appeared stiff or tense.

"I was beginning the passage." Phyna was unsure exactly what the issue was but was starting to feel a little nervous.

"Yes, yes of course. Please, start over." Alop's stiffness did not abate.

"We were…" Phyna was again interrupted.

"From the beginning!" Alop seemed like… well Phyna was not sure. It was not like there was anger in there, maybe it was an emotion closer to frustration. But that did not quite fit either.

" 'The first time I met Gunzgakaphunchistiolanwendug we were on opposite sides of the Great Hall. A friend of mine at the time, Yertloachantorgvunqualea, had dragged me there to join in the discussion of succession. I did not know anyone who was vying for the position so, to be honest, I was not that intrigued by the process. Others certainly were, and the discussion was becoming heated. I was staring at various other Gaens at the meeting, thinking of little, when my gaze crossed with Gunzgak's.' " Hinto used Gunzgak's full, but truncated, name the entire passage, along with Yertloach's, but Phyna decided against doing that. " 'We stared at each other for some time, before Yertloach realized I was no longer paying attention to it. 'Do you know that Gaen?' 'No,' I replied. 'Would you like to?' And so I was quickly introduced to the future Beleg by Yertloach.' " Alop was staring unmovingly at the wall. It was not just the lack of movement, but it was also hard to identify lack of intent. Phyna felt that Alop had lost interest, so it stopped speaking. It took several moments before Alop realized and was shaken from its internal reverie.

"Sorry, I was…" Alop paused for a moment. It was certainly no longer tense. Its mood was more… confused. "Maybe we should find the passage that I came here for."

Phyna was a little taken aback. Gaens were, as a general rule, very patient compared to other Yavens. Alop was always a little more scattered, a little more spurious, a little more chaotic than most Gaens that Phyna knew, but this seemed a little odd. Did Alop not request to hear the passage?

"And what did you come here for?" Phyna did not mean to seem frustrated.

"Do you remember, near the beginning of Fatilzhov's reign, during the Duxintrol revolution, when there was a raid on the First Barracks that was pushed back by the Lukhoan Guard?" Alop had started to roll towards the center of the library. "I wish to read whatever passage that was written during that brief time."

Phyna thought long and hard. It was such a specific moment. Phyna was alive and well during that time, however, and remembered quite clearly what it was doing. It just had to piece together what Hinto was doing. Phyna slowly rolled towards the latter half of the library. Thinking... Phyna was in the derlian realm during the beginning of the rebellion or, as Alop had put it, the revolution. It was serving a Fluen mage, Astyr maybe, at the time, working on some caves at the tidal breaks near the Clatsvol Sea. Phyna had asked hundreds of times but was told the same thing hundreds of times. "No, the caves had nothing to do with the Fluen Temple for Lembin." It was good, clean work and one of the more enjoyable times that he had served in the derlian realm. Thinking... What had Hinto been doing before Phyna had been summoned...? Nothing came to mind. Certainly nothing to have written about. But afterwards... Phyna thought back to its homecoming. Hinto was unhappy about the rebellion, they had spoken about that. This was why, combined with the fact that Hinto had not been personally involved on either side, there was nothing written about the rebellion itself. Hinto wrote about things it did not personally experience only in the digression alcoves. Phyna could not recall anything significant that Hinto spoke of that might have happened during its time in the derlian realm, so it had to find the next significant thing. A while after Phyna had returned, they had attended a coupling ceremony of some friends of Hinto's. Phyna was rolling towards where it thought the ceremony was written. As long as Phyna was remembering the correct friends...

Phyna stopped at the passage with the ceremony that it had been thinking of. It began reading backwards by small chunks, attempting to fit each section with a chunk of known time until it felt that it found the section that Alop was looking for. Alop, for its part, silently rolled alongside Phyna, patiently waiting.

"Ah, I think it is here. Please understand that every moment is not written and that Hinto only wrote what it personally experienced. All I can do is read what is shown here. I do not know if it will be the assistance you are looking for." Though not intimately familiar with the passage, Phyna knew enough about it from deepening the etches to know it contained nothing special. It was worried that Alop would feel let down if the passage did not contain whatever it was searching for.

"Do not worry, Phyna. You have been a most gracious host, and I knew the difficulties and limited chances of success when I asked you for this favor." Alop nodded its head slightly at the end of its speech. Another derlian gesture.

Phyna read for a good derlian half hour, reading all the way back up to the coupling ceremony, but Alop did not indicate it had heard what it was hoping for. At Alop's urging, Phyna started to reread the passages. It was about halfway through when a quiet chanting became audible. Phynalloinchtaghoureack… Phynalloinchtaghoureack… It started quietly and slowly became louder and more insistent.

"What I want is not here. Again, you have been most gracious." Alop started to roll towards the entrance but kept its "torso" pointed towards Phyna. "I know that you are not always receptive to a derlian summoning, but I do not wish my presence to affect your decision." It gave a short bark that may have been meant to be a derlian laugh. "I would not want anyone in my home if I were being summoned away."

Phyna rolled behind Alop, trying to figure out the other Gaen's mood. It seemed quite happy and upbeat, especially considering they were completely unsuccessful in finding what it was looking for. It also seemed *un*shocked and *un*surprised by the derlian summoning, rolling blithely along towards the entrance foyer. The insistent chanting had certainly shocked and surprised Phyna. It had been many, many derlian cycles since the last time Phyna had visited the derlian realm. Certainly there were no derlians left alive from when it was last there. How did derlians get the names of Yavens anyway?

"Yes, thank you for understanding. To be honest, I am not sure if I plan on struggling against this summons or not." They finally reached the foyer. "It has been quite a while…" Phyna trailed off.

"Of course. The decision is yours and it is a personal decision. Thank you again for your time." Alop went to the far corner of the foyer where the linkage was and began to sink into the floor. Phyna tried to think of something more to say, but Alop dropped out sight before it could come up with anything decent.

Phynalloinchtaghoureack… Phynalloinchtaghoureack… The whispering chant was increasing in volume and power. What to do? It had not yet become demanding. Sometimes, in the past, Phyna had just ignored the summons and waited the mage out. Oftentimes a mage would have several names to choose from and would try a Yaven that was more eager to travel to the derlian realm. While it thought about the situation, it did just that. Phyna was easily able to ignore the summoning for what must have been half a derlian day. But the mage was incredibly insistent. Phyna was unsure if the mage just did not know another name, or it specifically wanted Phyna and no other Yaven. Phyna had gotten all of its simple affairs in order, letting a couple friends and neighbors know that it may be visiting the derlian realm for a little while. Phyna led a fairly quiet and simple life. It decided, once it realized that the mage was not going to simply summon a different Yaven, that it would travel to the derlian realm and find out what was going to be asked of it. It could always continue to struggle against the summons once it was there if the proposed task was too long or abhorrent.

Phyna let itself be pulled from the Yaven realm. It always felt like moving upwards, like being lifted. Phyna wondered what would happen if it stood on its head, or even just oriented its "head" downwards—would it be pulled through the floor instead? The mage was powerful enough to pull Phyna along with no assistance but was smooth and gentle as well. Some mages yanked so hard that there was a feeling of stretching, of straining as you were pulled through the Void. But this was comfortable, just like traveling through the Gaen realm, but without having to think about where you were going, how to pull the next linkage over to you. Then Phyna was in the Void proper. It gathered a thin veil around itself as it was gently pulled along. It seemed to take a little longer than normal, but Phyna was no expert and it had been a very long time since it had last been summoned. *Each mage pulled at different velocities,* thought Phyna. Something else happened, however, that could not be explained away by lack of experience. There was a definite atypical warmth that flowed around Phyna as it traveled. It was disconcerting, to say the least. Phyna relaxed and allowed itself to drift along, ignoring all else with an empty mind. And then... crash!

Phyna always stayed spherical during summoning travel, it softened the inevitable impact by leaving no protrusions that could get damaged. It cracked a stone floor, much like it had in its own home, except that this crack spiderwebbed in all directions in a much larger pattern and would never heal itself. Never again be whole. The room it landed in was tiny and cramped, though it may not have been considered so by derlian standards. It made Phyna wish to stay a sphere, all curled up and protected and small in this tiny room full of wide-eyed derlians. It knew that was not an option, however. It quickly sprouted a torso and a few fingerless arms and the requisite head that all derlians spoke to as if that were the only part of a Yaven that could sense the world. Derlians were so stuck with their own realities that they often did notice that others might not be. This frozen understanding of the physicalities of bodies was in stark contrast, in complete dichotomy even, with the constant chaos that they were surrounded by. It was rich enough in irony to be humorous.

There were several derlians in the room, but no Yavens that Phyna could sense. It would have to remember its humorous irony for a later time. Derlians could be oddly sensitive about their own blindness. There were three derlian Gaens, a Fluen, a Luften, and a Pyran. They were an odd mix of races, to be sure.

"Why have you summoned me?" Phyna asked the traditional question in the traditional way. Sometimes it was easier to rely on rote statements than it was to create something specific to an unknown situation. The chaos would begin soon enough.

He did it. He did it! Croy wanted to run in circles and shout with joy. It had seemed to take forever. It took most of the day. It would not have surprised him to know that the sun had set almost an hour ago. Nothing had happened for so long that he had almost given up... several times. Every other hour or so a great despair would settle on his shoulders like an impatient vulture. Claws gripping and relaxing to the rhythm of Croy's chanting. Phynalloinchtaghoureack... Phynalloinchtaghoureack... It was a constant noise. It was said so often that Croy was not even sure if he was saying it correctly anymore. His voice cracked and crumbled, and Clerin would bring him some more water. He would swoon with the constant drain of magic, and Feyazki would push a river of energy back into him. Feyazki never helped with the spell, no. The Blind One never helped either. But they would help him to be able to keep up his own casting. And he had done it! He had cast his mind beyond the derlian realm and had been heard. And he had been responded to! It was a curious mixture of giddy excitement and heavy exhaustion. Then, through it all, he realized he had been asked a question. The Yaven that he had summoned was speaking to him.

"I have summoned you to assist our coterie in our mission." Croy cast his mind back to what he was supposed to say. The day had been so long and draining that he was having difficulties recalling everything. "We are a band of all races. There are several Yavens that have already joined our cause. You would be our third, and we may gain several more before we reach our goal."

"What is your goal?" The Yaven interrupted Croy's spiel with a deep rumbling voice. It was gigantic. Not that it was larger than the Pyran or Fluen Yaven that Croy had encountered. No, the perimeter of this Yaven was similar to the others. But there was a heaviness, an unbelievable density, that emanated from it, that encompassed it, that could only be described as gigantic.

"Our goal is the destruction of the Cabal of Lochom." Croy was again interrupted.

"So, this is a combat mission? There is to be bloodshed and magic?" It turned more completely towards Croy. Every time the Yaven moved there was a grinding, crushing sound. It was much more disconcerting than watching living water or fire move. Movement for those elements felt natural, felt normal. They were always moving in the derlian realm after all. But the shifting stone that was the Yaven's body had a heavy, grating feeling that made him think it should be moving in a halting and herky-jerky gait. It appeared to move quite smoothly and without effort, however.

"There will be some fighting, some casualties." This came from the Blind One. He who had promised to be completely silent during this first meeting.

"Then I do not wish to participate." The gigantic Gaen rolled backwards. The bottom of it was a sphere of stone that appeared to be able to roll in any direction. A torso protruded upwards from the center of the lower sphere, no matter how the latter shifted and rolled. The arms protruded vaguely from each side of the torso. There were hands and fingers, but they seemed to be melded together. Or maybe they just looked that way until they were individually used.

"The Cabal of Lochom destroys Yavens by trapping their essence into dead items to be used by derlians for eternity." This was Trela. She had made no promise to be silent such as the Blind One had, but her interruption was still jarring.

"If we fight them, will they not be tempted to capture the Yavens that you bring with you?" The Yaven was positioned facing halfway between Trela and the Blind One. Reacting to both, but eerily looking at neither. "No, I am not participating." It raised a hand to no one. "I do not kill others and I do not wish to die. There is nothing else to be said. We are at an impasse."

"We could keep you here against your will." The Blind One quickly broke in again.

"You could try. You could risk nemesis. But…" The Yaven turned to face its torso to the Blind One.

"No one will hold you against your will. The old Gaen over there does not speak for all of us." Trela's thumb jerked over to where the Blind One was standing with his back as straight as a placid lake. "We just wish you to hear us out. We feel that this mission is of utmost importance to both of our races and we have need of your special skills. Please, just listen to our mission. If you wish to leave afterwards, no one will stop you." She glared over at the Blind One.

"I suppose I could take some time to listen to you." The Yaven rotated its torso to Trela. "I am known as Phyna, and I await your tale of woe. Impatiently, but with anticipation. Convince me of your plight."

"I am Trela. The mage who summoned you is the illustrious Croy Sie'tin. The other two mages are Feyazki, the Luften to my left, and you have already met Narst Dea'jin. Aedon Dea'sol is the last one over there." Trela brought her hands back to rest in front of her. "I will not waste your time, Phyna, the situation is dire. The Cabal is destroying Yavens at an alarming rate. And not just destroying them, but trapping them as a mindless husk for all of eternity. A never-ending torture. They kill other derlians as well, but that is of smaller importance. Even to us! But they are also somehow increasing the number and veracity of the Tlana. We are still searching for the link between those two chains. This will affect thousands of derlians, each realm has villages and outposts that call the transition between the Northern Desert and the foothills their home. So, they are killing us, torturing you, and flooding the world with evil. Does that not deserve death?" Trela immediately raised her hand to ward off any of Phyna's protestations. "Spare me. This is not what we wish you to be doing. You will be far from any action, far from prying eyes and angry guards. We do not wish you to kill, we have others who excel in that arena. No, we just wish you to create some tunnels." Trela stopped and stared at Phyna for a moment.

"Go ahead and continue, I am listening." Phyna's body did not move at all, not a twitch.

"Their lair, we think, is at the border of the Gaen and Fluen realms. If it is close to the ocean at all, we wish to construct a small network of tunnels underneath their lair and lead the main entrance to the beaches to be able to enter secretly and at our leisure." Trela's voice unconsciously sped up as she talked about battle plans.

"And what if it is away from the ocean?" Phyna was as still as stone.

"Well... Then we will want a small network of tunnels that lead out amongst some mountains. Or hills. Or whatever." Trela smiled at Croy, he was not sure why.

"Then why...?" Phyna trailed off. Then Trela interrupted.

"Well... Your specialty, your skill, your art, is to make tunnels at the confluence of stone and water, is it not?" Trela looked over to the Blind One for corroboration, for it was the Blind One who had attested to Phyna's skills.

"I was working for Fluens." Phyna paused for the briefest of moments. "Did you hear of my work?" Phyna turned its torso towards Clerin.

"Me? No. I do not know the exploits of any Yavens, really." Her cheeks turned a lighter shade of pink.

"It really was the Blind One... A Gaen, not a Fluen." Croy spoke up just to be able to speak up more than anything else. Provide some useful knowledge, maybe. He was giddy from the summoning and even of Trela's use of the word "illustrious" to describe him. The Blind One stiffened a little, which Croy had thought to be impossible.

"We have left the trail. None of this is pertinent anymore. Please understand, Phyna, we are not asking you to get involved in bloodshed and magic. We need your peaceful expertise, that is all." Trela brought them back.

"Promise me." Phyna's voice was deep and, no pun intended, quite gravelly, but there was also a strange lilt to it.

"I pro..." Trela started to speak but was interrupted.

"No, not you. I want the mage who summoned me to promise." Phyna shifted its torso towards Croy. "I do not take the lives of others. I do not wish to be destroyed, whether it be by death or the torture of eternal entrapment. You must promise me that no matter what this Pyran demands, no matter what any of these other derlians demand, no matter your own personal desires, you will not allow me to be placed in a position of killing or dying. You, my summoner, must promise to be my protector."

Croy had his mouth half open, prepared to immediately acquiesce to the request, surely the simplest solution, the path of least resistance, when he froze up. His mind tripped over itself, that was his only explanation. There was a gravitas that he was missing here. This was not a light request. This Yaven would completely expect him to protect it. Him?! What could he do if they were being attacked, being overwhelmed? The thought was… overwhelming. But what else could he do at this point? He could not let the only Yaven he had ever summoned just turn and leave. His mind began to attempt to justify itself. Surely, being the protector of a Yaven was not any worse than being alone. If he was to be overwhelmed and killed, would it matter much that Phyna would be killed soon after? Would that make Croy strive more or less? Would that make him worry more or less? How could any motivating factor trump the innate desire to keep oneself alive? They were all staring at him. His mouth was still stupidly open. No matter the fear, no matter the consequence, no matter the trepidation, there was no way that he could refuse this promise. Maybe Trela was right and one should not paralyze themselves with useless thought. It was not like he had even come to a conclusion. Just thoughts whizzing and racing to nowhere…

"I promise you, Phynalloinchtaghoureack, that I will do my best to protect you from others and from any need to hurt others." Croy nodded to himself.

"Do not promise me to do your best. Promise me you will die before I do." Phyna's voice sounded like a metal shovel digging gravel. It was unnerving. But as with a moment ago, Croy did not really have a choice, only whirring thoughts.

"I promise to die before you do." What were the odds that he could outlive a Yaven anyway?

"Good. I will agree to work in this derlian realm, I agree to assist all of you in your quest to destroy this Cabal, but I will not harm another, and this Gaen must accompany me at all times as my protector." Phyna rolled back a little.

Croy was sure that the motion was meant to be more inclusive to all the others gathered around, but it just made him more uneasy. As if things were already fading away. He shook his head to clear it.

They were finally back on the road. Croy had enjoyed the respite of the Forgotten Junction quite a bit and was not particularly excited about attempting to hunt down some violent Cabal powerful enough to destroy Yavens, but he had been getting antsy and bored as well. A mixture of emotions only exacerbated by living in tight quarters with the same derlians day after day. Luckily, he had been able to avoid the Blind One for most of their time there.

Phyna was able to change shape easily and could get quite small, small enough to fit in his pocket if need be. It had a hard time reducing its mass, however. Therefore, it rode in one of Wesduin's wagons. Since Croy had somehow become a Yaven's protector, he also rode on that wagon. The driver was a rough and scarred Pyran by the name of Yasku. Croy spent most of the time up with the driver, swaying along with the ruts in the road. Yasku was typically taciturn, leaving him with his own thoughts. During their brief and infrequent discussions, he learned that Yasku's natural paranoia extended quite heavily to foreigners. Yasku was quite forthright about his distrust of Gaens and the fight at the inn had only solidified his preconceived notions. Croy had tried to explain that it was the Tlana that they were really fighting, that the Gaens were just a proxy, just the muscle being controlled by the central mind of the Tlana. It did not sway Yasku's opinion. Oh, he did not mind the Gaens in the coterie too much, they seemed a quiet and helpful sort, but he refused to think they represented the vast majority of the Gaen populace. They were the exceptions to the rule, not the rule itself. That was nothing compared what he thought about Fluens, however. They were a hundred times worse than any Gaen, or so he had heard. Croy tried to point out that they had a Fluen traveling with them, and in his opinion, she was one of, if not the, nicest derlians in the entire coterie. Yasku fell back into a terse silence. Croy found comfort in the quiet and he practiced his own version of detente. Some things were best left alone.

At camp, he would set up Phyna in his tent and attempt to wander away. There were many times that Phyna was content to be hidden away, unprotected. Other times Phyna would insist that Croy stay in the tent all night, barely allowing him to set up the campfire and cook a small, lonesome meal. It would position itself next to the door, watching his back as he cooked. These were times when Phyna "felt something watching them," but he thought it was just being nervous. And though he had not met many Yavens, he thought that was not a common emotion for them. It was a bit perplexing.

Nights like those were spent tightly together, much like the days sitting next to Yasku. They were generally quiet and lonely affairs, with Phyna not feeling like talking but not wanting to be alone. Luckily Phyna's natural paranoia did not overtly extend to foreigners, though it did have some general misgivings about all derlians. But then again, Croy did as well. He did learn some things about Phyna and the Gaen realm, but mostly Phyna would want him to tell the stories. It particularly liked the ones about Ilana, which filled him with an enjoyable nostalgic feeling, so he did not mind too much.

They soon put the Forgotten Junction far behind them. They kept to the main road that somewhat skirted the Northern Desert. Croy thought it was mainly for the wagons. He knew Trela was concerned that they were stuck out in the open, but she did not want to dump her provisions and equipment too early either. After a week of uneventful travel, they neared another inn.

Trela was wary of inns after the Forgotten Junction, so they planned on skirting this one and camping just out of sight. To make sure that no one at the inn noticed or became suspicious, she wanted to send a small group of derlians to the inn to check it out and stay there for the time it would take for the coterie to slip by. She wanted only Gaens to rent rooms at the inn, for obvious reasons. She was fairly particular about who she wanted to go. She explained to Croy that she was worried about the Gaens who had joined up with them at the Forgotten Junction, those who were under the geas of the Tlana. She explained to him that she was concerned about the Blind One and those under his employ. She explained how she needed him to be one of the few to go.

"You are my most trusted Gaen advisor, Croy. You have to go." Trela had plied him with a fantastic dinner and as much beer as he cared to imbibe. She sat across from him and stared intently into his eyes. He did not wish to admit it, but she sometimes unnerved him with her stare. Her eyes could get hard and intense, somehow squinting with wide eyes. He did not understand it. Of course, this time he wanted her to convince him. He would rather spend the time in a comfortable inn, surrounded by other Gaens, sitting next to a fireplace instead of a fire pit. With nothing to be concerned about, no worries about being attacked at night, no need to look over his shoulder, no chores to accomplish, a bed to sleep in, a real bath. Though they had only left the Forgotten Junction a week ago, he was quite ready to be won over.

"Phyna will not want to be apart from me." Croy smiled wryly over a thyme-encrusted sage hen. "Though I am sure the Yaven will be much safer at camp, amongst all of the warriors." Croy figured that if there was any derlian who could convince Phyna of its safety away from Croy, it would be Trela. He was not quite sure why the Yaven insisted on him being its protector. He could barely protect himself.

"Well, at worst case, I will allow you to take Phyna to the inn. I need you to take one of the wagons anyway. I'll also be sending Aedon, Verin, and Tesjuk. Yasku will have to drive the wagon, but he will stay covered and sleep in the stables if need be. Oh, and Knill will be going with you as well." Trela took a deep breath. "Keep an eye on Knill, won't you?"

It happened that fast. Croy was not even sure if Trela had tried to talk Phyna out of traveling with them. It hid in the back as a tiny but immensely heavy rock, centered over the wagon's rear axle. As was typical, Croy and a thankfully silent Yasku were up at the front of the wagon. A gray cloak and cowl covered most of him; it looked to be sweltering. The wagon itself had been mostly emptied, with only enough items left in it to appear less suspicious. The others all rode singular horses. Croy felt himself missing Buttercup, his own horse. Saddles were certainly not comfortable, especially on those long days, but he was beginning to think the wagon's flat board seat was some sort of fiendish torture device in comparison.

The inn was called the Desert's Cusp and had several signs along the main road before it even came into full view. Of course, since there was only one road running along the Northern Desert's edge, there was no way to miss the inn even if there had not been any signs. They looked weathered but well kept, much like the road itself. Croy wondered if the inn's owners maintained a stretch of the road near their business. If not, he was unsure of who did.

As they approached, Croy could see another road running perpendicular to the one they were using, slowly sloping from the hills to the south down towards the inn, to cross this one on its way towards the desert. Croy wondered where it originated. He also briefly wondered how far it crept into the desert before fading into nothingness, but the inn was soon in full view.

The inn was large and sprawling but appeared to be only one floor unlike the Forgotten Junction. He could not yet make out the main doors, but they were obviously smaller than the ornate steel-bound ones at the Junction. The buildings appeared a drab brown, as if to match the desert barely visible to the north. There was no smoke visible from the chimney, but it was after lunch and before dinner, so that was not unexpected. There were a few outbuildings as well. One was obviously a stable and one looked like a storehouse, but Croy was unsure of what the other two were for.

The closer they got, the more Croy expected to see someone. If nothing else, he expected to see a stablehand as they arrived. But there was no one. No sound. No movement. No signs of life. It was beginning to get eerie, but he did not want to be the first to voice any concerns. He just kept hoping to hear a door opening, or the patter of boots on the dusty ground. But there did not even seem to be any wildlife in the area.

Finally, the wagon came to a halt. The horses danced sideways a little. Not necessarily scared, but maybe a little nervous. The silence grew as they all sat silently, staring back and forth between each other.

"Hello! Hello, innkeep!" It was Verin who finally broke the quiet. "You have guests!" She looked around at the others, her right eyebrow cocked upwards, as if she were asking them a question.

"They are all probably just drunk in the commons." Tesjuk swung his stocky frame off his horse in one motion. "Or maybe they're cleaning the rooms."

Tesjuk walked his horse, a muscular chestnut-colored quarter horse named Firestomp, over to one of the varied hitching posts at the front of the inn and tied her off. Verin silently followed. Then Knill.

"You two stay with the wagon." Aedon pointed to Yasku and Croy. "We are going in to investigate. We'll holler if we need you."

"Maybe Knill should wait with us." Croy hopped down from the wagon. He did not want to be stuck up there if something happened.

"I'll be fine, don't worry yourself." Knill turned and marched past Aedon and the others. If Verin had not already been at the front door, he would have been the first one to enter the inn.

Verin turned towards him and the rest of the group and held up her hand in a gesture to halt. Everyone in motion, even Croy, halted. She then pulled a long dagger out and held its blade upwards against the back of her arm. It would be hidden only if no one was paying attention. She stood in front of the left door and swung the right door open wide. And... nothing.

Croy could not tell if everyone was as tense as he was, but he let out an inaudible breath that he had not realized he had been holding when Verin opened the door. He gripped the hilt of his own small dagger as Verin deftly swung herself into the building. Part of him expected her to suddenly laugh as she came face to face with an innkeeper, and part of him expected her to scream as she attacked something or was maybe attacked herself. But... nothing.

Tesjuk unhooked his half-moon axe from his belt and followed her in. Knill, weaponless as far as Croy could tell, quickly followed them. Aedon took one more glance at Croy, smiled wide showing her bright teeth, and ducked herself inside. He stood there motionless, waiting for some sound to emanate from the open door, but it did not happen. Yasku, as was his habit, sat silently staring off into the distance, reins loosely held in his hands. Croy wondered briefly if Yasku was watching the road for anything in particular, maybe dust pillars kicked up by travelers in the opposite direction, but he could not tear his eyes from the black hole that was the open door. The silence was excruciating.

Seconds ticked by. Then minutes. Still no sounds emanated from the inn. Croy felt like he was straining the muscles in his ears, but he was unsure if there were any. Either way, he had given himself a headache by the time he heard a loud but dull thud from behind him. It pained him to shift his gaze from the expectant blackness that lay in front of him but he could not ignore the noise. Unfortunately, by the time he looked behind him there was nothing to be seen. He walked towards the back end of the wagon, turning to peer at the silent doorway every so often just to make sure nothing was still happening.

There was nothing there. Croy fully took his eyes off the empty doorway to examine the scene behind the wagon more carefully. The wagon itself looked undisturbed, there was nothing any more askew than could be expected for a couple of hours on the road. He stared down at the dusty ground and noticed what looked like a small, shallow bowl in the dust. From that bowl a trail meandered off and out of sight. The bowl looked like a large rock had fallen off the wagon while the trail looked like a small stone had rolled through it. It reminded Croy of the snows he had experienced as a child outside of Serif, when he would roll a small snowball down the hillside and watch it grow into a boulder before exploding upon a tree trunk and the trail left on the hillside was a concave rut. That was exactly what the trail in the dust looked like.

"Phyna." Croy whispered it frantically. "Phyna!" There was no response. He could not believe that Phyna would have wandered off, but nothing else could have made that trail. "Phyna!" It was like a whisper-scream.

"What are you doing?" Yasku's head peered around from the front of the wagon.

"I… I have to investigate." Croy did not even want to mention the name Phyna to Yasku, did not want to say that he had lost the Yaven. So he left it there.

"What? Are you stupid?" Yasku's question was not necessarily out of line. "We are supposed to wait here until the others are done investigating."

"I have to investigate." It was all Croy had, and he knew it was woefully inadequate. Instead of arguing however, he began following the trail of the rolling stone.

"It's your burial." Yasku gave up quickly and turned back around to watch his nervous team of horses.

Luckily the trail was not the least bit hidden or hard to follow. Phyna had just rolled along with no thought to what might follow. Soon Croy was behind the stables, ears still straining to hear anything besides himself and an occasional horse. The trail, unfortunately, disappeared through a chink in the wooden slat wall. He would have to find a more typical and mundane entrance. He crept all the way around the back and most of the side before he found a small door. He was not sure what he was doing. He did carry a small dagger with him but had never really trained in close combat. He unsheathed his weapon to at least give himself something to grip and took a deep breath. There was nothing left to do but open the door… so he opened it.

It was a weird mixture of dark and light inside. He stood at the doorway for a moment attempting to let his eyes adjust. The darkness in that portion of the stables, which he figured was just storage, maybe for hay and some tack and tools, was cut by bands of light that sliced through the gaps between the horizontal wall boards. He figured that if he went around to the other side of the stables there would be many open stalls, but here it was small and cramped and it stunk. There was something wrong with the stink. It was too copious, too thick, too… oily?

"You do not wish to investigate further." Croy spun around to see a tiny Phyna rolling away from him. If the Yaven would not have been moving he probably would not have noticed.

"Why?" Croy knew before he asked but was still a little put off by the smell. Certainly death, probably even derlian. It may have been under the hay, or even just on the other side of the slatted wall. Lurking and waiting for Croy to discover it. But there was something more to it than that. The oily smell did not belong to just dead bodies, it was not a typical dead body smell. Maybe rancid olive oil? Or rancid mink oil used to make leather more supple? There was something…

"Follow me. I am on a trail and you are my protector." Phyna began to roll away from the doorway, from the stables. "I grow tired of staring at senseless death."

Instead of poking through the hay piles which, though Croy could not place exactly why, he truly felt a compulsion to do, he followed the tiny rolling stone that was Phyna.

"You are on a trail?" Croy was speaking more to himself than actually asking a question.

"There is something amiss. Something that warps what should be into what should not." Phyna rolled around a corner and gained momentum as it sped along a long, straight, horizontal wall. They must be towards the back of the inn, or at least a rarely used side. There were half dead desert plants clinging to the rocky soil all around. Croy jogged to keep up. "It is… unique to my experience. I have not felt this type of disturbance before. It is… intriguing."

If ever Croy wished for Phyna's characteristic paranoia to take hold, it was at that moment. But somehow it was more intrigued than concerned. He jogged quietly along, wondering what else they were going to find, trying to ignore Phyna's cryptic descriptions. He thought that maybe they should find the others before exploring too far. "Maybe we should get the others before continuing. You know… just in case."

"Here. We are here. Open that door." Phyna had rolled around a corner and had stopped in front of a low angled cellar door.

"But…" Croy did not want to open the door. Images turned to worries turned to fears.

"You are my protector, are you not?" Phyna stayed a tiny stone.

Before he could think twice about it, Croy flung one of the doors open. Nothing happened. There was darkness below and another stench. It was even more oily but held less decay. Croy was unsure if that made him feel better or not.

"Help. Help me…" A voice as soft as the hot breeze wafted up from the cellar.

Croy looked at the tiny stone that was Phyna, but got no words of encouragement, nor any words that would alleviate him from having to enter the cellar. He turned back to the door, took a deep breath of the last fresh air he would have for a while, and began to descend the stairs. He did his best to ignore the quiet pleas of whomever was down there. They were eerie and kind of pathetic and did nothing to boost his desire to descend farther into the cellar.

At first, he took his time at each tread, trying his best not to let it squeak. However, the tiny stone rolled after him making loud thudding sounds as it dropped onto each next step. So he soon sped up, ignoring the thunderous sounds of his own feet. He reached the bottom landing, breathed deep the last semi-fresh air he would have for a while, and swung around the corner to see the cellar proper.

"Help…" The strong whisper, the weak shout, kept repeating itself, as if it were a chant.

The room was poorly lit. It appeared to have been ransacked. There was stuff strewn everywhere. Tables and chairs knocked over, barrels of beer, broken barrels of beer, shelves that had been toppled with their various sundries scattered on the floor. He did not want to stumble too far into the room, and since there were no more wooden treads to sound off of, he could no longer hear Phyna's location. There was a weird sound of iron being drug on stone.

"Nudepito!" Croy's hand glowed with a small flame dancing just above his outstretched palm. He knew there was a less draining way to create a light source, but he thought he could use the flame for minor defense if needed in a pinch. His thoughts stopped at the sight before him.

"Help me…" The voice came from the lump of a body against the far wall. The body was wrapped in chains and rags and appeared to be much too small.

Croy could not help himself. His feet slowly carried him over the detritus strewn on the floor to the pile of rags that the voice came from. It was an eerie feeling and yet strangely compelling. Like pushing on a bruise or wiggling a loose tooth until it falls out. Finally, he got close enough to see what it was. To see why the pile of rags appeared too small. There were pieces missing from the body.

"Great Gunzgak." The oath escaped from his lips with no more conscious thought than breathing.

"Hello…? Is someone there?" A Gaen face peered up from the rags. A face with empty holes where the eyes should have been.

The chains were wrapped around the Gaen's torso, but there were manacles laying on the ground nearby as well. The Gaen was missing a leg, but Croy could see a severed leg with a manacle still clamped around its ankle off to one side. The Gaen was also missing its left arm and its right hand, but they were not immediately visible. The wounds seemed fully cauterized over.

"Stop!" The voice was certainly Aedon's, it had that air of authority running through it. "Don't move any closer to that thing."

"Help me…" Croy stared at the tiny husk that lay before him. He thought it appeared to be male but was not fully positive. In any case, there was no way the Gaen had any fight left. It was hurt and that was all that really mattered, so he knelt down and scooched just a hair closer.

"Wait!" Croy could hear several others moving around behind him. Aedon was not alone. "Check its tongue, see if it's black."

"We don't know if that works with the living. That may only be a sign once the host has died." That sounded like Verin, but Croy could not tear his gaze from the mutilated creature in front of him.

"I heard some say they saw black tongues before we were attacked at the Forgotten Junction." That had to have been Tesjuk. Croy slowly reached towards the wounded Gaen, though he was unsure of what he was planning on doing. Force open its mouth?

"And I heard from others that they noticed pink tongues until the fight was over." Verin was being obstinate about the argument.

"To be honest, I am not sure either way, but if it does happen to be black, then we can take that as a bad sign and leave the wretch chained up." This was Aedon again, clarifying her original position.

"Please… Please! You have to help me. You have to set me free. What if it comes back?" The last sentence finally rose above a whisper. The orbless sockets of its eyes were a thousand times worse than the cataracts that the Blind One carried with him.

"Stick out your tongue and maybe we will set you free." Verin was crouched near Croy at this point. She had her long dagger out, tapping the tip on her knee, as if she were getting ready to use it to pry the wretch's mouth open.

"PLEASE!!" The scream was long and loud. Croy thought the poor thing was in pain, how could it not be?

"Muliderarc!" The healing spell rolled easily off Croy's tongue and out of his mind. He was paranoid enough to not want to touch the tortured creature, so he used Arc in lieu of To.

Croy felt bad about that for the briefest of moments, but it turned out the paranoia came with good cause. The healing spell did nothing of the sort. The Gaen burst into screaming flames. Croy felt someone pulling him backwards, or maybe he was being pushed by the small fireball in front of him. In the moment it was impossible to tell. The screeches seemed to go through several stages in the split second they were audible. There was certainly shock followed by anger and frustration, but at the end, they evoked nothing but pain.

The room was like a tinderbox. Flames began to lick the overturned furniture. Croy struggled to regain his footing. He was definitely being pulled by someone behind him. It was by the collar of his shirt, somewhat choking him in the process. He could not see what had happened to Verin. He could not really hear either. There was a loud buzzing sound that lowered in volume and in pitch the farther he was dragged away from the burning corpse.

"I never saw the tongue." Croy was talking to whomever was pulling him along but was unable to hear his own voice, so he was unsure if he was actually speaking aloud.

It was when he was finally outside and dragged around a corner and placed next to the most incongruous tree he could imagine, a large apple tree that must have required well water or irrigation or some form of derlian assistance in this dry climate, that he finally noticed who had pulled him to safety.

"Trela told me to keep an eye on you." It was all he could muster. It was odd, but Croy had not been burnt, nor even attacked really, but he felt as drained as if he had just been in a week-long siege. The tree cast a wondrous cool shade.

"Funny, she told me the same about you." Knill's infectious laugh filled Croy's ears. His smile was still in place, but his head cocked slightly and his left eye narrowed. "Did she really ask you to keep an eye on me?"

"Yes. Truly." Croy watched his friend's face stretch into an even broader smile.

"That's... kind of sweet." Knill was nodding to himself. He sat down next to Croy in the shade. "Yeah... I like that."

The bark was hard and rough through Croy's shirt. The shade was cool but contrasted against the heat attempting to infiltrate from all sides. It was as if the apple tree had cast a sphere of protection around them but he could still feel the attacks shaking the barrier. Knill was laughing and talking about Trela. It was a story that Croy had heard many times before, after Knill and Trela first escaped Serif and joined up with Iventorn's warpack and he had to pretend to be a ghulzan. It was a comfortable story, one that Croy felt he could completely ignore, and he could just listen to the rhythm of it. They sat that way for a while as the inn was engulfed in flames, the familiar tone and cadence of Knill's voice mixing with the crackle and the roar of the immolation happening before them, and Croy just... felt... good. He had a lazy smile on his face as Tesjuk and Verin finally gave up trying to stop the fire, as Aedon paced frantically, as Yasku unhitched the horses to help calm them in front of the blaze, as the dust kicked up by Trela's approaching coterie finally overshadowed the diminishing smoke in the sky. It was weird, there was no real reason for it—in fact there were several reasons against it—but he felt better than he had in a long time.

Chapter 11

Bisquailanchuftungtorshunqui flowed through the surrounding flame simply and easily. It was all around everywhere. Unlike some of the other realms that Bisquail had heard of, the flames did not come in different densities. Any direction was available. Always. There was something that differentiated parts of the realm from other parts. This was known as "intensity" and consisted of color changes, louder sounds, and more energy. The simple flames, the most common flames, were a red-orange color to Bisquail. They would turn yellow, then white, and then blue as the intensity increased. The sound, the background white noise, would roar and gain in volume as well as deepen in tone with greater intensities. The energy level was difficult to describe as to how it affected Bisquail. It was an odd mixture of excitement and panic—the closer you would get to intense flames, the more you felt like standing straight upright, of running, of moving faster, and usually well away from the intensity. But at times in the past, Bisquail had used the excitement and panic that built up to make itself burst through the intensity across to the other side. It just took incredible willpower to overcome the natural urge to turn and flee.

The flames would be more intense around private areas of small groups, or families, of Pyrans. This did not mean you could not enter where you wished, if you could control yourself, but that most would find the main entrance to the compound and announce themselves before entering. That was the intensity's main goal, to ensure communication and reduce surprises, to make it physiologically difficult to bypass an entrance. That was the job of culture, making certain things psychologically difficult.

The vast majority of the Pyran realm, however, only had differing intensities as a separation of space, not necessarily to create entrances. There were vast red plains and plazas. The majority of what would be called a public building in the derlian realm was red with slivers of yellow separating out rooms like walls. The yellow was easily seen through and simple to walk through, however. No one was required to find a particular entrance and, in fact, many rooms did not have a specific entrance at all—you were expected to enter through a wall. These comparisons to the derlian realm were not from Bisquail, no, for it had never visited the derlian realm. Bisquail was, in fact, the youngest Yaven that it knew. It had an insatiable curiosity about the derlian realm, and every single Yaven it spoke with had been there at least once. So words like "building" and "wall" were explained to Bisquail in terms of the intensity of flames, not the other way around.

For what seemed like an incredibly long time, Bisquail had yearned to visit the derlian realm. All mysteries, all unknowns, all other types of elements and even the derlians themselves were common knowledge to every being that Bisquail could communicate with. It seemed that this was the one thing that separated it from all the others. That it was the only one lacking in this knowledge, that it was somehow deficient. Disturbed may have been too harsh a term to describe the way that Bisquail felt, but certainly bothered. Yes, it bothered Bisquail that it had never visited the derlian realm. It wished to speak with a confident attitude about all of those ideas, to agree in a knowing manner when another spoke of some foreign derlian thing, to mention something that others did not immediately recognize. Bisquail, correct or not, imagined that only a visit to the derlian realm could give it that pride. Yes, more than anything, Bisquail wanted to feel prideful.

Following close behind the desire to feel included in the vast conversation about a realm it had never experienced was the very real desire to have its curiosity satisfied. One could hear about other elements, but without the direct experience, it was impossible to be able to really fathom them. Bisquail understood that others had achieved just this seemingly impossible task. The Belegs themselves were so intelligent and imaginative that they were able to understand enough about each other to conjure a place to meet without destroying themselves. But they had time, Bisquail told itself. They had spent aeons on that singular task, that ultimate feat of imagination. Bisquail did not have that much time behind itself, nor did it have the patience to stretch that much time out in front of itself, whether or not it had the other faculties and capabilities that such a feat would require. Neither did any of the other Pyrans that Bisquail spoke with. "Why imagine when you can experience?" or some such similar sentiment was always tossed back. What was the point of pondering or wondering when all one had to do was to be summoned? That would put an end to the debate. Bisquail could find out for itself whether or not it liked the derlian realm and wished to go back. And after that, it would be able to participate in all of the constant discussions. Bisquail could finally feel like it belonged.

So, how to go about being summoned? All Bisquail really had to do was ask one of its progenitors to pick their current, favorite mage and provide the mage with Bisquail's name to have them summon it. A simple question, a simple favor. But for some reason, Bisquail hesitated over this simple decision. It did not like asking for favors, and besides, it felt that one should be able to be summoned without an intermediary. By some random and chaotic and oh so derlian chance. Not some other's choice, imposed upon Bisquail by some well-meaning relative.

The main way to get summoned was to place your name down in the derlian realm somehow. Oh, there was certainly a time, way in the ancient past long before Bisquail came into being, when a derlian mage would recite a million random syllables in the hopes that it could communicate across the Void to some being of sentience, to some Yaven. That time seemed to be over by now, however. There was certainly no one who had randomly called to Bisquail, at least not that it had ever noticed. There were times that it would sit quietly, all alone, and listen. Listen for the faintest of voices to cross the nothingness and beckon it. But it had never noticed another calling to it, never noticed a derlian mage. So Bisquail had recently taken to sending its own name down through the only way left to it. It scattered its name through the Void.

The theory was that things scattered into the Void sometimes filtered into derlian minds as they slept. Apparently, the derlians were prone to imagining an impossible life for themselves in their chaotic minds while their bodies became useless and limp. These were called dreams. Bisquail was unsure of the mechanism, the reason, or the capability behind some derlian minds wandering through Chaos to stand at the frayed edge of the Void. This was what the theory posited, however. This was, supposedly, how the original Yavens who were the first to be summoned got their names to the lips of derlian mages, those that were not found by chance. This had the ring of random chance to Bisquail that it thought it wanted. So it would sit on its own side of the frayed edge of the Void and chant its own name out towards the eternal darkness. Over and over, sometimes whispering, sometimes screaming. Bisquail would never be able to satisfactorily explain why it wanted its first trip to the derlian realm to be mired in randomness—not to itself, nor to any others—but it added a delicious feeling of excitement to the otherwise overriding boredom of waiting.

The problem with this particular theory was that Bisquail was not quite sure if it was real. It had an air of impossibility, which was the main selling point of all things derlian. And though several different Pyrans had told the same story, the same theory, to Bisquail, none of them had ever experienced it themselves. They had heard of the theory from some older Yaven who said they had been summoned in that way. This shook Bisquail's confidence in the theory a little, but it still added the delicious feeling of excitement.

The main Pyran to tell Bisquail about the theory was Yibteralyshnickwoulsta. Yibtera was a progeny of one of the same parents as Bisquail's parents. In the Pyran Yaven realm extended family members would often travel together in small groups, roaming the realm in a meandering and somewhat aimless way. They did not have the same type of permanent structures so often found in the Gaen or Fluen realms, which made the concept of "home" a bit quaintly irrelevant. It was during some of these travels that Yibtera and Bisquail became close conversationalists. And Yibtera conversed nonstop about the derlian realm. It told incredible stories of its adventures, embellished or not, that piqued Bisquail's imagination about the realm. In fact, Bisquail could probably trace the beginning of its wanderlust back to those conversations.

"You cannot imagine the ocean, simply cannot imagine it." Yibtera often started its stories like that. "You cannot imagine…" It was a needling mantra that got under Bisquail's skin. Yibtera would do its best to explain it, to explain the ocean and what it entailed. What it *meant*. The vastness was easy to understand. The immersion, the engulfment, was easy to understand. But the teaming life, the variety of what Yibtera called "animals"… the frothy crashing waves, with their arrhythmic consistency… the salt, which somehow differentiated the ocean water from the water found in rivers and lakes… and the water. Of course. The water. "You simply cannot imagine water." It drove Bisquail a bit mad. Not crazy, not angry, but frustrated. It was a circular frustration, one that spun like a derlian mage's mindtrap—beginning at curiosity and wonder, traveling along the struggle to understand, the effort of imagination, but always ending with the taint of frustration for the failure to fully comprehend. But somehow… somehow it was delicious at the same time. The way Yibtera would explain things, the way it would act out its conversations with various derlian mages, the way it would get excited about a particularly interesting experience… It kept Bisquail coming back for more. Despite the frustration.

The story about the summoning theory concerned an unrelated Pyran friend of Yibtera's called Jafrazichealsuntwopkloiski. Jafraz was ancient. Ancient even by Yaven standards. It was much older than Gorbanax, but that had nothing to do with it learning how to be summoned. It told Yibtera that the first Pyrans to be summoned were summoned randomly. That somehow the derlians had found a name, found a path, found a spell. It was Jafraz's opinion that the Belegs had instigated this. Jafraz was not one of the first to be summoned, but rumors of it happening spread quickly. Whispered gossip whose truth was tenuous at best. This was before Menels were created, before there was any considered benefit to the experience. It was viewed by most as an abduction, something to be feared and avoided. But Jafraz and some of its friends at the time had a desire to visit the Belegs' creation. They did not know any of those who had already been abducted, so they pondered the conundrum. Not knowing derlians, not knowing dreams, not understanding magic in the slightest, they worked on the only thing they did know. The rumors were all clear that what had happened was a calling, that the name of the Yaven was important. Those that had been abducted had heard their own name being chanted repeatedly as they crossed the Void. So, according to Yibtera, Jafraz and its friends invented void dreaming. They sat on the edge of the Void and chanted their own names repeatedly. Until …finally… Jafraz got summoned.

That was not, of course, how Yibtera first came to be summoned. Yibtera was summoned by a mage that Jafraz knew. It was often difficult, since the derlians lived for such short amounts of time, for a Yaven to get to know any mage at all. After a summoning, however, if everything went well, the derlian would often write the Yaven's name down for future mages. Jafraz was being summoned constantly, or at least what seemed like constantly for a Yaven, according to Yibtera. Yibtera had offered to introduce Bisquail to Jafraz, for it should have known several mages of summoning age and would know enough about them for Bisquail to choose which sounded the most compatible. Yibtera often spoke of compatibility issues. That was, apparently, the most important consideration of your first summoning. Not where, or for how long, or what the mission entailed, but this all-encompassing idea of compatibility. According to Yibtera, compatibility was based upon the idea of mutual respect. That being summoned was much like choosing a friend in the Yaven realm, except that these things that encompassed the idea of mutual respect were unable to verify across the vast Void. You would not know, until you were there, in the unfamiliar derlian realm, whether or not you were compatible with the mage that had summoned you. The unfamiliarity was disconcerting and overwhelming on the first visit. It made any type of struggle difficult. This was why, amongst other reasons, that Yibtera wished to introduce Bisquail to Jafraz, or if Bisquail did not want to put its trust into a stranger, that Yibtera itself would get itself summoned with the express purpose of feeling out a mage. Bisquail did not want to be summoned that way, however. That was the core issue. Though, oddly enough, it could not satisfactorily explain, even to itself, exactly why it did not wish to be summoned that way. That was just the way it felt.

In its own way, Bisquail could have waited an aeon before being summoned that first time. It wanted to know, it had an insatiable curiosity, it truly wanted to experience the derlian realm for itself. But it was not an impossible desire to control. It was not overriding; it did not consume every waking thought. At least not until Bisquail met Utalsenpojachastinfulwudan.

Utal was utterly amazing to Bisquail. There was a quiet grace to each movement. The way Utal flowed around obstacles, through open fires and intense wall-like infernos, was mesmerizing. Utal moved with its whole body, with every tiny piece in complete unison. And each piece was in constant motion. There was always a twist and curl in the outstretched limbs. Bisquail knew Pyrans that moved as spheres. Balls of fire rolling along the striated intensity of the hallways. How boring! Not Utal, though. Utal stretched and flowed in long tendrils, smoky wisps wrapping around obstacles, feeling and gripping each object in its path. Just experiencing the beauty and grace of Utal, just watching Utal flow through the simplest of rooms, made Bisquail wish to modify its own movements. It made Bisquail strive to make a grace of its own. Not necessarily to mimic the exact grace that Utal showed, but to find a form that fit itself perfectly. It made Bisquail pay more attention to itself, to examine why it moved the way it did, what it could do to make the motion feel more comfortable. It was not something that had occurred to Bisquail before. It had just moved. There was nothing conscious about motion before Utal.

And smart! Utal was amazingly perceptive about the Pyran realm and its denizens. It understood what other Pyrans were thinking, even if they themselves did not. Utal would play a game with Bisquail. They would make small obstacles in the middle of a well-used pathway, nothing difficult or that would take too much thought or time to bypass, but complicated enough that several steps would have to be taken to get around the obstacles. They would hide themselves nearby, within viewing distance, but not necessarily within communicating distance. They would guess at how a Pyran was going to pass through the obstacles, betting only for bragging rights. They based their guesses only on the appearance of the Pyran and the way that they moved towards the obstacles. Utal was almost always correct, even when Bisquail was the only one setting up the obstacles. But it was not just that, not just guessing how others would react to random situations. It was also how Utal understood itself. How it understood Bisquail. How it understood the realm. The insights were real and amazing. Utal could somehow make Bisquail think of the answer just through conversation, not just say what it thought the answer should be. It made the insights seem that much more powerful.

And inquisitive. It knew nooks and crannies that Bisquail had never heard of before. But it was not just geography, it was everything. Utal had a pure hunger for knowledge. No, not just knowledge… but experience. Utal wished to experience everything. It was a beautiful burning desire. It almost had an energy all on its own. Utal was always on its way somewhere, always meeting with another Yaven, always doing something. Perpetual motion. Long limbs twisting and flowing towards the future.

And strong. And fierce. And funny. And kind. And insatiable. And imaginative. And… everything. Utal was everything. Bisquail desperately wanted to be one of Utal's friends, Utal's only friend, with the full Yaven connotations that accompanied that word. To do that, it felt that it should—no, that it needed—to be summoned to the derlian realm. To become, in Utal's language, "experienced."

Utal did not discuss the derlian realm as often as Yibtera, not by a long shot. But it did converse of the realm often. And when it did, it was to illustrate some obscure point, to make an effort of explanation that Bisquail just could not comprehend. It frustrated Bisquail to be missing such an integral part of being with Utal, such an integral part of Utal itself. It seemed to frustrate Utal much more, however. It did not necessarily seem to cause anger, there was nothing palpable, but it seemed to bring about a low-grade disappointment. That some things just could not be shared, not be discussed. It always seemed to be in the middle of something, as if they were getting close to some invisible, non-corporeal destination, when—bam!—they hit the wall of Bisquail's ignorance. It was jarring, that disappointment, and it hung over the rest of the conversation like a dirty shroud. There was really only one thing to do. There was really only one cure. That was to get summoned.

So Bisquail sat on the Yaven side of the Void, chanting and hoping. It poured all its energy into this, all of its time. All of its time that was not spent with Utal, that is. It was not difficult to do—in fact it was probably one of the simplest things to do, just chanting—but it was quite disheartening. All of that time and energy for… what? For nothing. Nothing ever happened, nothing changed. It became somewhat difficult to for Bisquail make itself go and sit there and waste its life. Half the time it was chanting its name it was thinking of other things. Like why did it not just ask Yibtera to introduce it to Jafraz. Why not? What stupidity was this, trying to become summoned "naturally?" Even for just a tiny amount of time, to just immerse itself in the derlian realm for the briefest of moments. To experience water, stone, air. To experience derlians, to experience magic. Then it could come back and live the rest of its life without returning if it wished. Just to be able to converse with others, to be able to fully converse with Utal. That was what really stuck in Bisquail's craw. All of this time that it could be communing with Utal, and here it was, on the edge of the Void, wasting its life chanting. Repeating. Redundant. It started to become unenjoyable. Bisquail stopped believing it would work, that the rumors, the old tales, were all lies. Intentional or not, it did not matter. Maybe it had worked at one time, but certainly not anymore. With the change in attitude came the change in essence. It started to become a waste of time. It started to weigh upon Bisquail. A frustrated depression set in. Bisquail thought that full capitulation would be better than the… waste. Bisquail had decided to meet with Yibtera a little later. It was staying and chanting out of habit more than anything. It was over, the decision had been made, Bisquail was going to quit the useless, wasted, effort. That was when it happened.

"Bisquailanchuftungtorshunqui… Bisquailanchuftungtorshunqui… Bisquailanchuftungtorshunqui…" It was faint, but unmistakable. It was unmistakable not only for what it sounded like, but also for what it did not sound like. It did not sound like a fellow Pyran Yaven was attempting to commune. There was a taint of …accent?… that hinted at something different, but it was not just that. There was an undeniable difference to the *feeling* of the attempt to commune. It was a bit indefinable, a *zing* within a faraway echo. It was somewhat of a new sensation and, therefore, it was hard for Bisquail to describe. And that made it unmistakable. Was that not what Bisquail was searching for? A new sensation? A giddy thrill of enthusiasm charged through it.

How to respond? How to commune with the unknown? Bisquail did not want to just succumb, to be dragged into, and through, the Void. But it was unsure of how to open a discussion. Did it push? Could it even do so? Did the derlian mage have to pull? Would the mage even try to pull, would it even want to? How mutual was this arrangement? There was a thrill of fear that ran through Bisquail about the unknown. Maybe it should have had Yibtera find a friendly mage. Maybe it should have asked more about the first communication. Maybe…

"Bisquailanchuftungtorshunqui!" It was becoming insistent. It was starting to tug at Bisquail. There was the small feeling of movement.

"Who are you?" It was all that Bisquail could think of. To push, with all its available energy, the essence of the question across the Void. In the general direction of where the calling came from. Did it work? Did the mage receive any signal? There was no way to tell.

"Bisquailanchuftungtorshunqui!!!" It was becoming urgent. It started to repeat with forcefulness. It was no longer a distant echo. "Bisquailanchuftungtorshunqui!!!!!" The name became a command. Not simply something that signified uniqueness, no. It demanded something of Bisquail. It demanded obedience. It demanded movement.

Bisquail began to be pulled. It did its best to stay put. It resisted with all of its might. Bisquail no longer wished to see the derlian realm. Not in that way. Not under duress. A panic began to well up as the pulling became more insistent. The pulling caused movement of part of Bisquail, but part felt like it was still well rooted.

It turned into a stretching. Bisquail resisted with all of its power, but the stretching continued. It became painful. Bisquail wished the pain to indicate a tearing, a rupture. Bisquail wished to be shredded into pieces, as long as the majority of it, the conscious part of it, could stay there in the Yaven realm forever. It screamed and howled against the agony. Against the movement. But to no avail.

There was a horrendous POP. The noise and the feeling rippled through Bisquail as the stretching snapped back and it was no longer rooted to the Yaven realm. Faster and faster it sped, through the fire and into the Void. Bisquail reached speeds it had never experienced before. It did all it could to slow itself down, gripped all of the nothingness at its disposal, but nothing could slow the movement. Nothing could stop the summoning. The howling did not escape into the Void, it just echoed in Bisquail's mind. And then… pain.

Parts of Bisquail felt as if they were tearing apart. Other parts felt pinched and crushed. It barely noticed the darkness, the stone floor it had struck during the summoning, the quenching tubs nearby filled with the most foreign of liquids. It did not notice the air that surrounded it, the metal anvils, the wooden beams. All Bisquail really noticed was the pain. And the rage. The rage pounced upon Bisquail and bit into it. The rage scratched and clawed, it howled alongside Bisquail; it swallowed, devoured, ingested Bisquail. In the end there was no sensing the strange, foreign, derlian realm. There was no "Why have you summoned me?" There was no conversation, no sensation, not even pain anymore. The rage consumed all. It was pure. It was nemesis.

Bisquail needed to destroy. All other feelings, desires, intellectual curiosities, all of those useless things that keep a being busy during the long stretch of eternity… They all fell away. The only need was destruction. Bisquail needed to find the mage and needed to kill the mage. Only then could it pretend to be a Yaven again.

Bisquail reached out with all of its being. It could sense fire somewhere in the distance. Not real close, maybe not in the same room, but somewhere. Bisquail called to it, drew it in like a derlian drawing a breath, like the inhalation before a deafening scream. It reached out as if it were back in its own realm, surrounded by its own element, living the only life it had known. Bisquail felt the energy moving, felt the distant fire's desire to be with it, felt the movement.

Then, just before it could coalesce into a larger being, just before it could attack with all of its might, just before it could bring all of its power to bear, just before the nemesis peaked… it was shut down. There was no other way to describe it. The fire stopped listening, stopped moving, stopped coalescing, and with that, the energy stopped moving as well. Bisquail looked up in the direction of the emptiness, the direction that it felt the snuff emanate from, and saw what had to be derlian mages. There were some that scurried in the peripheral senses and some that sat and stared. Bisquail was being stymied and stifled.

The next instant the chanting began. The next instant the pain began. The next instant the nemesis took full control over Bisquail. There was no thought. But there was no power, either. That one instant when it had first appeared allowed Bisquail the useless luxury of a thought. That instant it had been building power allowed it the useless luxury of hope. Bisquail was no longer a conscious being, no longer understood such high concepts as hope. It reached out to one of the scurrying figures before it and shot itself into the figure. The fires of the derlian realm would not come to Bisquail, but it had brought some of its own. There was a delicious scream as Bisquail boiled the blood of one of the evil mages. It leapt upon another as the chanting reached a fever pitch. It was melting the eyes out of their sockets as an unnerving cooling sensation enveloped Bisquail. It had never known water before, so it was unable to fully understand the slick sensation, but it felt the *weakening*. The chanting increased in volume, increased in power. Bisquail had never known steel before, so it was unable to comprehend the stiff sensation. The immobile sensation. The numbing… the numbing.

The sword was quenched. The screaming was deafening. The screaming was maddening. The screaming came from Bisquail itself, though it did not understand. It was like hearing torture from another room. It could not pinpoint the direction, the distance, it did not realize the screams emanated from itself. The memories of Bisquail were being seared away. Peeled like layers of flesh from a flayed derlian. It had a hard time thinking of anything. The rage was fading. It forgot why it had come to this realm. Bisquail saw an image of Yibtera in its disintegrating mind and wondered why. Why an image? Why a Pyran? Why fire? Fire? Bisquail saw an image of Utal in its frayed mind. It no longer wondered. There was a sadness, yes. There was a frustration even. But there was no rage, there were no thoughts. The screaming was distant now. It was nicer to be distant. It was nicer to be in the quiet. The image of Utal faded. No images ever returned. The idea that there was such a thing as an image faded. No more sadness. No more anything. No more nothing. Nothing. Not a thing. The sword was quenched.

Trela sat there with Strife across her lap and a scowling Taglo above her. Not that she could quite see the scowl but she could certainly feel it. Strife was unsheathed, naked. It was heavy but cold. She had thought it should be hot. *It should, at the least, emanate warmth from the Pyran Yaven trapped inside,* thought Trela. But no. The chill in the metal brought heat from her knees into it. She could feel the transference.

Trela had not wanted to be there, certainly not with an angered Taglo. She had argued quite loudly, but unsuccessfully, that only the mages needed to be there. It seemed that Taglo did not trust mages in general, and those it did not know in specific. Accordingly, only Feyazki, Ryshial, and Serghno were present. Croy was not considered powerful enough and the Blind One was not trusted by anyone, so the Gaens were not represented. The only one who Taglo would allow to touch the sword, however, was Trela. She had never learned to cast a spell in her life. So she was, basically, a piece of furniture to rest the sword on.

"Let me try to commune with it." Feyazki was staring at the back of Taglo. The other two mages merely nodded their heads.

Taglo ignored Feyazki and scowled at the cold sword. Taglo had not wanted to be in the same room it. Had insisted upon keeping it wrapped in layers and layers of cloth and sheepskin. It had certainly never touched it. Trela had wondered when the investigations would begin but had had the good sense not to bring it up.

"I am able to sense something. Something Pyran, something in pain, something that wishes the release of death. I should be able to commune, but it is… too far. You can see someone on the horizon, but cannot hear them, yes?" Taglo did not turn towards Feyazki.

"Yes." Feyazki's reply was quiet and unobtrusive.

"It is like that. But they cannot wave their arms, or jump up and down, or make any visual communication of any kind. It is like attempting to talk with a derlian who has no ears, no mouth, no lungs, no throat. All there is, is pain." If a Yaven could sigh, Taglo did so. "There is nothing… coherent."

Taglo started to hum a little. The humming became deeper but did not get louder. Ryshial and Serghno quietly looked at their feet while Feyazki continued to stare at Taglo. The humming raised and lowered in volume, in intensity, in pitch. It went on like that for some time. It felt like a good hour, but Trela knew it to be much shorter. Probably only twenty minutes or so. She was not sure if it had been trying to commune but that was her guess. Taglo was silent for a while after the humming had stopped.

"Fine. Try magic." Taglo dejectedly shifted to a corner. Feyazki deftly and quietly shifted out of the way.

Clap! Feyazki slapped his hands together and rubbed them for a moment, standing just in front of Trela. His brow was furrowed, but in concentration not in a scowl. His hands slowed, stopped. His lips pursed for a second. "Lumsidpiarc!" His face drained of color, but he just stood there staring intently at the sword. Nothing happened.

"That was quite interesting, yes. Quite clever. But you are going to need to know the Yaven's name if you are attempting to summon it out of the sword." Ryshial walked forwards to stand behind Feyazki. "Let me try something." Ryshial paused while he got out of the way. She also rubbed her hands for a moment and stared up at the ceiling. "Lumfintotarc!" She waited there, hand held up for others' silence, for quite some time. They all waited patiently until, finally, "Nothing." The sigh said it all. "I was hoping, if we could somehow commune for a moment, we could get the name of the trapped Yaven."

"Let me try one. You may have had the pillar tilted the wrong way." Serghno moved to the foreground. Trela sat there patiently, Strife held steadily on her knees. His long, waxed mustaches were curled upwards, quivering with his concentration. "Lumfinpiarc!" He waited there, with his own hand up for a little less time than Ryshial. More nothing.

They tried various spells for quite a while. Every once in a while they would huddle and discuss something heatedly. Some finer point of visualization or emphasis. But nothing they cast could allow them to get commune with the trapped Yaven, let alone get the Yaven out. Finally, Trela spoke what she had been thinking.

"What if the name is hidden in the steel? Not a spirit, not a mind, but try to commune with the sword itself." She smiled as each of their faces lit up.

"Lumsidheparc!" Feyazki was the first to try.

"Lumfinheparc!" Ryshial followed almost immediately.

They waited for a couple of minutes for those spells to have whatever effect that they might have had. For any effect at all.

"What if we just changed the steel to fire? You know, used -traheprefpi?" Serghno spoke up into the silence.

"Quite clever, yes." Ryshial gave out praise but did not condemn or condone the idea.

"So... Do we know if these items can be destroyed?" Feyazki had turned back towards Taglo. It was still in the corner. Trela could not tell if it was sulking or thinking.

"No. We know nothing. That is why we are here, to learn all we can." Taglo slowly wafted over to the group. Trela had to look up at all of them.

"I thought the reason we were here was to kill the Cabal and destroy all of the items." She knew that it would not help the situation, but she had gotten tired of sitting there, merely being Strife's display furniture.

"We could learn a few things along the way." The terse and irritated response came from Ryshial. Trela ignored her glare.

"No. The queen is right." Taglo shifted slightly, back and forth. "While we do need to learn as much as possible, we cannot do anything that jeopardizes our primary objective. I would really like to know what would happen if you tried to turn the steel sword into fire. I really would. Part of me thinks that if that particular spell were cast, the Yaven would be extracted from the item like water drawn up a siphon. That is the part of me that has spent too long amongst you derlians. That part is still quite happy to cling to hope and unknowable promises." Taglo shifted towards the door, towards the exit. "Part of me thinks the spell will just not work. That more time and energy will merely be frittered away. While the final part of me, the older, wiser, more cynical part, worries that you will ruin everything by testing that spell."

"If our primary objective is to destroy the items, then how can anything be ruined by trying the transmutation?" Feyazki walked towards the door, not quite placing himself in Taglo's way. "If the item is destroyed then we will know of an easy way to destroy the others."

"What if we have to show some of the Cabal that we have an item? What if that is the key to gaining their trust?" Trela was ready to let them cast the spell and let Taglo walk out the door, she was quite ready to be done, but she could not help interjecting. It was, at that moment, their only bargaining tool. Their only physical link to the ideals of the Cabal. Maybe if she had thought the odds of the spell pulling the Yaven out of the sword were higher she would have kept quiet.

"Then why didn't you bring that up before?" Serghno interjected himself into the conversation.

"I thought you were just trying to communicate with the doomed Yaven, I didn't think you were trying to destroy the sword." Trela was not enjoying being the only one in the room sitting down. They all hovered expectantly over her.

"We are not destroying anything today." Taglo began to shift out the door. "You all can keep casting whatever other spells you wish to. I am done. I need to rest. Or at least I need to leave this room."

They all stood over her in silence for a little while longer. Feyazki kept his eyes on the doorway, Ryshial was sort of glaring at Trela still while also sort of staring off, and Serghno was looking down, whether at his own feet or at Trela's, she was not sure.

"So... can I sheath Strife?" Trela looked expectantly up at them all. They all looked as tired as she felt. So she stood and sheathed the sword. "A good day to you all." She left in much same humor as Taglo. She was done.

As she turned down the hallway, she wondered why. She had not had to cast any spells. It was not one of her kind that was trapped. She had only sat there. There was no logical reason the mood that had crept into her should be there. Maybe Taglo's mood was infectious.

She turned down another hallway. After the Desert's Cusp Inn had burned down, they had wandered for some time along... well, along the cusp of the desert. Just yesterday they had found this tiny, abandoned village. Trela was not even sure she could call it a village, there was only one building of size and four smaller ones. There were a couple of outlying farmhouses, but those appeared to be abandoned as well. Her day scouts should be returning shortly. In another hour or so dusk would be settling in.

There was nothing there, nothing alive at least. There were no signs of a struggle, no horrific blood stains, no dead animals. Nothing. It was as if the entire village just decided to up and leave at the same time. The carts were gone, the tack and harnesses and saddles were gone, the pets were gone, the clothing was gone, the tools and utensils were gone. Nothing looked ransacked, however. The doors were all closed nicely, the sheets were still on the beds, the closets, though partially empty, did not look disheveled. They had plenty of time to leave. It was a conscious choice, not a panic. It was an orderly retreat.

Trela had set up their main camp in the main building. It was a kind of catch-all governmental building. It had a small section that was used like an inn, and it had a small section where the governor or mayor or constable or whatever the Gaens used above ground to keep their citizens in line had their meetings. It housed a large enough kitchen for her coterie and a public house that still had kegs of beer, and it also had a tiny library. This was all packed into a fairly small building. Trela had not really thought of it before, but she wondered why the main Gaen cities were underground, while the farming villages were above ground. She would have to ask Knill or Croy about that later.

She decided to leave the building and wander around outside. The sun hung low but was still bright. There were bodies moving in the distance. Her own warriors took on a blurred and grayish appearance. That one could have been Estfale or Dartsyle, that other one could have been Zira or Escha. It was with an odd, disconnected aura around herself that she walked down the main street. It felt as if nothing had a spirit, nothing contained any meaning. A cold rushed into her. She could feel it slip into her spine like a fine thread. Thin, almost imperceptibly so, but long. The freezing thread went from her lower hips to the base of her skull. She looked around her; no one seemed to notice her. No one acknowledged her existence. Did she want them to? She could have yelled, swung her arms around, started to bark orders. But no, she enjoyed being invisible for a moment. Maybe enjoyed was too strong of a word. She certainly didn't not enjoy being invisible. It was a mood of negating negatives, not of positives. She continued wandering down the main road. There was a bleakness to the sun, as if it shed light but no warmth. It felt like nighttime. It felt like everyone should be asleep. It felt like she was walking into a dream. But it was too bright. The sun kept trying to pierce the bleakness. She turned to her right, away from the dying sun, into a wide alley. Or maybe it was a narrow street. She did not care enough to examine the doors on either side of her. Were they back doors? Were they front doors? Why could no one commune with Strife? What use was magic if it could not perform the impossible? What use was this mission if they were unable to save any Yavens? What use was she if she were unable to find the Cabal? What use was she?

The thread kept trying to pierce into her skull. She walked in a straight line, not looking left or right. It was like a frozen needle, twisting and turning, pushing, pushing, pushing. Trying to break into jail. Trying to pierce, to penetrate. Trela stopped walking. That was the exact problem. There was no use. It was not just that they were on an unobtainable quest, that they were just chasing phantoms, just chasing smoke, but that they were performing no function. No good could come from the quest. There was no use to any of it. Trela stopped walking. She was staring ahead, surely, but she saw nothing. Nothing of use. It was all blurred and grayed. She knew there were buildings nearby, but they were like blinders on a horse, keeping her useless vision forwards without adding any detail. The needle in her spine rammed against the base of her skull. Repeatedly. It should have been painful, somewhere in her fog-ridden mind she understood that. A frozen needle ramming the base of your skull should be painful. That was a fact. She dropped to her knees, her spine still straight as an arrow. She thought she could see her breath. She tried to remember how cold the day was. Was it cold enough to see your breath? Through all the numbness came a foreign thought. What if she just let the needle in? There was no pain, so why not? There was not a struggle, per se, but a strong desire to end the ramming, the pushing, the twisting and turning. The only way to stop it was to give in to it. That was what she was told.

Just what told her that? She was unsure. But it came from outside of her. She felt that to be true. And that nagged at her. Just a little. The needle nagged at her as well. Why should she let anything enter her skull? She was the Kriishan. She was the Kriishan! The bleakness began to nag at her. Why was she bleak? She tried to remember but could only recall the failure with Strife. That did not seem like enough to make her bleak. At least not for who she thought of herself as. Who was she? She was the Kriishan!

She started to batter back at the needle. Her quest was not useless, it was one of destiny. Her coterie was not useless, they were great conquerors. She had defeated Qizern, she was the Queen, she was the Kriishan! Then the real struggle began. The thread thickened into a string and spiraled around her spine. It stopped trying to slip into her skull and began to constrict her spine. The pain was incredibly intense, but she could not move. She just stayed there, kneeling upright in the dirt. The cold increased until it almost seemed like fire was wrapped around her spine. The chill should have started her shaking, shivering, but it was if she were paralyzed. But she could still feel pain. The string turned into a rope. The rope was so thick that it felt as if her spine were fully wrapped, fully engulfed. Why could she not scream? Why could she not lie down? She did not need to feel the pain, she thought. She could overcome the pain, she was the Kriishan. Wasn't she?

Trela tried with all of her might to think of herself as an agent of destiny. She tried to think of anything to push back against the frozen rope. It came down to one statement, only one thing that she could chant in her mind. Only one way out. *I am the Kriishan. I am the Kriishan.* She began to feel a little solace in her chant. She began to be able to feel the rocks under her knees. She began to feel something besides the icy pain. That was when the rope truly began battering at the base of her skull. It did not try to pierce, to sneakily insert itself, no. It fully rammed. Repeatedly. Fast and continuous. She was unsure of what it was banging against. What hard piece of bone was stopping the rope from smashing through, from breaking and entering, from wrapping itself around her brain, from squeezing the life out of her?

The fact that the rope had not yet penetrated did not really make sense. But Trela was unable to contemplate such things. She was incapable of complex thought. In fact, she was unable to think of anything besides four words. *I am the Kriishan. I am the Kriishan.* It was all she had. All she could cling to. It was all that she *was*. It was the essence of her being. That she could boil her essence down to one thought, one idea, one word, did not bother her. The simplicity of it was soothing amongst all of that paralyzing pain. Ram, ram, ram. Bang, bang, bang. She was not even sure she could feel the cold anymore. She had lost all sensation outside of her spine, her skull, her brain, and the rope. The horrible, relentless rope.

Whatever bone was in the way was getting pulverized. Surely it should have been dust by then. Trela was no longer able to think four words, to string anything into something resembling a sentence. A cognitive thought. It was merely *Kriishan, Kriishan, Kriishan.* Repeating endlessly. Repeating to the rhythm of the rope. They beat at the same time. It was all that she understood. All that she was. There was no other life. There were no other derlians. There was no world beyond her spine, her skull, her brain, and the rope. Nothing else existed anymore. It seemed that nothing else had ever existed. The only other thing was the chant. One word hung in the void of pain. One word that pulsed to the same rhythm as the pain. If asked, she would have been unable to come up with her own name, been unable to come up with speech at all. There was nothing more. Ram, ram, ram. *Kriishan.* Bang, bang, bang. *Kriishan.* It would have been maddening if she had any mind left. Just then she started to cough. A great hacking, wheezing, racking cough. Her eyes burned and teared up, her nose ran snot, her throat felt scraped raw. She lay there in the street, in the alley, on her side in the fetal position, while her lungs exploded. She could not see but felt something oily escape her mouth. She coughed for what seemed like forever. Finally, she could breathe again. Finally, she could feel the world again.

"Trela? Trela! Are you all right?" It was Rewista, her short black hair framed her face, framed her piercing raptor eyes. Her face was the only thing that Trela could focus on.

"What... what happened?" Trela wondered briefly if she had vomited. There were others, other shapes of bodies surrounding her, but Rewista was all that she could focus on. She thought her head was resting on Rewista's knee but was not sure.

"I was walking by... You were walking in a daze. I tried to talk to you, but you did not look over at me. It was as if you did not hear me." Rewista gently pushed Trela's sweat-soaked hair out of her face. "You dropped to your knees. You dropped to the ground. You coughed up the most amazing amount of jet-black smoke. It floated in a thick bulbous line for a moment and then ...it just... dissipated."

"I saw the smoke as well." Kryhir spoke up just beyond Trela's vision.

"I hate to sound weird but show me your tongue." Rewista was smiling down upon her. Trela opened her mouth wide and stuck her tongue out, trying to touch her own chin. A sigh of relief rippled through the tiny crowd. "Nice and pink, not a touch of black." Rewista giggled a little.

That was when Trela fully realized what had happened. She had known a little bit, had an inkling. The talk of smoke had brought it to the front of her mind. But Rewista checking for a black tongue really solidified it. She had been attacked by a non-corporeal Tlana. In broad daylight. And she had fought it off on her own.

"We have to warn the others. Everyone must be on guard." Trela tried to stand but her legs were still quite rubbery. "Kryhir, gather the others. Get Feyazki to *whisper* to the scouts, bring them back in. Let everyone know that we are under attack." Trela wished that she could recognize the others around her to give out more specific orders, but everyone began to scatter anyway. She lay there and just breathed for a while. She could have rested there for an hour or more. She almost closed her eyes, but she knew she had work to do. "You are going to have to help me up. I need to get back to the main building."

"Of course, my Queen." Rewista shifted and slid until she was able to get Trela's arm around her neck. "Ready?"

The close call worried Trela to no end. She gathered her warriors and compressed them into the main building's common room and pub areas. There was a folding set of doors that she fully opened so that all could hear her and still be comfortably seated, or at least comfortably standing. She had an idea to explain the feeling of the attack, to explain the slow grip before the real struggle began. She wanted the others to recognize the signs. She was not even sure how long she had been… stalked? Steered? Attacked? Did it start when she left the building? At least. Did it start while they were attempting to commune with Strife? She doubted it, but could not be sure. She wished fervently that the Tlana had not been around Taglo. But why not? She would need to talk to Taglo about what it had sensed, but that was for later. Now she had a room full of expectant derlians.

She told them her story, from entering the street to kneeling in the alley, in as much vivid detail as she could recall. Mainly the feelings, what she considered to be the warning signs, the bleakness and the gray, the thread and needle, everything before the full attack. Once she was under attack, she knew she was being attacked. She was not sure what had allowed her to survive that, to be able to resist. She was not sure if whatever she actually did could be replicated by strangers, or even by herself at a later date. She would certainly cover that part but thought it would sound more like she was bragging rather than imparting information. No, it was the insidious portion that concerned her, made her want to explain it to her warriors. They needed to be able to sense the beginning. That would be the only way they might get help in time. Though in what form the help might come in, she did not know.

Trela explained all she could, in as much detail as she could. She was going to open the floor to questions when a youthful Gaen stood up. She did not recognize him and so assumed, correctly, that he was with Roqural Mur'jin at the Forgotten Junction.

"I would like to point out that you were attacked during the daylight hours, though near dusk. You were attacked on a public street." The young Gaen took a breath. "Their attack is more effective at night. It is more effective if you are alone, if you are already afraid, if you have already lost hope…"

"So… You are saying I might not have survived if I had been attacked at night?" Trela raised an inquisitive eyebrow. She had not meant to sound defensive. "Certainly, I survived through luck more than…"

"No, that is not what I am saying." She was quickly interrupted by the young Gaen. "Well, not really. I do not know if you would have succumbed if the attack was more focused. You are a great warrior-queen, and I am just a young recruit. I know that my capacities are minor compared to yours." He held up a hand to stave off her attempt to interrupt him. "That is not what I am saying, however." He took a deep breath. "They specifically targeted you. They want you. They want you bad enough to try to ambush you in broad daylight, to risk an attack when you are surrounded by allies. They have tipped their hand because they thought the element of surprise was enough to get to you, to catch you off guard. This will not be their last attempt to assassinate you."

"What is your name?" Trela wanted to deflect where the conversation was headed. She did not want to spend an hour arguing against being shadowed by guards everywhere. She already had precious little alone time.

"Caephin Beo'jin, my queen." He performed an odd bow. Trela was a little concerned that Gaens who she did not really know were showing fealty to her—*shouldn't their loyalties lie with their own lord?*—but the concern was fleeting. There were always larger concerns, and besides, she definitely needed their loyalty for the specific mission.

"Caephin, what was your experience? Did you not also get attacked? Please, tell me what your warning signs were." Trela decided she would have every Gaen from Roqural's group tell their individual stories if she had to.

About four of the Gaens told their stories before most of the details were repeating. It took two more to satisfy all who wanted to come up and share their story. By then all those in attendance were ready to move on. Trela felt good wrapping up the meeting. She should have let the Gaens explain their attack by the Tlana a long time ago. She wasn't quite sure why she hadn't done that yet. Knowledge was power, she truly believed that. But some sort of pride led her to think that the Gaens' succumbing to the Tlana negated some of that power. That because they had been overwhelmed, their information would not be useful. In fact, it was quite the opposite. Though her story was filled with as much detail as she could recall, theirs had that one additional piece of information. The piercing. The fall. The succumbing. Each had a different point of departure, a different point in the story when they had succumbed, and that rounded out the warning signs nicely. Yes, as the meeting was wrapping up, she felt good about the information imparted. They all left a little better equipped to deal with future attacks.

By the evening, Trela was still a little shaken up and decided to spend some time amongst friends. She found Estfale, Dartsyle, and Aedon drinking beers. She thought she would just share a quick mug, some fine company, and then head to bed. Instead, she ended up having more to drink than she had anticipated, though she still avoided any heavy or difficult conversations.

"Where do you think Iventorn is?" The thought crossed Trela's mind every once in a while, but she rarely voiced it. The fuzziness of the beer made it come back around. "I would have certainly given him a just reward."

"You know, I've heard this name mentioned previously. He was a leader of an opposing warpack, correct?" Aedon squinted over her own mug of beer, trying to piece together various tales she had heard of Trela's campaign to become queen. Estfale and Dartsyle nodded in unison to her question. "So why did Iventorn not join forces with Trela? Was he an ally of Qizern?"

"Oh, no, Iventorn did not like Qizern at all. He just didn't believe in the idea of the Kriishan or, if anything, that he hoped *he* was destined to be king, not Trela." Estfale chuckled lightly to himself.

"True. Iventorn wanted the power to be his. He wanted the biggest warpack, to be the most feared and admired leader, to be the one to defeat Qizern. But he was too much of what he would call a 'realist.' I agree that he did not believe in the idea of a Kriishan, or really, even of destiny. He would have loved to have defeated Qizern and been crowned king, but he knew the limitations of his warpack. He knew he could never have gained enough warriors to force Qizern to cross swords with him. He knew he would never have had enough to get across the Dekhan plateau." Dartsyle was chuckling alongside Estfale.

"Luckily Trela was unable, or unwilling, to read the warning signs of reality." As Estfale spoke, they both laughed loudly.

"So, he did not believe in himself?" Aedon was nodding to herself.

"Oh, no, he thought very highly of himself. But it takes a certain kind of self-belief to defy reality. Iventorn prized reality above all other ideals." Estfale was still grinning as he tried to explain himself.

"Whereas I prize destiny above all other ideals." Trela inserted herself more assertively into the conversation. She knew that Estfale and Dartsyle were two of her most trusted and loyal warriors, but they were dangerously close to implying something quite impertinent.

"Of course, my Queen." Estfale's grin did not slip but did look slightly strained. "And you have proven, time and again, to be destiny's most favorite vessel."

"Remember when Iventorn tried to take Qizern's arms shipment headed to Dun Frething?" Dartsyle deftly deflected.

"Oh, yes, where we tried to destroy the bridge over the Nikin Chasm? That's a good one." Estfale stood and began to refill everyone's mugs.

"You see, Dun Frething was a tiny keep close to the chasm. Which is where all the goods from the main roads, from Agoge, came across. Iventorn knew of a lesser road that wound up to Dun Frething, and he assumed if we could destroy the bridge, we could grab the weapons and armor, and Qizern would unable to send warriors to hunt us down in time. The only warriors of Qizern's in the area would be at Dun Frething and they would be outnumbered, and without their new arms shipment, would be poorly equipped. They could defend their keep, certainly, but they would have a hard time sending sorties out beyond the walls. Especially as Iventorn was planning on high-tailing it out of there before they knew the shipment had been raided."

"We were not in the contingent to attempt to destroy the bridge, so we had no idea what was going on down there. We were spying on the keep, making sure that the warriors there stayed there." Estfale sat back down.

"This was before *whisperers* were used all the time." Dartsyle nodded to Aedon as he spoke since she might not know about the Pyran military tactics of the time.

"It all seemed to be taking a long while, but that may have been because we were bored stiff staring at the guards walking along the cat-walked parapets. Suddenly, with no alarms or changes in the visible guards, the drawbridge started to be let down. We wasted valuable moments arguing if we should immediately ride to find Iventorn." Estfale looked sideways at Dartsyle while pausing.

"Admittedly, I was on the wrong side of the argument. I thought that maybe it could have been a merchant caravan heading out, or a hunting party, or anything really. There really is no way to tell what's behind the drawbridge until it's lowered enough." He placed his hand on his heart to show his sincerity. "Besides, it only took a couple of minutes to lower and then to raise the portcullis."

"So, eventually, we got on our horses and charged out of there, hoping to kick up as little dust as possible." Estfale picked up the story where he had left off. "The problem was, and this is in Dartsyle's favor for staying to see who came out, the amount of warriors that exited the keep was much larger than Iventorn had anticipated. And they looked fairly well armed."

"And fast. They came out very fast and we were only so far ahead of them. We should have left as soon as the drawbridge started lowering." Dartsyle lifted the hand that was on his heart.

"We got to Iventorn as quickly as we could, and they were just finishing their fight with the arms shipment guards. We yelled and waved our arms as much as possible, trying to get their attention. We figured we were about to be slaughtered with the keep's warriors hot on our heels and nowhere to go." Estfale paused as he drank from his mug.

"We had assumed the bridge was out and we needed to turn and fight." Dartsyle interjected briefly and then took a sip of his own, letting Estfale pick the story back up.

"We got to Iventorn and Cavish as they were examining the wagons with the weapons. Three of Qizern's wagons had suffered damage during the melee. One had a broken axle and the others each had a damaged wheel. It was bad enough luck that we've always wondered if the guards had damaged their own wagons on purpose. We explained that the warriors from Dun Frething were only a couple of minutes away and everything was dropped. That's realism right there. We didn't even try to shift any weapons from the broken wagons to the good one. The one wagon that was still serviceable was hastily driven away and we all followed."

"I thought there was no escape?" Aedon appeared totally engrossed, glancing between the two narrators.

"That's the best part! You see, the group sent to destroy the bridge had failed. Utterly failed. We were able to get across and hold the other side." Dartsyle laughed and slapped his knee.

"Once the warriors from the keep realized we only had the one wagon, they grew less zealous to try to cross the bridge under a rain of arrows. Iventorn did not get nearly as much as he had hoped, but we got away fairly unscathed." Estfale sat back. "And that is when Qizern and Iventorn really started to hate each other."

"I am glad they were enemies, that certainly helped me later. And, wherever Iventorn is right now, I wish him only the best." Trela raised her own mug. "To Iventorn!"

"To Iventorn!" They all joined in the chorus.

They stayed another two days at the tiny village to gather up what intelligence they could. Trela felt somewhat uneasy there and so had been hoping to leave earlier, but there was too much left unanswered to escape right away. Her scouts returned the night of the meeting but had to be sent out again the next day. Trela herself went to investigate some of the nearby farmhouses. They searched everywhere they could, but never found anything of note. The Gaens had just left. They had to finally do the same.

The road out of the village meandered into the hills a little. She was happy to pull away from the desert's cusp a little more. There was some minor hunting to be had and they had finally found a small stream. There was almost a week of travel that was fairly bucolic. She let them use campfires every night. They even had some leftover beer from the tiny village that they had absconded with. All in all, it was an enjoyable week.

They were traveling on a narrow path through some shade trees, Trela was riding towards the front of the column, when Escha came pounding back down the path towards them. She had been scouting ahead with Pejal and a Gaen named Evicaol Ona'jin. They had obviously found something. She pushed her horse partly off of the path to squeeze past a few other riders. She did not want Escha yelling information to her through others, even though secrets were not easily kept with a group as small as the coterie. Eventually she handed her reins to Kryhir and dismounted to be able to get to the head of the column quicker. Escha waited for Trela to arrive before she spoke.

"We have found what appears to be some abandoned ruins. Pejal and Evicaol stayed back to do a little more reconnaissance. We figured it was best if they stayed together. You know, just in case." Escha smiled her crooked smile.

"How long did you investigate before heading back to us?" Trela paused for a moment. "Is it completely abandoned?"

"I did not stay long to investigate, but it does appear to be completely abandoned. The amount of vines covering the entire structure is amazing. It is a little off the main path. I can show just you or we can take everyone?" The last part of her sentence turned into a question.

Trela looked back at her small train. There was no real reason to split up, but the wagons were already having difficulty on the path they were on. She squinted back at Escha.

"How wide is the side path?" Escha's eyes traveled back to where Trela had just been looking.

"Hmph. Not wide enough for the wagons. We can all travel to the branch in the path and then split a party off on horseback?" It was another half question.

"Yes. Good. Lead the way." Trela was hopeful there would be enough room at the branch to park the main coterie. So much for the idea of secrets.

Trela remounted and followed Escha, and the coterie followed her. One foot after another. One hoof after another. With her eyes trained on Escha's back, it seemed to take no time at all. They reached a bulge in the path, with a dirt track leading off into the trees in a mostly perpendicular direction. The track quickly disappeared amongst the foliage. She did not want to make any more noise than was required, and the track looked barely wide enough for a skinny horse. So, she dismounted while trying to think of the group she wanted to bring with her.

She ended up grabbing Estfale, Tweltas, Gyllhelon, Tesjuk, and Feyazki. More due to their proximity than any complicated calculus. She left Kryhir "in charge" since she did not want to have to find Rewista. Escha led the way up the small sidetrack. Trela felt she could have followed the narrow path fairly easily, but it was nice to not have to pay too much attention to their direction. This did not mean she was lazily plodding along. She spent most of her energy listening into the trees for an ambush. Her struggle with the Tlana had left her quite paranoid. It was exhausting.

They walked for much longer than she had thought they would. It made her wonder how far off the main path her scouts usually wandered. How did they find anything? Did they just get bored and wander off? Did they ride a certain amount of distance, walk a certain number of paces, at each crossroads? She thought about asking Escha these questions when they came to the rise before the ruins.

Escha stepped to the side to give Trela an unobstructed view. There was a small cluster of towers, maybe three, maybe four, that were half disintegrated and covered in vines. It was difficult to tell that there were even stones anywhere, anything at all made by Gaen hands, the green clawing leaves shrouded everything so completely. If Escha had not been standing off to the side, if the viewpoint were not so pointedly shown to her, she might have missed the ruins completely. Scouting did have its own set of required skills and natural abilities. Though she fancied herself as having many of those abilities, she wondered a little about the cultivated skills.

Escha made a high-pitched whistle that trilled up and swooped back down. It sounded exactly like a bird, though not necessarily a bird that Trela had ever heard before. She gave a small wink as she walked past Trela again, heading down the small hill towards the ruins.

"Pejal should definitely recognize the call... I'm not sure about the Gaen." Escha spoke over her shoulder at Trela. They had a little distance to go downward before the next rise where the crumbling towers were situated.

Maybe another fifteen minutes and they were standing before the mass of green foliage that marked the towers. They seemed more impressive close up. The vines crept into the crumbling window openings. They sifted in and out of the rock walls like sewing thread. They sprouted from the tops of the towers like unkempt hair. Trela tilted her head back to take in the full, crumbling height. She thought of Clerin praising dilapidation, how she would say that there was a hidden destiny in the triumph of nature. Trela, on the other hand, felt that the transitory nature of derlian creation was a bit lamentable. That everything she strived for would eventually disappear... The corner of her eye caught a brief motion at the top of the middle tower. Was it the vines wafting in the wind? Was it Pejal? Was it black smoke? She could not be sure.

"Shall we enter?" It was Feyazki. Always eager to push ahead.

"Allow me." Estfale slipped past both of them and Escha. He disappeared quickly into the darkened interior. He was soon followed by Gyllhelon and Tweltas. Trela knew that she was not allowed to be the first to enter anything anymore—in fact, it had been quite a while since she had been given that freedom—but sometimes it still took her body a moment to recall what her mind knew. Especially when she was intrigued by something. She stepped back from the entrance, but no one else entered. Tesjuk and Escha were staring intently into the trees behind them. That left a smiling Feyazki.

"After you." He made a sweep of his hand.

Instead of trying to think up something witty, she entered. It was somewhat dim in the crumbling interior. The windows, though large and plentiful, were stuffed with invading vines. The ceiling was high and she did not immediately see any holes in the floor above, though the creaking induced by her companions was a little unnerving.

As she wandered in a slow circle on that lower floor, Tesjuk placed himself in the doorway. She heard the others clamber around above her. Escha kept herself outside, and Feyazki leaned against the wall next to the rickety stairs heading upwards. It was as if they all talked to each other, planned it out. She found herself trying to find a corner, trying find a pool of darkness. Something unexplored.

She wandered over to a choked window. The light that splashed through was colored with a green hue. The smell was green as well, full of life amidst the cold stone tower. She parted the vines to let the light in more than anything. To get some fresh air circulating. She breathed in deeply, her eyes barely open in the sudden brightness. There was just the tiniest twitch of movement out there in the distance, the most minor of discrepancies, maybe a bird, maybe a rodent, but some unknowable instinct took over. She dropped to the floor with the speed of a bag of rocks, and with about the same amount of grace as well. The arrow, or maybe it was a bolt, skittered across the far stone wall. It made a tingy, clangy noise amongst the shocked quiet. Then the noise rushed back into the air along with a second arrow.

Trela slid herself against the wall, under the window, still clinging to the floor. Tesjuk clambered noisily over to the other side of the window, though he was careful not to place his head near the opening or his feet near Trela. Feyazki rushed over to the window as well. "Narteclufclo!" Escha's fleeting form was seen running outside. Two more arrows struck Feyazki's clear shield just as Estfale came running down the stairs.

"Quickly! Escha is out there alone." Trela yelled to no one in particular, but both Estfale and Gyllhelon slid out of the front door in a blur. Tesjuk clambered noisily behind them. Trela tried to remember if Tweltas had a bow, but she did not think so. They had not run into Pejal or Evicaol that Trela knew of, but both of them should have some form of a missile weapon. She pulled herself up off the floor and dusted herself off absentmindedly.

"Nope." Feyazki was peering through his invisible shield at the window. Some of the vines had been chopped off when the shield went into position, but the greenery seemed difficult to see through.

"I didn't say anything." She glared at him. Hard.

"I know. It doesn't matter. The answer's still no." He would not look over at her glare.

"What if I don't listen to you?" She was losing interest in the argument, however.

"You'll lose." He stopped peering for a moment and looked over at her. "I can stop you without hurting you. You'll have to cut me or stab me or at least kick me. You'll lose because you aren't willing to go the lengths you'll need to." He smiled over at her. "Or at least that's what I hope."

"Then at least we should go to the top of the tower. See what we can see?" She smiled back. He was right, of course. She just felt so impotent while her warriors were scouring the area.

She picked up one of the arrows on her way to the stairs. There was a sticky liquid clinging to the head. It was somewhat thick and reddish, like a chili paste. She did not need to smell it to realize it was poisoned. Whoever they were, they had definitely been lying in wait. She carried the arrow loosely in her right hand as she climbed the stairs.

They passed two small floors in the tower before they popped out through the top into the open air. Tweltas was kneeling down near a low crenellated wall, peering over the edge. He glanced behind him and waved them over. Trela and Feyazki crouched as they walked over. Before she got to the edge, she noticed a derlian on a nearby tower top. It seemed like Pejal, but it was hard to tell. Whoever it was had their arrows aimed down at the ground, not across the tower top towards her.

"Can't you just protect me or something?" Trela had a hard time telling what was going on down there, between the towers. It was not walled off, so she could not refer to it as a courtyard, but it was not raised either, so she didn't want to call it a terrace either. "I can't see anything. I want to be... down there... helping." She waived ineffectually at the space between the towers.

"We do not know their strength or numbers. We do not know if they have a mage with them... or worse. In fact, the only thing we do know is that you are their target." Feyazki's head was twitching back and forth, scanning the terrain. He kept looking back nervously at the empty stairs as well. "Whoever is down there is attempting to assassinate you."

"Ugh, then what can I do so that you can help?" Trela realized that in her selfish need to be helpful she was keeping one of her greatest assets off the field.

"There is just too much camouflaging greenery in the way. Wait, let me... Mekfinderclo! Meksidpanclo!" He stared downwards, then at the other towers, then towards the stairs of their tower. He then came back and stared at the space between the towers. "I think there are only two left... Out there..."

"Then go. I promise to be safe and guard the stairs. I won't even peek over the edge of the tower." Trela drew her short sword and squat-walked over to the stairs, just to show him she meant what she said. That she would stay safe. It was incredibly difficult.

"Then... at least go down a level. I don't like you exposed out here. What if a *bird* came by? What if that is their entire plan?" He did use the euphemism for Tlana but exaggerated the word so much he overemphasized it.

Trela ran down the stairs because she knew that if she stayed up there, the fight would be over before he could even fly down there. It was only once she was down there that she began to wonder how he knew there was no one waiting in ambush. He had cast two spells, which surely would have provided some insight, but... Then her mind wandered onto why he had cast two different spells for the same end. The room she was in had no furniture and no one was waiting in ambush. She positioned herself so she could see both sets of stairs and was away from any windows. She sat on her haunches with her sword out in front of her, tip resting lightly on the floor, and she waited. And she waited.

"We captured one!" Gyllhelon came bounding up the stairs on her long legs. "We caught one alive!"

Trela immediately began to move towards the stairs. It had taken so long for anyone to come up that she had already re-sheathed her sword. They had a prisoner they could question. It was amazing.

"They were all Pyrans." Gyllhelon stopped just at the top of the stairs and shifted to one side to let Trela run past. The statement caught Trela so off guard that she stopped as well. They both stood there for the briefest second, taking up the stairwell.

"Qizern's?" Trela had truly thought they would be Gaen. At this point in their travels they were closer to the Fluen realm than the Pyran one. Who would have tracked her this far into the Gaen realm?

Gyllhelon just shrugged. Trela had not really expected her to know but was just asking to ask. Whoever they were, they were probably not wearing any insignia. But they had a prisoner! She regained her enthusiasm and shot down the stairs past Gyllhelon.

Round and round she went, down to the bottom floor. She had expected to shoot out the front door, to have to find her warriors out amongst the foliage, in between the towers. But there was Tesjuk and Tweltas just standing there, waiting for her. Either they had been incredibly quiet, or she had not been paying very good attention.

"Where is the prisoner?" She found herself speaking directly to Tweltas, rather than Tesjuk. She was not sure if that was because Tweltas was a Pyran, or that he outranked Tesjuk, or that she had known him for longer. Either way, she attempted to make a mental note of it. She did not want any faction of her coterie to think they were lesser than any other.

"Estfale insisted we hold the prisoner in another tower, one that he swept himself." Tweltas smiled a lopsided smile at her. "The mage is with them."

Tweltas had been the leader of the Guard before she gave that job to Lishean. Tweltas was a consummate professional, and she never felt that he was wary of her. He had never seemed to warm up to Feyazki, however. She thought that he disliked foreigners in general and Luftens in specific. But then Gyllhelon sauntered down the stairs and his smiling eyes watched her head towards the door rather than continue his conversation with Trela. So, she coughed to get his attention.

"Of course, follow me." He somehow kept himself from looking embarrassed.

They all hustled over to the adjacent tower. Trela felt excited and slightly nervous, though she was not positive where the nervousness came from. The attempt on her life did not come very close and she had been kept from most of the action. When she had gotten to the tower, though, she understood her instinct better. Estfale was already pulverizing the trussed up Pyran.

"Ah, Tesjuk. Just the Gaen I was hoping to see." Tesjuk let his wide shoulders fill the doorway for a moment before stepping in, darkening the room a little. Trela wondered about how warriors were trained in the Gaen realm. Or was that type of thing just natural. Surely Torpalin would have paused as he entered through the door as well. Estfale was grinning like a maniac. It made Trela think of when

Lishean had Feinsley tied to a chair of a warehouse in Parthia. She wondered if that maniac stare just came from punching someone who was tied up in front of you. As if the stare came from the part being played, not from the actor playing the part.

"Wait up a moment, Estfale. I worry that, in your zealousness, you will render our friend here unable to communicate." With that she kicked the prisoner in the stomach. He moaned and rolled over. She needed all her warriors, as well as this one lying before her, to know that she understood the gravitas of an assassination attempt. She knew that this Pyran would not survive long. Nor would it enjoy the little time it had left to it. Those who organized the coup knew the price for failure. She hoped to make this one take as little time as possible. It was the dragging it out that she did not enjoy. The making it last as long as possible to make sure every nuance was removed from the prisoner. She would prefer to start removing fingers than to make it last three days.

"Who sent you?" Estfale got in a quick swipe before fully backing away. He knocked the prisoner's face against the stone floor. His limbs moved too sharp and exaggerated, even while backing away. He usually had his adrenalin under more control.

"Let's start with something much more basic." Trela knelt down next to the crumpled-up prisoner, but still far enough away he could not bite her or lash out. "What is your name?"

"What does it matter? You will kill me anyways." The broad-faced Pyran grimaced at her, showing bloody teeth below a bloody nose. "Just skip to the end."

"Of course we will kill you. You attempted to assassinate the queen. But not before we get the information we need from you. We won't let you die before then, no." Trela had her long dagger in her right hand, bouncing against her left. She needed to figure out what to say to shorten this up. "So why don't you just tell us what we ask you? You know… so we can skip to the end. You are not going to enjoy this middle portion." She figured honesty to be the best policy. It truly was in all of their best interests to skip to the end.

"My name is Mynthur, the Eastborn." He paused for dramatic effect. "Great nephew to Qizern." He paused again while they nodded amongst themselves. "So, this part is pretty well moot, don't you think? It is obvious why I am here. My only regret is the trouble that has befallen my companions." His tied-up hand swept vaguely in a circle. "I had conned a couple of my dear friends to follow me to my doom, you see. My vanity and the strongest sense of my own destiny led me from the Pyran realm to this forsaken ruin. Following you by staying ahead of you, a most arduous task I can assure you. The difference between us is that the voices in your head, cheering you on to bold and noble conquests, are correct—whereas mine are not. Yours led you to vanquish my uncle. Mine led me here. To my untimely death." He laughed sardonically.

"I wish I could leave it at that. And, truly, it could end up being as simple as that. But this part is far from moot. We have plenty of questions left to ask. You still have plenty of answers you will beg to tell me." Trela stood and nodded over to Estfale, who kicked Mynthur quickly in the stomach.

It only took about a half-hour or so. They did not have to cut him up too badly; he was already eager to confess his own crimes. He was also eager to confess about all of the friends that he had conned into following him. It was the names of the money that was difficult to get out of him. Trela knew that someone, someone who stayed back in Agoge safe in the midst her own warriors, had given Mynthur the resources to follow her through countless leagues of rough Gaen territory. The first fifteen minutes he babbled uncontrollably about himself and his friends. The next ten minutes or so got ugly. Trela truly did not like torture. He did finally name his own grandmother, Qizern's sister. They all had figured that she would be involved. Trela could not ease up on him until he had given her something difficult. She was also of the opinion that his own immediate parents had to be involved. He stated that his father had died years earlier, in a campaign for Qizern. That could be checked once they got back. If Mynthur was lying, they would just arrest his father. The last five minutes were excruciating. Nothing they did could get him to implicate his mother. Mynthur was barely screaming anymore.

"Can't Feyazki just look into his mind?" Gyllhelon sounded annoyed. She had her arms crossed and was glaring at Estfale and Tweltas.

"Feyazki!" Trela yelled to his back. He had wandered off and was chatting with Escha. What to Pyrans seemed like a cruel but necessary part of interrogation, especially for an attempted assassination, it seemed that the Luftens had little stomach for—at least some of them. Trela found herself wishing that Malghain was with them. He would have made Mynthur sing.

"Aren't you finished with him yet?" Feyazki took his time returning to the main group.

"Just to make sure, we would like you to enter in his mind and see if anyone other than his grandmother has assisted him in this matter." Trela nodded towards Gyllhelon, though she doubted Feyazki would have any idea why. "Do not worry about the friends he brought with him, but if there is anyone left in Agoge or anywhere else in the Pyran realm, we need to know." She paused for the briefest of seconds. "Oh, and make sure he does not know of another planned ambush."

Feyazki paused, looking at her. Glaring at her really. Then he looked over to Gyllhelon, who nodded to him.

"Well, if it will speed this up any faster." Feyazki knelt next to Mynthur and placed a hand on his sweaty forehead. "Eqefintotto!"

Chapter 12

Voytriluphmajnickluhnwereg let itself waft through the realm. The air currents were not chaotic even though they were constant. They flowed along set paths of direction. A Luften could spend very little energy moving from one part of the realm to another as long as it knew where all of the currents were. They did not cross, so there were always sections that one would have to travel through under their own volition—the static areas. The currents were strong in the middle of the stream but got weaker the farther away from the center you got. In this way one could affect one's speed by shifting where in the current they were. The size of the currents varied widely, and they rarely took a perfectly straight path, which is why the memorization of their locations and sizes were important to those who wished to get somewhere quickly. Of course, memorization was generally centered around the areas that one typically traveled. Due to the vastness of the realm, there were few who bothered to memorize every main current, let alone the countless tiny currents that encompassed much of the realm. Those who tried were referred to as "explorers," constantly drifting the various currents, rarely stopping to converse with others let alone taking the time to engage in friendships, to participate with the public bureaucracy, or to get summoned to the derlian realm. The pockets of stillness, the static areas, could be incredibly vast depending upon their location, and these were rarely memorized, even by the explorers.

Voyt was an ancient explorer, as old as any Yaven it had encountered since its youth. Not that it had encountered many other Yavens lately. It had taken up an odd cause. Voyt had decided to find the edge of the realm, to find the farthest extent, to find some type of barrier. Or, and this was a very real and distinct possibility in Voyt's mind, it would find a way that wrapped back to the center. The problem was that the main currents, those with the greatest velocity, were never fully straight. They had sweeps, arcs, and curves. In the center, where most of the Yavens were, where most of the main currents were, one could tell the sweeps and curves by watching the scenery shift. Also, as one traveled along the curve, they would shift from the center of stream towards the edge. Keeping a straighter line than the current itself. When Voyt was first learning to explore, it would travel the main central currents and watch the scenery intently, paying utmost attention to the feeling within itself when it sensed the shift from the center of the stream. It was this feeling that Voyt had carefully cultivated through aeons of experience, that allowed it to gauge the straightness of the currents out in the middle of nowhere. It took a large amount of concentration and could be tiring, but it was the only way known to Voyt.

It was on the straightest current it knew of. Heading in one direction for as long as it could before it would have to cross a static area. Voyt was concerned that once it left a current it would never cross one again. So, it wanted to get as far away from the center as it could before leaving the ease of the currents, before it had to stop wafting.

How to explain the passage of time? Voyt did not ponder or wonder or think fanciful thoughts as it wafted. Its mind did not wander to other Yavens it had known. It did not recall its own past, other explorations it had performed. It did not wax nostalgic. It did not even attempt to gauge distance or speed. It only concentrated on the straightness of its path. One thing. It was not even a concentration that happened over and over again, for there was no ending to it. It was a constant push of energy, a constant awareness. Time and distance flowed unnoticed by the ancient explorer. There was nothing but straight.

Eventually, Voyt wafted from the center of the stream. It kept up its vigilance, of course, but it started to put some energy into its forward momentum. It was concerned about slowing slightly. It knew, eventually, that it would reach a static area, that its straightness would pull it out of the current, that it would have to move itself with its own volition. This, while not necessarily a worry—maybe a concern—kept it from allowing itself to slow at all.

Eventually, Voyt wafted to the edge of the stream. The current was slowly curving away. Voyt knew that this was a dangerous moment. It had to keep itself moving straight almost entirely under its own energy, for the current was mostly flowing in the wrong direction, and that made it incredibly difficult for Voyt to tell how straight it was moving. Once it was in a static region, it felt that it would be able to sense direction more simply since it would be providing its only impetus. It poured a vast amount of energy into sensing its straightness during this dangerous time. Making the transition from in the stream to out of the stream seemed to take an agonizingly long time.

Eventually, Voyt was out of the stream completely. It did not know how vast the static area was for it had never been there before. It spent most of its energy in movement but kept a small amount in sensing directional changes. Eventually, Voyt would probably cross another current, get swept up into another stream. Voyt needed to be able to sense that immediately. It might not happen for eons, however, so the energy mix was set up to be infinitely sustainable, rather than perfectly accurate. Voyt might even stop periodically to rest, even though stopping would make measuring straight difficult. At the least, it was not ruling that option out.

It was a long, long time before anything else happened. Voyt enjoyed the silence, the solitude. It enjoyed the movement and the minor constant vigilance. It was all it had ever really wanted to do. To explore. Many Luftens were quite content to waft around each other; to build their governments, their cities of frozen wind, their lives, surrounded by others. The interruptions of vapid speech were seen as a break in the monotony. They traded ideas back and forth, refining and expounding. Old and obsolete "structures" were dismantled and rebuilt better. Better. The constant swirling of energy and effort for betterment. And who feels that now is better than before? Who is the arbiter of the hierarchy of time? That was much of the conversation, the argument, that the Luftens were constantly having. One could feel vindicated about one's life if only it could convince another that its own idea was better than a previous one. Which previous one? This appears to matter little to the clamoring masses. Pick a subject, become an expert, argue your point of betterment for eternity. Voyt figured it was not a bad system, it was certainly the only system that it had ever known. What better arbiter of truth than a consensus of experts? It was just a system that Voyt did not enjoy. Voyt was the rare Luften who did not like argument, did not like the cajoling and the compromising that it entailed. Of course some things were better than others—to a specific Luften. Voyt assumed, not entirely incorrectly, that what was considered better was often decided by the loudest, most energetic arguer. Though Voyt certainly had opinions as to what was better, it did not care enough to struggle with others about it. Maybe "care" was not the right word. In fact, Voyt knew that it was incorrect, but it did not care enough to attempt to clarify it. Not to itself, at least. Maybe if it had another Luften to explain it to, to refine the idea against. But no, Voyt just enjoyed the silent movement.

Eventually, Voyt nicked the edge of a current. It felt proud of itself for noticing the slight pull immediately and compensating for it. It passed through the edge very quickly, considering the amount of energy it needed to sense its straightness. It nicked three more currents before it began to yearn to enter another stream. To be able to travel without the energy required for movement. What if, Voyt thought, there just happened to be a straight current going in the same direction that it was? What if it led exactly where Voyt was headed? Much time was wasted on this foolish notion. But what did a Yaven have besides time?

Eventually, even the yearning for ease of movement faded. Voyt certainly never found that perfect current. But Voyt pressed on. Moving as fast as it felt it could while keeping itself straight. Ever onwards. Into the unknown. Except that it was always the same. How to embark into the unknown when you were surrounded by everything you have always known? There was no change in scenery. No change in motion. And no change in Voyt itself since it had partitioned all of its energies into movement and in sensing direction, meaning it did not have the leftover energy to let its mind wander much. Certainly not enough to change itself appreciably.

Eventually, Voyt had difficulties recalling why it was doing this. What was the end goal, what was the point? To show that it was wrong? To show that the realm extended infinitely? How would it know when it reached its goal if the goal did not exist? Voyt knew these feelings to be an enemy to be conquered quickly. It could not afford the effort it would take to conquer them if they gained in power and magnitude. Even just incrementally. For what if it was about to find the edge, or to find that it had wrapped around and was headed back to the same current it had started in? To never know would be worse than finding out that there was no end. Wouldn't it? Would it? Certainly, Voyt could turn back and return to the inhabited portions of the realm and tell its story. Find another expert explorer and argue the infinity of the realm until they reached a consensus. No other being would care that Voyt had, in its own mind, given up. Failed. Luftens were not known for their consistency, for their steadfastness, or for their perseverance. Most Luftens were experts in many different things, calling into question whether they could be

354

called an expert in any single particular subject. Voyt was not a typical Luften, however.

Eventually, Voyt was recharged, had gained its second wind so to speak. That lasted for an incredible amount of time. Eventually, Voyt again had difficulties remembering why this was important, why the impetus, why exploration at all. Most importantly, what made Voyt choose that particular current? Why this direction? What if it was the wrong way? But then, Voyt would get a third wind. And another bout of doubt. And another wind. And so on, ad infinitum. Except, as all eventuallies turn into eventualities, there was an end. Voyt did not travel straight for all of eternity. Nor did it wrap around back to the original stream, its beginning current. No. What Voyt finally found was a boundary.

The boundary was not necessarily an invisible wall. It was not visually detectable, that was true. It did not allow Voyt to travel continually straight, that was also true. But it was more of a deflection than a stopping. In fact, Voyt could have missed the fact that it was being deflected if it had not been paying attention. The deflection was slight; it was a gentle curve. It had almost seemed like a current when Voyt first encountered it. Merely like a slight shift in momentum, a slight push sideways. Voyt pushed back slightly, attempting to keep its straightness, but it… couldn't. No matter how hard it tried to keep true, it kept being deflected. Since it was continuing to move, but just not quite going straight, Voyt felt it had to stop. It pierced long, straight tendrils of itself up and down, side to side. These were partially to keep its knowledge of straight intact. Voyt found that the longer it made itself, the easier it could sense if it was wafting off course. The tendrils were also there to feel, to sense the boundary.

It was like a wall in the sense that Voyt's tendrils were unable to penetrate it. But it was more dynamic than that. It pushed the tendrils sideways, ever so slightly. Like some impenetrable and constant current. And the more that Voyt pushed directly against the wall, the more it, itself, was shifted sideways. As if the harder Voyt pressed perpendicular to the wall, the faster the parallel current pushed it. There was some sort of direct relationship between the two.

Voyt kept its long tendrils out in all directions except directly in front of it. It created the thinnest tendril, the thinnest thread possible, a threandril if you will, and slowly felt the barrier in front of it. The threandril extended straight and then started getting pulled to its right. Voyt pulled it back and tried again. It moved the threandril straight up as high as it was able to and barely touched the barrier. The threandril was pushed to the right. Voyt tried below it, diagonally, off to the side, everywhere it could from its vantage point, everywhere it could reach without moving. It was loathe to shift its main position, even in the slightest. But what else was there to be done? It had reached what it had been searching for. Or at least, it had reached something.

Voyt brought all of its tendrils back in. It oriented itself perpendicular to the barrier. With all of its might, it pushed out against the barrier. Whoosh, it was shot off to the right a huge amount of distance. Pulling back, Voyt again oriented itself towards the barrier. It made itself into a cone and tried to pierce the barrier. Whoosh. It made itself a spear. Whoosh. It backed up and got as much momentum as it could. Whoosh. It made itself into a club, a battering ram. Nothing worked.

Voyt tried over and over to breach the barrier. It was not discouraged, however. It could leave and bring a hundred other Yavens to this place and prove, not by intellectual guessing or by consensus, but truly prove that their realm had a barrier. It was what Voyt had lived for, felt it had been created for. It was a pinnacle of explorative achievement. And it did not really matter to Voyt if anyone else knew. It did not matter if it never made it back to the inhabited portions of the realm. It had found something no other had. It had experienced something unique. It exalted.

So why, then, did Voyt stay at the barrier? Why did it not return to its own home, whether for accolades or rest? Why did it not bask in its own glory? That was what most other Luftens would have done. Voyt was not a typical Luften, however.

Voyt found in itself, in the very center of its being, another goal form. Another impossible dream. Another task before it. It found an insatiable curiosity about the barrier and what lay beyond. It stayed for a long time at that spot, contemplating and trying various ways to break through. After a while, it began to think that the barrier was shifting it away from something. It began to travel along the barrier, to its left, away from the sideways motion. It kept a tendril out to periodically touch the barrier. Just to make sure that it was still there, that it was still flowing to the right.

The flow began to move a little downwards, as well as to the right. Voyt shifted its movement up a little, to keep itself moving exactly opposite of the barrier's current. It flowed this way for quite a while. Still jubilant, still excited, but still vigilant. It tried to sense its motion, to keep track of where it was going compared to where it had been. The huge amount of time it spent throwing itself against the barrier, however, made it difficult to tell where it had actually started from. Voyt had very little idea of where it had made first contact with the barrier, though it could certainly find the original current that aimed it in the correct direction if it reached the inhabited region of the realm again. That, in itself, was another reason for the new goal of penetrating the barrier. Voyt knew, in general, which direction the inhabited region lay, but it was not completely positive. And as it traveled along the barrier, it was becoming less and less positive. The barrier seemed to undulate slightly. No, there was really only one way to go. There was only the new goal to be pursued. Voyt felt that it could travel this way into infinity. Maybe there would be no end to the barrier. Maybe the barrier would wrap around and bring it back to where it had started, like the interior of a sphere, not that it would even know. Maybe it would find another Luften, another explorer, traveling along the barrier. That thought, though it was quite ridiculous, made Voyt even more jubilant. At least all its energy could be put towards movement. Voyt no longer needed to be concerned about direction, for the barrier itself provided that.

Another countless amount of time passed. Voyt did not lose its excitement. Not one iota. It had found the barrier; everything beyond that was extra. Bonus. It traveled along the barrier, changing its course slightly every time the current changed. Almost all of its energy was allocated to movement. It flew at a furious pace through the static scenery.

Eventually, Voyt found a dimple. It had almost missed it, almost passed it by. It was not a dimple so much in the barrier, but more in the current. The current began to shift slightly. It was still going to the right, but just below the dimple, it was going downwards, and just above the dimple, it flowed upwards. Voyt stopped in jubilant contemplation. It had found an anomaly in the barrier.

Voyt waited for some time before deciding what to do. There was no reason to rush this moment. It felt all around the area, examining all it could. It felt well above and below the dimple. It felt to each side. The left side had the same curious shift in current that the right side had. There was definitely a central point, a location of focus. Voyt examined that point as closely as it was able. Visually, just like the barrier, there was nothing there. When Voyt pushed on it, it pushed sideways, just like anywhere else along the barrier. There really was only the one small anomaly. After every passive version of investigation that Voyt could think of had been performed, it prepared itself for the attack.

Voyt bunched itself up into the smallest shape possible, the densest form, with zero empty space between any of its solid essence. This took an agonizingly long time. It went quickly at first, the shrinking. Towards the end, however, it seemed to take an incredible amount of effort for any noticeable effect at all. Finally, it had shrunk itself to a miniscule size, spherical in shape. It knew it should be able to pierce better if it were at least a little cylindrical, so it flattened itself further, creating a tiny point at the front of it and lengthening itself as required. It positioned itself perpendicular to the dimple. It took its time, making sure everything was perfectly lined up. Voyt then backed up. It moved very slowly, with some of its energy being used in keeping itself dense, a bunch of it being used to keep itself straight, and the tiny amount left over was spent on movement. It backed away far, far into the distance. It hummed with power. It hummed with energy. It backed away as far as it dared, but it knew it needed distance to gain enough momentum with the limited amount of energy it could spare. Voyt had, in its youth, spent a large amount of exploring time moving as fast as possible. It was a pure and exhilarating experience. They used to have races. It would build up the speed slowly, but ever increasingly. As it gained in momentum, it would slowly pour more and more energy into movement. Voyt never won a short race. If it were completely honest, it had probably never won a long race, either. But there was no other Luften who could build up more speed. Voyt was able to, eventually, move faster than any other. The trick was in the build-up. How to keep yourself constantly increasing. This was what Voyt began.

The motion seemed quite fast at first. It had been a long time since Voyt moved for speed alone. It just wasn't used to the feeling. Especially during this last exploration that had taken so long, so many eons just to get where it was headed. To get to that one moment. Soon instinct took over. Soon all that useless time racing, all that time training, all that time striving, took over. It was a different type of memory. It was almost opposite of what Voyt did while memorizing the myriad currents in the realm. It was a forgetful memory. It had to forget what it was doing, had to forget what it was, to recall the old skills of speed. Eventually, Voyt was moving faster than it ever had before. Eventually, it was difficult just to keep itself together, to keep itself dense, to keep itself straight. Eventually, so much energy was spent just keeping itself together that all else faded into nothingness. If Voyt had been asked something as simple as its name, it might not have been able to respond. There was nothing but forward. There was nothing but density, keeping its point sharp. Finally, eventually, there was an impact.

Then... nothingness. Voyt was still moving, or so it appeared amongst the Nothingness. It had a hard time telling. It could not sense any air around itself, could not sense any drag. It was more that it did not feel that it had stopped, or even slowed. That it was still moving at its incredible velocity. Voyt was about to experiment, to splay itself out from its needle shape, to attempt to make itself rotate, to try to stop or speed up... But before it could make up its mind, before it could decide on exactly what to try first, what experiment to begin with... The unthinkable happened. Voyt struck another barrier. No, more than that, Voyt pierced another barrier. Another impact. And after that impact, Voyt was convinced it had gone completely insane.

There was air again. Voyt immediately felt the drag against itself. But it was not just air that Voyt sensed. There was a brightness to the air that felt foreign, almost painful. But that was not all. There was a moisture in the air that surrounded Voyt. Not that it felt moist at the time, but more like an extra drag. An extra mass, an extra viscosity, an extra... stickiness. Contradictorily, there was a dryness to the air that seemed to come from the brightness, or maybe from the passing air itself. How could these dichotomies happen at the same time? There seemed to be a war that went nowhere. These things battled and so they canceled each other out, and yet they were still individually... experienceable? The war, the conflicting experiences, appeared to make the air currents variable. They buffeted one way, then the other, with no discernable rhyme or reason. Voyt could have spent an eternity pondering such things. Wondering just what these individual experiences were, why they interacted with such struggle, to somehow make peace with all of the contradictions. But Voyt was not given that time. There was a huge dark blob looming in front of it. A dim shadow amongst the too harsh brightness; its outline was a misshapen, jagged triangle. And it was getting larger by the second. Voyt felt a sudden urge to slow itself; to, maybe, reverse its momentum. To somehow avoid the gigantic blob. It did not want to crash into something that appeared so… dense.

The crash did not hurt Voyt at all. It was incredibly startling, certainly. Even quite scary. But Voyt just—whooshed—against the stone mountainside and flattened out. It took a much longer time to pull itself back together than it did to flatten out, but that was more due to the constantly shifting air currents and the utter shock of it all. Voyt coalesced into a small ball and wafted in front of the cliff face for a while, attempting to coalesce its own thoughts.

This must be the derlian realm, thought Voyt. It was the only possible answer, outside of having gone completely insane. Voyt had never been in the realm before but had been told about it numerous times. It had been told about moisture and stone and fire, it had even been told about trees and iron. It was another thing to experience them. Voyt had never imagined… But, of course, that was the point. That was why the Belegs had made the derlian realm, to allow the Yavens to experience the unimaginable for themselves. Even more mind boggling than being there, of being in a constructed, mixed, chaotic realm, even more astounding than being able to experience the other elements, what really shook Voyt to its core was the question of *how* it got there. It had heard tales of the realm. Many, many boring tales. But it had never heard of a Yaven reaching the realm without being summoned. Never. Did that mean this was a unique experience? No, Voyt could not say that for sure. It did not communicate with other Yavens that often, even when it had roamed in the more populated areas of the realm. It had spent much of its ancient life exploring the realm. Alone. No, this might not have been a unique experience. But if not, it was certainly a rare one.

Voyt stayed at the mountain top for the rest of the bright day. Floating. Just experiencing its own surroundings. Tasting the moisture, the rock, even the air. Then the night crept in. Voyt enjoyed the dark even more than the bright day.

Moons passed, maybe a full derlian cycle. To Voyt it was just the slow digestion of the elements. Time meant nothing. It knew there were many other things to experience besides that mountain top, but it was already overwhelmed. It felt it needed to understand all that surrounded it there before experiencing anything else. Ever so slowly, Voyt let the intensity of the experience wash over it, wave after wave.

Voyt was not a Yaven used to stillness. Voyt was an explorer, was used to being in constant motion. From one end to the other, it had traveled to the limits of its own dimension. It had been unable to stay still for long in its own realm. Here, however, it enjoyed the stillness. Stillness calmed the overwhelming waves of unknowable experience.

Eventually, Voyt felt so comfortable at the mountain top that it began to worry just a little that it would be unable to get back to its home realm. All the other Yavens that it had communed with never had a story of returning. They were merely unsummoned by the mage who had summoned them. Voyt was not overly concerned. It truly thought that it could just get sent back by some derlian mage. After all, that was what mages did, wasn't it? No, more than the panic of never being able to return home, the feeling was one of comfort. Voyt had been so inundated with the elements, with the constant chaos, that it was now saturated and able to let its mind wander. The majority of the digestion, the bulk of the difficulty, had been accomplished. The time for further exploring, of actually traveling and investigating the realm, was finally at hand.

Voyt wafted down the rocky and snow-splattered peak. Quite soon it encountered trees and stopped to examine them in full. It encountered birds and followed them. It encountered lichen and moss. Undergrowth and mountain lions. Deer and grass and flowers. The farther down the mountain Voyt traveled, the more crowded and varied the life became. And not just life. The rock that made up the top of the mountain was dark and hard. The soil farther down was much more diverse. Then there were the streams. And the rocks in the streams. Each little way farther down the mountain, Voyt had to stop and examine and ingest. It took many more derlian moons for Voyt to travel towards the base of the mountain, towards paths and roads, towards derlians.

The first derlian Voyt encountered was approximately halfway down the mountain from the peak. At the very first, Voyt was unsure if it was an animal or derlian. Listening to it whistle as it walked did not help. But the bipedal form, walking upright, carrying things, struck the idea home fairly quickly. Voyt flew amongst the tree branches, high above the oblivious creature. Finally, the creature got to what Voyt rightly assumed was a horse from the tales it had been told and mounted. Horse and rider trotted down the mountain for a ways until they got to a structure of felled and stripped trees. There was as much green moss growing upon the logs as there was hanging and dripping from the standing trees. It made everything seem so alive, but Voyt knew that to be an illusion. The horizontal and limbless trees were dead. Derlians used their carcasses to construct things with, that much Voyt knew. Of course, in a land full of death, they had to find some use for all the different carcasses.

Voyt would float down the chimney while the derlian was at home and float back out when it left. For over a moon Voyt shadowed this lonely derlian and never once did the derlian glance sideways at Voyt. It had kept itself thin and dispersed on purpose, taking up most of the lofted ceiling area, but still, it would have thought that the derlian could sense it at some point, on some level.

The creature kept itself quite busy. Walking and riding, eating and sleeping, working the garden and hunting the forest. Even sleeping appeared to take a large amount of energy. There was a lot of tossing and turning and, occasionally, some throaty screams. Voyt wanted to know what the derlian was thinking. Wanted to crawl inside its head and peek around. It had heard that this was not possible. That the derlian mind was too foreign, that magic was required, that the inside of a derlian head only contained goop and was unreadable. But Voyt had been told that there was no way to leave the Yaven realm at all, that all the wormholes had been gated over. It had been told that the only way to reach the derlian realm was by a summoning. But there it was. And there the derlian was. Voyt did not wish to destroy the creature, to accidentally kill it or the like. Every derlian that ever lived was doomed to die, however. Would one premature death even be noticed in this realm that reeked of it? How could the derlians even gauge what premature was? Voyt took its time and studied the situation as patiently as it dared. It came to the logical conclusion that the experiment was worthwhile and intriguing enough to perform. The next time the derlian screamed during its sleep Voyt would slip inside its head and see what was there for itself. It felt a strange pleasure in anticipation.

The first time Voyt was so careful as to be called timid. It explored the mouth and nasal passages. It allowed itself to be drawn into the lungs as a vapor. Bits of Voyt got dispersed through the bloodstream. Inside the derlian's head was indeed a bunch of unreadable goop. The first time was disastrously useless.

The second time Voyt was more adventurous. It pushed on boundaries. It stuffed itself into every corner, partly as a dissolved gas and partly as, well, air. It somehow fit all of itself into the comatose derlian. Somehow there was room for the both of them. Voyt could feel itself being pumped through the toes and fingers, filling every alveolus in the lungs, swirling amongst the goop in the derlian's head. It did not try anything, it was still timid, but it completely saturated the derlian's physical body. Completely. It stayed there most of the night. Flowing and breathing along with and throughout the derlian.

The third and fourth times were the same as the second. Voyt enjoyed filling the derlian, saturating it. All the chaotic movements, being pumped hither and yon, being pushed out and sucked back in. It was oddly invigorating. If asked, Voyt would have been unable to provide a coherent explanation of the enjoyment, but... there it was.

By the fifth time, Voyt became even more adventurous. It began to push itself around. It would gather in different areas, coalesce densely and then let itself be dispersed again. It tested gradations of dilution.

By the eighth time, Voyt had gained some control over the derlian's body. It could make the fingers twitch or a foot flatten out. It needed to coalesce a little bit, and fatten itself in the area of control. But it did not need to coalesce very much. It was still fairly evenly dispersed within the body. Voyt had become much less timid, but it did not feel it was damaging the derlian. At least not such that it could perceive. The derlian did not scream any more than usual during its sleep, and it did not seem slowed the next day.

Voyt became so used to entering the derlian that it began to do so each night, whether or not the derlian screamed during sleep. It began to move the limbs of the derlian more and more. It eventually began to make the derlian walk around while it was still asleep. This all took several derlian moons, though Voyt was not keeping track of time. Then the happy accident happened.

Voyt was coalescing in the goop when it happened. The derlian had begun to scream in its sleep and the goop began coursing with chaotic energy. Voyt focused itself intently upon the energy, attempting to make some sense of it. It began getting flashes of images, as if it was looking through the derlian's eyes, if the derlian had its eyes open. There was one of a different derlian with long flowing hair and a warm smile. The image of the face repeated several times. Sometimes the face would laugh, sometimes it would be whispering something, but it always looked happy. Then the flashes of images would turn to a red-splattered axe. Lifting and dropping. No one held the axe, the axe did not strike anything, but a great panic would build up in Voyt. A great and urgent fear would shiver through it, reverberating throughout the derlian's body and, therefore, throughout Voyt's. Then the flashing images would connect the two. The axe struck the derlian. The red splayed out and splattered the vague background. The image of the derlian screamed as the axe fell again. The sleeping derlian screamed and shook Voyt to its core. It was a terrible experience, but also a joyous one. It made Voyt realize what the goop was, what it did. If Voyt wanted to experience the sensory input of the derlian, it needed to coalesce in the goop. That was where the exterior senses lay. Even touch.

Vrric was in Mynthur's mind. Could he have entered without Mynthur's express consent? Who knew? Surely, knowing a mage was trying to infiltrate your mind would affect the spell. Vrric assumed there was a reason the Blind One performed his experiments surreptitiously.

It was an odd feeling, being in another's mind. It felt… dirty… oily… tainted somehow. He was not supposed to be there, he could feel that throughout his being. He was unwanted by the lay of the land. He was an intruder. He wondered what it would feel like if the victim did not provide consent. Even Mynthur's "willing" mind felt much different than Clerin's.

It was a very visual experience for Vrric. He was in a room, not very large, that had hefty doors scattered about its perimeter and a cold-looking metal table in its center. There were four metal chairs scooted against the metal table. There were no windows. Vrric could not see the ceiling and he could barely perceive the floor. The room, even without sound, felt hollow and echoey. Once tried, the doors appeared to be locked.

"Mynthur!" Vrric felt that he should be able to travel alone through Mynthur's mind, but was not sure how to get his questions answered.

"Of course. I'm here. Sorry." Mynthur appeared before Vrric and seemed to be out of breath. As if he had been doing something strenuous.

"Your grandmother." Vrric's question was a statement.

"Of course." Mynthur closed his eyes briefly, and an old lady appeared beside him. She had a stiff neck and wore expensive clothing and jewelry. She frowned at Vrric, then turned to Mynthur.

"You were always my favorite, Mynthur. You were always Qizern's favorite as well. You know what you have to do." She frowned at Vrric again.

"So, this is supposed to be a memory?" Vrric looked back and forth between the two.

"Yes. Of course." Mynthur glanced at his grandmother and then back to Vrric. "I mean, not exactly. This is not the entire thing, it is not… real. It just a representation of my memory."

It was like watching a horrible play. Put on by children. Who were just trying to distract you while their friends picked your pocket. The oddness of it just added to the oily feeling. Mynthur's grandmother turned back to him and opened her mouth to speak.

"Bring your mother." Vrric interrupted whatever tripe the grandmother was going to say.

"What?" Mynthur looked put out.

"Your mother, bring her before me." Vrric waved his hand in a rolling motion. "The culprit is either your mother, your grandmother, or both, yes? I want to see both of them at the same time."

"Well, I…" Mynthur kept looking about him. Almost as if he did not know how to summon the memory.

"Do it!" Vrric roared into the hollow room. He brought the spell that he cast back into his fore-mind. There was no reason for debate.

Mynthur shook when Vrric yelled, then closed his eyes. For the briefest of moments, Vrric imagined a grin slide across Mynthur's grandmother's face. A much younger Pyran appeared before them. She seemed to be just slightly older than Mynthur himself. Vrric wondered how much of memory was true. For anyone.

"My dearest…" Mynthur's mother reached her hand out towards Mynthur's face.

"We have company." Mynthur interrupted her and nodded towards Vrric. Vrric wondered at the interaction. He was just in

Mynthur's mind, was he not? These were only thoughts or memories or impressions that all came from the same derlian, were they not? How could one entity argue with itself? How could one being interact with itself in this way? It was not fully making sense.

"Of course." She smiled a large and beautiful smile at Vrric and nodded to him.

"How do you feel about Qizern?" Vrric spoke to her directly.

"He was the Kriishan." Her dark eyes flashed briefly between Vrric and Mynthur. "But he was defeated." She smiled again and turned more towards Vrric. "That is the way our realm works. That is the way our rulers are changed. We do not have a constant dynasty of inbred weaklings. By all accounts, the girl killed him in a fair fight."

"And you, how do you feel about Qizern?" Vrric directed his gaze to the grandmother.

"He was my brother. I grew up with him." Mynthur's grandmother stared intently into Vrric. "Do you have any siblings?"

"None that I know of." The pause and question took Vrric off guard.

"Then maybe you do not understand." She smiled at his own cryptic response. "Sibling relationships are... complicated." Mynthur almost took a step towards her. She smiled again. "But no matter how much you may argue with, or complain about, your own sibling, you do not allow another to argue with them. You cannot bear to hear complaints about them. They are to be protected. They are to be cherished. They are to be revenged." Here Mynthur's grandmother approached Vrric, stopping only when she stood directly in front of him. "I did it. I alone. I ordered my grandson, my Mynthur, to destroy that usurper. I gave him coin enough to bring some friends with him. I even offered him my favorite horse."

"And you had nothing to it." Vrric turned towards Mynthur's mother.

"Of course not. Qizern lost of his own accord." Her smile showed her white teeth.

Vrric walked straight up to Mynthur. He stared into his eyes. First one, then the other. Mynthur just stood there.

"And is there another ambush? Is there another ambush?" Vrric brought his spell back into his fore-mind. He did not want to tiptoe through rounds of misdirection. "Is there another ambush? Is there another ambush?" He yelled until Mynthur broke down.

"No. No! It was just me, just my miniscule chance, just my failure." He did look quite distraught. "It was just me. It was just me."

Vrric returned to the world and removed his hands from Mynthur. He stood slowly while Mynthur recovered. He did not hesitate in his speech.

"It is just the grandmother. There should not be another ambush, either." He nodded amongst his companions. "Or, at least, this one does not know of another."

Vrric nodded again and started to walk away. He did not want Trela's obligatory "Are you sure?" He did not want to listen to them beat on Mynthur further, nor did he want to hear them slit his throat or whatever was going to happen. Even more than that, however, was that he could be convinced that Mynthur's mother was actually involved in the ambush in some way. It was the odd way it was all presented to him. He certainly did not want to mention it while Mynthur was still alive. That would just start the protestations and then more torture, ad nauseam. But he was not sure he wanted to mention it later, either. That was what Trela wanted to know. That was what she ordered him to find out, if such a strong word could be used. By all accounts, his mother should pay for her actions. But what would that really serve? She lost her son and uncle, and would soon lose her own mother. Would she try again? Would she hire another, maybe more capable assassin? Maybe Vrric was even incorrect in his assumption of her guilt. He certainly did not learn anything definitive, not from Mynthur. They had tortured him for some time and he had not admitted her guilt. Maybe it was the odd sensation of being within Mynthur's mind that made it difficult to tell. Maybe it was because she was female or that she looked beautiful in Mynthur's mind, a glowing image of motherhood, but Vrric allowed the niggling doubt to stay within him for a brief while, churning and roiling.

Vrric walked past a wall of ivy that was clinging to the dilapidated stone. No, he thought to himself, Mynthur's mother was definitely involved. She was clinging to an old, dilapidated world order. But did that mean she should die? Did that mean she should be tortured? He was not typically overly squeamish, so he was a little taken back by his feelings. He hurried past the ivy, hurried down the path, but he was unable to get far enough away that he could not hear Mynthur's quick death screams. Maybe he should have flown.

They reached another tiny empty village. It was not eerie in the same way that the previous one was eerie. The previous one had been completely empty. All the doors were closed, all the horses and pets were gone, the sheets were still on the beds. The current village was ransacked. The doors were busted open and lay in piles of splinters. The few small buildings were half-burnt husks. The ground was churned with hooves long gone. And there were plenty of bodies. Horses and cows, dogs and cats, even dead crows and ravens. The main difference, however, the main component that made this village so differently eerie, were the Gaen bodies. They were all over. They were spread all over. There was an arm laying in the street, a leg draped over a porch rail. It made it impossible to tell how many derlians had been killed, how many "whole" bodies there had been. It was beyond eerie. The scene was horrific.

The Gaens amongst the group were adamant about burial. There was a somber need to provide at least a modicum of respect to the abused bodies. Trela allowed great latitude in that regard. They set up camp outside the village proper and they stayed for almost a week. Cleaning what they could, burying what they needed, and dismantling the broken structures that remained hazardous. There was even a certain amount of wooden structure that could only be burned.

Trela used the time for investigation. All the non-Gaens of the group assisted with that part. Everyone was busy though no one was frantic, each main group working around and through each other seamlessly. Each lending a hand when necessary.

"Rewista, what did you find?" They were in Trela's large marquis tent. She gathered all those who had investigated during the day.

"The damage was done by steel. All of the bodies looked as if they were attacked by simple weapons." Rewista was in charge of a small group of investigators who were helping bury the dead. She had the undesirable position of examining the bodies without distressing the Gaens burying them. "Not tooth and nail. Even with the large amount of scattered parts, nothing was torn apart."

"Any signs of farming implements, or just weapons?" Trela was seated at the head of a long wooden table, so that she could stare at each of them as they gave their reports.

"Maybe some kitchen knives and wood axes. It is hard to tell due to the advanced state of the decomposition, but no hoes or rakes, no hammers or rocks. It appears that they were killed militarily." Several derlians began chiming in at her statement, causing Rewista to cut them off with her hand before she continued. "They were at least killed by derlians swinging swords."

"But derlians controlled by what?" Tweltas broke in before the others.

"That was not mine to investigate, Tweltas." Rewista rarely raised her voice, but that statement came out a little louder than most.

"That is a good segue, thank you." Trela glared at both of them. "Feyazki, what did your investigation turn up?"

He had been dreading this moment. Try as he might, he had been unable to find a trace of anything out there. No scent of Yavens, which was not surprising since they were difficult to detect after they were gone, their spoor dissipated so quickly. But no scent of magic, either. He had been with Escha and she had not found any derlian tracks. No trampled vegetation going to or from the village. Nothing.

"Nothing, I found absolutely nothing." Vrric inwardly grimaced as Tweltas took in a mighty inhale.

"So, of what use…" Tweltas was the sort who was naturally distrustful of magic, like many Pyrans who had never used it but had to pick up the charred remains of their fellows from the battlefield. It was a dangerous tool. It was a double-edged sword. It was to be eyed warily from a distance.

"And what did you find?" Vrric interrupted Tweltas before he could start.

"We are doing this in order!" Trela interrupted the babble that was bubbling up.

"How about everyone who found nothing of value, raise their hand." Tweltas stopped glaring at Vrric to glare at Trela instead. *A dangerous move*, thought Vrric.

Everyone's hand shot up, however. It kind of killed the whole argument against Tweltas and added a heaviness to the air.

Vrric had been wondering how long it would take before the Pyran warriors began to resent the mission. How far away from their home realm would they follow their queen before becoming disgruntled? If there had been any sort of progress or...

"Arnasta, why isn't your hand up?" Trela had spotted Arnasta sitting to the side of Serghno's portly frame. Vrric had not realized that she had not raised her hand, had barely known she was in the room.

"I think I found some blood from someone who was not killed in the..." Here she waved her hand around uselessly for a moment. "...battle. From someone still alive. From someone who may be close enough to track down."

"Well, why didn't you say so?" It was Tweltas again, but he was grinning.

"We were going in order." She leaned forwards to give him a smile with too much teeth. Serghno pushed his chair back a little so that she could better eye the room. The chair scooching back sounded extra loud in the deep silence that engulfed the room. All eyes were craning to see Arnasta as she spoke. "It was near the back door of the burned-out inn. It was smeared on the remaining wood wall, dropped on the clay brick walkway, and splattered on many of the nearby plants. There was, of course, some in the soil, but that is almost impossible to notice until you know it's there. It was a little odd since there weren't any bodies near that part of the inn. That was what had got me interested." She glanced at Serghno who just smiled silently back at her. "Anyway, I tried to sense a direction and followed it for a little while. It was quite late in the day and we were all to meet here at dusk to discuss our investigations, so Serghno and I came back before we could find anything."

"So..." Trela held up a hand to silence the rest of the table. "...how do you know that the derlian who left the blood is still alive? How do you even know it is derlian blood?"

"When I sensed for a direction, I could kind of hear a heartbeat." Arnasta got quiet and looked down. "It is how I trace things." Trela's hand was still up, keeping the others at bay.

"No one here doubts your abilities, Arnasta, if it wasn't for you, I would not have found Qizern." She slowly lowered her hand. "I just didn't realize how your tracing magic worked." Trela looked around the quiet table for a moment. "I would love to head out tonight to try to find what you felt..." Trela paused as she looked around again. Vrric was worried that if anyone spoke, she would have them all out in the dark, looking for what could very well be an angry Tlana. Luckily, no one spoke. "…but we should wait until morning." A collective, but silent, sigh released into the room. "I will meet you all at dawn."

As the others began to shuffle out of the room, Trela grabbed Vrric and Arnasta. Serghno, of course, stayed behind as well. She let the door get shut and secured before she spoke up.

"I understand this may be a trap, I do, but we have nothing else to go on. We have nothing else to do here." She smiled warmly. It took some of the feral out of her eyes. "Is there a way to cast something now, tonight, that might give us a better feel of where the derlian might be hiding? Our best estimate is that the massacre happened almost a week ago. If someone were truly wounded, it is hard to imagine that they have not either succumbed or escaped the entire area. I just… I don't see how someone is still holed up."

"Well, I can certainly try… but we are not fully investigating until tomorrow morning, right?" Arnasta laughed for the briefest of moments.

"Of course not." Trela waived her hand towards the closed door. Towards where the others had just left. "We will want a full contingent of warriors and mages with us when we investigate. I'm just curious, that is all. I just thought we could see the inn. Where the blood trail starts."

Serghno looked between Arnasta and Vrric. Arnasta was smiling at Trela while Vrric was scowling at her. He knew her well enough that he doubted she would just stand there at the inn.

"Seriously. We are not going to follow the trail in the dark." Arnasta's right eyebrow shot up for the briefest of moments. "We are going to wait until dawn before wandering down the hill and into the brush." Vrric wondered if they should grab a bunch of warriors on the way down, just in case.

"Of course, of course." Trela's smile could be disarming if she wanted it to be.

"Lead the way." Serghno opened the door for Arnasta.

By the time they arrived at the burnt-out inn it was getting quite dark. Vrric had his head down, trying not to stub a toe on the myriad of rocks in the road, so he did not see the two figures waiting by the door frame.

"We knew you wouldn't be able to resist." It was Pejal and Gyllhelon. They laughed and slapped each other on the back as the Trela's small group arrived.

"We are not going to follow the trail in the dark." Arnasta spoke up as the two warriors chuckled.

"Well, I don't know how long you have known Trela for..." Gyllhelon was punched lightly in the shoulder by Pejal and she stopped speaking.

"Have you been drinking?" Vrric had always found Gyllhelon's smile infectious, but never more so than when she had been drinking. She spent much of her sober time quite serious.

"Maybe just a little bit." Pejal held his thumb and forefinger apart just enough to squint between them.

"How did you even...? I mean, we just left the meeting." It was Serghno who interjected.

"Ha! I told you they wouldn't notice." Gyllhelon grinned from Pejal back over to Serghno. "We weren't even there. We ran into Rewista as she left the meeting."

They were certainly not sloppy. Vrric did not think he had ever seen Gyllhelon get truly sloppy. But they were definitely enjoying the evening. He felt a tiny pang of jealousy. He would have rather skipped the meeting and had a beer with Gyllhelon as well.

"We are wasting our time here." Trela silenced them both with a quick look that was not quite a glare. But almost. They both stiffened a little and grew more serious. Then she slipped into an easy smile. "At least now we have some warriors for an escort." She turned towards Arnasta. "Could you get a direction and assure us that there is still a beating heart at the end of this trail?"

"Of course, my queen." Arnasta turned away from the group and felt around the charred door jamb and, eventually, the ground. She seemed quite intent before casting, trying to find the perfect object in the dark.

Vrric almost asked if she wanted some light but assumed she could make some if she wished. Or, if she actually needed assistance, he thought that it should be Serghno who offered it, not himself. He was lost in his own thoughts when she finally cast her spell.

"Narfintotarc!" Her voice was quiet but strong. Her face was serene as she stared down at the dark walkway bricks. Everyone had quieted down to let her concentrate.

Vrric imagined he could see her nostrils flare slightly, as if taking in the scent of the hunted. She slowly stood, her eyes still downcast. She breathed in deep, rolled her hands out in front of her, and then let then her arms swoop out. Serghno had to sidestep out of her way. She had her eyes fully closed and her arms outstretched, and she began to walk along the clay bricks, down the path. They all fell in behind her.

Arnasta continued slowly with her hands held in front of her, palms inward but only touching at the wrists. Her fingers were splayed out as if she were attempting to catch a large ball. She walked slowly but purposefully. Every once in a while, she would stop and sweep her arms, still held together at the wrists, left and right in front of her, then she would continue walking. Vrric, being behind her, could not tell if she had opened her eyes finally, but she did not trip or stumble. She had a long stride that kept her voluminous curly hair from bouncing too much.

They walked for some time in the dark. They were cutting through mild and scattered brush, having left the clay walkway a little while back. Finally, they came to an edge. While certainly not a cliff, the somewhat rocky path was steep enough that it would probably take using hands and feet to make it down unscathed. This was where Arnasta stopped.

"This is as far as we can go in the dark." She let her arms drop to her sides as she turned around.

"But what's down there?" Trela sounded quietly excited. "Did you sense the heartbeat?"

"Yes. Yes, I did." Arnasta crossed her arms in front of her chest. "We had a whole meeting about this and you agreed to wait until dawn. In fact, the only reason I agreed to bring you this far is that you agreed to wait until dawn once we followed the path a little ways."

"What if I did just a little reconnaissance work for you, my queen? Just to see where the path leads?" Pejal spoke up from the back. Vrric had always kind of liked Pejal. He was a true believer. In Trela, the idea of the Kriishan, the Pyran way of life, of everything. He believed, utterly, in everything he surrounded himself with.

"Well, that would keep Arnasta and me from going further. You can't argue against that, can you?" Trela smiled wide. It was a smile that made Vrric think she had planned it, but how could she have known that Pejal and Gyllhelon would be waiting for them?

Arnasta, for her part, just glared at Trela, though he did not feel that the glare had much heat behind it. It seemed more that she felt she had to glare, had to play her part, than that she felt actual animosity about it.

"I will stay with my queen to ensure her safety." Serghno spoke so that it was difficult to tell if he was indicating whether Trela or Arnasta was his queen.

"Well, Pejal should not be forced to go alone." Gyllhelon stepped forward.

So, it was left to Vrric. Should he stay up at the top and be bored with Trela and a couple of mages, or should he descend into the unknown with a couple of thrill-seeking warriors? He had almost made up his mind when Gyllhelon winked at him. That clinched it.

"You should have at least one mage with you." He had unconsciously smiled at Gyllhelon and then turned towards Pejal to speak, meaning he was grinning like an idiot while offering his assistance to the Pyran warrior.

"Perfect. Be quick but thorough." Trela nodded to each of them in turn. She was also grinning widely. Vrric could tell that it took all of her willpower to not insist on coming along, on leading the expedition. "If there's anything interesting down there, I want you to come back up and get me."

Pejal clambered down into the darkness and Gyllhelon followed quickly. Vrric let them get a little ahead, so that he would not kick rocks down on them. He wanted to cast a simple flight spell for himself but would have felt bad that he had not included them. Besides, they should only have to climb down so far. It took him a little while to get back to flat ground in the dark. He decided to fly them all down the next edge if they found one.

"We need some light down here." Pejal was whispering from somewhere up ahead.

"Mekmorflufrefpi!" Vrric immolated a small sphere of air near him, tilting the power towards duration instead of intensity. He floated the ball of light past Gyllhelon and towards Pejal's voice. She shielded her eyes as it went by. Vrric followed while trying to keep his senses trained outwards. He did not want to get caught unawares. His mind, however, was wondering why Arnasta had been so adamant about not coming. She really should have come down there, letting them know that they were going in the right direction. Of course, she had given them all fair warning that she was not going to follow the trail to its source until daybreak, so it really was his expectations that were more incongruous than her refusal.

The ball of light stopped near Pejal, who was stopped near a hole in a hillside. A dark yawning cave opening. Vrric let the ball float into the entrance. Pejal immediately followed with a long dagger held in front of him. This made Vrric follow closely behind, so that he could steer the light more easily. Gyllhelon brought up the rear. He was not sure if her sword was out, but he assumed so. The thought made him step carefully so as not to slip and impale himself.

The cave started out a little narrow, kind of like a hallway. The path angled downwards, taking them ever deeper. The roof of the cave stayed straight the farther down they went, making the hallway larger and larger.

Vrric tried to examine the floor as they were walking, to see if there were tracks or blood droplets or spoor of some kind, but the light was up with Pejal and there were lots of shadows bouncing around, making it impossible to examine anything. A part of him wanted to stop, if only for a moment, to take in some of their surroundings. He thought of asking Pejal to slow his purposeful stride but did not. He again wished that Arnasta were with them, providing her invaluable assistance. Maybe he should have wished they had waited until dawn.

They turned a shallow corner and Pejal slowed to a stop. Vrric peeked around his shoulder to see what was there and almost gasped. The hallway opened up into a large cavern, but that was not all. The cavern had, at its center, a long rectangular wooden table with about thirteen or fourteen chairs around its perimeter. There appeared to be a myriad of unlit candles along the table, but no discernable food or drink. Gyllhelon had her hand on Vrric's shoulder as she peered around both him and Pejal. She looked at the lack of movement between the two and nodded towards the table while giving Vrric a small push. He did not budge.

"Well?" Her loud whisper made him look around furtively, but he could not sense anyone else in the area. "Figures." Gyllhelon stepped around both Vrric and Pejal and strode into the, hopefully, empty cavern. She had her right hand on the hilt of her sword, but it was still sheathed.

Several quick moments after she boldly walked forwards, Pejal followed her with his naked dagger in his hand. Vrric waited another quick moment before heading out himself. He looked around for a moment but was soon drawn to the table. There were four silver candelabras scattered along its length, all with light brown candles in various stages of melted. Some were mere stubs, while others barely had their wicks blackened. Each candelabra had five candles in it. One was lying on its side, directly on the table, candles still held in their sockets. Vrric walked over to that one to investigate further. There was some wax on the tabletop but no blackened scorch marks. He glanced directly down in front of him while looking at the candelabra. Lo and behold, there was a small book sitting closed on the seat of the chair he was directly over. While Gyllhelon and Pejal were scanning the cavern's perimeter, Vrric noisily slid the chair out to pick up the book and sit down. He successfully ignored the looks he got from the warriors as he slid the chair.

The book was untitled, with no wording or marks of any kind on its exterior. The interior was purely handwritten in a flowing and ornate script. It appeared to be a journal of some kind. Vrric flipped past the pages somewhat nonchalantly. He had intended on just reading the last entry, but there was a bloody thumbprint on a page near the middle which caught his attention. He started at the top of the left page, which started in mid-sentence.

...where the tracks left off. The wall before us was solid stone, but we knew there was something behind it. Where else could the handcart have gone? We tapped along the surface of the wall with our hammers, listening for a more hollow echo, but found nothing. We were about to give up when Tulfigner found an odd rock on the ground, near the wall. It was roughly pyramidal in shape, its edges rounded and dulled, but seemingly dust free. It stood at the juncture where the wheel tracks terminated at the wall. Tulfigner, whether in a fit of anger or genius I'll never know, kicked the rock as hard as he could. There was a huge rumbling sound and the wall, which was more like a slab lid of a sarcophagi, but vertical like a door, slid upwards of all directions. Upwards! Vrric was so engrossed in the brief narrative that he did not realize Gyllhelon was hovering near him until she pulled out the chair next to him. She smiled as he looked up.

"Read it aloud." Her eyes were wide and bright, brown irises flecked with bits of gold.

Vrric could hear Pejal muttering to himself in the background. There were three doors at each end of the cavern and he was trying to open one. He was certainly no spy. Rather than getting up to help out Pejal, Vrric cleared his throat to read to Gyllhelon. He started at the beginning of the page again.

"…Upwards! Tulfigner led the way, holding his torch low so that we could see the wheel tracks. After we had passed and continued down a long hallway, we could hear the door crashing down behind us. Stopping what we were doing, we returned to the stone doorway. We kicked every rock, pushed on every outcropping, slid our fingers around every crevice, but we could not find a way to trigger the door from the side we were now on. There was no turning back anymore. No way out but forward.

"We followed the tracks for some time. Not that it mattered, there was only the tunnel, only one way to go. No branches, no doors, no way to get lost beyond how we already were. Eventually we stopped looking for the tracks and just walked. We felt a great despair settle upon us, or at least I certainly did. Tulfigner was never much for that type of conversation. How were we ever to find the Hammer of Petros? How were we to find our way out of here? Why did we even listen to the Old Hag? No amount of pebbles was worth this trouble." Vrric paused as Gyllhelon laughed.

"I'll never get used to Gaens referring to money as 'pebbles.' It's ridiculous." She was sitting sideways on the chair, facing Vrric, with her sword almost horizontal behind her.

Vrric was about to read more, it was an intriguing style of writing, almost story-like. He wondered when it had been written. Not as in "what cycle it was written in" but more of a "when, during the ongoing adventure, was it written" vein. Who has the time to keep a journal? Of course, if they were lost in these caverns, Vrric could imagine it was something to stave off the boredom with. Gyllhelon's right eyebrow started to lift, signaling he was taking too long to muse during the interlude. Vrric was about to read more, that was his intent, but then Pejal began yelling.

"Quick, quick! Help me barricade this door!" Pejal had his shoulder pressed against a wooden door which jumped periodically as something struck it from the other side.

Gyllhelon hopped up and toppled her chair sideways with her sword as she ran over to where Pejal was. Vrric dropped the journal on the table and ran over there as well, dragging two of the chairs with him. There was a loud thumping sound every time the door was struck.

"What is it, Gaens? Are we intruding?" Gyllhelon asked Pejal several rapid questions as he tried to hold the door closed and shift his body around so that Vrric's chairs could be propped up under the door handle.

"I don't know, I don't know." Pejal's face was sweaty with exertion or maybe fear. Vrric wished he had been paying closer attention to what Pejal had been doing or muttering while he had been reading. He felt woefully unprepared.

There was a deafening pounding sound and the door shook mightily. Vrric realized it would not last long. What they needed was some time to be able to talk, to think.

"Move back. Everyone move back." He racked his brain for a brief moment. *What would dishearten them quicker, a shield spell or turning the wooden door to stone?* he thought. A sword pierced the wooden door. "Narmorfpanrefge!" He decided on the stone in the heat of the moment. There was a brief strange quiet that settled over the cavern. The sword was sticking through the stone wall. Suddenly the metal handle started rattling as whoever was on the other side jiggled it.

"If the hinges are still metal, can they just pull the stone door over?" Pejal was backing further away from the door as they talked.

"We have the chairs bracing…" Vrric was starting to argue, though he was not exactly sure why.

"Just throw another spell on it. Just in case." Gyllhelon shook her fingers at the door as she backed up as well.

"Mektecgeto!" Vrric touched the stone door before backing away as well. He was suddenly concerned about conserving his energy, so he kept the shield spell to a minimum.

Shuffling noises began to emanate from the door just to the left of the stone one. Pejal and Gyllhelon were dragging the gigantic table towards the bay of doors. "Eqetecpanarc!" He cast a more powerful shield spell on the door he heard shuffling behind. "The door on the right." Vrric pointed to the door that did not have a spell on it. He had to clamber over the table as they positioned it. It was long enough to cover all three doors. Pejal began tossing chairs against the end of the table at the third door. There was a sound of an axe striking the wood of the third door. It did not shake much, but Vrric did not think it would take too long for them to break through. There was not much he could do but cast a shield on that door as well. "Eqetecpanarc!"

He did not really stagger, but maybe swayed for a brief moment. They headed to the other doors on the opposite side.

Locked. All three of them. Vrric began to muster himself, but Gyllhelon put a hand on his arm.

"We'll come back tomorrow. With reinforcements." She nodded to Vrric, Pejal nodded to her. They all nodded in agreement.

"Nukmorflufrefpi!" Vrric cast another light spell so they could more easily find their way out. He did not stagger that time either, but Gyllhelon tucked her shoulder under his arm and gripped his waist. He did not feel that he needed the help, but he enjoyed the closeness, so he let her lead him along. Pejal ran forwards with the light.

They soon reached the surface and the small hill. Vrric did not wish to try to clamber up the steep slope, so he cast a minor flight spell. "Nukinderclo!" It was really more of a jump spell than a flight one. Trela, Serghno, and Arnasta were waiting at the top of the hill for them. It did not seem like they had been waiting patiently.

The next morning, after a quick wash and a good breakfast, they all gathered back at the top of the hill. This time, however, they were joined by Jalin, Estfale, Rewista, Malghain, and Verin. It was not a huge force, but much larger than last night. Trela, against the wishes of her advisors, took the lead. Vrric, Pejal, and Gyllhelon were nearby since they were the ones who had already done some exploring. Arnasta was next to Trela to track the trail they had originally been following and, of course, Serghno was close to Arnasta's elbow. That left the newcomers at the back.

They found the cavern with the long dining table quite quickly. It had seemed to take longer to get there during the dark, when there were only three of them moving cautiously. The long table was still against the far wall and the doors looked intact; the sword was now sticking through wood. The three doors at the opposite side were still locked. Everything seemed exactly as they had left it, as if their attackers had simply given up and went back from whence they came.

Something nagged at the back of Vrric's mind while they milled about in the cavern. He stared at the ground while Trela and Arnasta decided which door Jalin should start working on. Gyllhelon appeared near his shoulder and whispered to him.

"Did you get the journal?" She, too, was staring at the ground. He had not been sure of what he had been unconsciously looking for until she had said it out loud.

"No, did you?" He knew it was a stupid question the moment it left his mouth. She just shook her head and continued peering around.

"Should we tell the others about it?" Her voice was still quite soft.

"Don't know why we would." He thought about it for a moment. "I guess it means that this room was searched after we left." He looked about himself. "Any tracks they may have left have been ruined by now." He swung his arm about the room. It was not necessarily crowded, but it was certainly well trod. As he looked about the others, he realized that Verin was the only Gaen with them. Seemed kind of foolish.

"Conspiring?" Pejal walked over to them.

"Not really. Just trying to figure out if they walked through this room after we left." Vrric let his voice rise in volume to match Pejal's.

"Well, not through the doors with the table against them. They must have opened and relocked one of these." Pejal began walking over to the doors he had pointed to. Vrric looked over at Gyllhelon. She just shrugged and followed Pejal, so he did the same.

He had crouched down and was peering at one of the locks. Vrric was unsure if Pejal could tell if it had been opened just by looking at it. He, himself, surely could not. Trela and Arnasta, Serghno and Jalin, all made their way over to the doors. Trela's voice carried in front of her.

"…should leave a few warriors, just in case. Pejal, step away from the door and let a professional take a look." She shooed him away while Jalin moved into position. "Feyazki, I was thinking of trapping those other doors. You know, just in case whatever tried to attack you comes back while we're winding away through the tunnels."

Vrric just nodded and headed back over to the doors. He was a little concerned that they would have to open them. Maybe, if they were being chased and the exit was blocked, they would have to go through the doors he was about to trap. He had practiced unraveling a delayed spell while with Revkin once or twice but had not tried it since. He had certainly not tried it under duress. He was not worried about not being able to do it, but more that he would not be able to do it quickly while axes and arrows rained down upon them.

"Can you cast a trap that doesn't hurt anyone?" Verin interrupted his reverie.

"What?" Vrric's ineloquent reply did not phase Verin. She quietly stared at him until he was able to think up a proper one. She was not scowling, but her arms were crossed in front of her. "I was just going to release a little fire at the doors. Maybe something more impressive if they get into the room."

"And here I had assumed you would be more thoughtful than a Pyran mage." She still was not scowling, but her eyebrow was up.

"Well, we want to scare them away. At least while we are investigating." Vrric was not really sure where she was headed.

"Who do you think is down here? In these caves." Her right hand rose briefly and then settled back across her chest. "Who do you think 'attacked' you last night?" She made air quotes with her fingers for the word "attacked."

"I don't know. It could have been anyone. They could have been controlled by a Tlana." Vrric squinted at her. He hoped it did not appear that he was glaring.

"I'll bet you they were just Gaens." Verin paused for a brief moment before continuing. "Some Pyran and Luften invaders enter their caves, their last bastion of sanctuary after their above-ground village has been ravaged, so they send out a group of guards to investigate. They see Pejal being …Pejal… and they overreact. They draw weapons and try to get into this cavern. Suddenly magic is being thrown around at them, probably at a level they've never seen, and they realize it is a true threat that they are facing."

Was she right? They had seemed very quick to try to kill Pejal, to burst into the room brandishing weapons. But what had Pejal been doing to the door anyway? At the time, Vrric was certain they were being chased. But were they really? Certainly no one followed them out of the caves.

"We weren't a threat. I was sitting at the table, reading a journal." Vrric pointed ineffectually towards the upended table.

"You don't understand how Gaens feel about foreigners in their caves, in their sanctuary. And so how do we respond? We bring in a small army the next morning." She was still not scowling, but she was close.

"I'll set up the trap to set off a shield spell." He did not want to antagonize her further. He wondered again why there was only one Gaen in the advance party. If even just to help while wandering around in caves. Trela was typically much more cognizant of these types of things. He wondered if she chose those who were down here, or if they were just close to her during breakfast. "Just for the record, however, we do not know who is down here with us. We really don't."

"Noted." Verin turned and walked over to the main group by the other doors. He wondered why he had tossed in those last words. It was some weird attempt to make himself feel better. It did not work.

"Nartecpandel! Nartecpandel! Nartecpandel!" He cast three spells on three doors. He looked around a bit absentmindedly for the journal, or anything of interest really. Finding nothing while slowly walking in front of the turned-over table, he went to join the others.

"So, it's agreed, no one will be left behind to defend this cavern." Trela and the others were nodding to each other. Vrric wondered what the conversation was. He was sure she was going to leave a couple of them behind to guard their exit. He pulled her aside, away from the main group after she was done.

"Why is Verin the only Gaen here?" He whispered and pointed with his eyes, not his hands.

"To be honest, she wasn't even supposed to be here." Trela kept her voice barely audible. "I am a little concerned that we may have to kill some Gaens here. Maybe get some information from some civilians. I thought it would be best to not test our new friends' loyalty."

"Well, then at least Knill or Croy. These caves…" He was not really sure where he was going with the conversation, so he was fine when she interrupted.

"Don't be daft." It was quick and to the point. She walked past him towards where the others were gathered. Waiting for them.

Jalin had the door open and Arnasta, Trela, and Serghno disappeared quickly. Vrric waited around until it was just him, Verin, and Gyllhelon. He started walking while they were still hovering near the entrance.

"I thought you would want to be near the front, just in case we run into any Gaens." Vrric kept slowly walking by. "You know… for diplomacy."

"We will not run into any Gaens who do not wish to be found. Up front is not where diplomacy will be needed." Verin waved her arm for Gyllhelon to follow Vrric. She was, apparently, going to bring up the rear guard. It was comforting.

Vrric trotted a little to catch up to Rewista, who was the last of the main pack. She did not have any weapons out but appeared to be examining everything along their way. At least her head kept swiveling and tilting around. He had always thought of her as a commander rather than a fighter. A tactician and strategist. He wondered if that was justified, or if she was just as dangerous in single combat. He had never seen her actually swing a sword. He watched her short cropped black hair fade in and out of the shadows as other warriors passed in front of Serghno's light spells. He had a couple placed amongst the pack, so Vrric did not feel he needed to add to the brightness.

They traveled through the winding cave system that way for some time. Trela following Arnasta and the rest of them following Trela. Vrric lost track of time and direction. His mind began to wander. Eventually, Gyllhelon got in front of him and he plodded along behind, his eyes fixed on her swaying, lithe body. It was hypnotic. Then… slam!

A pile of rocks fell between Rewista and Gyllhelon. Vrric was glad he had not been in front because she immediately sprang backwards out of harm's way and he doubted he would have reacted that quickly. He could have been crushed under the stone that now separated them from the main pack. He had automatically grabbed Gyllhelon's elbow as she hopped back into him and Verin immediately grabbed his.

"Run. Now. We have to go." Verin pulled on his arm for a split second and then took off in another direction.

Vrric did not have time to be stunned. He thought he could hear the clash of steel behind the wall of rubble. But instead of attempting to move the rocks, instead of attempting to help, he immediately turned and ran after Verin. It sounded like Gyllhelon was on their heels.

"Mekmorflufrefpi!" Vrric did his best to keep the light sphere next to Verin. He was not completely sure that she needed it, but he did.

So many questions bounded through his mind as he bounded after Verin's fleeing form, but they could not be properly contemplated. He attempted to keep a small list in his mind to bring up once they had stopped, but each question led in a different direction, diffusing his list. They turned several corners during their run. He would try to see if they were taking one side of a "T" or if it was a true corner, but he was having a hard enough time just keeping up. Verin was amazingly quick and agile for her short stature.

Suddenly she stopped. There was a stone wall in front of them. It was a dead end. Literally. He barely halted in time and bent over with his hands on his knees, just trying to breathe. Gyllhelon came to a rest next to him. She barely seemed to be breathing, the running had not fazed her in the least.

"Why have we stopped?" Gyllhelon split her time between watching behind them and looking at Verin. Verin was scowling and pushing on the stone wall in front of them.

"There should be something here. I…" She stopped herself from talking but kept feeling around the wall.

Vrric was staring at the floor, trying to get the spots out of his vision. He was not out of shape, per se, but he was obviously not as fit as Gyllhelon or Verin. He wanted to blame it on the suddenness of the exertion, but he was typically wont to cast a flight spell before trying to jog or run. As he stared down, catching his breath, he noticed tracks in the stone floor. Wheel tracks. His eyes flashed around the scene in front of him as he began to hear running behind him. It sounded like a lot of feet.

"There. That stone, kick the stone." Vrric tried to point. Verin backed up with her hands up, trying to see what he was attempting to show her. He took a step and kicked the pyramidal shaped rock with all of his might.

The sound was quite loud, as if stone were sliding against stone. It rumbled so loud that it seemed to vibrate Vrric's sight. The wall in front of them began to slowly raise. Verin slapped him on the back and quickly ducked under the small but lengthening space. Gyllhelon waived him to be next and then immediately followed. They stood there for a moment, with the wall completely raised, listening to the footsteps in the hall. Vrric prepared himself to cast something. Something devastating and violent. Luckily, the wall lowered itself before the following footsteps got too close. They waited there in silence, barely attempting to breathe. He was positive that whoever was following them would know what rock to kick. He assumed this was their cave after all. But... nothing. The wall did not raise again. They were not attacked. Eventually his light spell dissipated.

"Mekmorflufrefpi!" Vrric stared hard at Verin. Gyllhelon was also looking at her.

"You read Inschuspar's journal?" Verin was the one who broke the silence.

"What is going on here? What has happened to the others?" Gyllhelon spoke before Vrric could.

"You were looking for the stone described in the journal. You led us here." Vrric spoke before Verin could, though it did not appear she was preparing to answer Gyllhelon anytime soon.

"You have to understand that I am trying to help you. All of you." Verin stepped back with her arms crossed. No one made any moves for any weapons. Vrric did not feel threatened at all. It was more of a confusion. Maybe a somewhat frustrated confusion.

"You can see how we would be concerned if this was all planned. Right? Was this all planned?" Gyllhelon's body appeared relaxed during her tense speech. Oddly enough, that relaxed posed made Vrric more nervous than if she had been clutching at her sword's hilt.

"Listen, I... We don't have time. I should explain everything, I really should. You both deserve that. But we don't have the time." Verin held her hands out in supplication. Her chest heaved during a sigh. Her cheeks raised in a pained expression. "I am going to have to blindfold the both of you."

"Nope." Gyllhelon's back was the only thing that was rigid on her. She still did not reach for a weapon, but her back conveyed her intransigence.

"Listen, I appreciate your concern, but if your death or even your capture was my goal, we would not be here discussing this. I would not be asking you. I am not even asking to tie your hands, just the blindfolds." Verin kept her arms out, away from her own weapons. "You have to trust me about this. They will not talk with you without the blindfolds."

"Who are 'they'?" Vrric could not help himself.

"If you could know that, we wouldn't need the blindfolds, now would we?" Verin went back to crossing her arms.

"Is it safe to assume that 'they' consist of angry Gaen warriors?" Gyllhelon had a wry smile on her relaxed face.

"Listen, they are coming soon. They are on their way. If we could just get the both of you blindfolded…" Verin looked plaintive.

"Show me your tongue." Vrric interrupted her. He was ready to acquiesce, just to end the conversation, but wanted one last tiny piece of assurance.

Verin walked straight to both of them, closing the distance in two long strides of her short legs. Her hands were clasped behind her back. If they wanted to kill her, that would have been the moment. She tilted her head back slightly and stuck her tongue out and down.

"Well, at least it's not black." Gyllhelon turned her wry smile over to Vrric. He smiled back.

He was never sure where they had left off on that theory, the coterie in general. Was a black tongue while the victim was living really indicative of Tlana control? In any case, it was a vulnerable position that Verin immediately put herself in, just to reassure them. She still had her tongue out, looking at them over her cheek bones.

"Fine. Whatever. Blindfold." Vrric spoke the words that he doubted Gyllhelon could. He figured he would have to capitulate first. "But if this is some sort of trap, some sort of ambush, I promise you I will destroy everything within a twenty-rod radius." Too much? Probably. He felt better for saying it out loud, however.

"Of course. I'll be the first to die." Verin made a turn-around motion with her forefinger.

He turned around. Gyllhelon turned around. She smiled slyly at him. "Just remember who your friends are when you start laying waste to everything around you."

Vrric had to squat to let Verin blindfold him. It just seemed simpler. He stood back up and listened to Gyllhelon and Verin go through something similar. It was tight and he certainly couldn't see, but there were comforting gaps in the bottom so that a little light still penetrated. If he strained, he could see the scuffed and traveled-stained tips of his boots. He wondered how long they would have to wait. Then Verin whistled a high and piercing trill. It was followed by another whistle off in the distance. Vrric was glad to have his back towards the sliding door. At least he would hear it open if it did.

They waited for what seemed like a quarter hour, but he knew it could not have been more than three or four minutes. The sound of footfalls slowly gained in volume. There were several gaits and Vrric counted at least five individuals. The echoey tunnel made it difficult to tell for sure. The footsteps came to a staggered halt and there was a small bit of whispering. Before Vrric could get impatient, however, one of them spoke.

"I understand you are Feyazki, the Luften wizard who defeated a Tlana." It was half a question and half a statement. Vrric only nodded shallowly. "I am Havolin Cru'tul. I am no 'jin, so you can relax. We… we had to hide ourselves down here, away from what ravaged our village. We lost a lot of loved ones when the evil showed up. I could tell you stories… That is not why you are here, of course." Havolin clapped his (his?) hands and rubbed them together lightly. "We have become quite nervous, almost scared of our own shadows, you might say. We even had the main entrance in this cave system sealed off until a couple of days ago. What I am trying to say is that we should have not attacked you when you came investigating, we understand that now. You must understand that our only intention was to secure our system, to protect our meager sanctuary." The hands rubbed as Havolin paused again. "You returned with a full contingent of foreign warriors. You sealed off our main civilian tunnels and wandered through our escape ones. You made enough noise to rouse the dead, let alone to strike fear into our poor, overwrought hearts. We would have either attacked you or, more likely, herded you into one of our pits, but we were contacted by some of your Gaen companions last night. They explained your situation. We explained ours. They explained how we could assist each other. Does this all make sense so far?"

"So, the others of our group are safe?" Vrric wondered how many of their Gaen companions contacted this group. Obviously more than just Verin.

"Yes, though they are a little contained." More hand rubbing. "We were concerned that they may lash out. We are attempting to keep everyone from getting harmed, you see. We are quite zealous that no Gaens are hurt, but we see no reason to hurt any foreigners either. At least without provocation."

"Why the blindfolds?" Gyllhelon broke in.

"Merely an overabundance of precaution. There may be some in front of you now who do not wish to be recognized. It may be a gentle nudge to keep you from pulling your sword and slashing through our group. It may just be a small capitulation on your part, a peace offering of a weakened state. It might be that we are all horribly disfigured and shy. There are many possible reasons. But please understand that it is not intended to be a projection of ill will towards you. We... need something from you." A small cough echoed through the tunnel amongst the sudden silence.

"And what is that?" Vrric did not care much why they were blindfolded. He wanted to know how they could get the blinds removed. Havolin seemed like he would talk forever if allowed.

"We need to speak with the Great Communicator. The one who speaks with Belegs. The one called Clerin Toswin." Vrric tensed at the thought. There was no reason to endanger her.

"It is not like I can teleport out and get her, bring her back in the blink of an eye. You would need the Blind One to do that." Vrric had a hunch at who was involved, who was hidden in front of him.

"We have that part covered." It was the Blind One himself. It had to be. The voice was just too close to be anyone else.

"What we need is someone to convince her to travel with the Blind One. From our understanding of the situation, you are the one we need to convince her. Is there someone more suitable to the task?" More hand rubbing.

"No. Not even Trela. Though if you are looking for one whom she feels would never intentionally betray her, you might try Croy. He is as innocent as a newborn babe." Gyllhelon spoke before Vrric could open his mouth. "But if you are looking for the one most qualified to convince her that a bad idea is good, look no further."

"Hey..." Vrric was immediately interrupted by Havolin.

"We are not trying to trick her in any way. We just wish to speak with her." Vrric could hear movement but could not tell exactly what was going on beyond his blindfold.

"Then why all this? Anytime I am blindfolded by someone other than myself, I have to wonder..." Gyllhelon sounded like she was beginning a tirade, so Vrric jumped in.

"I will speak with her, I will. I will try to convince her to talk with you. I will even try to convince her to travel with the Blind One." He knew where they were headed and did not wish to drag it out any more than necessary. "But her safety is my number one priority. If you go to retrieve her, I go with you. If you wish to bring her here, I stay by her side. If I feel that she will be harmed, I will attack. If you even make her feel uncomfortable with your questions, I will require you to stop. She is not a warrior and had nothing to do with our investigation into your cave system. She is completely innocent."

"That is for us to judge." It was the Blind One again. Just his voice made Vrric nervous. "But do not worry, we are under strict orders not to harm her by one we respect and fear much more than yourself."

Chapter 13

It was faint at first, the *whisper*. Clerin had not been expecting it, had not been listening for it. It was more like an itch in the back of her mind than any real form of communication. Finally, she realized it was Vrric. He was calling to her from somewhere distant.

"Clerin… Clerin…" It was a long, thin tendril. Like a jellyfish appendage.

It took her another couple of moments before she could separate herself from chatting with Escha and Torpalin. Her name merely repeated in her mind, getting louder and louder. Finally, she found an empty house in the empty village. She sat on an empty chair.

"Lofintotarc! Feyazki, it is me." Typically, Vrric did not need any help, but she cast the tiniest response to his *whisper* more to let him know she was available than to assist him at all.

"Clerin, good. Are you alone?" His voice was quite strong at this point.

"Yes. I stepped into an empty house. That is why it took me so long to respond." She found herself whispering a little, even though there was no one around. She wondered if that affected her volume at the other end of the communication.

"Uhm, hold on." Vrric got quiet for a little while. She stared around at the small parlor room she was in, trying to imagine the Gaen life that used to take place there. There were two short bookshelves, one on either side of a fireplace. She sat in a large, overstuffed chair and there was another one opposite her, with two smaller wooden chairs against a wall. Several doors led off into different areas of the house. All in all, the room looked a little Fluen to her. It was odd. Before she could get too distracted, however, Vrric's voice returned. "It appears as if we have a lock on your location. We will appear shortly."

"Well… Okay." Clerin meant to ask Vrric what he meant by "we," but did not get the chance.

Suddenly he was in front of her and the Blind One was beside him. She doubted that she had even blinked. They just appeared. She let out an embarrassingly awkward yelp.

"That was completely unfair, you should have warned me." Her hand clamped uselessly over her heart.

"Yes, he should have." The Blind One's head swung between them as if he could see. "Apologize to the lady."

Vrric was silent a moment as he glared uselessly at the Blind One. The Blind One was patiently waiting with a tiny soft smile on his lips. Clerin waited patiently as well.

"Listen, I am sorry that we startled you." He stopped glaring at the Blind One and turned towards her. Suddenly his face softened. "Truly. I should have *whispered* to you for longer. I was not thinking of how shocking it would be if we just appeared." The corner of his mouth curled up in a mischievous smile. "I'd like to make it up to you. I'll tell you what… Tonight, when everyone else is bored and listless, I'll make you a nice dinner here, in this house. How does that sound?"

"That sounds nice." Clerin could feel a small smile creep into her lips as well. He sounded so sincere.

"Perfect." The Blind One interrupted them. "I come to ask a great favor of you. Rest assured that I do not ask this just for myself. I ask for the last of these villagers, the elders who have sunk into the safety of their warrens. There is a consensus amongst them that they need to speak with you."

"Of course." Clerin did not think about why. She did not wonder if Trela was being held captive, or if this was a trick, or if Vrric wanted to speak with her in private before she agreed. She heard a plea and responded. It was her nature. It was only after she responded that her mind began to wonder. She attempted to reassure herself with the thought that Vrric would not have brought the Blind One to her if he did not believe in whatever they needed. His very presence was comforting.

"Excellent." The Blind One was nodding to himself. "Please, take my hand and we shall be off."

As was often the case, Clerin did not pay attention to the Blind One's spell. She knew he was about to cast a Minora syllable. So, what did it really matter what it was? She would never attempt to cast such a thing. Then, suddenly, they were elsewhere. There was no feeling with it, no rushing, no motion, not even a queasy feeling in her stomach. They were just in one location, then in another.

They were underground. Before her eyes adjusted to the flickering torch light, she could tell. There was a smell, though not unpleasant. There was a drop in temperature as her heat left her body towards the walls. There was a hollow echo to the silence.

Her eyes did adjust quickly. There were plenty of torches circumscribing the large room emitting plenty of light. There were two stone chairs on a dais, ornately carved. Or sculpted? These were across the room, but large enough to be the first real objects to catch her eyes. There was a large, round table in the center of the large room. There were at least four closed doors near where they had appeared. There were about five groups of Gaens milling about in small clusters, or maybe six. One of the groups quickly gravitated towards them. Clerin was happy to see that the group contained Gyllhelon and a Gaen that she certainly recognized. Verin?

"Good, good. You have arrived." An ancient-looking Gaen with a long white beard that was tucked into his belt spoke. He appeared a little nervous because he kept rubbing his hands together. "My name is Havolin, and I am very pleased to meet with you."

"I told you it would not take them long. Now will you admit it was better to bring the mage to the meeting room before teleporting?" The Blind One was talking to some other Gaen, off to the side. Clerin could not take her eyes off of Havolin, however.

He had a kind and wrinkled face. The wrinkles gave him a permanent smile. There was an amazing amount of sparkle in his eyes. Maybe with a hint of mischievousness in them, but not too much. He had on wrinkled robes made of a wide and thick thread that made the garment look scratchy. He was short to begin with but was also bent at the back with a small hump to his shoulders. He looked safe. He looked… benign. Yes, against her better judgment, Clerin took an immediate liking to Havolin.

"And I am pleased to meet you." Clerin shook his outstretched hand. He did not let go and began to lead her towards the table. His stature made her stoop a little to hear his murmuring as he walked. It gave a conspiratorial air to their conversation, though he was mainly talking to himself.

"First time that I have seen a Fluen. What a beautiful girl you are, you must make your mother so proud." He was pattering on, almost mumbling. Shuffling towards some of the wooden chairs.

He pulled out a chair for her and waited. Clerin did not want to keep him waiting, so she sat down. He reciprocated quickly.

"You are wondering why we brought you down here?" He posed it as a question.

"Well… yes." It had seemed rude to ask it, so she had been resigned to make some small talk first. But if he was just going to tell her directly…

"We were not planning on it. We were going to attack your Pyran warriors in the village during the night. But we worried about our losses. We were going to attack the group that entered our caves, for simple self-defense if nothing else. But then we were told you were friendly. We were then going to just leave you alone, to hide farther and farther into our underground maze. But then we were told that we had to speak with you. Not the others, mind you, just you." He smiled a little and rubbed his hands together. "You are the Great Communicator, correct? You speak with Belegs?"

"Who… who told you to speak with me?" Clerin began to get a tingle in her stomach.

"Why, Gunzgak, of course." His grin widened.

It hit Clerin like a fist. She had not been expecting that. She was supposed to visit Gorbanax again after they had destroyed the Cabal of Lochom. She had not even been thinking about Gunzgak.

"Does Gunzgak wish to commune?" What if Gunzgak could take Clerin's messages from her? What if she could end her quest and return home? She had even wondered if Gorbanax was to send her to Gunzgak after it spoke with her. At the very least, maybe she could shorten her trip.

"No. Or… maybe." Havolin was staring at his hands. "Gunzgak definitely wants you to speak with someone specific. Whether or not it will speak with you through that Gaen, or whether it will wish to commune with you afterwards, I know not."

"Please. Yes." Clerin tried to keep her enthusiasm on an even keel. "I will speak with whoever and wherever, just lead the way."

"It must be without your friends, without your guides." Havolin stared directly into her eyes. "You must follow me deep into our caverns alone. The… someone specific is unable to move, you understand."

"Surely, the Blind One…" Clerin was interrupted.

"No." Havolin shook his head while still staring at her. It was a little disconcerting, the way his eyes moved. "You must be the one who travels. Alone."

"Of course." She nodded to him. What choice did she have? And besides, this was a great opportunity for her. She would have done anything at all if it was to shorten her overall quest, even in the slightest. "Lead the way."

Vrric, of course, tried to insist upon coming with her. In fact, and this took Clerin aback, the Blind One offered to come as well. Havolin was adamant, however. Only the two of them could travel to meet with the "someone." No others.

As she was leaving, Vrric stopped her. He smiled warmly at her and tilted his head, so she tilted hers in the opposite way. She had thought he was going to whisper something in her ear. Something cute. Or considering the way his hands were on her hips, perhaps something daring. His lips hovered not next to her ear, but at her neck. She could feel them softly moving against her but could hear nothing. Was it a kiss? He took her face into his hands, smiled warmly into her eyes, and bade her good luck. It was the most contact they had had for some time, and Clerin was certainly willing to stick around to soak up a little more, but Havolin was becoming urgent. Vrric turned and walked away. Clerin, also silently, turned and walked over to Havolin. Her mind swirled.

The interaction with Vrric created such a cloud of confusion around her that she was not paying attention to any of the turns in the tunnel. She was not even sure if they had passed other passages. She was sure that they had passed some doors. It did not take too terribly long once she had started paying attention, but she was not quite sure how much time had passed in total. They stopped before a door and Havolin nervously rubbed his hands together. This small gesture made her feel more nervous herself. It was odd, but it made her want to rub her own hands together.

"After you." He opened the door and swept an arm in front of his bow.

Clerin suddenly became nervous. She hated entering a room with someone behind her. Or at least a stranger behind her. But since she could not just stand in the corridor, she entered and turned slightly to keep Havolin partially in her view.

The room was not large. It had a small table with several chairs centered in it. The table had a lamp that kept the room fairly well lit. There were two other doors leading out of the room besides the one they had entered through. But all of these things were barely noticed. There was a Gaen Yaven engulfing the back part of the room.

The Yaven reminded Clerin somewhat of Phyna. It had two boulders being used as wheels for its legs instead of one, with a central torso rising up from them, leaving the connection point hidden. The massive chest and arms looked more derlian than Phyna's. Its head was a helmet with face plate, with the eyeholes bored deep. Since there was no mouth carved into the plate, she was somewhat taken aback by its sudden projection of voice.

"You are the Great Communicator, are you not?" Clerin had forgotten all about Havolin and walked towards the Yaven.

"I have been called that, yes." Elange's stone immediately grew warm against her skin, so she removed it and dropped it into her pouch.

"Then I have a message for the messenger." The large Yaven shifted sideways as it spoke, farther away from the table.

"Please." Clerin decided against trying to finagle a chair from the table.

"Communication is desired, you see, but we are concerned about the nature of the conversation. Gunzgak has typically kept in touch with Lembin, not with Gorbanax, but Gorbanax has sent what was most probably a warning. It was… quite perplexing." The Yaven seemed to be getting agitated. It did not introduce itself, nor it did not explain itself; it just launched into its questions. "Do you carry messages?"

"Yes, but not any for Gunzgak. That I know of." Clerin stood with her legs shoulder width apart. The conversation felt somewhat confrontational.

"Who did Lembin send you to? Surely not Gorbanax." The Yaven had stopped shifting and stood square towards Clerin.

"Lembin sent me to Linchon with only one message." Clerin paused for a moment. "That I know of."

"It was Linchon that sent you to Gorbanax?" It was hard to tell if the sentence was a statement or a question.

"Yes." She thought hard for a moment. "In fact, Linchon did want me to give the original message, the message from Lembin, to both Gorbanax and Gunzgak. Then I was to give Linchon's reply to Lembin. But Gorbanax refused to listen to the message. At least until we have destroyed the Cabal of Lochom." It all came pouring out. Should she be secretive? She had been entrusted by Lembin to deliver one message. Had she already betrayed that trust? Was she about to betray that trust? It was a quandary that was wending its way through Clerin when she was interrupted.

"So, you truly speak to Belegs? You are their vessel?" It was Havolin. His voice sounded odd and out of place. She had forgotten that he existed. She turned towards him. "You are the harbinger of change. After you the world will be unrecognizable. We have decided against that, though we may increase in power because of it." It was the strangest feeling. She was listening to him. Sort of. But her eyes, her visual perception, had taken up all of her energy, all of her resources, and his voice faded to a whisper. As Havolin babbled to her about a coming revolution she noticed something strange in his mouth. She saw, with absolute clarity, that his tongue was as black as pitch. It sent chills down her spine. His diatribe was reaching its crescendo. "…and that is why you must be destroyed!"

Time stopped as he yelled that word. His mouth hung open, his black tongue curling slightly. Then, "Eqedepiarc!" The room brightened with the pillar of flame. A huge stone cage descended swiftly upon Clerin. This redirected her attention. One of the Yaven's hands had morphed into a large stone cage, with mere slits for her to see through, that crashed into the ground around Clerin. The vertical slits were only a finger width wide, but there were many of them, each "bar" in the cage was about three finger widths wide. The overall result was that she could still see much of what was happening beyond the cage, but she did not even feel the heat from Havolin's fire spell. She was somehow fully protected despite the slits. The Yaven's "face" was turned towards her, all but ignoring Havolin and the licking flames. The cage was boring into the hard rock cave floor, somehow pushing the plug of rock she was standing on down with it, sinking her into the floor. As she was descending, she looked out through the cage's "bars" and, in the midst of the intense brightness of the fire, thought she saw Vrric and the Blind One blink into existence. Lightning began to flash amongst the flames as she was pushed below the floor level while the mages battled whatever it was that Havolin had become. She forgot to scream.

It was incredibly dark. The yelling from above faded and it would have been quiet except for the sound of grinding stone. Oddly enough, no chips or dust seemed to strike her or fill her lungs. It took several moments of motion before she popped through into a lower cave. It was still dark but the grinding had stopped, and soon afterwards, so did the feeling of descent.

"Hmph. Birds think they are so very clever." It was the low rumble of the Yaven. Clerin reached out blindly but could no longer feel the cage in front of her. "If you wish light to continue our conversation, you will have to perform that service yourself."

Clerin did not necessarily need light to speak, but she already felt somewhat panicky about the darkness. She thought back to her magic teacher, Olwinn. Light was such a simple spell, but it was one that she seldom used. She typically just ignited a candle or campfire. The word was finally summoned from her memory. "Numorflufrefpi!" A small ball of flame hovered in front of her. She did not need much light, just enough to make herself feel better, so she tilted the pillar towards duration and away from intensity. The Yaven in front of her appeared smaller than in the other room, but it could have just been a trick of the light.

"Do you mind if we continue our conversation down here, where we will not be disturbed?" There was a gentle courtesy in the Yaven's voice, as if she really could have requested the conversation to end. It was more similar to talking with Wil than with Taglo.

"Do you know if my friends are safe? Should we help them?" Clerin was not entirely positive that she had seen them. "I don't want to leave them fending for themselves."

"The bird's vessel was fully engaged with me as we left. I believe your friends were able to catch it unawares while it was distracted. There is little we could do at this point to help in any case. I do not hear more combat through the stone, if that is any consolation." That speech sounded more like Taglo than Wil.

"Well, if we are to converse, I am at a disadvantage in that you know who I am, but I do not know who you are." Clerin paused for a moment, listening to the silent stone. "How are you called?"

"You may refer to me as Nolkrung. And though I do know who you are, I do not know what you are called." Whenever Nolkrung stopped speaking, it echoed briefly, but then a full silence descended.

"My name is Clerin Toswin. I am pleased to meet you, Nolkrung." Not knowing what else to do, she gave a small curtsey.

"I am pleased as well. Surely." There was an awkward pause. "How did you know that Gorbanax did not hear the messages from Linchon or Lembin? Were you explicitly told? How would Gorbanax know not to listen to them?"

"How did Gorbanax warn Gunzgak?" Since Clerin did not know, she figured it was best to answer with a question of her own.

"Hmph. So, you assume Linchon warned Gorbanax? But why then would it provide you with a message? Why not just provide the warning?"

"Well, I…" Clerin paused. She did not want to mention her father, did not want to discuss the varying modes of communication she had endured. She did not know Nolkrung like she knew Wil. "I do not know. I do know that Gorbanax insisted that I keep a certain distance. That I keep all the messages within me. We did not truly commune… Gorbanax showed me images, distant charades, to convey its intent that it would receive the messages once the Cabal of Lochom was destroyed. Only after that."

"So, if you did not commune, did you convey meaning to Gorbanax, or was all meaning in only one direction?" The Yaven did not pause as often as some others did. Certainly not as much as Phyna did. Clerin paused herself to make sure that what she spoke was true.

"I attempted speech at the end of it all, to let Gorbanax know my understanding of the situation. But I was under lava and, truly, have no idea if my words were conveyed." She paused for another moment, attempting to recollect fully. "Gorbanax did nothing after I spoke, gave no indications whatsoever. It was not like we were standing together, in air, conversing, like you and I are doing right now."

"And what was your communication with Linchon like? Did you converse, in air, like we are doing?" Clerin assumed that Nolkrung was attempting to make a joke about the air and Linchon. Instead of enjoying it, however, she made a knee-jerk response.

"I would rather not discuss Linchon." That was still a sore spot. She did not like to talk to anyone about that conversation, least of all someone she had just met.

"Is there anything physical thing I could provide you with? Diamonds? Is there any creature comfort at all that would convince you to explain your communication with Linchon?" The stillness of the Yaven was slightly unnerving. She was used to staring at the constant motion of Taglo and Wil. Speaking with Nolkrung was like talking to a statue.

"No, nothing." Clerin racked her brain trying to think of a way to change the subject.

"Is there any threat that I could make? What if I promised to kill you?" Its voice did not change in volume or tenor. It was merely stating possibilities.

"No, nothing." Would she have said that if she had truly felt threatened? She would like to have thought so but was not positive.

"Well, that is unsatisfying." There was a small pause. "Gunzgak wishes to converse with you. Not to truly commune, like what I assume you did with Linchon, but to talk at a distance, like what you did with Gorbanax. Would that be agreeable with you?"

"Of course... Of course, I would like to converse with Gunzgak." Clerin thought for a moment. "But how long would that take? We are nowhere near the Gaen Temple, are we?"

"No. We are not. But we can travel quite swiftly through the ground. No turns to make, no obstacles to avoid, no elevation to raise and lower. Just straight and swift travel." It paused again, silent and motionless, like a statue. "From our location here, I will say it should be several hours, but certainly not longer than a quarter day of travel."

"Well, I did not bring a waterskin..." Clerin was muttering, mainly to herself, out loud.

"We will pass more than one underground river during our journey. I will stop whenever you are thirsty. Will you need food?" The Yaven seemed quite impatient for a Gaen.

"I should probably only eat fruits or vegetables anyway." Clerin patted her pouches and pockets uselessly. "I'll be fine for the rest of the day. But yes, we should stop at the nearest underground river."

"Good. I am elated." The Yaven did not sound elated. "Step inside."

Nolkrung grew and then opened a section of itself, revealing a small hollow chamber. Clerin did not hesitate but crawled inside and sat down cross-legged. There was not a lot of room, so she left her light spell in the main room, she could always cast another. She took in a deep breath and closed her eyes. She was quickly sealed up in darkness and the feeling of motion engulfed her. She did not think about how worried her friends might be that she would be gone for a couple of days until she was well on her way. That horrible panic-filled thought was quickly pushed aside by her realization that Vrric had not whispered to her after he had defeated Havolin. Of course, that meant she assumed he had defeated Havolin. Of course he had. How could he not have? He even had the Blind One with him at the time. These thoughts swirled uselessly in her mind while barreling through the solid stone ground. Quite comfortably as well. It was not like lying on stone, which she figured would be the default setting, and it was certainly not like lying upon mud. No, it almost felt like leather. It was soft and forgiving, but still strong and supportive. She never did thank Nolkrung for being so accommodating to her. Nolkrung, for its part, was quite quiet during their journey. She wondered how much effort it took to steer them towards the Temple. It was hard to tell anything because once they got up to speed she could no longer feel the motion.

It took what seemed like a couple of hours before Nolkrung began to slow. If she were honest, Clerin thought she slept for much of the journey. When they finally came to a stop, part of Nolkrung opened up. Into darkness. "Numorflufrefpi!" She gripped the edge of the opening and peeked over. They were floating in a tight cavern. It would have given her claustrophobia if she had not spent the afternoon cocooned inside of a Yaven.

"To my understanding, this is the cleanest underground river along the way." Nolkrung's disembodied voice echoed hollowly in the small cavern.

Clerin reached over and took several small drinks with her hands. It tasted incredibly refreshing. She realized she was going to immerse herself anyway, so she got undressed and pushed herself over the edge into the water. It was bracingly cold. She had just had her hands in it and, yes, it had seemed somewhat chilly, but that was nothing compared to dunking her whole body. She had planned on drinking gulps of water while she was treading, but in the moment that seemed more like drowning than drinking. She dunked her face and hair several times and then tried to clamber back up. Nolkrung was kind enough to form a small ledge for her to sit on. She rested for a while, her feet floating in the freezing water, while she slowly scooped water in her hands. It took a lot longer to drink that way, but she felt better about doing it. Soon she was satiated and re-hydrated. The river water evaporating off her skin began to truly chill her. No matter how much she enjoyed the water, how much she missed swimming and bathing, it was just too cold for her to continue to dangle her feet in that river. With a heavy sigh, she climbed back into the—very comfortable—tomblike vessel. She kicked her boots and dusty clothes to one end of the chamber as Nolkrung closed up and began to build up speed again.

"Thank you very much. That was refreshing." Clerin was not trying to start up a conversation, but she was not trying to avoid one either. "Is the water comfortable?" She did not ask about the fire from her light spell since it was not touching the Yaven. She did not ask about the air because she did not even think of it.

"We are no longer against the water. We are traveling through the ground again. I find this much more comfortable than the water, but…" Clerin waited for some time before Nolkrung spoke again. She wondered more than once if she should prompt it with more than a grunt or a hmm. "…the reason I am here is to experience these other things. To understand things that make me uncomfortable. To understand something as foreign as water."

"I suppose that is why we are all here. To understand things that make us uncomfortable." Clerin enjoyed the sound of the sentence. It brought her mind to another path, though. "Do you have a Menel?"

"Have you seen other Menels?" The Yaven posed a question in answer to her own.

"Yes, a couple." Lying in her sarcophagus, it was difficult to tell where to direct her speech. She felt like she was talking to a room rather than to anyone in specific.

"Then mine will be much of a disappointment. Though I am almost as old as Gunzgak, I rarely travel to this realm. And when I do, it is typically only to commune with Gunzgak. And Gunzgak is completely surrounded by only stone." There was a small pause. "We share a parent, Gunzgak and I."

"Wow, you are sibling to a Beleg?" It seemed obvious to Clerin that they should exist. In fact, it was quite probably that some, or even most, of the Belegs' parents still existed. She had just not specifically thought of it before.

"Half-sibling, yes." A small glow emanated around Clerin, like phosphorescence from moss. A portion of the stone in front of her face gained in translucency, as if it were morphing from basalt to a clear quartz crystal. A small disc slowly spun next to the stone window. The amulet was approximately the same diameter of the ones she had seen before but was thin. Easily less than half the thickness of Wil's Menel. It was amazingly beautiful, however. The three sections were so intense in color that they appeared to vibrate slightly. Bright orange red for fire, a deep aqua blue for water, and a slightly rainbow-tinged opalescent white for air, like the inside of an oyster shell. It made Clerin gasp under her breath. "Do you like it?"

"It is so vivid and vibrant. Its beauty is breathtaking." She grinned openly while staring at the slowly spinning Menel.

"It makes me proud to hear you say that." The quartz section of Nolkrung began to become more opaque. Clerin's hand twitched in an urge to reach out and touch the fading amulet. "It is not too small?"

"No. No, not at all." Clerin was quite shocked at this admission of... of what she was not quite sure. Not quite shame. Not embarrassment. But maybe just a twinge of self-effacing guilt? Well, not guilt either. Maybe just a small feeling of inadequacy? In any case, it was certainly an emotion that Clerin never thought she would get from a Gaen Yaven. "It might be thinner than some, but its beauty more than makes up for that." She hoped that she had picked the correct words. If there were any correct words.

"Good. Yes. That makes me proud." Nolkrung paraphrased its earlier response.

They traveled for so long in silence that Clerin put out her light and fell back asleep. She was not sure how long they had traveled when she woke back up, but they were definitely slowing back down. She assumed, correctly, that they were nearing their destination. She could not think of how she had slept for the vast majority of the journey. She had been tired, for sure, but that did not explain it. Maybe it was the dearth of fresh air that had left her so languid, though Nolkrung obviously did not allow her to suffocate. She had not noticed any real lack of air; it had just seemed a little stale.

They slowed for quite some time before they finally stopped. Clerin waited patiently before Nolkrung opened itself up for her to sit up. It took a while for her to clamber out and stretch enough that she felt derlian again. She had not really been uncomfortable in her journey, just a little cramped. She was in a tall, domed room that was lit with the same phosphorescent glow as Nolkrung had been.

"We are near what you would call the Temple. Gunzgak has been waiting." Nolkrung swept a stiff arm towards one of three hallways but appeared to be waiting for Clerin to lead the way. Its spherical legs seemed poised to begin rolling.

Clerin spun on her heel and started walking in the direction that Nolkrung had pointed to. The hallway had a barrel vault ceiling that was lower than the dome in the central room. Though the hallway had several large radius turns, there were no branches or offshoots, making it impossible for her to lead them in the wrong direction. She wondered why they had not just popped up in the Temple proper. Maybe it was protected against intrusion?

It felt good to walk. She enjoyed stretching her legs down the hallway. After another slow curve, she could see in the distance that the hallway ended and opened up into a large room of sorts. Her heart and her feet sped up unconsciously as she neared the hallway's exit.

"Wait. I must apologize, but wait." Nolkrung stopped Clerin about a hundred rods from the end of the hallway. "We had so much time earlier, but I did not explain the requirements for this meeting. Part of me was concerned that you would refuse to come or, at least, that it would dampen your enthusiasm for the meeting. I see now that it was foolish to waste that time."

"No matter, Nolkrung. I will speak with Gunzgak under any circumstances. Tell me your requirements." She turned towards Nolkrung. She meant it, she really did. She would have done anything at all to have the chance to speed up her return home.

"You will not be speaking with Gunzgak, you will be speaking to me. I will interpret between the two of you. You must not try to reach out to Gunzgak in any way. You must use only words. And you must direct your words and your thoughts to me only. You must not attempt any magic. You should try not to thrust outwards even with something as innocuous as emotions. You will be in proximity to Gunzgak, but we do not want any communication between the two of you whatsoever, even unconscious communication. This may sound foolish, but we do not want you to even use Gunzgak's name while in the Temple. And try not to think it. I will ask you direct questions. Please answer them to the best of your abilities. It would be best if you spoke in statements. We do not wish to preclude you from asking questions, but we ask that you keep them simple and in the vein of our line of questioning. Gunzgak decides when we start and when we finish. Do not be alarmed or offended if we must cut our conversation to an abrupt end. If there are any questions you know that you might ask, you may tell me now and I will let Gunzgak know during our meeting." Nolkrung ended abruptly.

"Just… if you know, or if Gunzgak knows… anything you could tell me about the messages I am carrying would be appreciated." She wished she could think of something else to ask. Something random and innocuous. Something light and superficial, maybe even humorous. But she was tense and could think of nothing but her messages.

"Ha! That is what we are here to ascertain." Nolkrung became silent and immobile again, like a statue. Clerin wondered what it was thinking. "To be honest, we do not wish to taint the vessel. We will be unable to share any thoughts we may have about what your messages are, even if they are mere wild guesses. We are concerned that any nudge from us will affect them in some way or, at the least, affect the preservative qualities of the vessel. We wish you to remain pure, even if that purity can only be achieved through ignorance. I apologize to you, but we will not be allowing your question." They waited a while in silence.

"That is quite all right." Clerin waited another few moments. When Nolkrung did not speak again, she slowly began walking towards the end of the hall. It did not stop her.

Clerin peeked into the Temple proper from the edge of the hallway. It was vast. That was her immediate impression. Just gigantically vast. There were pillars in the distance and they appeared to have complicated carvings on them. All in all, it gave the impression of appearing most like the Fluen Temple than any other. Except that it was not underwater. She peered ahead, staring around, trying to find any details she could before entering, but it was just too vast. More than anything, she found she was ignoring Nolkrung until they could enter. Why? She could not answer. It was not as if she was worried about any of the requirements. It was more that she could think of nothing to say, could not think of the appropriate icebreaker to open their re-frozen silence. Finally, Nolkrung spoke.

"It is almost time. You must leave all of your possessions outside of the Temple." Nolkrung did not move, did not twitch. The voice seemed to emanate from nothing, ghostlike.

"Of course." Clerin piled up her clothes and slipped Elange's stone, burning hot through its leather pouch, into her boots. She had brought no other possessions. They waited another couple of minutes in silence before Nolkrung began to move.

"Follow me." So she did.

The floor was not necessarily soft, certainly not as soft as Nolkrung while she was traveling, but it was not as hard as it looked. It was also immaculately clear. There were no stones, no gravel, no pebbles, not even any sand on the floor to get stuck in her feet. They walked for some time across the smooth floor towards a group of pillars in the distance. At first Clerin's mind swirled with questions. Questions about the Temple, about Gunzgak, about the Gaen realm. With a monumental effort of will, however, she was able to quash them long before they got to the pillars. By the time that Nolkrung stopped, she had achieved a pristine, clear mind.

"Wait here." Nolkrung rolled back and forth a little, situating itself between the pillars and Clerin. A short amount of time passed quietly while she stared up at the pillars. "I, Nolkrung, greet you."

"Uhm, yes. Greetings to you from me, Clerin Toswin." It was oddly awkward, consciously not thinking of anything unconsciously. If Gunzgak was going to speak through Nolkrung, and she was not supposed to think about it, then Gunzgak needed to hide better.

"I would like to know some things about you first. To start slow before we begin in earnest." Nolkrung had stopped moving during and after speaking. Back to the disembodied voice coming from the statue. "Were you a commissioned translator for Lembin?"

"No. I only communed with Lembin the one time."

"How did Lembin know to commune with you?"

"My mother was a translator."

"Your mother recommended you to Lembin?"

"I don't think so. I believe Lembin asked my mother about me."

"How did Lembin hear of you?"

"I do not know. Maybe my mother mentioned me earlier?"

"Did your father or any other family member commune with Lembin?"

"No… Not to my knowledge."

"Do you know if your mother has continued as a translator?"

"I would assume so. It has been over a cycle since I have last seen the Fluen realm."

"Ah, yes. The Pyran queen can be a distraction. But you have her following you now, don't you?"

"I'm not sure that Trela follows anyone but herself. But, yes, we are on a quest given to me by Gorbanax."

"I did not mean to jump so far ahead. May I ask about your communication with Lembin?"

"Of course."

A long pause.

"What was the point?"

"What?"

"Exactly. What was the essence? What did Lembin commune to you?"

"I don't know… pain?" She laughed.

"No, not emot… Well… then, yes. What type of pain did Lembin commune to you?"

"Maybe that of becoming a Beleg? The pain that comes from the chaos induced by the mixing of elements? It was strange, but every time the image of one element was absorbed by another, there was a… searing… feeling."

"Any other pain?"

"Nothing of note. That of receiving the messages, that was painful. For me. But that probably has more to do with the method of transference than with any emotional response. But there was something at the beginning now that I think about it, certainly not a pain but, maybe a… sorrow? They used to communicate freely. The Belegs used to send messages to each other with impunity. No, not impunity. With love. They sent these love messages back and forth with no filter. No proxy. No messenger. You should understand that. There was some definite sorrow about the loss of that communication."

"Is that what you think the messages contain?"

"I used to think that they contained that. That the messages were a request of some sort. Some beseechment or supplication. Just that they conveyed the desire to rekindle the open communication that used to exist."

"Used to?"

"Well… Now I don't know."

"Don't know? What don't you know?"

"How would I know?" A pause. "I haven't come up with a different theory. But I can say that I think it odd that Gorbanax did not wish to receive the messages. You obviously think the same."

"We have never been warned of communication before. It was… alarming. The only Beleg to receive Lembin's message was Linchon?"

"Yes, yes. In fact, that was the only thing I thought I had to do. That was my mission. Lembin did not request that I commune with Gorbanax, Linchon did."

"But you refuse, even under the threat of death, to provide me with information concerning your communication with Linchon. Is this still correct?"

How could she not? This was not some side conversation with Croy. This was not Chiavel trying to get information or Vrric trying to be sympathetic. This was not even just a Yaven trying to glean information about Beleg communication. She knew she was not even supposed to think it, but she knew that the question was coming from Gunzgak. How could she refuse?

"Well, I…"

She did not want to do it. It was not as if she feared it, it was not like being flung into an invisible cave entrance. It was not as if she was ashamed about it or embarrassed about it. It was not as if she were a child being scolded and pressured by adults to admit some transgression. It was just… sad. She just did not want to think about it, as if ignoring it made it not exist. But maybe it did not even happen. Maybe, when she finally made it back to the Fluen realm, made it back home, her father would be there waiting. That was the hope, the dream, a dream she kept alive by not speaking about Linchon. She knew it was foolish, but that did not make it any easier.

"…I suppose I owe you that." Clerin paused to gather herself. "Linchon did not communicate much to me. I was spun around and opened up, and the message was taken from me. It was hard to tell how much time was passing. I do not think much passed at all, but… after the message… Linchon became angry. Or something akin to that. I do not think it was necessarily mad at me, but the reaction was quick and fierce. I… I think I passed out." She paused once more, this time for much longer. She was grateful that Nolkrung did not prod or interrupt. "When I awoke, my father was standing before me. I had to cast a spell to be able to speak with him, something he kept mouthing to me, because at first he was mute. Or an illusion. Or a figment of my imagination. Or something. I finally realized that the spell I had cast was to speak with the dead. He told me that Linchon had killed him just so I could speak with his spirit. To commune more simply. By proxy." Clerin waved her hand around the gigantic hall of the Gaen Temple, encompassing the distant ceiling, the gigantic pillars, Nolkrung, et cetera. She did her best not to think the name Gunzgak while Nolkrung nodded its statue-like head at her. "Proxy." It was barely spoken aloud that second time. Clerin breathed in deeply through her nose and exhaled slowly through pursed lips. "So we talked. He said things that only he could know… Anyway, he said I needed to take Lembin's message to Gorbanax and you and that there was a message for them from Linchon as well. Then, and only then, could I take Linchon's reply back to Lembin."

"So, it was the death of your parent that made you hesitant to tell the story. Hrmm."

"What? Yes. Why? Was that not enough?"

"Of course. Any reason that is a cause is enough. That would have been my furthest guess is all."

She could not tell if she was being subject to some subtle jab.

"These conversations always seem to take so much longer to have, in the moment, than to explain to someone later. That is all I can tell you about my conversations with Lembin and Linchon."

"Of course. I understand the amount of energy that goes into these things. I do not wish to tire you out. You have been incredibly helpful, truly. I have just one last question."

"Sure."

"When you defeat this Cabal, when you have accomplished your mission, when you return to the Pyran Temple, do you really think that Gorbanax will accept your messages?"

"Well, I… That was what was promised."

"Or that was what you interpreted."

"Gorbanax allowed me to summon a Pyran Yaven that spoke to me about the need to destroy the Cabal. I am fairly sure that the interpretation is correct."

"I am not attempting to argue with you. We all certainly agree that the Cabal must be destroyed and we will do everything in our power to assist you in this matter. I will return you to your friends and then have some errands, but if we meet again, I will offer what aid I may."

"Thank you."

It was not until she was back with her companions that the thought came to her. It was wrong, of course. It had to be. But it was a little tantalizing as well. What if Belegs could appear as Yavens? What if Nolkrung was actually Gunzgak? It was absurd. The Belegs were ethereal. But weren't Yavens a bit ethereal as well? The prevailing wisdom was that the Belegs were tied to their temples. Clerin, herself, had communed with several, if not all, of the Belegs, and it was definitely not like conversing with Yavens. But why not? They had been Yavens, though they were certainly more powerful than Yavens. Why could they not communicate like Yavens? Surely, they could trick a derlian into thinking they were a Yaven if they wished. She did not quite think it was true, but it was a thought that nagged the back of her mind for quite some time. She decided to keep the tantalizing absurdity to herself.

"Did you find the bird?" Clerin was finally alone with Vrric and she wanted to know what had happened as Nolkrung had stolen away with her.

"No. Not even smoke escaped from Havolin as we killed him, I watched for it. I wish we better understood how they control derlians. It would help immensely." His smile was slightly crooked, giving it a wry tinge.

"I wish we understood them at all." The thought suddenly made her think of Altrond. She had not spoken to him for a while and was not really sure why.

"I think the Gaens are going hunting tomorrow. Want to crawl through some tunnels?" His eyes were soft and his smile was warm. He was impossible to resist when he was like that.

"Sure. Is it a big expedition?" She was not sure which she would have preferred. Safety or privacy.

"I think there will be many smaller ones. They are going to try to flush out anyone who has been turned. And you never know, maybe we will find that bird." He laughed a little. Like it would be fun. It made Clerin hope that they were in a decent-sized group. "Only once they feel the cave system is cleared will the Gaens provide us with any warriors or provisions. So, the sooner we get that done, the sooner we can be back on our way. You know how Trela can get if she's not on the move."

Did he ask her about Gunzgak? Did he ask her about being gone for half a day? No. She could not figure out if that was out of consideration for her privacy, that maybe he thought she did not want to discuss it since she had not brought it up, or if he was just being oafish. Did she ask? Did she investigate? No. She decided to provide him with the benefit of the doubt and assume he was biting his tongue trying to be gallant.

They had two Gaen guides that Clerin had never met before. One was thickly muscled, Daszhel Mur'cha. Clerin had originally thought that he would be the one to walk behind, that he was the dangerous one. She eventually found out that he was a blacksmith, not a warrior. This pleased Vrric to no end, who chatted with Daszhel about hammers, bellows, and what the differing color of the forge fires meant about the temperature, et cetera. The warrior was skinnier, though she was certainly not thin. Nanjiol Fyr'jin was quite tall for a Gaen, though still shorter than Clerin or Vrric by a full head. Vrric was, of course, their mage. Trela had insisted that each team had at least one competent mage. Malghain was with them, which made Clerin more comfortable, and Jalin, Kryhir, and Pejal. There were about ten other teams, and half of them were purely Gaen.

"And what do we do if we find the bird?" The question came from Jalin as they were walking along a wide tunnel. "I'm not trying to sell myself short, but I am a bit useless here."

"We let Feyazki blast it into leaves." Malghain's grin had some mischievousness in it, which was nice since it toned down the enthusiasm for the fight that tinged his eyes with a bit of madness.

"Sure, fine. What happens if another team finds the bird?" Jalin would not be deterred that easily.

"Well, hopefully, they will have a mage to blast it into leaves." Malghain was a little less gleeful. Just barely.

"And everyone else? Are we just along to distract it? To give it more targets? To give the mage enough time?" Jalin did not sound annoyed, just… persistent.

"You are along in case we need to circumvent any obstacles along the way. If we find anything corporeal, you should hide in the shadows." Kryhir brought his crisp, but dry, analysis to the conversation.

"No, no. That's not it all." Nanjiol turned and stopped the group. "We are not hoping to corner the thing. We are not hoping to blast it into leaves or whatever. We are flushing it out. We just wish it to leave our caves. We do not want it underground. They can attack our animals, our farms, our inns, our villages, what have you. What can we do about that? They just fly away if we get the upper hand." Nanjiol stared at Kryhir. "This here, our underground caves, are our sanctuary. This is where we escape to when we are under siege. We have nowhere else to run to. We have nowhere else to hide." She took a deep breath and glanced between them all. "We need a place to flee to. We need one place to feel safe or else we are just animals roaming the hillsides. We need these caves to feel clean, safe and impenetrable." She nodded while she talked. Not to anyone or anything outside of herself, but just to herself. "If it gets cornered and kills us, that would be terrible, but that would be preferable to constantly looking over our shoulders in our own sanctuary."

"Speak for yourselves." Kryhir stared back at Nanjiol.

"Oh, no. We speak for you as well. We are all in this hunt together." Daszhel spoke up.

"What if it just stays hidden? What if we scour this entire sanctuary and are unable to detect it?" Malghain still had a small smile on his lips. "Or, not that you would know, but what if it has already left? What if it left when that…" He snapped his fingers as he sought his answer.

"Havolin." Clerin filled it in for Malghain. She only knew what he was searching for since she had been thinking the same thing.

"Yes. What if it left when Havolin died? How would we even know?" Malghain's eyebrows were high.

"We don't know if it has already left, you are correct. However, if it is still around, I do not think it will be able to stay hidden. With all these tasty morsels wandering around?" Nanjiol waved her hand around. "I am sure it will try to hide, but I think temptation will overcome it, and it will attack a group. When that happens, a mage will *whisper* to the others, and all the other teams will come running. Hopefully it will sense that rush, it will realize we have lain a trap, that we are ready and hoping that it will attack. That is the most dangerous moment. That is when it will decide to maim and kill all that it can before it is destroyed, or to flee. Personally, I hope that it flees."

"You don't hope that it is finally destroyed? No matter the cost?" Malghain looked between the two Gaens. "What if it sneaks back in later? What if it brings friends?"

"They are attracted to certain areas, to weak derlians, to derlians with evil in their hearts. There are many other interesting places to go and plunder. Besides, we will try to barricade the entrances with magic." Daszhel spoke up while Nanjiol's eyebrows furrowed.

"So… you're hoping it gets bored and wanders off to destroy some other village?" This came from Pejal. Clerin kind of liked Pejal because he was typically so enthusiastic and optimistic. He was a true believer, a true follower of Trela as the Kriishan. That statement, however, she had expected from Kryhir or Malghain. Someone with more cold cynicism coursing through their veins. For some reason it disappointed her just a little, even if she could understand the cynicism.

"That is what they typically do. They ravage a village, and those who make it to the cave sanctuary survive. They then fly off to find easier pickings in another unsuspecting village." Daszhel's eyes grew a little dark. "We are not positive why this one has stayed this long. They do not like to be hunted. They do not like to be expected. They do not like their presence known at all."

There was a brief moment of silence before Nanjiol spoke back up. "The prevailing theory is that it is sticking around because of you." She pointed at them vaguely, encompassing all of the foreigners. Clerin knew that. It seemed to her, however, that Nanjiol was talking directly about her. That the Tlana was waiting for Clerin in specific. Hiding. Biding its time for the perfect opportunity to pounce. She got an unconscious shiver in her spine.

They searched. They all searched hard. They searched for three days but found nothing. No one found any sign of the Tlana whatsoever. Clerin silently agreed with Malghain. It would have been better if they had found it, cornered it, and killed it. However, she was not staying. She would not be trying to sleep in the dark, wondering. Maybe it was Nanjiol who was correct in the end. Maybe the Tlana was hunting Trela's coterie. Maybe it was hunting Clerin in specific. Who really knew? All that was known for certain was that the Gaens assumed whatever debt Trela had racked up had been paid off. They could leave with good conscious and the Gaens were to provide them with food and equipment and even some warriors. Trela could finally get back on the road again.

"Why are we even here?" Clerin glared at Vrric. Was she really mad? Meh, maybe. Was she annoyed with him? Not necessarily. It was not really his fault that they were stuck there, waiting in the chilly air of the cemetery, amongst the multitudes of ancient Gaen dead. When Clerin took the time and truly thought about it, she could not say that she was mad at anyone in particular. Maybe she was just mad at the situation. Her… annoyance… carried through into her voice, however.

"Because Altrond's an idiot." Vrric was not shy about his dislike of Altrond, at least not at this point. Daszhel and Verin ignored them both.

It was not the dead that bothered Clerin. She did not have some irrational fear that they would rise up and begin gnawing her flesh, though if a mage could make them do that, a Tlana probably could as well. No, it was the desolation. The quiet. The somber mood. The boredom. They had been waiting for hours and would have to wait a while longer. Was it Vrric's fault she was bored? Not necessarily. She had certainly not been helpful on that front.

Altrond, Trela, Ryshial, and Aedon were on a separate, but related, mission. Vrric had been told specifically not to *whisper* to Ryshial, that they were merely to wait patiently. To hold tight. Eventually, Ryshial would *whisper* the name of a dead Gaen whose grave they were to find. Daszhel was supposed to be able to help them find the grave so that Vrric could speak with the corpse. Verin was there, as always, for muscle. Clerin had no particular job. She supposed she was there to keep company more than anything else, but she certainly wasn't doing that very well. It was not her fault really, at least not in her opinion. When they had finally arrived at the cemetery, Vrric immediately began to question why they were there. That in itself was not typically obnoxious since simple complaining was a favorite pastime of most members of Trela's coterie, but he somehow blamed Altrond for every moment that they waited. Clerin was simply tired of the tirade.

True, it was Altrond who had suggested talking to the first Gaen who had died under the control of a Tlana at the adjacent village. The village was about two days' ride from Daszhel's, and this seemed to have happened several moons ago. The neighboring Gaen villagers had hung the dead Gaen for his crimes, so his body should have stayed mostly intact, comparatively speaking. Since Daszhel had not been there during the trial, he could not say for certain whose body they were looking for, but he used to live in the village, so he was their best bet in finding the grave quickly once they had a name. Apparently, the cemetery was divided into vocations first, then families. He and Verin were huddled conspiratorially, waiting a stone's throw away.

"What don't you like about Altrond?" Clerin had not really planned on asking that question, it merely slipped out.

"He's an idiot." Vrric's reply was quick and curt.

"What does he do that makes you think he's an idiot?" Though she did not necessarily want to continue the conversation, it annoyed her that he just dismissed Altrond out of hand.

Instead of responding verbally, Vrric lifted his shoulders slightly and panned around with his torso. His hands were held out flat with his palms up. As if what they were participating in was idiotic, and if it was, that it was purely Altrond's fault. It did not matter that the same thought had passed through Clerin mere moments ago. The premise coupled with the comedic image defied basic logic. Vrric did not think his answer through, it was not derived from any evidence. He was merely pantomiming his opinion. And the opinion was not even necessarily about what was happening at the moment. He had simply decided a long time ago that he did not like Altrond.

"Seriously? You can't articulate anything so you just shrug?" Her own mind skipped thinking the situation through and leapt towards Altrond's defense. "Now that... is idiotic." Her mind had raced to find another word, another argument. But... nothing. She began to wonder if she was the idiot.

"You want to giggle and hold hands with him, go ahead. Why aren't you with him now? Why are you even here?" He looked to be actually getting mad. It was odd, he did not normally get mad around her.

She hadn't even wanted to start this conversation. She had just been bored, just been trying to kill time. She knew she needed to end it, to capitulate with a laugh, and then maybe he would laugh as well. There was no reason for her not to end it, but... now she was kind of mad. *Why are you even here?* Who even asks that question?

Who questions the validity of another's existence? In fact, Vrric had been acting quite annoying himself lately. What gave him the right to question her like that?

"You know what your problem is?" Her face grew heated and her fingers clenched unconsciously into fists. And luckily, thankfully, she was interrupted. She did not even know what her next sentence was going to be, had no ready response as to what she thought his problem was. It would not have been pretty, she was sure about that.

"Wait, wait." Vrric's hand went up to stave off her assessments into his character. It could have been construed as rude, his interruption of her opinion, but somehow it wasn't. There was nothing personal about it all, no animosity, not even any annoyance. It was just business. "Ryshial is *whispering*."

He listened quietly to the voice in his head, unconsciously nodding while staring at the ground some distance in front of him. He had his left hand poised near his ear, as if he might need to plug it to better hear Ryshial. His face softened as he listened intently. It amazed Clerin how a derlian's moods affected how she thought they looked. He had been almost ugly a moment ago and now his soft face and unfocused eyes grew in beauty by the moment. She knew it was also her, her own shifting mood, but it amazed her just the same. She felt her own annoyance melt back into boredom in the span of a few seconds.

"Okay, we have a name." Vrric smiled warmly at her and then turned to walk over to the Gaens.

She followed him without a word. The small crunching noises faded as they left the gravel and walked onto the grass. Verin and Daszhel saw them approaching and started to lean back away from each other as they continued chatting. They stopped speaking before Vrric and Clerin arrived.

"So, do we finally have a target?" Verin hopped off the stone bench she had been sitting on.

"Yes. We are looking for the grave of Aweroih Fyr'lak." Vrric stopped, so Clerin stopped.

"Hmmm. The merchant section." Daszhel stood while rubbing his reddish beard in concentration. He silently began walking in a direction, staring down at the ground. The other three followed in silence, as if speaking to him would break his concentration. And who knows, it might have.

The cemetery itself was situated on a rolling hill. There were winding gravel footpaths that crisscrossed almost randomly through the groupings of graves. There were some nice shade trees scattered about to break up the skyline. Verin whistled a quiet tune as they walked. It was quite an idyllic scene. Jylohan, Clerin's poetry teacher of youth, would have enjoyed the scenery immensely. He used to find little picnic spots for them to camp out at and make her improvise poetry while he nibbled on their meal and drank copious amounts of wine. The hilltop made Clerin slightly homesick. There was even the tiniest little stream that had reeds growing along it. Reeds!

"I think… I think the merchants are over there." Daszhel picked up his pace.

They walked for a while in silence. They were in a rough single file, snaking their way through the headstones. Clerin brought up the rear, after Vrric. She tried to keep her boots in the same footprints as his. At first it was a little unconscious—no one wanted to tread over the bodies of the dead—but then it turned into a bit of a game. Another way to break the boredom of the long day. She wondered, briefly, if someone were tracking them, would they have difficulty telling how many had passed through? Or would the double footprints be utterly obvious?

"I had always thought that Gaens buried their dead in caves, in stone mausoleums and sarcophagi." Clerin engaged Verin as she dropped back more as a matter of boredom than out of curiosity.

"You are thinking of Serif, where I am from. We are closer to Hifrim here. The Gaens of Hifrim are more comfortable amongst the hills than in mountainous caverns. Their soil is soft and easily plowed. Some hill Gaens live their entire lives on farms above the soil. I hear tell that some have never even set foot in a cave." Verin kept her voice low and one eye on Daszhel.

Clerin wondered about having two seats of power for one race. It did not make much sense to her. Sure, the Fluens living on the Eidyon peninsula were far enough away from Tureyn that they probably did not think about the monarchy much. But they still swore fealty to the throne. They still kept the same social observances. And even if they did not, the peninsula was sparsely populated and economically dependent upon Tureyn. No, there was no split in the Fluen realm, not even with a city as powerful as Vatlisi. The idea of Serif and Hifrim struggling against each other boggled the mind. Daszhel suddenly stopped in front of a grouping of headstones and Verin fell silent once more. Clerin thought she should chat with Verin more about the subject later, her curiosity was suddenly strong and it appeared that Verin had some opinions about it.

"He should be here somewhere. These are all the merchants." He waved his hands in front of them vaguely.

Each of them dutifully spread out and began walking down individual rows. Clerin read only the first names, ignoring the last. It was then she realized she was not positive on how to spell Aweroih. Vrric had spoken the name so quickly. She assumed, correctly, that it was a common enough Gaen name that Verin and Daszhel immediately knew what had been spoken. She thought about asking for the exact spelling aloud but Verin hollered from a nearby headstone. They all rushed over.

There it was, Aweroih Fyr'lak, carved deeply into the stone. There was an image of a pile of coins on one side of his name and a small still life of grocery items on the other. They stood there a moment in silence.

"Do we have to dig him up?" Daszhel's question took Clerin aback for a brief moment. Then she thought about it. Did they?

"Let's hope not." Vrric smiled at Daszhel. The squinty eyed look that Daszhel gave him did not betray any amusement. "Sorry. The last time I did this the body was exhumed. However, I feel fairly confident that we can get this to work without going to that extent. Hopefully."

Vrric always sounded so confident, so even the slightest bit of hesitation appeared glaring to Clerin. She wanted to say something supportive but all she could think of sounded insipid in her head. So she merely backed away slowly along with everyone else.

"Eqesidtotarc!" Vrric's voice sounded strong and robust. It made Clerin worry that the ground was about to burst and the corpse was to spring forth, but only a yellowish-green glowing image appeared. The image of a short and portly shopkeeper. Clerin had no idea what type of clothing a Gaen shopkeeper would wear, what their typical "uniform" was, but the apparition was too archetypical to be anything else. "I wish to ask of the last weeks of your life. I wish to ask of your possession. I wish to ask of your memory of your deeds and your trial."

"I know not of any possession but I will gladly speak of any time of my life you wish to hear about. The only thing that has filled my mouth lately has been soil and worms. It feels good to have it filled with words again." The apparition clasped its hands in front of its ample belly.

Verin and Daszhel wandered off a small distance once the spell was cast. She was not sure if they were attempting to give some modicum of privacy or if they were just unable to sense the apparition. Gaens had notorious difficulty with magic and were considered natural jinxers. In any case, Clerin could sense the apparition quite clearly and was curious enough about the conversation that she felt quite comfortable staying put.

"Then let's work backwards." Vrric's bright eyes reflected the glow of the apparition. It was slightly eerie. "Do you recall your trial? Your execution?"

"Ahh, that. That is like a dream to me. Or more precisely, like a nightmare." His downcast eyes raised and stared forth with great intensity. "I am innocent. Innocent! They executed the wrong Gaen. I was framed!"

"Do you recall being arrested?" Vrric pressed forwards. Or more precisely, backwards in time.

"Yes. Yes! They were quite rough with me. They hurled insults at me before hurling my body to the floor. Why would it take eight 'jin to arrest a shopkeeper, I ask? Did I struggle or resist? No. I would have gladly walked but no, they had to carry me out like a sack of flour. With all of my neighbors watching. All of my customers. Everyone." The apparition looked somewhat dejected. It was hard to tell with only the outline of the glowing figure moving, but the shoulders definitely slumped while it explained the humiliations it was put through.

"Do you recall the murders?" Vrric's voice was quieter, more somber.

"No. Never!" The apparition's shoulders sprang up as his spine, if he had had one, went rigidly straight. "I would never do such a thing. I never could do such a thing. That is a thing that one would remember, correct? How could such an image slip from mine own mind? They told me the first one was my sister's daughter. My own niece! How could I not recall that, if that were true. Even a worthless drunk awakes with remorse the next day. He will not look at his wife's bruises for he has a bright inkling in the darkest recesses of his mind of what had happened. Like a sliver of sunlight peering down through a deep crevasse. I begged them to let me see her body. I explained how I was framed. I wished, more than anything, to find some exonerating evidence on her. Something that would wake me from the nightmare." The apparition paused. The first part of his speech was an impassioned rant—it flew from his mouth like bats from a cave at dusk—but the last part was spoken quietly, to the ground in front of him. "They told me she had already been buried on the hill. Weeks before. They told me that three others had been buried since then. They told me that I attended her funeral and wept with such conviction that they had not considered me a suspect. And how could they? How could anyone suspect such a horrible thing of me? I shoo spiders from my home rather than stomp on them. I would die rather than harm my own niece."

"Do you recall going to her funeral?" Vrric's right eyebrow twitched up, but his voice kept its somber tone.

"No… No, I do not." The apparition stood still for some time. Clerin wondered what it was doing. Was it thinking? Was it trying to remember? How did time flow according to the dead? The apparition seemed to be completely alive. She did not know this Aweroih—she only knew so many Gaens—and yet she knew deep down that this was how Aweroih would talk. How he would have acted when he was alive. It was… eerie. "Truly, that time is blank to me. It is as if it never happened. It was as if I went to sleep a moon before and only awoke as they were arresting me. I would not have thought that the time even existed, but the whole village agreed. My wife herself told me of the funeral. It was as if they were all trying to make me crazy, to drive me insane. But why would they do that? Why would everyone you've ever known lie to you about the passage of time? But that is how I felt. That is how I feel. Even now, even unto death, it feels that those weeks did not exist. Not that they were missing, not as if they were blank pages of a book, but that the pages were torn out. Gone. Without even a ragged edge left behind in the spine. I…" The apparition trailed off. It was silent for an even longer time than before. Finally, almost imperceptibly, it shrugged.

"Well, I guess that answers that part." Vrric glanced at Clerin, then glanced back at the dejected apparition. "When were you arrested? How long before your execution?"

"Ah, that, I remember that. Yes, I was arrested a fortnight before they executed me. They had all this evidence, you see. They had the knives they said I used. The leather apron worn to absorb the bloodshed, the boots that the murderer wore going to and from the houses, the black scarf they said I wrapped my face in as I stalked the night. As I stalked my victims." The apparition's back snapped back up. "I was framed! Just because they found these things under my bed, did they know they were mine? Did they know, without any doubt, that I wore those boots just because they fit me? Just because I had purchased them sun cycles ago? Who would leave all that evidence under their own bed? I know what I know! I know who I am. I know what I am capable of. I know I did not do these things. To my own niece? No, not I! I know who I am! You cannot tell me I am someone else. You cannot confuse me into thinking that I am… that I am capable of what I am not. I was framed! Even as they put the noose around my neck, I declared my own innocence. They could not convince me of what I am not. Neither will you. I know who I am!"

"But you cannot recall where you were during that time. You cannot recall what you did. If you had any exonerating evidence whatsoever, any alibi whatsoever, do you think they would have executed you within a fortnight?" Vrric's voice took on a stronger tone. One that was quite unnecessary in Clerin's opinion. They all knew what had happened, at least all of the living did. In her mind, the Gaen was completely innocent. It was the Tlana that was guilty.

"I know who I am. I know what is in me, in my deepest heart. I know what I know. You cannot… Your tricks…" The apparition slumped again. "I know who I am." The last one was barely a whisper.

"You are innocent. You were attacked and you were possessed. You did not mean to do these things. You were being controlled by another. Your only crime was not being able to fight off an ancient evil. There are few derlians who can." Clerin could not take it anymore, so she tried to absolve the Gaen. She glanced over at Vrric, but her eyes were drawn back to the apparition as it slumped to its knees.

"So… You're saying I did it? You are saying I killed my niece? Slowly. Painfully. With five different knives." The apparition started to sink into the hard packed ground. "I'm guilty? I tortured my own niece?"

"I'm saying it's not your fault. I'm saying that whatever happened was not because of you. That you would never do such a thing. Never could do such a thing. It wasn't your fault." Clerin wished she had kept her mouth shut. The apparition just stared at her with accusation staining its glowing eyes. As if it were her own fault. She struggled to say something more eloquent, something soothing, something that could ease the dead Gaen's pain. But instead, it sank into the ground, back into its own grave, accusing her with its glowing eyes while she stared silently back.

"Wow, thanks for deflecting the heat on that one for me." Vrric was grinning from ear to ear, as if he just made the funniest joke in the world.

"I was trying to be nice." She was not amused.

"See where nice gets you." He was still smiling.

"I didn't see you trying to soften the blow." She was starting to get annoyed. Again.

"What, why? He's dead." His mouth was smiling, but his eyes were getting wary. "What are you even worried about?"

"I don't want him to think badly. Of me, of himself, for his niece. I just want him to rest in peace." Her eyes started glaring.

"Well, I guess you shouldn't have mentioned the..." He stopped himself in the nick of time. "Listen, we got the date for his arrest. We got the information that Altrond wanted about his memory of his actions. We got everything we need. I consider this a success." He put up his hand as she was about to say something. She wasn't really sure what she was going to say, it was sure to come out angry in any case, so she let herself be interrupted. "It could have been handled much more eloquently, surely. We will learn from this instance and move forward."

"Why did we need the arrest date anyway?" She let herself leak the anger, the annoyance, out into the air, away from herself.

"There were other murders after this Gaen was executed. We are thinking the bird jumped and wanted to see if that happened right at the arrest or if it happened a little earlier." His smile had decreased to a smaller, more genuine size.

"Well... what if the bird didn't jump. What if it was in someone else the whole time and he *was* framed." She thought hard about it.

"Why didn't he remember anything about those weeks? Why could he not come up with some sort of defense, some alibi?" His brow was furrowed as well. At least he was considering it, not just dismissing her idea out of hand.

"I'm not sure. Where did we leave off on the idea of more than one attacking at a time?" She looked up at the sky, looking at nothing in particular. "Was that in the plausible column, or the probable column?" It was certainly not in the confirmed or highly likely columns. It was certainly somewhere in the middle.

"I'll check when I *whisper* the trial date." He nodded. Whether to her or to himself, she could not be sure.

Chapter 14

Croy had never been that far west before. Never even close. The above-ground villages and farms of the Hill Gaens were an oddity, a curiosity. They made Croy think of some of the tiny Pyran villages that Trela's warpack traveled through. Or traveled by, to be more technically correct. They did not seem completely Gaen, but that did not make them any less derlian. He would have said he would defend Hifrim more ferociously than Tureyn or Agoge, but in truth, he would defend wherever his traveling companions were at. His home away from home was his friends.

The underground sanctuaries—that felt weirder than the farms, however. Almost every single village of size had one. A place to hide during times of struggle. A place to escape to when the weather was uncooperative. A place where the young could explore without supervision against the wishes and advice of their parents. But they were not a place to live. Everything felt temporary about them. Too many hallways and not enough rooms. Unfortunately, they made for the perfect location to hide a Tlana, or to hide the bodies that followed in their wake.

They were in one such place currently. Searching for a Tlana, or at least trying to flush one out. Croy couldn't remember the village they were near. Ilushkin or Askushin or some such. He had never been explicitly told the name of the village, he had only overheard it in other derlian's conversations, so he did not feel too bad about his lack of knowledge.

He was with Haswyxe, which always made him feel safer. Sure, there were other warriors stronger or more dangerous. There were mages more powerful, though supposedly, Croy was becoming quite powerful himself—he was certainly becoming a decent healer. No, Haswyxe made Croy feel safer due his *attention*. Even when Croy was not paying attention to his surroundings, Haswyxe was. And not obtrusively, either. Croy, in the back of his mind, kind of wanted to try to walk off a cliff just to see how far Haswyxe would let him get before pulling him from the brink. That would have been both stupid and mean on a couple of levels so, of course, he never tried.

There were also Tweltas, Vulthrim, and Baltuz Fyr'jin. Tweltas was one of the most dangerous individuals with a sword in Trela's coterie, and Vulthrim was considered quite competent, though his loyalty to the Blind One made Croy distrust him on principle.

Baltuz was a decent fighter by all accounts, but her true talents lay in giving commands and overseeing battles. She was on a similar ladder as Kryhir or Rewista, though maybe down a couple of rungs. Crawling through a cave looking for a Tlana did not seem to be her strong suit, but it was certainly not Croy's, so who was he to judge. Baltuz was built like a warrior with dark eyes and brown curly hair. She seemed to have a serious temperament but was quick with a smile.

There were five other teams in this one tiny cave complex. They would pass each other periodically, each to or from some other dead end. They had not found any villagers in the above ground farmsteads, so they had no one to help them navigate the caves. The caves, too, were eerily quiet. He hoped that they were as empty as the tiny village above. He had no desire for heroics, but they did not have enough mages for him to get out of every search. He was ready to *whisper* to Feyazki or Serghno at the first sign of any trouble. At least the complex seemed small enough that it should not take too much time for them to arrive once he called.

Tweltas was leading, his large sword filling the hall in front of him. Croy wondered if a smaller weapon would have been a smarter choice, not necessarily an axe, but at least a short sword. Some Pyrans could be quite sensitive about what swords they wielded, however, so Croy was certainly not going to broach the subject. He was near the middle, with Haswyxe behind him and Baltuz taking up the rear. They were all walking slowly, all looking around them intently. They had been in the complex for a while already and he was getting a little fatigued.

He was staring at the floor rather than looking around, that was probably why he noticed it. The floor, the solid stone beneath his feet, flickered. It was as if he could see beyond it for just a brief moment. He started to shake his head, to check or reset his vision, when he felt a splash of cool water wash over him. He had felt that enough times that he knew what it meant. The floor flickered once more and then disappeared.

"Mekkinderclo!" It was not strong enough to keep them all where they were, to levitate them or fly them back out, but it slowed all of them enough to make the drop harmless. Croy was not used to encompassing so many derlians with one spell, especially at such a short notice. By the time they reached the spikes littering the floor he was completely out of breath. The spikes were about the size of

Croy's arm, in length and in thickness at their bases. They appeared to be made of cast-iron and tapered to a cruel point at the top. Everyone was able to avoid them nicely during their slow decent.

"How quickly can you fly us back out of here?" Baltuz immediately weaved her way around the spikes over to Croy.

"Wait, there is a door over here. Shouldn't we explore this area first?" Tweltas was at the other end of the pit.

"My question does not affect searching the area. His answer may be now, in five or ten minutes, or in an hour, whatever. I am not trying to dictate anything, just to know what our parameters are." Tweltas looked annoyed but did not respond. Baltuz's eyes were slightly feral, but her smile was wide and genuine.

"Five, ten minutes?" Croy was breathing heavily.

"Is that after you *whisper* to the others?" She was obviously not the type of Gaen to let something be assumed.

"Yes, yes. Five minutes and I'll *whisper*. In ten I'll be able to fly us all out." Croy had his hands on his hips, though he was unsure of how that helped his breathing.

"Perfect!" Baltuz smiled again and turned to leave, but then turned back, her smile still in place. "That was amazing Croy, simply amazing. You saved us all with your quick magic, thank you." She gave him a small pat on his shoulder before she wandered off towards Tweltas's door. It was oddly reminiscent of something Trela would have done.

Croy sat down amongst the spikes and rested his spine against the cold iron. The slope of the taper was actually quite comfortable against his back. He closed his eyes and breathed. He doubted that he had fallen asleep but a sudden commotion made him jerk to attention.

He staggered to his feet and wound his way through the maze of spikes towards the open door. It was not necessarily screaming, but definitely some yelling. The deafening crash of steel striking steel. Several voices clamored for attention, vied for dominance. It felt like it took minutes for him to just get to the door though he knew that hardly any time had passed.

What greeted him was a scene of chaos. The room beyond the door was much larger than he had imagined it would be, with chairs and tables scattered about. Some were broken and some knocked over, adding to the mazelike feeling. Behind a table resting on its side at the end of the room were three shouting Gaens. Behind them was a short, stout door. He saw at least one axe and at least one crossbow peaking over the table edge. Tweltas was behind another table, facing them, yelling incoherently. Vulthrim was next to him, pulling thin throwing knives from a stiff leather sheath. Haswyxe was at another table, sheathing his sword and readying his bow. That was when Croy noticed Baltuz clutching a bolt stuck in her left shoulder. Her shirt was getting soaked with blood but the white fletching of the bolt stayed pristine. Once he realized he was needed somewhere, doing something he felt confident at, he sprang into action. He was by her side almost immediately. The yelling that engulfed the room faded as he began to focus upon his task.

Croy knew he needed to remove the obstruction before healing her too much. He did not want to leave her with any permanent scars or anything. Of course, he did not have his full complement of instruments with him either. He typically had a pair of gardening shears that he used for small diameter wood obstructions. Snip the end and pull it through while casting a small healing spell for the pain and any important blood vessels. Then the real healing spells could be invoked. He stared at her for a long moment before pulling out the small portable kit he had brought. There were plenty of sutures, gauze, and bandages, a bone saw, pliers, and even a pair of scissors, but nothing that would quickly go through a wooden dowel. At least not without damaging the underlying tissue excessively. Baltuz was waving him off with her good arm, trying to get him to pay attention to the fight behind him, but he would not be deterred. He would much rather heal than harm.

Suddenly Haswyxe was next to him. He stared at Croy for a tiny moment before raising his short bow and firing off an arrow towards the Gaens at the back of the room. He glanced at Croy's meager kit and at Baltuz's protruding bolt.

"You'll have to chop the head off the bolt with magic. There's no way you'll get that out without doubling the size of the hole." He nodded to Croy and began nocking another arrow onto his string.

Of course! Berating himself silently, figuring that Feyazki never had these problems, he began to think through his options. He wished he was more familiar with the Majora syllables. His mind raced so fast that it felt like it was just spinning.

"Lokinpanto!" The head protruding from Baltuz's back immediately sheared off the shaft. "Loliderto!" Croy slowly pulled the shaft back through her. "Narliderto!" He cast as large a healing spell as he dared, considering the circumstances.

He sort of sat down, sort of teetered back while Haswyxe was nocking another arrow. Croy's eye was drawn to the back of the room, to the three Gaens. Their heads bobbed around and kept ducking down, it made them difficult to track. Haswyxe was on one knee with his bow drawn taught, waiting. His left hand, that which held the wood of the bow, would slowly move back and forth as he glared just over the top of the table the Gaens were hiding behind. His right hand, that which held the string of the bow, was pulled back with his fingers lightly touching his own cheek. Croy was tired, just plain tired. He leaned back farther, his shoulder barely touching Baltuz's.

It was only because he was already staring at the Gaens at the opposite side of the room that he saw what happened. The one with the crossbow spun his weapon over the top of the table and attempted to take aim. Haswyxe's arrow immediately jumped from his bow. Another Gaen leapt upwards with an axe high over his head and ran towards Tweltas and Vulthrim. The third was barely stirring when the arrow struck the crossbow wielding Gaen in his left eye. It was the most amazing shot Croy had ever witnessed. The Gaen's head jerked back and his arms jerked upwards a little, ricocheting the bolt off the stone ceiling, and his mouth opened wide in a silent scream. And that is when Croy noticed the smoke pour from the dying Gaen's mouth. It was like a black rope slid out of his mouth. A spineless, wriggling snake. But it did not dissipate; it did not float up and disperse. No, it extended sideways and slipped into the third Gaen's ear. It happened so fast that he was not quite sure that he saw what he saw.

The second Gaen was swinging his axe at Vulthrim, while Tweltas was skewering him with his sword. Croy could not quite see what had happened, but somehow Vulthrim missed the parry and the axe dug deep into his neck. Croy struggled to his feet even though he was too tired to cast anything amazing, even though the strike looked ghastly from across the room. Another spineless, wriggling black snake escaped from the dying Gaen. Tweltas's sword drew back out of the second Gaen and a gush of blood poured forth. Maybe not as much as seemed to come from Vulthrim, but enough that it covered Tweltas's hands. Tweltas staggered back. Vulthrim staggered against him. The third Gaen was over the table and running towards Tweltas. An arrow from Haswyxe flew past Croy as he stumbled towards the melee. Vulthrim was grabbing at Tweltas and falling at the same time. Tweltas held his sword only in his left hand as he was attempting to brush the dying Vulthrim off with his right. His parry was probably only successful due to Haswyxe's arrow striking the Gaen at the same time. Vulthrim was now gripping Tweltas's belt, now falling. Tweltas counterstruck the Gaen with the sword in his left hand. Croy had barely taken two steps. Then, almost too quick to notice, the smoke from the dying Gaen's mouth slipped into Tweltas's left ear and some smoke from Vulthrim entered his right. Or did it?

Tweltas stood straight as the bodies fell all around. Haswyxe relaxed his bow. Croy stopped walking. He truly thought that Tweltas would scream and charge at them with his sword held high. But that didn't happen. Tweltas grinned at them as he did his best to wipe the blood from his sword and hands.

"I didn't expect an attack like that, wow." Tweltas was typically very stoic and laconic. Croy was still half expecting some sort of attack. "Too bad about the Gaen. He was a good fighter." Tweltas indicated Vulthrim by nodding his head in the body's direction.

Haswyxe put his bow over his shoulder and started walking towards Tweltas. Croy was not sure what he was doing, but he grabbed Haswyxe's shoulder and held him back. Haswyxe squinted a little as he turned his head towards Croy.

"Where are you going?" It just popped out of Croy's mouth; it wasn't what he was intending to say. Of course, he was not sure what he had intended to say. He had not even intended to grab Haswyxe's shoulder.

"Just... my arrows." His brow knitted together and he shrugged an arm towards the other side of the room. "What is it?"

Tweltas started walking towards them. He still had his sword in his hand. It was limp and pointed downward, swaying naturally with his gait. Part of Croy wondered if there was still enough blood on his hand, or maybe on the hilt, to adversely affect his grip.

"Stop. Stop!" Croy threw his hands up. "Everyone just stop!"

Everyone stopped.

"What's your problem little Gaen?" Tweltas was lightly swaying his sword. It may have been unconscious. He had stopped moving towards them, however.

"I saw smoke enter Tweltas." He just said it. He had to say it. "You have a Tlana in you. Or… whatever happens when that happens." He knew he was not supposed to say the word "Tlana," but it just popped out. Besides, there was no way that could have drawn more attention to them than actually fighting one.

"Ha! That's ridiculous." Tweltas took another two steps forward. "Don't you think I would know if I was attacked?"

"If Croy says he saw it, he saw it." Haswyxe drew his short sword, stopping Tweltas at about the middle of the room.

"You think that little toothpick would stop my Reaver? She could snap its neck with one swipe." Tweltas swayed his sword a little but did not take another step.

"Only if that heavy chunk of steel connected, my toothpick is pretty swift." Haswyxe grinned as if he was enjoying himself. Maybe he was.

"I was the leader of Qizern's Guard. I could cut a mosquito in half in mid-flight if I wished." That part almost sounded like a typical Tweltas comment, compared to the previous one.

"Since Qizern is dead now, I wouldn't brag too much about that." Haswyxe laughed at his own joke, which happened fairly often. What was odd was that Tweltas also laughed. Heartily.

"This is stupid." Tweltas placed his sword on top of the only table still upright. "I would sheath her, but she's still wet." He held up both his hands and took another step towards them.

"Stay where you are." This was Baltuz. She had finally stood and staggered over to where they were standing.

"What? Did you see smoke too?" Tweltas turned his complete attention to her. It was an oddly intense second and a half.

"No, I had my eyes closed." She placed a hand on Croy's shoulder to steady herself. "But I trust that Croy saw the smoke."

"How can you even see something like smoke from that far away?" Tweltas pointed behind him.

"Show us your tongue." Croy tried to think of some way to alleviate the situation.

Tweltas, hands held out to each side, stuck his tongue out and took another step forward. In his defense it looked pink, but it was a bit difficult to see from that distance.

"Stop moving forward." This was from Haswyxe.

"I am unarmed, what are you worried about?" Tweltas took another step. "I thought you wanted to see my tongue?"

Haswyxe took the last four or five steps to Tweltas and held the point of his sword to his chest. They each paused for a split second. Glaring at each other. Tweltas with his hands out to each side and Haswyxe with both hands on the hilt of his sword. Tweltas suddenly stuck his tongue out again.

"Well… That definitely looks pink." Tweltas pulled his tongue back into his mouth but Haswyxe did not lower his sword.

"Do we know if that is definitive? Does it take a certain amount of time before it happens?" Baltuz was wondering aloud.

"This is stupid, I'm fine. I'm not possessed." Tweltas sounded almost sad.

"We want to tie your hands behind your back." Baltuz cut to the chase.

"What!?!" Tweltas moved back a step. "What if we get attacked on our way back to the others? What if a possessed Gaen attacks us and all I can do is get stabbed?"

"I think we will have to risk that." Baltuz stood between Croy and Haswyxe. The Luften still had his sword out, pointed at Tweltas.

"Of course *you* don't mind that risk!" His eyes narrowed as he glanced back and forth between the others. "What if I said I saw smoke entering the Gaen? Will you tie him up?"

"Did you?" Baltuz sounded serious, though Croy was hoping she was only humoring Tweltas. He certainly did not want to wander back through the cave system with his hands tied.

"No…" Tweltas looked dejected. "It's just not fair, though. Really."

"Are you completely sure, Croy? Are you absolutely certain that you saw smoke enter Tweltas?" Baltuz had turned to Croy. With her shoulder bothering her, it was an odd, wooden, jerky sort of turn.

"I'm one hundred percent positive. I saw what I saw." He was completely sure he wasn't lying, but could he be completely sure he wasn't mistaken? If Tweltas was killed on their way back to the others due to his hands being tied, Croy would never be able to live with himself. But that was a risk he was willing to take. Of course.

"Then I'm afraid we are going to have to insist." Baltuz woodenly turned back to Tweltas.

"If I die, it'll be on your heads." But he turned his back and crossed his wrists behind himself.

Haswyxe sheathed his sword and wrapped a thin cord around Tweltas's wrists multiple times. There was a barely audible "sorry" as he finished up, followed by a barely audible "this is stupid." He grabbed Reaver afterwards and cleaned the blood off of her fairly meticulously before sheathing her in Tweltas's scabbard.

Croy had walked around them and stared at Vulthrim and the other Gaens. While the others definitely had black tongues, Vultrhim's still had some pink to it. That did little to ease his concerns.

"Don't worry about the bodies. I'm sure Trela will send a team down here to search the area and for clean up." Croy was not sure if Baltuz misunderstood what he was doing over there or not. She had a wry smile on her face. Tweltas was facing the opposite direction, towards their exit.

They all moved into the room with the spikes. Though not a lot of time had passed, Croy was feeling good enough to cast a flight spell. He had to be, he told himself. He did not want them to stay down there for any longer than they had to. But he just… pondered for a moment. He was not necessarily nervous, but something felt off. Tweltas was glowering at the floor, Haswyxe was behind him with an arm half outstretched towards him, and Baltuz was staring up at the steep pit walls. Everyone was a bit… lackadaisical. The low fog in his mind did not feel as if it were going to dissipate soon, so he decided that there was no time like the present.

"Narkinderclo!" Just then he remembered what it was he had unconsciously been trying to think of. He never *whispered* to Feyazki about what had happened. Of course, they were close the coterie anyway. And if he had *whispered* it would have probably taken more time before they could have left the pit. Croy was feeling pretty good about the situation as they started to rise into the air.

They were about halfway out of the pit before it happened. He had heard a short commotion but, for some reason, he glanced over to his right at Baltuz, instead of behind him. Suddenly Tweltas was on his back and the rope that still held his hands tied together was pulled tight against Croy's neck. They stopped in mid-air while he choked and gasped for breath. Tweltas's cheek was held close to Croy's. The smell of old grog and the bristle of a two-day beard greeted him.

Then, almost inaudibly, Croy thought he heard something. "You're going to have to kill me." It was whispered in his ear almost tenderly. Like a declaration of unity from a lover.

Croy kicked back against Tweltas's legs, but they just bounced around. He clawed at the hands clasped together against his neck, but they just pulled back harder. He swung his head back wildly, hoping to connect with Tweltas's face, but he missed. Tweltas's face was now further away. One knee had been brought up and was jammed against the middle of Croy's spine.

A panic began to creep into Croy. He was not yet seeing stars, but he could not breathe. Not through his mouth, not through his nose. He could feel his heart beating in his chest. What could he do? He was unable to get his mouth close enough to Tweltas to be able to bite any part of him. He swung his head back again and missed again. The knee was folding him up, backwards and sideways. It was excruciating. He wanted to cast a spell. Even something as simple and stupidly dangerous as setting fire to the rope around his neck. Anything. But he could not gasp for a thimble full of air, let alone enough to get words to exit from him. No, he could not move forwards. He was stymied. He could only move back, could only stop actions, not start them. He could only negate.

So that was what he did. He knew he was taking a risk, not only with his life but with the lives of the others as well. If he could not create a way out, he needed to destroy his way out. He canceled his flight spell. They plummeted. Everyone screamed.

Croy landed on Tweltas, who did not land on a spike. The impact loosened Tweltas's pull on his neck, but only for a moment. That brief moment gave Croy some much needed air. He tried to put an elbow into Tweltas's ribs and landed a blow that did not seem to do much. He kicked and flailed with his legs and got several solid hits in, but they could only damage Tweltas's legs. He needed to cause some serious damage to something more sensitive. He was beginning to panic and his pride and sense of decency waned with his consciousness. He suddenly thought of Haswyxe telling him he had to show his enemy who was uglier. He squirmed sideways to get part of his body off Tweltas. This actually pulled the rope tighter around his neck. He removed his left hand from the rope, while leaving his right to attempt to keep the rope from severing his head from his body. He smashed his left hand down as hard as he could on Tweltas's groin. Still he was being choked. He felt down there and directly grabbed testicles through pants fabric and squeezed with all of his might. He felt his vision blurring. It felt like forever since the last time he had taken a breath. He got one testicle between his thumb and forefinger and pinched for all he was worth. He felt himself passing out. He saw Baltuz flash into his vision and stab towards his head. All he could do was close his eyes, stop squirming, and hope for the best.

Baltuz's dagger barely missed him and plunged into Tweltas's right eye. The rope loosened just enough, and he coughed and hacked. He wanted to roll over onto his right side, but the dagger was still there, straight up with Baltuz's fist still pushing it down. It vibrated slightly as Tweltas bucked and kicked and swung his hands towards her and then went back to pulling on his throat. The death throws did not take too long, however. Croy was soon able to pull Tweltas's tied hands away and roll far enough to get off the dead body. He was not sure why—he certainly was no longer scared for his life—but he started crying. There was something cathartic about being able to breathe again. To not having to struggle. To still being alive. He did not cry for long, but it felt amazingly good to do it.

Croy finally realized there screaming going on. Baltuz hobbled over to Haswyxe, who had his left leg impaled on a spike. She was apparently trying to free him, but he was not cooperating. Croy hobbled over to where they were. His throat felt both closed and on fire. It made breathing in anything besides staccato bursts too painful to endure. When he finally got over to them, Haswyxe looked up at Croy plaintively. Like a puppy who doesn't understand why they've been scolded.

"You're going to have to knock me out. I... I can't stay still through this. I just can't. I'm going to shred my muscle, if I haven't already." He was as white as snow. Croy was shocked that he was not passed out already.

"Where did the smoke go?" Baltuz interrupted them, glancing back and forth.

"What? Who cares? We need to get my leg off this spike!" Haswyxe was looking more panicked by the moment.

"What if Croy knocks you out and then turns on me?" Baltuz's eyes narrowed.

"Then you'll put your dagger through his eye. It doesn't matter. If Croy turns, I will be unable to help you. Me being conscious right now doesn't help anyone!" His eyes were wide and wild. Croy had never seen him like that before.

"Nufinderto!" It was difficult for Croy to speak the word, but he could not stand the continued argument either. Haswyxe was right. He would be unable to help or hinder anyone. Baltuz just raised an eyebrow. He could not tell if she was smiling slightly.

"Nukinderto!" Croy placed his hands under part of Haswyxe's leg and slowly raised his entire body, stiff as a board. It did not take long before he had Haswyxe back down on the ground. The blood was pouring out of his friend's body. He wondered if this was what Feyazki always felt like. Constantly casting spells while others bickered around him. Croy was so incredibly tired, he just wanted to lie down. He knew, however, that if he did that, Haswyxe would surely die. Quickly. At least healing was something he was good at.

"Eqeliderto!" It was wrenched from his hoarse mouth. Luckily, he was kneeling next to Haswyxe's body, for he felt himself topple over. Just before he passed out, he heard Baltuz say, "Better hope the smoke didn't enter into me." Or at least he thought that was what he heard. It was hard to tell as he was losing consciousness.

When Croy woke up he found he was unable to move. It took him a couple of quick moments before he realized what had happened. He had been tied to one of the spikes. He shook his head while he opened his eyes, which was a mistake. His head ached as if he had drunk a gallon of beer the night before. There, before him, was Haswyxe tied to a spike. Off to the side, not really struggling, but wriggling vigorously enough to wake Croy, Baltuz was removing the last of her ropes.

"What happened?" Croy expected to see someone else down in the pit with them, or maybe that Tweltas was still walking around.

"Vulthrim was killed and then Tweltas was taken over and…" Baltuz was prepared to explain the whole thing. Croy did not have the energy for that.

"I know that part. Why are we tied up?" Croy did not like interrupting other derlians, but sometimes it had to happen.

"Sorry, I wasn't sure how much you lost when you passed out. I tied us up. I couldn't tell where the smoke went, so I figured it was safest if each of us were incapacitated." Her smile looked sheepish.

"You tied yourself up? Why would you tie yourself up? I mean, wouldn't you know if you were being taken over?" That was not the most puzzling part about it all, however. "Wait, how did you tie yourself up?"

"Well, I got to thinking about Tweltas. Why did he not attack us right away? Why did let himself be disarmed? He seemed to be genuinely confused about why we were worried. Didn't he?" Croy assumed these were all rhetorical questions, so he waited her pause out. "As for how I tied myself up, I had it a little loose and tightened it with that end in my mouth. Then I dropped the end." Her little laugh was melodious. "Obviously it didn't work very well. If I had actually been invaded, it probably would have taken me less than a minute to escape."

"So… why are you just now untying yourself?" Croy started squirming against his own restraints.

"I wanted a certain amount of time to pass. To make sure, you know." She shed the rest of her ropes and walked over to Croy. He was soon free as well. "You were not out for that long, actually."

They stood over Haswyxe's body for some time. His face looked so relaxed and peaceful that they did not bother to wake him. So Baltuz left him tied up. They investigated Tweltas's body and his tongue was definitely darker. They went into the anteroom and found Vultrhim's body. His tongue was pitch black. They discussed those ramifications briefly, and then Croy *whispered* to Feyazki.

"Well, they'll all be down here soon. Do you want to wait for them or…" Baltuz nodded her head at the short door behind the overturned tables at the back of the room. Her curly hair bounced towards the door quite cutely.

Croy almost immediately said yes. That was his knee-jerk reaction. But then he thought of what horrors could lay beyond the door, what dangers. He knew that he could not take another fight. He had not even really participated in the first one and the second was just one long strangling session. Baltuz's smile was too much to resist, however. It was odd, her eyes were always so serious and dark and piercing, that her smile could be so effortlessly infectious. Croy found himself smiling in return.

"Can we run at the first sign of trouble?" He knew he had to quantify it somehow.

"Sure, I'll even give you a head start." She laughed, but at the same time, she was walking over to the tables and the door.

Not sure what he was really doing, and certainly not sure why, Croy hesitatingly followed Baltuz over to the closed door. She stopped. He stopped. Her left arm was held tight to her side, the dried blood on her jerkin the color of rust. She used her right to open the door, but the latch appeared stuck. She slowly put her weight against it, then she slowly put her shoulder against the door. Nothing. She squatted down and examined the keyhole.

"Do you know how to pick locks?" She was still half kneeling. "I have some tools, but I doubt my left hand is dexterous enough for the delicate work."

"You pick locks? I thought you had other 'jin following you." Croy was incredulous.

"Not all members of the 'jin are just warriors, you know." She smiled and stood.

"So, you were a spy? But I've seen you swing a sword." Croy could not recall if he had actually seen her in combat, he had just assumed it. She had been with them since the Forgotten Junction. He had certainly noticed her but had never really talked with her before.

"Well, you have to be a competent enough warrior, that is true. But it takes a certain mind to read a battlefield, and that mind is not always a great fighter." She smiled a crooked smile, her eyes still piercing black holes. "So, you are saying no, yes? You are unable to pick locks?"

"No, I mean… Yes, I am unable to pick locks." He frowned to himself briefly. "If you don't care about the lock's usefulness afterwards, I am sure I can get the door open."

"Well… Seems silly, but I *am* awful curious…" Then the commotion started.

It came from the pit room with the spikes, not from behind the door. Whether that was good or bad from Baltuz's position, he was not sure, but it certainly made him feel better. He had not realized how tense he had become. He turned and fled towards the refreshing sound of others. He thought he could hear Torpalin's booming voice echoing into the room.

It took a whole day before Trela had a debriefing. This was a little abnormal, but the rest of the small cave system had to be thoroughly checked. They never did find where the smoke went, or at least there was not another attack.

Croy and Baltuz arrived at the same time from opposite sides of the camp. Haswyxe showed up a tiny bit later. He had spent the evening with Nochiel. She was, by far, the coterie's most skilled healer, and he was looking quite well. He walked with a slight limp, but that was the only indication that he had recently had a giant cast-iron spike through his leg.

Trela had a small square table set up in the middle of a small tent. They were standing around until Haswyxe arrived, and then they all sat at separate edges of the table. Croy was sitting across from Baltuz. She unexpectedly winked at him while Trela started speaking.

"You look like you're recovering well." She smiled sincerely at Haswyxe.

"Ah, yes. The benefit of being the only wounded warrior in the coterie." He laughed with them. "The individual attention has been fantastic. But really, it all started with Croy." He waved his hand at Croy.

"Well, we'll… We'll get to that." Croy was grateful that Trela interrupted Haswyxe. His first thought had been that he had dropped Haswyxe on the spikes to begin with.

They talked through the entire encounter, one by one. Trela was certainly not as thorough as Ryshial had been back at Agoge, but she did delve deeply into some areas. She would ask confirming questions and get them to agree on something before letting the story continue. Mainly it seemed she was concerned about how the smoke traveled, how the Tlana would flit from derlian to derlian. And she asked an inordinate amount of questions about the tongue color. She seemed to be frustrated that it took some time for it to turn black. What really intrigued her about the whole situation, however, was that it appeared to take a while for the Tlana to take control. Was that real or was it just trying to throw them off, pretending to still be under its host's control? How could one know for sure? As was the coterie's custom, if the Tlana already knew where they were, the usage of the word was sanctioned.

"So, Vulthrim was taken over immediately, correct?" Croy thought this might have been the third time she had asked this same question. He knew her next question as well.

"Yes, he seemed to hang and drag on Tweltas as he was dying." Croy got ready for his next answer.

"Wait… He didn't attack Tweltas?" Trela stopped and squinted at him. That was not the question that he had been expecting. He tried to recall what he had told her the last time, just to figure out what changed her response. Her head tilted a little, indicating that she was waiting.

"Well, no. He completely hampered him, though." It sounded idiotic to his own ears.

"How do you know that he was possessed? I mean, really know." She sat back a little, giving him some more room. He took the hint and thought about his response before delivering it.

"So, I thought, maybe, that I saw smoke enter Vulthrim. But to be honest, maybe not. Also, I'm not sure if his 'hampering' of Tweltas was due to Tlana possession or if he was just dying. He could have just been dying." Croy used air-quotes over his restatement of the word "hampering." As if to contradict himself. "I am fairly positive, however, that I saw smoke leave Vulthrim and enter Tweltas after Vulthrim died. It was much more wispy than the smoke from the other Gaen, the one who was definitely possessed, but it was there. Mostly, however, I know that Vulthrim was possessed because his tongue eventually turned black."

"Hmm. I'm not sure I'm convinced." Trela drummed her fingers on the table briefly. "How black was it when you checked? You checked when Haswyxe was tying Tweltas up?"

"About halfway. It was splotchy, with pink mixed intermittently with black." Croy did his best to recall the image in his mind. "Seemed to happen fairly quickly when compared with Tweltas."

"But Vulthrim was already dead when you checked, correct?" Trela continued to stare at him. "Tweltas had a perfectly pink tongue after the smoke had entered him, but before he attacked you, correct?"

"Correct on all accounts." He nodded to himself as much as to her.

"Hmm. Clerin told me that she saw that Havolin's tongue was completely black while he was still alive." She glanced at the others in the group, as if looking for collaboration. "I was really hoping we could nail this down."

"How long had Havolin been possessed?" Baltuz was looking at Croy while she asked Trela the question.

"No one knows. It may have been for some time, but he did not attack anyone or even make any illogical statements until he was alone with Clerin and the Yaven. At least, that is what I am told." Trela turned her gaze from Baltuz to Croy. "And how long did Tweltas take to turn?"

"Maybe two minutes?" Croy scrunched up his nose trying to think of it. It was difficult for him to fully recall the time measurements. Everything seemed to happen so fast, and yet a lot of stuff happened. It would probably have taken Haswyxe a full two minutes just to tie Tweltas up. Wouldn't it? "Maybe five?"

"And he gave no indication, no outward sign of the Tlana, during those brief minutes." Trela was slowly shaking her head to herself, staring at the table in front of her.

"No, none. It did not appear that he was struggling with anything, certainly not for control of his own will." Haswyxe finally spoke up.

"So, the tongue turns black after death. Definitely. But maybe it stays pink during the struggle. Maybe the amount of splotchiness has to do with how much of the victim is under control of the Tlana?" Trela directed her question to no one in particular.

They all nodded in agreement. The silence stretched. Croy was not sure about adding anything. He did not want to modify the unstated feelings left hanging over the truncated conversation. Best to leave that to Trela.

"So, I guess the last thing I have to ask is… Were there two Tlana or just one?" She was not quite done, however. She turned pointedly to Croy. "You saw smoke enter Tweltas from two directions, correct? One from the Gaens that attacked you and the other from Vulthrim?" She drummed her fingers on the table as he nodded silently. "So does one Tlana control many derlians, or can several Tlana control the same one?"

"The first answer is obvious, of course. One Tlana can control many derlians. Not sure about the second one. But I think that poses yet another question. What is a 'corporeal' Tlana made of? How does it gather enough strength to create a body that walks through swaths of dead warriors? How does it do that and still leave enough 'smoke' in each individual derlian that it maintains control over them?" Baltuz used air-quotes to designate the different types of Tlana she was describing.

"Unless it takes many 'smoke' Tlana to create one 'corporeal' Tlana. Is it that the whole is split amongst us, possessing us individually, with enough of itself left over to be corporeal? Or is the whole greater than the sum of its parts? Meaning that as the individual Tlana join together and become corporeal, they become stronger than they were when separated." Trela was frowning to herself. "I'd like to think that you are correct, Baltuz. That there is a corporeal Tlana hiding somewhere in this cave system, controlling each individual portion of smoke that it uses to infest us. I do not know why that idea feels more comfortable than the alternative, but it does."

Croy had to admit that the thought made him more comfortable as well. He also did not know why that was so, but there was little time to contemplate it. Trela stood to dismiss them, with Haswyxe immediately following. When Croy glanced over at Baltuz, she unexpectedly winked at him again. That sent his thoughts careening haphazardly about his skull, making further contemplation impossible.

They arrived at another abandoned and destroyed farming village, Kayaf, he thought it was called. They were getting quite close to the Fluen realm. Croy was not really sure where Trela was headed. Was she going to turn south and head towards Hifrim, or skirt the border and continue to examine the Gaen villages, or enter into the Fluen realm? He kind of hoped for the latter, mainly because he had never been. He supposed he could just ask, but it had been a while since he had been around Trela when she was not completely surrounded by others.

He had probably been spending too much time with Baltuz. They were certainly not an item—he still thought of himself as handfasted to Ilana; he still *was* handfasted to Ilana—but Baltuz was a lot of fun, and he enjoyed just being around her. It had been a long time since he had allowed himself to chat with someone outside of Trela's inner circle. The warpack had taken up so much of his time. His time at Agoge had been his to spend as he pleased, but he had not felt comfortable enough to branch out with his friendships. This last foray, the coterie, was similar to the warpack. There were always so many little things to do and old friends to talk with that he did not spend any time out of his comfort zone. Baltuz definitely took him out of his comfort zone. But in a good way.

That morning he had woken up thinking of Ilana. It was not a true dream, certainly nothing memorable happened, but she was on his mind. So he was avoiding Baltuz. He knew that was probably not healthy, and it certainly wasn't fair, but it was all he could think of. It was a poor solution to a complicated issue, but it was his solution.

He missed Ilana terribly. He missed her scent, her smile, her touch, her laughter, the way her hair bounced as he followed her from room to room, the twinkle in her eye, their banter and conversation. He missed their conversation. Not while they were at the well, but back in Serif. When he had first met her they would stay up all night speaking of nothing. Later, after they were handfasted, they could spend as much time together as they wanted, but their lives became busier. Even so, after she had come home from Larelt and he had been released from Rycher, they would chat while lying in bed well into the night.

Croy had heard about the phenomenon of a "phantom limb." Sometimes a warrior would get so grievously wounded that something needed to get amputated. Throughout the rest of their lives the warrior could feel an itch or a pain in the amputated limb. By all accounts the sensation was maddening. There was nothing to be done about it, no ability to scratch it, nothing could fix it because nothing was there. That was how he felt about Ilana at times. He missed her terribly, but she was gone and nothing was going to fix that. She was not going to show up and surprise him. He might never find the well in the Northern Desert again. They might never see each other again. He might never smell her again. It was… maddening.

So here was Baltuz. He was still handfasted to Ilana. He still loved Ilana. He could not be with Ilana. But he might, one day far into the future, see her once again. Was he to stay faithful to a memory? Was he to ignore every beautiful flower along the roadside so that they did not outshine the dead and dried ones in his mind? He did not know what to do. Truly. He wanted to do the right thing and he wanted to be happy. Why were those two things mutually exclusive?

Since he was unable to come to a conclusion, he decided to avoid Baltuz. He tried to think of someone to talk with about it.

Feyazki was absolutely useless when it came to these types of conversations; he could not even figure out how much he liked Clerin. Trela would just tell him to do whatever made him happy. Knill would probably tell him to stay true to Ilana's memory. He already knew what Haswyxe thought—he had already told Croy that he should go for it, to be with Baltuz, without any prompting from Croy whatsoever. There were others that he could not guess their opinion. The other Luftens, Trela's inner circle, et cetera. But he did not feel comfortable with all of them. Gaens, as a general rule, were very lifemate oriented, so he could guess what most of them might say. But he did not feel very comfortable around all of them either. Not even Verin, really. Certainly not the Blind One. He was concerned that Tumu would think he was trying to get something prophetic out of him, rather than just some advice. The only derlian he could think of that he was comfortable with enough to talk about something so sensitive, who would provide a thoughtful answer *and* which he could not already guess their opinion, was Clerin. The more he thought about it, the more he felt it was true. He decided to get himself assigned to her search party if they were all going to split up again.

There were search parties combing through the caves near the abandoned village, but Croy was not amongst them. Clerin was somewhere above, looking through the stone and wood farmhouses. At first, he had tried to nonchalantly run into her while she was alone, but he had lost track of which house she was at. Riverlightening was unsaddled and grazing in the grassy village square. Croy decided that Buttercup would enjoy some unbridled time as well. He took a little while getting all of her accoutrements off, and he was prepared to brush her down when she trotted a little ways off and began to roll around in the grass. He swore her lips pulled back into a smile as she wriggled on her back. He wandered into a nearby house, avoiding the small inn that Trela was using as her headquarters.

He was not really sure what he was looking for. Well, he was looking for Clerin, but he unsure of what was *supposed* to be looking for. They rooted through these villages, rummaging through these abandoned lives, for… what? Was there going to be clue as to what Trela was looking for? Croy doubted that he would be able to recognize a clue even if it were staring him in the face. Was she hoping that someone had written down a map or some instructions? Some diary that explained the Tlana raids and how to defeat them? He certainly wanted to help, he certainly rummaged as thoroughly as he was capable, but it all seemed a little pointless. Wandering through the caves, acting as live bait for Tlana, almost made more sense than the invasion of privacy aboveground.

He absentmindedly opened and closed drawers and wardrobes. He dutifully looked under beds and in closets. He knocked on the walls as he was shown to listen for hollow spots, for hidey-holes or secret passages. He was not paying very close attention. He wandered from room to room with an almost bored affectation. His heart was just not fully into it. He sat on the bed and stared out the window for a few minutes. There was a naked blackthorn tree in the unfenced back yard. Then he lay back across the bed and stared at the ceiling. He did not mean to, but he soon fell asleep. And he dreamed.

It was dark, pitch black. Croy was not sure how he knew this. Was it that he was awake with his eyes closed? He tried to look around, tried to wake up. But it was just black. Eventually, however, a small outline appeared. It was as if there were a thousand thin layers of silk before his eyes. One was removed. Another removed. The light slowly, ever so slowly, increased. How many layers before he could see clearly? After what seemed like several minutes, the outline became recognizable. It was a head with soft curls in its hair. The face was turned away, so he had to wait more agonizing minutes before he could recognize the head. By then the illumination had increased such that he could see the outline of shoulders as well. It was Ilana, definitely Ilana. She was turned away from him. She appeared to be crying, her shoulders moving up and down slightly but rapidly.

Croy tried to reach out to her, to comfort her, but he could not move. He was unsure if he could not move because he was frozen in place, or paralyzed, or maybe he just had no body at all. He looked down and saw nothing. He looked back at Ilana's form as more layers of silk were removed, more light illuminated her. He tried to scream, tried to blow air against her hair, something. But nothing. Finally, when most of the layers had been removed, when he could see as if he basked in the summer sun, she turned towards him. Though there were old tracks of tears down her face, he realized she had recently been laughing, not crying.

He tried to wave his hands, he tried yelling again, but she just looked through him as if he were not there. The last of the silken veils was removed. Ilana smiled into the distance, through Croy. He tried to turn, to see what she was smiling at, but could not move. She backed away, slowly, still smiling. She used her forefinger to make the come-hither motion, but he still could not move. After an agonizing wait as she backed farther into the distance, Lemniscate walked through Croy.

How did he know it was Lemniscate? The white wispy hair was similar once he had passed through Croy, and Croy could see him. But the skin did not look as leathery, nor did it have any age spots. No, Croy did not necessarily recognize Lemniscate by sight, but more by feel. When Lemniscate passed through him, he could *feel* it was Lemniscate. He could feel the age, the history, the crushing weight of countless experienced cycles. He could feel further back than that. In the dark distance there was a bright and blinding star, shimmering like a diamond, that he could feel was *Yaven*. There was no other way to describe it. He did not feel that Lemniscate had been a Fluen, just that he had been a Yaven. Had been, and still was in a stunted way, eternal. Did he *feel* that Lemniscate left anything behind, inside Croy, as he passed through? No. But that did not mean there was nothing there.

Lemniscate walked through Croy, sped up for a couple of steps, swept up Ilana in his arms, and spun her around and around. They both looked as if they were laughing, but he could still not hear anything. When they kissed, at that brief moment, he felt the sharp pang of jealousy. But it faded almost immediately. They were torn apart, Croy and Ilana, separated forever. That was due, in part, to his own choosing. He had chosen to leave the shanty town, had chosen to show Clerin the location of the Luften Temple. Did he not still love Ilana? Did he not want her to be happy? Was he not, in fact, wrestling with his own desires? She was gone, they were apart, they would stay apart. It was as simple as that.

Croy felt he could wake up then. He had seen what he needed to see, that Ilana was happy without him. He certainly hoped that she missed him as he missed her, he certainly hoped that they would embrace when they met again, but she was happy without him. And that was okay. That was more than okay, that was good. It was more than good, it was wonderful. It was fantastic! But he did not wake up. He stood there motionless, veil-less, passively watching. Lemniscate put Ilana back down on the invisible ground. He held her face with both of his hands and stared into her eyes tenderly, as Croy used to. He kissed her tenderly and then swept an errant tress of her hair across her brow. He smiled at her and she smiled back at him. He then punched into her stomach. Pierced into her stomach. The violence of it took Croy by surprise and he attempted to scream. But Ilana did not react as if it was painful. In fact, her face was raised upwards and had a joyful ecstatic look upon it. Her lips were parted, her chest heaved upwards, her eyes were smiling, her arms were outstretched, she looked every bit as if she were in the throes of passion. Lemniscate then stepped back and pointed at Croy. Ilana turned and appeared to notice Croy for the first time. Her smile became huge and she ran over to him but stopped just short. She blew him a kiss. He tried to blow her one back but could not move, did not seem to have arms.

Lemniscate walked over while she was animatedly trying to tell him something. Try as he might, he could not read her lips. She seemed so incredibly beautiful to Croy in that moment. She was obviously very excited and… happy. She seemed so incredibly happy. It made Croy's heart fit to burst with love for her. He thought he was grinning like an idiot but was unable to feel his face. Lemniscate cupped his hand at her ear and whispered to her. She listened intently for a moment and then nodded. He spoke again and she nodded again. When he was done, she smiled back at Croy and gave him the come-hither motion with her forefinger, then she turned and ran in the other direction. To Croy's surprise, he floated along with her.

They traveled like that for some time, her running on the invisible ground and him floating. Finally they seemed to be heading towards something. At first it appeared to be just a lump, then a pile of clothes, then a derlian. The derlian was curled up, lying on the invisible ground, facing away. Croy could not even tell what race the figure was. Ilana stopped at the figure and Croy stopped behind her.

Ilana knelt next to the figure and stroked its hair, which appeared to be in tight curls. She bent over and whispered to it for quite some time. The figure did not move but just laid there while Ilana whispered. Eventually the figure raised itself on one arm and faced Ilana. It was Baltuz, and there were old tracks of tears on her face, but she smiled hesitatingly at Ilana. Ilana continued to talk and occasionally Baltuz would nod and say something back. Ilana stood and held out her hand to assist Baltuz. They smiled at each other and Ilana held Baltuz's face with both of her hands. Ilana kissed her tenderly and then swept an errant tress of her hair. Then Ilana punched into Baltuz's stomach. Croy immediately awoke with the image of Baltuz's upturned face searing itself into his mind. It was beautifully ecstatic.

Croy wiped the sweat from his brow, sat up, and glanced out the window. Clerin was outside walking around the blackthorn tree. He jumped up and quickly found his way to the backyard. She was still there, fingering the bare branches.

"Ah, Clerin. Just the derlian I wanted to talk to." He trotted up to her.

"Oh, did you find anything interesting?" She motioned towards the house.

"No, no. Not that. I just ah… Well, maybe it has resolved itself." He suddenly realized he no longer needed to talk to Clerin. He tried to think of what else he could ask her about. He felt that his dream had absolved him of any external guilt, so he could not fully explain why he jumped up and ran outside at the sight of Clerin. He supposed it was just that he had been looking for her before he had fallen asleep.

"No. You've piqued my curiosity now. What did you want to talk about?" She had stopped touching the tree and now crossed her arms over her chest. She looked oddly serious.

"Well, I…" There was nothing to be done. He had started and, therefore, he should finish. Stammering and wasting time would not help him get out of it. "I'm handfasted, you see. But my wife is… gone."

"Oh, yes. I remember her yelling at Trela at the well." Clerin's smile only worked for half of her mouth and he did not think it touched her eyes.

"Well, you cannot judge her from that one meeting." He suddenly felt defensive of Ilana, and he shook his head to clear it. There was no reason to bring any of that up again. "Listen, all I was trying to say is that I love her very much."

"That is what I like about you, Croy." Her smile, still lopsided, reached her eyes.

"But we may never see each again." He decided to forge ahead. "So, if we are unable to be together, does that mean that I can never be with another?" It sounded so bad when he said it aloud. Like he was being callous and cruel. "Since we're handfasted."

"Well… how did you part? Does she know you think you'll never see her again?" Clerin's arms were still crossed, but her stance had softened.

"Yes. She knows that we may never see each other again, I was warned of that by the guardian of the well. And even if we did meet again, it may be cycles and cycles later." His brow was slightly furrowed. He was trying to avoid speaking about his dream, to keep this conversation as he had originally intended it. But why?

"Would you be cross if she were seeing someone else?" Clerin seemed to be skirmishing around the issue, testing his defenses.

"No, no. I would want her to be happy." He crinkled his brow. "As long as she is happy, I could let myself be happy. But it would feel like a betrayal if I was happy and she was not. I guess I just want to know that she has moved on. Not just physically, but emotionally." He paused and thought about it. "I think if she has moved on, it would allow me to do so also."

"So you are saying that even if she is having sex with another derlian, if she has not emotionally given up on your relationship, if she is still holding out hope that you will return and sweep her off her feet, then you will stay miserably single out here." Her hand waved towards the spiky blackthorn. "You are doomed."

"Wait, what?" He had been nodding along with her. He had felt that she had a great underlying grasp of what his issue was, that she understood.

"You are completely doomed." Her dimples pulled back into a grin. "Listen, you cannot base your happiness upon another's. Especially if you may never see them again, never communicate with them again. Especially if they have 'physically' moved on." Clerin made little air-quotes around the word physically. "How will you ever know? What thing would happen that could allow you to 'be happy'? You are setting yourself up for a life of misery based on your imagining that your wife is unhappy." Clerin held up her hands to stave off Croy's automatic reply. That they were *handfasted*. That was what made all the difference. "It would be different if you could talk with her. If you could ask her if she was happy, ask her if she had emotionally 'moved on,' whether or not that meant being with someone else. But you can't. You can't know Croy. You can only base your *now* on what was last said between the two of you. If you both knew you were never going to see each other again, if you both wanted each other to be happy, if you both agreed that you were parting." Croy could not think of anything to add, so he let her pause last long enough that she continued. "I think I know you well enough, Croy. I would certainly call you a friend. You are the type of derlian who is full of hope and kindness. You are the type of derlian who would keep themselves miserable forever if it meant not making another derlian miserable for a moment. Your hope and kindness, in its darkest aspect, can be called a form of masochism. This is why you are doomed. You cannot base your happiness upon another's or else you will never be happy."

"But isn't that the basis of handfasting? Isn't that what relationships are? Isn't that the foundation of love?" He suddenly felt that he should just tell her about his dream, let her know that their entire conversation was moot. Instead, he said one more sentence. It was as if inertia had a hold of him and continued him on his course. "Isn't that why you are so miserable over Feyazki?"

Clerin stopped. Her smile stopped, her hands stopped, her back straightened. She did not look mad or sad or anything. She looked completely neutral. Croy wanted her to yell at him, but he was afraid she was just going to turn and walk away. To never speak to him again. It was an agonizingly long and silent moment. It was only broken by something more agonizing.

Escha burst around the corner of the house. She seemed to have an instinctual read of the situation. The silence, the tension, the two derlians just standing in a backyard staring at each other. She paused for the briefest of moments. But Escha being Escha (and this is what endeared her to Croy, truthfully), she ignored the social aspects of life. And she burst forth with her agonizing message.

"It's Baltuz. She's been horribly wounded and I can't find Nochiel." Then, without waiting for a reply, she turned and ran.

Croy felt like he had been kicked in the gut. But he had no time to worry and ponder about what had happened, no time to apologize to Clerin, no time to let the shock of the news digest or dissipate, no time for any thoughts at all. His body reacted while his mind spun. He immediately ran after Escha. He had to get to Baltuz. He had to fix it.

Croy had cast three healing spells upon Baltuz before Nochiel arrived. He collapsed against the cold stone wall and gratefully let her examine Baltuz. There was blood everywhere. Some of it was Baltuz's, of course, but some of it was from the possessed Gaen and a lot of it was from Trivusch Mur'jin. He was a Gaen warrior they had picked up at the Forgotten Junction, and by all accounts, he had been a skilled fighter. Zira had been there as well, It was she who had finally killed the possessed Gaen.

Baltuz awoke while they were healing her, which was typical. They still carried her to one of the rooms of the inn rather than making her walk. Rest being the lion's share of recovery, she slept while Croy stayed beside her bedside for the rest of the day, casting occasional healing spells on her. It was not until the middle of the night that Baltuz awoke for any length of time. Croy was shocked when she told him of her experience.

"I thought I was going to die. Truly. I should have died." Croy had given her water, but she had laid back down on her side while talking. Croy sat in a chair opposite her, hating himself for not being there when she had been attacked. "As I lay there on the ground dying, with the fighting still going on above me, I... it is almost as if I dreamed. I felt myself blacking out. I was... I was at peace, but very cold. I curled up to try to warm myself but it wasn't helping. I just... I was tired. I was tired of fighting, tired of the struggle. I was ready to slip away. Does that make me weak?" There were tears in her eyes.

"No, never." What could he say?

"Well, I was ready to die. I think a part of me wanted to die. It was just so..." She shook her head slightly and some of the tears loosened and fell onto the bed. "But then a voice came out of nowhere. It whispered to me, it comforted me. It... it brought me back from the brink of death. It was so strange, lying there and feeling and hearing things that weren't in the same room with me. I could hear the voice much more clearly than I could hear the fighting above me. I was just... hallucinating, for the lack of a better word."

"What did the voice say?" Croy wanted to tell her about his dream, but was unsure of how to broach it.

"I... I don't know." She paused and stared at Croy for some time. Her dark eyes, almost pure black pupil with just a little brown at the edge, appeared to be magnified by tears. They were no longer shedding, just vibrating slightly. He could not tell what she was thinking, what gave her pause, but he knew it could have been one of any number of things, so he did not begrudge her that. "It is like a dream that you remember having, but cannot recall what it was about. I know that a voice spoke to me, I am just unable to recall what it said."

"Do you know if the voice was male or female?" He pried only a little.

"I don't know." Baltuz blinked a couple of times. "I think I want to say it was female." Her mouth twitched. "I'm… I'm really tired, Croy. I think I just need some more rest."

"Narliderto!" Croy nodded to her as he cast another healing spell. "We can talk some more tomorrow."

He sat there watching her for some time. She had a dainty nose that had a cute valley between it and her upper lip, the philtrum, he believed it was called. He watched that as her chest and head slowly moved during her breathing. It was hypnotically soothing.

Chapter 15

Trela knew they were getting close but was not quite sure how long it would take to get there. The haunting and desolate abandoned villages, coupled with the ever-present threat of Tlana attacks, had everyone on edge. It was that low constant pressure that was going to break them. Not that the pressure was even very low. And it hung over everything like a cloud. It blocked the sun, it smothered the lungs, it disoriented the senses. It brought a malaise to her coterie. A miasma.

She wondered how long it would take for her coterie to heal itself if they could just sit in an occupied, normal, cheerful town. Not very long, she thought. But would that be leading them further from the final goal? It would certainly not get them any closer to the Cabal. She decided to call a meeting.

She needed Aedon since she was the one who knew where they were headed. Trela also needed Arnasta to find someone. Did she need Serghno just because Arnasta was coming? Did she need Croy to bring another Gaen voice to the meeting? Did she need her Fluen princess just because they were getting close to that realm? Did she need Feyazki because he was a great mage, Rewista because she was a great Second, Estfale because he was a great warrior? It amazed her how quickly her meetings became large social gatherings. Soon half her privy council would be there, then half the coterie. She wanted as much great advice as she could get, but did she really need all those voices? She decided to only gather Aedon and Arnasta. She would let the others wonder what they were talking about.

She pried each of them away from their typical gatherings with as little fanfare as possible and brought them to an abandoned farmhouse that had been thoroughly cleared. They sat on the floor in a small circle.

"I know we are heading towards the village where you sent your spy... To be honest I have forgotten the name of the village and the spy." Trela hated to admit that. At the time she had promised herself to memorize them, but so much had happened since then.

"Ah, yes, Pulthrim. The spy's name was Gyaer." Aedon answered with a helpful smile on her face.

"How long ago did we set out for Pulthrim, several weeks?" Trela was trying to straighten it all out in her head. "Ever since the Forgotten Junction, we have been zigzagging around. I just want to make sure we are heading directly there." The idea, unbidden, of Aedon using her coterie to investigate every abandoned village along the way popped into her mind. It gave her a moment of pause. She trusted that Aedon was helping them track down the Cabal. But did she trust that it was going as quickly as possible? She liked Aedon and did not want to feel suspicious. "How long do you think it would take us to get there from here? If we marched hard."

"Maybe... three days? Maybe four?" Aedon's face gave away nothing. She seemed to genuinely be gauging the distance in her mind. And, to be honest, they had come a long way. Maybe they had not zigzagged as much as Trela had assumed.

"Once we get to Pulthrim we will need to do our best to find Gyaer. We need to get the investigation back on the scent, streamlined." Trela nodded over to Arnasta. "I know you can track better if you have something of your prey, but I do not think that will be possible." She cast an inquisitive eye towards Aedon, hoping against hope. Aedon quietly shook her head. "So, I think we are going to need as much of a description as possible. Maybe Aedon could write down everything she can remember about Gyaer while we are traveling to Pulthrim."

"Yes, that would help." Arnasta looked over at Aedon.

"And we should have Narst write a thorough description of Vuildan as well, just in case." Both Trela and Arnasta stared blankly at Aedon. "The Blind One... Narst is the Blind One."

"Ah, I had forgotten that he had assisted you with your research." Trela nodded absently.

"Yes, it is easy to forget, but he can be quite helpful when he wants to be." Aedon grinned.

They laughed about that. They planned their route to Pulthrim. Arnasta created a list of questions for Aedon and the Blind One to answer, an outline of the description she required. They weighed the merits of seeing Lethos first—Lethos was a doomed city that lay along the Yulhpin river, just before they would reach Pulthrim. Aedon reminded them of Jeschet, the Cabal member, of the Stone Shield she had been trying to purchase, of how long it had been since she had last heard from her spy. There was a synergy there amongst them. The feeling that the whole was greater than the sum of its parts. It made Trela realize that she had been missing that, the rush of collaboration. It energized her. It made her think that she should spend more individual time with some of the lesser known and newer members of her coterie.

It was then that Trela realized she had no idea what Aedon made. She was an assembly member for the 'sol guild, the artist guild, but Trela had never asked what she created. She felt sheepish for a moment.

"So, what, exactly, is your art?" Trela looked at Aedon's long fingers. "A painter, perhaps?"

"Ha! No, nothing that delicate. No, I am a sculptor. Though, admittedly, I mainly make smaller statues. Nothing like the massive carvings that encompass the Great Hall of Serif. Though I have done some detail work there. Small animals and filigree. For the Hall, everything must be larger than life itself. Personally, I am fine with my art being the same size as nature, sometimes even a little smaller. I like to get up close and personal with detail." Aedon squinted at the last of her speech, as if staring at something minute.

"I had just thought, no offense, that you had to be big and bulky to sculpt." Trela glanced again at Aedon's fingers, as if she could see calluses from a distance.

"Not if you're doing it right." Aedon laughed. "If you are forcing the stone to break where it does not wish to, then yes, you need mighty muscles. However, if you see the shape hidden within the stone, the way it wishes to cleave, then you just need to hold your chisel at the right angle and strike true. There is plenty of shaving and rounding and smoothing that takes a lot of time and a decent amount of pressure, but I'm also stronger than I look."

Aedon stood and held out her hand for a handshake, so Trela obliged and clasped her hand. The grip was like a vise, crushing down on her own hand. She had been anticipating such a move and kept her own hand taught, not allowing the bones to roll slightly. Trela swung swords almost every day of her life. Her grip was nothing to be scoffed at; she had her own vise working. There they stood for a moment, both testing the other's grip, not moving but spending enormous amounts of energy, forearms tight but not yet vibrating. Aedon's easy smile did not slip, but neither did Trela's. Then they both suddenly stopped and Aedon withdrew her hand.

"Impressive." It was a shared word and a shared sentiment. Trela had never thought Aedon's grip could stand up against her own. The realization was slightly shocking. Not that she was annoyed or jealous, but more like she had just learned something secret about someone she had known for a while.

"You know, it is often thought that females are weaker, by both sexes. And for breaking a stone where it should not be broken, that is correct. But strength comes in many forms, and it is often the smaller things that are the most important." Aedon sat back down, so Trela followed. Arnasta was silently watching them both. "You do not know, why should you, but I have a twin sister. My mother carried us around all the time, one in each arm. She cooked for a group of Sie'wir, lumberjacks, making massive cheap meals for the lot of them. Hundreds of eggs, pancakes, anything they could afford. So, between the constant cooking, pot scrubbing, and the constant carrying us around, she had incredibly strong arms. She was not skinny, by any means, but she did not look overly muscular. I remember the day as if through a fog, but I do remember seeing it for myself even though my mother told the story a thousand times. Some of the lumberjacks, maybe a little older, maybe a little soft in the belly, began to complain about how hard they worked, how difficult it was to be them. My mother turned from the dishes and challenged them to arm wrestling. She was not one to take complaining well. Not from her own little girls and certainly not from a full grown lumberjack. She beat both of them!" Aedon smiled widely and clapped once. "Not at the same time, of course, but one after another. I am sure there were those in the camp who could have easily beat her, but no one else took her up on her challenge. It was better to have the outcome of the bet unknown than to be whooped by the camp cook. She was treated with much more respect after that and, of course, no longer had to listen to the lumberjacks complain. She had hit them where it hurt the most—their egos."

They laughed about that as well, all three of them. The male ego was something they could all enjoy a chuckle about. It was a good evening, and Trela felt much better knowing they were only a couple of days from at least one their goals. She had been worried it was much further out.

It took most of two days to find the Yulhpin river. The road would wind closer, then meander farther away, allowing them only periodic glimpses of the water. Not that the river was incredibly grand, but just that it was something. Not that Trela thought it should

454

have even been called a river. More like a stream. It took another day to find the shell of Lethos.

She hated to do it, but she ordered them past the broken stone buildings. The village she really needed to find out about was Pulthrim. That was where they might pick up a trace of Jeschet. Or of Gyaer or Vuildan. She could not afford to waste any more time, she could not afford more distractions. Another day and they had reached their destination.

Pulthrim was a fairly small village. Fire had gutted the only four stone buildings. Oddly enough, most of the wood buildings were still intact. Devoid of life, scarred, and thoroughly ransacked, but intact. It took Trela a moment to realize what was wrong with that. Ransacked. Most of the villages they had investigated emitted a quiet serenity from the vast majority of their buildings. As if their owners were due back at any second. Or at the least, that everyone had left at once. Without any warning to pack. No, something had definitely torn through Pulthrim. Searched every nook and cranny with no regard to the mess left behind. Drawers and their contents scattered about as if a small tornado had wound through every room. It felt more violated than abandoned.

Trela moved herself into the largest intact wooden structure left in the town—her headquarters on the ground floor and too much room for herself and Knill upstairs. The kitchen was always busy with her chef, Kolaf, in a constant state of motion. She doubted she could live without him; it would certainly be a much drabber existence. She had meetings in the old parlor, with warriors grabbing a plate of food on their way in or out. There was a large front porch that she used when she wanted some fresh air and the dining room table held her papers and maps. She could not have asked for a better headquarters. Considering.

The remaining wood buildings filled up quickly. It was a bright early evening and Trela allowed them enough time to settle in. They searched their immediate living quarters and that was all. She watched through the dining room window as various warriors traveled from one building to the next. Some were more inebriated than they should have been, laughing too loudly and staggering, but she really wanted them to enjoy the night. To relax. She smiled at the sight. The only thing she had been strict on had been the sentries. It was their first night in Pulthrim and they were on high alert.

***

Trela awoke in the middle of the night. There wasn't a noise that she could place that might have startled her. No feeling of dread. She did not sit up in fright, covered in sweat. She merely passed from asleep to awake. She opened her eyes and saw the dim gray outline of the dresser in the distance. There was no urgent emotion that drew her out of bed but she got up just the same. It was odd but she felt completely refreshed, as if she had slept in until noon. She silently gathered up her boots and clothes and sword belt and headed downstairs. She got dressed in the soft shadows of the curtainless room. The bluish silver moonlight was soft, if a bit cold. Once dressed, she sauntered out into the village.

She walked the perimeter, stopping and chatting with each sentry along the way. Some were staring intently out into the trees when she walked up on them. Some heard her coming from a long way off. One had wandered from his post to visit a latrine, which was a fairly reasonable excuse. One unlucky sentry, a young Gaen named Silvadhin, had dozed off under an elder tree. She was in a deep enough sleep that that Trela was able sneak up and slip the sentry's sword from her scabbard. Trela chastised her thoroughly for that. The rest of her loop was fairly uneventful until she came walking back towards her headquarters.

There, backlit with the soft moonlight, was the unmistakable image of smoke. Twisting, turning, boiling, writhing; an angry black stream of smoke that snaked upwards and then looped down and into the chimney of a building. Of her headquarters. Her heart stopped.

Trela dropped into a dead run. The building was still some ways away. She pulled her short sword from its scabbard even while she wondered about its effectiveness. She wondered if anyone might be wandering around the first floor, the office area of her headquarters, looking for something. Or if Knill would be the only occupant. She tried in vain to look for candlelight through a window. She tried in vain to remember if there was a fireplace on the second floor as well as the first. But did a Tlana really need a fireplace? Could the smoke just seep through holes in the walls? In any case, it could certainly float up the stairs from the first floor's fireplace and be on top of Knill in no time at all.

"Code black! Code black!" She yelled as calmly as she could. She needed to be quick, but she also needed backup. She got Ryshial,

Escha, Trasdou, and the Gaen sentry, Silvadhin. Maybe not her first choices, but more than she had hoped for on such short notice.

Trela waved Escha over to the back door as she ran around towards the front. She ran low alongside the side of the house. She peeked around the last corner and glimpsed into the dark front room. Nothing. Or at least, she could see nothing. She wanted to check to see if everyone else was with her. Trela already knew that Ryshial was right behind her; she made enough noise to be heard from across the village square. Trela had to consciously not get annoyed by that. Ryshial had other skills and was essential to the current mission. Trela could sense another presence behind her, but this one was much quieter. She couldn't quite tell if it was Trasdou or Silvadhin, but it was definitely there. It was the third member of her party that she was unsure about. Had they wandered off? Were they really that quiet?

Since the building looked empty, she glanced back at her companions. Everyone was there. Good. She swung back around and quick marched to the front door. She had to open it with her left hand since she refused to sheath her sword.

The only light she could see came from the moon. The empty fireplace seemed cold. It was sucking heat from the room, unless Trela was imagining that. Instead of examining each room she jogged upstairs. Time was of the essence. She burst forth onto the landing with little regard to her own safety. Nothing. She jogged up the last few steps and could see the silhouette of Knill at the far wall, outlined by the window. It appeared as if he was just staring outside, lost in his own mind. He did not even turn around after they all had clambered upstairs. Trela slowly walked over to him. She kept her sword out but left the tip down.

"Knill? Knill." She kept herself just out of striking range, if he were to spin around swinging. But he did not respond. "Knill!" Nothing. She slowly reached out her left hand and took another step and a half. She touched his left shoulder.

"Aigh!" Knill flinched and managed to hop towards the window all while attempting to turn around. Trela took a couple of steps back to let him get ahold of himself.

She could hear the others behind her jockeying for position. Someone pulled a sword from a scabbard. She thought it was odd that anyone would have gone up the stairs with their weapon sheathed. For a fraction of a second, she wondered where Escha was.

"What… What are you doing here?" Knill waved his hand at the warriors behind Trela more than at Trela herself.

"What were you doing staring out of the window?" It was Trasdou from behind her.

"I'm not sure." Knill frowned as he looked back and forth between them all. "I think I woke up and found myself alone. Maybe I was looking for Trela."

"You think…?" This came from Silvadhin. "Did you just wake up when Trela touched you?"

"While I was walking outside, I saw smoke enter the chimney." Trela interrupted those behind her. She wondered, for just a moment, whether it had been wise to bring warriors with her. She did not want Knill to feel awkward or that he was being attacked. She had never seen him sleepwalk before, however. It was disconcerting that he did not answer the first question with more assuredness.

"I feel fine." Knill looked between them and then centered his gaze back on Trela. "Seriously."

"Maybe you cannot feel you are under attack?" Trela instantly recognized Escha's voice. She must have finally come up the stairs.

"Maybe the smoke came from the fireplace. Maybe it was going up." Knill squinted at her, somewhat ignoring Escha and her comment. "Maybe there was no smoke and you just imagined it. I mean… How do you even see smoke in the middle of the night?" And he laughed just like Knill always laughed.

Trela thought about it. She thoroughly mulled it over in her mind. The fireplace was cold, she knew that, she had felt that. But what if she had imagined the smoke? It *was* dark out. Or maybe it was still there, hiding. Or maybe it flew back out the chimney when they entered the building. She thought back to when she had been attacked by a Tlana in smoke form. It had been an excruciating ordeal. She doubted she would have been able to converse through it. But how long had it really taken? Maybe the fight was already over and it was the Tlana talking. That was what scared her more than anything.

"I think we are going to have to tie you up." This came from came from Trasdou. He was in the back, next to Escha. Escha moved farther into the room, attempting to spread out a little more.

"That's ridiculous." Knill narrowed his eyes at Trasdou. Trela knew there was still something between Croy and Trasdou and briefly wondered if it could have spilled over.

"Ryshial, can you look into Knill?" Trela did not necessarily want to tie Knill up, but she wanted to feel assured of his safety. And hers too, for that matter. She understood the tongue did not turn black immediately. Maybe they should just tie Knill up for the night and check on him in the morning.

"Maybe, I have never tried…" She was quickly interrupted.

"There! Smoke!" Knill pointed past Trela. She whirled in the direction of his outstretched arm without thinking. She chastised herself later for that. If Knill would have attacked her at that moment she would have fallen for the oldest trick in the book. Embarrassing indeed. But he did not attack. Nor did she see smoke. Ryshial and Silvadhin were directly behind her and they both turned to look at the only derlian left way in the back. Trasdou.

"The smoke just entered Trasdou!" Knill's voice was frantic and his arm was still outstretched. Trela backed up to the side, so that she could keep both Knill and Trasdou in her vision.

"Liar!" Trasdou shouted and pointed at Knill.

Both Ryshial and Silvadhin turned and backed up, each to a different side, to keep both Knill and Trasdou in their sights. Ryshial joined Trela while Silvadhin gravitated to the opposite side.

"He's trying to trick you!" It was as if they both yelled the same thing at the same time. Trela was sure that they spoke slightly different sentences, but the gist was the same. The voices were at the same volume and vehemence, the arms were both outstretched with fingers pointing accusingly. They were both staring at each other with fire and hate in their eyes. It made Trela's head hurt.

"I say we tie them both up." Silvadhin was smiling as she said it.

"Never!" Trasdou swung Cobra at Silvadhin and she immediately parried. Her smile never left her face.

"Stop!" Trela yelled and swung her sword at no one in particular. It was more of an exclamation point than anything else.

"He's obviously lying, he just repeated the exact thing I had said!" Trasdou pointed at the unarmed Knill with his sword. "Did anyone else see any smoke around me?"

"Nobody saw smoke around me, either." Knill was calm, but almost patronizingly so. It seemed as if he was enjoying himself. That, in itself, gave Trela pause.

"Maybe we do need to tie both of you up." She needed time to think everything through, and all the yelling and sword waving was not helping.

Trasdou yelled at Knill and he yelled back and Trela was starting to get angry. She knew that when she got angry she had a harder time being impartial, and she was already inclined to think that Knill was telling the truth. But she knew she could not just assume anything based on personality. Something about the control of the Tlana left enough of the victim visible that detection through simple conversation was difficult to accomplish.

Trasdou suddenly rushed towards Knill. His sword was swinging more because of his run than because he was getting ready to stab someone. At least, that was Trela's first thought.

"Mekkinderarc!" Ryshial's arm flung out and Trasdou flew against a far wall. She then turned towards Knill, but he just raised his open hands in surrender. There was a weird smile on his lips.

"Sit." Trela pointed to one of two chairs in the room with her sword. It was wood with a high back and was askew to a small wooden table. She had been trying to read there before she had tried to sleep. The book "Consequences of a Life in Battle" lay upside down and splayed open on the table. Knill sat.

Trela went over to Trasdou. Silvadhin had already taken Cobra away from his dazed hands. He certainly had the wind knocked out of him but did not appear to be bleeding. Trela sheathed her own sword and attempted to get him up. With Escha's help she was able to get him into the other wooden chair. In lieu of rope they used the sheets, a couple belts, even one of Knill's shirts to tie both of them up. They left Knill near the table and had Trasdou on the opposite side of the room.

"Should I grab Feyazki?" Escha glanced at Trela. Trela glanced at Ryshial. Ryshial shrugged. The shrug was not just noncommittal but conveyed the sense that she really did not care. Her dark brown hair moved along with her shoulders. It was held back with her characteristic leather thong, like a tiny tiara.

"Sure, but be quiet about it." Trela thought the more magical strength that they had on hand the better, but she did not want Ryshial to feel marginalized. She also did not need a gaggle of warriors crowding the room with their weapons out, threatening either Knill or Trasdou. Or both, knowing some of her warriors. It was already tense enough in the room without the escalation.

"So… Are we going to just wait until dawn and then check their tongues?" Silvadhin was squinting slightly at Trasdou. As if she was contemplating pulling the truth out of him. Both Knill and Trasdou were silently glaring at each other from across the room, seemingly ignoring all the other derlians in the room.

"That is the back-up plan." Trela smiled at her. "If all else fails."

"And what is the primary plan?" Silvadhin did not pace but began walking away from Trasdou.

"Ryshial is." Trela turned her smile towards the mage.

"Not that I am not willing, but are you asking me to remove the Tlana from whomever is afflicted?" Ryshial's dark eyebrow rose into a sharp peak as she spoke.

"No, no… Not unless you think you could do that." Trela paused hopefully. Ryshial's eyebrow did not relax. "I am just hoping you can detect the presence."

"Well… I'll try." She walked over to Knill and then hunkered near his chair, her butt resting against her boot heels. He just smiled weirdly at her. She seemed to take a couple of deep breaths before speaking quietly to him. "Mekfintotto!" Knill stiffened slightly but gave no other outward signs of the spell. He then closed his eyes and looked meditative. Ryshial kept her hand held lightly over his strapped-down arm for a while, maybe three minutes. Trela stared intently at Knill's mouth, waiting for any signs of black smoke emerging. Nothing.

Eventually Ryshial stood and walked over towards Trasdou. She did not look at Trela at all, just stared intently at the wooden planks before her boots. She then hunkered down next to Trasdou and cast the same spell. Trasdou stiffened slightly and then closed his eyes as well. Trela stared intently at his mouth the entire time. Nothing.

Ryshial stood and walked over to Trela. She stared at the ground the entire time, her brow furrowed intently. Silvadhin excitedly hurried over.

"I… I can't seem to get a read on anything. To be honest, I am not sure what I am looking for. Even if I knew either one of them better, it might be easier to ascertain if there is something abnormal going on in their minds. But as it is... Nothing." Ryshial lifted her hands as she shrugged.

"I have an idea." Silvadhin glanced between Trela and Ryshial. "You watched them in turn, correct?" She nodded to Trela, who nodded back. "You didn't see any smoke or anything?" Trela shook her head. "I was watching Trasdou while Ryshial was looking into Knill and vice versa. I swear that the other twitched when the first was being probed. They looked at the other intently the entire time, never once glancing at me or anything else while the one being probed had their eyes closed. It was eerie." She paused for a moment and gesticulated with her hands, fanning her fingers outwards. "I think you should look into both of them at the same time."

Ryshial shrugged. Trela had been expecting something more out of her. She was not sure if she had expected a positive or negative response, but something more. She, herself, felt fairly ambivalent about the idea. She was fine waiting for Feyazki, or worst case, waiting until morning. So she had thought to leave the decision to Ryshial. Since that was not happening, she decided to be enthusiastic about it. For better or worse, Silvadhin had the only idea.

"Sounds great." Trela broke into a grin. "Should we move them closer?"

"Yes... Maybe over to the corner of the bed there." Ryshial breathed out slowly and shook her hands as she wandered over to the bed. Trela wondered briefly if they were taxing her, but she was one of the strongest Pyran mages from the guild.

They moved Knill over to Ryshial quite easily. He was a feather. Trasdou was heavier, but they did not have to drag his chair along the floor or anything. Once they were in position, Trela and Silvadhin stepped back. Trela promised herself that she would watch both of them intently. She unconsciously crossed her arms over her chest and spread her legs to be shoulder width apart.

Ryshial breathed in deeply several times. She placed a hand on each of their strapped-down arms. She closed her eyes. "Narfintotto!"

Trela stared intently at both of them while nothing happened. Several minutes passed but Ryshial did not give up, so neither did she. Time stretched. Then, when the odd pangs of boredom had just begun, Knill coughed. Nothing visible happened, she had been staring. Then Trasdou had a small cough. These were tiny. Like the type of cough let out while hiding in a basement. A tight-chested cough. Another minute went by. Ryshial still had her eyes closed and her hands lightly resting on their strapped-down arms. Then Knill coughed again. It was louder this time, more forceful. Trela imagined some smoke. Then Trasdou started coughing. There was definitely a wisp of smoke. Knill started to jerk a little while he coughed. Trasdou was shaking. A thin stream of smoke passed from one to the other. Knill was racked with a fit. Trasdou began a low moan. The smoke thickened as it shot between them. Knill began yelling in between the coughs. Trasdou was yelling. A thick black stream of smoke raced back and forth between their open mouths, adding an appropriate visual to the deafening screams. Trela stood there helplessly.

"Eqetectotarc!" Feyazki appeared out of nowhere. The black smoke swirled around Knill's head for a moment.

"Eqetectotpri!" Ryshial flung herself away from the chairs, further onto the bed. The black smoke shot itself back into Trasdou.

"Eqetectotsfe!" Feyazki gestured towards Trasdou. The smoke shot back out but cupped in front of Trasdou and swirled there. An invisible sphere was centered around Trasdou and made visible by the tendrils of smoke as they whisked and wisped around for a full fifteen seconds. Then they shot back into him.

Everyone was quiet for a few moments. Knill looked passed out. He was completely limp. Ryshial climbed further up the bed until she was at the far corner. Her hair was plastered about her face but she straightened it quickly. Trela's feet felt as if they were made of lead. She just stood there, staring at Trasdou. Feyazki was breathing heavily. Escha stayed invisible in the background. It was Silvadhin who broke the silence.

"So you chose to doom the Pyran?" She walked over and knocked heavily on the invisible sphere before turning fully to Feyazki. "You decided Tradou's life was worth less? Was worthless?"

"I wouldn't say worthless, but I had to do something." Feyazki crossed his arms over his chest and turned to face Silvadhin. "I could not figure out how to save them both. To be honest, I was not even sure this would happen."

"But you cast the first shield on your friend. You knew you were not saving Trasdou." Her eyes narrowed.

"I would have if I could have. But of course I cast it on the one I know better. What other criteria is there? Did you want me to attempt to weigh the merits of their contributions to the coterie as a whole? Was I supposed to let them discuss it, to argue their cases? To allow them the opportunity to volunteer? You are mad. I entered the room and did the best I could in the allotted time." Feyazki waved his hand dismissively. "I will not feel bad about that."

Suddenly, Trasdou began to shake. His eyes widened in pure terror, pure horror. His strapped-down arms pulled and strained. His chair made a couple of small hops. The smoke pushed a couple of tentative tendrils from his mouth and one from each nostril. He began yelling, but it seemed to be muted by the shield spell. Trela was pretty sure he was saying, "Get me out of here!" There were some tentative tendrils wisping about his ears. She could have been imagining it, but there seemed to be tiny threads of smoke wafting out of his tear ducts at his eyes.

Trasdou was shaking so violently that his chair overturned. The smoke began pouring out of one area, mainly his mouth and nose, then swirl around the sphere for a moment before entering back in, mainly through his ears, but it appeared that some of it entered through his eyes. His body bucked and trembled as the chair hopped against the floor. He was screaming wordlessly now. He banged his head repeatedly on the wooden planks. Trela was glad that the sounds were muffled by the shield.

It took a short while for Trasdou to die. Trela forced herself to watch it. Feyazki cast the shield spell again. Ryshial took Knill downstairs and Escha followed. Silvadhin did her best to stare holes into Feyazki. That did not seem to bother him at all. Trela tried to feel bad about Trasdou, and she did to an extent, but she could not make herself wish that it was Knill. Not in the slightest. So, in a bizarre attempt to appease that guilt, she forced herself to watch Trasdou bounce and buck until he was finally still. She watched for a time after that, waiting for the smoke to show itself again, but it seemed to be hiding. Still, staring at Trasdou's lifeless face was easier than arguing with Silvadhin.

"Do you think it's still in there?" Silvadhin made a half-hearted kick towards the shield. "Do we have a trapped Tlana?"

"I didn't feel it leave, but I really didn't think I could trap one, either." Feyazki frowned to himself for a moment. "Maybe it slipped out. Maybe it dissipated."

"Maybe it's incubating." Trela did not really want to say it, it just popped out.

"Maybe it is slowly devouring his innards." Silvadhin switched her angry gaze towards Trela. It was a little frustrating because Trela had thought she had been calming down a little.

"Maybe. But since he is dead now, I suppose it doesn't much matter." Feyazki interrupted her with his own angry gaze. He squared his shoulders to her. "Why are you still here, exactly? Shouldn't you be guarding something?"

"Ah, yes, I have a task for you." Trela grasped Silvadhin's shoulder conspiratorially and turned her away from Feyazki. As they slowly walked down the stairs, she racked her brain. "I need you to get Serghno up and bring him here. I think we need some Pyran mages to help us investigate."

"Of course, my queen." Trela could not tell if she was buoyed by the sentiment, but at least she had a task. It was always a little odd when a Gaen of the coterie called her queen.

"Ryshial, we need you back upstairs." Trela spoke loud enough that Silvadhin could hear her on her way out. But, hopefully, not obviously so.

"I cast a healing spell on him, though I wasn't really sure if he was hurt. I think he's just sleeping normally at this point." Ryshial walked past her and up the stairs.

Instead of following, Trela walked over to the couch that held Knill's tiny body. She sat down in a chair near his head and watched his chest peacefully rise and fall in the slow rhythm that meant he was in deep slumber. How often had she watched him sleep? Typically, he would try to stay awake with her to help her strategize, or more likely, just to keep her company. He was typically full of energy and did his best to keep her optimistic. Well maybe not optimistic—Trela was not a natural pessimist by any means—but he was always trying to make her smile, to keep the mood light, while she was concentrating over some specific problem. He used to joke that her head should catch fire, she was thinking so hard. She had not realized it on her own, but she apparently had the habit of frowning when she played different scenarios in her head. So he would do his best to distract her. He would inevitably end up curled into a tight ball at the foot of a bed or in a large chair or even on the ground. He could sleep almost anywhere under almost any circumstances. Trela had always envied him that. She reached out and wiped a lock of hair from his forehead. A warm feeling of nostalgia came over her. She wished she had spent more time with him during the relative peace and calm of Agoge. She always had so much to do. And now there was Knill. Sleeping peacefully after coming as close to death as she had ever seen him. She would have to thank Feyazki the next time they were alone together. The loss of Trasdou was difficult, but the loss of Knill would have been devastating. She scooted her chair over to be able to rest her fingers in his hair as he slept. She closed her own weary eyes. She did not think she fell asleep, but her body jerked when a loud Serghno entered the building.

He instantly realized that he had startled her. He smiled his apologies and walked over while Silvadhin went upstairs. Presumably to harass Feyazki some more.

"Sorry, my Queen. I am sure your night has been trying enough without me bumbling through it." He smiled and nodded, his mustaches bobbing double time with his head. "Here… Mekliderto!" He knelt and laid a hand on Knill's forehead.

Knill stirred for a brief moment. Serghno smiled at him and then at her. He made a shushing motion with his index finger and slowly got up. He then comically walked away with high knees so as to not make any noise. It looked rather ridiculous with his portly frame. Trela knew she should head upstairs as well but wanted more than anything to go back to resting.

Knill stirred again and opened sleepy eyes at her. He frowned for a moment. "Trasdou?" It was only one word, but that one word held a lot of meaning.

"He ah… did not make it." Trela was unsure of how much detail to get into. "We might have trapped the Tlana, however."

"It was me. The Tlana entered me first, while I was alone. Trasdou was innocent." His eyes were brimming wet when he reclosed them. He completely ignored her latter sentence. "I even knew that I was lying while talking with you. I don't know if I could have told the truth, but I knew I was lying."

Trela waited for more. Knill kept his eyes closed and his head down. It almost appeared that he had immediately fallen back asleep. She knew there was no way that had happened and yet… she also knew that he was done talking. He had made his confession and did not want to think about it anymore. She certainly could have pried, could have forced him to talk with her. But to what end? She stood and slowly walked upstairs. She tried not to make too much noise but could not bring herself to tiptoe like Serghno had done. She walked softly, but somberly.

Between Feyazki, Ryshial, and Serghno, they kept the shield spell in place until dawn. Trasdou's body decayed quite rapidly within the shield. Trela and the others kept a close eye on it but were unable to see any smoke. It was incredibly disheartening. Trela wondered if it was consuming Trasdou. By the time the sun was shining the corpse looked as if it had sat out in the sun for a week. It did not bloat and rupture but seemed more like it had just desiccated. It was a dried husk.

They brought others in to examine it. Trela had them move the shield enshrouded corpse outside. They placed it in the middle of the main road. She had the thought that sunlight might do something to the smoke, she was not really sure why. She had every mage in her coterie help. When dusk began and still no one had seen any smoke, she got a little concerned. She did not want to release the shield during the night. She made sure everyone was comfortable with the decision and kept it going through that night as well.

The next day brought more conjecture. Finally, around noon, she began to tire of the exercise. And she had not really assisted. She could not imagine how tired all the mages were. Knill had made the suggestion to shrink the shield as small as possible before allowing it to dissipate. Not that he would look at the corpse. He would not even go outside, not even leave the couch. Once the corpse was dealt with, they would have to make sure he was untainted. She was not really sure how. At least they made sure his tongue was not black. Everyone gathered outside to watch the shrinking of the shield. Everyone helped to watch for the smoke. In the end, however, Trela could not order the corpse to be completely crushed. She had the mages check for any signs of Tlana through the shield, but no one could sense anything, not even Arnasta. The entire ordeal had taken way too long. Finally, the shield spell was allowed to fail. And... nothing. Who knew how long ago the Tlana had escaped? Maybe it sank into the ground at the moment Feyazki allowed the shield to dissipate. Maybe it oozed out after destroying Trasdou sometime during that first night. They could not sense anything in the corpse either. They had certainly tried, they had to, but no new knowledge had been gained. What had started horrifying and then turned tantalizing, now just felt like a waste of time to Trela. They gave Trasdou a burial with full honors. It was the least she could do.

***

Trela hated the time wasted, but she could not overly disturb the somber mood. Especially since Knill was involved. Silvadhin, oddly, did not talk about it with anyone. Or at least, not that Trela ever heard about. She had been so vehement at the time. It was odd but Trela did not want to look a gift horse in the mouth, as the saying went. The next day would not be somber, however. Trela decided to wake everyone at dawn to begin their search of Pulthrim in earnest. They needed to find some trace of something. This was where they had been heading for so long and it was completely deserted. First, they were going to scour what was left of the buildings. Then, they needed to find the "hidden" underground cavern system that she had come to expect at these villages. If they still had not found anything, they would need to search every farmhouse in the area, radiating all the way out to Lethos if need be. They needed some sort of a break, something that could lead them to where they were going. Something that could lead them to the Cabal.

She wanted to make them all breakfast. To have a big meeting at dawn and gather them all for a rousing speech. To send them off to search with high spirits and full bellies. Searches could be so tedious and she needed them to stay vigilant. To put every iota of energy they had into it. And then do it again tomorrow, and the next day. Typically she would get Knill to help her, he always woke up before dawn anyway, but he was listless and despondent. She would certainly attempt to get through to him later, but she needed to assume he would not be helping. So, to help her and Kolaf, Trela enlisted Torpalin which meant, of course, that Escha was enlisted as well.

It was an incredibly comfortable time in the large kitchen. The jovial atmosphere made her miss Knill's presence. She knew he would have enjoyed it immensely. The warriors came in waves and then loitered around afterwards. They knew what it meant when Trela was cooking. Finally, they had all been fed and she was able to give her speech about how important the day's search was. She told them that if they found a cavern system to merely post guard. That was how important it was to stay focused. She did not want them missing anything above ground because they splintered their forces. To be honest, there were enough abandoned buildings within the village proper to warrant two days of heavy searching. It was always difficult to keep the warriors out of the caverns once they were discovered, especially the Gaens, but she figured she could keep them above ground for at least the first day of searching.

As she had anticipated, they found nothing of note that first day. Arnasta found a few ghostly trails, but they were merely marked for future reference. Trela did not have full confidence in anything based off of another derlian's verbal description. She wanted Aedon or the Blind One to verify the spoor, or for Arnasta to be given something more concrete to work with. Something besides the vague feelings of comings or goings.

So, the next day they prepared to enter the caverns. They began at dawn again, with the vast majority of her coterie participating in the search. Typically, she would leave over half of her warriors above ground. Part of her reasoning was for safety, part was for diplomacy in case they ran into any Gaens, and part of it was simply to keep an easy flow underground—many of the cavern systems were quite small and could be a little claustrophobic for the taller warriors. But today she needed to turn something up, she needed something to happen. She was going to force something to happen if need be.

The first cavern was large and round. There were four passageways radiating out from it, five if you counted the entrance. There was absolutely no furniture in the room. Typically, there was a large table in the entrance hall, many times rung with chairs. But there was nothing this time, nothing smashed or broken like aboveground, there weren't even splinters. There was, however, a lot of scratch-marks in the stone, a lot of footprints in the sparse sand on the floor. There had been a lot of traffic through there. And somewhat recently.

Trela tried to figure out which passageway had more footprints, but they all seemed heavily used. She split her large group into four and decided to take the one farthest from the entrance, thinking that would lead deeper into the cave system. She knew that tactic did not work all the time, that the Gaens often twisted and turned the caverns in odd directions to be intentionally confusing. She certainly missed the massive, but straight forward, construction of Serif. The systems by the hill villages were almost always made for defense and, therefore, were much less predictable. She had to base her decision off of something, however. The odds that she, herself, would find what they were looking for were quite low. She knew that in her mind. But she still yearned for it in her heart. What were they really looking for anyway? Anything. At this point, she would take anything at all.

She brought Aedon with her to increase the odds that if they found something, it would be recognized as such. Estfale, Feyazki, Malghain, and Jalin were with her as well. Along with a myriad of other warriors, including Silvadhin. She had wanted to bring Arnasta with them too but felt she should split the mages as much as possible. But no Knill. He had refused to come, refused to delve underground. She was not sure if it was out of fear or depression, but she had not wanted to argue about it.

Feyazki had a glowing ball of fire in front of them, leading the way. Trela had wanted to be out front, but Estfale had refused. He and Malghain led while Feyazki and herself followed. It was oddly boring for a while. She thought that maybe she had chosen the longest tunnel. There were not too many turns but enough to make it difficult to see what was up ahead. They reached a notched door in the side of the tunnel. Jalin made quick work of the lock but there was nothing in the tiny room. Only scratches and footprints. They went on for a while like that, finding small rooms off to one side or the other, but they were always empty. After about the fifth one, they found a T-intersection.

She did not really want to do it, but she left three warriors to guard the intersection while the rest of the group went on. She did not want to split her group up but did not want something to be able to come up from behind either. She took the side passage hoping it would terminate soon and they could quickly meet back up.

The side passageway went up and down, twisted and turned. She would have been lost had there been more than one way to go back. The walls seemed much more rough-hewn than in the main part of the system. There were heavy gouges and sharp protuberances along the walls; even the floor was quite uneven. It went on for much longer than she had hoped, though she was unsure if it just felt that way or if the tunnel really did extend that far. Finally, they reached the end. It appeared as if there was a large boulder jammed into the tunnel. It implied that there had to be a room beyond, somewhere for the rest of the boulder to be. The seam between the aperture and the boulder was subtle, but there was certainly more boulder than tunnel. There was a deep-set hole near the floor on the left side of the tunnel wall. They stared dumbly at the boulder for a moment until Silvadhin wormed her way to the front of the pack.

"You'll have to turn it." She pointed at Feyazki.

"What, how?" He squinted at her.

"Magic. They have removed the mechanism." Silvadhin pointed to the deep-set hole. "It must have been quite the emergency."

"So, I just rotate the boulder?" Feyazki looked from Silvadhin to Trela, as if he was making sure she was okay with the directive.

"Yeah, there is a hole through the center of the boulder. It is probably just perpendicular right now." She made a twisting motion with her right hand over the flat palm of her left.

"Do you think whoever removed the mechanism will be waiting on the other side? As in, 'prepared to murder us' waiting?" Malghain threw his always sunny concerns into the mix. "I mean, they are not expecting the boulder to start turning since they removed the mechanism. Hearing that grinding around will certainly arouse their fear." He made the same twisting motion.

"Well then, spin it real fast and they won't have the time." Silvadhin narrowed her eyes at Malghain. He smiled broadly back at her.

While this was happening, Estfale was on his knees staring into the deep-set hole, no doubt attempting to figure out the mechanism connection point. Trela wanted, more than anything at that moment, to just be simply intrigued. To kneel there next to Estfale and poke around in a hole that *might* be dangerous, but probably not. Instead, she had decisions to make. She thought, for the briefest of moments, about just leaving whatever was behind the boulder alone and reuniting with her sentries back at the main tunnel. But the insatiable curiosity that had Estfale kneeling was the same that would make her find out what was behind the boulder. She knew herself well enough to know she was unable to abandon it.

"We'll turn it quickly. Everyone up and at the ready." She shook her foot towards Estfale and then turned towards Silvadhin. "You are going to have to be at front and center."

Trela truly thought Silvadhin was going to argue or at least ask why. She had a whole list of reasons, besides the obvious "you're a Gaen," prepared for the argument. But Silvadhin just nodded slightly, repeatedly, with her lips slightly pursed and twisted, as if she were thinking of the arguments on her own.

"Of course." And that was that.

Silvadhin did not unsheathe a weapon, but Estfale and Malghain did, both of them behind her. Feyazki was to one side and Trela, weaponless as well, to the other. The rest of her warriors were gathered behind. She was unsure of where Aedon or Jalin were, but assumed they were in the very back. She nodded to Feyazki. He nodded back.

"Eqekingearc!" The sound was horrendous, but the boulder did spin pretty quick. Silvadhin was correct; it was just a ninety-degree turn and then the tunnel continued through the boulder to a large room at the other side.

Silvadhin strode purposefully through the tunnel, not too quickly, with her hands held high and speaking clearly in a strident voice. "It is I, Silvadhin Fyr'jin, from Serif under the leadership of Narst Dea'jin. We are here to help, we come in peace. We have traveled…" She trailed off as she entered the room.

Trela soon realized why as she walked through the boulder. There was a pile of bodies off to the side. And they were rank. In fact, she was unsure of how she did not smell them right when the boulder turned. Maybe she had been holding her breath.

The bodies were stacked neatly and respectfully, but definitely so as to take up as little room as possible. It immediately made Trela think that there were survivors somewhere. If a Tlana had killed all those Gaens their bodies would have been strewn about the room.

"Search!" Trela twirled her left hand above her head as a signal to her warriors. Her right hand brought her cuff up to her face so she could breathe through the fabric. The familiar stench of her own unwashed body was a welcome relief compared to the rotting corpses. She wished she had a perfumed vinaigrette with her.

There were three doors leading out of the room. Other than that, it was devoid of any furniture or embellishments. Each door was about the same size and shape, thick wood with iron bands. Each was locked tight. Silvadhin gave a small speech in front of each door but none of them were voluntarily opened. Trela was pretty sure that if there was anyone behind the door, they would have heard her. At least they were forewarned. She chose the door farthest from the corpse pile and had Jalin pick the lock.

Jalin was so silent that Trela could not even hear the mechanism turn. Of course, they had already announced themselves to whomever was in the room, so being silent was more of a professional pride issue than a security one. Jalin quickly stood and shifted out of the way.

Silvadhin opened the door and then shifted out of the way. Estfale was the first through the door and Trela followed quickly behind. It was horrible. There were what she assumed to be a total of three bodies. They were completely torn apart and strewn about the room. There was also one body, whole but bloody, lying in the in the middle of the floor.

"Feyazki, we need a sweep." Trela wished she had brought Arnasta with her. That made her wonder, briefly, about the other portions of her coterie. Hopefully, they were having more luck than she was. She left the room as he came in.

The second room they checked, the middle room, started the same. Jalin picked the lock, Silvadhin opened the door, and Estfale entered first. This room, however, was completely empty. It was refreshingly clean.

The last room started the same. But when Silvadhin opened the door, a blur escaped. It was incredibly short and incredibly fast. It shot right by Estfale. Trela lunged so hard for it that she came crashing down on the stone floor. It zigged past some warriors and then turned a hard zag as others lunged for it. Feyazki was yelling something. Trela suddenly panicked.

"Don't hurt it!" She was still in the process of getting up.

Jalin had almost caught up to it, but it turned hard and ran straight for the tunnel. Trela looked up, despondent that it might escape, and noticed Aedon crouching at the entrance, hands held up in front of her, bracing for impact. Whatever it was crashed into Aedon, who bowled over but seemed to have gotten a grip on it. Jalin pounced and Malghain was not far behind. Soon everyone was around the small pile.

When the commotion died down, they found they had a scraggly Gaen boy. Trela was not great at guessing the ages of young Gaens, but he certainly appeared to be younger than Knill was when she had met him and even younger than any of her classmates when she was in Serif.

Estfale and Silvadhin examined the room the boy had escaped from. Aedon was worried she had been bitten by the boy, so she and Feyazki went to the clean room so he could heal her if need be. They made the boy sit cross-legged in the middle of the room while several of her warriors protected the exit. Malghain sat next to the boy. He was not touching the boy, but close enough that he could grab at him if need be. He was kind of leaned back on his arm, with his hand just slightly behind the boy.

"Can you tell me your name?" Trela was sitting cross-legged in front of him, attempting to be as non-threatening as possible.

"Pylor." He stared at the ground in front of him, not looking at her at all. "My parents named me Pylor, after the smallest lake in Hifrim."

Trela wanted to ask him if his parents were alive. She wanted to ask if they first met at that lake. She wanted to ask if he had ever been to Hifrim, ever seen the lake, or if he had lived in Pulthrim all of his life. She wanted to know about him, his family, his life. She wanted to pry. But she was unsure of what she could ask. Well, she knew she could not ask about his parents.

"Have you ever been to the lake?" She smiled warmly.

They spoke inconsequentially for some time. Once she had gained his trust, she wanted to ask about the bodies, about the assumed Tlana, about what had happened to his parents. But all of that would have to wait. It had taken too long to get him relaxed. Trela charged Jalin with watching him, since she was near the back of the pack and mostly out of harm's way. Plus, Pylor seemed to take a liking to Jalin. Trela was not positive if it was her demeanor or the fact that she was one of the least obviously armed warriors of Trela's group, or maybe a mixture of several issues. Regardless, it was long overdue for her portion of the coterie to get to moving again.

When they reached the T-intersection again, they found two of the warriors that she had left behind dead. Both of their throats were slit and there was no sign of the third warrior. She racked her brain trying to think of the missing warrior's name but was having difficulty even thinking of the names of the dead ones right in front of her. And she was much better putting names with faces. All three were, or had been, Gaen. And fairly new recruits as well. The one slumped down on the left was... Raiquette? The one on the right might have been... Havesh? She knew they were somewhere near the Mur ranking. The killings seemed almost mundane; they might have been performed by the missing warrior. It was an odd feeling, that of hoping she had a murderous traitor in her midst. To be honest, she was just tired of fighting with Tlana every step of her way.

"Tulkan is missing. Do you think he did this?" Silvadhin pointed her short sword at each of the bodies.

Trela wondered if Pylor could see what had happened. Of course, this was nothing compared to what he had been trapped with for who knew how long. Besides, they needed to walk past the scene to be able to investigate further. *Why did I leave anyone behind?*, she thought. It made her think of the other portions of her coterie. Were they all getting picked off, one by one? Maybe by the time they left the cavern system, there would only be those warriors surrounding her left alive. She shook her head to clear it.

"In any case, we will have to track Tulkan down. He's either a captive or a traitor." *Or possessed by a Tlana*, but Trela did not speak that thought aloud. She did not really want to give the Tlana any more of her time or energy than necessary. "Weapons out."

Though most of her warriors already had their weapons in hand, a few more were unsheathed. She did not typically like that many melee weapons out in the tunnels, especially the axes. There was just not a lot of room to swing anything. The warriors needed to space out more evenly just to walk around. For herself, she kept a long dagger, point up, against her forearm to keep it out of the way.

They walked as quickly as they could while keeping spread out and hypervigilant. Trela let Estfale lead again, she followed close behind. There were no offshoots, so they made good time as the tunnel slowly curved, even though that kept the visibility limited to less than eight rods at best. At the end of the rough-hewn tunnel was a gigantic set of wooden doors. No large boulder to turn. No lock to pick. It appeared that the doors were held fast by a large timber across their backs. At least that was what the shadow looked like as Trela peered at the crack between the doors. She pushed on the dark spot with her long dagger. It definitely felt like wood and was definitely not going to budge.

She backed up to whisper with her confederates. The odds that whoever was behind the door had not noticed them yet were not great, but she had to try for the element of surprise.

"We need to cleave the timber lock-bar in two and then rush into the room." It was not much of a plan. She pointed at Feyazki to explain how she wanted the lock-bar to be cleaved. Everyone nodded and got into position as quietly as possible.

"Mekdeheparc!" Feyazki split the timber behind the doors. Estfale and Malghain each shouldered a door open. Trela and Silvadhin led the charge into the room.

There were four of them, and they were prepared for the charge. Three had crossbows and one threw an axe as Trela and her warriors entered. She did not really get to see what happened because, embarrassingly enough, a bolt slid into her right thigh immediately and dropped her like a sack of potatoes. She had not dodged, had not even tried to evade or weave, but had run straight forward into the fray. She had not even been able to toss her dagger but had just crumpled to the stony floor. The only thing that she was able to remotely do correctly was to roll onto her left leg as she fell, sparing her right. Luckily, the Gaens who ambushed them were unable to reload before her warriors fell upon them.

One was dispatched immediately during the fight. Another had almost been run through by Silvadhin but Aedon had recognized the warrior and was able to stop her before the irreversible had happened. Trela was staring at the ceiling, trying to regulate her breathing through her lips, when she heard their exchange.

"Wait, stop! That is Gyaer!" She went on to say complicated sentences explaining who Gyaer was and why he should not be harmed, all of which were lost on Trela and, she assumed, on everyone else in the room.

Somehow, Silvadhin was able to realize that she was the warrior being yelled at and shifted her sword at the last moment. She still struck Gyaer but it was only a small slash compared to what it could have been. The others were wrestled to the ground amongst the deafening pandemonium. She squinted through her tears to see Feyazki approaching her.

"Go. Go make sure Gyaer is okay." She tried to wave him away but couldn't remove her hands from the shaft protruding from her leg.

It took what felt like an eternity, but was likely less than five seconds, for Jalin to appear. She examined the wound carefully before yanking the unbarbed bolt out. Trela's natural reaction was to strike out at Jalin, but her hands were busy clamped around her thigh and she could not have kicked with either leg to save her life.

"Mekliderto!" The pain began to subside. Jalin was still staring intently at the wound. Trela leaned back so that she would have been looking at the ceiling had she had her eyes open.

"Mekliderto!" It was Malghain's voice the next time. Trela could almost breathe again.

It took a little more time. Someone placed a wadded-up piece of clothing under her head. She listened to the quietening sounds of the struggle coming to a close. Jalin cast another healing spell. She did not want to wear out her warriors. She did not really need any more healing spells cast on her. She just wanted to continue to lie there. She just wanted to relax in peace.

"It's good. I'm good. Thank you." Trela opened her eyes and waved her hands slightly to show just how fine she was. "I just… need a moment. Just a moment." Jalin and Malghain both quietly wandered out of her vision. She just wanted to stare at the ceiling.

They were back at the house she was using as her headquarters. The other teams had little to report. It was Trela's that saw the only fighting. Gyaer's companions were slain, but he had been healed up nicely. He was also heavily trussed up and waiting for Trela upstairs. She had been downstairs, trying to get Knill excited about looking after Pylor. It was not going well. She had explained the situation with a warm smile, but they both kept a dour look on themselves. They had stared at each other for quite a while before Trela decided to break the silence again.

"Please, as a favor to me. I am sure you two would get along if you just let it happen." She tried her warm smile again.

"He knows." Pylor held a somewhat shaky finger towards Knill.

"What? What does Knill know?" She had been trying to get them to use their names. To get them friendlier towards each other.

"The taint…" Pylor cocked his head askance. "It never quite leaves, you know. It is like a thin film of rancid oil that coats the inside of your mouth. Forever. You know." He was still looking at Knill.

Trela surmised it had something to do with the Tlana. Knill had been despondent and listless ever since Trasdou had died. She had thought it was his death that had slowed Knill down, but now she wondered if it was more serious.

"I was attacked by a Tlana once as well. Mentally." She had wanted Pylor to open up about his experience. Maybe it would open Knill up about his. It did not work, however.

"You don't know. He knows." Pylor shook his head slowly. Knill just stared at him in silence. It was becoming a little eerie. "This will be fine. Thank you." Pylor walked over and took Knill's small hand in his smaller one. "We will be fine. Do what you need to do."

Trela wanted to stay. Even if she didn't talk, she wanted to hear them converse. Even if they didn't talk, she wanted to be there for Knill, to make sure he was all right. But he had not been talking with her lately. At all. And besides, she really did need to get on with interrogating Gyaer. Aedon was up there with him. Trela had made Aedon promise not to talk with him until she arrived, but she wasn't sure how unreasonable of a request that was. Silvadhin was up there in guard capacity. She seemed to be a constant fixture for some reason. Feyazki was up there as well. Trela knew the Blind One should be present, but she wanted to get some information out of Gyaer first. Just to have the upper hand. She knew she should trust the Blind One at this point, but she had just never gotten over him stealing Croy. It stuck in her craw.

So Trela wandered upstairs, not even saying goodbye to Knill or Pylor. She wandered off, staring at the floor thinking, in much the same way that they wandered off into an adjacent room. It was an amiable ignoring of each other.

Feyazki was sitting next to a window, his wooden chair at an angle compared to the room. Trela had burned the chairs that Knill and Trasdou sat in during the unfortunate incident, so that one was new. Silvadhin was standing with her arms crossed, glaring at everyone. Trela had wanted Estfale or Malghain or the like, but she had also wanted to keep the group as small, and as Gaen, as she could. Aedon was sitting in another new chair across from Gyaer. His torso was heavily wrapped with ropes, his hands behind the back of his chair. His gag hung loosely around his neck like a bandana. He was glaring at Aedon and barely glanced at Trela as she topped the landing.

"So, now that the Pyran is here, can you tell me why you killed my companions? Or at least explain why I'm tied up here?" He kept his steely eyes on Aedon.

Gyaer was tall for a Gaen, though it was difficult to tell with him sitting down, covered in ropes. He had salt and pepper hair, but his beard was heavily streaked with gray, especially in the front. It made Trela wonder why a dog's muzzle went gray before the rest of it. His eyebrows were quite bushy, which made the hairs take on a life of their own as he glared.

"You attacked us as we entered the room." Trela walked over to stand next to the seated Aedon.

"There were Tlana about now, weren't there? We'd been attacked on 'n off for nigh a moon. Nothing major mind you, just enough to keep us on edge." His gaze traveled to Trela but settled back on Aedon. "Those were good 'jin and good company. You hired 'em, though I suppose you never actually met 'em."

"I told you we were just defending ourselves." Trela tried glaring at him, but he wasn't looking.

"I don't blame you, little filly. Not really. You were lying on your back, squealing at the ceiling during the fight." He smiled a little but did not take his eyes off of Aedon. "So, how's about you untie me now that you remember we're all friends? I can barely feel my hands."

"Did you find the Stone Shield?" Aedon glared back at him.

"What do I have to do to prove that I ain't tainted?!" He rocked back and forth violently but his chair stayed upright.

"Stick out your tongue." Trela still wasn't sure how long it took to turn black, but if he was tainted, it had to have been a while ago.

"Well, we just met, but if that's what it takes." He dutifully stuck his pink tongue out. He wiggled it around a little and ended with his mouth open. His eyes glanced back and forth between Trela and Aedon. It made him look comical.

Trela realized that he was just not going to be helpful until they had untied him. Willfully so. She glanced over at Feyazki at the window. He merely raised an eyebrow. Bored, but alert. Gyaer still had his mouth open and tongue out. She glanced over to Silvadhin and nodded. Silvadhin took her time before she walked behind him and started sawing at the ropes with her dagger. Trela would have preferred her to untie him to save the rope for later, but she let Silvadhin add her own drama to the situation. The town was abandoned and there were an odd amount of supplies left behind.

Gyaer rubbed his hands and wrists for a little longer than Trela was comfortable with. He glanced at Feyazki more than once. Silvadhin, for her part, stayed behind him, just out of his sight, her dagger held at the ready.

"You were telling us about the Stone Shield." Aedon's eyes never left him.

"You know, you would be quite beautiful if you weren't so obsessed." He smiled. She scowled. He leaned back a little and spread his hands out. "Of course, of course." He took a deep breath and glanced at all of them before beginning. "Vuildan and myself got along great, which is weird considering my history with mages." He smiled at Aedon as if she knew something. She did not blink. "Well, we ended up chatting together more than I did with Evroil and Raghosh or the other warriors, at least until I was trapped with them underground. See, he was always flying with all seven of us. We would pop up in the morning and go for as far as he could get us, then we'd land and rest. Then we would pop up in the noontime, and then land and rest. Then once more before evening. We ended up fashioning a stretcher to try to get some walkin' in during his rest, but that didn't work so good for him. It took us a solid week to get down here. I'm sure that it was faster than riding, but I'm not sure by how much. Anyway, I don't know if it was because we were chatty together or what, but when we arrived here, when we were attacked, well ol' Vuildan and me got shot off in one direction and the other warriors were shot off in another."

"So, you were attacked immediately? You were unable to speak with anyone from Pulthrim?" Trela interrupted him, looking for clarity.

"Don't be daft! Of course, we were unable to talk with anyone. The whole town was already destroyed. Well, not destroyed, but deserted and ransacked. That was the whole reason we were sent over." Gyaer squinted at her.

"Then why did you fly in?" Feyazki perked up.

"What?" Gyaer turned his squint over to him.

"If you knew the town was already destroyed and that there might be enemies there, why would you fly directly in? Wouldn't you want to land outside of the town and sneak your way in?" Trela was not sure, but it seemed that Feyazki was squinting back at Gyaer.

"Ah, yes. Yes, that was truly a monumental mistake, one that I chide myself for. But I place most of the blame for that one at the foot of Raghosh. He was insistent that we come in fast and furious, thumping our chests and the like. I think the rest of us were hoping the area was deserted. I know I was." Gyaer paused for a moment and looked up at the ceiling. "He had a flair for the dramatic, he did. If it makes you feel any better, I chided him about that almost every day that we were trapped. But I, ah… Where was I?"

"You were telling us how Vuildan and yourself were separated from the rest of the group as you arrived." Aedon kept her gaze on him, as if willing him to stay on target.

"Yes, we had a soft landing. I heard that one of the warriors broke her leg and another broke his arm as they crashed. Neither of the wounded made it to nightfall. The other group was attacked soon after landing and had to scatter. Vuildan and myself got attacked as well, though from the stories of Raghosh and Evroil, we were attacked by a smaller force. We didn't realize they would be hostile when we first saw them, they just looked like good 'tin Gaens. Farmers coming to help those who were arriving to help them. Vuildan was able to scorch them when they attacked, and we were able to escape to a nearby farmhouse. We holed up there until dawn. We rested a bit then, maybe a bit too long, before heading out to find the others. It was around noon when we finally met back up with the other three. Therioyle was wounded pretty bad. Vuildan did what he could for him, but he didn't make it. The last of us made it a couple of nights before we finally had to seek shelter underground. Safety in numbers you know. The villagers were pretty agitated down there. They had been hiding out for a week or so already. We heard down there that Jeschet had made it back to Lethos. I, being a Gaen of my word"—here he winked and thumped his chest lightly at the same time— "wanted to head out immediately, to investigate. Vuildan had taken up with a cute young farmer, which made him lose all interest in anything else. So, I gathered Raghosh and Evroil and tried to set out. We were attacked immediately at the entrance to the cave and so hastened a retreat. We tried a couple ah times, and we got attacked in the depths of the cave a couple ah times. We were losing hope. We'd even stopped trying to see Vuildan and the group of 'tin he was protecting. It was… disheartening. To say the least." He glanced between Aedon and Trela. "Then you showed up and murdered the last of my friends."

"So, what you are saying is that we have to circle back to Lethos?" Aedon glanced quickly from Gyaer to Trela.

"Aye, if you still think you are looking for the Stone Shield. There's not a chance we can head back to Serif?" Gyaer looked squarely at Trela. "Even if it was just me alone?"

"No. No, we must all go to Lethos." Gyaer had already looked defeated, so Trela did not feel she was giving out unexpected news or anything.

"What about Vuildan? Would you recognize his body?" Feyazki spoke up again. "There was quite a pile back in the cave system. Maybe his body is amongst them, but maybe not. He may have attempted to escape on his own."

"Good thinking, Feyazki. We should definitely make sure if he is dead or not. He would be a great resource to have if he is still around." Aedon nodded towards him.

"If he was alive, don't you think he'd have already contacted you all?" Gyaer went from looking defeated to looking nervous. There could have been many reasons for him seeming nervous at that moment, but it seemed odd enough that Trela made a mental note of it. She wondered, briefly, if Gyaer was hoping to never see Vuildan again. That was not what mattered at the moment, however.

"Yes, we will get some good rest. We'll go back through the cave system for another round, and we should probably search the village one last time. Then it is off to Lethos." It felt good to be moving towards something definitive.

482

Chapter 16

"You are positive that none of these are Vuildan?" Vrric squinted at Gyaer. Hard. Gyaer would not be deterred in his assuredness, however.

"Nope." Vrric almost interrupted, but Gyaer raised a hand immediately. "Nope, not here. Yep, I am positive."

It was a little frustrating since they had laid all the bodies out for easier identification. Twenty-two dead Gaens in varying states of decay were splayed out on the cave floor, each on their own blanket. A few of the blankets contained the assumed body parts of an individual Gaen, laid out in the proper order. It was not a pretty sight, or smell for that matter. Vrric supposed they would be easier to get out of the caves to bury them separately up above, interred in the soil, so it was not a completely wasted effort.

"You said he was interested in a young farmer. Do you see her body here?" Vrric figured Vuildan would not have escaped without his interest, but he really had no idea what type of derlian Vuildan was.

"His body, not hers. And no, I do not see Wiquen amongst the dead." Gyaer turned away from the scene. "I know it must seem odd to you, you being a Luften and me being a Gaen, but I have to get out of these caves and into the fresh air. I've spent too much time down here."

"Of course, of course. You've been most helpful." Vrric was not completely convinced of how helpful Gyaer had been, but at least they could cross some more items off their list of possibilities. There was something small in the back of Vrric's mind about Gyaer and Vuildan, but he could not place it. Could not even trace the thread back to the source. It was just an odd feeling, a small itch. It certainly would not be solved while he was standing there staring at, but not really seeing, the bodies in front of him.

He waved his hand in the air to the Gaens around him. They then began the unfortunate task of loading the bodies into wheelbarrows, though the blankets certainly helped. They only had two wheelbarrows, so the entire operation would take some time. Vrric had offered to help but was told that the Gaens would rather take care of their own. He wandered back to the three small adjacent rooms. For no particular reason, he started in the same order as before.

The first room was empty but with a copious amount of blood splattered about. He did his best to examine each surface with diligence. He could find nothing out of the ordinary. He tried the second room, which was much more pleasant to search through, but he could not find anything in that room either. The third room, the one that Pylor had been locked in, was clean of blood splatter as well. He looked it over once and did not find anything. He was getting a little frustrated. There had already been others through this room, so he was not really sure what he had thought to find. Maybe he was just not ready to leave the caves, but he did not want to be in the main room with the bodies and their slow extraction. He lay back on the cold hard floor and closed his eyes. He breathed in and out for a while, not really meditating but balancing his energy. He relaxed like that for several minutes.

When he opened his eyes again he thought he saw something on the ceiling, near the corner. It was not a true corner due to the large radius of the fillet, but where the ceiling started to turn down into the wall. It was like a group of scratches. "Lokinderpri!" Vrric floated up to the ceiling. It was not too much taller than he was, less than an additional rod, but he wanted to get a better look.

They were not just scratches but fairly deep grooves that had been gouged out of the rock. He wondered why he had missed them before, but he supposed he had not been looking up very much, and in his defense, from a distance they sort of looked like the chisel marks that all the Gaen caves were covered with. He could not recognize them. They did not appear to be any symbols that he understood. They were almost too random to be artwork or doodles, let alone any type of writing. Out of an overabundance of curiosity, he took out some parchment and meticulously scratched out a copy with magic. "Mekmorfpanto!" He would ink over it later once he was aboveground.

He showed it to several Gaens, thinking it was some form of shorthand. He tried Trela and Ryshial. He figured once they had stopped between the towns of Pulthrim and Lethos he would try some more mages, maybe Arnasta and the Blind One. The final sweep through Pulthrim quite distracted him from this little side task, however.

***

"Feyazki, come quickly!" It was Silvadhin and she was jogging between two buildings towards him.

Vrric picked up his own pace as she slowed hers. Between them they ended up at a fast walk. He was unsure of where they were going or who had sent her, but he had a solid trust in the full members of the coterie. Though Silvadhin was not from Agoge, she was definitely a full member. Since he was suddenly presented with the opportunity, he decided to investigate something that had been circling in his mind for some time.

"How come you've never beaten me up about Trasdou?" He did not mean physically, of course. He meant verbally, mentally, in public, et cetera. He realized, after he had spoken the words, that they could have been somewhat confusing.

"Why would I?" Her breathing was light, as if she were sitting in a chair around a fire, just chatting. He wondered briefly how far she had jogged from.

"Well, if I recall correctly, you upbraided me quite profusely at the time." His crooked smile only lifted half of his mouth.

"Of course. We disagreed. I told you why at the time." She glanced over at him as they turned a corner. "Why would I bring that up again? Is there new evidence? Why are you bringing it up now? Did you think of a new argument?"

"No, not at all. Just…" He thought hard for a moment. Why was he bringing it up? "I guess I just want to say thanks. You really could have stirred up some vexation if you had wanted to. Some would say justifiably so."

"How would that have helped?" They turned a final corner and fast-walked straight towards the remains of a large single-story building. "I saw what I saw and I voiced my complaints at the time. To be honest, it *was* a messed up situation, one that does not have a simple answer. You were correct on that point. Those who were not there would not have added anything constructive to the discussion. They did not, do not, need to be involved. I said my piece and then I was done." She smiled a little as they stopped at the front door. "You're welcome."

Silvadhin raised her hand to knock but the door flew open before she could tilt her wrist. Ryshial was there, standing in the opening, and Vrric thought he could see Aedon talking with someone in the room beyond.

"You were told speed was of the essence." Ryshial was smiling, making the tone of the words incongruous. She stepped aside and waved them in.

"Next time you try to find him. He just wanders about aimlessly." She smiled back and strode through. "He was just standing in the street, staring."

"I was thinking…" Vrric was not sure what he had been doing, really. He had been thinking about the scratches he had found, but that was not an actual task. He had been told, along with all of the others, "to make one last sweep." The vagueness of the order had left him a little aimless, he had to admit to himself.

"That's your main problem, Feyazki. Always thinking." There was something mischievous in Ryshial's brown eyes. "Please, the others are waiting."

Vrric walked through the empty main room towards a cramped room beyond. He supposed it was originally a dining room. There was a large table centrally located that nobody was sitting at. There were empty shelves lining the walls and a dresser-like piece of furniture that Vrric assumed once held and semi-displayed dishes. There were a ring of derlians around the table, orbiting a couple of beer casks. Silvadhin vanished into the room beyond and Ryshial handed him a mug of beer. It looked more like a social occasion than a meeting.

"We've decided to have one more enjoyable evening before traveling to Lethos." Ryshial's laugh was contagious. "We've been trying to get Trela over here, but I doubt that will happen, what with Knill and all."

Rewista and Aedon wandered up to the two of them. It sounded as if they were discussing serious matters, but when they reached Vrric they stopped talking. Aedon nodded seriously to Vrric, shook her empty mug, and then reached over to the table for a refill, before wandering slowly back into the crowd.

"Do you know what I am tired of?" Rewista was talking to Ryshial but looking askance at Vrric.

"No, what?" Ryshial's contagious laugh rang back out.

"Feints and dodges. Really. Why can't someone just take aim and swing?" They both laughed heartily.

"We'll see." Ryshial shook her own empty mug and turned away.

Rewista took a conspiratorial step towards Vrric. She was staring into the kitchen, which made him glance over there, but he could not tell what she was looking at. She elbowed him lightly in the ribs.

"See anything you like?" Her raptor eyes were soft with the beer and her laughter.

"What?" Vrric began to drink deeply from his mug. He was obviously far behind all the others.

He could see a couple of derlians in the kitchen area, all holding mugs of various sizes. As he was taking a quick inventory of them and the room beyond, trying to grasp Rewista's hint, Clerin looked through the doorway over to them. He thought she might have winked, but it was difficult to tell at that distance.

"You were a blacksmith's apprentice, were you not?" Rewista pushed his mug upwards while she talked, so that he had to take another drink or let the beer spill. So he just murmured in acquiescence. "Then a word of advice: strike while the iron is hot. Because if you don't, someone else will." She took a drink of her own mug, her eyes regaining a bit of steely raptor. "Even I might." It was said so quietly that he could have imagined it.

"What?" He understood, but was still confused. Of course, that only made sense to himself.

Rewista gave a quick, exasperated sigh. She grabbed his hand and led him over to the kitchen doorway. They stopped directly in front of Clerin.

"Feyazki has something he wants to say to you." She then promptly disappeared.

"How intriguing…" Clerin's mouth curled up into those cute dimples. They had the instant effect of disorganizing his brain. His mind raced. He almost stammered. What could he say? What was he doing here? He almost cursed Rewista, but took another sip instead.

"You're the most beautiful thing I've ever seen in my life." It just burst out of him, without any forewarning to his mind whatsoever. His mouth just… spoke. Somehow her smile got even larger. He felt he had to follow it with something. Something elegant. But his brain betrayed him further. "Not just of derlians, but of everything, everything I've ever seen. The stars, the moon, trees, horses." *Horses!?!* If he could have curled into a ball on the floor and disintegrated right then and there, he would have.

"Wow, you are really bad at this, aren't you?" Luckily, she laughed. "You would make a horrible Fluen."

"Well, I just... I wasn't really prepared, you see." He stammered while she stared through him with her ice blue eyes. They were like staring into the afterimage of lightning as it hangs there in the air after it's gone. Her large pupils the black sky behind. There were almost twinkling stars hidden in their depths. But he was struck dumb as if hit by actual lightning. All he could do was point in the general direction that Rewista had escaped to.

"That's all right, I'm feeling generous tonight. Why don't you think of something by the time we get outside?" Clerin took his empty mug from him, glancing around looking for reinforcements.

His mind was utterly useless. All he could do was watch her as she moved. It was mesmerizing. She had on a travel-stained shirt, one that had started white but was now a more ecru color with long and somewhat free-flowing sleeves. It was loose at her neck with the ties half undone, but it was tight at her waist as it dove under a wide leather belt to flare out slightly over skintight doe-skin breeches. It was the type of shirt where one could almost see the side of her breast through the neck as she tilted forwards to set their empty mugs on the table. Her knee length boots were also travel stained, flat-footed for comfort and durability. She moved with the grace of a deer, sliding from one keg to another, tapping their wooden torsos to check for fullness, before she topped off their mugs. She may have noticed him watching because rather than turn to hand him his mug, she sauntered out the back door with a delicious swagger. It took all of his willpower to simply break his gaze and follow her out.

Still nothing would come to him. No poetry, no seductive lines, not even anything as tripe as his earlier comments. He could only watch her back as it moved and flexed under her shirt while she walked. Her bottom would lift, tilt, and shimmer as it settled with each step. He was utterly mesmerized. She kept walking, beyond the backyard, towards the tree line of the surrounding woods. There was a silver fir attempting to distract him at the top of a hill, awash in the colors of the dying sun, but it was no match for Clerin's shimmering radiance. She just barely penetrated the trees before stopping and turning.

"What do you got?" She handed him his mug, took a sip of hers, and listed provocatively on one hip.

What *did* he have? Nothing, he had nothing. His mind, useless for this type of ordeal in the best of times, was completely blank. All he could think of was how fantastic she was. Not just physically, though she was, by far, the most beautiful derlian he had ever met, but in all ways. Her dimpled smile, her piercing eyes, the way her head tilted back as she laughed, her... wait, that was still all physical. The way she talked, the way she could see to the center of the problem before he could, her amazing healing skills, the way she could make him laugh. She could make him laugh at any time, even in dangerous situations. He found himself smiling around her even when she wasn't doing anything. It was like he had air bubbles in his blood, lifting him. He felt giddy at times. He felt he could confide in her, that he could tell her stupid things about himself and she wouldn't laugh at him. She was his closest friend. Yes, he just felt comfortable around her, close to her. Like if every time he reached out for her, if she was there, he could stay that way forever. Outstretched. There were a million miniscule things that were perfect, like the stars above that made up the night sky. How does one explain the entire sky by describing the beauty of an individual star?

So he could not speak, could not express himself. He was overwhelmed with his thoughts and emotions such that he was useless. He had nothing. His mind attempted to salvage itself by dreaming up his one skill. Magic. He could show her phantasms that would amaze her, delight her. But which ones? Could not words provide as much amazement and delight? Was not destroying a Tlana with lightning as it held her by the throat amazing? He was a derlian of action. One is what one does when it counts. So he could not think of a fantastic illusion to create for her to show how he felt, the same as he could not just tell her.

He began to feel the crushing weight of the silence. He began to realize how long they had been standing there. Still. He thought he could feel her boredom, her impatience, her disappointment, emanating from her. He had nothing. She took another sip as the glint in her eyes dimmed. He had nothing to lose. He downed half his beer and tossed the mug into the trees. He reached for her face with both hands, as a drowning sailor reaches for the only log in the sea. Her own mug tilted, spilled, and then slipped to the ground. He half pushed himself, half pulled her, into a deep, drowning kiss.

Some things obviously changed. He certainly spent more time with Clerin. They began to share a tent or a room in an abandoned building periodically. But he enjoyed his space and it seemed that she enjoyed hers, so they would set up two tents side-by-side at times. Whenever they were invited anywhere, it was as an assumed combined unit. Warriors clapped him on the back for no reason and standoffish females were more friendly. However, some things that changed were harder to notice. For instance, it took him quite a while to realize that Gyllhelon would no longer come up and talk to him if he was alone. He missed their conversations. Since they had been sporadic to begin with, they were harder to notice when they completely went away. Overall, he was pretty sure he was enjoying his life much more than before.

It did not take long to travel to Lethos. Trela had let them leave Pulthrim late and stopped them about halfway there, along the road near the Yulhpin stream. She kept a large contingent of guards out, rotating often so that almost a third of her coterie held a two-hour shift. It seemed a little excessive, but Vrric did not balk when his turn came. He let Clerin sleep through the night. Splitting the travel time like that had the benefit that they arrived at Lethos around noontime. The sun was high and it would be easy to search through the abandoned buildings and to set up camp. They would still be on high alert again for the night, he was sure. Trela would probably not relax until they had thoroughly searched through the cave system the next day.

Instead of starting at the largest building with the most warriors as usual, Vrric and Clerin decided to search a small house. Just the two of them. They picked a house that was close to the other buildings, but was certainly just a small dwelling. Small enough that they could claim it for themselves after the search. The roof had burned off, so they planned on setting up their tent in the large common room. They would have to try to figure out where the fire started, but it appeared to have mostly consumed the roof and left the lower portions, the stone walls and wooden furniture, charred and scarred, but not consumed. Which was odd, but not too odd. The floor was packed soil, so they did not have to worry about a basement or damaged joists. The walls were still fairly intact, thick stacked stone, and somehow the door was undamaged. The windows were all broken, however, so the door was certainly not a safety feature. More like a privacy feature. Most of the furniture that had not been devoured by the fire had already been rummaged through, so he felt it was unlikely that they would find anything of interest. They would check of course—they were not attempting to shirk their duty—but they were both hoping to not find anything to share with the main group. It would be nice just to enjoy a quiet evening together.

"Mekkinhepclo!" Vrric started by floating the glass shards away. It did not seem too odd that every window had been broken, but it was of interest that they had all been broken inwards and with little other debris. There was not typically a huge percentage of Gaen buildings that they checked that had glass windows anyway. Most of them merely had shutters. He would have guessed that less than a quarter of the houses, of the smaller family dwellings, had glass windows. But when they did have them, and when the majority were broken, the glass was often split between laying outside of the building and inside. Sometimes it was obvious that someone had broken the glass to escape from the building and, therefore, the glass was outside. Much of the time an object, such as a rock, had been tossed through the window, scattering the glass inside. He had not completed his investigation, but there did not seem to be rocks or bricks or any other typical implement to shatter glass laying around. Still… nothing really unusual. It was odd, but not too odd.

The house had a few other things going for it as well. The fireplace was fairly intact and had some iron cooking utensils that had survived the fire. There was a small cauldron and a swing-arm that could shift the cauldron in and out of the flames. There were other kitchen items that survived as well, pewter plates and wooden spoons were still on display in the dining area. The kitchen seemed to have avoided the most damaging effects of the fire.

It took about two hours to completely clean out and rummage through the house. The bedroom was the most damaged and they piled a fair amount of debris in there. As hoped for, nothing of significant interest was found. No strange notes or orphaned keys. They had their tent set up and a small cooking fire warming up the fireplace before anyone stopped by.

It started with a loud banging on the door. There were a couple of incoherent statements bellowed in a deep voice, followed quickly by some giggling. By the time Vrric had gotten to the door he had figured out it was Torpalin and Escha.

"I can't believe you have a door, this is fantastic!" Torpalin turned sideways to enter through the narrow door. He clapped Vrric on the shoulder as he walked past.

"Sorry, he insisted that we make an entrance." Escha shook Vrric's hand vigorously as she walked past.

They sat and got comfortable before chatting. They spoke of nothing for a few minutes before Clerin suddenly asked Torpalin, "How did you get so big and strong?"

"It's from all those years of bodyguarding, right?" Escha nudged him lightly with her elbow.

"No, I've already told everyone about my bodyguarding days, they don't want to hear about that again." Torpalin turned from Escha towards the others. "First of all, my father was a large guy, so some of this is natural." He lifted his arms and flexed his enormous biceps briefly. They were like cantaloupes sticking up and stretching his skin. "But what I really wanted to be as a child was a baker, like my father. He always wanted me to be a warrior. 'You'll never meet anyone important as a baker,' he used to say. He wanted me to be surrounded by royalty and great leaders from the guild branches. His bakery was on the ground due to the weight and heat of the ovens. I remember it being such a gigantic kitchen. He had six clay brick ovens running at all times, and these were not small ovens."

He paused for a moment and tilted his head slightly as he looked at Vrric. "You certainly know the difference between Groundborn and Airborn, all Luftens do." Vrric nodded silently, his eyes narrowing slightly. Torpalin then turned his gaze to Clerin. "Well, no one wants to be Groundborn, certainly not my father. And even more than that, he did not want his son to be Groundborn. Since it was too late for that, I think he then decided to make sure his grandson was Airborn." He laughed to himself a little wryly.

"So, he was always trying to teach me to fight. To be a vanquisher of bullies when I was young." He smiled over to Escha. "It didn't work at first, not really. I still just wanted to be a baker. I was good at it, don't get me wrong. You have to get good at something you practice constantly, at least eventually, right? But I kept begging him to let me help him in his shop. So, once he felt I was old enough, he brought me into the bakery. But did he teach me to cook? Not at first, no. He had me bringing wood in for the ovens. Chopping wood for the ovens. Unloading the gigantic sacks of flour from the mill wagons. Carrying water back and forth. Anything to make me stronger, to make me bigger. When I complained that he wasn't teaching me his trade at all, that I was just a pack animal to him, he finally showed me how knead the dough, which is a workout all of its own, ha! He also kept up my sparring and warrior training, of course. Eventually, I began to like that as well, especially since he made baking as obnoxious as he could. I really was just manual labor to him at the bakery. He never did show me the secrets of the yeast, never let me create my own sourdough starter. No, the only way to make him proud, to put a big stupid grin on his face, was to win some fighting competition. I loved my father and wanted to see him proud of me, so I became the best warrior I could, practicing in between chores. My younger sister ended up taking over the bakery and I ended up working for Hulgert and Vanelia. My father never appeared prouder, more choked up, than when I brought them down to his shop. They were incredibly kind to stop by for some scones, just to appease me, just to make him happy. He never forgot that. 'You see where your muscles have gotten you?' I remember him saying that more than once. 'I gave those to you. Without me pushing you all the time, you would have given up.' And maybe I would have. Who knows?"

"Is your sister still running the bakery in Ariellyna?" Clerin's warm smile placed a grin on Torpalin.

"Yes, she is. Or at least, she was when we left for the well."

"Then we'll have to get some scones once we make it back there."

"She'd like that." Torpalin paused for a quick moment. "But really, *I'd* like that."

There was a longer pause. Vrric felt he should probably tell a story, something about being Groundborn maybe, and was still trying to think of something when Clerin turned to Escha. "You've got to have some stories. I never get to hear yours." Her smile beamed infectiously.

"Well, it's not as if I don't have any stories, it's just that I don't like talking about myself." Her shoulder gave a small involuntary twitch and she looked down slightly.

"That's all right, just tell a story about others." Torpalin smiled widely. "How about one of your hunting stories." He glanced over to Clerin and Vrric. "She's the most amazing hunter, of course, and used to lead King Hulgert's expeditions into the woods outside of Ariellyna. Remember that one…"

"So who is going to be telling the story?" Clerin was grinning at his enthusiasm, but interrupted just the same. He held his hands up in surrender and comically squished his lips shut.

"You didn't happen to be there when Hulgert fell from his horse, did you?" Vrric had not even thought about that before. They had traveled so long together, he assumed he had already heard everyone's good stories. But there were those talkative derlians who'd tell you everything all the time, there were those in the middle who'd bring up a good story when it was relevant, and then there were those who never spoke at all and you had to forcibly drag their stories out of them. Escha was in the latter group.

"Yes, but not the time you're thinking of. I would have told you that gossip after we left the Luften Temple if I had been with Hulgert during the fateful picnic before his incapacitation." Escha smiled softly towards the ground.

"Would you have?" Clerin got a small good-natured jab in.

"It was in the early winter, after the rut. Hulgert liked to hunt stags, the bigger the racks the better." Escha ignored Clerin's jab. "The problem with mature bucks is that they don't always bed near food sources, not like a doe or young buck. The one I was tracking had bedded himself on a ridge. There was no way to get close, just no way. Hulgert was getting impatient, he was always on a tight schedule, and kept threatening to just bring in a pack of hounds to flush the buck out. I told him I'd find the trail from bed to water source and, if not, then I'd let him use the hounds."

"He didn't want to flush it out with magic?" Vrric grinned as he spoke, knowing he was being a bit ridiculous.

"Where's the sport in that?" Escha looked genuinely aghast. "Why don't you just float the buck down and hold it splayed out in front of your bow?"

"Where's the sport in a pack of dogs?" He knew it was not comparable but could not help bringing it up.

"Well, that was what *I* was arguing against. I had tried to find the water path the buck was taking but was having a difficult time. The buck seemed nocturnal. Eventually, impatience won out and, as you say, sport was thrown to the wind along with all caution." She did glance up and smile at Vrric, showing she was not bothered by his interruptions. "The hounds were brought out in force and other hunters were there on horseback to help with any corralling required. Chiavel was there, though not being a hunter, I kind of assumed he was only there to be close to Hulgert, rather than for the stag itself. He had a way of inserting himself next to power. Hoping to siphon some of it for himself, if you ask me."

Vrric kind of liked Chiavel, but Escha's description did not bother him. Chiavel oozed ambition, it was true. If one were to walk up to him and say that to him, he would probably even agree. There was something honest about his naked hunger for power.

"Hmmph. He always did think he was better than everyone else, except when he was sucking up to the king." Torpalin's disparaging thought caught Vrric off guard. Not so much what he was saying about Chiavel, but because Torpalin rarely disparaged anyone.

"Well, he did come from a royal branch. The Branch of Largon, was it not?" Clerin's interjection caught Vrric off guard even more than Torpalin's. Before Torpalin could respond, however, Escha pressed on with her story.

"So we were scattered about, most of the hunters were in a wide semi-circle. I was in the middle, attempting to find more spoor, and Hulgert was following me on his horse, Old Red, and Chiavel was following Hulgert. The hounds were all around, waiting to be told which scent to pick up on. We were approaching what had to be the stag's water source. Once I felt comfortable with the beginning of the trail, up towards the stag's bed, I thought I'd turn them loose. I remember it was in the morning, long after dawn but long before noon as well. We crept forwards for a bit, heading uphill a little. Then, from out of nowhere, there was this big 'crack!' sound. I remember it distinctly, though I'm not fully positive of which direction it came from. I think from in front of us. Then the hounds started a chorus of chaotic barking and running in different directions. I glance behind me and I look past Hulgert and see Chiavel back there. It looks like he is casting something, seriously. Suddenly, Old Red rears up and Hulgert goes tumbling to the ground. No worse for the wear, mind you, nothing broken, but angry at his horse, yelling at the hounds. He was definitely worked up, maybe not scared, but maybe a little worried."

"Do you really think Chiavel was casting something? Something to make the horse spook?" Vrric wondered about the various implications. Quite a low level spell could be cast to cause a derlian's death if it was done through an intermediary, especially through an animal. He had never thought of that. There were, of course, other more sinister implications as well.

"I can see it in my mind right now. His eyes mostly shut, his lips moving, his fingers waving slightly. I'm unable to sense magic, but I'd been around Chiavel enough times when he'd use magic that I feel fairly comfortable with saying he could have been casting something." Escha almost answered the question.

"Well, that is certainly some juicy gossip you failed to mention." Clerin laughed, then they all laughed.

It was still late afternoon and Vrric had a hard time telling if they were there on a purely social basis or not. After about fifteen minutes, however, he found out.

"So, have you looked for the lid?" Torpalin suddenly switched topics and pointed upwards.

"I don't... The roof seems to have burned off." Clerin seemed taken off guard by his sudden shift.

"You'd think that, wouldn't you? Apparently, several of the other buildings have their half-burned roofs tossed about a hundred rods away. Like they were blown off." He pointed a thick thumb towards the trees, beyond the stone walls. "Have you looked around the outside much?"

"No, no. We've just been making it cozy in here." Clerin's smile was infectious.

"Well, we should check it out. If yours is the same, the privy council will want your opinion. Even if not, they'll probably want you to see the other houses." Escha spoke up with her eyes looking serious, but she was smiling warmly at Clerin. "Oddly enough, none of the larger buildings have the same roof issue. It seems to be just the smaller houses." She nodded to herself and a small unconscious twitch went up her left cheek.

Sure enough, barely visible through the trees now that they were looking for it, the charred lumber of the roof lay off in the distance. All four of them set out for a closer look. It took some effort to weave through the firs, but they were soon staring at the upturned roof. It was misshapen and broken, burnt and splintered, but it was definitely the roof from the house that Vrric and Clerin had staked out as their own.

"It seems to be all here." Clerin was walking the opposite way around it than Vrric. "Like it was lifted in one piece and only broke apart due to the impact of hitting the ground here. Doesn't it?"

Vrric had to agree that was what it looked like. But he was still walking around it, staring at it, examining it, even smelling it. Some of the collar-ties were intact, attempting to keep the V-shape of the now inverted gable. Most of it, however, was just shattered and splintered wood, collapsed piles of misery. It made him wonder if objects felt pain at being unable to perform their original task, at their loss of utility, loss of purpose. He shook his head to clear it, but then realized that Clerin was watching him, waiting for his response.

"Yes, completely, I agree." He did not want to give the wrong impression.

"How many others?" Clerin's voice went up in pitch just slightly at the end of the sentence.

"Four." Escha held up four fingers to illustrate.

"Making this one five…" Clerin's voice dropped in volume as her eyes scanned the roof debris in front of them.

"Are they all the same distance from the house? The same direction?" It just seemed so odd to Vrric. Not impossible, not unfathomable, just… weird.

"Umm, well all of the roofs are in the nearby trees. So, not the same direction per se, but the same direction away from the roads, if you can call these roads. The same direction to keep them less noticeable. As for distance, I have no idea." Escha started walking over to where Clerin was poking around while she was absentmindedly speaking with him.

"How about the window glass? I only noticed it in passing earlier, but… is all the window glass broken outwards or inwards?" He had kind of stopped and was staring at nothing, just the blur of the ground in front of him. Trying to think. If there had been equal pressure in the house, enough to tear the roof off, it would make sense that all the glass would be outside, not inside. But if the roof was torn off so quickly that the air was pulled off with it… or if the air in the house was used to push upwards on the roof… but what of the fire…? Nothing made sense to him. He could not bring it all into line.

"How about we get you to see the other houses, the other roofs?" Torpalin was hovering around the perimeter of the roof. Not really investigating, but more like staying out of the way.

"Wait, Feyazki, come here." Escha was waving him over.

Clerin was crouched down near the peak of the gable, now a valley, at the far edge of the overturned roof. Escha was standing over her, not looking at him. They were both looking intently at something out of his view.

"Lokinderpri!" Vrric decided to just hop over there, rather than taking ten minutes traversing the broken tree branches.

It was hard to see. There was a small hole in the half-broken roof, that much was readily visible. But there was something beyond that. There was something liquid on the ground that the roof was over. Black and shiny. He only thought it was liquid by the way the limited light bounced off of it when he shifted his head back and forth. It shimmered in its blackness.

"Lomorflufrepi!" A small sphere of burning air lit the area. He floated it towards the hole but off to one side so he could still see directly. Clerin and Escha were leaning over and craning their necks along with Vrric. He could tell by their gasps that they saw exactly what he did. The black fluid coalesced, thickened slightly, then shot off out of view. It all happened in less than a second but he was sure of what he saw.

"That was liquid, wasn't it? That wasn't smoke." Escha was backpedaling somewhat gracefully, staring at the roof and the ground. She finally stopped a rod or so away from the edge of the roof.

Clerin turned and jumped off, jogging a little past Escha. Vrric floated himself off the roof. He felt an odd sensation of fear. Like awakening to a large spider on your pillow when you are a child. It was not a rational fear. It was otherworldly.

"Lift it, lift the roof. We need to see under there. We need to see where it went." Clerin was still backing away a little. Her right arm outstretched, pointing a quivering finger at the roof, her left hand half covered her mouth.

"Do you know how heavy that is?" It just popped out of his mouth, unbidden.

"I don't care. Find it." She was looking around at her own feet.

Her attitude was insidiously seeping into Vrric. His own fear was increasing with each passing moment. Escha was standing her ground, but she had her arms crossed over chest tightly, almost hugging herself. Her eyes were on the ground as well, staring at the edge of the roof, waiting for the liquid to come pouring out. Torpalin had his axe in his hands on the other side of the roof.

"What are we all doing?" He had not seen anything, had not been paying attention. But he was now. Vrric could see the tight grip he had on his weapon's handle.

"We just saw something, honey. Nothing to worry about, but come over here." Escha pointed off to the side. "The long way around, come over here." She went back to hugging herself. Torpalin began to teeter through the broken tree limbs and underbrush on his way over. She had pointed to the higher side of the ground, maybe assuming the liquid would run downhill. "It wasn't smoke, was it?" She turned towards Vrric.

"Just lift the roof. Please. Just find it so we can see what it was. What if it was nothing? What if it was just a dark pool, or an animal, or what if we just imagined it?" Clerin had stopped retreating, but was probably a rod behind Vrric and Escha. "Just find it."

"What if it was smoke?" Escha turned back to glance at Clerin. There was something weird in her glance.

Torpalin slipped as he was coming around the roof. Not enough to fall, but enough to leave him standing for a moment with his arms out to maintain his balance.

"Narkinpanarc!" Vrric tried to lift the piecemeal roof smoothly, but ended up just flipping the whole thing over.

There it was. It was probably more smoke than liquid. But a smoke of solid dots, like black and silent bees, swarming together. It reared itself up into a shadow, a silhouette, of a derlian. Vrric had never seen so much smoke in one place. It was typically a physical Tlana, made corporeal with Vijen leaves, or there was just a little bit of smoke escaping into or out of a derlian host. His mind was reeling. He had never seen smoke shape itself. He had not known it was even possible. There was even still some daylight out. Clerin screamed behind him.

"Eqedepiarc!" He could think of nothing but attack. The fire spell came quickly and easily to him, shooting a horizontal column whose diameter was approximately as large as Torpalin's head. But the fire seemed to shoot straight through the smoke without damaging it at all. It was like a hole in the smoke appeared just as the fire reached it. The trees behind the smoke, those caught in the column's swath, burst into flames. The smoke shape, the shade, turned towards Torpalin and rushed him. Its shape faded slightly as it fled, becoming more amorphic with wispy tendrils flailing about it.

Vrric felt a little light-headed. He had just cast a fairly powerful spell and it had done absolutely nothing to the non-corporeal Tlana.

"Surdeelearc!" He poured everything he had into that one bolt of lightning. The Tlana had just passed Torpalin before it was struck. The lightning seemed to shimmer and flash between each dot, each black bee, and it seemed to push them farther apart, to separate them with each ricochet. It all happened so quickly, but he was able to see how it bounced and split between the constituent parts quite clearly. It was burned into his mind for that tiny fraction of a second, as if time had stopped and allowed him the luxury of uninterrupted observation. The smoke burst into a shapeless cloud and dissipated, like breath on a cold morning. Torpalin leapt, or was thrown, off to one side. Vrric was hopeful that the lightning had not touched him but was unable to tell.

He knew that it would be a long time before he could cast another spell like that, and that the Tlana could easily circle back around if it were able and inclined to do so. He half leaned on a tree, teetering on his knees. Feeling the scratchy bark against his skin was somewhat soothing. The roughness on his cheek at least brought his mind around to his physical body. Eventually. He was not even sure if he could stand.

He could hear Escha trying to get Torpalin up. It sounded faint and echoey, like at the end of a long hallway. He smiled to himself as she gently cajoled Torpalin wondering, from down the long hallway of his mind, if Torpalin had escaped unscathed. Suddenly Clerin was tugging on his own arm.

"We have to leave." She was quite physically strong, actually. Others assumed she was weak since she was not as bulky or obviously muscular as most of the warriors, but they did not know her like he did. And she was not only strong, but tenacious as well. "We have to go, get up! Nuliderto!" A refreshing wave washed over Vrric.

After a small amount of cajoling, both Vrric and Torpalin got up and staggered back to the road. They held onto each other like a couple of drunks at the apex of an evening. Clerin was in front, yelling something at someone, while Escha was on the other side of Torpalin, assisting in the meandering stagger. The thought of the sight of them gave Vrric pause for concern. He knew why he was useless, but he was unsure as to the extent of Torpalin's injuries.

"Why can't you walk?" He had meant to say something more poignant. He had meant to voice concern over casting his lightning so close, to make sure he had not caused the stagger that afflicted Torpalin. But his speech seemed to suffer from the same ersatz drunkenness that his legs did.

"It touched me." It was faint, ever so faint. If Vrric's head had not been hanging near Torpalin's at the time, he might have missed it. There was a certain resignation to the statement. A certain capitulation. He had never heard Torpalin's voice sound so defeated. It sent a chill down his spine.

Suddenly they were surrounded by too many derlians. The voices were all familiar but the faces were a blur. They were separated and carried swiftly to various corners of the little village.

He was laid down somewhere soft. Clerin cast another healing spell, and he began to feel better but was still too tired to move. The sweat dried on his brow. He kept still for several minutes, consciously breathing, relaxing, resting. He no longer felt ill, but he was hesitant to sit up. He knew that once he sat up, the race, the struggle, would be back on. He took another selfishly gratifying moment before righting himself and opening his eyes.

Clerin was there, of course. So were half a dozen others. He wondered briefly if more time had passed than he had supposed during his rest. But looking around the room it appeared that it had already been set up, that the others had already been there when he had been brought in, he just hadn't noticed them.

"Clerin explained how useless the fire spell was." Trela immediately sat in a chair opposite the couch he was laying on. "Do you think it was the power level, the skill level? Or do you think they really are immune to fire spells?"

"It certainly wasn't the power level, but I don't know if they are immune. It was not like it was hit directly and the fire was absorbed or deflected or anything. It was more like it dodged it." Vrric wondered if he should explain exactly what he saw, but he was interrupted.

"But the lightning worked…"

"But the sun was still up, wasn't it…"

"But fire has worked in the past, hasn't it? Hasn't it…"

"But there was no corporeal body, only smoke…"

"But Torpalin was grazed..."

Vrric was unable to tell who was speaking which part of what sentence. They all ran together in his dazed and tired mind. It was not until Torpalin was mentioned that his head cleared.

"Is Torpalin all right?" He tried to stand but was waved back down. It was just as well. He doubted he could have stood right then anyway.

"We are doing what we can. Really, you both just arrived, there is still a red glow at the edge of the sky. We have him with Nochiel at the makeshift infirmary." Trela was leaning forwards slightly, her forearms on her knees. "If anyone can help him, it's her."

"What we really need from you is whether or not you think fire will work on a Tlana. That will make a huge difference. That will make all the difference. We will not survive if all of our other mages are useless against them." This came from Aedon.

"How would I know?" Vrric glanced between the myriad of faces leaning towards him. "Personally, I am not going to try fire again. But what does that mean for all the other mages? Does that mean they should all just not try? Does that mean I have to be in every single expedition? None of this is appetizing to me. The problem is that we run into them so rarely that it is difficult to try different tactics, especially while under heavy attack. We need a way to experiment or else we are just guessing blindly."

"Haven't the other mages attacked a Tlana before? Is this the first time a mage has shot fire at them? Is it the first time that you have?" Estfale's glare bounded around the room until if fell upon Ryshial. Vrric decided to interrupt.

"I had never even seen the smoke in that form before. This may have been a unique configuration of events."

"No. No, I have not attempted to throw fire at a Tlana. But... I think that Serghno has. At the Forgotten Junction, maybe?" Ryshial went ahead and responded to Estfale even as Vrric offered her an exit.

"Well, we should get him over here." Estfale pressed his advantage.

"What do we do now that nightfall is upon us?" Zira spoke up.

"That is what we are trying to find out. Is there one mage who can help, or are there several? I think that is the real question. The only one." He had stood and waved his arms at his last sentence.

Vrric was not used to seeing Estfale agitated. He was never as calm as Malghain, especially where Trela's safety was concerned, but he was not typically that dramatic either. It made Vrric briefly wonder where Malghain was.

"We've only seen the one fully formed Tlana. Or at least I have." Ryshial was glaring at Estfale. "We have generally dealt with them in smoke form, attacking derlian minds. With that, a warrior is about as helpful as a mage, whether or not the mage can cast lightning. These are all things we should know." She held up a hand to ward off Estfale's response. "I am not arguing against speaking with Serghno about this. And I truly hope he has helpful information. But what I am arguing against is this sudden panic, this sudden loss of confidence. If we can no longer use Serghno, or myself, to assist the warriors as they comb through the caverns and search the towns, then we should head back to Agoge. We cannot only use Feyazki."

"I am not suggesting we turn tail and run, just that we investigate the new evidence. Fire may not work against the Tlana." Estfale turned his gaze to Trela.

"It is not any evidence, new or not, that concerns me. It is the new form of Tlana that I find troubling. Has anyone heard of the smoke being so prolific that it can take on a derlian form, a Shade?" Trela looked at the mute audience, one by one. "I share Estfale's concern, and I do wish to speak with Serghno further about the Forgotten Junction, but I cannot shake that we are getting close to the volcano's edge here. I can feel the heat on my face as much as the dread in my heart. The closer we get to the Cabal, the more defiant, the more brazen, our enemies will become. We must find a way to spend the night safely, and then we must enter the cave system tomorrow. We must find Vuildan or, even better, Jeschet and the Stone Shield. We must find the Cabal and we must destroy it. There is no other alternative. Yesterday was easier than today, and it will only get worse. Each day from here on in. Much, much worse."

The night passed without anything out of the ordinary happening. Lethos was quiet for all. Serghno did arrive and filled everyone in on his failed attempts at destroying the Tlana with fire at the Forgotten Junction. That did not mean much to Vrric. The circumstances were much different, with the Tlana being fully corporeal, and besides, Vrric only got his spell off due to the amazing amount of distraction that the Tlana had been under. Maybe Estfale was right, but maybe not. Vrric tended to agree with Trela. It was the realization that the smoke form of the Tlana could be that dense, that copious, that coherent, that was most worrisome. There were other, somewhat random, thoughts as well, *Had it been lying in wait for them? Would the sunlight have affected it if it had not been so diffused by the trees? Was Torpalin okay?* But mainly Vrric relaxed and let the others argue. He was tired, even with the myriad healing spells cast upon him. What he really needed was rest, so he stole it when he could. The next day would take a lot of energy, that he was sure of.

After half-listening to the arguments for a while, he got up to leave. To head back to his quiet tent with Clerin and get cozy, to fully rest. Of course, Trela insisted that he sleep closer to the center of the town, just in case they were attacked. They ended up sleeping just upstairs. They got a small room with a comfortable bed and attempted to sleep through all the commotion downstairs. He was quite worried about it, and honestly, it took him some time to fall asleep. But once he was there, he went deep for a long time. He woke up feeling quite refreshed with the scent of breakfast teasing his nose until his eyes realized how bright the room was.

Clerin was quietly eating at a small wooden table near the bed. He was sure that it was the smell that woke him, not any noise. He rolled around for a minute before deciding to finally get up. Once she realized he was conscious she brought his food over to him. He did not normally like to eat in bed, especially not a rope strung bed, but figured he could manage it the once. Besides, if he made a mess, he could just leave it for someone else. He pushed the pillows behind his back and attempted to sit up to eat. That necessitated that he hold the metal plate just below his mouth—precisely why he did not enjoy the experience. It made him feel like he was just shoveling eggs into his maw.

Clerin was about finished and mainly sat at the edge of the bed, letting him shovel in peace. Most derlians, or at least Vrric himself, slouched while sitting on a sloping, too cushy surface. Clerin, however, kept her spine straight while allowing her plate to stay on her lap, a league away from her mouth. It consistently amazed him how she always had proper posture, like a boat on calm seas, with its mast plumb against gravity. It did not matter what surface she was sitting on either. She kept a rigid and plumb mast even while riding a horse. It seemed to take too much effort for Vrric to achieve such serenity. The only time he had a straight spine was during meditation. Currently he was half crouched over his plate, eating like a starved dog. He was sure he would have snapped at her hand if she had tried to move his food away. *Must have been that royal upbringing,* he thought without a trace of annoyance or jealously. Just pure admiration—her grace was an ever-flowing continuum.

They were soon at the entrance to the caves of Lethos. Almost every member of Trela's coterie was there, armed to the teeth. She left a few guards up above, just enough to notice an intruder or raise the alarm if attacked. The rest were bristling with anticipation. It was a little before noon, leaving plenty of time to investigate the caves and still exit into sunlight. It was at the entrance that she laid out her plans.

"We are going to move as a unit. At each cross-path, I'll leave a guard contingent that will be reabsorbed once the main group travels back through the area. If ever any of you feel that I am leaving too few at a cross-path or that there are not enough of us in the exploratory group, let me know. I do not want anyone to feel vulnerable or left behind. I assume we will be attacked today, as Torpalin was yesterday. Whether in smoke, corporeal, or even Shade form, we must expect an attack. An all-out assault. We are as close to our goal here as we ever have been. Be on high alert, all of you." Trela nodded back to those warriors nodding to her. "We are looking for several things beyond survival. We are looking for a Gaen mage named Vuildan, who may or may not be here. He was traveling with Gyaer, hired by the Blind One and known to Aedon, and he may now be traveling with a young Gaen farmer named Wiquen. Gyaer would be the only one to recognize the farmer. Our main goal here is to find a Gaen named Jeschet. He knows of the Cabal and it is very important that he is taken alive. Of utmost importance. Finally, if we are able to, there may be a Stone Shield to be found within these caves. Aedon?"

"I have only met Jeschet once, and he kept his identity hidden as much as he was able. But here goes." Aedon took Trela's place at the head of the group, in front of the cave entrance. "He is tall for a Gaen and of a medium build. Somewhat like a skinnier Tesjuk." There were a couple of small laughs from the captive audience. "He had brown curly hair, though only a little peeked out from his hood. He had a piece of cloth over the lower half of his face and his eyes were somewhat hidden, but his eyebrows were wild and bushy. Like large black spiders." Another small chuckle rippled through the warriors. "His hands were heavily calloused, his fingernails were bitten very short, and he had a large scar on the back of his left hand. It started at the confluence of these two fingers and extended back under his sleeve." She held up her left hand and drew the location of the scar on it with her right. "He had no visible weapons and nondescript clothing. I guess he had some nice leather boots on." Aedon's brow furrowed for a moment of concentration, then relaxed. "That is all I can do. It was very dark in the pub when we conversed."

"Did he drink?" Vrric was unsure of who asked the question, someone in the middle of the crowd.

"Yes, yes. We each had one mug of beer." She nodded almost imperceptibly while talking.

"What did his voice sound like? At least in general terms. High and squeaky? Low and gravelly?" Another anonymous question.

"Low, but more raspy than gravelly." She peered about into the crowd for another question, but was met with silence.

"Gyaer, do you have anything to add?" Trela turned towards him, making everyone in the group look at him as well.

"Nothing helpful. I never saw him. When we talked with those who had seen him, really seen him, without a cowl or in a shadowed bar or whatever, they all had the same different thing to say about him." He paused while everyone stared and tried to figure out what he was talking about. When he realized no one was going to prompt him, he continued. "His eyes, not his eyebrows mind you, but his eyes were always described as hypnotic. Piercing. Luminescent." He paused again with his hands open wide near the sides of his face. Again, no one prompted him. "But they all gave a different color. Some said blue, some said green, some brown, every natural color there is. One even told me hazel. What color is hazel supposed to be?"

"Thank you, Gyaer, that's very helpful." Trela started to kind of shoo him back into the crowd.

"What about the scar on his left hand?" Aedon perked up before he was swallowed by the other warriors.

"Oh, that was still there. They mentioned that, his curly hair, his height. All the other stuff, which is why I assumed they weren't lying to me. But I never figured out the eyes."

"What color was his tongue?" Trela raised an eyebrow as she asked her question.

"Oh, that again? No, no one mentioned that. No one would mention that. Who notices someone's tongue while they're talking with them?" He stepped back into the group.

"Are there any further questions?" She scanned the crowd quickly but they all stayed silent. "Then let us enter." She clambered down the rest of the hillside to enter into the cave.

Estfale went quickly after her and then Vrric, who cast a light spell even though they did not quite need one yet. The others filed in behind them. The entrance was quite wide, and the hall eventually narrowed until only four could walk abreast. Vrric liked the openness of it, though he knew it would not last. The hall finally opened into a large room. Vrric always thought of these as a Great Hall, there was typically a large table surrounded by chairs in the first room of the cave systems. There were typically at least three doors, wood with cast iron banding, that led out of the room and deeper into the cave system. Oftentimes there was a large fireplace, sometimes two. It was comforting to see the similar layouts. Like they could know they were in the right place. It was in that first room that Trela stopped again.

She began to separate out a small but strong group to leave there, at the largest cross-paths. It was at that moment that Vrric realized Torpalin was not with them. He found Escha and sidled over to her. She was at the edge, her back resting against a stone wall, arms crossed in front of her, watching Vrric as he walked towards her.

"Where's Torpalin?" He swept a vague hand towards the room and then leaned back against the wall next to her.

"He's with Knill and Pylor." She kept her eyes on the mass of derlians in front of her. They jumped back and forth to random warriors, but did not alight on Vrric. "I think Nochiel is trying to be helpful, or something."

"Oh, so he's not feeling well?" He meant it as a statement, as in he understood what she was saying, but it came out like a question.

"He'll be fine, don't worry about it. He's as strong as an ox." She barely touched his elbow with some outstretched fingers and she gave him a small side-glance. "Thanks for noticing, or asking, or whatever, but I'd prefer not to talk about it." Her fingers shrunk back into the crook of her elbow and her eyes went back to eternally scanning the crowd.

"Of course." He wanted to say something more. He wanted to be helpful. But he knew that when she said she didn't want to talk about it, she really meant she didn't want to think about it. And she was doing just that, standing there and thinking about it. But she did not appear to want to engage in useless small talk to distract herself, either. Try as he might, he could not think of anything to say which would not make her think of what she was already thinking about. At least not without being annoying or sounding inane. He wondered if she would prefer to stay behind, there in the Great Hall, or would prefer to be with the lead group, scouting. The latter would probably distract her the best, but maybe not. He thought about asking her but she was steadfastly ignoring him. It did not seem that she was annoyed, but he felt she was close. He decided it was best to just walk away. So he did.

It seemed that Trela was leaving a larger group in the Great Hall than he had thought. Almost half her warriors were suddenly making themselves comfortable. Some sat at the table, some on the hard stone floor, while others stood around and either looked menacing or chatted amongst themselves. Most of the sitters pulled out weapons to sharpen, or oil, or whatever. To Vrric, warriors always seemed to be doing something with their weapons.

"Looks like we'll be traveling together." Malghain had walked up to him as he had been staring vacantly at the bustle of the room.

"What?" He had been caught unawares.

"Trela's orders." Malghain pointed vaguely behind him. "Or are you saying you would prefer to walk alone?"

"No, no, of course not." And he fully meant it. "I just… wasn't paying attention."

"That's why I'm here." He gave Vrric a quick smile. "Besides, getting to walk with you means I won't miss any of the action."

"Or is it the other way around?" They both started heading towards the door that Trela was opening. Vrric often wondered how she could be so concerned about everyone but herself. He saw that Serghno was nearby and Estfale shadowed her even when she expressly forbade him to, but she always seemed to hand out bodyguards to others while putting herself at the front lines of the battle. He guessed that was part of her charm.

Vrric and Malghain were allowed to sift towards the front. They were still about six derlians back by the time they were walking through the tunnel behind the door. The tunnel was fairly wide, they could have fit three in a row, but it was quite comfortable with just the two of them.

They walked in silence for a while, tense with anticipation. They reached a cross-path, and Trela chose who and how many would stay behind. Repeat. Finally, after about four cross-paths, though Vrric was admittedly not paying complete attention and could have been slightly off in his count, they were down to eight. Trela, Estfale and Dartsyle, Vrric and Malghain, Serghno, Jalin, and Escha. Escha did not always make it that far, so he wondered if Trela was trying to keep her busy or keep an eye on her. Or maybe it was just a coincidence.

Suddenly the path widened back out—it had gotten narrow enough that they had been walking single file. It turned a corner and bulbed out to a terminus with three doors. Trela placed a silent finger to her lips and motioned Jalin to the door to their right. Jalin nodded, kneeled down, and got to work. Once the lock was picked, she moved back to the back of the group. Estfale got his shoulder to the door while all the others stared hard at him. He threw it open and Trela was the first in, followed quickly by Dartsyle. The room, as far as Vrric could tell by looking between shoulders, was vacant. Estfale and Serghno piled into the empty room as the other two doors burst open.

Malghain leaped forwards and stabbed a Gaen in the chest. Escha slashed the air in front of an exposed neck, only missing because its owner leaned back so far that he fell over. A knife from Jalin spun between Malghain and Vrric, finding another target. Vrric himself only paused in the shock of it for a moment.

"Eqedepiclo!" About seven Gaens in the back burst into flames. Trela's warriors in the empty room did their best to turn back to assist. There were several attacking Gaens in front of him, but his eye caught a Gaen in the back. It just stood there, not on fire, and stared at Vrric. It struck him as odd, both the stance and the stare. *That must be a mage*, thought Vrric. He had decided to cast something specific at the mage, to neutralize him or at least test him out, when he got stabbed.

The pain was excruciating. It was in his gut, not really at his skin, where he felt the pain. He remembered thinking that was odd, thinking that the outside of him should be in more pain than the inside. Malghain quickly decapitated the Gaen warrior who had been grinning in victory as Vrric fell back with the momentum of the stabbing. He curled up on the floor and tried to think. Should he heal himself and then pull out the weapon, or should he remove the obstruction before attempting any healing? It was a bit moot since he was unsure if he could even speak.

"So sorry, so sorry." Malghain was almost chanting as he took the handle of the sword and extracted it. He was unsure if Malghain was apologizing for letting him get stabbed or for the pain caused by removing the steel. To be honest, he did not even care and would not have even thought about it if time had not slowed to a crawl. He attempted to shift his focus as far away from his guts as possible.

Malghain pulled the sword out perfectly straight, relieving any further injury. He quickly cast a healing spell. The fight was over fairly quickly, though it seemed to take an incredibly long time to Vrric. Serghno was soon next to him, casting another healing spell. Vrric could only recall bits and pieces later. The Gaen mage, the sword, Malghain's apologies, Serghno's healing, Trela screaming at Malghain, Dartsyle wrapping makeshift bandages around him, the feeling of floating as Serghno levitated him, the cave walls flying by overhead as he was run back to the main room, back outside, back to the headquarters building, to Nochiel.

Vrric was unsure of how long he had lain there. Was it an hour, a day, a week? He had certainly been asleep for a while. He did not have a headache or dizziness, even if he moved his head too quickly. He could tell, without moving, that he would be unable to move his torso. There was a tightness stretched over a soreness, though he was not feeling any real pain. He glanced at his fresh-looking bandages. He glanced at the curtained windows. He attempted to get the lay of the land, but the beds near him were empty. Judging by the orangish glow behind the curtain, he guessed it was either dawn or dusk. He hoped that he had only been asleep for a few hours, rather than a few days.

It took a while before he got bored enough to try to holler. Though he did not really get a yell out, he made enough noise that Nochiel finally came wandering up some stairs. Not that he could see any stairs, but the way the sound of her footsteps echoed upwards made him think he was on an upper floor. Her leisurely but almost methodical steps slowly brought her from behind the bed and into his view.

"So, the master magician wakes." There was something odd in her voice and in her smile. Something... annoyed?

"Only thanks to the greatest healer in Trela's warpack." He smiled up at her, attempting to head off any issues, even if there were no issues.

"Greatest healer in all of the Pyran realm." She smiled back down at him.

"Let's just run with greatest healer." He lightly patted his bandaged belly. Truly, there was no discomfort at all.

"We don't have to go that far, but I thank you." She paused for the briefest moment. "The Gaen mage they found in the caves will only talk to you, apparently. He, along with Trela, figure you to be the greatest mage, without a quantifier." Her smile seemed sweet and genuine, which was quite relieving, but it also made him wonder if he had been mistaken at the beginning.

"It is odd how most derlians appreciate death more than life." The thought to explain how much better of a healer she was than he flashed through his mind, but he did not want to overdo it. He was already walking a fine line.

"Too true." She was somewhat ignoring him, running her hands over his bandages, squinting as if she could see through them. She kind of hummed tunelessly to herself while she felt around. "Eqeliderto!" It was like he was dunked into a cool pool. It was a refreshing feeling, not a cold one. "A little excessive I know, but you should not have to worry about your injuries as you argue death with strangers." She tilted her head slightly, her short brown hair moving in unison. "And with friends." Her smile stayed sweet as she patted his shoulder. "Trela will be waiting at the bottom of the stairs for you. Probably Malghain as well. He was incredibly apologetic, go easy on him. The wound was not grievous, and I'll make sure you are none worse for the wear." She stood back and rubbed her hands lightly together.

"Thank you. Sincerely." Vrric swung his legs out of bed, happy to realize he still had his trousers on. He stood up gingerly but had not needed to. He really did feel great. "I think I feel better now than before the stabbing."

"Ha! Don't worry, that will fade with time." She started to wander off as he started to wander towards the stairs.

He wondered where his shirt ended up. *Probably ruined,* he thought. And then he began to wonder where he could find another one. It was not too cold, and the bandages covered most of his torso, but he felt a little naked. Even though he felt great, he took great caution as he descended the stairs. Trela was there at the bottom as Nochiel promised, waiting somewhat patiently.

"Vuildan will only talk to you." She spoke before he hit the bottom stair. "Which is weird because the Blind One hired him and he traveled with Gyaer for over a moon. I even offered him Aedon to talk with." He finally reached the floor. "Nope, nothing. No one but you."

"It's good to see you as well." He smiled at her as Malghain approached.

"You've been out for over a day. It is sunset again and he will not even eat." She shifted her stance while complaining to him so that Malghain could be in front of him.

"I have failed in my duty to you. I..." Malghain was going to continue, Vrric could tell. He was going to go on and on about honor and failure and shame and punishment and on and on. He could sense it and did not have the stomach for it.

"Phthhp! Are you crazy? There were like eight of them and they all rushed us at once. I'm not helpless and I failed to protect myself. Even Trela was looking the other way when I got skewered." Vrric interrupted him immediately and tried to wave away his hard feelings, his self-loathing. If Vrric had been out for over a day as Trela stated, then Malghain must have been raking himself over the coals about it. Trela's scowl at his bringing her into it made Vrric smile.

"But I..." He was attempting to not be deterred.

"No. Seriously. I can't have it, I won't have it. We are friends and we were both trying our best. I'm not going to waste my time worrying on it like a dog with a bone and I would appreciate it if you did not either. In fact, the best thing you can do for me is to ignore it and be yourself again. Swallow it. That will be your punishment. Not mentioning it again can be how you flagellate yourself over whatever it is that you think you've done. I fully forgive you for everything." Vrric smiled and clapped Malghain on his shoulder. "Really, I just need you to keep being you."

"Of course." And his smile held nothing but good humor in it.

Vrric was not quite sure if he was being cruel or not, but at the moment, he was unable to dwell upon it. Besides, if there was a derlian alive who could take any cruelty, it was Malghain.

"Come, let me take you to Vuildan." Trela, still scowling slightly, turned towards the front door.

Vrric smiled again and clapped Malghain's shoulder again. Malghain handed him a rough linen shirt that he had not noticed earlier. He tried to don it himself but had a hard time getting it over his head. Malghain helped him put it on after watching the struggle for half a second. Just long enough to not assume Vrric needed help, even though that was obvious.

"Thanks." It was half muffled in the shirt.

"Of course." Then he turned to the stairs.

Vrric walked after Trela, his boots sounding hollow on the wooden porch and then crunching along the gravel. Even though he was unable to dress himself, his stomach felt great. He knew he should be careful not to overexert himself even though he was feeling good, so he consciously walked slowly, keeping his stride in check.

"It would have been better if you had let him apologize." Trela did not look back.

"Would it have?" They traveled the rest of the way in silence, which was fine with Vrric.

They cut through the town, into another building and up the stairs. There, bound and gagged, was the Gaen mage Vrric had seen in the caves. His eyes smiled when he saw Vrric and Trela, but it was hard to tell what his mouth was doing. Serghno had his chair leaned up against the wall and looked languid and lazy, as if he had just woken up when he heard them climb the stairs. He righted his chair and stood.

"I've ungagged him and tried to get him to talk every hour as you asked. I received nothing for my efforts, though we had some lovely one-sided conversations." He nodded to Trela as he started to head down.

Trela walked over and untied Vuildan's gag. "Are you going to cooperate?" She glared at him and toyed lightly with a dagger in her hand. Vrric was not sure if she was threatening him or if she was just fidgeting.

"Is that the one who has destroyed Tlana?" He nodded towards Vrric. "The one who casts lightning?"

"Yes, as I promised. He was brought here right when he woke up." Trela glanced over to Vrric. "He hasn't even eaten."

"I only have a minute, do not untie me. Mage come back!" He yelled down towards the stairs and then looked wildly at Vrric. Then he turned towards Trela. "Jeschet is in the Fluen realm, near the ocean, near Vatlisi. The Cabal is nearby." He turned his crazed gaze back to Vrric. He held out his tongue; it was inky black. Serghno had just come back up the stairs but then leaned backwards, almost tumbling down the stairs, when he saw Vuildan with his tongue out.

"Why do you think fire doesn't work?" Vuildan's eyes were too large and wobbled around as he spoke.

"Umm, the Tlana are immune to fire?" Vrric was not sure where he was going with his question.

"No. No!" He rocked his chair slightly. "They are immune to damage. They cannot be hurt, you see. They are immune to pain. They feel nothing, which is part of the problem, but that is for another conversation. How do you destroy nothingness?"

"Fill it with something?" Trela added her opinion.

"No, but you are getting close. Nothingness needs a vessel, does it not?" He nodded his head way too vigorously. "The vessel must be shattered. But what if the vessel is also immune to damage? Ha! Why do you think they use Vijen leaves? The leaves are also invincible, though they rot almost immediately once removed."

"If the Tlana is immune and the leaves are immune, how come lightning works?" Serghno's question was a bit plaintive.

"No idea. None. That was why I wanted to speak with you, but I do not have the time to satisfy my curiosity. I have something else that has worked, albeit only temporarily." His eyes bounced between the three of them constantly. "Wind, yes wind! It came to me once I realized they used leaves. Blow them apart, from the inside out. Scatter the leaves, scatter the smoke!" He made a weird, half-strangled sound.

"How did you find out about the Tlana being made of leaves?" Vrric could not quite wrap his mind around that, but

Vuildan had been hunting the Cabal and had been trapped and surrounded by Tlana in both Pulthrim and Lethos.

He rocked violently back and forth on his chair. His eyes bulged in their sockets as they kept glancing between the three of them. His mouth was clenched and his lips quivered. He appeared on the verge of a seizure. "I…" His lips peeled back but his teeth were still held tight. "I… can't." His chair fell sideways and he went crashing to the ground. "Kill me…" It was so faint that Vrric was not positive he heard it. Then… "Surdepiclo!"

They were engulfed in flames, all of them. When Vrric heard the "Sur" he started to cast a shield spell. But luckily, Serghno had started to cast one just before that. Vrric wondered, a little later, whether or not Serghno could sense magic like Croy seemed to be able to. Between the two spells, they got away with singed hair and clothing. Trela had immediately pounced on the Gaen and thrust her dagger under his throat, up into his brain stem.

It all happened so incredibly fast that they held their positions in stasis for a while. Vrric's own muscles were so taught that he was not even sure that he *could* move. His eyes darted around, however, looking for the smoke. He was terrified of watching that drift towards someone, or into someone, or into him. He did not see any smoke at all, try as he might. Maybe it was the double shield spell. Maybe there was very little of it. Maybe it escaped, trying not to be blown apart by a magical wind.

Eventually Trela stood. Serghno then shifted his stance. It all allowed Vrric to relax himself slightly. The shields were still up and he had seen no sign of smoke, but he was still tense and nervous. If a loud noise had occurred, if someone would have yelled at that moment, he would have probably shot lightning through them without a second thought, without a first one. Eventually Trela began to laugh. Nothing crazy sounding, just a low chuckle to let the tension out.

"Whoo, wow. I'm a… I'm glad that both of you were here for that." She stared down at the dead Gaen. "That one took me by surprise."

Serghno just stared down, thinking. Trela wiped her blade on the dead Gaen's clothing before sheathing it. Vrric kept looking around the room for smoke.

"We could probably drop the shields now." He was not really in a hurry, but as long as they were standing there together, he felt like he should keep an eye out for the smoke.

"How do you think he gained his knowledge?" Serghno was still staring downwards.

"Like... knowledge of the Cabal... the Tlana?" Trela asked just to spur him to speak further.

"Yes. The Tlana. How do you think he knew so much?" He would not look at either of them.

"I wondered that earlier, but he had been following Jeschet. He had been attacked by Tlana." Vrric felt a little foolish that he had let the subject drop so quickly in his head.

"But we only figured that after fighting them. After beating them." His brow furrowed a little.

"Well, didn't Aedon talk to a Vijen that mentioned that? Something about the Tlana trying to trick them into dropping their leaves or something? Maybe she mentioned that to him, or to the Blind One, who then told him?" Trela's brow furrowed soon after Serghno's.

"Maybe... Maybe." Serghno looked up at them. "But what if, and I am just completely guessing here, what if there was something else. What if, when a Tlana enters a derlian and takes control, what if the derlian gains some knowledge about the Tlana? Like if their minds must meld to gain control, then maybe there is some transfer of thought that happens in both directions, not just the one."

"No, I was attacked by a Tlana like that. I felt nothing of its thoughts besides it wanting to destroy me, to destroy what makes me me." Trela shook her head slightly.

"But the attack didn't work, now did it. The Tlana was rebuffed, there was no melding." While Serghno was talking the idea occurred to Vrric.

"What about Knill? He was controlled for some time before we were able to help him." He was not sure if Serghno was leading the conversation there or not, but he had to speak once the idea popped into his head.

"Hmmm. Pylor mentioned something about the taint lasting. I've just been so busy..." Her eyes were on the dead Gaen in front of them but her mind appeared to be with Knill. "You would think he would have said something, though. You would think he would mention being able to see into the Tlana's mind as it was peering into his."

"Well, maybe Vuildan was an incredible mage. He had enough willpower to assert control over himself. I have yet to see any derlian speak so lucidly while being possessed." Vrric thought for a moment. "Well, speak lucidly about something the Tlana would not want them to say."

"Maybe the Tlana did want Vuildan to say those things." Trela looked between them both. "What if fire does work and it was just trying to get us to abandon that."

"I don't know. That part seemed genuine." Serghno stared at Vrric for a moment. "And maybe Vuildan was able to see things that others were not privy to. I don't know that either. But maybe one of us should chat with someone who has experienced this from the other side." He waved his hand slightly towards Vuildan.

"All right, all right." Trela threw her hands up.

"You do not typically take this much prodding." He smiled at her.

"Well, Knill is not going to like it. *That* much I know." She smiled ruefully.

Trela, Vrric, Serghno, Aedon, Ryshial, the Blind One, and Escha all met with Knill, Pylor, and Torpalin. It was seven against three, and that was how the room was laid out. The three to be questioned were on a comfortable couch pushed up against a wall. The seven were in individual chairs opposite the couch. Vrric had begged Trela, *begged her*, to have fewer questioners. He thought that Serghno, Ryshial, and the Blind One were not required at all. He doubted Aedon or even his own necessity. Escha was just there because Torpalin was there, everyone knew that. Torpalin was there because he felt odd after the brush with the Tlana smoke, Pylor was there because he was odd, and Knill was there to be grilled. Vrric had suggested that they just have a couple of derlians talking to Knill alone, maybe even just Trela at first. She had not liked that idea, however. She thought that having several of them might jar different memories, might make them explain themselves more clearly, if not to her, then to someone who had a similar experience. She thought they might feel safer amongst each other, that they would not allow anyone to question the others too vigorously. That it would somehow keep some sort of balance. He remained unconvinced.

Knill looked so unutterably unhappy that it pained Vrric to look at him. Torpalin had a desperate look on his face, so Vrric avoided him as well. He just looked at Pylor while the silence weighed on the group. The child, for his part, just stared dead straight back at Vrric. He did not even seem to blink. It was eerie. Just the soft brown eyes of a doe staring holes into you, daring you to loose your arrow in an attempt to make them lose their life. There was a… struggle there, a conflict that Vrric did not want to be involved in. So he blinked, he looked to the side, he looked down, he capitulated, and often. Mainly, he did not want to stare at the others. Mainly, he did not want to be there.

"We are here to attempt to understand what you, any of you, felt while being controlled, or touched, or anything, by a Tlana." Trela was smiling and glanced between the three on the couch, giving each a similar duration and weight. Knill just stared back at her, only her, with his arms crossed aggressively. Vrric could not recall seeing Knill look aggressive before. He was sure it had to have happened at some time, but no specific instance came to mind.

Nothing. Silence. Silence, like a wet blanket, smothered the room. Radiating anger from Knill, twitchy eyes from Torpalin looking plaintively at Escha, and Pylor's unnerving stare. It was already a disaster, and the worst part was that Vrric knew it would be a disaster and he had shown up anyway.

"Pylor, you mentioned a constant feeling of oil in your mouth? Afterwards?" Trela tried to zone in on the middle participant.

"Yes. Rancid oil." He did not look at Trela while he talked, only at Vrric. "I can feel it now."

"This is stupid. Who cares how we feel now? You want to know something about Tlana, something you didn't before. Well, I can't help you. I don't know anything about them. I was not conscious while being controlled. Well, I was conscious but paralyzed. I felt nothing, purely nothing. How does nothing help you? How does lining us up against a wall help you? We are, what, supposed to feel so grateful to be interrogated that we think up something that we didn't tell you earlier?" Knill's face got a dark cloud over it while he was speaking. He was livid. "We don't know anything about being attacked or controlled. That is like asking a sheep to describe a wolf by the feel of its bite. It's stupid."

"Well, I agree with the rancid oil part." Torpalin raised a finger and then trailed off.

"So, you were conscious of it." The Blind One spoke up. "Was it a compulsion? As in, did you feel that you just had to do something, so you did it? Or was it like you were being controlled? Like that you would try to not move your arm, push your muscles against it as hard as you could, exert your mind against it, but your arm moved in front of you anyway?"

More silence. Finally, "It was like I wasn't there. Like I was watching someone else. And watching someone I did not care about, doing things that did not matter to others I cared even less about. It was neither of your two options. It was a non-state." Knill sounded defeated.

"But... did you know it was you doing it?" Aedon's voice was gentle and caring, but she asked defining questions anyway. "I mean, it just *felt* like someone else, correct?"

"Yes. It was Knill doing it. It was Knill walking across the floor, Knill being tied to a chair. Knill lying to Trela and Feyazki." Knill's chest was half-collapsed. He was no longer staring at Trela, but was staring at the floor. "I knew, somewhere, that I was supposed to be Knill. I had all these memories of myself, lurking in the back. The derlian who was acting was Knill, and I had a sense that I was Knill, but really, I was just watching someone else go through motions. It was like I was sitting on this couch, all alone, here in Lethos, tired but not sleepy, and somehow I could see, from the vantage point of the very eyes of another, like I was tiny and standing in another's skull, Knill there in Pulthrim. He was facing with Trasdou, he was talking to Trasdou, he was openly lying about his situation." He closed his eyes for a moment, his voice was low and emotionless. "It was like that spyglass that Feyazki enchanted while Escha was spying on Iventorn. I was seeing it like that. I was far, far away. I was surrounded by quiet and stillness even though everything around Knill was loud and frenetic." He stopped, opened his eyes, and breathed out slowly.

"That is what I like less than the rancid oil. The feeling of knowing that I am me, but of no longer feeling it. I no longer feel far, far away, sitting in another village, like I did that night. I no longer feel that I am tiny and in another's skull. When I wish to move my arm, I move my arm. But I have forgotten how to forget to act and just be myself. I think, 'I should eat now so that I do not perish,' not 'I feel hungry.' I feel the sun on my face and think, 'that should be pleasing, I should smile.' And, oddly enough, it still is pleasing. I do like it. There is just some sort of leap I need to perform now, from cause to response, that I did not have to do before. I did not think about it before. I don't want to wonder if I am normal. I don't want to have to think. I just want to enjoy being myself. I just want to be." He waved his hands around in front of him. Not violently, but it was unexpected, so Vrric and the others tensed up. His voice stayed the same, however. "It is like I am waiting to wake up. It is like I am watching an illusion of life played out before me, and others ask me about which illusion will pop up next and… I just don't care. It doesn't matter, it's all fake. Why even waste the time guessing at the illusion? I just… I just want to wake up. I want to feel like myself again. I just want to be me."

They all sat in silence for a moment. Vrric had no idea of what to think, let alone what to say. In fact, he was proud not to have said anything at all. The Blind One shifted slightly in his chair, took a small breath, and lifted an arm.

"Nope, that's it. I'm done." Knill stood and started to leave. "I told you I didn't want to talk about it." The Blind One's hand slowly lowered as the sound of Knill's heels diminished into the distance.

"Let me just say that I experienced nothing like that." Torpalin stood as well. "In fact, I feel bad for saying that I experienced anything at all. Whatever I went through pales in comparison." Escha left with him.

To be honest, Vrric was never sure why Torpalin had volunteered anyway. He was certainly shook up when they were walking back from the encounter. He was certainly attacked in some way, he certainly felt tainted. But, as far as Vrric knew, he had not been controlled. The meeting, apparently, was what he needed to free himself from the concerns that he had about himself. At least someone gained something from it.

All eyes then shifted to Pylor. Who, for whatever reason, was still staring blankly at Vrric. Vrric, for his part, did not want to break his silence now. At least with the others gone he was able to stare to the side of Pylor, rather than down at his feet.

"Well, we have not heard your story yet." The Blind One sallied forth.

"That is not why I came here." He stood as well. "I have told Jalin my story, you can ask her."

The others left with the slow gait of the dejected. Soon it was just Trela and Vrric sitting in silence. For some reason he did not feel like leaving. After some time had passed it got back to being comfortable again. They each just stared at the empty couch. Finally, Trela spoke up.

"Go ahead and say it, I know you are dying to." She sounded more depressed than angry. "Fiasco. *Fiasco.* Fia*sco.* Fia*s*co. Feeassscohe." She emphasized different syllables and then ended by drawling the word out languidly.

"It could have been worse."

"Ha! No, there's no use trying to walk it back now. Just say it and gloat."

"Well, what were you hoping to accomplish? I guess I never understood that."

"You were there when Serghno suggested it. It sounded great at the time, didn't it? Where is he anyway? I should demote him."

"I'm not sure that *this* was what he was suggesting." Vrric's hand waved towards the couch.

"Plus, I wanted Knill to finally burst. He festers like no other."

"In that case, you can call this a success."

"Thanks for trying to make me feel better." She finally glanced away from the couch, but it was away from him as well. "But, no. This, in no way, could be categorized as a success."

"Feeassscohe." He drawled the word out as she had earlier, but it didn't seem that funny. He stood and swung his arms back and forth for a moment in a caricature of stretching. "We should be heading out. Want some company walking back to your quarters?"

"No, I think I'd prefer to fester here for a while." She smiled weakly over at him. "I foresee a rough night ahead of me." She spoke in a haughty voice and waved her fingers in front of her, mocking the charlatans at the bazaar of the Blaze. It seemed like such a long time ago that they were resting peaceably at Agoge, with nothing to do but wander the maze of city streets.

"I'm sure he'll come around soon."

"Only if he can be himself again."

It took them a couple of days before they packed themselves back up and headed out. Trela took her time on the road, allowing everyone leisurely breakfasts and stopping to set up camp well before the sun went down. It was almost another week before they started skirting the border of the Fluen realm. It was lush all around, so it was difficult to say exactly where the border was. They had not run across a town of any size since Lethos, but they were not really trying to. Vrric assumed Trela was tired of searching through cave systems, waiting for Tlana to pounce. He certainly was.

As they were setting up camp Escha noticed smoke off in the distance. It had been so long since they had encountered other derlians, especially above ground, that the discovery rippled through the coterie with a wave of curiosity.

Vrric flew over Trela, Estfale, and Serghno to investigate. It was not far, so they could have walked, but Trela wanted to reach the fire before nightfall. She decided to bring warriors rather than diplomats, just in case.

The smoke was not prolific, certainly from only one fire, it was amazing that Escha had spotted it at all. As they got closer to the campsite Vrric realized there was no easy way to sneak up on it. There were no visible roads, no nearby clearings other than the one the smoke was emanating from.

Trela motioned for the decent and Vrric obliged. Serghno glanced around for a moment before casting a shield spell, "Narteclufclo!" Though it may not have been required, the feeling of something solid under his feet made Vrric feel better. They landed near the fire and kept a lookout for any derlians. He stepped off the shield and turned in a circle, peering into the trees. There was a small tent off to one side that used to be white. The slow and smooth color gradation went through several shades of beige, from the darkest at the bottom to the lightest at the top. Estfale cupped his hands to his mouth and let out a fairly sizeable, "Hello!"

Vrric was still turning, expecting to see something crash through the underbrush, when the tent flap opened and out stumbled a nondescript middle-aged derlian. But he was not completely nondescript. Surely, he was homely and had the physical features of one who could easily be lost in a crowd. He did not seem perturbed, even at being intruded on by four dangerous looking derlians. At least, some of the four looked dangerous. His black curly hair had some wisps of gray in it, his facial hair was trimmed short enough to be considered intentional, and his clothing was well worn and stained but did not look vagabondish. No, everything looked nondescript except for where he was. He was definitely a Luften in the Gaen realm! Or at least as far into the Fluen realm as possible. Vrric was still not positive of where the exact border was.

"I am being called Voyt." He smiled at each and gave a tiny bow. The verbiage was odd, but the emphasis only clouded the verbiage. Vrric turned the words over in his mind. Was that *a being* called or just *being* called? He was not sure.

Trela walked straight up to the Luften and held out her right hand. "I am Trela, pleased to meet you." The Luften took a moment staring at her hand before he clasped her forearm and shook vigorously. "What brings you here?"

"I am living!" What struck Vrric most about Voyt was how happy he looked. He had a constant smile on his face, and he nodded a lot while he spoke in his short, clipped sentences.

"You are a long way from home." Vrric wanted to shake his hand as well, though he was not sure why. There was just such a positive energy that emanated from him.

"Yes, yes. You speak a great truth." Voyt nodded to Vrric and held out his hand.

Chapter 17

Clerin was excited to finally be at the border to the Fluen realm. Or at least near it. Or maybe they had already passed it, it was difficult to tell. She was definitely as close to her home as she had been in well over a cycle, since she had last traveled with Wil. She had no say on where they were headed—she never did—so she had resigned herself to merely follow at this point. They were headed towards doom in her opinion, and there was nothing she could say that would deter anyone. So she just held on to a silent hope of being able to see the Fluen realm before that doom happened. Even just to be able to smell the sea again. At least she had Vrric.

Clerin had been spending as much time as she could with Wil, which meant that she was spending less time with Taglo, even though she was technically the carrier, the summoner, for both. But there were times when Taglo specifically sought her out. This time it was traveling with Trela, which might have meant that Trela was seeking her out, but she knew which was cause and which was effect.

"We need to speak in private." It was Trela who spoke.

Taglo was tiny and inconspicuous, but Clerin knew it was with Trela because she had been carrying Elange's stone around her neck. The warmth carried through the cloth and into her chest the nearer that Trela got. There were times, especially when more than one Yaven was speaking with her, that the stone became too hot to wear. She would typically just toss the necklace into a leather pouch at that point. The stone was a fantastic boon to her; being able to sense Yavens without them knowing, before they were ready to reveal themselves to her, was incredibly helpful. Though she doubted she would ever see Elange again, she was prepared to thank him profusely for his gift. Embarrassingly profusely.

"Where does Taglo wish to speak with me?" Clerin sounded bored, even to her own ears. She smiled a little inwardly when Trela narrowed her eyes at her.

"Just… come with me." Trela turned hard and walked towards the tree line, away from the scattered tents of their encampment.

They went well within the trees, then through the trees and through some yellow-flowered gorse bushes, and finally into a tiny clearing before they stopped. It was more of a cross between a meandering path and a game trail than a true clearing. Taglo leapt from Trela, whether from her hand or pouch or belt Clerin could not have been sure since it had started so small. All she knew was that it was suddenly growing in size right in front of her. Its heatless fire looked odd surrounded by dry undergrowth, not igniting anything. She wondered if it took Taglo energy or concentration not to set anything on fire.

"You are correct that Taglo wishes to speak with you." Trela did not necessarily look annoyed at Clerin, but she did not look happy either. Clerin wondered if it was Taglo that was causing her grief. Or, maybe, Knill. Clerin had heard about the fiasco from Vrric.

"Yes, it is I who has requested this audience." Taglo did not stop growing until it was a good head taller than Clerin. "We are getting closer to the Cabal and must fill in some missing pieces."

Clerin thought hard for a moment. "You want a Luften Yaven to be summoned?"

"Yes, exactly. And we would like the summoning to happen soon, before we fully enter the Fluen realm. We would like any residual void spoor to have dissipated before we get much closer." Taglo looked like an oversized warrior. She was not sure if it was supposed to appear intimidating. If it was, it was not working. In fact, it had a bit of the opposite effect.

"Why is it so important to have Yavens with us? It is widely known that none of you have ever been helpful around the evil birds. I'm not even sure if you have been around an evil bird." Clerin crossed her arms and stared Taglo, who started increasing in size as soon as she started talking. It was soon taller than Clerin and Trela put together. She had thrown in the word "evil" in front of "bird" to better indicate a Tlana while speaking with a Yaven. They had not been attacked by one for a while, and though not overly superstitious, Clerin avoided the word when things were peaceful.

"We need a full contingent of Yavens to obliterate the Cabal. That is why we are here. That is our only purpose." Bits of non-igniting flame shot off the Yaven in small angry bursts.

"So that is a 'no' on the birds?" She had to crane her neck to look at up Taglo's head, but that did not deter her. "All the Yavens we have summoned will only fight derlians? No offence, but we could probably manage that on our own. It is the birds that…"

Taglo interrupted her by engulfing her. There was still no heat, she felt no burning pain, but a brightness seared through her eyes and directly into her brain. It was like staring into the sun. No, it was like staring into a thousand suns. She clasped her hands uselessly over her squeezed-shut eyes. Nothing blocked out the blinding light. She dropped to her knees, she tried to bury her face in her thighs, anything to reduce the light. She was in the fetal position, sure that her vision would be useless for the rest of her life, when it suddenly stopped. She had not realized that she was screaming until the light went away. It was an odd sensation, that light could drown out sound. She coughed once and peeked around her legs. Trela was also on the ground as well, peeking around, though Clerin did not think she had been screaming.

"I must apologize." Taglo was back to a normal-sized warrior outline. "You are actually correct. Yavens may not interact with the evil birds, as you call them. But make no mistake, we are not here for them. We are here to destroy all of the Cabal, every derlian who has ever helped them, every derlian who knows any of their secrets. We must do that, we *must!*" Though bits of non-igniting flame still shuffled about in a rough halo around Taglo's body, they did not have the annoyed energy they did before. "You must understand; once we destroy the Cabal, the birds will fade back to their typical energy level. These things are linked and though we can help with but one part of the equation, it is the most important part. It is the cause *and* the catalyst. We will not abandon you to the birds. It is just that we must help with that particular issue indirectly."

"I should not have pried so." Clerin offered her own apology, though it was a bit weak and not very heartfelt. She stood and dusted herself off, though a bit absentmindedly and insufficiently.

"No, you have every right. This should have been explained to you from the beginning. I, like many other Yavens before me, am somewhat proud of my capacities. Therefore, there is something akin to shame in me that I am unable to help with one of the more vexing issues that you face. I had, foolishly, thought to avoid the subject all together." Taglo was now slightly smaller than Clerin. "There is more than the request of summoning the Luften Yaven, however. In the midst of the argument I fear I had forgotten the reason I had pulled you aside."

"Of course." She waved it on.

"I need you to unsummon me and then resummon me." It had shrunk to the size of Trela. "The resummoning should be first thing tomorrow morning."

Clerin could think of no reason to refuse. It did not really matter—Taglo should be quite easily summoned with its eagerness and their familiarity at this point—but it was a little confusing. She wanted to ask questions, to pry. That was the only reason she hesitated, the swallowing back of her curiosity.

"Of course." There was nothing else to say, so she repeated herself.

Her mind was not on the conversation, however. She was desperately trying to recall how to unsummon a Yaven. She could see Olwinn, her old magic teacher, in her mind telling her that it was the same word to unsummon as it was to summon. But that did not quite make sense. She wanted to say the word backwards or something. What if she bound Taglo to this realm even stronger, rather than releasing it? However, many spells, with somewhat different effects, used the same word but the caster's mind was used to steer them. She thought of healing a burn versus healing a cut. The both used the same word, but the images in one's mind could direct the flow. At least they were both healing, however. Summoning and unsummoning seemed like complete opposites. They were complete opposites by their very definition. She kept imaging Olwinn, trying to get him to say something different or at least provide a further clue, but she had not actually summoned anything with him. The first being she ever summoned was Taglo itself. She had no experience with that sort of thing, and Trela and Taglo seemed to emanate impatience as the silence stretched. She wished Vrric was with her. He would know what to say to her, how to explain what needed to be held in her mind as she spoke the word.

"As you know, you are the first Yaven I have summoned. So, of course, you will be the first that I unsummon as well." She decided to come clean, but the nervous laughter that accompanied her statement happened by accident.

"Ah, that explains it." Taglo was half her size at this point. She briefly wondered if it would be easier for her to unsummon if it were tiny, but then decided it should not make a difference. So it probably wouldn't. "No offence, Communicator, but your summoning was incredibly weak to begin with." It held up a hand to divert her response. "I only say this because you should not worry how powerful or perfect you may cast your spell. I will assist in the unsummoning with all of my strength reserves, just as I had assisted your summoning. You will not even have to say my name this time."

That did make her feel better. Much better. She smiled and nodded to no one in particular. She just had to recall what the word for summoning was.

"Meksidpiarc!" It came to her in a flash and just rolled off of her tongue. Taglo shrunk into nothing and disappeared.

"Well, that solves that." Trela nodded approvingly.

Clerin wandered about for a while before she found Vrric. He was with Malghain, Haswyxe, and the odd new member of Trela's coterie, Voyt. He was relaxing with Luftens. At least Gyllhelon wasn't there as well.

Clerin did not know what to make of Voyt. He seemed fine for sure, but that was part of the issue. She could not get over the fact that he just appeared out of nowhere and everyone seemed to accept him. He was a Luften in the Gaen realm! That alone should ring alarm bells. And Voyt himself did not have any type of convincing story of why he was there. He just woke up there? No explanation, no recollection of travel, no plan to visit the realm on the opposite side of the world. That was the worst story she had ever heard. In fact, it was not even a story. That was not all, though. It was not just that Voyt woke up in the opposite realm, but that he did not have a good idea of what he did before that. The answer was always just one word: farming. Clerin had never met a farmer who could not explain reaping and sowing, milking and slaughtering, feeding and caring and animal husbandry. Voyt was a blank slate, a non-entity. Voyt's story was not just built on nothing; Voyt himself seemed to be built on nothing. If the Cabal, or whoever, was trying to plant a spy in their midst, just having someone show up and start traveling with them seemed to be the easiest solution. Vrric had argued that the obviousness of it, the weirdness of it, was what made him think Voyt was not a spy. That was because he immediately took a liking to Voyt and was willing to accept whatever non-story was handed to him. Clerin, admittedly, did not take an immediate liking to Voyt—that was part of Vrric's argument against her.

Elange's stone got warmer the closer she approached the group. She was not sure which Yaven was hiding where, but she slipped the stone into her leather pouch so it would not keep bothering her. She wished it grew warm around Tlana or something more useful.

"Clerin, come, visit." Vrric stood and walked over to her just so he could walk her the couple of paces back to the group. Sometimes he acted like a Fluen. It was cute.

They talked about useless things for a while. No one seemed to notice that Voyt would not speak fondly of the Luften realm as the others did. He did not mention Ariellyna, or Queen Vanelia; he did not even mention Helioarc trees by himself. Clerin, for herself, kept mostly quiet and let the conversation roam free of rein.

Eventually she began to get a little bored and the others a little restless. She estimated that they were getting close to disbanding for supper and there was something she still wanted to bring up.

"So, I learned some juicy gossip today." She grinned as they all perked back up. "The Yavens will definitely not help us with the evil birds. We are on our own."

Haswyxe cursed just as Malghain said, "I knew it!" Vrric laughed and shook his head. It was Voyt's reaction that she had been looking for, just to see if he would react dramatically, but he did very little. His brow furrowed and stuck that way. His hand slowly went up to touch his mouth and rub his cheek and chin. He looked down for a long moment.

"What a... What exactly are these evil birds?" He squinted between them amongst the uncomfortable silence. Clerin thought he did not understand the nomenclature, that he did not know they were speaking of Tlana. It made her experiment difficult.

"They are what we are fighting. They infest us. They kill us." Vrric looked at Voyt askance.

"They are evil, pure and simple. Coalesced evil." Haswyxe looked more serious than typical.

"They are noncorporeal. They are smoke." Malghain chimed in as well. Voyt snapped his fingers towards Malghain.

"Closer. Closest." He then snapped his fingers in front of himself. Staring oddly intently at them. "When I ask 'exactly,' I wonder what are they made of. How do they exist? How does their essence exist?"

"Well... When I say smoke, that is just because that is what they appear to be to me. In their most basic form." Malghain frowned a bit. "It is not that I necessarily think they *are* smoke."

"So, wait, you are asking what element they are made up of?" Vrric glanced between them all. "We've had this argument before, haven't we? They aren't any particular element that I know of."

"Maybe air?" Clerin found herself intrigued enough. It helped that Voyt knew what they were talking about.

"Oddly enough, Vuildan mentioned using an air spell to disperse the smoke, to blow away the Vijen leaves." Vrric looked incredibly serious for a long moment. "I don't know. I thought it was the act of separating it, of un-coalescing them. Not that it was damaging them because they were air."

"So… to attack a Luften Yaven, you use air in your magic?" Voyt kept his hand near his mouth and his eyes on the ground.

"No, no, not at all. That would be foolish. You would just make it stronger." Vrric immediately discredited the theory.

"Do you know that?" Malghain glanced around before settling his eyes back on Vrric. "Has anyone tried attacking a Yaven? Besides summoning or unsummoning? Or… trying to make it do something it does not want to do?"

"Have Yavens attacked derlians?" Voyt looked genuinely curious.

"Of course. Derlians can be destroyed quite easily by Yavens." Clerin spoke quite assuredly, though she had very little experience of watching Yavens in actual combat. Vrric quickly backed her up, however.

"Derlians are made up of each of the elements and require each of the elements. Since Yavens have complete control over their element, they have an incredible advantage over derlians."

"So, if the birds are not an element, then how would a Yaven affect them?" Malghain was looking directly at Vrric while speaking. The look turned a rhetorical question into a real one. "Maybe that is why they refuse to assist us?"

"Closer. But I think I know what scares Yavens. It is not to be ineffectual, it is not fear of a struggle or a clash of elements. There is only one thing that scares Yavens, truly frightens them, and that is Nothingness. That is the Void." Voyt nodded into his hand.

"Are you saying that they are beings of the Void?" The question escaped Clerin's mouth before she thought of it. It happened so quickly that it bypassed her mind completely and thrust itself into the world. They were all quiet for a while. All of them nodding unconsciously and staring at the ground. There was nothing but Nothingness on all of their minds. But it did not last for Clerin. "And then what are Vijen? Are they the opposite of the birds, or are they merely different sides of the same coin?" Vrric was right earlier.

They had argued all of this fruitlessly before. Even the part about Tlana being from the Void.

"But what if the birds are creatures of the Mind, or what if they are more directly Chaos? Pure Chaos." Vrric squinted at Voyt. Apparently, it did not last long for him either. "Surely Yavens fear Chaos more than they fear Nothingness? Nothingness has been around them forever, Chaos less so."

"But do they know or understand Chaos?" Voyt responded to Vrric with a thoughtful look on his face. Maybe they had not discussed *all* of this before. "What is fear? Is it of the unknown or the known? Is that answer different for Yavens or derlians?"

"Let's ask." Clerin brought Elange's stone out. It was hot in her hand. There was definitely a Yaven nearby. "Come out from your hiding place, Yaven!" She held the stone above her as she yelled into the dying sun. "I can sense you, I know you are near!"

"I... I must go now." Voyt stood and walked away back towards the camp.

Clerin did not think it overly odd at first, though it was quite abrupt. It only seemed odd when the hidden Yaven left with him. *It must have been following him*, was her first thought. Maybe Phyna or Wil was following Voyt around for some reason. Then she wondered if he had summoned his own Yaven and kept it secret, hidden away. She wondered if it would be loyal to the general Yaven cause, or if its loyalties would lie with Voyt. She assumed it would have had to have been a Luften Yaven, the very kind she was going to make Vrric summon. Or more correctly, the kind that Taglo was going to request Vrric summon. Would they not have to summon one if there was already one there? She wondered what Taglo would say if it knew they had a hidden Yaven in their midst. That struck her as a little odd as well. Why wouldn't one Yaven sense another? *Or*, and this idea just popped into her head, *maybe it was a completely new Yaven, unknown to all of them. Maybe it was hiding from them. Maybe it was a spy from the Cabal. A traitor.* Yes, it was all very odd indeed.

She put the thoughts from her mind, but back at their tent, alone together and sipping another terrible batch of stone soup, the thoughts came swirling back like a "D.C. al coda," the repeating end of a song that recaptures the theme. She had almost forgotten to tell Vrric that he would have to summon a Luften Yaven the next morning. And that she would have to resummon Taglo. That tomorrow was going to start with a lot of effort and early. She had, thankfully, found the piece of parchment that had Taglo's name on it that Croy had given her so long ago. She was not really sure what she would have done if she had lost it.

Vrric had not taken the news that he was to summon a Luften Yaven very well. It was not the spell itself, no. He had an almost infuriating amount of confidence in his spell casting capabilities. No, it was the name. He had never summoned a Yaven before and had no idea of where to begin to find a name. He had even asked her last night if he should just start rattling off syllables and see what showed up. He had not been helpful. There were no other Luften mages amongst them, no one else to ask, so she was not exactly sure where he was headed off to after they had their quietly cordial breakfast.

Clerin, for herself, was off to see Trela. They were to go to the same spot as before, the tiny clearing surrounded by spiky, vibrant gorse. They waited a couple of moments for Clerin to feel confident and calm. She slowly unfolded the parchment.

"Meksidpiarc! Taglochprefwaskintruld!" She had her eyes closed and expected to open them to the proud and vibrant Taglo. But there was nothing there. The last time she had summoned Taglo it had all happened so quickly.

"I don't mean to be pessimistic, but wasn't that supposed to do something?" Sometimes it was difficult to read Trela. She would joke around about serious matters at the oddest times.

"Yes, yes, of course." Clerin took a deep breath to bring her confidence back up. She carefully re-read the name, sounding it out with her lips before attempting another try. "Meksidpiarc! Taglochprefwaskintruld!" Nothing still.

"Could you be reading it wrong?" Trela's voice was gently chiding her now, without a hint of true annoyance. Her words, however, were completely obnoxious. Clerin did not need to be chided at that moment. She glared hard at Trela for a moment before turning her attention back to the shakily written name.

She tried several more times, at approximately ten minute intervals, but with no luck. They were there for almost an hour before Trela forbade her to try again. It was incredibly frustrating for Clerin, it was just not her area of expertise.

"Would you like me to fetch Feyazki?" It was probably supposed to sound helpful but it only frustrated Clerin more. Though she did not necessarily mean to, she found herself glaring at Trela again. "How about some bread and cheese? We'll make it a picnic."

And wine, thought Clerin. What she would have given for some wine at that moment. To have been able to truly sit down and enjoy a proper picnic. "Yes." She waved her hand noncommittedly. "That sounds great." Her voice did not sound like she thought it was great, she heard that herself, but Trela smiled and trotted off just the same. Clerin lay down and closed her eyes and tried to relax. To think of nothing, to meditate. Anything. But she just kept thinking that she had personally failed the coterie. Taglo was the Yaven with the mission. Taglo was the entire reason behind their quest. She did not think they could continue in good faith without it. The only thought that eased her despair was that Taglo had requested to be unsummoned.

She waited quite some time before Trela came back. It certainly felt like an hour, but she could not be sure. She did not like the burning quiet of nothingness. Finally, though she moved quietly, the sounds of Trela getting near filtered through the birdsong. The forest had been idyllic, really, but Clerin was definitely ready for Trela's return. Apparently her glare had conveyed something because Trela came back alone, and was laden with picnic supplies.

They chatted and nibbled into the afternoon. They discussed whether or not they should head back. They chatted a little about Vrric and less about Knill. They even discussed whether Tlana were creatures of Chaos or the Void. It was actually quite a lazy and relaxing day. Each hour or so Clerin would try again. She began to wonder if the location really meant anything. Why shouldn't she be back with Vrric in the main camp trying to enjoy some warm Gaen beer? Trela could still pop by periodically and harass her. Trela, however, was a stickler for previously agreed upon parameters. Eventually, she even brought more food and a couple of sleeping bags. It appeared that Clerin would be sleeping under the stars. At least Trela was sharing the discomfort.

It was in the middle of the night and Trela was shaking her. Clerin had been deeply asleep and had a hard time realizing what was going on. She waved her hand ineffectually as her shoulder was shaken.

"It's time. You've got to try again." Trela was whispering somewhere near her ear. "Let's just do two or three in a row and then you can sleep for longer."

"Can I sleep until dawn?" She did not open her eyes. She wanted to refuse to open her eyes.

"Of course not. But I'll let you sleep more than an hour after this, surely." Trela laughed a little, but the shoulder shaking was gaining in intensity.

Finally, Clerin sat up. She kept her eyes closed for a while longer, but did not want the shaking to start back up, so she eventually opened them. There was certainly enough moonlight that she did not have to cast a light spell to see the letters on the parchment. Not that she really needed it at this point, but she did not want to leave anything to chance. Trela moved back a respectful distance.

"Meksidpiarc! Taglochprefwaskintruld!" Nothing. She waited a minute or two. "Meksidpiarc! Taglochprefwaskintruld!" Nothing. She moved to lay back down, but Trela made some motions and grunted towards her. So, rather than attempt to argue her tiredness, she tried a third time. "Meksidpiarc! Taglochprefwaskintruld!"

Suddenly, a burst of light appeared before her. It grew in height and intensity as Taglo manifested between Trela and herself. It may have been the stress and lack of sleep, but she almost cried she was so happy that it finally happened.

"Taglo!" The word escaped from both Clerin and Trela at the same time.

"I have returned." It grew to a regular derlian size. "I had forgotten how the time flows differently between the realms. I appreciate the vigilance, but will probably be more cognizant of my limitations. There was no way for me to return sooner than this."

"We're just glad something terrible didn't happen." Clerin was unsure of how to express her concern.

"What would have happened…?" Taglo spun itself in a quick circle, as if looking for some sort of danger. "No matter. Has a Luften Yaven been summoned as I requested?"

"No, not yet…" Clerin was about to explain that Vrric was unsure of who to summon.

"Yes, one has." Trela quickly interrupted her. "Voyt knew a name." She spoke quietly, almost conspiratorially, to Clerin behind her hand.

"Good." Taglo spun a little again. "It is your resting time, is it not? This appears quite late at night, or quite early in the morning, depending on your point of view." There was a pause that Clerin was unsure if she was supposed to fill. The question appeared rhetorical. Taglo spoke again before the silence stretched too long to ignore. "Then we should convene tomorrow after resting. Bring the new Yaven."

Clerin was only too happy to oblige, she was still half asleep anyway. She gathered her meager belongings and followed the other two out of the tiny clearing and back towards the main camp. She dumped her bag outside their tent and crawled inside to a warm and unrousable Vrric. He gave a small grunt and twitched a little when her chilly toes touched his leg, but he did not wake. She fell asleep almost immediately. It had been a highly obnoxious day.

They awoke and had a leisurely breakfast. It was fantastic. Clerin had gotten to sleep in while Vrric cooked. They ate in the tent, and she laughed and joked with him. It was light and airy, and she did not bring anything up that was bothering her—until after they had eaten and relaxed for a moment. She just could not understand how a derlian who was unable to cast a spell could know the name of a Yaven to summon. It was bizarre, as simple as that. She had swung back and forth as to how she felt about Voyt, but she did not think that was the issue, she really didn't. It just did not make sense. Of course Vrric did not care. Voyt had saved him, in a way. It was just what he had needed at the time he needed it, and Vrric— though she loved him, she had to be honest—had the utmost confidence that everything would work out for him. And it typically did, so maybe it was Clerin who was wrong. Oddly enough, it was not like the belief in destiny that Trela had, but it could be just as obnoxious. He did not want to think anything bad about Voyt, who had just helped him, so he completely ignored the obvious fact that Voyt should not have known the name of a Yaven. They argued a little. Clerin, not wanting to sour the day, eventually had to drop it. She did not always like having to drop something she believed in, sometimes it felt like capitulating, but she had learned how to pick her battles and this one was just not worth the price. To make things even more curious, the new Yaven, named Yinnis, was with Voyt, not with Vrric. They had to go to Voyt to get Yinnis so they could all meet up with Taglo and Trela. Still, Vrric thought nothing of it.

Trela had her large marquis tent set up in the middle of the camp. They all met there in the late morning. Included in the group were Aedon and Serghno and Ryshial. Clerin felt a little outclassed by the amount of mages and experts around her. Maybe having someone as simple as Voyt around would make her feel better, though she was concerned that he was not so simple. Elange's stone was so hot that, even though it was already in the small leather pouch she typically put in, she had to put that in her main leather pouch hanging off her belt. Thereby double-pouching it, as it were.

"Friends, we are here for a brief meeting today. To be honest, there are probably too many of us here, but today is also a leisure day before we begin our journey to Vatlisi. So, as long as all goes well, we can all have a little beer afterwards. Soon we will officially be in the Fluen realm." Trela slow-walked over to the table in the middle of the tent. The others followed her like water being siphoned up a straw. "And believe me, I tried to get you a little wine, Clerin. But it appears we will have to wait for that." She spoke a little softly, as if she was only to be heard by Clerin. Then her voice raised again as she stood in front of a chair. "Please, sit. There are a few formalities we must address first."

They all shifted their chairs around a little. Clerin had some slight difficulties with the plush carpet, but got herself seated before a few of the others. There were two empty areas on almost opposite sides of the table for the Yavens. Taglo stood in between Ryshial and Serghno, while Yinnis was between Vrric and Voyt. Trela was at an apex of the slightly oval table and flanked by Aedon and Clerin. They all seemed to be in some pretty specific places for each derlian choosing their own seat. Clerin did not have enough time to ponder the order of chaos, however.

"First, I would like to thank Feyazki for bringing Yinnis to us. Thank you." She nodded obviously towards Vrric. "I would, of course, enjoy speaking with you a little later today, if you do not mind." She was looking at Yinnis, but Clerin was unsure if it noticed. Yinnis was like a mist, a whitish fog that was partially transparent. Taglo took aims to appear derlian shaped, even if it did fluctuate in size and form quite often. Yinnis was more of a cylindrical blob, which made it incredibly difficult to tell if it was "looking" in a specific direction, which made it impossible to tell what it was paying attention to. Maybe everything.

"Secondly, I would like to thank Clerin for bringing Taglo back. I know they will need to converse together later, but while we are here, I want to express my gratitude." She then nodded to Clerin.

Trela had more thanks to cover. Serghno for helping with Vuildan, Aedon for something or other. Clerin's mind began to wander the second Trela had mentioned Taglo wished to speak with her. Apparently privately. She was not even sure why Taglo had needed to go back to the Yaven realm. She should have guessed that it wanted to communicate, the raw idea of it was not shocking, but her mind tried to figure out what the conversation could have been about. It was running over useless guesses rather than listening to Trela. She came back to the conversation as Trela was discussing Vatlisi because she heard her name.

"…Clerin will have to lead us through the town." Clerin had no idea of what came before. She wasted precious moments thinking about how narcissistic it was that she only started paying attention when her name was brought up, but she would have to beat herself up about that later.

"I have never been to Vatlisi before, so I don't know…" They all stopped and stared at her. It was unnerving. Had they even been talking about Vatlisi? "Of course, I would be honored." She tried to smile endearingly.

"Good." Trela stared at her for another moment before continuing. "Then, once we have made contact, we will bring the others."

"Are we sure about the tunnels under the city?" Aedon asked the question as she leaned forwards, bringing Clerin into her strong gaze that seemed mainly aimed at Trela. "They lead directly to the sea?"

"According to the Gaens from near Hifrim, yes. We will have both Wil and Phyna make sure once we are near. I do not wish to leave anything to chance, any more than you do." Trela nodded to her, then to the others. "We have a new guest with us today. Would you like to tell us how you came to know Voyt, Yinnis? We are all very curious."

Yinnis may have turned towards Trela, it may have not. "I have served one who knew of one who employed Voyt." It may have nodded, it may have not.

"Voyt?" Trela turned her gaze to the derlian. Clerin was happy that she was not going to let it slide. Maybe Trela could ferret out some answers from Voyt concerning Yinnis. Clerin had certainly not gotten any from Vrric. There was another small pause. "Would you care to expound?"

"Ah, yes. Of course." His curly hair bounced slightly as he nodded into his speech. "I was not even an apprentice, my learning is so small. I was an errand fetcher. The mage, my master, was summoning, summoning…" He looked a little lost, which did not lessen as his pause extended. Finally, his face brightened back up. "Yes, unfruitful. He knew another mage with which to share learning. This other had Yinnis to fetch errands. We talked much while the mages talked much. Then another Yaven, then an argument, then Nemesis. Mages destroyed and Yinnis left." Clerin wondered what was wrong with him. Something must have happened, or maybe he had started out like that. Maybe it was a Mindtrap? Maybe he belonged in an eshram? He sounded… damaged. She felt a burning shame for even thinking it, but there it was. There was no denying her thoughts. "Lucky for me, lucky for Feyazki, the name of Yinnis was written down. So was the other, but I did not take that name." He continued to nod and smile widely.

Clerin glanced over to Trela. Trela had an incredibly intense look on her face. She was quiet and immobile, just staring directly at Voyt. It looked like she was weighing something and the scales were flat even, without a tilt in any discernable direction. Clerin was unsure of what, exactly, she was weighing, but she had her guesses and was performing her own measurements. It took several seconds of uncomfortable silence.

"Yes, well, good enough." She leaned back in her chair, her face still tight with thought. "Thank you." She finally glanced at the others before smiling widely.

"Before speaking with Yinnis, I must speak with the… Clerin. Alone." Taglo began to shift around the table.

"Of course, Taglo." Trela had her hands half up as if she were going to say something else. "I suppose this is as good of a stopping point as any."

Clerin was taken a bit aback by the abruptness of it, but nodded to no one in particular and stood. She did not care to argue, and honestly, there was not much to argue about, though she certainly wanted to hear Yinnis speak more than one sentence. She moved away from Vrric and then let Taglo lead her out of the tent. She had no idea where they would be able to be alone, but knew it certainly was not going to be nearby.

They ended up in the same spot that she had unsummoned and then resummoned it. Clerin tried hard to listen for any others, and Taglo swiveled around for some time before they were satisfied that they were truly alone. Trela's coterie could be counted on to at least feign disinterest when Yavens were about.

"I need the message to come from you." Taglo shrunk a little so that it was about Clerin's size, maybe a little smaller.

"What message?" Clerin felt the sudden urge to flinch but kept her posture straight and plumb.

"I have it, but it is encapsulated. It cannot come from me, you see. I do not wish to distress you, you who hold so many different messages. You are the only one, however." Taglo did sound a bit contrite about it.

"So, you just give me the message and then take it back?" Much of her mind was concentrating on her posture, which was a welcome distraction.

"Well… You must decapsulate it." Taglo paused for a brief moment. "Maybe an hour of your time." It paused again, longer this time. "I do not think you will need to do anything conscious with it. I feel, and Gorbanax feels, that the decapsulation will occur just due to you being the Great Communicator. You did nothing to Lembin's or Linchon's messages, correct?"

"Not that I know of." Clerin thought hard, but could think of nothing. "Of course, they were with me much longer than an hour."

"Yes, well, maybe a couple of days." Taglo almost sounded nervous. "We are getting close to the Fluen realm, close to the Cabal. I do not wish to be caught unawares. If there is any feeling or sensation that you may have that indicates the decapsulation, you will tell me, yes?"

"If I know of anything, I will tell you." She nodded once and brought her head back into alignment with her spine. Her arms were straight at her sides. The anticipation was the worst part about it.

"Again, if there was another way…" Taglo thrust its hand into Clerin's stomach and dropped something in her. It was a little odd since Taglo gave off no heat whatsoever as they were talking.

Just because Taglo was made of fire did not mean it would typically burn. This time, however, Taglo's touch felt terribly hot. It was as if she had been seared open with its hand and a hot cinder had been placed in her stomach. The burning sensation was so intense that she felt nothing else. She would have described it as being so intense that she thought of nothing else either, but her mind was more blank than focused on the pain. As Taglo withdrew its hand, she fell to the forest floor. Blank.

She was unsure of how long she had lain there. Taglo was above her, somewhat twirling in place, when her mind receded from the emptiness. Taglo appeared nervous or restless; it had a way of shedding tiny sparks when it wanted to do something but was unable to. She rolled over on her side and tried to speak reassuringly. Then the cinder took over. The smoldering burn, the soldering heat. It tore the blankness from her.

She had carried messages before. For all that she knew, she was still carrying every message placed in her care, placed within her. They had hurt, yes, at least some of them had. But this was different. It burned with an insistence. It was incessant. It was incandescent. The pain was small in area, not all over her body, but the cinder was a white-hot ingot of… damage. She felt like she was being permanently damaged. The other messages tingled or shook to let her know they were there. It was disconcerting, to be sure. It bothered her sometimes during those quiet mornings or when she was trying to sleep. But they did not hurt like this. They did not burn.

She had, at first, tried to say something soothing to Taglo, but now she just wanted it to get help. She wanted Vrric or Nochiel or anyone, she wanted help. She wanted to ask for help. She wanted to speak. What came out was: "Ungh."

Taglo twirled and sputtered nervously, but did not rush off for assistance. Clerin did her best to marshal her strength. The scratching of her cheek on the forest floor helped bring some focus.

"Feyazki!" She was amazed at herself, so proud of herself, for saying Feyazki instead of Vrric. It was a hollow and short-lived victory. All she had managed was one word, one name, and the burning pain had silenced her once again. At least it made Taglo pause for a moment.

"I am not sure I can allow magic." That was it, a simple sealing of her fate. "It is just that I am unsure of what Chaos will do to the message. Do not worry, we will not wait days. We may even curtail the hour that I had originally estimated. Yes, we shall shorten that." Taglo somewhat engulfed her. It spread over her as she lay in agony, still quietly apologizing. "I had assumed that only the first moment would cause you pain. I had not realized it would continue like this."

The pain became all-consuming as the ingot seared inside her. She could not form words, could barely form thoughts. Taglo babbled incessantly in the background but that did nothing to her. It did not help, but it did not necessarily make things worse either. The searing felt as if it were piercing her, yet it stayed stationary. It floated within her and swallowed up every tiny fraction of her mind. It churned and burned. She would have vomited if she had been able. She would have yelled if she had been able. She just wanted help, why would no one help her? Why would Taglo not help her? But even that faded under the constant pain. That was an order higher than emotion; it was almost a thought. And even raw emotion finally faded under the constant pain, under the crushing weight of the miniscule ingot. There was only nothingness wrapped in agony. And then, quite suddenly, it stopped. The ingot was white hot one moment and then cool the next. It was over.

She was unsure of how long it had lasted, how long she had had to endure the unendurable. She was wrapped in cool flames, curled under a blanket of Taglo. She began to loosen, to unfurl. She rolled onto her back and just breathed for a while. She stretched out her legs. They felt fine. Her arms felt fine. Her face was scratched where her writhing had rubbed it against the forest floor, but her head felt fine. No headache. She had not bitten her tongue or anything. Her stomach was still cramped up into a knot, as if it were making an angry fist, but it no longer burned. Finally, even the stiffness went away. Taglo shifted so that she could see the sky.

"Again, I must apologize. I had not known the amount of suffering involved beforehand. But there is one more thing." Clerin nodded to Taglo since she was unsure if she could speak. It punched through her stomach and withdrew the decapsulated message. "Better to finalize things now than to revisit anything."

She agreed. She was also quite numb at that point. She barely registered the removal. It was over. She was just so happy that it was over. Though happy may not have been the best word. She was ecstatically relieved that it was over.

"So, if you had known the amount of suffering… would that have changed anything?" She lay there, staring at the sky, engulfed in full ecstatic relief.

"It would not have dissuaded me. This is a necessary part of a necessary mission." Taglo was an amorphic shape, a mound rather than a derlian. "But I would have more properly prepared you, prepared the setting. There must have been something I could have done to alleviate the roughness of the process. You are most appreciated, Communicator. Though you do not understand the problems you have instigated, you are indispensably instrumental in some of the solutions. I doubt it is much comfort at this moment, but long after Chaos disappears along with this world, when Yavens are the only sentience once again, when all else is forgotten, you will still be remembered. I will do my best to make that remembrance a fond one."

Clerin nodded again, though she was not quite sure why. She was not in pain, not still stiff and locked up, but she did not really feel like standing. She did not wish to be around other derlians for a while. Taglo, for its part, waited in patient silence until she finally stood. It felt as if Taglo would have waited a year if that was what she needed, though she knew that not to be the case. It was a comfortable time, to be watching the sky without any pain. Ecstatic relief indeed.

When they finally arrived back at the tent, Clerin was surprised to learn that they had only been gone for an hour. It had all seemed to have taken longer; the travel to and from the clearing, the pain itself, the recovery. Each piece felt as if it could have lasted an hour. The others were well into their cups and enjoying themselves immensely. At first that made her angry, but it did not last. The enjoyment was contagious and the ordeal was over. Snapping at Vrric or Trela would not have changed the past. So she grabbed a mug of beer and joined in.

The next day they were on the move again. And the day after that, and after that, and so on. They were no longer passing abandoned villages, so they were no longer stopping every few days. There seemed to be no villages at all. Clerin was unsure if it was due to being farther away from the Northern Desert or just because they were farther from any source of civilization. Clerin had wanted, more than anything in recent memory, to find a bustling Fluen village full of the sights and sounds of home. They were slowly aiming for Vatlisi, so at the very least, in a week or so she should be around a large bustling Fluen town.

She finally got around to speaking with Wil about Vatlisi. She was supposed to after the party, but had not been feeling much like being around Yavens. Not that Wil was anything like Taglo, not even close, but that was definitely part of it. She just felt… better… around derlians. Not even just derlians, but mainly around close friends, around Vrric. She felt she deserved to feel comfortable for a little while, and comfort meant easy. Part of it was out of an overabundance of caution. She felt that if she talked to Wil she would automatically complain about Taglo, which would compromise whatever secret Taglo was attempting to keep with the message. Did that matter? She wasn't really sure. Another part was the timing of it all. They were traveling most of each day with little besides food and sleep in the evenings. And finally, she was procrastinating, she could admit that. But no more.

"So, have you traveled to Vatlisi before?" They had stopped early enough that the tents were up and the food was eaten before the sun set. Just barely. They were in their tent, Vrric, Wil, and Clerin. Wil was tiny, sloshing about within a wooden bowl when she asked her question.

"Not in several derlian lifetimes." The answer was not necessarily useless, but…

"Well, as you may have heard, we are heading towards Vatlisi and Trela will want a scouting mission, as it were. She is hoping that you can get some information about the town and surrounding area before we arrive." Clerin paused for a moment. She was suddenly worried that she would have to accompany Wil and leave Vrric, and all the rest, behind for a while. "And, of course, it will have to be done without raising an alarm or leaving a trace."

"Easy. I would want good direction, the exact information that you are looking for, no ambiguities. All you have to do is get me to the Clatsvol Sea, and from there I can travel with the deep currents and riptides, undetectable." Wil zoomed around the bowl a couple of times, demonstrating its abilities. It was quite comical.

"Perfect, that's great!" Clerin clapped her hands together and then thought better of it and stopped, her hands stuck together in front of her. She did not want to seem overly excited, though she was not sure why. "We will certainly get a good list together of what we need before we get too close to the Clatsvol Sea." She paused for a second, trying to think of what they might need. Certainly Trela would want a map, but that seemed a little out of the way. Could Wil carry and use writing materials without ruining them? If Taglo could stand amongst dry timber and not start a forest fire, surely Wil could carry some paper. As her mind wandered into the silence a little further, a sudden thought popped itself into her head. "Have you been spying on Voyt?"

"What? No, why would I do that?" Wil stopped its circling swish in the bowl.

"Well, I... There have been times when I have sensed a Yaven near Voyt and was wondering if one of you had been following him at times." She hated to lump all of the Yavens together but was unsure of how else to explain it.

"Wait, how do you sense Yavens?" Wil got large enough to be "standing" in the bowl, about two hands high.

"Well, that's..." She had not wanted to bring up Elange's stone with a Yaven and silently chided herself for backing herself into a corner for no good reason. "Can you not sense derlians?"

"Well, yes, but I sense derlians by sensing the water in them. I can sense water, through all of its forms and with all of its personalities, from quite a far distance if pressed. I am unable to sense Phyna or Taglo with anything besides a direct line of sight." Wil paused for a moment, its tiny face looking up at Clerin. "Though I could hear them around a corner, of course. And in hearing them, the more mental forms of communication could be established..." Wil began to trail off.

"Which is why we began traveling together so long ago, to leave as little trace as possible." She knew that line would not help redirect Wil but she felt she had little hope of that working anyway. Maybe Wil would wax nostalgic about their first time together. She wished she could segue into Lembin or something. That subject always sidetracked Wil. "Remember when you brought Midinarre and I to Tureyn, before I spoke with Lembin?" It was a bit forced, but hopefully not too noticeable.

"So how do you sense Yavens? That seems very difficult." Wil would not be deterred, however.

"Magic, of course." Vrric jumped in to her rescue. He nodded at Wil so assuredly that she wondered if he really could sense

Yavens. "Sometimes we just like to sense what else is going on and we just basically stumbled upon the issue with Voyt."

Wil was good at keeping secrets, as far as she knew. Out of all of the Yavens, she doubted that Wil would really care about the stone, one way or the other. They truly got along very well, the two of them. She was just trying to keep it a secret to… keep it secret. In any case, she was glad Vrric had intervened and flashed him a quick smile of thanks.

"Ah, magic, of course." Wil paused for a moment. "Is that good for tracking?"

"No, no. Just sensing one that is attempting to hide." Vrric replied quickly, still nodding. "Once the Yaven is gone, there is nothing I can do."

"Does it detect items that have a Yaven trapped inside?" Wil seemed to be getting excited about the prospect.

"I… don't… know…" Vrric drew out each word, appearing to be truly puzzled by the question, as if he had never thought of it before. Of course, Clerin had never really thought about using magic to sense a Yaven before since she had Elange's stone. It made her wonder if it could sense a trapped Yaven as well. "We tried destroying or freeing a Yaven from an item, but did not check about sensing it. We even tried to communicate with the trapped Yaven, but to no avail."

"Trela still carries Strife, does she not?" Wil recalled the name of Qizern's sword before Clerin did. It made her wonder what the Yavens talked about when the derlians were not around.

"Yes, I believe so. We should investigate that tomorrow, before we begin our travels." Vrric appeared to be trying to delay the test, maybe so that he could figure out what to cast. Clerin was going to join in to help him, but Wil quickly acquiesced.

"Good. I look forward to being there for the experiment, as will the others. I have already agreed to meet with Phyna and Croy tonight, however. I must leave you for now. Until tomorrow!" Wil hopped out of the bowl and flowed out of the tent, leaving a very small trail of moistness behind it.

They sat in silence for a while. Clerin was wondering if Wil was outside, listening in, hiding, waiting for Vrric to cast a spell to sense it or to eavesdrop. She assumed Vrric was thinking the same thing since he just furrowed his brow and stared down at his lap. She eventually pulled out Elange's stone from the leather pouch near her pile of blankets. It was cold and lifeless. She smiled and held it aloft for Vrric to see. He smiled warmly at her, but then furrowed his brow in silence for a little longer. Rather than interrupt, she waited as patiently as she could for him to start the conversation.

"I'm just not sure what to cast… I want to use an element, but how would I have known which to use? Would I have cast them all? Wil is the only Fluen Yaven, so I would have known who was spying on Voyt if I cast a detection spell based upon Fluens." He rubbed his forehead for a second. "Why did you even bring that up?"

"There is just something that bothers me about Voyt. I just… I don't think that I'm the only one who is bothered by him. In fact, I know I'm not. You were there when we sensed a Yaven near him. Someone is spying on him. I just can't believe you are so chummy with him." She waved her hands in front of her somewhat uselessly. As if flailing around would convey something beyond her words. Unfortunately, she was a little unsure herself as to just why Voyt bothered her so, which made explaining it quite difficult. She just sounded petty instead. But it was not that. She was not being petty, Voyt really did bother her.

"What about Voyt bothers you?" He lifted his head and straightened his spine.

"I don't rightly know… His existence." Her voice ended the word with a question mark and a half-exclamation point, making it seem just like a period. All that confusion and self-doubt just ended flat and true. It should not be that way, but Voyt's mere existence bothered her. Greatly.

"Well, there is nothing he can do about his existence." Vrric shook his head.

They sat in silence for a moment. Clerin could think of nothing that would explain herself more clearly, to Vrric or even to herself. Therefore her mind wandered. It shifted from one useless thing to another. She needed something to change the conversation. She needed a distraction. Then, out of nowhere, it hit her.

"If you can't know the element, then you have to cast the spell on yourself." She knew there was a better way to say it, but she didn't have to think of one.

"Of course!" Vrric snapped his head back straight and smiled brightly at her. "I've been thinking of detecting a specific thing, not of expanding my observational powers." He tapped his finger on his chin for a moment. "I'll have to think that through, but I like that."

The rest of the evening went smoothly, without another word about Voyt and his annoying existence. They had a great meal and Clerin spoke with Trela about meeting with the Yavens and Strife in the morning, to which she enthusiastically agreed. Vrric poured over his spell books or meditated or whatever he needed to do to come up with a spell to sense Yavens. All in all, it was a pleasant evening.

They woke in the morning with the sun attempting to make the walls of their tent glow. They did not rush, but got cleaned up and even ate before heading over to Trela's large round tent. The scalloped edging and red piping would have been ostentatious on a smaller tent, but it seemed necessary there. The red was a proper dull color, stained by weather and time, looking a bit like dried blood. They entered into the main tent with zero fanfare. Trela had not had a guard outside of her tent for at least a week. Clerin wondered if it was complacency or confidence. If she were honest with herself, she had become quite complacent herself since they were no longer stopping at every abandoned village. She had not even realized, well not consciously at least, how much the daily worry had been wearing on her. They had not been attacked, had not even seen a whisper of a Tlana in a fortnight. She entered the tent with her spirits high.

All the Yavens were there: Taglo, Wil, Phyna, and even Yinnis. There was a wide audience of others as well: Trela and Knill, Serghno and Arnasta, Estfale, Aedon, Croy, Malghain, and Ryshial. There were so many mages that Clerin was a little shocked that the Blind One was not there. At least Voyt was not in attendance.

She had brought Elange's stone with her, wrapped in several pieces of leather, just in case Vrric needed some extra assistance. Seeing how many others that were there, especially each and every Yaven, she realized that was not going to work. They were trapped, surrounded, and Vrric's demonstration lay completely with himself.

"We are all here for a couple of reasons. One, an enlightening demonstration. The other, a hopefully equally enlightening experiment." Trela had barely allowed them to enter the tent before diving into her little speech. No welcomes or handshakes, no greetings or salutations, just a quick and friendly ambush. Clerin found herself wondering how long the others had been sitting there waiting.

"First, we would like to see the Yaven-sensing spell." Trela shooed her hands at the Yavens and they all floated off in different directions. "Here in a moment, only one of the Yavens will be near the tent. I'll want you to point to the direction and tell me who it is."

"It doesn't work that way." Vrric motioned to Clerin that she could sit with the others while he spoke to Trela. Clerin shifted off a ways to give him room, but did not sit with the others. She felt it would have been, well certainly not a betrayal, but… something.

"What?" Trela's inelegant reply accompanied her shifting her feet to shoulder width apart and crossing her arms. Clerin recognized the stance immediately. Trela wore it often when she was getting comfortably confrontational.

"Well, I cannot tell who it is. I cannot tell what element it is. In fact, I can only tell that it is not a derlian and not an animal. So, by the process of elimination, the living spirit I sense must be a Yaven." He paused and frowned for a moment. "It is more deductive than actual truth."

"Still… That's something." She waved her hand and sat down with the others, leaving only Vrric and Clerin standing. "You can still tell us the direction, yes?"

Vrric nodded to her and closed his eyes. He took a visible breath and exhaled slowly. He raised his face to the roof of the tent, eyes still closed, and intoned, "Narsidtotpri!"

There was utter silence for a moment. In fact, other than Croy jumping his shoulders slightly at the word, there was very little movement from anyone for a moment. All eyes were on Vrric. He clapped his hands together in front of his chest and tilted his head to stare down at them, his eyes still closed. He slowly spun in a circle, fingertips raised. He started to speed up. He spun around four, five times. Finally he stopped, feet spread apart and one hand flung in an obvious direction, his face still looking down, eyes still closed. The silence finally ended with Trela, then the others, slowly clapping.

"Bravo, bravo. Wil should be in the direction that you have indicated." She smiled at him and walked over. He had lowered his arm, shaking it slightly, and finally opened his eyes. "Now for the experiment."

Clerin was so excited for him. Whether or not he had been, she had been nervous that it was not going to work out. She smiled at him askance while he rubbed his hand absently. He glanced at her for the briefest moment and smiled back. Trela was wandering over to a long table that had a dark cloth over the top of it. Clerin had not really noticed it when they had come in. It was a bit in the background. Now that she was looking at it, she realized there were long lumps under the cloth.

"So there are five swords here under the cloth spaced somewhat apart from each other. One of them is Strife which, according to Taglo, has a Yaven trapped inside. We feel fairly confident that each race of Yaven can sense their brethren in an item. This is part of the reason we need one of each Yaven with us when we confront the Cabal. If we ever find the Stone Shield, we will put Phyna to the test. However, it would be incredibly helpful if a derlian mage could sense a trapped Yaven as well." Trela swept a hand over the cloaked swords and smiled. "I know you've never done this before, but since the success of our mission may very well rest upon it… no pressure." She smiled and the others gave polite chuckles, but it made Clerin realize how much Trela leaned on Vrric for things like this. She did not expect Serghno to come up with a foreign spell. In fact, if Clerin recalled correctly, Arnasta was supposed to be the expert at detecting derlians. Shouldn't detecting Yavens be part of her burden? Vrric, however, did not seem to look at it as a burden. He was grinning, eyes dancing across the veiled weapons, eager to perform the experiment. Eager to perform. Eager. He did not appear to notice the audience behind him. He did not appear to notice the weight of their stares, the heaviness of their expectations. It was a strange juxtaposition. He looked incredibly handsome at that moment, but he also had an effervescent boyish glow to him.

Trela moved back out of the way, while Clerin kept her stance off to the side. He clapped his hands together and rubbed them lightly. The others craned their necks in relative silence, attempting to glimpse… something. He took a deep breath.

"Narsidtotpri!" He cast the same spell as before. He closed his eyes and waved his hand slowly above the covered swords. He sort of shifted back and forth so that his hand could cover the long table. The silence stretched into a small agony. A lot more time passed than earlier, when he was sensing Wil. He finally opened his eyes and lowered his hand. "It's no good. I'd just be guessing."

The others starting commiserating and making small encouraging noises. Trela stared seriously at him and tapped a finger on her chin. Not as if she was glaring or anything that confrontational, not even in true annoyance, but maybe a little frustration. And not even frustration with him, just with the situation. Her gaze did not waver. Clerin decided to walk over to him, to say something nice and touch his shoulder, but he raised his hands, still looking at Trela.

"Let me try something more specific." The others quieted, Trela cocked an eyebrow, and Clerin stopped after only one step. "I just think the spirit is too weak for me to open my senses to. I'll have to sense directly." He turned and clapped his hands together again, rubbing them lightly. "Narsidpito!" He placed his hand on each one, over the cloth. He did it again, then once more. Suddenly, amidst the still silence, he flung the cloth off with a flourish. He pointed to the second one from the right. "That one, that's Strife." Trela's face broke into a grin and the others started clapping. It was if they were at a show.

Vrric went over and sat amongst the others, Trela followed soon afterwards. Clerin savored the moment for a little bit, slowly walking over. His face was ebullient, chatting with the everyone. They congratulated him to varying degrees while he nodded at them all. This was what he adored, and Trela knew how to bring it about. Clerin was not really listening to the others, she was just watching him enjoy the attention. Finally, when she was fully upon them, the words unscattered themselves into some semblance of sense.

"I almost couldn't believe it when you cast the spell to sense a Yaven, Sid-Tot. That was the same spell the Blind One uses to speak to the dead." Croy's small voice was clear amongst the clatter. "Though he uses Clo instead of Pri at the end."

"Where is the Blind One anyway?" Vrric voiced the same question that Clerin had thought of earlier.

"He has gone ahead or, more correctly, gone sideways, scouting out the Gaen border near Vatlisi. He should not be gone long. He'll be back with us before we reach the Clatsvol Sea." Aedon turned to Vrric as she overheard the question. "Though there are doubts about his invitation even if he were here." The last sentence was said quietly enough that Clerin doubted Vrric heard it, as his attention was already diverted. But she easily noticed and Croy glanced sideways at Aedon, so it was meant to be heard by him at least.

They chatted for a while. Croy, Serghno, Arnasta, and Ryshial all cast the two spells a bunch of times. The Yavens seemed to enjoy hiding about, checking each mage's skill and various ranges. The ranges were dependent upon power levels, of course, but it appeared to vary a little between each of them even at the same static level. There were little variances due to who was sensing whom. Arnasta sensing Taglo seemed to be the combination with the longest distance for medium power ranges, but Vrric was impossible to beat at the most aggressive power levels. He did not seem to favor an element, either. They made a day of it. Even Clerin participated a little. Though she always worked with low power spells, it was good practice in case she was unable to use Elange's stone for some reason. It was, by all accounts, a great day.

They slowly made their way towards the Clatsvol Sea. It was nice, the foraging easy, the water simple to find. They avoided most other derlians, which just meant some small farming villages really. Clerin felt a little annoyed that they were avoiding Fluens when they had seen every location in the Gaen realm that had more than three houses grouped together. But she also enjoyed traveling peacefully with Vrric, so she did not attempt to rock, or even steer, the boat.

They were only a couple of days away from the sea when Clerin made an incredible discovery. It was dusk and they were heading over to several of the Luftens that Vrric liked to visit with. She liked most of them as well. She certainly enjoyed Queen Vanelia's warriors whom she had spent so much time with earlier. They were walking up on several of them sitting around a fire when Clerin noticed it. Elange's stone grew hot as they approached the others, but she did not notice a Yaven around. She slowed a little and looked around more thoroughly.

"What is it?" Vrric, sensing her slowing, stopped and turned towards her. His words could have certainly been interpreted coldly, but she knew that he was just asking her why she was slowing down, so she did not let it affect her.

"There is a Yaven nearby." She stopped where she was, forcing him to take a couple of steps back towards her. She patted the stone lightly.

He cocked his eyebrow. "That, uh, doesn't indicate direction, does it?"

"No, just intensity." She cocked her own brow back at him. "Which I think is basically distance, but when there is more than one around it just becomes uselessly hot."

"That's interesting. The spell does better with direction than distance. Let me try." He took a deep breath and turned back towards the group milling about in the distance. "Narsidtotpri!" He paused for a moment, looking at them all. "Hmm, I can't tell. Certainly over there somewhere. I tell you what, I'll try to find the direction and you find the distance. We'll hone in on whichever Yaven is sneaking around."

She giggled and started walking again. He walked beside her with a measured and deliberate pace. As they got closer, it became clear to Clerin that the Yaven was somewhere in the midst of the derlians.

Normally, Clerin would sit and chat with Escha and Torpalin while Vrric talked with Malghain and Voyt, but both of them stayed standing. Standing was probably not the right word; they wandered in slow motion while talking. Clerin started and ended a couple of conversations just to be able to walk through the group. She took her time, she did not want to be obvious about it, but eventually she assumed she had figured it out. Voyt must have Yinnis hidden on his person. It was the only logical conclusion. The stone was warmest near Voyt, from every angle. It appeared that Vrric agreed by some subtle and some not-so-subtle winks, nods, and finger extensions. She doubted anyone else knew what was going on, but they may have thought he was being weird. Luckily, everyone was being a little bit weird as evening wore on into night and the last of the Gaen beer was being passed around.

Eventually, others started to peel off and head to their tents. Escha and Torpalin went first. Clerin typically took that as an opportunity to begin to nudge Vrric towards the exit, but she held back this time. Haswyxe left and, finally, Voyt said his farewells.

"Oh, please, let us walk you back to your tent." Vrric steered Voyt away from a slightly confused looking Malghain, and Clerin eagerly followed. Once they were away from everyone, somewhat equidistant between Malghain and the tents, Vrric stopped Voyt. "We know you have Yinnis with you."

The look on Voyt's face was priceless. There was a flash of pure panic, followed quickly by confused stammering. Through it all, however, he was adamant that Yinnis was not with him. Clerin was willing to drag it out as long as it would naturally go. It shamed her, just slightly, that she enjoyed Voyt's discomfort so much.

"We can sense Yavens." Vrric put his hands up to calm Voyt's protestations. "I've cast a spell. We know Yinnis is on your person." Then Vrric thought for a brief moment. "Or another Yaven perhaps?" His voice notched up in pitch a little at the end of his question.

The stammering stopped. Voyt's eyes darted between them, at times looking frightened and at others looking dangerous. There was a serious fight or flight response running through him. Clerin felt herself clenching up in anticipation for whichever route he chose. Instead, he stopped and straightened his spine. He looked directly into Vrric's eyes. "I am a Yaven."

Clerin was so stunned she could not even react. Of all the things she had expected him to say, that was not it. Other things drifted through her mind. Could she still refer to Voyt as a he? What element was Voyt? Why did it look derlian? So many untethered thoughts careened around in her head, without one resting long enough to bring her out of her stunned state.

"But… you are covered in flesh." Vrric brought forth the semblance of a sentence.

"I am inside. Hiding." Voyt's head bounced up and down, and his bizarre grin was still stuck in place. "I control the derlian from inside."

"So… there is a derlian trapped inside with you?" Vrric's eyes narrowed slightly.

"Not sure. It is difficult to ascertain anything amongst all this decay." Voyt paused. "No, I believe I am alone at this point."

"So… this derlian summoned you and then died? You took over the body? I… I had no idea this was possible." Vrric furrowed his brow and stared downwards. "This does not make any sense."

"Please, you must understand my fear. Do not explain my secret to the others." Voyt held his hands out in supplication. Such a derlian gesture. "Please."

Vrric stopped for a while and thought about it. Clerin knew him well enough that she could tell he was really thinking about it. Sometimes he would pretend just to placate somebody, it could be infuriating really, but this was not one of those times. She wanted to know something else, however.

"Did you kill him? The derlian, did he die because of you?"
She was worried this was going to be glossed over, that Vrric would
just understand Voyt's fear and agree to keeping the secret. "When
you entered that body, did you push something out?"

"I do not believe I was the cause of its leaving, no. Was it
there when I first arrived, did we share the body for some time? Yes."
Voyt dropped his hands back down while explaining himself. And
yes, Clerin was quite aware that Voyt was a Yaven and that Yavens
were sexless. In her mind, however, derlian or not, Voyt was male.
As clear as day, standing before her, Voyt was male. She could not
fully wrap her mind around it. She wondered if she could not see
him, if it would change her feelings, but the voice that escaped from
the derlian throat even sounded thoroughly male. These side
thoughts made her hesitate to follow up her questioning.

"So you entered and it left? How can that not be cause and
effect?" Luckily Vrric was paying more attention.

"It started at night, during what I know now to be called
dreams. I would enter, just to see what was going on during the
body's twitchings. Then I would leave. At first, it was for short bursts
of time, very quick. Then longer. Then came some simple motor
abilities, tests, learnings." Voyt paused for a moment and then raised
its hands in supplication again. "I feel that when I finally took over
during wakefulness, the derlian had passed. I do not believe I caused
it to do so."

Clerin did not believe him, as simple as that. She felt that
Voyt was realizing they would be less apt to assist him if they knew
he had killed the derlian. The story was veering just ever so slightly
while they were talking. Of course, she had always had a weird dislike
for Voyt, which may have been coloring her opinion, but... A
thought about Taglo dashed through her mind for no reason. It was
when Taglo was yelling about letting every last derlian die if that
would also destroy the Cabal. The lack of interest or concern in most
Yavens, or at least of Taglo, of damaging or killing a derlian had been
shocking. It seemed to think that since derlians die all the time, death
could not be a horrible thing for a derlian. That it was an inevitability
and, therefore, should be met with the same dispassionate worry as
about eventual rainfall. She did not believe Voyt would be worried
about murdering a derlian, did not believe he would feel the slightest
remorse or sadness if he had accidently killed a derlian, and just
seriously did not believe him. Another thought dashed through her

mind, of when Voyt said he was not sure if the derlian was still alive in there with him, and she decided to keep up the attack before she was pre-interrupted.

"We will, of course, keep your secret for you." Vrric dove past her and made the promise she did not intend to give.

She decided to let him have that. *She* had not given her promise, *she* was under no obligation. She was tired of the conversation anyway. Better to discuss all these things in private, with Vrric. At least the mystery of the hidden Yaven was solved.

Another couple of days and they had reached the Clatsvol Sea. Clerin was ecstatic. It had been so long, so incredibly long, since she had seen the sea. The smell of the salt air, the sound of the crashing waves, the blue-green rolling waves. The Clatsvol was warmer and more sheltered than the ocean outside of the Eidyon Peninsula but could be chilly at times. Still, it was Clerin's ritual to wash her face in the salty waters every time she saw them anew, and she ran the whole way down the long and rocky beach to get to a small enough tide pool to safely squat next to. It was the perfect temperature and she splashed and scrubbed for some time. By the time Vrric moseyed over to her she had decided to take a dip. They found a tiny sanded area and she made him hold her clothes as she waded into the water and then dove into the waves. It was fantastic. She frolicked for some time before realizing there were other derlians around.

It appeared that Trela had, thankfully, decided to set up camp near the beach. As Clerin looked back at the shore, she could see tents going up in the distance. They were somewhat sheltered at the bottom of an escarpment and there were some straggly trees, but she knew it was not very protected, militarily speaking. She wondered if Trela was cursing her name right now, but if she were honest, she did not care that much. It had been too long, and she was finally back in the salty water.

There were already some others who had decided to swim as well. They were in small groups, clustered about. Clerin was happy being alone, however. The feeling of resistance as she kicked her legs back and forth was delicious. As a child she used to hover a little under the surface and roll sideways like a log. All it took was undulating like a snake, arms in and legs held together. With her eyes closed, she could still sense the light sky and then the dark sea floor below her. Rolling and spinning. She did this for a while until she got dizzy and headed up for air. Her hair was swirled around her face, clinging to her in long strands like ribbons. She tossed her head back to sweep it all behind her. Her eye found Vrric at an outcropping near the shore. She waved heartily and he waved back. Good, he was watching her.

She frolicked a little more, going to the shallow bottom and then popping back up, floating on her back, rolling sideways. She looked back after a little while to check on Vrric again. He was wandering a little, staring down, still holding her things. She decided to head back in a few more minutes. She was diving down into the shallows, hands picking through the goopy mud looking for treasures or at least shells and pretty rocks, when she suddenly felt... encapsulated. It was quite shocking for that first split second, the feeling of water separating from water, leaving her in a pocket of air, before she realized it was Wil.

"Greetings, Clerin." The voice came from all around her, encapsulating her as much as it itself was.

"Greetings, Wil." It felt weird, breathing air at the bottom of the shallow sea. It was almost claustrophobic. "You certainly surprised me."

"I must apologize, that was not my intent." They seemed to be floating farther away from the shoreline. She trusted Wil completely, surely more than any of the other Yavens, but the feeling was a bit disconcerting. "I merely wished to speak with you alone before I travel to Vatlisi. It seemed like a good hidden location, hidden time, and hidden departure point as I will just seep into the sea once we are done."

"Of course, yes. It is all very hidden. You just startled me is all." Clerin shifted around so that it felt like she was sitting up. It was more comfortable that way, especially with Wil's slow drift. She crossed her legs into the lotus position. "Did you wish to talk about Vatlisi?"

"I believe I have received a full description of the desired information to gain and the requested tasks to perform from Trela. She can be quite thorough about her requirements of others. No, I have another conversation in mind, one that requires more secrecy."

"Which is?"

"Do not trust Taglo. Do not trust any of them, any of us, but specifically do not trust Taglo." There was a small pause. "Taglo is obsessed. That is the word I believe most describes it. Obsessed. There is nothing that Taglo would not do, there is no pain that Taglo would not inflict, there is no betrayal too large, no sacrifice too big, no destruction too great. Taglo is obsessed with eradicating the Cabal. Completely."

"You do not have to warn me of Taglo's obsessions." Clerin was thinking about explaining Taglo's outbursts, of how it watched her writhe in pain with nary an apology, but Wil continued.

"Taglo would gladly obliterate this entire world if it was the only way to eradicate the Cabal. Truly. It has been discussed." There was another short pause. "I understand that you know how far Taglo is willing to go, but there is another item as well. Taglo has the full backing of Gorbanax. Completely. Taglo has been given free rein in this mission. I have never even spoken with Lembin, and yet I must listen to the triumphs of Taglo. There has been discussion of gaining something from Gorbanax. Something that would assist in unravelling this world, to be used if the Cabal proves too difficult to best." A final pause. "This is what I need to impart with you in secrecy, in hiding. You must not, under any circumstances, let Taglo go to the Yaven realm and come back. This is of vital importance for your world. I have grown fond of derlians and of your world even with perturbances such as the Cabal. It would distress me to witness its obliteration. Make up some excuse, create some lie as to why you are unable to assist Taglo. Stall for time if you must and contact me and I will try to return from Vatlisi. Anything at all, just do not let Taglo leave and come back with Gorbanax's message. It will surely be a message of destruction."

Clerin thought quietly for a moment. She wanted to tell Wil that it had already happened, that Taglo had already left and returned. That she had "digested" Gorbanax's message and that Taglo was in full possession of it. The warning, the secrecy, it was all for naught. But she could not bring herself to do it. She could not bring herself to speak the truth. To admit weakness, to admit failure.

"Do not worry, I will not let Taglo return to the Yaven realm." She lied. It slipped so easily from her mouth. After it was said, she thought of the statement she should have said instead: *I will do what I can to stop Taglo.* But the lie left her lips before her mind had the opportunity. Her only thought of comfort in the swirling guilt of lying to her good friend was that if the world *was* obliterated, she would not have to face Wil afterwards. It was a small comfort, but it was warm.

Chapter 18

The beach, aahhh, the beach, thought Croy. He knew it was a bone of contention between Clerin and Trela, but he didn't care about Trela's arguments, he just enjoyed the beach. It was not just that it was idyllic, though it certainly was. It was not just that it was easy and relaxing and fun and drunken and secluded.   It was what it represented. *The last respite,* thought Croy. They all knew they were getting close to the end, close to their goal, the finish line, the moment of truth, the Cabal. They all knew this was probably the last time that Trela would let them drink and carouse with impunity. To slip from tent to tent in the darkness of night without being stopped by a sentry. Or wander wherever for that matter. The previous night he had just strolled along the surf with Baltuz, watching the moon with one eye and the waves with the other. This night he was planning on doing the same, even with the clouds rolling in.

Shared hardships solidify lasting friendships quicker than anything, but Croy thought that shared respite was a close second. It brought about a certain harmony. Everyone wanted to enjoy themselves one last time. There was an agreement in the air, unspoken but not silent. As long as you were not infringing upon any other, the sky was the limit. Quick apologies were followed by quick forgivenesses. No one wanted to begrudge anything, to add bitterness to the nectar of the shared respite.

The respite was so enjoyable, mostly, because it was shared. Baltuz was fantastic. They would stay up half the night just chatting about nothing useful, then they would sleep in. Trela had made the privy council meetings non-mandatory so, since he was really only part of the council due to circumstance versus merit, he had been skipping them. He just enjoyed it, the harmonious respite, and he enjoyed it more immensely since Baltuz was there. She was certainly not Ilana and he was still certainly in love with Ilana—there were a myriad of reasons that their moment together should have soured— but he enjoyed his time with her immensely.

Of course, Trela would only let it last three nights. Which, actually, was quite generous of her, considering the circumstances. He could not think of a previous time where they had stayed in a more conspicuous spot for three whole nights. There was really nothing defensible about their position. It was at the beginning of the third night that Trela pulled him aside.

They went to a small tent surrounded by small tents. Aedon was already cramped into one edge and Taglo burned on the end of a candle, tiny in form, almost camouflaged. Trela came in behind him and gestured him into sitting on a pillow near the entrance. She stared at him and inhaled deeply. Then Aedon stared and inhaled the same. It was a little odd, as if no one knew where to start, and it made Croy want to stare back and inhale at them.

"We want you to pose as the buyer of the Stone Shield, along with Aedon." Trela broke the silence.

Croy's first thought was, *why me? Why should I have to do this, I'm not even a warrior.* But that faded quickly. There were probably many different reasons all weighed carefully against each other. He almost opened his mouth to say something neutral. Some quiet but begrudging acquiescence. But then he stopped himself. He was going to end up doing it, that he knew. There was no way he was going to leave that tent, after being talked to by Trela, Aedon, and Taglo, without agreeing to do whatever it was that they wanted him to do. So, in the face of certainty, he just smiled at them as said, "Even though I am no warrior, yes, of course, I would be honored."

Though Trela looked a little stunned, she quickly transitioned into praise for Croy, how brave and selfless he was, while Aedon merely sat back in pensive silence. He wondered briefly if they had spent time on speeches made to convince him to agree.

"You are correct that you are no warrior, that is obvious to anyone who has seen a warrior before." Taglo interrupted Trela's flattery with words that were meant to have an opposite effect. Croy, however, felt zero shame for not being, or even looking like, a warrior. "The Shield will not be for you. You must pose as a buyer, a merchant. You contacted Aedon, she contacted Gyaer who contacted Jeschet, and so on. Now the both of you need to know what happened to the large sum of gold already spent and what to do with the large sum to finalize the payment. We feel that this should be enough enticement to get a meeting brokered. Do you agree?"

"Gold usually works." Croy nodded dutifully.

"And the desire to fulfill the previous contract. Which is what you need to sell to them. That you are annoyed and expect restitution." Trela leaned towards Croy. "That is our main concern here. Or, at least, it's my main concern. Can you bring up a pure and righteous anger?"

"So, why I am being asked to do this again?" It just popped out, it was purely reflexive. "Surely there is a Gaen warrior amongst the coterie who can let their anger issues aid a situation for once."

"Right, that!" She snapped her finger twice in rapid succession. "That is what I want. Something hidden under the surface, just waiting to breach the calm waters of consciousness. Something quiet and silent, but rumbling like a distant volcano. If you can bring that hidden smolder with you, we can't fail."

It was weird. The comment made him more annoyed, which made him squint, which made Trela smile, which annoyed Croy some more. It quickly spiraled out of control. Which made Croy suddenly smile at the absurdity of it, which made Trela frown, which…

"You see. He's inherently too nice." Aedon cocked an eyebrow over to Trela.

"Maybe you're right. Who else was on the list?"

They were smiling a little too much. Were machinations *machinations* if they were done out in the open, if there was no intrigue? The odd thing was that even with him seeing through the ruse, it was working. At least a little bit. He felt a compulsion—well maybe that was too strong a word—he felt an urge to help. He wondered if that was natural, that urge to help, or if other derlians were casting tiny un-worded spells with their desires. It made him realize that he had never seen, or even heard of, Trela casting a spell. Croy had been so far from his sheep for so long that it struck him as mundane to have never cast anything, even though that was the norm from where he came from. Plus, Trela's life was about as un-mundane as they came. Speaking of un-mundane, Croy had then come to the conclusion that he needed to convince the others he could act angry enough for them to let him do what they wanted him to. So he stood. He wondered if he should throw something. So he did.

"Great Gunzgak!" He upended a nearby empty table and then stomped his right foot just once and quickly. It was hard to do in a cramped tent. "I won't tell you again, I am not leaving here without recompense!"

"No, no. Too much, way too much." Aedon's lips twitched into a tiny smile mostly hidden behind her hand.

"Recompense?" That was Trela. She was not smiling, but just stared at him with one eyebrow cocked.

Croy inhaled slowly and looked at the ceiling. He did not want to lose any momentum, even as he was trying to scale back. He did not want to smile with Aedon, did not want to feel that dread of embarrassment from knocking over the table, did not want to dwell on just how fake the situation was, did not want to disappoint Trela, did not want to overact and did not want to underact. He exhaled slowly. He realized he needed fear to conjure anger. That was just something in his essential nature, that required link. He doubted that same link was required in others. He knew he would be scared when confronting the members of the Cabal. He just needed to summon some of that right at this moment, just to show them that he could be trusted to perform. But did he want to perform? He glanced between them briefly.

"Listen, there is no way you can force me to do something I don't want to do." He needed to bring it closer to a truth. "Maybe I don't want to go and get trapped by a bunch of evil mages. Maybe I don't want to be sent as a distraction, just so that you can come in and mop up afterwards. Maybe I don't want to die, to be sacrificed, just to make your job easier." Trela narrowed her eyes at him. He could not tell if that was from some annoyance at his speech, or if she was merely paying more attention to him. It made him feel nervous though.

"You are always picking others to do your dirty work for you. What, did Estfale tell you no? Did the other mages turn you down?" Aedon had stopped smiling. "You tried all the derlians you thought would perform well for you, didn't you? You tried everyone before me and they all told you where you could stick it, and now you're desperate. That's what's happening here. Now you need me. Now you need me and you're realizing that maybe I'm not going to help you." Trela's eyes started to get some heat behind them, her jaw tightened.

"Do you think you can just snap your fingers and all the puppets will dance for you? Why are you so special? Why do you get to treat others like puppets? Why don't you do something for once." That one did it. Croy watched in fascination as ripples moved up and down her arm muscles. Her right hand clutched the hilt of her ever-present dagger with white knuckles. *To keep herself from throttling me,* thought Croy. His tiny outburst brought danger, which brought fear, which he shifted into anger. It took a monumental amount of effort, like trying to steer a galloping horse, but he found his anger. "You have abused me for the last time, my patience has finally crumbled. I have provided you with everything you asked for and you are just...

somehow… unable to deliver. That is unacceptable! I do not, I will not, accept your continued failure. I will not leave here. I will be a continual thorn in your side until you have conjured up the Stone Shield. Do you hear me? Are you deaf or just stupid? I will not lift a finger, not take a further step, until you have finally provided what was promised to me!" By the end of it he was gesticulating wildly.

There was a moment of silence. Then, clapping. As Croy stood there trying to slow his breathing back down, both Trela and Aedon were clapping and smiling. It was fantastic.

He did not want to do anything without Baltuz, though he was hesitant to put her in any danger. Aedon insisted that she be involved at all times, since she was the only one who had communicated with anyone near the Cabal. So there was argument as to who else would come along. It had to be a Gaen. Croy thought Gyaer was a good candidate, but there was some concern about his trustworthiness. Aedon mentioned the Blind One, but Croy refused to entertain the thought. He would have been the perfect choice, really, but Croy simply could not trust him. It agonized him even as he argued, refusing to listen to logic and only to his own fear. Vuildan was dead. Verin was a great warrior, but Trela wanted the sexes to be more balanced.

It took an entire day to come to a decision. There was a lot of arguing and wondering aloud. Trela said more than once that, "There are no stupid questions." But, of course, there were. Croy had always thought he had an abundance of patience. But eventually, he just got worn down. They discussed every Gaen in the coterie, at least every male that he could think of. Merits were weighed and discussed. Towards the end, he just did not care anymore. He wondered if they had planned this beforehand. As if the entire day had been planned with, as Baltuz was fond of saying about Trela, "malice aforethought." He supposed it did not really matter, in the end. He was eventually given an ultimatum, after all other options had been thoroughly discredited. Either he left Baltuz behind and just went with Aedon, or the additional member was the Blind One.

He could see their point. The Blind One was a powerful mage, certainly the most powerful Gaen mage they had. And his specialty in magic was escaping places even when trapped. He was not easily swayed or easily fooled. He could lull others into a false sense of security due to his handicap, but he could easily switch to an imposing figure. He knew all of the Ata' of Serif and some from Hifrim. He could certainly show more anger than Croy had just mustered up. Part of Croy wondered why they just did not use the Blind One as the buyer. But Croy still did not trust him. He wondered, not in the light of day and certainly not out loud, if the Blind One was a secret member of the Cabal, just biding his time to get Croy alone.

So there it was. He wondered which option they wanted him to pick. He figured he would choose the opposite at this point. Just for a bit of spite. He mulled it over and decided that they must have wanted him to leave Baltuz behind. Why else poison the well with the Blind One, the only derlian they knew he would never choose? He mulled it over some more. Did he really want to choose to travel with the Blind One just to be defiant? He could not read their patient faces at all. He was tired and wanted to be done, to go back to his tent and be with Baltuz. And that was the thought that solidified it for him.

"Yes. All of us. You, me, Baltuz, and the Blind One." He had nodded to Aedon as he spoke. He felt a little smug about his decision for a moment. The glance between the two as they thanked him, however, made him wonder if that was what they had wanted all along.

They left the next day. It was later in the morning, well after breakfast, with enough time to repack once or twice. Of course, they were not on much of a time schedule since the Blind One whisked them directly to the outskirts of Vatlisi. They were far enough away that it took them an hour to walk, but it would have taken days otherwise. The city looked amazing from a distance. They had been skirting small Gaen villages for so long that Croy had almost forgotten the size of a real city. It was certainly not as large as Agoge, but it sprawled from the sea to as far as the eye could see. He had never seen a Fluen city before, or a Fluen village for that matter, and so he had been unsure of what to expect. More than anything, it gleamed. There were forests of white stone spires and minarets sprouting up from behind the tall, crenelated walls. There was nothing near the outside of it. The guards could probably see all the way over to where the four of them were standing, though there was at least some brush around to help dot the landscape. The walls seemed to extend into the sea a short distance as well, it was a bit surreal. Some of the spires bulbed out while others were quite straight. They all had pointed tops and steep roofs that splayed out at the bottom with a kind of red-orange tile covering them. If Croy would have been asked about capping the gleaming white towers with red-orange roofs, he would have laughed at the suggestion. But he was stunned at how well it looked together. It was breathtaking. The gate, a color within proximity of the red-orange of the roofs, was the only non-gleaming portion of the walls. Its juxtaposition was less breathtaking than the roofs, but it certainly drew the eye appreciatively.

"So, we are going to have to go through the gates?" Baltuz had a habit of asking what Croy wanted to, but was afraid of looking foolish for.

"We have to, just to get our names on the roster. It will look odd to the Cabal if we snuck in. They do not know Croy's name yet, but once I walk past those guards, they will know that I wish to speak with them." Aedon explained her reasoning without making Baltuz look foolish.

"Don't we *want* to sneak up on them?" Baltuz persisted in her line of questioning.

"We do not know where to sneak. They do not have a sign hanging from their headquarters like a common merchant." The Blind One was less concerned about niceties. "We could wander around the city for days attempting to get their attention."

"Also, as Gaens, we will stick out in the city. It will be much better if the guards do not think we are trying to hide something." Aedon nodded to Baltuz, smiling and full of patience. Croy was happy to stay silent.

They stood tall and proud and walked slowly over the barren landscape towards the gated, gleaming walls. Croy kept his eyes on the visible parts of Vatlisi, marveling in its beauty. Baltuz slipped her hand in his and walked beside him, face turned towards the dirt below their feet. Aedon led the way with the Blind One taking up the rear. The melodious crashing of the waves helped Croy forget the smell as they plodded along. He did not mind the taste of fish, but was not overly fond of their stench.

They finally reached the gleaming white walls. Croy was forced to look away, or at least, at the ground like Baltuz. It was too much to stare directly at. He wondered if the interior was like that, or if the jumble of spires cast enough shadows to cut down on the glare. He certainly hoped so.

A guard opened a small door in the large gate and walked confidently out to meet them. There were a couple of other guards milling about in the thankfully shady interior, but they were not ready to attack. There was no militant danger from any of them. The guard who approached them was smiling widely and carried several rolls of parchment. It was a far cry from the Pyran realm where the guards all carried swords instead.

"All Gaens?" He was nodding to himself before Aedon had a chance to reply in the affirmative. "Names and business?"

"I am Aedon Dea'sol from Serif, and this is Croy Cru'tin, Baltuz Fyr'jin, and Narst Dea'jin. We are here to peruse your famous merchant streets and bazaar." Aedon had not told him of his incredible promotion beforehand, but he assumed he needed to represent monied interests somehow. It was interesting that she left everything else as it was. He knew that Aedon wanted the Cabal to recognize her name and, probably, the Blind One's as they entered the city, but he suddenly wished they had discussed everything more thoroughly. He had gotten used to Trela's obsessive planning style.

"All from Serif, no one from Hifrim?" He was busily scratching his roll with a quill, not really looking up. He would kind of wind the parchment with his left hand while writing with his right.

"I am originally from the low hills to the south of Hifrim." Baltuz interrupted with a nice vague statement.

"What are you, a bodyguard?" His smile had a tiny bit of cruelty to it for the briefest of moments, then it was gone. "Both of you Dea are from Serif?" His eyes slid past Croy and Baltuz.

"Yes." The Blind One merely nodded in the guard's general direction. That seemed to satisfy the guard.

"Well, let me be the first to welcome you to Vatlisi. It has been some time since anyone of consequence from Serif has visited." He smiled to all of them, but Croy almost heard the word "to" as "two" in his welcome. It certainly did not seem that Baltuz was someone of consequence to him. "Please, follow me."

They followed. They walked past a couple of lazy seeming, poorly armed guards, and off to their right, there was a round turret. It appeared to be built into the wall, but only on the inside. The was an unbroken straight line at the exterior of the city. The shade of the interior turret was a nice respite. The guard handed the parchment to another, robed Fluen. Croy was certain something was being cast, but was unable to make out the exact syllables since the original guard had started speaking again.

"You will need to stay in the Gaen quarter for at least two days before venturing into the main Fluen quarter. As you probably know, you can still reach many shops at the cusps, but if the specific merchants you are looking for are fully within the Fluen quarter, you will have to wait to gain an appointment." He had wandered back behind a small standing desk, or a large lectern, Croy was unsure.

"They have not been previously listed." The robed Fluen spoke quietly to the guard and then turned to take the parchment back behind another door.

"Ah, first time visiting?" He seemed to be nodding to himself more than to them. "Would you like a rough map of the Gaen quarter?" He rummaged around in his desk for a quick moment, not really paying attention to their nodding heads. He pulled out a small parchment map and a long thin stick, well-sanded and tapered to a rounded tip. He began pointing at the map with the stick. It bobbed about quickly with his words, as it was obviously a well-practiced speech.

"You are here and will leave through this interior gate. The Gaen quarter is quite large, at least compared to the other two. I would recommend staying at one of the inns along this street." He leaned forwards conspiratorially. "They really are the best for first timers. Then you have the main cusp. The Fluen quarter abuts the Gaen here and here and… a little over here. The cusp shops are along these streets and those. And here is the tiny Pyran cusp over here. We ah… well, we do not get many of those kind around Vatlisi, so it is mainly Fluens who are prepared to offer hospitality. Though there are some interesting shops run by far-ranging Gaens as well. I guess you are all from Serif, so the novelty is probably minor. We do not have a large Luften quarter either, certainly not like Tureyn, but after a couple of days, if you would like to head down there, they do have some interesting items. Whichever inn you choose will have further information about the Gaen quarter, many of them are even run by Gaens. After the requisite two days, we will send a guard over to inform you that you are free to roam most of the rest of the city, providing everything checks out." He leaned forwards briefly again.

"I am sure Dea such as yourselves will fly through the process." Then he held out the map.

"Thank you so much…" Aedon paused and was fishing for a name, Croy could instantly tell, but it took the guard a moment to realize that her sentence had not ended.

"I am just one of many civil servants here at the gate, really. No need to thank me for performing my duties." He shook the map again lightly.

Aedon took it and smiled a large and warm smile. It looked quite sincere. Croy smiled warmly as well. The Blind One ignored everything and Baltuz tried a smile but gave up halfway through. They left the turret in a line following Aedon, following the map. They passed through the aforementioned interior gate, past several smiling and poorly armed guards, and entered into another world. The Gaen quarter of a Fluen city.

The buildings were mostly one to two stories, almost crenelated like the exterior wall. And like the wall, they were also grammatically separated by towers and spires of punctuation. It was a haphazard rhythm, but it was definitely a rhythm. The street wandered somewhat left to right, like a meandering stream. The overall effect added random splotches of shade that detracted nicely from the white gleam. It made the walk quite pleasant.

Most of the derlians they passed were Fluens, but almost a third were Gaen. It was intriguing. They had finally left the Gaen realm and they were still surrounded by Gaens. In Agoge, there were no other quarters, no bastions of other races. It was a Pyran city made up of Pyrans. Certainly there were some foreigners thrown into the mix, but they were scattered haphazardly throughout the city, with no rhythm whatsoever.

It seemed that the largest streets were those at the cusps, which meant they were surrounded by merchants as they wound their way to the street of inns. Each merchant had a way of hawking their wares, but they all noticed the strangers' travel-stained clothes, and they all zoned in on them. Aedon played the deflector there, warding off their aggressive advances by waving her hands. Of course, she was also holding the map, which only made more obvious their recent arrival. She did pull out an intensive glare when she needed to, and to her credit, they did make fairly good time before reaching the street of inns.

The entire street was two-story buildings, all lined up flat and straight. There were no gaps in between, no discernable alleyways, no ways to get lost, no varying punctuation. The street was wide, though certainly not as wide as the cusp street they had been on, but there were many chairs and tiny tables that spilled out of each inn, narrowing the street further. The chairs were mostly empty, with a few scattered Gaens clustered here and there. Whatever custom they were fulfilling was not a Gaen one.

There were about ten inns to choose from, and Croy wondered how they all stayed in business. Surely there were not that many Gaen visitors at any one time. They walked to one end of the street and then turned back. How to choose?

"Should we stop in and chat with each innkeeper? Maybe find one with the most pleasing personality?" Croy was trying to be helpful, but all of them furrowed their brows at him, even Baltuz.

"Let us stay at that one." The Blind One threw a hand out, pointing dead center between two buildings.

"You're not even sure which one you're pointing at." It was Croy's turn to furrow a brow.

"You are in between two of them." Baltuz interjected herself helpfully. "Do you want to stay at the Sunlit Cave or the Sapphire of the Mountain."

"Oh, those both sound horrible. What is on the other side of the street?" He shifted his arm, and this time, pointed directly at only one building.

"Hillside Heather." Baltuz seemed to be enjoying the inanity of the names. Or, at least, enjoying the unspoken reactions she was getting.

"Maybe we shouldn't be choosing based on the name alone." Croy figured they had all day to decide where to stay, they may as well investigate.

"That will be perfect." Aedon quickly betrayed Croy. "Having the word 'hillside' in the name implies ties to Hifrim."

"All of these inns should have ties to Hifrim." He was still not convinced and was willing to argue, but he was cut off.

"That settles it then. Lead the way." The Blind One lowered his arm and made a couple of quick, shooing motions. Aedon turned and led the way. Baltuz gleefully, but warmheartedly, put her arm in Croy's and made him follow.

The front room was a two-story atrium with a large circular couch under a round cupola with a giant bunch of heather stacked on top of itself, sprouting from the center of the couch. Croy was instantly attracted to it and wanted to sit down, but followed Aedon to the front desk at the gentle urging of Baltuz.

The front desk was small and tucked off to the side of the entrance. It was on their right as they entered, which was the direction that Croy preferred turning after an entrance. It was made of sturdy oak with a golden stain, and had a skirt that rested on the floor, making it more of a small decorative wall rather than an actual desk. The legs of the desk protruded like ornate columns while the skirt crept around beyond them. There was a stolid, somewhat grumpy looking Gaen behind the ornate desk.

"May I help you?" The question was posed as if it were the last thing the Gaen wanted to do. There was some boredom mixed in with the grumpy, but their arrival did not appear to fix that portion either.

"We would like two rooms for two nights. We might stay longer if we are impressed by the service." Aedon flashed her smile.

The grumpy Gaen looked between each of them in turn. It took longer than it should have, especially for someone who looked that bored, but maybe she was attempting to spread her mood onto them. She eventually gave them a price, took their money, handed out keys, and waved a porter over. Having nothing to take from them, he led them to their rooms and left without waiting for a tip.

"You have two days to explore the Gaen quarter. I doubt we will be contacted before we are allowed to roam. If we do, I'll let you know." Aedon flashed her smile at the two of them.

Croy and Baltuz dropped their own meager belongings in their room and flopped on the bed. It was strange, but just the feeling of the bed below him made him tired. He could feel his eyelids growing heavy as he stared at the ceiling. Before he could convince himself that a nap was a good idea, however, Baltuz jumped back up.

"We can sleep anytime, let's go explore." She grinned and held her hand out to help him up. He let her pull on his arm for a moment before he roused himself.

They wandered the quarter at a slow, leisurely pace. It was entertaining as much as they were in a new and unfamiliar city as it was that they were together. Early on they enjoyed a very small lunch, appetizers really. Nibbleys. They had a small carafe of wine to split between themselves and sat out in the weird chairs and small tables at the edge of the street. They watched the derlians walking by and the derlians walking by watched them. It was a mutual curiosity, a mutual invasion of privacy. They walked several of the larger streets, leaving the smaller side streets for the next day. The buildings were low and crowded everywhere they went. There were lots of shops and plenty of derlians walking around. There were more Gaens than Croy had expected, about half really when one started to pay attention. The other half were Fluens. He did not think he saw a single Luften or Pyran. Some of the Fluens were shopkeepers, but many appeared to just be wandering around, browsing the shops, sipping wine at the little street tables. And that was where they ended their short afternoon of wandering, outside of their own inn at a little table. Croy half expected Aedon to show up, but they finished their salmon alone, laughing about the little things they had seen on the street, nothing in particular. It was a wonderfully relaxing day.

The weather was an odd mixture. It would rain for an hour or two almost every day and be cloudy for about half the day, but the other half was somehow mostly sunny. It made Croy wonder how the farming and grazing was in the area, though it was hard to judge a season off of a couple of days

The two days whizzed by. Croy utterly enjoyed every moment with Baltuz. He had not felt that way since... well, since Ilana. They had barely seen Aedon and had not even passed by the Blind One. Croy wondered if he was hiding in his room the whole time. While Croy enjoyed the too dry and somewhat sour wine, he did miss his bitter beer. So, since they were in the middle of the Gaen quarter, they would drink wine during the afternoon meal and have beer in the evening. That way they could enjoy the diversity of the city and he could still have the taste of beer on his tongue as he got ready for bed. They laughed at the thought that the most difficult decision they had was in what order to imbibe their drinks. It really was the most carefree he had felt in a long time, even more so than at the beach. He wished it would never end.

They were outside the inn when an unarmed Fluen guard walked by, slowed, and finally stopped as she was almost past them. "Are you Aedon Dea'sol?"

"No, but we are traveling with her." Baltuz smiled up at the Fluen, her fingers just lightly touching the long stem of her glass.

"Ah. Is she in her room?" There was a small pained look on her face. Croy could see her struggle with leaving a message with such an obvious underling. Duty won out and she entered the inn after they both shrugged at her.

They laughed about it, nibbling on some sort of pungent cheese. It was certainly not sheep. Croy had been raised on sheep's cheese. Maybe goat? Finally, Aedon came down and told them the news they had already assumed, that they were now allowed to wander into the Fluen quarter.

"Please sit. Chat." Baltuz scooched a chair over from an empty table with her foot hooked on a leg.

"There's nothing I can say. They would not have contacted us before now, and it will probably be another day or two now that the guards have fully vetted us. Really, you should enjoy the city while you can. Once contact is made, it will get very hectic." Aedon lifted the chair and put it back at the other table.

"We don't have to chat about that, certainly not here." Baltuz waved a somewhat dismissive hand at the empty tables and sparse cobblestone street. "I want to know about Aedon. What gives Aedon joy?"

"Knowing that everything is going according to plan." She smiled a truly warm smile at Baltuz. It seemed to Croy that they could have been friends. Aedon took her glass of wine and downed it in one gulp. "I promise I'll try to make it out here for dinner. But unfortunately, I have some things to set in motion now that we have been vetted." She nodded to both of them and walked into the darkness of the interior of the inn.

They split Croy's glass and finished the nibbleys before heading out. They headed to the cusp street directly. Part of Croy wanted to walk along it for a while and savor a last look at the Gaen quarter, but the other part wanted to see what was beyond immediately. Baltuz had no such internal argument that he could tell, and headed straight for one of the crossing gates. He followed.

"I have not seen you here before. Names?" The poorly armed guard was bored, and obviously so. He actively projected it.

"Croy Cru'tin and Baltuz Fyr'jin." Baltuz almost interrupted Croy in her bid to speak first, but placed his name front and center.

The guard spoke to a robed Fluen behind him, who cast something and then whispered something back. "That was quick. You've just been vetted." There was almost a glimmer of interest in

the guard's eyes, but whatever it was faded quickly. "You may cross."
He stepped aside.

They hustled over to the Fluen side and kept moving for a few moments. Croy felt like he just wanted a little distance from the gate before examining his surroundings. It was also a cusp street, with the Fluen and Gaen shops creating the dividing line. But the Fluen street was wide and open. The opposite side of the street had many gaps, almost ruining the street effect. A small hut would be there, then a gap, then a shop, then another gap, then… a stage? There were low platforms scattered amongst the buildings that held Fluens on them. Croy and Baltuz walked adjacent to the row of buildings that was the cusp while taking in the various sights. One stage had a Fluen just talking, one was reciting poetry with expressive hands, another had one singing. Several platforms had musicians, either alone or in small groups of three to five. One even had two virile looking Fluens using sticks as swords to spar with each other. There would be a loud clack and then one participant would shuffle forwards, their boots making a distinctive scraping sound. Clack, clack, scrape. Another platform had a puppet show booth, a castelet, surrounded by laughing children. That was one thing the platforms had in common—a small crowd. Some Fluens walked by quickly, tossing a coin into the slotted box at the front of every stage. Others sat down on the ground to watch the entire performance. A couple of the platforms even had benches in front of them.

The rest of the Fluen quarter appeared to be similar. Gaps, small buildings, lots of platforms. There were larger structures and many scattered towers with red-orange roofs, but the ground level was like an open maze. It boggled the mind. Croy wondered how anyone found any particular building. He had not thought the quarters would be organized so differently, it was just one city after all. It made him want to see the others, just to check.

They had a brief discussion on how they would find the gate back to their street of Gaen inns. They decided to hug the cusp so that they would recognize the way back. They wondered aloud why there weren't maps for the Fluen quarter like there were for the Gaen quarter, but no one ran up and provided them with anything. They finally found another place to eat nibbleys and drink wine. They chatted and watched other derlians walk by, mainly Fluens. They talked about how every single Fluen they met working seemed overcome with boredom and some tinge of annoyance.

They watched a couple of musicians and a puppet show and wandered away from the cusp, in a straight and repeatable line, towards a giant plaza. The square was empty of buildings, but filled with derlians lying around on a lush lawn. There were a couple of fountains, statues, and some rows of hedges, but mostly it was just a flood of bodies on a sea of green. Behind it all was a gigantic castle or palace or cluster of red-orange topped towers. Or maybe it was all three, it was hard to tell. They commandeered a small patch of grass in the shade of a distant tower and sat down. They sat there until just before the evening, when the light was still bright and the colors still vivid. It came much sooner than either had hoped. They had only lain there for about an hour. The walk back was quick enough. They reached the gate before the sun got too low. They had not made it as far into the Fluen quarter as they had thought. The strangeness of it had stretched the distance in their minds. They found their own inn again as the sun was dropping behind the city's walls.

They got cleaned up and hustled back down to the tiny tables. They only ordered a little bit of food since they had snacked all day, but they got three beers, the extra one for Aedon. They had almost finished theirs by the time she finally came down.

They happily explained their day in bursts of details and gaps of laughter. Aedon ordered a large plate of food and listened quietly as they regaled their stories. When she had finished her meal, she ordered another round of beer. "As expected, no news today. But I have a feeling it will be soon." And she was correct, relatively speaking.

It took another day and a half before they got first contact. Croy and Baltuz had gotten back to the Gaen quarter and had just finished a quick lunch. They were huddled together and reminiscing about their morning when Aedon came walking by. She made some weird hand gestures, gave them a squint that might have been intended as a wink, and headed upstairs. The inscrutability of the interaction did not matter as they had been waiting for any sign whatsoever. They swiftly followed.

They found Aedon in their room, not hers. They had only knocked on her door twice, quietly but to no avail, before searching elsewhere. The Blind One had not been seen by either of them for most of their time in Vatlisi. He was certainly not answering any door.

"I told you to come straight here." The strong whisper imposed its urgency upon Croy as he slowly closed the door to his and Batluz's room. He was closing it slowly, in his mind, to do it quietly. But it just seemed like something else odd that would attract attention after he had thought about it. *Trying to be sneaky is the surest sign that you are up to something,* Croy thought.

"Was that what all that was about?" Baltuz caricaturized Aedon's earlier gestures and blinked in rapid succession. It was kind of funny, but Croy could sense when it was a bad time to let slip a smile. The icy stare that Aedon passed over each of them was enough of a hint for him but barely dampened Baltuz's low chuckle. They all sat down and she got her serious face on. "Sorry." It was quick and blithe, but it was more than Croy would have gotten, so he hoped it would suffice for Aedon.

"The Cabal has made contact." Aedon started with a statement of the obvious. "They know what we are here for and wanted to let us know that they are setting up a meeting. I think they are trying to track down the Stone Shield before the meeting, which is probably why it took so long for them to make contact."

"So, we should assume we'll be under surveillance until the meeting?" Croy was not so sure it had taken them too long to make contact. He was enjoying his time with Baltuz.

"Yes. And you've probably already been under surveillance, and probably will be after the meeting as well. Probably until everything is over." Croy noticed that Aedon did not explicitly say that they planned on destroying the Cabal. He wondered if that was on purpose, if she thought they were under surveillance at that very moment.

"But we haven't done anything…" Croy was going to continue. He was not sure how or with what words he was going to continue, but it had been his plan to do so. Luckily, his long pause was interrupted.

"You two have been great, really. Wandering, day drinking, tipping street jugglers. You're the perfect tourists, I couldn't have asked for better. Please, just keep doing what you're doing. It's Narst that I'm worried about. He's been acting oddly and I haven't even seen him the last couple of nights." Her voice dropped a little in volume at the last two sentences, more conspiratorial.

"As you well know, I voted against bringing him in the first place." Croy beamed to himself.

"Yes, you're very smart." She waved somewhat dismissively. "He is still necessary, however."

"So what do we do this evening, tomorrow morning?" Baltuz did her best to keep the conversation on the scent. "Should we prepare?"

"No. Don't worry about that. I'll handle the prep. Just keep enjoying yourselves. Publicly." Aedon's brow furrowed for a brief second. "Before you head out this afternoon, could you *whisper* to Feyazki? Just have him let Trela know we've made contact. I'd rather have you do it than to ask Narst."

"Of course." Croy nodded to her and then, for no real reason, he nodded to Baltuz as well.

"Great, wish I had more to cover, but we'll know more soon. I promise." And with that she stood, opened the door, and strode into the hall. Presumably to her own room.

"I think she's warming up to us. She used to be so formal." Baltuz's laugh was lilting.

Croy found a quiet corner and *whispered* to Feyazki. Apparently, the coterie was already on the move, but the going was intentionally slow. Feyazki sounded excited to be getting closer to danger. He never seemed like he enjoyed sitting still. He was a little like Trela in that regard. They kept it formal and short, not saying anything that could provide specifics to anyone who might be eavesdropping on Croy's end. Croy left keeping the *whisper* itself private up to Feyazki, since he had more power and control.

They left for a quick walk through the Fluen quarter of Vatlisi. Nothing major, nothing new, just some wandering peppered with stops at the various stages. They were back in the Gaen quarter before the sun went down and lingered for a while at a table, but Aedon did not reappear. It took another day and a half before she encountered them again.

The first meeting with the Cabal was set up. They would all go, Croy bringing Baltuz as a bodyguard and Aedon bringing the Blind One in a similar capacity. Aedon was excited since she assumed the Cabal had taken so long to set the meeting up, that they had to have found the Stone Shield. Croy was actually hoping they had not found it. He felt it would have given them a distinct advantage if the Cabal had failed. They would then be on the defensive.

They prepared for the meeting by getting as armed as possible. Even Croy had a couple of daggers scattered about himself. They were, of course, not going to see where the headquarters were, but were set to meet at an old warehouse near the northern edge of the town, far from the sea. They were supposed to pay the remaining fee and then try to set something else up, to see more merchandise. Assuming, of course, that the Cabal had the shield. If not, they were supposed to track whoever they met with, maybe work their way up the food chain if need be. He was not really sure how much planning was actually happening versus just improvising. At least he trusted Aedon and Baltuz.

Speaking of trust, or the opposite thereof, when they met outside of the inn at dusk, it was the first time he had seen the Blind One since their arrival at the inn. He wondered if the Blind One was armed as well, but he doubted it. Their greetings were short and gruff.

Aedon led the way out of the Gaen quarter. Croy followed so that Baltuz was between himself and the Blind One. They were obviously walking with purpose, but he doubted that mattered at this point. Any spies would know where they were headed, and why. It took quite a while to get to the warehouse, certainly longer than he had anticipated, and the sky had faded to dark. Though, since he was not exactly sure when they were supposed to meet, he was not sure that they were late. Aedon had taken care of all those details.

The warehouse itself was a large wooden structure with many bay doors. He could not quite see the wood clearly with the distant street lamps, but it seemed like it would be that peeling gray that old cedar got, weathered and checked. There was an eerie light peering from underneath each of the doors, escaping from a gap about as high as Croy's fist. None of the doors were open, but Aedon strode towards one with great purpose, as if she had been there before. They bunched up together before she knocked loudly.

There was a silence that followed the echo of her fist that Croy strained his ears towards. It took a couple of moments before the scratching of boots on a stone floor became audible. Another moment passed before the clang and scrape of door barriers being removed, of locks being opened, assaulted his ears. He took an unconscious step back at the noise. The door opened to a world of light, with six long derlian-shaped shadows thrust into the night.

Aedon strode in and the rest of them followed. The six derlians parted in front of them, three to a side, and channeled them towards the center of the warehouse. Croy's eyes finally adjusted by the time they got to a long table. It was incredibly long, stretching almost a third of the length of the entire warehouse, which made it seem narrow even though Croy and Baltuz could have lain head to toe across its surface and barely reached the sides. There were three other derlians there, two Gaens and a Fluen, sitting at the far side of the table. Aedon sat across from the middle derlian, the Fluen, and Croy sat next to her. Baltuz flanked him while the Blind One flanked Aedon. The derlians from the door audibly followed them and stopped back a bit, but Croy was not sure how many were Gaen and how many were not since he had walked past them so quickly. At least two of them were still noisily closing the door. He kept his eyes forwards.

"It is a pleasure to finally meet you, Aedon Dea'sol. You may call me Tarolle. I believe you already know my colleague Jeschet, or at least know of him." The Fluen was quite tall between the two Gaens. Croy almost wondered if his chair was a little taller just for dramatic effect but quickly discarded the idea as foolish.

Tarolle was dressed in white robes, with a complex light blue embroidered design around the neck, shoulders, and wrists. He had long blond hair, straight and past his shoulders, held back by a simple braided leather circlet. His eyes were blue but not the eerily bright kind that Clerin had; they were a darker shade, a stormier shade. His teeth were a pearly white and he smiled weirdly with them. It was a wide and warm smile in his mouth that never touched his darker eyes. Jeschet and the other unnamed Gaen were full warriors, proud 'jin. They both had curly brown hair and beards and appeared well armed and armored. They grunted and squinted harshly while Tarolle flashed his fake smile.

"I would say it was a pleasure to meet you as well, but I have had an incredibly long and arduous journey just to find what I have already paid handsomely for." Aedon did not attempt a fake smile. Croy was not sure if he should burst in, but he had not been introduced as the fake buyer yet.

"This is a very difficult line of business, you must understand. We are constantly under attack and must be very careful of who we do business with. There are those who would see us destroyed." Tarolle stared only at Aedon as they talked. He did not even glance at Croy once the conversation started.

"So… you do have the shield?" She stared back at him impassively.

"We do not. At least, not here." His smile twitched for a second but then settled back into place.

"For some reason I had thought you wanted to sell to Gaens, those from Serif. That was my understanding. If you have enough business through the Fluens or Hifrim, then fine, steal my money. If, however, you do want to be allowed in Serif, you will have to explain your failings and then, most importantly, you will have to fix them. Am I clear? You have two Dea, two Assembly members, in front of you right now. You will never be allowed in Serif if you do not produce what we have paid for. Do you understand me?" Her impassivity began to give way to anger. Slowly though, almost subtly, as if she did not want it to give way.

"Of course we understand, Aedon, of course. That is why we are here. That is why we are speaking with you." His hands splayed themselves on the table and he breathed out slowly. "We understand this is the first big order placed through an Assembly member of Serif and that our reputation is on the line." His smile kept its fake rigidity. "This is it, pure honesty…" He paused for a long moment. "We need to make you a new one. I wanted to have it with me, for this meeting, I truly did. But due to circumstances beyond our control, we must create a new Stone Shield."

"I want to see it. Your process, your creation. I want to watch you make the shield." Croy spoke up even though no one was looking at him, completely out of turn. He caught the others by surprise. Aedon seethed at him in her half-a-second side-glance, and the Blind One made a bizarre grunting noise, the first noise Croy had heard out of him since they had sat down. But he had also caught himself by surprise, which was even scarier. He had, in his conscious mind, decided to let Aedon do all of the talking. His unconscious had other ideas, however.

"Uhm… Well, that is a most unusual request." Finally, Tarolle's dark blue eyes turned on Croy. "Normally I would refuse immediately, just on principle."

"You will not refuse this time." The Blind One spoke plainly, impassively.

"This is not up to me. I might not be refusing, you understand, but I cannot agree without discussing this with my superiors." He coughed out a short, nervous laugh.

"Then you had better discuss it with your superiors." Aedon almost smiled at him.

"Yes. Yes, of course." He nodded back at her, his fake smile back in place.

Darkness, emptiness, desolation. Then movement. It was a similar enough beginning that Croy knew he was dreaming. It just felt… unreal. He slowly moved towards a pinpoint of light. The light became larger and began to illuminate the walls of a circular tunnel that he was moving through. The walls were rough-hewn rock, like the tunnels at the fringes of Serif. He could see long shadows cast from the heavy toolmarks of the irregular surface. The light soon became so bright that it washed out the tunnel walls, making his motion, once again, only detectable through his gut. Pure light and pure darkness provided the same level of blindness, especially when it came to obscuring detail.

The sense of motion switched directions on him. Instead of flying face first through a tunnel, he was now falling. The tunnel was beneath him. As he slowed, the blinding light faded. Soon he was standing in a room surrounded by stone walls. Not hewn from solid rock, but stacked and pieced, like a building above ground. He still felt, for a reason he was unable to explain besides a lifetime of experience, that he was still underground. His feet touched the fitted flagstone floor. There were many low arches built into the walls, many openings that were almost doorlike, but they just led from one giant room to another. The ceiling was a series of corbelled stone domes, supported by the walls perforated by arches. The light was a little dim, but since it seemed to come from everywhere at once, he was still able to see everything. Except there was nothing to see but for the rows of arches extending in all directions.

Croy started to walk and wander. There was an odd echo that emanated from every one of his footsteps. It bounced rapidly from floor to ceiling such that it took a while to diminish down the archways. He played with the sound for a moment, even rapping his knuckles against the columns while stomping around. He was unable to find a piece of metal on himself to assist with his echo experiments.

However, he was quickly distracted by a light source off in the distance. He walked towards it, having to zig-zag in perpendicular lines for something diagonally away. It did not take too long before he was able to see what was exuding the light. One small section, one domed ceiling surrounded by arched walls, was dripping teardrop-shaped globs of fire. It was like a slow rain, with each glob about half the size of Croy's fist. The drips were quite constant and were close enough together that one could certainly not run through the area without getting struck. The fire just extinguished, or disappeared, once it hit the stone floor. When he got close enough, he tried to peer up at the ceiling, to see where they came from, but they just sort of dropped straight from the stone. There were no holes that he could discern. The other odd thing was that they produced no heat, at least not noticeable at arm's distance. There were so many drips falling in front of him that he was unable to see what was in the middle.

He stood and stared for a while before gathering up enough courage to touch the fire as it fell. He breathed heavily in and out a couple of times, steeling himself for the experience. He shot his arm out, placing the hollow of his palm directly in the path of the dripping fire. He expected it to be at least a little hot, but it was freezing cold. He immediately pulled his hand back out. The cold burned his flesh a little. He thought it odd how cold and hot sometimes felt the same to him, how opposites could be confused when they were at high intensities.

There, centered in the palm of his hand, was a good dollop of water. It quickly reached body temperature and about half of it dripped off the edge of his hand or through his fingers. It was definitely water, though. Clear and pristine. He turned his hand over to let the rest of it fall on the stone beside him. It stayed there, looking exactly like a wet spot on a dry stone. He looked into the area that was raining fire, but the stone looked dry after every drip.

He reached his hand in again. Again he felt the burning cold and pulled his hand away. He did this a couple of times, so that all of the stones around him had a wet spot on them. The first one appeared to be evaporating or soaking in or something. It was slowly disappearing. Croy was having difficulty telling the passage of time there, in his dream, but it did not seem that the water spot was evaporating too quickly or too slowly. He put his arm in and held it there, letting the burning cold hit his hand, his forearm, his wrist. He pulled it out and let the water drip from him. It had been a little painful, yes, but certainly not unbearable.

He took a deep breath. He felt compelled to run through the dripping fire, as a sort of gauntlet. It appeared that it might take about ten large steps, running steps, to get through the entirety of it. He took another breath, held it, and let it out slowly. He backed up two steps and then charged forwards.

The freezing fire was painful, but not unendurable. It seemed to be a little more intense when his entire body was being splashed compared to just his arm. But rather than put his arms up to protect his head and face, he ducked down a little and pumped his arms faster as he pumped his legs faster. He decided it would be best to just charge through. There was something else he hadn't realized when he was just putting his arm in the dripping fire. There was a large amount of smoke in the middle of the section under the dome. His eyes were squinted and his head was down, but he could see the cloudy white smoke swirling around his legs as he ran. More than that, however, was what it did to his lungs. It infiltrated them with a warm and wet heaviness, like breathing in steam rather than campfire smoke or, so he assumed, a Tlana. The heaviness clogged his lungs and made him want to cough, but did not make him have to. The warmth in his lungs contrasted with the cold dollops of the liquid fire. He was unable to ponder it all, however. He was running full tilt and concentrated on that. Just make it through, just pop out the opposite side.

But that is not what happened. About halfway through, though it was incredibly difficult to keep any sense of distance, he fell. He was not sure what he tripped over—he did not feel his foot hit anything—but his feet stopped running and his face plummeted towards the flagstone floor. In a fit of self-preservation, his hands crossed in front of his head. But he did not strike anything. He kept falling. The drops were now striking his back, which was better, but that did not slow as he increased his speed downward. He could feel a tunnel around him, but could only see the white smoke in front of him.

Then he slowed and eventually stopped. He was floating in the smoke; the drops had stopped falling. He found he could swim a little in the smoke. As he swam around, he found a smooth boundary all around him. He was inside of a sphere. It did not take long before he realized that the sphere was shrinking. It was so smooth that he was unable to get a grip on anything, meaning he just swam around until it shrank to his fully stretched out height, limbs extended. It stayed there for a brief moment, as if being held open by his strength. Then it shrank some more, though at a slower pace.

Croy struggled mightily against the shrinking sphere. He held it outstretched, then he held it while it touched his head. That actually lasted for a while, standing while the sphere stretched around his head and feet. Eventually he was curled up a little, with the sphere pushing on his back, making it hard to keep his legs straight. Then he was on all fours, pushing with all of his might. That stage lasted an incredibly long time. He seemed to have a lot of strength in that position. He had a little hope in that position. Finally, he was crushed against himself into a fetal position. He just wanted it to be over at that point. He had forgotten it was a dream, so did not wish to wake up, but he wished to die. He desired an end. That stage seemed to last forever, with the sphere straining against every fiber of his being, every tiny atom, crushing him into an even smaller space.

Then, out of nowhere, the sphere shattered. He had not stopped moving; it had just felt like that since the sphere was moving at his same speed. But not anymore. Now all was still. He looked about himself and saw the pieces of the shattered sphere were in specific interlockable shapes. It had been a puzzle ball, like the one his uncle had, that would fall apart when dropped. He saw himself, much much larger, trying to put the pieces back together. He saw a robed figure walk in and obscure one of the pieces with his foot. It was the same dream he had had many cycles ago, when Ilana was still at Larelt, but this time he had been inside the puzzle, getting crushed. He watched as his larger self, his younger self, finally finished the puzzle and disappeared. But he did not. He stood there, dumbfounded, before the robed figure finally bent down to look at him. The hood was pulled back to reveal... two white, cataracted, eyes. It was the Blind One, as clear as day. Croy screamed while the Blind One smiled. Adrenalin rushed through his veins like freezing fire.

He awoke to wonderment. *Was the cloaked figure always the Blind One, or just now? What did it mean? Was it that the Blind One had kept him from finding the piece by having his foot in the way, or did he help him find it when he moved his foot? And what was the crushing sphere?* In all, he was covered with a sense of foreboding, much like the sweat that soaked his body. That and he did not trust the Blind One, not the tiniest bit. Not even if he was being helpful the entire time.

Croy decided to talk with Aedon about the Blind One, one more time. He felt more comfortable with Baltuz there, so they visited her room after breakfast hoping to catch Aedon alone. No such luck. She invited them in, and the Blind One was sitting in the room beyond, on the edge of the bed, talking lowly with someone. Aedon was trying to get Croy to explain why he had stopped by, quietly and after she had closed the door, of course. He was too curious as to what was going on in the other room, however. In a fit of unabashed rudeness, he walked right past her. Baltuz attempted to run interference, but Aedon walked right past her to follow closely behind Croy, leaving Baltuz in the last position.

The Blind One got quiet and stiffened his spine as Croy walked into the room. But Croy was not trying to eavesdrop. He peeked his head into the doorless archway and looked at who was there. It was Arnasta, who became just as quiet and stiffened her own spine in response. Croy, now trying to not to appear completely nosy, smiled warmly at her.

"I was hoping to find you here. Do you know where Serghno is? I wanted to go over a couple of things with him." He then wondered how rude his ruse was. Was she Serghno's keeper?

"Why don't you just *whisper* to him?" This humorless statement came from the Blind One.

"I was trying to use magic as little as possible, at least for something that could link us together. You know, just in case." He just wanted to leave at that moment, to escape back to his room. He was not sure who he had thought the Blind One had been talking to, or why he had wanted to know so badly.

"We are at the Naked Hare, in the Pyran quarter. It would be good of you to drop by. He gets bored when I'm busy." Her smile was kind and genuine. He had always liked Arnasta. She had never been anything other than kind and genuine in his experience. Not just to him, but to everyone.

"Just don't get seen walking over there. You know, just in case." The Blind One then turned his head back to Arnasta, thus ending his portion of the conversation.

"Thanks, Arnasta." Croy turned to leave and gave Aedon a large smile as she was standing a little too close to him. She was squinting at him inquisitively, but he did not let it slow him down.

They escaped back to their room and Croy tossed himself on his bed. He wanted to just lie there for a moment, his closed eyes staring blindly at the ceiling. He breathed a couple of times, attempting to lower his heart rate.

"Smooth. I suppose we will need to go see Serghno now." Baltuz was giving him grief more out of habit than for any actual annoyance, or at least that was how it sounded to Croy.

"I needed to see who *he* was talking to. I hadn't realized that the others were already here." Croy opened his eyes. "They must be tracking the Cabal. Or trying to."

"Ah, yes, that is her specialty, isn't it?" Baltuz lay down near Croy, but from the opposite side of the bed. Their heads were adjacent while she stared up at the ceiling along with him.

"I wonder if anyone grabbed anything from the meeting? I certainly didn't." He was just wondering aloud, but was also kind of hoping that Baltuz knew something that he didn't. She did not.

As they walked through the Pyran quarter, heading towards the Naked Hare, Croy tried to figure out a way to tell her about his dream. But what was there to tell, really? That he didn't trust the Blind One? That he had felt cold fire and was squished in a sphere? He had not talked to her about it immediately upon waking and had lost the opportunity to discuss it with Aedon. The moment had passed.

They spent a little time wandering the Pyran quarter, visiting the shops that supposedly had the most exotic and bizarre wares. Of course, having come from the Pyran realm a few moons ago, Croy found it more gaudy than exotic. They had everything fire oriented that he had ever seen. Candles, lamps, braziers, little portable grill things made of cast iron, torches made of wood, torches that burned oil and you could stab into the ground, just everything. Of course, what he remembered most from the bazaars at Agoge were weapons. They sold every type of knife, dagger, sword, mace, flail, halberd, just everything. Admittedly, there had been some candle merchants at Agoge as well.

As they walked along, Croy thought he saw some members of Trela's coterie, but he was never quite sure. They always ducked away or he just saw them from the back or they ended up being someone he had never seen before and had only vaguely looked like someone. He was not really sure what he would do if he found someone he recognized anyway. Were they really all supposed to stay separate, "just in case?" He certainly did not feel confident enough to yell and wave at someone, but he was also on his way to see Serghno.

They decided against getting lunch before meeting up with Serghno. The decision was not really oriented towards keeping themselves hidden—it was too late for that—but mainly Baltuz wanted to eat at a new Fluen place they had found the day before. They found the Naked Hare fairly easily once they had decided upon it. The Pyran quarter was not very large at all.

The innkeeper was definitely a Fluen and sent up an errand boy to check if Serghno was accepting visitors. Croy and Baltuz stood on the far side of the lobby, watching the fire in the fireplace dance almost invisibly in the bright noontime sun. Eventually the boy returned and allowed them to head on up.

Serghno answered the door boisterously. His portly frame and overgroomed waxed mustachios gave him an air of the dramatic when he wished it. He slapped Croy's hand and practically pulled him inside the room. Once they were inside and the door was closed, he started to use his indoor voice. As he was talking pleasantries to them, half over his shoulder as he walked, they followed him farther into his and Arnasta's rooms. There, almost hidden in the back, sitting in an overstuffed chair, was Feyazki.

"I thought you had to wait a couple of days before you could leave your quarter?" He was slightly taken aback by seeing his old friend in the Pyran quarter.

"Those rules are for other derlians." He smiled and laughed for a brief moment. "Actually, I'm not even registered in the Luften quarter. I'm not registered anywhere. I just hopped the wall when no one was looking."

"And no one notices you when you're out and about?" Baltuz sat in the other chair across from Feyazki, leaving Croy and Serghno standing.

"Well, they only check at the gates. So, typically, I only switch quarters at night. Of course, I have only been here two nights anyway." He motioned for Serghno and Croy to sit on the small couch as if it were his room. Croy stayed standing. "What brings the two of you all the way to the Pyran quarter? Message from Arnasta?"

"I know I've said this before, but someone needs to keep an eye on the Blind One. At all times." It burst forth out of Croy.

"Has something new happened?" Serghno twisted a little on the tiny couch to look at Croy.

"No, not really. I just don't trust him." Croy could tell from the looks on their faces that he was going to have to bring more than that. "I had a dream about him."

"And in your dream, he was working for the Cabal?" Feyazki joined in.

"Well, no, not really." He squinted his eyes and tried to think. Was he really just being paranoid? "It just… It was the mood of the dream. It left a bad feeling behind, like a rancid oil stain."

So he told the three of them about his dream. He told them all of it, even the useless or weird parts, just so they would know he wasn't misrepresenting the feeling of it. However, try as he might, none of them thought the dream meant that the Blind One was plotting against them.

"He just did not do anything to you. Nothing ominous happened." Serghno had never really voiced any annoyance about the Blind One, so Croy had figured he would have a tough sell there.

"You're not even sure if he was trying to hide the puzzle piece?" He had been somewhat hopeful that Feyazki could have been swayed. Feyazki had voiced concern about the Blind One before, and he had been there when the Blind One had disappeared with Croy, stealing him away to watch his dreams. But Feyazki was hard to get to agree on anything, especially a common enemy. He always seemed to leave a tiny benefit of doubt open in any argument. He did seem interested in the crushing sphere, asking several follow-up questions and getting Croy to describe the feeling in detail. So at least that was something.

"The only time you saw his face was at the very end? As in, the second before you woke up?" Even Baltuz was not convinced. She, who should have supported him without even hearing about the dream, discounted his overwhelming feeling of dread.

He wondered, for the briefest of moments, if he should have lied about the dream, spiced it up a little. He was unable to do that, however. It would have felt wrong. At least he voiced his concern to someone, to several someones.

Feyazki left and Arnasta arrived. Croy thought about mentioning his dream to her, but so much time had passed that it took him too long to warm up to it. He had already explained it all and had mostly given up before she arrived. He did not tell anyone else, not even Aedon, who he had wanted to tell in the first place. He found himself missing Ilana. Surely, she would have stood by his gut feeling. Instead, Baltuz and Arnasta began chatting about Serghno.

"How long have I known him? I can't remember a time that I didn't." Arnasta's laugh was throaty.

"Our families knew each other. They'd get together a couple of times a sun cycle for some festival." Serghno smiled over at her, his mustaches quivering slightly.

"The real question is how long have I liked him." She laughed at that. "I'd say, off and on, at least fifty-percent of the time. So, yeah, I've liked him about half of my life."

He laughed as well. "Hopefully you've liked me a lot more lately."

"Oh, yes, definitely. There was a period there in our youth when I could not stand the sight of you." Her face softened a little in its mirth. "But now I can't fall asleep without listening to your soft snoring."

"Who was that big dumb warrior you used to date?" Serghno looked as if he was really trying to think up a name.

"Which one?" Arnasta laughed. "I have a terrible taste in lovers." She smiled a lopsided smile towards Serghno. "Had. I had a terrible taste in lovers."

"Oh, you know, the one when you were about twenty. I had just gotten home for a break from my magical studies and I was intent upon wooing you. I had this great image of you smiling at me before I had left and could not shake it. That simple image got me through many a night when I wanted to quit my training. When I got back, however, you were with this huge, ferocious... jerk, for lack of a better word."

"Twenty...? You must mean Skotruge." Her face squinted in thought. "Yes, that must be him. You are actually being quite kind by merely call him a jerk."

"Well, I decided one evening to sabotage him. We had met once, you see, outside the entrance of your family's farm. You know that long lane of trees? We both arrived at about the same time, though he may have waited for me briefly, watching the dust from my horse creep closer. He was there when I came up over the rise, so we gave each other salutations and small talk. He eventually asked me what I was doing there. Not thinking about it, I told him. And you know what he did then?" Serghno looked oddly serious suddenly, as if he were still offended by it. Arnasta merely shook her head. "He laughed. I mean full laughter, belly laughs, slapping the knee laughs. As if it was the funniest thing he had ever heard. And then he told me that you were already dating the handsomest, strongest, most skilled warrior off the Dekhan Plateau. Himself."

"He sure sounds like more than just a jerk." Baltuz nodded to Arnasta sympathetically. Croy was unsure of why she nodded to Arnasta and not Serghno.

"Well, so after you politely explained you were dating someone else that evening…" Serghno was going to continue, but Croy interrupted.

"You still asked her out? After that?"

"Of course. I had made up my mind. Why should I have let that jerk deter me? Maybe Arnasta was just waiting for someone else to sweep her off her feet? Maybe she had already tired of this Skotruge?" He looked a little shocked at Croy's questioning.

"I might have just turned around and headed home right then."

"Ah… I hope not," said Baltuz.

"Ah… That's so sad," said Arnasta at the same time.

"But you still spurned him. Right?" Croy looked from Arnasta to Serghno.

"She let me down easily. She was very gracious." His smile was a little sad.

"But the point…" Arnasta turned from Croy to Serghno. "The point was that I then knew. I knew your intentions after that. If I had not known, you would still be just an old childhood friend, just someone that I used to know." She stopped for a moment and then smiled. "You planted a seed that day.

"That's not all I planted." Serghno's grin sent his mustachios quivering. "He was in a jousting tournament later in the week. I let him do his worst on most of them, he really was a magnificent beast. But at the last joust, the one that would win the tourney, I quietly, but assuredly, planted his horse's hooves to the ground. I let it move towards the end, as the other jouster got close, but held it back long enough to not allow it to gather the necessary momentum. He was unseated and lost." He clapped his hands once.

"Wow, really? I remember that. You never mentioned that before." Her mind was lost for a moment in thought. When it returned, she was smiling. "No one could figure out what had happened. He never did trust that horse again."

Serghno suddenly looked serious. "He did not take his loss out on the horse, did he?"

"No, nothing bad. I think he gave the horse to his younger brother. But he always blamed his horse for that day. I guess he was right." She looked up at Serghno, still smiling. "But really, it was not his loss at some random tournament that brought us together. It was not your sabotage. It was the seed you had planted. You were so eloquent with describing your feelings. You made me feel beautiful. I remembered that often after you went back to your magical studies. Not necessarily the words, but how they made me feel."

The air was thick and Baltuz elbowed him, smiling at him as he turned towards her. He was unsure of what was meant by that. Was he to say something romantic to her? Were they to leave and let Serghno and Arnasta be alone? Was he to ask Serghno what he had said to Arnasta, to take notes as it were? He decided on the middle option. They stood, said their goodbyes, and left.

By the time they had meandered back to the Gaen quarter by way of the Fluen quarter, back to their inn, the Hillside Heather, Aedon was waiting for them.

"We have been contacted again. They will allow us to see their lab, to witness the creation of the Stone Shield." Aedon looked determined, but Croy felt ill. He did not want to witness anything like that. Besides, what if something went wrong? He had been getting his nerves primed up all day and now there they were, at the precipice. They had been aiming for this moment for so long that he had been able to block the enormity of it from his mind. But now there they were. His stomach churned. It did not help that it was his suggestion to be a witness.

"How long do we have?" Baltuz seemed unfazed by the prospect.

"Five days." Aedon gave them both a quick smile. "You have at least three of those to do as you please."

Chapter 19

Trela enjoyed Vatlisi, she really did. It rained too much, but that was certainly not the city's fault. She had come through the front gates with Clerin a couple of days ago. She provided a false name, that of Upsuhl, whom she had never met but who was supposedly a trader that might be known near the Luften side of the Fluen realm. Estfale and Kryhir had known her and they had assured Trela that it was a good enough name to get her access to the city. Clerin gave her real name, Trela had insisted. Clerin had been a little nervous about it, but there was no way that she was not going to use her Fluen princess, especially at Vatlisi. She wanted to get into the royal palace and Clerin would be her only chance. She knew it was a bit of a longshot but had decided to try anyway.

Unfortunately, she was going to have to head back out to where the bulk of her coterie was stationed for a couple of days. She was supposed to meet up with Arnasta who, hopefully, would have some leads on some of the members of the Cabal. As long as the Blind One had performed his duties satisfactorily.

Trela left in the middle of the afternoon, through the front gate on horseback. She let them know she would be back, though she did not give them a hard date. They marked it down somewhere in their seemingly endless archives. She arrived at the hidden encampment just before nightfall. She was proud of herself for timing it correctly.

They were at the edge of the sea, at the beginning of a cave complex. Phyna had known about it from work done long before Trela was born. Apparently, there were several distinct and separate cave systems around Vatlisi. Some were for rain water and storm surge run-off, dangerous to be caught in unawares. Some were escape tunnels that entered or left the city in case of emergency. Those were also dangerous to be caught in, because some were still used by some citizens. Some were just directly under the city. Those were smaller and more individual, many of them private, some just a small passage between adjoining basements, others much larger. Some were used for storage, others for secret rendezvous, others for youthful exploration, others as old haunts, but all could be occupied by someone at any time. Phyna had no information about that network.

The complex they were in used to be part of the escape routes but was most recently used by smugglers. Conceivably, there was a way to get from the complex into the city, though there was some talk of a cave-in a ways back into the rock. She had her experts search the immediate entrance area, and the Gaens told her that the old firepits and amount of dirt and dust piled up and the look of the footprints in said dust, all pointed to the cave not being used actively. She had been told that it had been well over a moon since the last major smuggling visit. She was a little concerned, but they were only here for another week or so, and she made sure there were several sentries on duty every night—they really did need a place for Wesduin to rest his wagons. In her opinion, no matter where they decided to camp, there would be a chance of them getting found out, and this place was more hidden than most. Besides, they were finally getting close to being able to track down the Cabal. She could not become timid so close to her goal.

Since Arnasta had yet to arrive, Trela spent her time making the rounds. She enjoyed visiting her warriors, whether they were Pyran or Gaen, and asking them little questions, putting them at ease. Personal enough that they knew that she knew them, but not so personal as to make the conversation awkward.

The Luftens were all in Vatlisi. They entered together as a group on a vague mission from Queen Vanelia. It seemed that, as prying as they were for their archives, the Fluens respected a fair amount of privacy. A mission that wasn't allowed to be talked about was allowed to not be talked about. Feyazki was the only Luften who refused to enter through the front gates. He had insisted on sneaking in during the night. Though Trela was not entirely sure why he was insistent, she herself had given a fake name, so she allowed him his covertness with the express requirement that he not get caught. The last thing she needed was to have to break one of her mages out of jail.

The Yavens, of course, were all in the cave. There was an incredible nervousness about some of them once they had gotten close to confronting the Cabal. Certainly not Taglo. Taglo did not get nervous, it got angry. She had stopped talking to Taglo so as not to hear, yet again, about how horrible the Cabal was. They were there to destroy them, weren't they? They had come all this way, she had put off being a queen, she was currently hiding in a cave in the Fluen lands—it boggled her own mind—and yet Taglo was ever insistent with its arguments.

That was what was on her mind as she was walking with Knill outside, heading to visit her sentries, to cheer them up or at least let them know they were appreciated. She had dragged the Pyrans across the world, into a completely foreign realm, for what? A completely foreign cause. In fact, since Yavens were not of their world, it was about as foreign of a cause that could be. And they followed her. They had fought Tlana for her. They didn't even complain that much. It was these thoughts running back and forth behind her eyes, ricocheting around her skull, that darkened her mood. Then, as if sensing what was in her head, Knill asked the question.

"Is this your destiny?" The sounds of the crashing waves in the distance gave an ominous tone to the question.

"You're usually more supportive." It was a thinly veiled dodge. He gave a quiet chuckle, which was great since he could have taken it worse. "I have a strange relationship with destiny, especially after defeating Qizern." She paused in both her walking and her talking. "Before it was so obvious, the road before me. Now… now it is more… It is like before I was telling destiny what I was going to do, where I was headed. Now I must listen to what she wants me to do, where she wants me to be headed. It is a more complicated relationship now."

"So, destiny is female?" His mouth curled into a small smile as he chuckled a little louder.

"Of course!" The question made her smile, but she pressed on, undeterred. "She has been very kind to me. I want to keep her happy. I want to make her proud. If she wants me to run across the world to a completely foreign land to help the Yavens, I will do so with a smile on my face."

"So, you are confident we are going to win?" Another wave crashed in the distance.

"Of course, I am the Kriishan!" She laughed at her own automatic response. "Seriously though, it doesn't matter. Even if I thought she was going to kill me, painfully and horribly, I would still go where I thought she needed me. I am her agent." It was odd that she did not feel a sense of peace at her first sentence, but she did at her last ones. Her mood immediately lightened even as Knill's brow furrowed.

"I suppose, at this point, there is nothing to be done about it." He nodded to himself as his forehead unwrinkled.

"We passed that point a long time ago." She took his hand and started to walk towards one of the sentries again. He smiled at her with a goofy grin. She rarely held hands with him, and it was even rarer that she instigated it. It seemed a small price to pay for his smile. It lit his face up, even in the dark night.

Arnasta did not arrive that night, nor the next morning. It was not until after Trela and Knill had eaten lunch that she finally showed up. They had been enjoying the shade at the cave entrance when she came into view along the beach. They let her come to them.

The greetings and exchanging of pleasantries took several minutes. Then the offering of hospitality, followed by the declining. Several guards walked through and started the pleasantries all over again. All Trela wanted to do was get Arnasta back to what they were calling her headquarters, a little niche away from all the others, to discuss the Cabal. Finally, protocol allowed them to escape.

Since the headquarters only had a curtain for a door, she made Knill stand outside while she and Arnasta headed in and made themselves comfortable. There were about seven wooden and canvas chairs scattered about in the room, some near a small table. Trela grabbed two and made them face each other.

"Did the Blind One get you what you needed?" It was a basic question to get Arnasta talking, but it was also one of concern. What Trela really wanted to know was why Arnasta was so late, but she felt she could not start with that direct of a question.

"Yes, yes, it was amazing. Somehow he got some hair from all six of the guards they met. The three main ones—Tarolle, Jeschet and Hegwan—he was unable to find, but we assume they will be there at the main meeting." Arnasta was visibly excited, which soothed Trela's worries immensely. "You know he can go places without traveling, right? That he can just disappear and reappear somewhere else?" Trela nodded in acquiescence. "Apparently, he cast a spell that did that with a couple of strands of hair from each of the guards."

"So, he stole their hair magically?" Trela was trying to figure out if it would have been noticeable. Did the hair get pulled out, or just cut, or was it just the strands that have fallen out but were still stuck with their brethren, like those hairs that come off in your brush?

"Yes, apparently he sent them to his room. Then they had their meeting, then they left." She was nodding and smiling to herself, her brown hair bobbing with her head. "So the Blind One and I spent all day tracking down where the guards live. We got the locations of their homes." She began to shuffle and grope around a little until she found what she was looking for. It was a piece of parchment folded into a tiny square. "I even have a map!" She began to unfold it with a bit of flourish. Her excitement was contagious.

The map was a little crude but the main roads were clearly shown as well as the pertinent offshoots. There were six clearly marked squares representing the houses. There were four in the Fluen quarter, two in the Gaen, and none in the Luften or Pyran quarters.

"I know it took a while, but we wanted to make sure we found the correct house in each case. As long as that hair came from those guards, I guarantee these are those derlians' houses." She sat back and let Trela ponder the map for a moment.

Trela stared at the map even though she did not really see it. Oh, she would figure out which order to go in, how many teams to send, who to place in each team. The map would certainly help with those decisions when the time came. No, she stared at the map more as a symbol than an actual object. The next stage was starting. She savored the familiar excitement in her stomach that she got when a new adventure was about to begin. It had taken them so long to get to Vatlisi that she had almost grown weary of the campaign. But now it was all coming to a close. In about a week the Cabal would be crushed. She did not let her mind wander to the other alternative. She was too excited to be nervous. The parchment felt rough against her fingers, the smell of damp soil touched with mold infiltrated her nostrils, the shadows from the candles dancing across the roughened irregular wall surface, she savored it all.

"Thank you, thank you, thank you." She was not sure what to say, so she just said what came to mind. "Is this my copy?"

"Yes, of course." Arnasta paused for a moment, a small smile formed in the corner of her kind face. "You never have to thank me for performing my duties. It is an honor to serve you, my Queen."

"Well. I just want you to know how appreciated you are. Your services have been essential on more than one occasion." Trela smiled back, but she doubted she looked nearly as kind. Arnasta was one of the nicer derlians she had ever met. Trela stood and half re-folded the rough map. "Please, you must have a little hospitality before you rest. We can discuss the six guards tomorrow, in the morning."

But Arnasta did not move. She looked down and bit her lip for a split second. "Actually, could we discuss them now? I was hoping to return to Serghno tonight."

"Of course, how inconsiderate of me." Instead of sitting back where she had been, she shifted over to a chair at the far side of the table. Arnasta quickly followed. Trela got some blank sheets of parchment and some ink.

"The thing is, I do not have a huge amount of information about them anyway. I tracked them to their houses, but you may want to talk with the Blind One about them as well." Arnasta picked up her chair to move it from the table, not dragging it on its hind legs. Trela liked that.

"So, how did you track them?" Trela got her quill ready.

"You mean, what spell did I cast?"

"No, no. I mean, how long did you hide outside of their houses, waiting for them to leave or return?" Trela unfolded the map again. "This one here," —she pointed at a random square— "how did it take for this one?"

"Well, we did not get a visual confirmation of them."

"What?"

"Well, I don't know what they look like. And the Blind One is, well… blind."

"But you confirmed the houses, right?"

"Yes, but it was more that we confirmed that the hair came from the house."

"I don't understand. Did you confirm the hair against what was found in a comb?"

"No, not really, though maybe. We never went into the house but would stay outside for a while, mostly at night. I would then make sure I got the same signature reading from something in the house that I got from the hair itself."

"So, what proof do we have?"

"Well… magic. It's what I do. We zeroed in to which house we thought it was during the day and then stayed outside of it for a while during the night, just to make sure." Arnasta had a tiny frown pass her face as they were talking. "Do you not trust me?"

"Of course I do. I trust you completely, Arnasta. You are correct, this is what you do." Trela had to think hard for a moment about how to fix it. She had not really thought to ask the question, but it came out because she thought she was going to get a description of each of the guards. She was obviously not going to get that without one of those who were at the meeting, maybe Croy or Aedon. They also did not know how many derlians were in each house. What if the guards had roommates, lovers, relatives, whatever? "So, if you cannot give me a description of the guard, can you give me one of the house?"

"Of course." Her kind smile returned. She gave detailed descriptions of each of the houses, which Trela dutifully copied down.

The group for the first try was as small as Trela could make it. Herself, of course, and Estfale, Jalin, and Feyazki. Jalin was required because she was the best spy Trela had at her disposal. Since they were breaking into houses, she needed a good spy. It was not just her skills that Trela admired about Jalin, though ample and unmatched, but it was that she kept a constant amazing awareness about her. She could sense movement a couple of floors below while concentrating on picking a lock. She could hear Trela speaking about her two tents over while whispering. She was just a natural. Feyazki was required because he was, well, Feyazki. Did she really need to include Estfale? Maybe not, but he was an incredible warrior with many of the same catlike abilities of Jalin. She did not want to have to worry about her back while she was rummaging through someone's house.

There was another thing that she was a little frustrated over. Arnasta and the Blind One had found the houses, but no effort seemed to have been made about figuring out the owner's schedules. She was going to have to enlist others in watching the houses she was not investigating so that by the time they got to them, there would be some sort of opportune timeline for them to arrive. Unfortunately, with the timing being what it was, she was going to have to go into the first one blind.

For the watchers, she had Croy, Croy's friend Baltuz, Aedon, Arnasta, and Serghno. Basically, everyone who had full access to Vatlisi. Except for the Blind One, who was doing other research, and Clerin, who was attempting to speak to the Prince of Vatlisi. He was a real prince, unlike Clerin. She kept reminding Trela that she was not a real princess, but that did not deter Trela in the slightest. Apparently, each of the large Fluen cities had a real prince or princess to rule over it, and other than Tureyn, there were few Fluen cities that could match Vatlisi's splendor.

Trela was a little frustrated with herself as well. She wished she had placed more warriors in the city. Aedon's plate was already quite full, and making her watch a house to mark each time a resident used the door seemed like a waste. Aedon, for her part, took the extra duties in stride. Escha and Torpalin were still going through the vetting process, but would hopefully be available soon. She thought that a couple would attract less attention than a lone, rough-looking warrior like Malghain or somebody.

Feyazki flew Estfale and Jalin over the walls at the darker hours that hung between late night and early morning. Trela had entered earlier, back under the name of Upsuhl. She took a short nap in her room at the same inn as Arnasta and Serghno—the Naked Hare—before heading out into the starry, moonless night to meet up with them.

They got situated outside the house Trela had chosen just before dawn. It was early, but she wanted to infiltrate as soon as the owner left. She hoped they were not a barkeep or some such that had gotten home just before they had arrived. They were in the Fluen quarter, since that one typically had more movement earlier and they should be less conspicuous. Of course, none of them were Fluen, which made her a little nervous, but that quarter also had the highest amount of foreigners. She had chosen the particular house because it was near a green space, a little public garden with a small sculpted park attached. They got themselves situated there, hidden from the casual observer but not so far back into the oddly placed aspen trees that they looked like vagrants. They could still see the front door of the house from where they were, but there was no way to watch the back door without calling attention to themselves.

She had Feyazki check to see if the house was occupied. He reported back that there were two derlians in there, somewhere. Definitely not moving. So she started phase two of her plan—she sent Jalin in.

Jalin was supposed to get the lay of the land, as it were. Not to go anywhere near the occupied rooms, certainly not to do the type of heavy snooping that Trela wished to do, but to get the general layout and any obvious information she could glean. Then the waiting game started. Trela hated waiting. Dawn came and Jalin followed shortly thereafter.

"Did you find anything?" Not that Trela thought that she would have, but it was just a good opening question.

"No, nothing of value. There are definitely two Fluens in there, sleeping. From the general looks of it, a guard lives there. Definitely a warrior of some kind. There are weapons hung, somewhat decoratively, around the walls. Not much art, not much to speak of for a kitchen, but I am not positive how communal Fluens are with their meals. So, from what little I saw of the aesthetics of the place, I would bet that the other derlian with the guard is a lover, not a spouse." Jalin looked back and forth between them. They all stared back at her, waiting for her to finish her report, not providing her with any input or feedback. "Anyway, there is definitely not a mage or a spy or anything other than a guard living there. There is a room off of where they were sleeping. Could be a large closet or small side room if my area calculations are correct."

"What are we hoping to find here, anyway?" Feyazki was as direct as ever. "We can't really kidnap or interrogate them, right? We do not want to warn the Cabal that we are here, certainly." It was his turn to glance amongst them, hoping someone would jump in.

"We are hoping to find some sort of further intelligence. Maybe one of them has a map, or a letter, or some form of written material about the Cabal or their superiors or their headquarters. Maybe one of them is more of a mage than a guard. Maybe they meet up with other members during their day. Maybe they lead us to the laboratory so we can scout it out ahead of time. Maybe a lot of stuff. I don't know, Feyazki, but I need something. Something more than to just hoping Croy will kill them all when he finally sees the lab." She was showing her frustration a little. There was not a lot to go on and they only had a few more days. She just hoped that destiny gave her something, and for that to happen, she had to be out searching for it.

"So, how are we going to follow them and search the house?" Estfale brought her back around.

"Oh, that's phase four, that's where you come in." She smiled at him. "I was going to have Jalin follow them but I might want her expertise while searching the house."

"And what is phase three?" Jalin was nodding to herself. "Must've been what I just did."

"No, that was only phase two. Phase three is when I get into the house." Everyone looked at her as if they were bored with her games already. It was going to be a long day.

They took turns lying around and wandering. It was almost midday before the door to the house opened. Trela froze, attempting to look nonchalant, forcing her head to stay staring in the wrong direction. She wanted to see what they looked like, but they turned and walked the opposite way she was staring, as if to spite her. Estfale lazily got up and wandered off, taking the long way around to get behind them at a safe distance. Feyazki had been grabbing food, so she was unsure of when he would be back, but Jalin was also nearby and might have gotten a look at them as they left. Not that it would make a dent in Trela's curiosity.

An agonizing minute passed before Jalin made herself obvious to Trela, just as she slipped around the back of the house. Trela figured that was her cue. She lazily got up and wandered off towards the house. At the last moment she took a hard right and walked past the side of it to get to the back. When she got there, there was a closed door up a short flight of stairs. Without hesitating she walked up, put her hand on the handle and pushed down on the latch. The door opened easily and she slipped inside, pivoting and closing the door quietly behind her.

It was pleasantly dark inside, with heavy curtains shading the windows. Trela let her eyes adjust before wandering too far into the interior. She decided to begin in the largest, simplest room—the parlor. There were some cupboards and several chairs ringing two sofas facing each other. The upholstery was simple in design, but was certainly worth a fair amount. There were crossed axes over the fireplace and an unwieldly suit of armor standing in a corner. What caught her eye, however, was a small standing desk, a secretary against a wall. She wanted, more than anything, to find something written, some correspondence of some sort. She ignored the rest of the room and flowed around the various obstacles before standing in front of the secretary.

The large and enticing main drawer was locked, but the main cover flipped over easily and two horizontal runners extended out as she lowered the cover, providing supports for it and creating the desk surface. The smooth mechanism made her think it was of Gaen origin. There were many slots and pull-drawers that she investigated, but there was not much with actual writing on it, nothing to really investigate. She had even found a secret drawer, hidden behind another, but it only had jewelry in it—two rings and a small necklace.

She closed the cover and fiddled with the main drawer for a moment before conceding to herself, silently of course, that she needed Jalin for the task. She was afraid she was going to gouge the wood with the small metal letter opener she was using, and that would have certainly been evidence of tampering.

She made a low whistle: *long, short, short*. It did not take long for Jalin to appear, but Trela was still messing with the desk and did not hear a thing. Suddenly, as if teleported by the Blind One, she just appeared. It was unnerving and comforting at the same time, though the comfort came from an ersatz pride by proxy that her spy was that skilled. She decided to try to listen for her next time.

"You need something opened?" Jalin pulled a pick and tension bar out of her sleeve, or somewhere, and splayed them playfully in front of her.

"Yes, I'm hopeful there's something useful in here." Trela pointed towards the main drawer.

Jalin popped it open quickly and effortlessly. In it were papers, stacks of glorious papers. Trela carefully pulled them out and began to skim them for any usable information. It appeared, however, that the warrior was just an aspiring poet. And not a very good one either. Though, if she were honest, she did not even get into what others considered "good" poetry anyway, so maybe it was just her. It was frustrating to have to glance through pages of trite allegory on the off chance that one of them held something of value.

After she fruitlessly rooted around for a while, she whistled Jalin back to relock the drawer. Still quietly undetected. They went through the entire house, Feyazki arriving about halfway through their search, and Estfale found his way back a little later. Maybe Feyazki was right. Maybe she should have an idea of what she was looking for before breaking into a home. They left disappointed.

Trela grilled Estfale about his shadowing over lunch. The couple ate and watched a couple of performers before heading to the palace. Estfale had tried to get in, but not too terribly hard. The palace was probably the most difficult building in the town to enter uninvited and they did not want to attract undue attention.

They hit another home that day since it was already empty. Fluens apparently lived very boring lives, or else kept very boring homes. They found nothing there as well, plus they couldn't follow anybody. It was suddenly dusk and Trela had nothing to show for an entire day of skulking. She wondered if she dared waste more days on the endeavor, but was a little unsure of what else she should be doing. They needed to find the Cabal's headquarters or laboratory or whatever before the big meeting. She needed some usable intelligence. She hated just waiting and doing nothing when she should be preparing.

So she went to see Clerin with Feyazki. Maybe she would have good news. And she did! Clerin would be able to have a brief lunch with the prince in two days' time. Even better, she would be able to bring her foreign bodyguard, so Trela could attend. Unfortunately, Feyazki was not invited, it would only be the two of them. While Trela was a little unhappy with that, she was glad to be able to go. Feyazki seemed a lot unhappy with that, however. He seemed to think Clerin had not tried hard enough to get more derlians invited. Trela admired Clerin's negotiating skills and doubted it was just because she had not tried. To keep Feyazki busy, she decided to hit some more houses the next morning.

The first house that morning was another boring one. The only papers that Trela found were full of bad poetry. At first she wondered if that was common amongst Fluen warriors. She decided to ask Clerin about it later. But then she began to wonder about these particular guards. There was nothing indicative of the Cabal in any house they had gone through. Of course, they would be minor enough to not be able to afford any of the items that the Cabal made, those were incredibly pricey. But there was nothing useful at all. The guards were at a high-level meeting, weren't they? Maybe that meeting was not considered that important. Or maybe the opposite was true and these were an elite squad who left no trace of their allegiance. It was just a frustrating blankness, a hole in her knowledge. She was afraid she would have to go into the next meeting blind. More than anything, she did not want to do that.

While watching the exterior of the next house, the fourth on her list, the fourth overall, she had Feyazki whisper back to the cave encampment at the outskirts of town. She had decided she needed the Gaens there, and Phyna as long as it would go on an adventure without Croy, to investigate the extents of the system. She had been worried they would draw unwanted attention to themselves by delving deeper, but she needed more than one iron in the fire.

One derlian left the house they were watching and Trela decided to move her team in immediately, letting Feyazki trail the owner as he had repeatedly requested. She wanted to hit three houses in one day and that meant moving as quickly as possible. Jalin had gotten them in and they started to split up, with Jalin taking the top and Estfale heading downstairs. Trela was walking down the hallway, as quietly as she could at the speed she was going, when she heard a scream. Part of her wanted to freeze where she was and wait for a moment to see if the scream brought anyone from the level of the house she was on, to watch their backs as it were. Part of her wanted to dash back and assist Estfale, since the scream seemed to come from below and definitely did not come from any of her troop. Her ears strained in the half moment it took her to make a decision. There was nothing but the silent echo of the scream, so she turned and ran down the stairs.

There, on the ground in the middle of the parlor—it seemed that every Fluen home had a parlor—was a Fluen female and Estfale was on top of her with his right hand covering her mouth and his left hand holding her right one at bay. There was a shiny dagger clutched in that hand, and her left was scratching at Estfale's face. Trela jumped into the fray, avoiding the Fluen's flailing legs and easily pinning her scratching arm. Her muffled cries emanated eerily from behind his hand.

Her blue eyes did not show fear or pain, only anger. She stared daggers into Estfale mostly, but would glaringly look at Trela periodically. It took several long moments before she stopped struggling. When she did so, Estfale slowly removed his hand.

"Now we just want to ask you a few questions, okay?" He put on a warm smile and attempted to shift his feet under him. Her eyes softened for the briefest of moments and Trela almost relaxed her grip a little.

"You have no idea of what you are meddling with. You will be killed slowly, your face peeled away from your skull!" She spat at Estfale and then began struggling again. Luckily his hand was almost back over her mouth as she spat.

They held her down for another long moment before her eyes opened wide in terror and went limp. Trela, her reflexes overcoming her judgement, turned to look behind them. There, looking abnormally tall from Trela's crouched position, stood Jalin. But it was not Jalin herself that struck fear into the Fluen's heart, it was that Jalin was holding a quiet infant in her arms, swaddled in a thin white blanket. Estfale was also halfway turned and stunned into silence, his hand shifting away from the Fluen's mouth.

"Look what I found upstairs." Jalin's voice was oddly soft.

"My baby, you can't hurt my baby." The Fluen glanced back to Trela. "You aren't monsters, are you?"

"Whatever happened to peeling off our faces?" Estfale's muscles were still taught.

"You have to let me go. You have to give me my child." Suddenly her head turned and she bit at Trela. Trela moved her arm out of the way, which led the Fluen to attempt to scratch at Estfale again, but Trela was able to wrest her arm back to the ground. This time farther out to both give her more leverage and to avoid getting bit. Estfale punched her in the face.

"I don't think you understand what is happening here." He held his fist pulled back and hovering above her, daring her to spit or bite again.

"You're right, you're right." She went limp again and her eyes lost a touch of their fire. "I was just in my own house, minding my own business, when I was attacked by a pack of Pyrans who are threatening my baby. Is that what is happening?" There was a trickle of blood that started to travel along the side of her face.

"We're not threatening the child, we're threatening you." Jalin's voice was still oddly soft.

"No one is threatening anyone." Trela spoke forcefully in an attempt to regain control. "We just have a couple of questions."

"You have questions?" The Fluen's eyes locked back onto Trela. "Then I need assurances."

"If you answer our questions, we assure you no harm will come to your child." Estfale's eyes snapped to Trela's as she spoke. He was clearly indicating that they should make no such assurances, but he did not contradict her.

"And why should I trust a bunch of thieves who have broken into my home?" Some fire returned to her eyes but her muscles stayed limp.

"What other choice do you have?" The Fluen tensed again for half a second, but maybe Trela imagined it.

"What is your first question?" She kept her eyes on her baby, not on Trela.

"What can you tell us about the Cabal of Lochom?" Trela knew it was a dangerous question. She might be dooming the mother if they were unable to keep her quiet until the meeting. But the oddest thing happened. She began laughing. Deep, throaty laughs.

"That's what this is about?" She laughed again. "Oh, you really don't know anything about anything, do you?"

"What do you mean?" Trela did not want to play into her hands, but had little choice.

"We're the Resistance! We've been infiltrating them for the last six moons or so, carefully biding our time." She nodded emphatically to both Trela and Estfale. "Let me up and give me my child, and I'll let you in on a secret. They're about to make another item. There's some Gaens who are going to buy a shield made from a Gaen Yaven, almost a twisted version of cannibalism if you ask me. Yeah, and they refused to just buy one, they're insisting on watching it get made. Let me up and I'll give you the details. You want to destroy the Cabal, don't you? You're part of the Resistance as well, aren't you?" The word resistance became capitalized in her voice.

"How do we know you're not lying." Jalin took a step back. The baby was amazingly docile in her hands.

"How do I know you don't work for the Cabal? Or want to purchase one of their items? I could be killed for what I've just said if I've said it to the wrong derlians. I am just laying down the truth here. I am at your mercy." She began nodding again.

It was a difficult decision. Trela did not trust the Fluen, but they could not hold her there on the ground indefinitely. It was unfortunate, but Trela would either have to let her up and listen to her, or just kill her right then. So Trela nodded to Estfale. He squinted his eyes at her and his jaw tightened, an obvious disagreement, but he relaxed his grip, nonchalantly picked up her shiny dagger, and stood. Forever faithful. Trela relaxed her own grip and stood. Her muscles were taught with anticipation. Part of her expected the Fluen to bolt, part of her expected a fight, and the rest of her hoped for a peaceful resolution.

"My baby." She held out her hands.

"First tell us about the Cabal and your infiltration." Jalin took another step back, almost reaching the stairs.

The Fluen tensed for a moment, but took a deep breath and appeared to forcibly relax herself. "Of course, of course. Laqual, my husband, became a low-level guard there, before he even knew what it was. Just hired to be part of the group, to pad their numbers, increase the show of force, you know. He's very gregarious and became fast friends with a few of the other guards. During one outing he ended up saving one of his superiors when a boat capsized, so he got promoted quickly, you see. Then, about six moons ago, he was promoted high enough to be told what they do at the Cabal. To be shown what they do. He was so disgusted by the process that he decided to turn against them and join the Resistance. So I got a job as a low-level guard and we began asking around. Discretely. That must be how you found us. Right?"

"I thought we didn't know anything about anything?" Jalin cocked her head to one side. "Now we're a part of this Resistance?" She turned to Trela. "There is obviously no truth to any of this."

Trela was staring at the Fluen when it happened, trying to sift through the story which, regardless of the premise being outlandish, all the details sounded quite plausible. The Fluen's eyes squinted a little and suddenly the docile baby started screaming for all it was worth. Then the Fluen's lips moved rapidly, but Trela could not hear her over the wailing child. The next thing she knew, Trela was drowning, the entire floor was flooded. All the water appeared in less than an instant. She could feel the wetness on her skin, the way her clothing stuck to her and then floated away from her. It clogged her ears with a muffled rushing sound. She had to squint her eyes to try to see through the strong current. But the Fluen was just running unencumbered through the room in the distance, and though Trela was holding her breath, it did not *feel* as if she had to. She was on her hands and knees, trying not to get swept away by the currents, when she tried to swallow a tiny bit of water. But she felt nothing. Then she tried to breathe a tiny bit of water but felt nothing. She did not cough or sputter or, thankfully, start to drown. Gripping the floor she steeled herself and inhaled deeply. Nothing. She could either suddenly breathe water or there was no water around. As she made that realization and/or decision, she could no longer feel the water surrounding her. Once she could no longer feel it, she could no longer hear it, could no longer see it. Suddenly she was just crouched on the dry ground.

Estfale and Jalin were also crouched on the ground, squinting into the distance, waving their arms around them in slow motion. It would have been comical if the situation was not so dire. Jalin was too far behind her. All Trela could do was kick Estfale as she ran past him towards the disappearing figure of the Fluen. She had wanted to get him in the stomach, to make him gasp for the air that surrounded him, but she had little choice of her angle as she ran past and he was flailing around a little too haphazardly for her to aim, so she ended up clipping him in the face.

As she exited the door, she saw the Fluen escaping the house. She ran down the hallway towards a door open to the outside. Estfale roared behind her, whether or not it was from her kick she could not tell. As she leapt off the porch, she caught sight of the Fluen struggling with a decorative gate at the side of the yard. The Fluen turned, yelled, and hurled something at Trela. Trela yelled as she flung herself at the Fluen in a clumsy attempt at a tackle. Estfale yelled from somewhere behind her. As the Fluen turned to escape, to try to jump a hedge rather than continue fumbling with the gate, Trela's right hand caught the Fluen's boot. She pulled up and out with all of her might, tripping the Fluen. It was then that Trela realized she had been stabbed. The Fluen had thrown a knife of some kind into her left arm and she only noticed when she tried to move it. Not only was her arm useless and not responding, but once she noticed the pain, it shot through her entire body, incapacitating the rest of her. Luckily, at that moment, she noticed Estfale launching over her and crashing into the Fluen as she was getting back up. Trela rolled onto her back while he half dragged, half carried the Fluen back into the house, one hand around her waist while the other tried to stay clamped over her mouth. The grass felt nice under Trela. Even the slight rain felt refreshing. She waited until she could not hear the struggles anymore before she found the energy to remove the blade. It took her another couple of moments to shuffle herself inside. Somehow all the commotion did not bring a bunch of guards or even curious neighbors. She shut the door behind her and hobbled down the hallway.

Trela got to the parlor and dropped herself into a chair. Jalin appeared a little dazed, but walked over to cast some minor healing spells on her. The Fluen was still yelling at Estfale as he was tying her to a chair of her own, but when she noticed Jalin on the move her ire shifted.

"You whore, that was my favorite vase!" She was soon gagged by Estfale.

Though Jalin completely ignored the Fluen, Trela's eyes wandered the room trying to figure out what she was talking about. Then they rested upon the baby's swaddling blanket. There, intermingled with the blanket itself, were a myriad of porcelain shards. Trela realized that Jalin must have been holding a vase the entire time they were talking to the Fluen.

"So, you're an illusionist." It was a statement, not a question. The Fluen would have not been able to respond at that point anyway. Trela was merely shifting stuff around in her own head, categorizing problems. She had yet to tangle with a good illusionist, so it had not entered her mind that the baby could be fake. It was only that the flood was so instantaneous, too instantaneous to be real, that she had even been able realize there was a disconnect between her senses and reality. Unfortunately, now she was going to have to examine and weigh everything that happened, just to be sure that it was all real. Which would make everything take a lot longer.

Estfale wandered over. "So, what do we do with her?"

It was a simple question, quickly and easily asked, but Trela had no idea. None whatsoever. They could not leave her there to warn Laqual, or whatever the warrior's true name was. Of course, it would raise a flag if she suddenly disappeared as well. Which meant that Trela could wait and ambush him, taking two hostages, and hope that would be missed less than if only one had gone missing. There just seemed to be no easy answers.

"Well, she is definitely not part of any Resistance." Jalin spoke dryly to no one in particular.

"I certainly agree with you, but to be fair, she could have been part of the Resistance and still tried to escape us." Estfale glanced over in the Fluen's direction. There was a wry smile forming on his lips.

"She is not part of the Resistance, we cannot leave her here, and we cannot take her with us." Trela cut Estfale off before he annoyed Jalin too much. "Do we ambush Laqual? For some reason, that is the only solution I can think of."

"I think we have to kill her." Jalin took a quick turn glancing at the Fluen. She had a different form of wry smile forming. Trela glanced at the Fluen—she did not appear to have heard Jalin.

"Whatever we do, we have to do it to both of them." Estfale looked back at Trela. "I guess you're right. We'll have to ambush this Laqual."

"What excuse could two derlians give that would alleviate them of duty without arousing too much suspicion?" Jalin was musing aloud, staring at the ceiling. But it was the question that Trela needed.

"They both have to be deathly ill. Like horrible vomiting and diarrhea. Bad enough that when they are checked on, the investigator leaves immediately." It came to her in a flash.

"But not so ill that they come back with mages and physicians. Like, borderline deathly ill." Jalin tilted her hand back and forth, emphasizing the word borderline.

"Maybe Laqual would not even know we were here? Maybe we could make her so sick that she can't talk to him, but keep Laqual at that borderline?" Estfale pointed with his thumb, through his chest, to the Fluen behind him.

"We only need them to be sick for a couple of days. Do we wait for Feyazki or grab some other mages? Who works with pestilence?" Trela cocked an eyebrow.

They were not sure. Pestilence was not an honorable Pyran specialty. Ages ago, long lost to the mists of time, warriors would coat their swords with rotten meat or feces to increase the odds of wounds going septic, but that was now considered a complete betrayal of honor. And had been considered such a betrayal for so long that warriors had been killed by their own warpack who had been suspected of such treachery. The whole idea of using pestilence as an attack was so despised that most Pyran mages did not even study the field, and those who did would certainly not admit to it. So Trela was hoping that some other race had less of an issue using pestilence against their enemies. Of the three Pyrans gathered in the Fluen parlor, however, no one knew of such a mage.

The other issue they had was getting more information out of Laqual's wife. Trela wanted to explain to her how close she was to being killed, how they were backed into a corner about her and needed her to be more useful to them alive than dead. But Trela was worried she would cast more illusions once the gag was removed. Plus, every time they looked over at her, she would yell into her gag and rock the chair around. She seemed to have an endless reservoir of energy and rage. It did not help that Jalin quietly, but continuously, argued to just kill her. Trela was more used to Estfale making such untenable suggestions, though she could not always tell if he made them in seriousness or in a conscious attempt to be annoying. He was easier to deal with than Jalin, however, because Trela could quiet him instantly by giving an order. It was more that he got bored during the decision-making process than that he really wanted the untenable suggestion to happen. It seemed that Jalin really could just kill Laqual's wife and be happy with any consequences that befell her. And Jalin was typically not very bloodthirsty; Trela could think of no other instance where her response was to just kill the prisoner. The illusion must have really bothered her.

So Trela wasted a huge amount of time not deciding anything. Laqual's wife stayed tied and gagged. Jalin and Estfale argued the futility of the situation back and forth amongst themselves. Trela's mind ran the same useless circle until, finally, Feyazki arrived. And he was not alone. For some reason, he had brought Clerin back with him. The excuse was that they had randomly run into each other while he was trailing Laqual, and once Laqual had disappeared onto the palace grounds, they had decided to get some lunch, et cetera. Trela was quite sure that it had been planned, which went a long way towards explaining Feyazki's sudden desire to shadow a Luften warrior.

The entire "Laqual's wife" situation was explained to them. Feyazki, ever helpful to learn something new, agreed that he could try some pestilence spells. However, Clerin's presence turned out to be quite serendipitous.

"I know a mage in the coterie who studies pestilence." Clerin smiled enigmatically. "I need to talk with them first, however, to see if they are willing for this to be known."

Both of them left. Trela didn't want Feyazki to leave so they could more thoroughly question Laqual's wife, but it was explained how much faster it would be if they could travel together. The explanation was supposed to be vague, but it was obvious that the mage they were looking for was out in the smuggler's cave, not in town. It made Trela wonder if there were members of her coterie she did not know enough about, like some of the Gaens who had joined over the last few moons, or maybe it was a Yaven, or maybe it was Feyazki and they were just playing for time, or maybe... The conjecture was useless.

Trela walked over to Laqual's wife and sat down next to her. She was both tense and intense. She squinted hate at Trela, flexed against her ropes, and chewed on the gag tied around her head. Trela wanted information from her, but was afraid to remove the gag. Surely she could steel herself against whatever fake dangers might appear, but the other illusions had been quite realistic. And besides, what if the Fluen could throw fire or untie her ropes with magic? Just because she was good at illusions did not mean that was the only magic she could cast. It was too risky, and for what? More lies? So, instead of removing the gag, Trela decided to explain her position.

"I'm really not sure how to get out of this situation without killing you." The Fluen did not look at her as she spoke, so her expression of concern and aggrieved acceptance that she had placed on her face went unnoticed. "It is not as if I *want* to kill you, though there are those here who do, but that I may *have* to. We need to have a way out of this situation, don't you agree?"

Laqual's wife glared and struggled. The chair rocked precariously back and forth but did not tip over. She tried to mouth something through the gag. It was difficult to tell, but Trela was pretty sure it had something to do with removing the gag, which was the one thing that she wouldn't do.

"The thing is, I can't trust you. Can I?" Trela paused for effect. The Fluen stopped for a second, and though Trela could not tell what was running through her mind, she could tell it was running fast. Suddenly the Fluen looked her in the eye, hard but not confrontational, and nodded. She thrust her jaw out, indicating the gag could be removed. All Trela could think about was the way she had talked about the Resistance. She had seemed so convincing. She ran so far between hot and cold, there did not seem to be any middle ground. "No, I really don't think I can. Which is why I think we are going to have to incapacitate you. Just for a couple of days."

The glare and the struggle came back. This time the chair tipped and she started to scoot herself along the floor. Trela watched impassively for a moment before she realized the Fluen was rubbing her cheek on the ground, attempting to get the gag loosened. So she hopped up, and careful not to be close enough to be head-butted, she hauled the chair back up. She had to move her own chair to be able to face the Fluen again.

"I'm not telling you this to be cruel." The Fluen's hair was plastered about her face, stuck to the sweat of her exertion. "Well, maybe a little bit. But really, what I want is your cooperation during your incapacitation. I understand this is not fair, but if you just lean into it, if you let yourself be so ill as to be mutely bedridden, it will all be over in a few days' time. And I promise you that both you and Laqual will survive this ordeal."

Trela wanted to continue, to explain how she was not in a position to let many of the Cabal live, that she needed to feel assured that they were just low-level guards and errand runners. That the coterie was there to destroy everything that the Cabal had worked for, every last asset to be immolated. That they were on a mission from Gorbanax, from the Belegs themselves. But she knew she could not. She knew she had already spoken too freely.

"So I am going to let you think about it. You understand the choice? Death or incapacitation." Trela leaned in close enough to whisper in her ear, close enough that she could head-butt her if she wished. If her rage got the better of her. "Think about it long and hard." She patted her knee as she withdrew. It was supposed to be paternal, not condescending, but Trela was not sure how it would be interpreted. The Fluen stared impassively at her, giving nothing away.

Trela walked back over to the others. They spoke of nothing too secretive, just in case they could be overheard. Jalin made several open threats, but Laqual's wife was calm and straight-backed the entire time. She no longer struggled or made noise. At that distance it was difficult to tell if she was glaring.

After a while, Jalin went upstairs, just in case Laqual got back before Clerin. Estfale and Trela chatted quietly, ignoring Laqual's wife. It took some more time before they heard someone else above them. Since Jalin was as quiet as a cat, they assumed the others had arrived.

Clerin came down first, followed quickly by Nochiel and then Feyazki. Jalin stayed upstairs. Trela had been unable to think of another powerful mage they had quartered down at the cave, but she hadn't truly expected Nochiel.

"I thought you were disdainful of all magics besides healing." Estfale said it almost immediately. Partly it was a great relief to Trela since now she did not have to say anything herself. A similar sentiment had shot through her mind the second she had seen Nochiel. However, it was also partly obnoxious that he burst out like that. Nochiel's face instantly hardened in response.

"Understanding pestilence allows me to heal better. You do not understand the complexities of the derlian body. The millions of chaotic nuances, all interlinked and interwoven. Besides, I've never made anyone sick that I didn't heal." She appeared poised to turn and leave.

"Estfale! Apologize and head upstairs." Trela turned on him before Nochiel could turn on her.

"Of course, please accept my apology, I meant no offense to your skills or your morality." He looked properly contrite through his obvious annoyance. He started for the stairs and Trela watched him for a moment, trying to think of how to soothe Nochiel. Just before he walked up, as everyone else was staring at her, he turned to her and winked. He had a wry mischievous smile on, and then he disappeared up the stairs. It took Trela another second to focus back on the others.

"I want you to understand how grateful I am for your assistance, Nochiel. Truly, you are saving lives here. If we are unable to incapacitate this Fluen and her husband, we will have to kill them. Which, while in and of itself would be regrettable, would also surely put the Cabal on high alert. I thank you for coming to assist with this." She hoped she was not pouring it on too thickly, but Nochiel brightened nicely at her words.

"My skills, all of them, are at your service, my Queen." Nochiel bowed deeply. She had been waiting for Trela with Lishean, had been there since beginning of the warpack. She was Trela's greatest healer and, arguably, the greatest healer of the entire Pyran realm. She had joined the coterie without hesitation, not content to merely run the hospital at the Blaze. She was a true believer. Trela felt humbled and was overcome with the urge, or reminder, to pay more attention to those who followed her. "You are the Kriishan."

Nochiel assured Trela she could incapacitate the both of them, though she would then have to stay at the house for much of the time. Though she might have several hours between castings, she felt she needed full oversight in case the pestilence was too heavy or too light. Trela left Feyazki with her, at least until Laqual returned and was subdued. Trela did not necessarily wish to watch the spell begin, though she would have certainly made herself if that was what it took. Nochiel waved her away, confident in her own abilities, to which Trela was quite grateful. She left with Clerin. Jalin and Estfale followed about ten minutes behind. Besides, she had to prepare for the upcoming meeting with the Prince of Vatlisi.

Trela did not want to run into more issues with the guards, so she sent Jalin in alone for the last two houses on her list, with explicit instructions to only enter if the building was empty. And if there was any chance of getting caught, if Jalin felt she was under observation or even just got a little nervous, the mission should be abandoned. Trela did not think anything was going to get found, certainly none of the attempts so far had brought forth anything interesting, but she had to try in case fate wanted her to get lucky.

For the meeting with the Prince, Clerin had many rules and regulations. There was a sort of dress code, even though Trela was going as a bodyguard. She was only allowed one short sword and one dagger. Both had to be fully visible, one on either hip, and they needed what was called a "peace tie." A nice thick and strong string, pure white for easy visibility according to Clerin, wrapped around the hilt several times and knotted through steel rings in the sheath. It all meant that not only did Trela have to waste time procuring the proper clothing, which she had figured she would have to do, but also to waste time trying to find new sheaths that fit her favorite weapons. In the end, she merely had steel rings added to her own sheaths. She had thought long and hard about trying to have fake, or at least flimsy, rings attached, but thought better of it. She was certainly not anticipating any trouble, and a meeting with Fluen royalty was apparently all about image and pageantry. No, she would do her best to appear the part.

Clerin seemed quite excited. She enjoyed the shopping and planning and dressing and all of it. But what Trela thought Clerin enjoyed most was that *she* knew what was right. It was her invitation, her colors that they would both wear, her house they were representing, her home realm. She forced Trela to try on four different shirts, all of a similar pale blue color, just to try to find the perfect complement to skin tones or something. At least she did not try to get Trela into a dress. It was all very foolish and time consuming, especially so close to their meeting with the Cabal, but Clerin appeared to be relishing each and every moment. Trela had to keep reminding herself that the guards they were tracking down had all disappeared behind the palace walls at one time or another. Was it a coincidence? It could be. But she would keep her eyes and ears open during their lunch, just in case there was any indication that anyone at the palace had anything to do with the Cabal. She had kind of hoped the meeting would be more public, with more derlians, so that she could get lost a little and wander. As a fellow servant, she assumed she could chat with the palace underlings more readily. They always knew more of the goings-on of a castle than those who supposedly ran the place. Unfortunately, with the tiny audience she assumed they were to be a part of, she would be unable to escape the table without being noticed.

"I'm glad we were able to find a way to keep from killing Laqual and his wife." They were getting dressed in Clerin's room at the inn. Clerin had on a long pale blue dress with a plunging neckline and wide strips of fabric dangling from it. Not like fringe at all, more like large ribbons. It was a style that seemed odd to Trela, especially in such a rainy city, but Clerin, of course, made it look stylish.

"You've killed plenty of guards before without a second thought." Clerin looked at her sideways while she was adjusting herself. "We're about to slaughter the entire Cabal. Hopefully."

"If any of those guards suddenly turn up missing, it could jeopardize the whole mission." Trela fiddled with her own shirt, but she was unsure if she was making it any better.

"Of course. But that's not what you said." She stopped. "You kind of like Laqual's wife, don't you? It's as if you could see the two of you being friends under different circumstances."

"Well, just because I don't want to kill someone, doesn't mean I want to be their friend."

"You know what I think it is." Clerin's smile became a little devious. "She's feral."

"What? I don't even know what that means. I mean, I know what the word means, but not what you mean by it."

"It's a Fluen turn of phrase. It means that she used to be civilized, but now she's not. She's lost the decorum that a Fluen comports herself with. 'Civilized' is a word heavy with connotation and responsibility in the Fluen realm. Etiquette dictates everything, or at least it's supposed to. Laqual's wife was definitely not civilized, especially from what I heard about her from Jalin."

"So, you think I'm happy not killing Laqual's wife because I'm also feral."

"Oh no, you're not feral. You're wild." Clerin laughed. "You have to be civilized first before you can be feral."

They finally finished dressing and walked over to the palace. It had taken way too long to get everything perfect for Trela's taste, but Clerin was happy with their garb so, all in all, things were going well. The perimeter wall was low enough that the turrets of the palace itself could be seen from all directions at quite a distance, gleaming in the early afternoon sun. In essence, you could see at least one tower on the palace from just about any street within the quarter. They arrived at the gates just when they were supposed to, which Trela thought was too late but Clerin thought was a little too early. Since they were in the Fluen realm, meeting with Fluen royalty, she probably should have allowed Clerin to walk around the block again, but she detested being late. Besides, if the Prince wanted to make them wait after they arrived on time, he was certainly free to do so.

They were allowed in quite quickly, with just a simple check of Trela's peace knots. They passed through the highly decorated iron gates into a wide plaza that separated the low perimeter wall from the palace itself. The flagstone on the ground had a pinkish hue, but the exterior walls of the palace, with their varied round turrets with red-orange roofs, were a stark white. The turrets were symmetrically placed but started on different floors, bulging out at various elevations along the wall, some not even reaching the top of the wall they were ensconced on, which created a little chaos amidst the order. There were packets of lightly armed guards wandering around, also dressed in white. Trela wondered if their peace knots were properly tied, or since they were there to protect the Prince, if they were just for show. In any case, the knots were quite obvious. Clerin led the way to two gigantic doors, painted a deep red in contrast to the lighter roof coloring, that stood wide open. There were at least ten guards around the interior of the open doors which, oddly enough, made her feel better.

They were given a small escort of three guards, two in front and one behind, to find their way through the palace itself. Though the Blaze and the palace were both mazes of interior walls separating rooms, stairs up and down, hallways, and the occasional open-air low veranda or high terrace, they differed in some obvious aspects. The most poignant was the thickness of the walls. The palace walls were only a hand or two thick, which made them seem brittle and flimsy. Each room of the Blaze was a defensible position in its own right, while the palace did not seem to care about defense at all. Many of the hallways were mere colonnades with at least one wall missing. Most of the doors to the rooms were open, and even when closed, were thin planks of wood beautifully polished with amazing stains and oils. She was fairly sure she could get her foot through them with a swift, hard kick.

They ended up at the top of a turret, sort of in the middle area of the palace. There were taller turrets on one side and shorter ones on the opposite, making an obvious viewpoint and making Trela want to consider the taller ones as behind her and the shorter ones as in front. The red-orange roof was held up by no less than sixteen round wooden columns, leaving the view mostly unobstructed. There was a white stone parapet that ringed the view about waist high that included a cantilevered bench smothered in fringed and multi-colored pillows. There was a circular wooden table with eight chairs centered under the roof, with several wooden bowls overflowing with fruit placed around it. The guards bowed and left down the circular staircase they had just come up, leaving Trela and Clerin on their own.

Trela grabbed a bunch of grapes, knelt on a bench, and leaned over the edge, staring down onto the plaza far below. The grapes were amazingly good, which helped her resist the urge to drop one to see what would happen. She did not want to be a bad guest.

"Did I ever tell you about the time Feyazki dropped me into the river at the Luften Temple?" Clerin appeared beside her and stared down over the edge with her.

"Only a couple of times." Trela chuckled to herself. The problem with traveling someone for a long time was you heard all of their stories multiple times.

"Well, I think it was from about this height." She chuckled herself. "Here, give me a grape so I can drop it."

"No, we are not doing that." Trela halfheartedly guarded her grapes. "That wouldn't be very civilized, now would it?"

"Enjoying the view?" The sound of the voice startled them both.

The Fluen behind them was covered in stark white robes, not a stitch of color. The robes were layered and copious; he even appeared to have a scarf. He had long blond hair and a closely cropped beard. He was smiling a bit too much, his teeth gleaming amongst his robes. His eyes gleamed as well. He was incredibly attractive, even with the amorphous robes, but he had a far-away look of smugness. A self-assured expectation of always getting what he wanted. Trela recognized the happy grin and swagger of one who never heard the word "no." Those types were usually rich or beautiful, and this Fluen was evidently both. She hated those kinds of derlians. Well, maybe hate was too strong a word, but her annoyance at their mere existence typically inured her to their charms. She glanced over to Clerin, expecting to see commiseration on her face, but she was batting her eyelashes at him. Trela knew she could turn her charms on and off in a heartbeat but, for the life of her, was unable to tell if this one was fake or not.

"I am as well." He finished the thought that Trela knew he was thinking, but had thought he would not dare to speak it.

She quickly stood to face him, her grapes still encumbering her hands. Clerin slowly turned and bowed deeply, stiff back and knees, bending only at the waist. So Trela did the same, wondering what she would have done if Clerin had curtsied. When she came back up, Clerin was already walking towards the Prince with her right hand outstretched but relaxed, her fingers dangling delicately. The Prince stepped forward to intercept her, held her hand in his and kissed it, bowing his head slightly as he did so.

That was when Trela noticed his guards. There were two fragile looking female guards flanking the only doorway. They were not exactly scantily clad, but they certainly did not have robes on and were certainly showing more skin than anyone else in the turret. Their blonde hair was pulled back into severe ponytails that hung to about the middle of their backs. Everything about them matched, making Trela wonder if they were related. All in all, they were just another reason to not like the Prince.

"It is a pleasure to finally meet you, Clerin Toswin, daughter of Aillel and the famed Midinarre. Tales of your beauty overshadow even your mother's important work and, I must say, they pale in comparison to the real thing." He smiled up at her, kissed her hand once again, and made a sweeping gesture with his left arm and then led her over to a chair. Trela took a deep breath in through her nose and let it slowly out as she walked over to the table. She hoped the entire conversation was not going to be in similar vein.

It was for quite a while though. He gushed about Clerin's tremendous beauty and her mother's reputation and her own storied work with Lembin. For Clerin's part, she gushed about how wonderful Vatlisi was, as if it had not existed before the Prince and popped fully formed into the world by his mere will. Trela understood that the pomp and the vapid compliments were a required part of the conversation—they were a required part of any parley—it was just that it seemed to last forever. Part of it was most certainly due to the fact that she was not involved at all; she was completely ignored by both of them. It was not necessarily a bad thing, certainly not something she would hold a grudge against, but it added to her burden of boredom. She had not even caught his name when he finally got around to inserting it amongst his list of titles and accomplishments. She figured she could just refer to him as the Prince until she could discretely ask Clerin. Finally, however, during the middle of what appeared to be an audible lull, she attempted to steer the conversation.

"You are correct about the importance of understanding the Belegs' communications." She had heard them talking about that earlier in the conversation. She hoped that too much time had not passed since then to make her segue as clumsy as it felt. "What I understand, from the Pyran realm at least, is the Belegs' total agreement on one thing: The horrifying nature of the Cabal of Lochom."

She had wanted to just bring the name, just to set it there on the table, and see what the Prince would say about it. But she had already put a spin on it. He could not, without outright contradiction, speak favorably of the Cabal. She cursed herself for not thinking through her words more carefully. The long boredom had numbed her.

"Never heard of it." He did not speak to Trela, did not look at her, but was speaking directly to Clerin, a glass half raised to his lips partially obscuring his face. His eyes and eyebrows were inquisitive. He obviously did not care what Trela thought, but was intensely attuned to Clerin, like he was trying to read her facial cues before her words were formed in her mind, certainly before they were spoken. Trela felt that the intensity of his curiosity was information on its own, a small betrayal of his own thoughts. She felt better about bringing the subject up.

"Well, I was not necessarily going to bring it up." Clerin glared a little at Trela out of the corner of her eye. "But I can assure you that Lembin is concerned about the rumors of this Cabal's existence."

"You simply must satisfy my curiosity. Just what is this hated Cabal rumored to do?" He seemed a little more guarded now. They were certainly not going to find out what his real feelings on the subject were. Trela was back to being worried that she had mentioned it. It certainly made the employment of a Pyran bodyguard by a Fluen princess more circumspect.

"They are entrapping Yavens into items, which apparently kills them slowly and horribly." Clerin's voice was calm and a bit dismissive, leaving the Prince plenty of room.

"Don't Yavens die elsewhere? Don't they die amongst themselves or here in our realm, serving some minor mage for some random purpose?" He kept his voice calm and dismissive as well. Trela fought the urge to retort, Clerin was clearly more skilled in getting the Prince to answer with less artifice.

"You bring up a fair point and are speaking of fairness. We do not know why the Belegs favor Yavens over derlians when it comes to death." Her smile was filled with knowing and cute little dimples. "But I assure you that they do. My family in general, and myself personally, have always strived to communicate freely with the Belegs, with Lembin." She paused and laughed a little, shaking her head slightly and keeping her eyes slightly downcast. "All I am saying is that Lembin is quite concerned about the Cabal."

"Well, let me assure you that I will investigate the existence of this Cabal." He did not take his eyes off of her. "What did you say it was called again?"

"Lochom, the Cabal of Lochom." Her eyes stayed away from his as she reached for a bright plum.

"Is that the name of a derlian or..."

"You know, I have no idea." Clerin was obviously done investigating him because her lips were now glistening and there was a small droplet of plum juice that attempted to reach her neck. The Prince eyed it eagerly as she laughed heartily and wiped it away with a long finger.

Trela stood to avoid the spectacle and nodded to both of them. She was ignored by them both, so she wandered over to the guards. She smiled as they stiffened at her arrival.

"Please don't take this the wrong way. I'm not trying to be rude, seriously, but this question is going to sound rude." She nodded to both of them and they just stared coolly at her. "So are you really bodyguards, or are you decoration?"

All four of their thin and manicured eyebrows shot up. Then all four of their eyes narrowed into a glare. Trela began to wonder if they were twins, they appeared to be mentally linked along with the physical similarities.

"Why can't we be both?" one of the twins asked.

"What is your specialty?" the other twin asked at the same time.

"Umm." What *could* Trela test them at? "Knife throwing."

Suddenly three knives were produced. One of the twins was surreptitiously eyeing the Prince while the other scanned the cushions. She slowly grinned mischievously.

"That one, the red and gold one with the concentric circles." They smiled and nodded to each other; one might have winked. One of the knives was quickly passed to Trela. "Closest to the center wins, on three. One… two… three!"

Trela barely had time to find the cushion, aim, draw back, and throw. They all threw on the word three, the knives spinning dangerously close to each other in flight. Then, thunk! The cushion was thoroughly pinned to the bench behind it. It appeared that all three knives were within the central dot. Trela wondered if the knives had different markings on them or something.

"Just what do you think you're doing?!" The Prince was already standing, his face puffed up with anger, fists clenched at his sides.

Both of the twins instantly pointed a finger at Trela. It would have been more comical if they were not trying to pin the trouble on her. But the angry Prince was their boss and Clerin was laughing hysterically, so they were probably assuming she would not be reprimanded as much they would be. If so, they were completely correct.

Before the Prince had the chance to fire them or even chastise them, another guard came breathlessly through the door. He was much less decorative than the twins, and Trela wondered offhandedly if he was as dangerous.

"The guards at the west tower have captured a mage trying to sneak into the palace." He was so tired from his run up the stairs that, evidently, he did not notice the Prince had company. He immediately flushed even further and straightened his back once his eyes locked on Clerin.

The Prince glowered for a moment before turning to Clerin. "Please excuse me, I shan't be long." He nodded his head to the twins and they followed him out with serious looks on their faces.

They were alone for a few moments before it felt like Trela could move. She kept expecting someone else to come up the stairs. If not to keep them from wandering around the palace, then at least for their own security or something. But no one arrived. She walked back over to Clerin, who was pulling the knives out of the cushion.

"How could you mention the Cabal? I mean, really?" Her eyes were on the knife she was yanking on, but Trela could still feel the intensity.

"How could you not? What are we here for?" Trela picked up one of the knives from the table, more to keep her hands occupied than for any other reason.

"If he is involved at all, even just the tiniest bit, they will be on guard for Croy and Aedon. I thought you were the one who keeps mentioning how important secrets are." She tossed the last knife onto the table.

"So you were just going to wait until he mentioned it?"

"Oh, there was no way he was going to mention it." Her hand fluttered dismissively, discounting the thought.

"Then what were we here for?"

"I don't know, to have some fun. To enjoy some hospitality." She reached for another plum, but just rotated it in her hand, watching it appreciatively.

"Well, at least now we know. He is definitely involved."

"Who do you think the mage was? One of ours?"

"I sure hope not."

Chapter 20

How could he have been caught? He ran it over and over in his mind. He knew he had been silenced somehow, that had to have happened before they began draining his flight spell. He had not noticed it, however. Not in the least. He was flying along, surreptitiously he had thought, floating amongst a row of yew trees, when he felt the magic begin to drain. Instead of fighting it, as he should have, he had disastrously decided to just recast the spell. Maybe he had been in the air for longer than he had thought. Maybe he had used more energy skirting along the walls than he had calculated. Maybe there was just an anti-magic shell around the whole palace. He had thought of all sorts of things besides the fact that there were several mages actively draining his flight spell. It adversely affected his reaction. But the real issue, the real reason he failed, was that he had not noticed they had already put a silence spell on him. That one thing completely skewed his reasoning process. He decided that, in the future, he needed to be able to sense magic being used on him better. The one derlian he knew who naturally had this ability was Croy. Croy would have gladly spent a moon's worth of evenings discussing this ability. Would it have helped? Maybe. But Vrric could not know because he had not asked. Had not given this simple victory to Croy, to ask for help with something magical. He could kick himself for his shortsightedness and hubris. What a powerful combination those two loathsome attributes were. And now where was he? Where did his shortsightedness and hubris land him? In a crude, damp, rusty, rough-hewn stone jail cell. It was nothing short of awful. It was certainly worse than Revkin's old "cell."

Clerin had explicitly told him to stay away from the palace while she and Trela were visiting. Did he listen to her? No, of course not. More shortsighted hubris. What had he really thought to accomplish by flying into the palace anyway? He did not really know. He had these fleeting images of himself coming to Clerin's rescue. Of popping over a wall and seeing her in distress, and he could just swoop in and save everyone. He had half-known that the images were mere delusions, but there were other images as well. He would sneak in and talk to some servants about the Cabal. Or meet some mages who hated its existence and would give him important information. Or find some member that he could kidnap or something. Where did these useless images, these fantasies, land him?

In an awful jail cell. Even more frustrating was that he did not normally fall prey to those types of whimsical fantasies. Or, at least, he did not imagine himself falling prey to them often.

At no time in the jail could he speak. He was not sure where the mages were, but they were vigilant in keeping his silence. He began to wonder why speech was necessary. So, no mute could be a mage? Was it merely because that was how he had learned magic? The Word controls the Will? He started to wonder if he could use the Word, completely in his head, unspoken, and still focus his Will enough to cast something. He folded his legs under him in the lotus position, breathed in slowly through his nose, and was promptly interrupted by a clanging at this cage door.

"Hey, none of that!" It was a Fluen guard with a Gaen crossbow. He rattled the cage again. "You're not allowed to think on anything. Besides, your visitor will be here shortly." He wandered out of view.

It took several long minutes before anyone else peeked their head into his view. He stood and paced and pondered. He still wondered about casting a spell without using his voice but he did not want to be seen concentrating. What would be the simplest spell to cast, the one with the least effort, but would still be easily noticeable? He thought, without concentrating, that changing a tiny pebble into a piece of wood for a moment would be the simplest.

Then the guard came back into view. He did not yell about thinking or anything, but stood there casually pointing the tensioned crossbow Vrric's feet. This made Vrric stop and stare at the guard. He waited unsatisfactorily for an announcement of the visitor. Instead, a Fluen slid into view behind the guard with zero fanfare.

It was a short Fluen with short blond hair. He stood at attention and frowned at Vrric for several moments. It took long enough that Vrric tried to ask him a question. The frown did not twitch, but the guard raised the crossbow to take a more direct aim. Eventually the short Fluen tapped the guard's shoulder to dismiss him. He pulled out an official looking scroll and slowly unrolled it in front of him. His feet were shoulder width apart, as if he were in battle. It would have been comical if the mood was not so serious. Apparently he had started the unrolling too soon because he had to stand there for several moments, looking to his right out of the view of Vrric, before he started speaking.

"I have a sworn statement, signed by no less than seven guards, that you attempted to fly over a battlement and into a tower of the palace." His voice was crisp, even being somewhat loud. This was, obviously, the sole purpose of the derlian's existence. "How do you plead?"

The absurdity of it was excruciating. He had planned on arguing that he was just flying by and had not realized his proximity to the palace before he was dragged out of the sky by the Prince's mages. But how could he argue if he could not speak? More absurdly, how was he supposed to plead without being able to speak?

"Just nod your head, prisoner." The Fluen lowered the scroll slightly so he could glare at Vrric. Vrric crossed his arms and shook his head in the negative, mirroring the wide stance of the Fluen in front of him.

"The statement includes your location at the time of interception. Were you over the exterior wall at the time your flight spell was drained?" His voice seemed to get slightly louder. Vrric shook his head again.

"Are you stating for the record that the esteemed guards who have signed this statement are lying?" The exasperation in his voice was palpable. Vrric had decided to be as uncooperative as possible until they lowered the silence spell, just to be able to argue his point. But this question gave him a pause. He was fine being belligerent, but did not necessarily want to make an official lie. He shook his head again.

"Are you even able to nod?" The scroll was no longer taut between his outstretched hands, but sort of half folded into a sinusoidal wave. Vrric nodded once, very shallowly, hoping it was not some sort of trick.

Something was said to the Fluen that Vrric did not quite hear. The Fluen glanced to his right again and nodded quickly. He snapped the scroll back to taut, the top hand rolled and the bottom hand unrolled the scroll quickly and seamlessly, until the bottom of the scroll was reached. His hands did not move up or down and his fingers worked quickly. Vrric wondered if he practiced that sort of thing in front of a mirror. He was obviously quite skilled at such an odd talent.

"If proven guilty of the crimes we have lain before you, you may be imprisoned up to one year or lose the pinky from your left hand. Your choice." He finished rolling up the scroll, bowed to

Vrric, then turned and bowed to his right. He left without further comment.

Vrric waited for another few moments, staring at the guard with the crossbow who merely stared right back. He strained his ears to hear something, anything. He knew there were Fluens around him, watching his reactions. So he just stood there until, finally, another Fluen slid into view.

This Fluen was tall with long blond hair and gleaming teeth, though his smile seemed fake to Vrric. His white robes seemed expensive, which was what Vrric thought the Fluen wanted to convey more than anything else, the outlandish cost of his outfit. *This was*, thought Vrric, *the Prince of Vatlisi*.

"I will ask you two questions, and think wisely before you answer. I have ten mages around you right now and at least four of them will be checking to see if you are lying. Do you understand?" The Prince's look quickly turned angry. He paced back and forth slightly, as if he were unable to stay still.

Vrric nodded and attempted a sincere smile. It was unfortunate, because he doubted he could answer the questions truthfully. He again cursed his own stupid hubris which had brought him there.

"Do you know Clerin Toswin?" He stopped and stared hard at Vrric once he had asked his question. Vrric, for his part, furrowed his brow in confusion and slowly shook his head. He could not bring her into this, and since she had no idea he was anywhere near the palace, there was no circumstance he could think of in which telling the Prince the truth could help her.

"Have you ever heard of the Cabal of Lochom?" His voice was loud and pointed. Vrric knew there was no way to answer that question truthfully either, though he was not quite sure why. Many derlians may have heard of the Cabal. How could that be dangerous? Yet, he could just feel it in his gut. Vrric shook his head again and attempted a little shoulder raise as well, showing the Prince the palms of his hands.

"Wrong, wrong, wrong!" The Prince clenched his fists and twisted his face up. "I told you not to lie to me!" He turned on his heel and walked out of view.

There were several moments of intense silence. The guard with the crossbow just stood back impassively. Vrric hoped Clerin and Trela had already left the palace grounds but he doubted he was that lucky. Then the pain began. It was a searing, pushing pain. As if a red-hot poker was slowly being slid up into the base of his skull, right where his vertebrae connected to it. He fell to the stone floor but did not feel himself hit it. All he could feel, his entire world, was just the searing pain. Wrapped in silence.

When he woke he had no idea how long he had been out, but did realize he was in a different cell. He was worried that a lot of time had passed but was able to logically conclude that Croy and Aedon had not met with the Cabal yet. For if they had, he would surely be dead. Or least tied up on a torturer's table. But there he was, alive but uncomfortable, stiff, head full of cotton, scraped and bruised, achy and tired, and with a feeling of impending doom that motivated him to ignore his myriad complaints. He looked around briefly. It was a similar type of cell to his previous one but seemed more isolated. He could hear nothing beyond the iron door, nothing down the hallway or around the bend. There was another guard outside of his cell, definitely a different derlian. He was quietly sleeping, cradling a crossbow similar to the previous guard's.

Vrric tried to hum, but heard nothing. He tried to yell, but heard nothing. He sat back and thought. There must be at least one mage near him, keeping him silent. He folded his legs into the lotus position. To be able to help Clerin, and to a lesser extent Trela and the coterie, he had to escape. To be able to escape, he had to be able to cast spells. To be able to cast spells, he had to incapacitate the mage silencing him. To incapacitate the mage, he had to find them. How to find them?

He decided to begin at the beginning. His only really useful tool was his magic. There was no way he was going to trick the guard into entering the cell and then physically overpower him, though his mind floated over that delicious thought for a long moment. He glanced around for a weapon of some sort and had to admit that there was not a rock larger than his pinky at the last knuckle anywhere around. They were certainly thorough. He decided to cast the simplest spell he could think of, completely silently.

He took a tiny pebble from the available multitudes and placed it in front of himself. He stared at it long and hard. He did not want to draw attention to himself, but needed to draw some energy, so he tried to do it slowly, as if through a long skinny snorkel.

Lotragereʃpan! He thought it as hard as he could, even mouthed the syllables. He was going to try it over and over, like a chant, but did not have to. To his immense astonishment and delight, the pebble turned into wood. He had done it. He had cast a silent spell. It quickly turned back to stone, but he had done it. He cast the same spell a couple more times. He did not want to call attention to what he was doing, but wanted to make sure he felt comfortable with the process.

To find the mage he needed a noise. He needed something loud enough that he could discern direction and a rough distance. And it had to be something natural, something that could go unnoticed in the dusty confines. Once he had narrowed down what he needed, the idea slid into place like smoke up a chimney. He needed a sneeze.

He had often wondered about the usefulness of the Kha syllable. Why would one need a random target? But there, surrounded by very few living objects, it was the perfect syllable. He did not need to see the mage, did not need to know where the mage was, he just needed to get lucky enough, just needed to have Chaos smile upon him. Should he move dust in the air and hope that a sneeze was induced? He thought that rather than creating the conditions for a real sneeze, he needed to create an illusion of the need to sneeze. He thought long and hard, but finally decided upon the silent syllables of his spell. He slowly drew energy into him through his long snorkel. *Lofintotkha!* He sent it out, tilting the pillar as far as he could to make a powerful enough sneeze happen. He did not need the spell to last a long time.

"Achoo!" The guard sneezed and almost dropped his crossbow. Vrric had worried that was a possibility, but could not stop there. *Lofintotkha!* "Achoo!" Vrric sneezed! And *he* knew it was an illusion. He had hoped he would have been immune. *Lofintotkha!* Finally, barely audible behind the stone wall, there was another violent sneeze. Vrric marked in his mind the direction it had come from and what distance it seemed to have been. "Achoo!" It was the guard again, walking over to the cell door. Vrric wasn't sure if that one was from his spell or what.

"You too, huh? This place is horrible for mold. I keep asking them not to stick me down here." The crossbow was dangling from one hand while the other roughly rubbed against his nose and mouth. "Hey, Yewathica! He's awake!" The guard yelled haphazardly behind him and walked straight to the bars, resting his elbow on a cross-tie and touching his face to one of the vertical bars. He still seemed tired but was quite friendly looking with a warm and ready smile. "They were wondering when you'd get up. They keep coming down here, checking on you. I tell them, I says, 'I'll holler for you when he starts moving,' but they're nervous. Seems like you've got some pretty powerful derlians mad at you." He blinked heavily. "What'd you do?"

"I lied to the Prince." Vrric stayed sitting where he was, mouthing his silent response. The situation was a disaster. Why couldn't the guard have just stayed asleep?

"What?" The guard's face scrunched up in momentary confusion. Vrric mouthed the words again, this time exaggerated for easier deciphering. "Oh, yeah, I forgot. You're saying you lied to the Prince?"

Vrric nodded.

"Hmmph. Must've been more than that." He pulled his face away from the bars and started meandering back to his seat. "I lie to the Prince all the time." His right arm flopped upwards in a rough closing salutary gesture and then dropped lifelessly down. He set his crossbow down and rotated slowly, ending up in his seat as if he were a corkscrew. A very lethargic corkscrew. "They'll be here in a while. Don't make any noise." He laughed briefly at his own joke and then his lids dropped to half-mast as if they were too heavy to keep open. He did not quite close his eyes, but there was no way he was really paying attention.

Vrric's mind raced. He made several quick calculations in his head. They all depended on two distinct things. One, how many mages were casting silence spells on him. And two, how quickly the guard would pick up the crossbow once Vrric started making noise. He felt pretty good about the second issue. It was the first that really worried him.

Nufintotclo! He cast a silent sleep spell that would surely encompass the location where the sneeze had come from. He did not hear a reassuring thump or anything, but had to assume it worked. He tried to hum a little, just to make a sound, and heard a beautiful sublingual buzz. He was not positive he could speak, but he could make a quiet noise. He had been worried that his spell was of such a low power rank that even with taking the mage by complete surprise they would be able to resist the spell. He might have benefitted from the mage being naturally tired but still felt he had gotten quite lucky. *Nutectotpri!* He decided to shield himself from the silence spell rather than trying to drain the magic from the sleeping mage, mainly because he was still unsure of exactly where the mage was.

"Narfintotclo!" Vrric cast another sleep spell, one that encompassed the entire room and beyond, just in case. The guard's eyes had opened wide at the sound, but dropped peacefully back down by the time the spell was finished being cast. "Lokinheparc!" The keys came flying over to Vrric's outstretched hand. It took only a moment to unlock the cage door from behind, but it sounded incredibly loud to him. The clanging, scraping, and rasping. He took the keys with him, just in case.

Just to his left, around the corner in a small alcove, another guard lay slumped. This was opposite direction that he had sensed the mage, and she had the look of a warrior, but it was slightly unnerving. He was glad he had cast the larger spell. He started to walk quickly down the only available hallway for he thought running would make too much distinctive noise.

He found a T-intersection. He strained his hearing as hard as he could, and there was certainly the soft sound of footsteps in the distance, but he was unable to tell which direction they were coming from. "Meksidgearc! Meksidgearc!" He sent a question through the stone floor in both directions. It was not long before he received his answer. He walked quickly away from the intersection along the empty hallway.

He eventually reached some stairs and found what he assumed was the ground floor of the palace. He popped up into what appeared to be a small foyer. The stairs continued up and there were three doors and plenty of windows. There was no one in the immediate room, no one saw him emerge from the lower floor, but he could hear voices all around. He had no idea where he was but just knew he needed to get off of the palace grounds. He needed to regroup with the others in Vatlisi, or even better for his nerves at that point, at the smuggler's cave.

"Eqekinderpri!" He flew through an open window. He skimmed along the ground for a while outside, just a little faster than he could walk, while he regained his bearings. There was a gate in the distance off to his right but he went straight for the wall. He stood there for several long moments. There were a couple of groups of guards in white meandering away from him to his left. It was open space on his right all the way to the gate. He was between turrets, at just the middle of the wall. It did not seem as if there were any guards on the battlements. He took several deep breaths. It was similar to how he had gotten caught previously, though he was at the perimeter wall now and had been at the palace turrets earlier. All he could really do was hope that no one was watching. He made one last scan of the area before shooting up the face of the wall. No one was at the top, and he flew over the wall and came down on the other side as quickly as possible. A few derlians pointed and exclaimed, especially a small group of children, but no one yelled for the guards, no one raised an alarm. He was merely a curiosity. He smiled and waved and walked away from the palace as quickly as he could and still be inconspicuous. His ears kept straining to hear footsteps behind him, or guards yelling, long after he had left the area.

Vrric finally found the Cascading Cataract, Clerin's inn. He was told she was not in and had not been seen lately. When he asked for more complete information, he was merely met with frowns. She had also apparently paid for a whole other week and, therefore, the innkeeper did not take kindly to Vrric's offer to assist her in her absence. All in all, he figured the next time he arrived there, it had better be with Clerin.

His next stop was the Naked Hare, the Pyran inn. He thought that Trela might be there, and if nothing else, Serghno and Arnasta should be. The innkeeper did not appear to know if Trela was there or not but did allow him to wander the halls and knock on her door since he knew her room number. The door crept open a tiny crack at his knock and Trela's feral yellowish eye peeked out and then squinted down into anger. She let him in and let him get settled before quietly, but forcefully, explaining what a moron he was.

"Why would you do that? What possessed you? Are you ill or malnourished? That was, without a doubt, the most moronic thing you have ever done. And I have seen you do some stupid stuff." When Trela got angry her whole body would emit it. Every muscle twitched with rage. Her eyes grew wild and unpredictable, alternating between wide-eyed disbelief to narrow dangerous slits. Her arms made slashing motions in the air as she spoke. Even her hair radiated a barely controlled rage. "You know the Prince still has her there, in the palace? She's a prisoner! Well, not necessarily a prisoner, but she can't leave. I barely made it out by bribing some twins and that is only because I'm inconsequential to the Prince. He's probably happy I'm gone." She got quiet for a second, as if it was the first time she had thought about the ease of her escape. "You've jeopardized our entire mission and gotten the derlian you love captured and... Argh! You've ruined all my planning. Just... just tell me you had a reason, a plan."

"I was hoping to find something, someone, who would help. I..." He tried with all of his might, but could not think of a good excuse as to why he had flown into the palace. He had just thought he could help out and Clerin would be grateful and nothing bad would happen. That at the worst it would have just been a waste of time.

"You're a Luften. You're a foreigner here, just like me. If you had been a Fluen, maybe you could have wandered the palace grounds looking for... I don't know what." She sat down heavily in the chair opposite him. Her voice got low and defeated, which was worse than getting yelled at. He was used to Trela being angry, even if it was not typically towards him. He was not used to hearing her sound defeated. "I could have imagined so many others doing this, being the thorn in my side. But not you, Feyazki. I need you too much for this to have come from you. And Clerin. What are we supposed to do about Clerin?"

"I'll fix it. Don't worry, I'll fix it." He tried to sound hopeful.

"You know you've been gone for over a day. Croy and Aedon meet with the Cabal tomorrow." There was a twitch of sadness in her eyes. "There isn't enough time to fix it."

Vrric went back to the smuggler's cave. Apparently, Phyna had found a tunnel that reached the interior of Vatlisi. They were to quietly sneak to the end of the tunnel at dawn. Once Croy and Aedon were on the move, Phyna should be able to bore directly to them, or at least near them. It was the vast consensus that the Cabal had their laboratory somewhere underground, hopefully within the confines of the city. When asked why they were not just camping at the end of the tunnel, certainly without fires or anything, it was explained to him that there was a concern of being sensed too early. The plans were already laid and he had already done enough damage, so he just went along for the ride.

He had kind of been hoping to speak with Croy a little. Somehow the Gaen could make one feel better about the largest of mistakes. It was an eerie, but beautiful, ability. Unfortunately, he was still in Vatlisi. Vrric supposed he should have stopped by the Hillside Heather before going to the Naked Hare.

It was evening by the time he reached the cave. Everyone was warm and welcoming. No one mentioned Clerin. He had a good meal and chatted with Serghno and Arnasta. They had left the city a little before he did.

The mood in the cave was an odd mixture. They had all finally arrived. The journey was over. It was only to finish the deed the next day. Would they all survive? Would any of them survive? There was the relief that they could be headed home soon blended with the impending dread that one feels before a battle. No wine or beer or grog was imbibed, nothing was smoked. Everyone was very serious even when they were joking. It was the calm before the storm, when all the birds fell silent and the horses trotted back to the barn. In its own way, it was nice.

Vrric typically did not have a hard time sleeping, even before battle. But he felt like he had slept for a couple of days, he was just not tired. So he packed everything he was not going to sleep in or wear the next day. It was amazing how little stuff he had. He helped others get ready as well. Then he wandered for a moment and found Voyt talking with Gyllhelon. Voyt had the odd habit of standing during conversation. Sure, if he was at a table and surrounded by other sitters, he would sit, but more often than not he could be found standing. His slightly vacant eyes and constant smile was somewhat refreshingly familiar. Gyllhelon was also standing, looking incredible as she always did. Of course, now that he was with Clerin, he did not allow himself to think things like that.

"Friend Feyazki, I greet you." Voyt's hand shot up to be shaken.

"Yes, friend Feyazki, how do you do?" Gyllhelon also shook his hand, though her smile looked more mischievous.

"Are you ready for tomorrow?" Vrric knew it was a bit trite, but he was never great at the pre-battle banter. He was also unsure of what to say to a Yaven who was pretending to be a derlian. He was not even sure if Gyllhelon knew the secret, though he supposed not.

"Oh, yes. It will be exciting to see what everyone can do. The moment has finally arrived." He nodded a couple of times.

"You might want to stay near the back, at least at first. It's ah… going to get ugly." Gyllhelon looked genuinely concerned for Voyt.

"Oh, no. I wish to experience it fully." He paused for a moment and looked intently into Gyllhelon's face. "I can see how you would be concerned that I would be in the way, however. I shall observe from the side, yes?"

It was her turn to pause. Vrric could tell that she did not want to be rude but did not want him rushing in as a lone shock troop either. She finally relaxed a shoulder and beamed a smile. "Perfect, yes. You should observe from the side."

She then half-turned to head off but glanced back at Vrric. Suddenly Voyt perked up. "I should be leaving to sleep. Thank you, both of you. I will see you both in the morning." He shuffled off as they were saying their own thank-yous and goodbyes.

"I guess it's just you and me." Her smile was still beaming.

"I… I really miss hanging out with you. Truly." Her black hair looked lush and full cascading down her back. He was always amazed at how it never seemed to be in her face.

"But…?" She was still smiling but had an eyebrow cocked. "I think I sense a but coming on."

"Well, it's just that you're too fantastic to hang out with." What was his problem? He tried to think it through, but was having difficulty.

"That is the worst compliment I've ever heard. And I have heard a lot of weird stuff."

"I just… I wish it could be like it was. Just hanging out, you know?"

"Me too. So what's the problem?"

"Well, it's like, the opposite of a problem. I enjoy it too much." He was going to continue but she put up her hand.

"It's fine, I understand. I'll give you a pass tonight." She darted in and kissed him on the cheek. "We'll see what tomorrow holds." She turned and left, looking as happy and as ravishing as ever.

It had happened so quickly, all of it. He had wanted to sit and chat with others, he had found some, they disappeared, and now he was all alone. He was not typically prone to melancholy, but he felt a little empty in the quiet. The feeling oddly reminded him of being alone at Agoge so long ago. So, instead of pondering further, he shuffled off to find his bedroll. He should at least get some sleep before they all got slaughtered.

Vrric was shaken awake by Serghno. It felt incredibly early and he was groggy enough that he wondered if he should have slept at all. He took his time gathering his meager things and wandered over to get breakfast. He could see stars shining out of the cave's mouth. It was still night, or at least it was not yet day. They had just about anything you could want for breakfast, hot and fresh. Sort of a last meal thing. He did not want to be too weighed down, even though it was going to be many hours before anything happened, so he did not overdo it. He always had some hard rolls and jerky on him if he got hungry later.

They gathered what they wanted but left whatever they did not need. They would either be coming back or not. He did bring a thick blanket that he assumed he could abandon if need be. He just wasn't sure how long they were going to sit at the terminus waiting for Croy and Aedon's directions. He left most of his spare clothes tucked away in the crook of a boulder. A lot of the warriors were doing the same, finding little hidey-holes.

Rewista was apparently leading them, though there was another group of warriors off to the side. Estfale, Jalin, Dartsyle, and the like. They were certainly following Rewista, but it felt as if they had further orders from Trela. Verin and the Gaens made another contingent, and the Luftens coalesced around Vrric. It was not completely cut by race—Silvadhin was with Vrric's group and Kryhir was with the Gaens—but it was a little striated.

As they moved through the tunnel system, the split became less obvious. Serghno and Arnasta were talking with Vrric, and Escha and Torpalin were chatting with Zira. Some of the Gaens seemed to lag in the back, but Verin and Tesjuk were up at the front. By the time they had gotten close to their destination it was fairly well mixed, though there still seemed to be a preponderance of Gaens at the back.

Rewista halted them and spoke quietly. "We are under some buildings now and will soon be at the tunnel's terminus. We are quiet and attentive from here on in." Everyone nodded to each other and then whispered loudly back and forth. Rewista seemed content with lip service at that moment.

Finally, they reached a large round room. There were a dozen or so crates stacked in one area and full sacks of flour or grain in another. There were also two large doors opposite each other. Vrric figured there were stairs behind at least one of them. They all gathered around and found as comfortable a spot as they could. At that point, the whispering was in earnest and the group was quite quiet. Rewista walked over to Vrric.

"So, you know the drill, right? Croy will *whisper* to you when they are on the move. You will take over the communication so that all magic is coming from our direction, not his. Then, between you and Arnasta, we will track them to wherever they head. Hopefully, it will be close and in a direction without many obstacles since Phyna may have to make a tunnel to get to where we need to arrive. At the proper moment we will burst through the walls and destroy the Cabal." Her raptor eyes narrowed at the end, though he was not positive if that was to emphasize the word "destroy" or if she was warning him not to contradict her.

"Do we have contingencies if the meeting happens outside of the city or above ground or if Croy is captured right away or...?" He could not help himself. He wanted to laugh at the simplicity of it all but knew that they were all being serious, so he only brought up serious concerns.

"We have dedicated Yavens and some of the greatest derlian warriors the world has ever seen. That is our contingency plan." She patted him on the shoulder and dropped her whisper even quieter. "Besides, all we can do is follow Croy and Aedon, right? You let me know if you have something better." At the word "better," which was barely audible, her eyes dropped in for the kill.

"Of course." He nodded and whispered loudly, no longer willing to have conflict over their lack of planning. She was right, in essence. They did not have any good choices. "Do you think we should start the tunnel lower? Will we run into anything if we shoot straight sideways?"

"Good. I'll let you speak with Phyna." She turned and strode off. Of course, the room was not that large, so she just strode to the other side.

Vrric decided to just get comfortable for the wait. He folded his blanket into quarters and laid it out partially on the ground and partially up the wall, making a rudimentary, but not incredibly uncomfortable, chair. After a few moments, Arnasta and Serghno arrived. They both sat near him, with their backs to the rest of the room.

"We hear you have some concerns about the tunneling portion of the plan." Arnasta began the conversation slowly before Serghno butt in.

"A word of advice about Rewista…" His mustaches quivered when he spoke. He was enjoying himself. He trailed off a little, as if he did not really have any advice.

"I know, I know." Vrric interrupted so that Serghno did not have to come up with anything. "It has been a rough couple of days."

Then a rock rolled out from under, or near, Arnasta's carefully laid out pouch. It rolled into the epicenter of the rough circle the three of them made. Phyna grew enough in size that it was obvious, but not large enough to be noticed by a casual passer-by.

"Please, I do not mind discussing concerns or contingencies. I was hoping to be traveling with Croy, but that was refused to me. It was explained that under no circumstances would a Yaven be allowed to try to sneak into the Cabal's laboratory, especially with one of the three performing the meeting." Phyna rolled to position itself in front of Vrric. "Also, I naturally feel more comfortable in the company of mages rather than warriors."

The word "three" took Vrric aback for the briefest of seconds. Everyone kept saying Croy and Aedon when they talked about the meeting. He had, somehow, forgotten that the Blind One was accompanying them. Well, forgotten was probably the wrong word. He had put it out of his mind somehow.

"Do *you* trust the Blind One?" Vrric looked pointedly at Phyna.

There was a small pause. "No." Another pause. "However, I am unable to tell if that mistrust is due to anything real or specific, or if it is just due to the fact that Croy does not trust the Blind One. While in the derlian realm, I tend to take on some aspects or affectations of my summoner. I am not sure if this is due to being in a strange realm, or if there is a deeper connection. I should speak with Wil about the relationship bonding it experiences with its summoner."

"How fast can you make a tunnel wide enough for us to walk through? I am a little worried that we'll have to move down to avoid other basements and the like." Vrric decided to voice his concerns. "We just have no idea how fast they are going to move up there. What if they fly? What if the Blind One teleports?"

"Well, if they travel on the ground, we should have no worries. I can certainly create a void in the stone as fast as a derlian can run, at least in bursts. I would not be overly concerned about starting lower, I should be able to slant the tunnel fairly easily. There is nothing these stones won't do for me." Phyna patted the ground with its tiny hand.

"And if they fly or worse?" Vrric pressed ahead.

"There is a speed at which they can move that will outpace me, even at my fastest. If that occurs, we would then depend upon your tracking skills and we would arrive after they did. If you are unable to track them, then I do not know what we would do next." Phyna turned towards Arnasta as it spoke. It obviously knew who had more skill in tracking.

They chatted about nothing in particular for a while until Vrric recalled something he was curious about. "So, the soil around you speaks to you?" He tried to steer the conversation without being obvious about it.

"Yes, and I speak to it. It is how I get the soil to do things. We communicate. I make requests." Phyna's speech sped up a tiny bit, which Vrric equated with it being excited, but he was not sure he wasn't anthropomorphizing, though that was not the correct word.

"But is it like you can see through it? Or do you have to ask the soil what is up ahead and then it describes it to you?" He did not pause long enough for Phyna to prepare its measured response. "And if you can't see through it, how about sound? Is sound the real sound or is it a description? I mainly ask because you can hear horse hooves many leagues away by placing your ear to the ground."

"Yes, I can see how you would expect a difference between how sight or sound travels through the ground, considering your limited experience. And there are differences, experienceable differences. Yet, since your second statement is most correct, in this case it does not matter if there are real differences. The sight or sound is described to me. This is a little misleading, since part of the description are flashes of what the soil actually experienced, the image of the sight as it were. But the essence is the same. The description is not fully complete. There are blurs and voids, problems with translation." Phyna paused for a moment but Vrric did not wish to interrupt. "As an added benefit, this form of communication is hard to trace or eavesdrop on. If we do not wish to be noticed, it is better to use description than direct experience."

"Good, good, that has certainly answered my question." Vrric smiled to himself.

They waited for quite a while, or at least it felt like a long time, chatting more and more about nothing in particular. Much of the group had split into smaller units as the time wore on. Vrric was shocked at how long Serghno and Arnasta stayed with him before splintering off to be on their own. He did not feel bad since he was fairly positive that was what he would have done had Clerin been there. It was while listening to Phyna tell the story of its great walls of history, its library, that the *whisper* came. It was so faint that Vrric almost missed it, as engrossed as he was in Phyna's tale.

"Feyazki… Feyazki…" Vrric found where the signal was coming from, triangulating on Croy's position as quickly as he could, then casting his own *whisper* spell.

"Croy, it's me, Feyazki." Vrric *whispered* back to Croy.

"Mm hmm." It was very faint, but undeniable. Vrric did not communicate after that. He knew Croy was too occupied to be bothered, he did not want to distract Croy in the slightest. They had established the link, as was required, and that was enough. Vrric got Arnasta's attention and then waved her over to him.

They were on the move. What was less sure was whether or not they were heading towards their destination. What if those above just wandered in a circle for a little bit, would that mean new torus tunnels would be created under the city? Since Croy was, somewhat, headed towards them, they all waited for a while longer. Croy eventually passed them by, so Phyna started making tunnels.

Vrric and Arnasta were right behind Phyna, and Rewista and Serghno were right behind them. Vrric did not concern himself with anything beyond that. The tunnel was completely neat and clean, not a rock to stub your toe on, not a pebble out of place, not even any dust. It made following Phyna a breeze. Vrric did not even have to look down.

The tunnel sloped downward slightly. Vrric just kept an open conduit between himself and Croy and Arnasta, while she did all the actual work. Her directions were quiet and simple, just left and right, speed up or slow down. Phyna decided elevation based on what it sensed ahead of them, or what the soil itself sensed and conveyed back to Phyna. They had decided to leave a decent gap behind Croy so that they would not actually ever be under him. Vrric had originally worried about the noise it would take to create such a large tunnel, but he needn't have. Phyna was completely silent. It was all the clanging and muttering of the warriors behind him that now concerned him.

They were underground and had been for quite some time, so he was completely turned around. He had not even been sure where they had originally stopped, the trip from the smuggler's cave had taken so long. He was not even sure which quarter of the city they happened to be under. So there was no way that he really knew where they were or were they were headed. And yet he could feel it, inexplicitly. He felt it deep within him, it came from his bones. They just had to be heading towards the palace.

Eventually they stopped, keeping their gap with Croy. Phyna did not widen the tunnel so they sat in line where they had stopped. After the clamoring of everyone sitting at once, an eerie silence blanketed the group. It only took a couple of moments of quiet before Vrric began to feel the oppressive weight of boredom settle upon him. Well, not boredom really, more like frustration at the inability to do anything constructive. He decided to take a small chance.

"Eqefinderarc!" Vrric placed most of the power of the spell into keeping itself hidden rather than duration, though a fair bit of the power was used in reaching Croy as well. It was just an open conduit, a way to hear the physical sounds that Croy heard, not to affect or change anything. He knew it was a risk, but they also needed a way to decide when to attack. He wanted to know, beyond realizing that it had already started, beyond being frantically asked by Croy or whenever Trela decided to have Ryshial *whisper* to him. Trela and Ryshial had another tiny contingent, following and spying up above. He wondered briefly if Ryshial had a similar eavesdropping spell going and, if so, if that made his spell more dangerously noticeable to the Cabal.

The sounds came in a bit faint at first, pieces of words at different volumes. Vrric slowly, carefully, focused his tilted pillar. The words started to become more coherent, the voices more distinct. He stopped improving the signal once he recognized Aedon speaking.

"…promised more than a walk through your laboratory. We were promised more than the shield itself which, apparently, you are still unable to produce. We were promised a demonstration. If you are unable to produce the shield, you must produce the demonstration."

"We know what we promised. We are having difficulty getting all of the mages required together, however. You must understand how much effort it is to confine a Yaven." The voice was strident, as if spoken from the diaphragm. Vrric, unsurprisingly, had never heard the voice before. "One of our mages is sick. You must understand, she is at death's door. We had sent several warriors to fetch her, but to no avail."

"That's the worst excuse I've ever heard!" Croy's voice boomed in Vrric's ear. He spun his head around, half expecting the others to shush him, but of course they could not hear anything. Arnasta cocked an eyebrow at him but that was all. "Sick?! This is a child's excuse. Don't you have other mages? You are really telling me this is the only mage who can confine a Yaven?"

"No, I am telling you it is a team effort. We have four of the five mages here. The one who is sick is not, individually, as important as the other four. She is not as powerful as the others. But she has done this before. She knows what is required of her and what to do to make things run smoothly and what to do if things become difficult. If we had a fifth mage…" The same voice argued back to Croy.

"Then let me assist." Vrric's blood suddenly ran cold. That had to have been the Blind One who offered help. It was… unexpected. He waited for Croy or Aedon to speak up against the idea, but the next voice he heard was that of the Cabal's representative.

"Hmmm. That might work. We understand that you are a skilled mage. I will have to confer with the others. Wait here." Footsteps faded into the distance.

There was a long period of silence. It seemed that Aedon and Croy did not wish to discuss the Blind One's proposal out loud. Of course, there could have been many other guards in the area, just standing there silently. Vrric did not have the same qualms. He whispered what had happened to Arnasta and let her pass the message on. It moved like a ripple down the narrow hallway.

Eventually the footsteps came back. "We will accept your offer of help. We understand that you have the gold with you?"

"We do. We will only hand it over once the shield exists, of course." Croy was playing the aggrieved purchaser.

"Of course. However, and let me stress that I am not attempting to be rude here, but we would like to see the gold before bringing your mage into our fold."

"Agreed, that's fair." Aedon was playing the helpful mediator.

It took a little more time before the distinctive chiming of gold coins, held within a sturdy bag that muffled them somewhat, reached Croy's ears. And, therefore, Vrric's. There was more than one grunt of appreciation, so Vrric assumed they had several watchers. Trela had been adamant that they bring the full amount, that it was all real, all legitimate. It was basically everything they had left and there had been some concern about the Cabal just stealing it. Her point was that it was all or nothing. If something was stolen before the attack, they would just attack sooner than they had wished. Vrric took a quick moment to wonder where she was. She had imagined attacking from above just as the main group attacked from below. But he wondered if the laboratory was anywhere near the surface. And she would have to dodge guards if it really was under the palace. This line of query made him wonder where Clerin was. Since he did not want to think about that, he turned his mind to other things. The Cabal was leading the Blind One away, to give him a quick lesson in the summoning process and what they needed from him. Aedon allowed it.

Eventually the Cabal returned with the Blind One and indicated they were ready to begin. There was a small ruckus as various derlians situated chairs and tables and whatnot. Once all the scraping and shuffling had ceased, the same voice explained to Croy and Aedon what they were about the witness. "See this normal shield? While it looks rather sturdy, with the iron banding about the wood structure, let me assure you that a crossbow from a rod away can pierce the wood. Once we have confined the Yaven within the shield, we shall show you how impenetrable it is to a bolt. Then a sword, a hammer, an axe. We will even allow you to cast spells on it. You will be amazed; I know you've never seen anything like it."

"We are excited to see the final product, especially if it is as impenetrable as you say." Croy sounded less excited than he should have, but that could have been chalked up to the long lead-up to the final moment. He had, as far as the Cabal knew, been trying to buy the shield for many, many moons and had traveled a long way to get it. In any case, no one seemed to begrudge him his lackluster response.

"So, we are almost ready, Croy. I hate to seem paranoid, but from here on out, we are going to have to envelop you with an anti-magic shell." There was a half-second of confused speech as several derlians began talking at once. Soon the original speaker spoke above the rest. "This is part of our requirements. This is not a negotiation. We are allowing Narst to remain in control of his magic since he is assisting us. You have to understand our position here…"

And that was when Vrric severed all magical ties. He dropped both his spells as "quietly" as possible and motioned to Arnasta to drop hers, though hers may have only been connected through him. He was soon surrounded by the same muffled silence as the other warriors. He took in a deep breath and explained what had happened to those around him as quietly as possible, letting it ripple to the back naturally.

"We should have Phyna dig us as close to the laboratory as possible. When we get the order to strike, we will need to strike quickly." All those within hearing proximity agreed wholeheartedly. It was a popular sentiment—do something to pass the time, rather than doing nothing.

"From here on out, we walk as silent as spies, and with as much awareness as well. We speak only as a last resort. We lead with our weapons drawn. This is our last chance for anyone's input. Any last words?" Estfale had his grim face on.

Vrric was sure that at least a few of them had questions. At least someone. At least about some subject. But no one spoke up. There was a moment of noise as they all pulled their favorite weapon, then silence floated back over to the grim Estfale. "Good." He nodded to Phyna who slowly started to silently dig. It took Vrric some time quietly walking behind Arnasta before he began to wonder why it was Estfale who had spoken up. Where was Rewista? Was he trying to usurp some of her power, or did he have orders from Trela? Or was Vrric just being paranoid? All unanswerable questions.

They moved quietly along at a walking speed for a while, then slowed to a crawl, then it became difficult to tell that Phyna was moving at all. At some point they all just stopped.

Vrric tapped on Phyna softly, getting its attention. "Communicate... soil... describe..." Vrric spoke as softly as he could, barely audible even to himself. Phyna made a silent, but obviously intentional, bow. It turned back towards the end of the tunnel and Vrric could only hope that it truly understood what he wanted, that the descriptions would be accurate, that no one from the Cabal would notice a Yaven spying on them, that Phyna would act with speed and decisiveness if needed and with stealth and prudence if needed. He could only hope. Those four words summed up so much of his life at that moment.

It was an agonizing wait. They all felt it. No one wanted to move or twitch in case a tiny noise was overheard.

Then the *whisper* came. "Now, now, now!" Ryshial's voice charged into his skull like an enraged bull. Vrric's body jerked at the intensity of it, the shock of it. At the same time, Phyna turned and gesticulated wildly, though silently. Vrric gesticulated wildly back, mainly throwing his arms towards the end of the tunnel. Phyna turned and burst forth from the last couple of rods of solid stone between the warriors and the laboratory. It was still done quietly as the tunnel was made by making the surrounding stone denser, shifting the particles from interior to exterior, rather than by pushing the stone outwards.

They poured out as quickly and silently as they could. They need not have tried so hard to be quiet however, since the Cabal was waiting, prepared for them. Phyna was unsummoned as soon it had left the tunnel. Vrric knew that would have taken an enormous effort, so he scanned the back of the room as he sidled to the right, just outside of the tunnel's exit. In a far corner there appeared to be three mages sitting in a circle, arms intertwined. He assumed they would try to silence him next, if they had not already. He decided to let loose.

"Lumdeeleclo!" The air around the mages burst into thousands of tiny lightning bolts, zipping around between them and through them. It was blinding and deafening, stunning most of the Cabal into standing still for at least three seconds as Trela's warriors did their best to leave the tunnel within that limited time frame.

Vrric tried to catch his breath for a moment. Looking away from the lightning storm in front of him, he turned left to watch the warriors pour out of the tunnel like water in a sluice-way. Then a derlian jogged into view, her hood thrown back and curly red hair bouncing, on the other side of the warriors. She dodged to the side and a column of fire erupted from her hands, creating a swath of burning warriors at the tunnel's exit. The screams were loud but short, the greasy smell of burnt flesh smothered Vrric's senses. He moved farther into the room, trying to see the mage beyond the wall of flames. He caught a glimpse of her, still shooting flames, as a burning warrior ran up and stabbed her. Then hugged her. They both crumpled to the flagstone floor, burning and writhing.

Vrric tried to cast a mass healing spell, something he had never done before but was willing to attempt on the writhing mass of charred warriors in front of him, but found that he had been silenced. A quick panic coursed through him like molten metal. He knew he could cast small spells while silenced but nowhere near the power levels that would soon be required of him. He needed to find the mage who was silencing him, and he needed to do it quickly.

He did his best to not allow his mind to dwell on the ramifications of the ambush. The Cabal obviously knew not only that they would get attacked and when they would get attacked, but where they were going to get attacked. There had always been a chance that the Cabal knew Croy and Aedon's visit was an excuse to infiltrate their organization, but Vrric had hoped that they would be spying from the outside. They knew what direction they were attacking from, which meant that they had obviously been tracking them. The effort was well coordinated, and they obviously had plenty of mages even though they had pretended otherwise earlier. The whole thing together, all that was happening, made him nervous that they had been betrayed, not just spied upon. And there was nothing he could do about it, which just made the thought of it a dangerous distraction.

Suddenly a familiar warrior sprang from the tunnel, sword out but pointed down. Malghain took half a second to swivel his head around before he caught Vrric's eye. He bounded over, clasping his left hand against Vrric's shoulder.

"This ambush stinks of rotten eggs. They were right here waiting for us." He was now glancing around the room, not really looking at Vrric, searching for the enemy. So it took him a moment before he realized Vrric was mouthing something to him.

Vrric mouthed "find the mage" as distinctly as he could, and pointed to his own silenced mouth. Malghain nodded but did not run off. He allowed Vrric to lead as they pushed their way farther into the room. There were still warriors streaming out of the tunnel, though they must have been nearing the last of them since the warriors were Gaen. Of course, over half of Trela's coterie was Gaen at that point.

"Do we need Arnasta?" The question caught Vrric by surprise. Which was quickly followed by embarrassment for failing to think of her himself. His eyes opened a little too wide and he nodded emphatically. "I think I know where she is."

Malghain pointed to a corner and said something too quiet to hear amongst the commotion. Vrric dutifully scuttled over to where Malghain had pointed, while he went through a separate large archway that led to a broad hallway.

The corner Vrric was in was covered in open-faced shelves, small rectangles that did not quite align, crawling over the wall like ivy. They were made out of wood and each had a glass bottle centered in the rectangle. They varied in size as much as the rectangles did. The bottles were all colored vibrantly and many had ornate stoppers. Instead of labels that described the reagents, each had an alpha-numeric code. It all made him wonder what the lab was like, really. Did they cackle and slap each other on the back as they enriched themselves on other beings' misery? Or was it relaxed and informal like Ryshial's guild back at the Blaze, filled with meetings and soirees? Were they good husbands and fathers, wives and mothers? Did they help when their neighbors' children got sick, even in the middle of the night? He could almost see one of them, patiently labeling and cataloging each individual reagent, mind buried in the task of perfecting the tiny world they were in charge of, nary a thought of what the others were doing. But it only took a glance around the room to chase all stray thoughts from his mind.

His back and a portion of his right side were protected by the walls covered in shelves. To his left was the archway and hallway that Malghain had ducked down. The archway was almost a separate room in itself, being so thick and wide. Straight ahead was the large room in tableau. On the same wall as the archway, but farther down, was the tunnel bored out by Phyna whose help they could have used right then. There was a large raised dais, almost like a stage, fully opposite Vrric. This was where several of the ambushing Cabal had been situated, including the mage with the curly hair. Vrric thought there was another hallway on the opposite side, but there were pillars in the way. To his right, a little farther up, the wall jogged out to open the room further, which held the open-sided room that the electrocuted mages had been waiting in. It only took a couple of seconds for him to read the area and memorize the moving parts.

He decided to try his own tracking spell, something weak enough he could do it silently and yet strong enough to check the entire surrounding area. He racked his brain trying to think of the least complicated solution when he suddenly realized the *sound* changed. The general clamor of the combat took on a different tenor. As if everyone in the room, as if the situation itself, was of one mind and was experiencing an amazing revelation. The shock of it pulsed out to Vrric and traveled through him. There were Gaen warriors at the back of the coterie, killing their own Gaen kin. The coterie was under attack from both directions.

He leapt to his feet and moved towards the tunnel entrance. He did not know what he was going to do or what he could cast. He did not know how many Gaens were back there, let alone whether they were originally part of the coterie or if they were the Cabal's warriors sneaking up from behind. What he did know was that they had to be stopped. He knew he could not find and then kill the mage he needed to, not while silenced, not in the allotted time. No, the only target that he really had was himself. And, really, all he needed was a couple of moments. Just enough to turn the tide.

Lotectotpri! The silence spell on Vrric was squashed, but not quite instantly. *Nutectotpri!* Then, directly afterwards, *Mektectotpri!* The last spell was almost audible, giving it greater heft. Then, there it was; he had bought himself an instant of using his voice. He wished he had thought of that earlier.

"Lumdeeleclo!" Vrric cast the same spell as when he first entered the room, but tilted the pillar such that the lightning did less damage but struck more victims. Oftentimes a mage would be tougher than a warrior when it came to resisting damage from a spell. A huge, muscular, fit and healthy derlian could be felled low by less powerful magic than a bedridden mage. That was not always true, of course, but it often seemed that a mage had thicker skin where magic was concerned. Like a natural set of invisible armor. It turned the image, even the definition, of "toughness" on its head.

The lightning flung itself at one of the more daring attackers, ahead of his peers. It struck him in the chest with a crackling sound. Three bolts shot out of his back, one straight behind and the other two symmetrically angled. It branched from one-to-three at each row, quickly disappearing back into the tunnel that Phyna had created. In the final row it might have only been felt as a tingle, but the front lines were devastated. Even the outer fringes who had escaped the triangular swath of destruction were soon being overrun with Trela's warriors.

Vrric, re-silenced, attempted to control his slow physical collapse. He was casting too much, and too varied, at once. He half toppled, half crawled, back to the corner of the reagent shelves. He propped himself up into a low slouch, back against the shelving, to be able to get a better view of the combat. He breathed in through his nose and out through his mouth in the slow cadence of recovery. He just needed to relax for a moment to collect himself. He was not tired yet, just… dizzy.

Suddenly, Arnasta and Serghno came running down the hallway with Malghain close behind them. His head would periodically glance backwards keeping an eye on their rear. Just as they entered the room, a Fluen mage bounded through the opposite hallway and shot fire into the midst of the Gaen portion of the coterie. Serghno shot a dozen tiny flaming darts back at the mage. Arnasta knelt and gripped Vrric's chin in her hand. She examined his face for a brief moment, one side and then the other. Vrric tried to mouth some words to her and pointed at his own face. He knew that she already knew, but he was unable to stop himself from pointing it out. He felt naked, exposed and vulnerable, without being able to cast his spells. She nodded kindly and smiled, placating him. At the end of it all, she cast a small healing spell on him, stood and began mumbling other magics. The healing spell cleared his head a little.

"The mage is over there, behind the wall." Arnasta pointed assuredly with her eyes closed.

"How far beyond the wall?" Serghno returned his attention towards them, mustaches quivering with anticipation.

"Five… to six rods." She paused in her speech, doing calculations in her head, eyes still closed and arm still raised

"Nardepiclo!" Serghno was methodical in his placement. When it came to fire magic, he was one of the most powerful mages Vrric had ever witnessed.

Suddenly, Vrric could speak again. "Thank you, thank you both. You have no idea…"

And he was promptly interrupted by Malghain. "We need to stay with the group." He then walked between them on his way over to the bulk of the coterie.

Up ahead, in the backlight of the opposite hallway, Vrric could make out Rewista and Estfale. They were both leading the others, swords out and moving cautiously deeper into the laboratory complex. Vrric sped up and followed Malghain.

He nervously glanced behind them as they joined the last of the group. Part of him wanted to cave in the other hallway, just to make sure no one was following them. Part of him knew that would be foolish if they needed to go in that direction later. He could not assume he would be with the group the next time around. The loss of Phyna was devastating on several levels.

He felt odd in the back but understood the plan was to stick together for as long as possible, not that he would have been overly excited to explore the other hallway on his own. They were supposed to meet up with Trela and then find Croy, or maybe vice versa. He wondered if Arnasta was searching for Trela. He wondered if he should *whisper* to Croy. The indecision created an odd malaise of impotency. He had thought better of trying to contact Croy and had decided to worm his way over to Arnasta when he saw it. There was movement in the far end of the room behind them. It was a brief glimpse, like the fleeting tail of a deer distant in the forest, but he was certain there was something shifting back there. He touched Malghain's shoulder as he passed behind him, ducking to the side as they rounded a corner.

Malghain turned and duck-walked back to the corner, peering around the opening. Vrric kept tall and was about to peek around as well when Malghain put up a fist. Vrric did not follow all of the hand gestures the Luften warriors used, but he certainly knew the one for "stop." His ears strained at the silence. Malghain tossed a glove into the air, just barely into the opening, and *whizz*, a crossbow bolt struck it in mid-air and pinned it to the wall behind. He then shifted into the opening himself and tossed a dagger. He immediately snapped himself back as another bolt went whizzing by.

Vrric thought back to the time Trela's warpack was fighting with Rewista's and he immolated their high-arching arrows before they dropped back down into the fray. He was not quite sure if it would work the same at this distance, angle, and velocity. Before he could come to a decision however, Malghain whispered a word to him. "Shield."

"Narteclufarc!" Vrric did not hesitate. Neither did Malghain. With a triumphant scream he turned the corner and drew his sword at the same time, charging headlong into a small barrage of bolts.

Vrric peeked his head around as all the attention was swallowed up by the attacking lunatic. Malghain was in the midst of several Gaens wielding crossbows. They were using them quite ineffectually as clubs, due to the tight distance and the shield spell. Since Malghain appeared to have the matter in hand, he scanned the room looking for more Gaens, taking his eyes away from the immediate fight. He was peering to the left, attempting to squint into focus some imagined movement, when the blast came from the right. Malghain and the remaining Gaens were engulfed in flames. The mage obviously had no compunction about killing their own warriors. The entire room was lit up with an eerie orange glow, casting bizarre shimmying shadows.

Vrric had two immediate choices. Increase Malghain's shield or attack the mage. He turned around the corner and saw his target. It was a tall Luften, imposing in stature, his wild grin underlit with the same orange glow as the room. "Nardepiarc!" Vrric was consciously trying to conserve his energy for later. The mage turned towards the source of the flame, swinging his own along with his gaze, bringing the two beams of fire in direct opposition. A wide disc of flame erupted where they intersected, reminding Vrric of the water spray at the bottom of a waterfall. The other Luften's spell had been cast at a higher power level, slowly pushing the disc towards Vrric. He worried for a split second that his frugality would be his undoing, but by then Malghain had reached the mage. With a mighty swing, he sliced through both wrists of the mage's outstretched hands, cutting off the flame spurt. The scream echoed throughout the room. Malghain flowed into a wide circle. The second swing struck the mage's back and it quite inelegantly stuck there. Vrric dropped his fire spell immediately, not sure how effective his shield spell could still be at that point and not wanting to accidently immolate his friend. It took a few long seconds for Malghain to free his sword. Eventually he had to place his foot on the dead mage's back and lever it out. Vrric took his time walking over to the carnage, glancing about the entire room as he moved, fully expecting to be attacked again. They both breathed heavily in the moment of peace.

"I think we'll have to go the opposite way of the others, to keep the back clear. We'll have to go it alone." As he spoke the words, a part of Vrric was hoping, in the dark recesses of his hind brain, that Malghain would argue. That logic and temperament would trump valor. Or at least that they could rest awhile while discussing the merits of various options.

"Agreed." Malghain merely nodded, his chest still swelling and ebbing from his heavy breathing. "Think we should do anything about our entrance?" He pointed towards Phyna's tunnel behind him with his thumb. Somehow it looked smaller now than when they had come pouring out of it. The dark opening appeared tiny compared to the vastness of the room. "We're either leaving through the front door or not at all, eh?"

"There is a scenario I can imagine where the Cabal is destroyed but we do not wish to disturb the Prince any further." At least he *hoped* there was such a scenario.

Malghain nodded again, squinting at the opening. He then turned towards the alcove area where the mages who unsummoned Phyna were and squinted in that direction. "Are we sure there is not another access point back there?"

"Lead the way." There was, indeed, a small wooden door dressed in cast iron bindings with simple filigree accents back there. The stench of burnt flesh was strong. It seemed odd that the stench could be worse with lightning than with direct fire, but many times Serghno's flames immolated things so completely that all that was left was the carbonic smell of char. While certainly not pleasant, it could be less nauseating than the oils and hair smell.

"Think we'll need this as an escape route?" Vrric thought briefly about just melting the lock with the bolt still engaged. Of course, that was what Malghain was really asking.

Without Jalin to jam the lock in a simply reversible manner, they decided on placing furniture in front of it. Luckily it opened into the room. The sounds of furniture being scraped against the stone floor seemed amplified in the otherwise quiet room.

"Need anything from there?" Malghain jerked his thumb at the reagents in the corner as they walked towards the hallway. Vrric shook his head.

The hallway turned soon after they entered. They moved quickly but cautiously for as long as the only option was forwards. Being careful not to make any noise to disturb the strange quiet. There was the distant sound of metal striking metal that wafted from behind them, presumably from Rewista and Estfale's contingent. It sounded as if it came from a different world.

After another turn, they were confronted with choices. The hallway continued silently ahead of them until it turned in the distance, but there were two doors along its left flank and one on its right.

"I don't like leaving access points behind us." Malghain nodded to the nearest door. "Do you think we have enough time to check them?"

"As long as they're rooms and not more hallways." They both smiled.

Malghain placed himself next to a door, back against the hallway wall. He held his sword upwards in his right hand and reached across himself with his left, grasping the knob and hesitating for half a second. He flung the door open and whipped around and stopped. Vrric peeked around and saw a large closet. It was full of sacks and barrels and shelves, packed such that there was little room to hide. They closed the door and moved to the next, the one on the right flank of the hallway.

Malghain again positioned himself and flung open the door. This time, however, there was a loud commotion emanating from the room. Suddenly a primitive-looking axe came flying through the open door, striking the hallway's left flank, clanging against the stone wall. A scream, sounding more scared than angry, though just as violent, emanated soon afterwards. Malghain waited for a heartbeat before spinning himself into the room, sword at the ready. Vrric followed him in as closely behind as he could and still maintain a safe distance for backswings and the like. As he spun into the room, he thought he could hear a commotion from the far end of the hallway. Was it merely an echo from the room, playing tricks with his ears? It was hard to leave any space in his mind to concentrate on the immediate task at hand. The room they had spun into had two Fluen warriors readily visible in it. They both looked scared and violent. Another axe came flying by, narrowly missing both Vrric and Malghain, clattering into the hallway. Malghain leapt over a small table and slashed the throat of one of the warriors, spraying blood in a misty arc. Vrric took aim at the other. "Nudepiarc!" The warrior dropped to the ground, engulfed in flame. He took a couple of quick moments to die, writhing. Vrric should have cast a higher spell to end it quicker, but he was trying to conserve his energy. The stench was quite unpleasant, worse than the bodies in the other room.

The room appeared to be a simple barracks or dormitory. There were several beds, some low tables, a couple of chairs and a large wooden locker at the foot of each bed. There were personal effects scattered about, playing cards and drawings, et cetera. It gave an air of youthful innocence to the room. Plus, the warriors they had just dispatched had not seemed overly skilled.

"Are we sure everyone in this area is part of the Cabal?" The question made Malghain look up from one of the open lockers he was rummaging through.

"Don't be stupid." His eyes narrowed down to slits as he measured Vrric. "You're not getting stupid on me, are you?"

"No, no. Don't worry." He started to slow walk to the door. "They just seemed a little green for this type of thing, don't you think?"

"Good, easier for us." Malghain walked over to him. "I know you like a challenge, but you can't second guess everything that is not an outright ambush. C'mon, we have to wrap back around to the others." He patted Vrric on the shoulder as he passed.

Vrric nodded to himself. He tried to think if the hallway they were in was somehow different than the one that Rewista and Estfale were walking down. The ambush was close enough that the Fluens had to have known about it, they had to be part of the Cabal.

"But it's kind of odd, isn't it?"

"You want to know what I think that was?" Malghain paused before leaving the room and took it in with a sweep of his head. "Those were deserters. They were planning to leave during the commotion and we found them in the midst of it. Simple as that. And if not deserters, they were cowardly laggards, hoping the fighting would be over by the time they finally 'arrived' at the scene."

Vrric smiled. It made perfect sense. "That's a good explanation, thanks."

"Glad to help. Now let's find some real warriors to tangle with."

That was when the real warriors showed up from the hallway. There was a blur of motion and Malghain slammed the door shut, but it did not have a latch. It was immediately struck with a sword. It wobbled and vibrated under the impact for a brief second, the force not quite perpendicular to the hinges. Malghain looked over to Vrric, his hand wavering near the bolt to bar the door. Vrric shook his head. He did not need anything in the way of what he needed to do. Then a shoulder pushed the door open and several warriors appeared.

"Eqedepiarc!" Vrric shot a pillar of flame through them. He then jumped over their falling bodies and into the hallway. With each hand pointing a different direction, he shot flames in both directions, immolating several more warriors. He had to dance around for a moment, avoiding the death throws and the last grasps made at his ankles.

"Yeeaah!" The drawn-out, overly enthusiastic yell came from Malghain behind him. "That's the Feyazki I know!" He came out of the room with a slight swagger, stabbing the bodies as he passed them. "This is how I like it. Easy." He stabbed another body before coming to the last door on the left. He took his place to the side of it and jerked it open.

They found another closet behind that door and continued down the hall. They took the corner and slowed, listening hard to the faint sound of fighting in the distance. As they turned the corner, however, there were just some stairs. Having no other direction to go, they went up.

As they went up a floor, their world changed from stone to wood. Wood stairs continued beyond the landing, wood walls surrounded it, and a wooden door sealed it off. There were windows up higher that spilled light somewhat haphazardly onto the landing. Vrric wanted to discuss with Malghain where he thought the warriors in the hallway had come from, but they needed to be as quiet as possible. So, while Malghain pressed his ear to the door and peered through the open lock mechanism, Vrric examined the landing itself. There was little dust, but what was there was definitely disturbed. He crawled on his hands and knees, examining the steps just above the landing to no discernable avail. No matter how hard he peered at them, he was unsure if the warriors had come from above or from the door. It was all just too disturbed to provide a clear story. He was about to give up when he heard a finger snap. He looked up to see Malghain moving as quickly as he could and still be silent. He was making a shooing motion up the stairs and his eyes were wide with alarm. That was all that Vrric needed, and he half-crawled up the stairs as quickly and quietly as he could.

Bang! The door at the landing flung open and about eight Fluen warriors crashed through and jogged down the stairs without a wayward glance. Their voices were a chaotic chorus, mostly unintelligible except for the word "intruder" repeated by several of them at once.

They had to be guards from the palace proper, reinforcements coming in by squad after the initial ambush failed. This solidified Vrric's opinion that the Prince himself was involved in the Cabal but did not want others to know about it. Though these guards may not have been true members of the Cabal, they would surely wreak havoc on Rewista and Estfale if they were to meet up with them. There was also no way that Trela's small coterie could fight off the entire palace. They needed to defeat the Cabal as quickly as possible and then escape. That meant that this entrance needed to be sealed. Since everything below the landing was stone, Vrric knew what to do. He just needed to do it quickly.

He grabbed Malghain and rushed to the door soon after the last warrior left it. The door was still open, still vibrating from its strike against the far wall, and Malghain ran through it. There seemed to be more warriors coming down the hallway but Vrric ignored them. He stood just inside the hallway, just off the landing, stared down, and took a deep breath. The last couple of warriors running down the stairs noticed them, stopped, and turned. They screamed, drew their swords, and ran back up the stairs towards him. At the same time, Malghain screamed and rushed headlong into the wooden hallway. Vrric ignored the commotion and the danger, keeping as calm as possible. "Lumdegeclo!"

The stones exploded and tumbled, the entire palace shook, Vrric fell backwards into the hallway desperately clinging to the floor. He couldn't quite tell what was going on behind him for he was staring at two hands clinging to the edge of the hallway floor. One of the guards had made the leap. He had done his best to keep the structure under the hallway intact, and it appeared to have worked. As the rumbling slowed and the warrior attempted to pull himself up, Vrric was able to scooch towards him and kick him in the face. Then again, and again. He would not fall, so Vrric dropped his heel on the warrior's fingers. The hand and face dropped out of sight, so Vrric worked on the other hand. By the time the warrior had fallen the shaking had stopped.

Vrric rolled over and slowly got himself up. He was a little woozy after the last spell but was able to stand without too much staggering. There were about three warriors left facing Malghain. They were the cautious ones, those who held their swords in front of them, those who parried rather than thrust. He squared his shoulders and faced them. He needed another few moments before he could cast anything but they did not know that. All three turned and ran. Malghain caught one, but the other two were very fast indeed. Vrric did not hobble, but did not run either. He slow walked down the hall as Malghain came to grips that they were going to escape. He turned and jogged back to Vrric.

"Well... you protected the others, but you've trapped us up here. There's no telling how many guards they have running around here." Malghain's sword was dripping blood as was the long dagger in his left hand. Vrric finally realized how many bodies there were in the hallway. There must have been another band of eight, and Malghain had cut down five of them in the time it took Vrric to kick a guard off a landing. The sixth was still trying to crawl away.

"Left. If I'm not turned around, we need to go left to get closer to the others. Maybe we can find another way down." They were facing down the hallway with their backs to the crumbled stairwell.

"Left it is." Malghain took a moment to stab the crawling warrior and then trotted down the hall to the next available door. He stood to the side, reached across himself, and threw open the door.

It was a long storage area, covered with wooden boxes and shapeless sacks half full of something. Maybe grain or flour. They shut the door behind them.

"They'll check this door soon. Can you cast a shield or something on it?" Malghain had his back leaning against the door while his eyes shifted about the room, examining the distance while chatting with Vrric.

"No, nothing of note. I need some more time to recuperate. I'll just melt the lock mechanism with the bolt engaged. That shouldn't take much effort." If he were honest, he probably could have cast a good shield spell, but he knew the day was only going to get more hectic.

"Well, they will definitely know we came in here then. Could you cast an illusion over the door to hide it?" Malghain paused for a second before arguing against himself. "No, at least one of the guards will know the door should exist. Ha, there's probably a trail of blood leading straight to it." He moved away from the door and farther into the storage room. "At least let me make sure we can get out of here before you melt that thing."

Vrric knelt and peered through the lock, playing with the mechanism absentmindedly until Malghain grunted something positive from the corner of the room. "Nudehepto!" It was as easy as that. He stood and wandered over to find Malghain.

There was a door at the other side of the room, half hidden behind a stack of crates, but that was not where Malghain was. He had gotten himself into one of the corners and was hunkered down poking at something with his dagger.

Vrric was about to say something but Malghain made a shushing motion with his forefinger over his lips. So he hunkered down as well. There was a faint sound of voices coming from below. It was impossible to make anything out. Malghain went back to trying to pry up a metal shroud-like object stuck to the floor. As he was poking, prodding, and quietly scraping at the metal object, Vrric was straining his ears to hear what was going on below them. He was about to cast a spell to allow him to eavesdrop when the metal thing audibly popped off the floor. The opening was dark, still covered by something on the other side. Malghain carefully tilted it up and out of the way.

"What was that?" A voice, still distant but much more clear, wafted up from below. There was a long pause during which Vrric held his breath.

"They are getting closer." Another, shorter, pause. "And they have at least one mage still with them, probably more. We should prepare."

There were some shuffling noises that wafted up that got quieter and quieter as the sounds' originators moved farther away. Malghain could have put the piece of metal back, but he didn't twitch a muscle. Vrric could have stood, but he couldn't move. They both squatted there, in a full hunker, quietly staring at the dark and empty hole. It was too much to be believed. The second voice had to have been the Blind One!

It all made so much more sense after that. The Gaens in the back attacking their fellow comrades. The supposed need to use the Blind One to help summon the Yaven for the Stone Shield even though they obviously had plenty of mages. It explained how the Cabal knew when and where to wait for the ambush. It explained the Prince's behavior. It explained everything. But it pointed to so much worse. It showed just how deep the Cabal had infiltrated Trela's little coterie. It showed how much of a trap they were in. At least since they had entered the Gaen realm. In fact, he almost worried if the entire mission was a trap.

"That was…?" Malghain stayed motionless, still staring downwards.

"It had to have been."

"Then Croy and Aedon are captured."

"And Clerin."

"Maybe he wasn't talking to a member of the Cabal? Maybe he was talking with one of the coterie?"

"That's more like something I would say."

"We're doomed."

"Yes, completely. Completely doomed." There was nothing else Vrric could say.

"You don't suppose that Aedon and the Blind One are both working for the Cabal, do you?"

No, Vrric had not been thinking that. He tried to think of it and just couldn't. Aedon did not seem untrustworthy like that. The Blind One had not seemed especially evil. Vrric had not imagined that he was planning something behind their backs, but he had never seemed completely trustworthy either. Vrric did not know what he would do if Aedon had been scheming with the Cabal too. It would be devastating. He knew it would crush Trela.

Malghain slowly put the piece of metal back. They both stood and stretched their legs a little. They took a couple of breaths.

"So… Want to make a hole in the floor or try out the door?" Malghain was still sort of looking down at the piece of metal.

It was at that point that they heard some scraping sounds coming from the door they had originally entered through. The guards must have been trying to quietly get around the lock. In the back of Vrric's mind he wondered how many guards were out there. Maybe another eight? Maybe a few more? He wondered if they should attack the guards head-on, if for no other reason than to alleviate being chased. He decided to do something small rather than burn through the door and the warriors behind it.

"Mekkinpanclo!" He quietly placed most of the wooden crates in the room in front of the door.

Malghain had opened the door on the opposite side while Vrric was moving crates. Malghain peered his head through it for a moment before entering. Vrric followed soon after, glad they were not trying to silently make a hole in the floor.

The new room was filled with more storage items, so he melted the lock and Malghain pushed crates in front of the door. There were three doors exiting the room, which was lucky since the one across from the one they had entered through exited to another hallway. If it was symmetric, there should be another stairwell to the left. They did not attempt that, but since that would lead them back towards the others, they also did not seal the door off.

The perpendicular door was tried. When Malghain swung open the door they could hear voices in the distance. They cautiously entered the room as quietly as possible. It was another storage room, but it was mostly empty. The voices had to be coming from below. Though Vrric could not really hear the voices, he imagined that the rhythms of the murmurs matched the Blind One. He made some hand motions to Malghain, and they exited that room back to the previous one.

"We should drop down through here somewhere and then get under that one. If we drop down there, they'll hear us coming," Vrric whispered a bit furtively.

"What if someone is under this room? What if the lower room doesn't lead over there?" Malghain pointed towards the room with the voices.

"Good points, but those are unknowns. I'd rather take a chance on getting lucky than to proceed on something I know is a losing bet." Vrric smiled.

"Me too, just checking." Malghain smiled in return. "How do we deal with the traitor? Should I distract him and allow you to stream lightning through him?"

"It has to be the opposite. He can sense magic really well, according to Croy, and he can disappear so quickly that he'll be gone before I can even speak the spell. I bet he could escape even if I were to cast it silently." Vrric paused for a moment, thinking. "No, I'll have to talk with him and you'll have to sneak a knife in him. Maybe

I'll try to cast a silence spell on him or a shield spell on myself or something. He might take a moment just counteracting me."

"I wish Jalin or Altrond was here. I'm afraid sneaking a knife into someone isn't my greatest skill. Even Escha with her bow might be helpful."

"Not sure about the bow, he seems to be able to sense danger, but maybe that really is just his hearing… We can only work with what we have, however, and right now all we have is the two of us."

They nodded to each other for a moment, listening to the faint commotion behind them slowly gain in volume. They finally decided on a location to make a hole in the floor and Malghain got a stack of crates pushed into position. Their plan was to shift the crates over the hole so those following them would not immediately know where they had gone. Maybe they would rush all the way through the room and into the hallway.

Malghain jammed his boot knife in between some floorboards. "Nudepanto!" Vrric made a large circle with his finger, centered around the knife. The plug of floor dropped for a second until Malghain was able to lift it up. Vrric had been afraid the plug would slip off the knife and clatter to the floor, but it all seemed to be stuck together. They dropped into a tiny empty room, or at least, empty of other derlians. "Nukinpanarc!" The stack of crates quietly slid over the hole above them.

The room was a small office or study. It contained a book shelf, a shelf of various items, an ornate desk with a lit candle flickering on it, three chairs, and a multitude of exit doors. Vrric naturally gravitated towards the desk to glance at a piece of parchment laying on it, squared out with the edge of the desk. The words were written in a smooth and deliberate hand. There was no salutation and no signature, just part of a paragraph.

"We will need the use of your deeper dungeon to detain the imposters. We will need access to the tools of the trade as well as to keep them out of public sight, even from your own guards. Unless, of course, you agree with the blind Gaen you sent us and you feel we should liquidate those assets immediately after the ambush." It was a little odd since the thought was finished, but Vrric truly felt that it was only half-written, that more argument was intended on being added, for one side or the other. Half-unconsciously, he folded up the parchment and stole it. He was going to rifle through the desk and discuss the note with Malghain but was interrupted by the door opening.

An unknown Fluen came walking through, his long blond hair held back by a simple circlet, his body covered in white robes. His head was down and he was saying something inconsequential to the short derlian following him. Both Vrric and Malghain froze as they recognized that derlian—the Blind One.

"This is not what it appears." Then he vanished.

Malghain hopped over a chair and had his dagger against the Fluen's throat almost immediately. Vrric ran over, eager to interrogate their abandoned captive, but the clatter of metal armor from the other side of the door brought him up short. A brief pause, then the sound of several swords being drawn from their scabbards. Malghain was forcibly dragging the Fluen backwards. There was a loud cry from the other room and guards began rushing in.

"Nardepiarc!" The fire engulfed the open door and chewed through the right side of the doorway. Though the main walls on the lower level of the palace were of stone, many of the partition walls were of wood. Vrric needed to hit as many of the guards as possible, so he swiveled his flame.

One guard, the first one, escaped the spell and rushed towards Malghain. Vrric was watching him but still swiveling the flame at the others, attempting to keep track of two things at once. He was not sure, but it seemed that the guard was not even looking at Malghain. Certainly his sword thrust was meant for the Fluen, straight through the robes, between the ribs and into the heart. Malghain pushed the body further onto the sword, swung around and jabbed his dagger into the guard's throat.

The room rumbled as the fire reached the furniture and licked the ceiling. Malghain ran to the unobstructed door, Vrric ran to Malghain. They emptied into a stone-walled hallway, seemingly a mirror of the previous one they had used. Malghain paused and looked about him. To their left, in the distance, was a corner reminiscent of the previous hallway's entrance to the stairs.

"Go turn the stairs to rubble, we can't keep having reinforcements showing up. I'll scout out this direction." Malghain started walking warily down the hallway.

Vrric, though typically reticent to seal off escape routes, jogged opposite of Malghain. They really could not afford more guards chasing them. He reached the corner and peeked around.

There, perfectly mirrored, was another staircase. Vrric silently thanked whatever force moved architects towards symmetry and then turned the stairwell to rubble. "Eqekingeclo!" There did not appear to be any derlians on the stairwell, so he hoped he could get away with just rearranging the stone supports. The sound was deafening and the dust cloud blinding. He did not, however, feel the extra drain of energy the spell should have taken if the demolition of the stairs had killed anyone. He smiled to himself. At this point he was just happy to not be unlucky.

He ran back down the hallway as Malghain was dispatching another two guards. He arrived as the second one was gurgling his last through the slit in his throat. Whatever one might say about Malghain, he was efficient.

They jogged down the hallway a little farther, leaving the fire behind. Vrric hoped that the fire was big enough to keep some guards busy, but not so big as to affect the structural integrity of the building. Though, he supposed, the collapse of the entire palace would finish off the Cabal.

A loud commotion stopped them in their tracks. It came from off to their left, on the opposite side of the hallway from the burning room. Vrric had been ignoring those doors since, if the building were completely mirrored, they should lead to closets. But the palace was much bigger than that, and the door they opened led to a balcony area. There was a long run of stairs that hugged the stone wall, leading all the way down to… a large underground courtyard? It was the only way Vrric could describe it.

The room splayed below them was gigantic. It had about thirty three-story columns spaced about twenty rods apart in a systematic array. The mostly empty floor was rough flagstone and was peppered with workbenches and cages. There looked to be a forge at one end surrounded by blacksmithing tools. The fires were hot but no one was bending metal. The walls were peppered with niches and lined with weapons and torches. There were about eight other balconies at their elevation, all with long stairs extending down, hugging the adjacent wall. In the center of the room, far below them, were two large groups of derlians. One of the groups consisted of at least some members of Trela's coterie, and other group assumedly consisted of the Cabal. Both groups were in a semi-circle shape centered on a Luften. It appeared to be Voyt. Vrric paused to listen to the yelling.

"You cannot unsummon me! I was never summoned!" A great wind began pouring out of Voyt's mouth, scattering some of the Cabal. Others, however, appeared to be unfazed.

The members of the Cabal appeared to be mostly mages, or at least, they were not heavily armed or armored. At that moment, just after Vrric and Malghain had arrived at their perch, guards came pouring out of several of the archways in the lower courtyard. There must have been a hundred of them, all well-armed and armored, rushing in from opposite sides.

At this, Voyt stopped exhaling and began to inhale, his arms outstretched to either side, open palms pointed at the waves of guards. Warrior after warrior clutched their throats in agony. Some kept running, these were cut down when they reached the coterie, but most fell to the ground and writhed for a few moments before becoming still. As Voyt was concentrating on the rushing warriors, the mages in the middle began to pick themselves up and reconvene.

Vrric hesitated for a second, unsure of who to target or how to help. Then he felt it. It was a huge upswelling of magic. It seemed to suck all the magic from the room just as Voyt was sucking the air from the guards' lungs. It was greater than anything Vrric had seen or even heard about. It felt like it was draining his entire essence. Every mage from the Cabal down there had linked arms and were shouting the same thing. There were at least twenty of them. Vrric did not know the spell, nor did he want to. The world seemed to explode with their collective voice. His head wanted to explode with it. He could feel the pressure inside swell, it felt like it was pushing his eyes from their sockets. Then, just as quickly as it had started, it stopped. There was an echoey popping sound at the end of it. Vrric was draped over the balcony railing, wondering what had happened, when he heard a great cheer well up from the mages. Voyt was gone. Vrric thought that maybe they had unsummoned Voyt, but there was a sphere that was now glowing on one of the workbenches. He thought, though he could not know for sure, that he had just witnessed Yavencide. Voyt was now stuck inside an object.

Vrric needed to pull himself together. They had not, as he had feared, drained him of magic. It was more that he felt the greatest of spells being cast. He wondered what that feeling would have done to Croy, who could sense magic to a much greater degree than he could. He breathed in deep. It was the perfect moment, the only moment. They would be weary from their casting and were still unwary of his presence. There was only one thing left to do. Cast the greatest spell he had ever cast. "Tordeeleclo!"

It was not a single bolt that bounced from victim to victim. It was many individual bolts that rained down from above, striking and restriking the mages. It was a giant thunderstorm sans the rain. It made the entire room glow with an eerie bluish tinge. The sound was deafening. Vrric could not stay conscious. He could only hope that the spell did not kill him or fade as he faded. But as he fell, first to his knees and then to his side, he glanced over to another balcony. There, just entering, was the Prince and Clerin and some blonde warriors. It was the last thing he saw before passing out. It was the most dreaded thing he could think of. He would have never casted a Tor level spell had he known she was captive just over there. How could he save her now? He was filled with regret and then filled with oblivion.

Vrric awoke being dragged down a hallway. He was unsure of who was dragging him, probably Malghain, but Croy was fast-walking behind and casting a healing spell on him. "Stop, stop. He's awake."

"What... what happened?" Vrric rested on the floor for a moment, staring up at Croy's face, which appeared enlarged due to it being way too close for Vrric's comfort.

"I thought you were dead, or at least out for the rest of the fight, so I was going to run down the stairs to add my sword to the coterie. But then Croy showed up and started casting healing spells on you. Kept rambling about getting you to the Prince's balcony. So... here we are." Malghain's voice filtered down from a more pleasant distance, somewhere behind Croy's.

"We have to capture the Prince. We need enough time to get Taglo and Baltuz together. Capturing the Prince won't help with the Cabal, but it should give the guards pause." He bobbed his head a little, it reminded Vrric of Knill. In the brief moment of calm that followed, Vrric thought he saw the tracks of tears in his Gaen friend's face. It took him aback for a second.

"You certainly gave the Cabal some pause, though. That was pretty impressive. You must have killed half those mages with that one spell." Malghain chuckled for a moment. Then, to Croy, "Should I keep dragging him?"

"Yes. We have no time. Mekliderto!" Another small healing spell. That one pierced Vrric's fog.

"No, no, I'm fine. I'll walk." He stood on unsteady legs. Croy hugged him from one side and Malghain the other. They shuffled down the hallway together. Vrric was not really walking; he was just trying not to trip them up as they carried him.

They turned a corner and there, in the near distance, were about fifteen guards milling about near a door, swords in hands, but their heads were together, talking. It did not take a full second for them to notice the three interlopers.

"Well, this should be interesting." Malghain grabbed the hilt of his sword.

"No, let me." That Croy spoke up at all shocked Vrric.

"I've never seen you cast an attack spell." It just popped out of Vrric's mouth. At the same time the guards began running towards them.

"Are you sure…?" Malghain was attempting to draw his sword and still support Vrric.

"Yes. I must." Croy took in a deep breath and dropped Vrric's right side. Malghain, apparently untrusting of Croy's untested prowess, dropped Vrric's left and pulled his sword. "Nardepiarc!" Just as Croy cast the spell, Vrric dropped to the ground.

The flames shot a swath through the onrushing warriors. Some were killed, some just set on fire, and some made it past the fire. Malghain cut down each who came near them, burning or not. Croy crumpled down next to Vrric. Malghain danced down the hallway, finishing off the rest.

Vrric was feeling well enough to stand if he clung to the nearby wall. So he did so. Malghain came back and cast a small healing spell on Croy. "I didn't know you had that in you. Seriously, that was great."

They all hobbled along to the door to the balcony. Vrric and Croy propped each other up while Malghain stood to the side of the door and breathed in and out for a moment. Then, with a quick jerk, he flung open the door.

There was Clerin, in a white and pale blue dress that was splotched with dirt. Her hands were bound tightly behind her, the rope wrapping up her forearms and even a little above the elbow. She was gagged and blindfolded. There were two dangerous looking but scantily clad blonde warriors. They both turned towards the intruding trio as the door opened. And there was the Prince. He stayed unmoving, staring at the carnage below, hands resting easily on the balcony's railing, back slightly bent so he could look down easier.

"I told you not to interrupt me for any reason! What is it with you today?" He turned towards them and then turned pale. "Kill them!" His voice jumped an octave.

Faster than Malghain could move, faster than Vrric could cast a spell, the twin Fluens flung their daggers. They struck their mark immediately. The Prince's head bounced back at the one that protruded from his left eye, while the other pierced his throat. Then, almost as quickly, they kicked him in the chest. He tumbled over the railing with a silent scream. Even without noise, many down below, in the midst of combat, stopped and looked up. He seemed to take a long time to fall and then... splat! It was a wet thudding sound.

"Nooo!" That was Croy. Vrric was too weak to move and Malghain appeared stunned into silence. "He was supposed to be a hostage. We were supposed to use him. He was necessary. Now the palace guards will fight to the death along with the Cabal."

"I think you misunderstand how his servants view him." One twin smiled a crooked half-smile.

"I think you misunderstand the Cabal's relationship with him." The other twin smiled the same half-smile, but this one was on the opposite side of her face. If you put their smiles together, they would have made one large, devious grin.

The fighting below resumed. The sound soon followed, wafting upwards. Vrric looked back and forth between everyone on the balcony before he realized he needed to untether Clerin.

They kissed, briefly. It was certainly not the time for such indulgences. Croy, for his part, kept raving. "We need to get Baltuz to Taglo."

"You keep saying that. What do you mean?" Malghain bit.

"She said she was dead. That she had already died back at the Gaen village of Kayaf, but she had been allowed to live for a while, to love for a while. That she had been given a reprieve so that we could be together. I told her that was nonsense, but she got angry and irritable. She will not listen to me. She says she made a deal with Gunzgak and that Taglo made a deal with Gorbanax. They are to combine forces or something. She rescued Aedon and me and then scorned me until I found you. She said she didn't need me anymore, that I would only get in the way." He looked downcast. "Like Ilana, her destiny has overshadowed our love."

"Well, we are all on edge here, you can't fault her for being snappy." Malghain tried to make Croy feel better about Baltuz but failed, which was more than Vrric could say.

"She's probably just worried for your safety." Clerin smiled warmly, though she was still trying to rub life back into her arms. "Where is she anyway?"

Croy pointed down to the fray, the actual battle. It had paused for the brief moment of the Prince's death, but was now back to full pitch. The clanging and screaming echoed throughout the room. Vrric was about to say something, he was sure of it. It would have been kind and consoling. But the twins each raised an arm and pointed to a balcony on the perpendicular wall. It was almost directly opposite the one Malghain and he had first entered onto.

"Your warrior Queen!" The one on the left spoke.

It was Trela, that much was obvious. What she was doing was less so. She wound up her arm and threw something as hard as she could into the last group of Cabal mages. It looked like a fireball to Vrric. It glowed the orange of molten metal and had a bit of a tail as it hurtled towards the ground. Of course, Trela did not cast spells. In fact, she was one of the few derlians that Vrric knew who had never cast a spell. So it took him a moment to figure out what it was. It was the Yaven Taglo.

It crashed amongst the mages and exploded in size. It quickly engulfed them, though many did not seem damaged. In fact, several of them began linking arms as they had done when trapping Voyt.

"You must clear a path!" Croy screamed in Vrric's ear. "If Baltuz does not reach Taglo, we will all die!" He then leapt over the balcony railing. Whether in grief or in a foolish attempt to help, Vrric was not sure. He originally assumed that Croy was going to cast a featherfall spell, but it was difficult to say afterwards. Luckily, Malghain caught him by the belt and kept him from plummeting.

Vrric could see Baltuz's tiny figure out there, in the distance. She was running like mad, weaving and dodging, still amongst the coterie but getting closer to the scorched boundary between them and the Cabal. He wasn't really sure what to do. Should he cast a shield on her so that she was not hindered on her way over? Would that affect whatever she was supposed to do with Taglo? If he were to clear a path, as Croy had so vociferously suggested, was that path to cut through the coterie? Taglo was so large at that moment Vrric was unsure where it would be when it became derlian shaped again. Should he drop lightning at the rear edge of the mages to distract them? Should he specifically target the ones linking arms? Should he just cast another sheet of lightning and hope that Baltuz survived as long as she needed to? It was pure chaos in his brain. Everyone was yelling something at him, some bit of advice or something to watch out for. It was too much.

He decided fire, since it could not harm Taglo. He decided to race it in front of Baltuz, attempting to move with her as she dodged around. He decided to let it wash over the front line of mages once it got there, hopefully centering on those with linked arms. He was, he knew, unable to cast another Tor spell. He hoped that had not been a mistake, but there was nothing to be done about it now. That was the first time he had ever cast that high of a power level and he had not recuperated enough, even with all of Croy's healing spells. It could not have taken too much time for his mind to come to a conclusion—Baltuz was still within the coterie—but it seemed agonizingly long. Time, fortunately, slowed, stretched, and almost stopped.

"Surdepiarc!" It was as grand as he could muster. A thick column of flame shot out of his hands in a straight line. Baltuz did not look up, did not look over her shoulder, she just kept running at full tilt. Vrric did his best to aim, to follow her path while staying in front of her, to anticipate her. Several of the mages down below directed their focus and intent upon him, trying to weaken his spell, trying to jinx him. Several kept trying to harm Taglo. Taglo, it appeared, was completely ignoring Baltuz and instead was killing the mages one by one. One would ignite into a pillar of flame, then another. None of them seemed to be paying attention to the tiny Gaen running towards them. Maybe Vrric's fire was helping to hide her, but maybe they were just distracted. As she began to cross the distance between the two groups, he decided push it into the mages who had their arms linked.

A searing pain jabbed into Vrric's skull. It was like a shard of ice being pushed into his left eye. He did his best to ignore it and roasted a Cabal mage. Another shard attacked him, this time in his right eye. He could feel the mages begin to concentrate on dissipating his spell. He engulfed another one. Taglo engulfed another one. The coterie was suddenly screaming and rushing away from the Cabal. The retreat made no sense to Vrric, but he was having difficulty staying conscious. Another shard stabbed at him, this time from behind, at the base of his skull. He torched another mage. This one had been centered amongst the linked mages, which Vrric hoped was a position of importance. Taglo began to shrink, began to thicken and coalesce. Baltuz was almost there, she was now running straight for Taglo. Vrric aimed at a mage who seemed to be tracking Baltuz, the only one who seemed to be paying attention. It was now as if his skull were in a vice. He was readily bleeding from both nostrils. It had been a long time since he last got a nosebleed while casting spells. He torched one more and then fell to his knees. His flames stopped. He could do no more. The vice did not ease up, however, but increased in intensity. Finally, after what seemed to be an entire epoch, Baltuz reached Taglo. Vrric fell to the balcony floor and felt Clerin kneel next to him.

Everything exploded. Fire engulfed all. It seared through everything, everyone. Vrric was unable to tell if the balcony had survived or if they were falling. His only ability, his only capacity, was to cling to Clerin as the flames roared around them. It was the beginning of the end.

Chapter 21 - Epilogue

The destruction was quite complete. On the Cabal side, at least. When Baltuz had reached Taglo the blast radiated out in a hemisphere, not expanding backwards at all. The fact that Taglo, or maybe Baltuz or even Gorbanax, planned it to keep the coterie's losses to a minimum shocked Clerin a little. She had assumed total devastation, utter carnage, especially as she had knelt there holding Vrric. Eyes shut against the blinding glare of the inferno, ears deafened by the roar of destruction. But there had been a reward at the end of it, or at least the lack of punishment. Most of the coterie who had made it to the end survived the final blast. That was something she was thankful for. That and the overall speed of the battle in the laboratory.

The victory dinner was at an inn, after a day of recuperation. Everyone needed a little rest, especially Vrric. They had it in the Pyran quarter since Trela wanted to be in charge, at the Naked Hare. The money that was handed over to the Cabal was gone, whether stolen or immolated, no one was quite sure. So they scraped together enough coin to make a massive feast, feeling fairly certain that they would be compensated somehow, at some point in the near future.

Most of the Gaen contingent had died, the majority slaughtered by their own kin as they were leaving Phyna's tunnel. Very few made it to the laboratory proper. Silvadhin and Gyaer were amongst the few to make it through to the end. Nyhan, Tumu, and Pylor had not been in the fight at all, staying behind in the smuggler's cove with Wesduin, and Verin survived the ugly battle at the laboratory floor. Tesjuk had not been so lucky, dying near her. "I could say that he saved me with his dying breath, that he leapt in front of me to take a killing blow, but he was just overwhelmed. They had rushed our position and there were too many of them. I tried to reach him, I truly did, but the only story here is that I failed." The others did not let Verin claim failure. They cheered her and toasted to her bravery and skill. Most of them had someone die near them. They could not all take the blame for someone who had died. It would be impossible to live that way.

Croy and Aedon had been saved by Baltuz, Ryshial, Zira, and Hygen. Hygen had died during the fighting, but the others had escaped. The two had been set aside as prisoners and were guarded by five or six warriors and only one mage. The Cabal must have thought they would not have been found, or they were saving their mages for the main battle. Though Arnasta did not help with the fight itself, she had pinpointed Croy's position for the others.

Several of the Pyrans also died. Kryhir's death was a great blow to Trela. He was an amazing Second, just barely behind Rewista in her esteem. Another blow was the loss of Pejal. He had provided her his sword to fight Qizern when no one else would. She had wanted to reward him with lands, but he had only wanted to follow her wherever she needed to go. His reward fell short of what it should have been. Olsfang also perished, throwing fire at the mages of the Cabal. Vrric felt bad about Olsfang's death even though he had not liked him while he was alive. They were still fighting for a common cause. Similar to that feeling was Altrond's death. Honestly, Vrric had liked Altrond more than Olsfang, personality-wise, but had been concerned about his interest in Clerin. It seemed petty when he thought back on it. Clerin was quite devastated, and he vowed to not say anything stupid or foolish, to only commiserate and comfort her.

Phyna and Yinnis had been unsummoned almost immediately, just as they were leaving Phyna's tunnel. Wil had been unsummoned quickly during the final battle in the laboratory, but praise about its valor was widely given. Wil had been the first Yaven to confront the mages in the lab and had killed several immediately, scattering the others. Unfortunately the Cabal was prepared, and they were able to remove Wil from the realm even as it was wreaking havoc.

There was much praise for Voyt. Almost no one had known that Voyt had been a Yaven. Not only was Voyt able to kill many mages before being destroyed by Yavencide, but it kept the mages from unsummoning Taglo by forcing them to focus their energies upon it. They combined their efforts at least once on the totally futile task of unsummoning the non-summoned. Many thought the Cabal had tried twice. Even those who knew Voyt was a Yaven had no idea that it had not been summoned. That was unheard of by derlian and Yaven alike. Voyt had made the ultimate sacrifice, becoming the last Yavencide performed by the Cabal, to ensure the success of the mission.

The most praise, however, was heaped upon Taglo and Baltuz. They, themselves, were obliterated during the fight. Though Yavens never left a body, and if Taglo had somehow escaped back to the Yaven realm no one would know, everyone assumed they had both been destroyed to create the inferno. There was certainly never a portion of Baltuz's body found. Not a piece of clothing, jewelry, or even a piece of her steel weapons or armor. Nothing, or at least, nothing identifiable.

The fact that Taglo had been planning it, had known that the destruction, the sacrifice, was coming but hinted at it to no one, was held in awe. Of course, Taglo did not trust derlians and would never have jeopardized the mission by hinting at anything. The fact that the Blind One had betrayed the coterie so completely showed that Taglo's distrust was not unfounded. But Taglo did not even hint to those it did trust, not even to Clerin. Baltuz, likewise, told no one, not until the end. But she had hinted at it to Croy and had explained it to him as best she could in the time allotted, just before she was to perform the deed. Croy made sure everyone knew of their sacrifice, Baltuz and Taglo's, and that they had planned it in advance. He wanted—no, he needed—everyone to understand the sacrifice. Baltuz was not known to everyone, and even for those who had heard of her she had been merely known as "one of the Gaens" picked up during their travels. Croy was insistent that the entire coterie know who she was and that she was the derlian chosen by Taglo to add her lifeforce to the inferno that saved them, that destroyed the last of the Cabal. That she was the derlian part of the equation. All glasses at the feast were raised in salute to those two, several times. Not a disparaging word was spoken about either of them the entire evening, and there were many who had complained loudly about Taglo during the campaign. All wrongs, real or imaginary, were forgotten by the survivors.

It took a little while for Clerin to realize that was what Taglo had gone back to the Yaven realm for. When she had been warned by Wil, she had assumed it would be for something more destructive, something that would wipe out the coterie along with the Cabal. Something that might wipe out more than just a city. But it had been something narrow and yet decisive. For that she would always be grateful to Taglo, or at least to Taglo's memory. She assumed she should be grateful to Gorbanax as well. If Taglo had been following any orders at all, they had to have been coming from Gorbanax.

The celebration was long and copious amounts of drinks were imbibed. There was wine, grog, beer, everything but mead, really. There were few enough left that everyone had a chance to tell their story. They filled their stories with valor and courage, amazing and daring feats, and no one corrected anyone. No one begrudged anyone's version of the truth that would become legend. They had made it, they had survived. They had, most of them, come all the way from deep within the Pyran realm, crossed the length of the Gaen realm, entered the Fluen realm, and destroyed the Cabal. The journey was so long and arduous that it had seemed to take lifetimes. But they were finally at Vatlisi, finally at the edge of the Clatsvol Sea. They could finally rest.

Appendix A (Races)

The general race descriptions given below are not absolute and are by no means considered exhaustive. Though rare, there are certainly blond Luftens and tall Gaens. Personality traits are even harder to pin exclusively to one race or another. These generalities are merely provided to assist in getting an overall flavor of the various derlian denizens of the world.

Race: Gaen
Element: Stone
Beleg: Gunzgak

The shortest of the races, the Gaens live in underground cave complexes and against rocky hillsides. They are simple and civilized, enjoying order and structure throughout their lives. They are skeptics and jinxers in general, and therefore are typically the weakest mages of all the races. Their hair is typically quite curly with mostly brown and red coloring. They are stocky bordering on pudgy. They love beer and are excellent miners, and colloquially refer to their coined money as "pebbles." They have a strict caste system based upon vocation. The last name of a Gaen consists of two syllables, the first denoting their rank and the second their guild:

Sie – Peasant	Tin – Farmer
Beo – Apprentice	Lak – Merchant
Ona – Member	Cha – Blacksmith
Mur – Overseer	Wir – Carpenter
Fyr – Teacher	Tul – Stoneworker
Cru – Guild Leader	Sol – Artist
Dea – Assembly Member	Rem – Physician
Ata – Assembly Leader	Jin – Warrior

Vyx – the Guild Lord

Race: Fluen
Element: Water
Beleg: Lembin

The blond, ship-building Fluens live around the Clatsvol Sea. Each royal family can trace their lineage back to the original Yaven they sprang from.   Their family name carries much weight and responsibility. Bastards are shunned. They are strict adherents to tradition and even call their coined money "crowns" in deference to the monarchy. They are generally tall and thin, with long, straight hair to match.   They are great cultivators of wine and masters of all manners of fishing. Magic is a skill much used in the Fluen realm by beggar and prince alike, though maybe not quite as specialized as in the Luften realm.

Race: Luften
Element: Air
Beleg: Linchon

There are two types of Luftens: those who live high in the cities amongst the helioarc trees, and those who shuffle along the ground. This demarcation means more than a family name or a chosen vocation, though those things may dictate where a Luften lives. They are somewhat thin with curly and mostly black hair, though there are also some browns. They are the tallest of the races, but are thicker than the Fluens, making for a more symmetric form. They harvest honey and ferment a deliciously sweet mead. They excel in woodcraft and magic. They are undoubtedly the most focused and engaged of the races when it comes to magic, as it is one of the most powerful guilds in the Luften society. There is a shaky monarchy, bound by a council of Branches, that has gone through so many kings of late that they have taken to referring to their coined money as "heads". There are both family Branches and guild Branches that make up the general council, balancing traditional aristocracy with meritocracy. In theory, at least.

Race: Pyran
Element: Fire
Beleg: Gorbanax

Pyrans are a nomadic race ruled by a caste of warriors. They are short and muscular and many of them travel in warpacks, fighting with each other and living off the land, sending what additional coins they can back to their families. The fighting is considered an art form, with warpacks growing and shrinking more from trading warriors than from actual death. A warpack is typically broken up into smaller units, a cohort having approximately forty warriors and a maniple comprised of two to four cohorts. They generally have straight, light brown hair. They drink grog by the barrelful, and there are more herders than there are farmers, though there are plenty of both. The king or queen rules with complete power, beholden to none. They have mages but they study, almost exclusively, destruction or healing magics.

Appendix B (Magic)

Magic is the art of sifting through Chaos to find a desired possibility, then willing that possibility into reality. A spell is comprised of one word, typically with four syllables: Power, Sphere, Element and Effect. This word defines the desired possibility in its simplest terms. The difficulty of the spell is estimated by adding the ranks of the syllables and then multiplying them by the Power's Multiplier. There are Majora syllables, those that are taught, and there are Minora syllables, those that are individually learned. The Majora syllables are listed below, separated into the four Pillars:

Power	Multiplier	Sphere	Rank	Element	Rank	Effect	Rank
Lo	3	Kin	2	Luf	2	Pri	1
Nu	5	Fin	2	Ge	1	Arc	2
Mek	8	De	3	Pi	3	Del	2
Nar	11	Tra	1	Flu	2	Sfe	3
Eqe	15	Tec	2	Der	3	Clo	3
Lum	19	Li	3	Hep	1	To	1
Sur	23	Sid	1	Pan	1	Kha	1
Tor	27	Morf	1	Tot	2	Ref	0

POWER:
Power designates a spell's effectiveness and duration. These are intertwined. A mage may make a spell shorter to increase its effectiveness, or they may decrease the effectiveness to increase the duration. This is known as "tilting the pillar." This list is simple since the Syllable is mainly defined by its Multiplier.

Lo:
Glyph: ●
Multiplier: 3

Nu:
Glyph: ● ●
Multiplier: 5

Mek:
Glyph: ● ● ●
Multiplier: 8

Nar:
Glyph: (three dots over one line)
Multiplier: 11

Eqe:
Glyph: (three dots over one line over one dot)
Multiplier: 15

Lum:
Glyph: (three dots over one line over two dots)
Multiplier: 19

Sur:
Glyph: (three dots over two lines over three dots)
Multiplier: 23

Tor:
Glyph: (three dots over two lines over three dots, double line)
Multiplier: 27

<u>SPHERE</u>:

Sphere designates a spell's action, its sphere of influence. The following descriptions are from Elange's book, *Principles of Grey Magic*.

Kin: Sphere of movement. This Syllable brings your Mind to the Realm of Movement. This Sphere is dependent upon the Element to be moved. This Syllable may be used with any Effect of the Caster's choosing. Movement is defined as changing an object's location through adjacent space over a period of time, meaning the object must move through all intervening space between locations and must take a certain amount of time to do so. Objects cannot be made to disappear and reappear, nor can they be moved through solid objects.

Glyph:
Rank: 2

Fin: Sphere of the Mind. This Syllable brings your Mind to Itself and to Others. This Sphere is Elementally limited for Majora use. The vast main Element to be used is Tot, though Pan occasionally and Der rarely may also be used. This Syllable may be used with any Effect of the Caster's choosing. The Mind is defined as all mental activities including thought, analytics and perception. This Syllable may not be used to affect anything tangible.

Glyph:
Rank: 2

De: Sphere of destruction. This Syllable brings your Mind to the Path of Death, Damage, and Destruction. This Sphere is Polymorphic, but most often paired with Pi. This Syllable may be used with any Effect of the Caster's choosing. Destruction is defined by causing injury to the living and demolishing the inanimate. The type of injury depends upon the Element and Power level, up to and including Death.

Glyph:
Rank: 3

Tra: Sphere of transmutation. This Syllable brings your Mind to essence modifier of Transmutation. This Sphere is dependent upon the Elements to be transmuted. This Syllable may only be used with the Effect of Ref. This Sphere is used to create the only typical five Syllable Majora Words. Transmutation is defined as changing one Element into another. This Syllable may not affect shape, but may affect density and thereby mass.

Glyph:
Rank: 1

Tec: Sphere of protection. This Syllable brings your Mind to the Path of Protection. This Sphere is Polymorphic, so most Mages use lower ranking Elements in the Word. This Syllable may be used with any Effect of the Caster's choosing. Protection is defined as the stopping of physical harm/damage from immediately happening. This Syllable may not be used to Ameliorate or Heal.

Glyph:

Rank: 2

Li: Sphere of healing. This Syllable brings your Mind to the Way of Healing. This Sphere only affects living beings and is therefore Elementally limited for Majora use. The vast main Element to be used is Der, though Pan occasionally and Tot rarely may also be used. This Syllable may be used with any Effect of the Caster's choosing. Healing is defined as the temporary Amelioration of damaged tissue. Temporary Amelioration may close wounds, bind bones, reconnect severed arteries, numb pain, and even cure some diseases, but the spell will always wear off. Only time-based cellular reconstruction has long lasting effects on the derlian body, making this Sphere act more as a time accelerant than true Healing.

Glyph:

Rank: 3

Sid: Sphere of communication. This Syllable brings your Mind to the way of Communing with Spirits. This Sphere may not be used to commune with a living derlian and is rarely used with the syllables Hep or Pan. This Syllable may be used with any Effect of the Caster's choosing. Communing is defined as transferring thoughts with Spirits. This Syllable is used to summon Yavens and commune with the dead.

Glyph:

Rank: 1

Morf: Sphere of change. This Syllable brings your Mind to the way of Changing Shapes. This Sphere is dependent upon the Element to be modified. This Syllable may be used with any Effect of the Caster's choosing. Change, in this instance, is defined as modifying a purely physical form. This Syllable may not be used to change Elements or the Essence of the object.

Glyph:

Rank: 1

<u>ELEMENT</u>:

Element designates what type of object the spell is acting upon. Its basic constituents, its Essence. Due to the amount of different types of objects in the realms, some of these elemental categories are quite broad, though the first four come directly from the Yaven realms and are, therefore, specifically defined. These definitions are considered intuitive.

Luf: The element of Air.

Glyph:

Rank: 2

Ge: The element of Stone.

Glyph:

Rank: 1

Pi: The element of Fire.

Glyph:

Rank: 3

Flu: The element of Water.

Glyph:

Rank: 2

Der: The element of derlians, of flesh.

Glyph:

Rank: 3

Hep: The element of metals, salts, and crystals.

Glyph:

Rank: 1

Pan: The element of nature: plants, animals and wood.

Glyph:

Rank: 1

Tot: The element of the mind.

Glyph:

Rank: 2

EFFECT:
Effect designates the target of the spell, the aim. This Pillar is highly affected by the Power level of the spell. The shapes of these Effects are intuitive and so are defined simply, below.

Pri: The target of yourself.

Glyph:

Rank: 1

Arc: A target in a line of sight.

Glyph:

Rank: 2

Del: The target of a sphere at a later time.

Glyph:

Rank: 2

Sfe: The target of a sphere centered around the caster.

Glyph:

Rank: 3

Clo: The target of a cube placed at the caster's choosing.

Glyph:
Rank: 3

To: The target of your direct contact.

Glyph:
Rank: 1

Kha: The targets are random living objects.

Glyph:
Rank: 1

Ref: The target refers back to itself.

Glyph:
Rank: 0

Appendix C (Map)

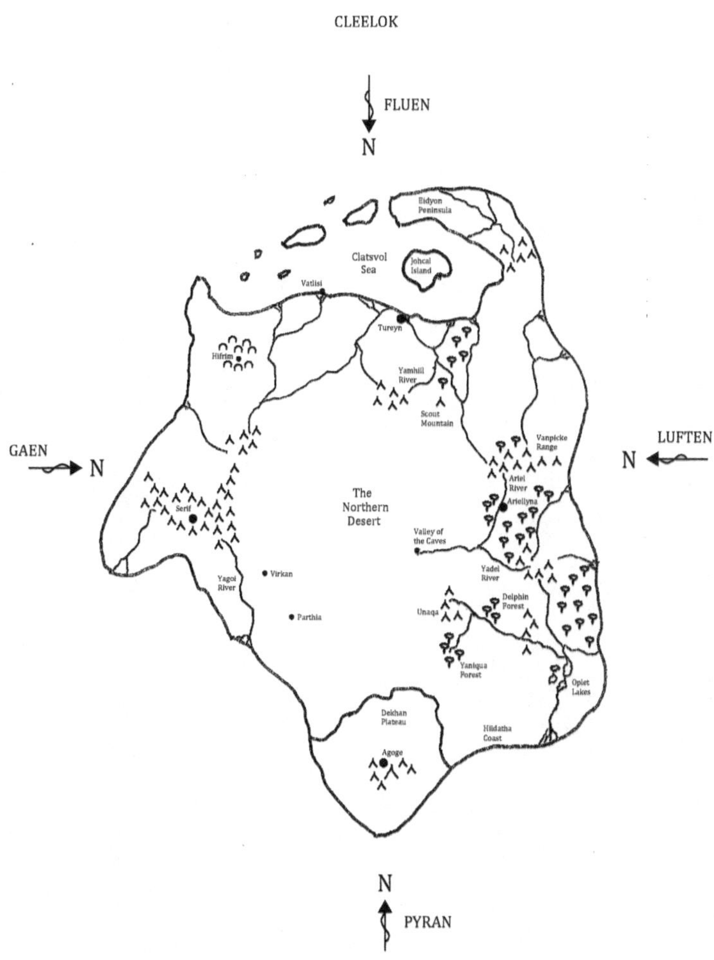